FIRE IN THE HENHOUSE

FIRE IN THE HENHOUSE

a novel by

Frances Grote

RULE BENDER PRESS
Marblehead, Massachusetts

Library of Congress Control Number: 2011902318
ISBN 978-0-9833341-0-1

Published by
RULE BENDER PRESS
38 Washington Street
Marblehead, Massachusetts 01945
rulebenderpress.com

*For **Rich**,*
who never doubted
for even the smallest n^{th} of a nanosecond,

and in loving memory of
Denise Dejianne Kelleher,
who set the standard for every
friendship that ever followed

1

From the first time she heard her son's heart beat over fourteen years ago, Maggie MacDonald was haunted by the possibility that something she would do, with the best intentions, would quietly go out of control and end up ripping him away from her. Even today that constant underlying hum of worry was there, like the buzz off a high-tension wire. But as she struggled to reach the zipper on the back of her dress reality hit Maggie like a sniper attack. Gary was the one she had lost. Her husband would never stand in this room again, never exhale his displeasure at having to stop what he was doing to pull up her zipper. That realization crushed her guts until a sound like a low howl squeezed out. She sat down hard on the bed and crossed her arms over her chest, rocking back and forth hoping for the numbness to return.

There was a light tap on the door. Albie peeked in, her red hair loose and wild. Even though Mac was fourteen, she was officially still his nanny. "The car will be here in a few minutes."

"It's time already?" Maggie's voice was a hollow whisper.

"Oh, look at you." Albie came into the room. She continued talking softly, her brogue more sounds than words, as she zipped up Maggie's dress.

Maggie floated away on Albie's voice for a moment before the grief caught her again, like a submerged branch. She shook her head. "Did you check on Mac?"

"He needs you to do that." When Maggie didn't answer Albie walked to the door. "Best finish getting ready," she said, not quite closing the door behind her.

Maggie made herself get up. She dug around in the porcelain box on her dresser, through the safety pins and unmatched earrings, until she found some clips to pull back her dark curly hair. Then she put on some makeup, looking at each feature with clinical precision, this eye then that one, skin, cheeks, lips. She did not consider them as elements of a whole.

Even though Mac's door was ajar she hesitated before going in. She felt like an intruder. His room was as neat as always. Why did it suddenly look so sterile? The only clue about the boy who lived here was some photos on the dresser. One of them had fallen over, its cardboard stand sticking up at an odd angle like the stiffened limb of some dead animal. Maggie walked over and picked it up. The picture had been removed. That was when she heard the terrible sound of Mac behind his bathroom door, crying.

She froze. She couldn't recall if she had ever felt it was safe to cry. Aloofness was as necessary to her success as a scalpel. It enabled her to face the families of her trauma patients without getting sucked into their pain. Now she was one of them, numb and confused. Gary's sudden death provided the only focus for her activities. She expected that once the funeral was over she would be incapable of figuring out what to do next. She just wasn't expecting to face that problem yet. But it had been so many years since she'd heard Mac cry she had no idea what would be the right thing to do.

Pushing aside the fears that sucked up all the air in the room she walked toward the bathroom door. As she reached out to knock, Mac fell silent. "Honey?" she whispered. "I love you." There was no answer. Maggie put both hands on the door and leaned her head against the wood. She ached for him, for her own inability to figure out how to comfort him. He began to cry again, quietly.

"Hey you two!" Albie called from downstairs. "The car's here."

r r r

Maggie wished she could sleep for more than a few minutes at a time. The days since the funeral had all blended into an indistinct impression, like a watercolor tilted before it was dry. She always said that being alone in this house that Gary's mother left him made her feel like she was trying not to get caught in the museum after hours. Now she was going to lose the house, and she grieved for it. The whole place was sadly quiet, as if the life in it had been wrapped up and put in storage. How could she have let herself overlook all the clues? The papers from the lawyer tore a hole through the remaining bit of illusion she had left about her life. At least thinking about it made her angry enough to get off the bed and go downstairs.

Albie was in the kitchen eating leftover potato salad, plucking large cubes of exotic-colored potatoes from a plastic bowl with her fingers. "Can't bring myself to throw it out," she said, her mouth full.

"You keep those leftovers much longer and we'll need another funeral in their honor."

"I'm not sure we could get anyone to come back."

Maggie sat at the island and rested her chin on her hand. "I guess I behaved badly."

"Depends how you define bad," Albie said. "Some of the nurses thought it was pretty funny when you told that old fart Taylor that Gary always said he'd make a good proctologist because he did his best work when he had his nose up somebody's ass."

"I don't get credit for that," Maggie answered. "I was just quoting."

"I'm sure I can think of something original you said that was inappropriate. Just give me a minute."

"Never mind," Maggie said. "I don't need to know."

Albie wiped her hands on a towel. "You really weren't that bad. No worse than anyone would expect, considering you put up with him for all those years. Besides, people will forgive quite a bit when you have a good excuse for not being yourself."

"What are you talking about?" Maggie asked. "That was as myself as it gets."

Albie put a hand on her arm. "You have no idea how sad you looked. Maybe you never won any awards for being nice, but those people care about you."

"No, they don't," Maggie said. "But they weren't meant to. I just needed them to follow orders." She paused. "The first time Gary bought me a coffee, when I was a resident and he was head of the department, he asked me if I knew the difference between a trauma surgeon and God. When I said no, he said, God never wonders if he's a trauma surgeon."

"You think you're going to win more blue ribbons for saving people if you stop to have a staff meeting about who's in charge?" Albie said.

"That's the problem," Maggie answered. "I'm just not sure anymore. I can't be standing over someone with a knife in my hand when I'm like this."

"Give yourself some time. You've just had quite a shock."

"No," Maggie said. "You don't understand. I don't even understand." She got up and poured herself some coffee. "Did you hear how the rabbi called me Mrs. Rifkin? You know why?"

"Because you were the dead guy's wife?"

"Because he saw something everybody else missed. I'm not Dr. MacDonald in real life. I never took charge of anything. I'm Mrs. Rifkin, who does what she's told. Even after I got smart enough to make up my own mind, it was easier to let Gary do it. So I never figured out what I wanted to be." Maggie's hand started to shake. She put her coffee mug down. "Now I'm not even sure I can. And it might be too late."

"You mustn't put this all on yourself." Albie moved closer. "He didn't exactly make it easy to stand up to him. He wasn't a nice man."

Maggie sighed. "I know. He wasn't easy to like."

"For crying out loud," Albie said, "he wasn't even easy to dislike. He was just somebody you wished you didn't have to ever be around. He was sarcastic and mean. He probably married you because he got a charge out of having someone so competent to boss around."

Maggie shook her head, looking at nothing. "I found out why he married me. He needed me to get his mother's money. It was in her will."

"Her will said he had to marry a shiksa?" When Maggie didn't laugh, Albie got serious. "What did you find out from that lawyer?"

Maggie took a moment before answering. "Gary couldn't get his mother's money until he had a kid."

"So MacDonald inherited all her money?"

Maggie nodded. "Yeah. For what it's worth."

"Seems to me it should be worth quite a lot."

"You know what keeps bothering me?" Maggie asked, turning her coffee mug around, then around again. "It just doesn't make sense to me that Gary stepped in front of an oncoming bus. That kind of accident should only happen to careless people."

"That's why they call them accidents," Albie said.

"Maybe my husband was such a legend in his own mind he didn't believe the laws of traffic and physics applied to him. But I think he was completely capable of going head to head with a couple of tons of speeding public transportation."

"Certainly neither of you was the poster child for respect for authority."

Maggie looked at her sharply. "What if Gary stepped in front of that bus on purpose?"

"Come on," Albie said. "What makes you imagine he would do something like that?"

"The money from his mother is almost all gone. There's not even enough for us to stay in this house."

"How could that be?" Albie was stunned. "I thought you said his mother left everything to Mac."

"She left it all to Mac in trust," Maggie answered. "Which just goes to show what a misleading word 'trust' is. Gary was his guardian. All he had to say was the money was for Mac and he could take as much as he wanted."

"Is there anything left?" Albie was holding her breath.

"Enough to put Mac through college with maybe a little extra. It's nothing compared to what he was supposed to get."

"What about this house?" Albie asked. "It has to be worth plenty."

Maggie shook her head. "Not after the mortgages are paid off. He refinanced it every time the value went up and took the equity out."

Albie wet a sponge and began cleaning an imaginary spill on the counter. "I don't get it," she said, rubbing hard. "He never parted with a dime without breaking a sweat. What would he do with all that money?"

Maggie's voice was full of anger. "I feel like an idiot. You know his unexpected trips, and those mysterious phone calls? I never paid attention because I never cared."

Albie stopped scrubbing. "You think there was another woman?"

"Right," Maggie said. "Like there might be another woman in the universe naïve enough to put up with his stuff. You know why he never let anybody in that mausoleum of a living room? He had lists all over in there. He didn't even make much of an effort to hide them."

"Lists of what?" Albie looked confused.

"Numbers. Gambling. He must have been in way over his head."

"And his mother left all the money to his kid to protect it."

"If so, it didn't work out the way she hoped."

"What kind of bastard would do that to his own son?" Albie asked.

"Stop." Maggie held up her hand as if deflecting something. "I don't want anyone saying anything like that. Whatever else he screwed up, he loved Mac."

"I can't believe you're trying to defend him."

"This has nothing to do with defending him," Maggie said. "This is about Mac. He can't know about any of this."

Albie went over to the refrigerator, but turned around before she opened it. "I know this is none of my business. But why did you stay with him? I'd look at the two of you and it just didn't make sense."

Maggie took a long time to answer. "When I met him I had a life nobody would want. He took me away from that. In the beginning I was afraid if I annoyed him he'd send me back. Once I finally realized I could stand alone, he was a habit. It was easier to stay in his shadow."

"So now that he and his shadow are gone, what are you going to do?"

"I'm working on it," Maggie said slowly. "I've never been in charge before unless somebody else already laid out the rules. This is a whole new thing for me to figure out."

"Promise you're not going to do something too stupid."

"Thanks," Maggie said. "I appreciate that vote of confidence."

"You bet," Albie answered. "What are friends for?"

🐓 🐓 🐓

Mac stood at the bottom of the stairs looking at his drums. They might as well be halfway across the state instead of right there in the middle of the basement. Before, all he ever wanted to do was come down here and play. He had this secret dream, ever since he was little, of being a famous drummer. Now it hurt too bad to even think about.

He went over to the leather-topped stool behind the drums, but when he sat down it made him think even more about his dad. His dad was never around much, but whenever he was home he came down here and hung out with Mac. He even said he liked listening to Mac because it made him feel like he was in a club somewhere. Mac would make stuff up for him, really soft and jazzy, and his dad would sit there with his eyes closed and this look on his face like he was riding on the music. When Mac would finish playing it always took a little while for his dad to come back from wherever the music took him inside his head. Those were the only times he was sure his dad was happy.

Mac touched the rim of the snare, but only for a second. Most of the time he still felt like his dad was just away on another one of his trips. But if he stayed down here too long with his drums it made him think about how he'd never see his father again.

He heard the door at the top of the stairs open. Albie came down. "How we doing?" she said.

Mac shrugged.

"You feel like talking?"

"I guess," Mac said.

Albie sat down and patted the bottom step next to her. "So what do you think of your mom's plan?" she asked as he came over. "Are you nervous about it?"

"Not really," he said, sitting down.

"Because if you are, you need to say so. You need to learn to tell your mother what you're thinking if I'm not going to be around to translate for you."

"I still don't get why you won't come with us," Mac said.

"Doing something just to please someone else doesn't make it the right thing to do, you know."

"Is that why you're not coming?"

"I wasn't talking about me," Albie answered.

"I don't do stuff just to please somebody else."

"People learn by example."

"You think Mom does that?" Mac was kind of surprised. His mom was so tough she never even cried when his father died. At least not in front of him. "Why do you think Mom wants to change everything so much now?" he asked. "I mean, I get it that we can't stay here, but she doesn't want to go back to work or anything."

"She just needs some time. She says she can't concentrate enough to be responsible for anyone's life."

"Did you tell her she'll get over it?"

Albie laughed. "I'm more her nanny than yours. I tried to sound supportive."

"Oh, man," Mac said. "That must've been good." He picked at a splinter on the edge of the steps. "Do you think it's because of me?" he asked without looking up.

"I think," Albie said, putting her arm around him, "that she can't believe how much she misses your father. I think that everything about this house and her job and this city hurts her, and she doesn't know why. It will be good for her to have more time for you, but none of this is because of anything you did. And you can't change any of it. But you're right that she won't feel like this forever. I wish she wouldn't resort to such desperate measures."

"You make it sound like that town she grew up in is a terrible place."

"Dooleysburg?" Albie said. "She's the one who called it the armpit of Pennsylvania."

"It won't be that bad," Mac said.

"Not for you, maybe. But she'll *hate* living in a small town. It'll make her crazy that everyone knows her business."

"You tell her that?"

"I tried. She said she needs to be someplace where people are normal." Albie snorted. "If people were normal there, how'd they turn out the likes of her?"

"Maybe it was weird when she grew up there," Mac said. "But it's pretty cool now." Albie looked skeptical. "No, really," he insisted. "It's got places to hang out and a movie theater that shows indie films, and some museums and stuff."

"And you found all this out how?"

"On the Internet. Here, I'll show you." He went over to the computer desk on the far wall. Albie followed him. "Look." He clicked the mouse a few times, then stepped back so Albie could see the monitor. "They have a webcam. This stuff is going on there live right now."

"What's that place?" Albie pointed at a two-story white building with arcade-style porches on both floors.

"It used to be some fancy hotel. Now it's called the General Store. They serve coffee and stuff."

As they watched the building's ornate front door opened. Whoever was coming out was hidden in the shadow of the overhanging porch. Then they walked into the sunlight and the shapes resolved into two people. One was a police officer, big and mostly bald. He had on the kind of sunglasses evil cops in horror movies wore, and his potbelly hung over his belt. He stepped off the porch, pulling the other person along behind him by a pair of handcuffs.

"Is that a kid?" Albie asked, her tone a combination of disbelief and dismay.

"I think so," Mac said. The grainy webcam image made it hard to tell for sure, but the person in the handcuffs looked like a teenager. Except he was only about the height of a ten-year-old.

"Oh, lovely," Albie said. "Welcome to Dooleysburg."

2

Roland Gamey balanced delicately on the edge of the clawfoot tub. It was no mean feat, getting a foothold with your tippy-toes. Good thing for him he was a man who valued precision. And caution. Even though up here in the second floor bathroom was the primo window for spying on his next door neighbor, since that time he slipped and had to call the ambulance he saved this spot for special occasions. Not like he got hurt, but it was not a pretty sight, the Rescue Squad having to unwedge him from between the tub and the wall. A man couldn't have too many accidents like that without jeopardizing his reputation.

The present situation justified the risk. That real estate bitch with the bingo winnings boob job was over there again, and if he wanted to get his nose over the sill of the privacy window it was either toes on the tub or learn how to fly. Why any fool would put a window up this high in the first place was beyond him. Even if somebody normal-sized was using the john, what were the chances anybody would be looking up from the ground at just the right moment?

He hooked his arm over the shower rod for extra safety and prayed it would hold his weight. This was the real thing. Old lady Morello, the human mountain of unrelenting aggravation who owned the place next door, was out there. Something pretty special must be going on if it got her to lift her bulk out of her favorite chair. The Carter Realty woman was walking along next to her, and even from up here you could see she was wishing she had a tow rope and a winch to get the old girl to pick up the pace. Gamey fought the urge to open the window and ask what the hell they were up to. It sure looked like the outside part of a walk-through, but the old girl didn't even have a "for sale" sign out front. Could she really be planning to ditch him? It was a depressing thought. The highlight of his days was figuring out some new way to be a boil on the backside of her life. He indulged in a moment of creative pride, remembering how surprised she was that time he put stolen license plates on her car and it got impounded for unpaid parking tickets. It was only a joke. Where was her sense of humor?

Gamey let out a noisy breath as the women poked along toward the front of the house. Even though the window was closed old lady Morello looked up in his direction. He would've ducked down, but he couldn't unwind his arm from the shower rod fast enough and she spotted him. Gamey was pleased that she couldn't get away with any of her usual gestures of greeting, not with the Carter Realty woman there, but he thought she'd at least shake her fist in his direction. Instead she gave him a grin so big he was afraid the sunlight glinting off her teeth might give him a headache. His heart started pounding and he jumped off the tub, shower rod be damned. He raced down the stairs and off his wraparound porch into the yard. He nearly threw his back out pulling open the big gate to his spite fence, and by the time he got it wide enough to squeeze through they were already out of sight. He ran around to the front of her house and stopped short. There they stood on the slate front porch, staring at him like they were just waiting for him to come whipping around the corner of the house.

"Can we help you?" Carter Realty said in a voice that made his nuts want to put on a down jacket and scamper off to warmer climes.

"He's beyond help," old lady Morello answered. "He's the demented half-pint from next door I told you about."

Gamey paused to catch his breath. "I was just coming over for a closer look. From up there," he gestured at his bathroom window, "I thought you were Laurel and Hardy in drag."

"What'd I tell you?" old lady Morello said. "I'm never going to be able to sell this place unless we find a way to get rid of him."

"Libby Morello," Gamey slapped his hand to his chest, "are you thinking of leaving me? What about my heart?"

"Unless it's going to stop right here so I can watch you drop dead your heart's no use to me."

"Just ignore him," Carter Realty interrupted.

"Ignore him?" old lady Morello spat. "Son-of-a-bitch is standing between me and a dream home in the Poconos, where decent people go to retire."

"Just finish the walk-through with me. We'll get you out of here."

"No need to waste your time on that," Gamey smirked. "My girlfriend here ain't going nowhere. I can make sure nobody in their right mind is going to buy this place."

"What a coincidence," Carter Realty said, all smug. "That's just the sort of person I happened to sell this house to."

"What kind of nut are we talking about?" Gamey demanded.

"That's something you can find out for yourself," Carter Realty answered. "I've never met her. She didn't even want to come see the place. Just called me up, asked me to post some pictures online and bought it." She opened the front door. "Come on." She pointed for the old lady to go in. "I don't have all day."

❧   ❧   ❧

Carl Bendz snatched up a used copy of *The Daily Intellectual* somebody had dropped by the door and settled himself in a chair. The overdone babe at the next table gave him a dirty look. Good for her. If she didn't like him sitting so close she could take her four bucks a cup Belgian Grande Mucho Mocha Skinny Ugly Latte and drink it somewhere else. They were all like that, the women in this town. They had perfectly good homes, but there wasn't a single thing they wouldn't rather do out in public, someplace they could be sure some other woman was watching. That was the only way they could tell if they were having a good time.

"Hey!" he called toward the counter. "Hobbit! Bring me a coffee over here!" He grinned, pleased with himself. Now that Joe Butts had finally busted the little weasel for extorting tips, the kid was only allowed to answer back with something polite no matter what anybody said to him. This made the game infinitely more satisfying for Bendz. "And don't give me any of that fancy crap!" Bendz yelled. The kid's mouth moved, but no sound came out.

Bendz snapped the paper open to the Automotive section. He nodded, momentarily content. His own face grinned back at him from a full-page ad, oozing friendliness and reliability. This week's copy read, "Carl Bendz over backwards to please you." It pissed him off that he had to pay somebody to write this stuff, but when he ran a contest to see what his employees could turn out for free, all he got was "Carl Bendz over for Mayor Frank."

The big wooden screen door screeched open then slapped shut. Bendz looked up and saw Carol Ann. His cheeks swelled with pride. It was a pity, he thought, that such a fine woman didn't have a bigger stage than Dooleysburg. She certainly knew how to make the most of her assets, and he enjoyed how she never felt bad about outsmarting a sucker. He especially liked meeting her in public so people could see them together. He waved a little self-consciously.

"Daddy," she said, walking over. She gave his cheek an air kiss, then sat down.

"I'm smelling victory," he crooned.

She made that smile, the one he hated, the cheap version of happy she learned from her mother. They claimed it helped prevent wrinkles. "You could say. I just sold the MacDonald house. You remember, the old stone place a few blocks from St. Agnes of the Precious Lambs."

"How the hell could I forget?" Bendz asked sourly. "MacDonald was such a cheap bastard he never bought a new car in his life. Drove whatever piece of crap he had until the wheels fell off and then he'd want to use it for a trade-in." Just thinking about it made his engine begin to rev.

Carol Ann gave him one of her looks that could cut paper. "We're here to talk about me, Daddy."

It was hard to pull the emergency brake on his rant, but a man had to be willing to sacrifice for his daughter. "I didn't know the house was for sale. The old dame who bought it from the MacDonald estate finally die?" He never forgot a customer. The woman was a Crown Victoria, needed a car as big and pushy as she was. Spent money on all kinds of upgrades, then one day she just stopped driving the damn thing.

"She's alive and kicking. Good and desperate to get out of there, too."

"Should be an easy sale. As I recall, the old lady put up a great garage, nearly took up the whole back yard."

"Believe it or not, Daddy, the first thing most people look for in a house is not a nice bedroom for the car. Everybody in town knows Roland Gamey lives next door. And if that wasn't bad enough, how about what crazy Mrs. Mac-Donald did? The place still feels creepy."

"So how'd you unload it?"

"I got a call out of the blue, some rich widow from New York. She wanted to know specifically about that house."

"You ask her why?"

"What the hell do I care? She's paying cash. As long as I get a cut of it she can have whatever house she wants."

"Seems to me it wouldn't hurt to show a little friendly interest. Help her figure out what she needs to get around town, maybe introduce somebody else to your widow too."

"For chrissake Daddy, my business is selling houses. You want to see if you can squeeze a car out of her, you're on your own." Bendz's cheeks sagged and Carol Ann eased up a little. "Stay awake when you go to cut a deal with her, though. She thinks she's a player. I told her my commission is six percent, just to see what I could get. And she doesn't even try to be polite, comes right out and says, this is a private sale, you're only entitled to three percent. So I say, under certain circumstances I might negotiate my commission, and she says, then pay attention, because that's what we're doing right now. Can you believe the balls?"

"So what'd you say?"

"I let her do the talking." Carol Ann forgot herself and smiled for real this time. "She tells me the house is worth tops $750,000, so if that's the best deal

I can get she'll give me the standard three percent. Then she tells me for every $100,000 I get the price down she'll increase my commission by one point."

Bendz shook his head.

"Our friend from New York thought she knew everything, but she never bothered to ask what the old lady wanted for the place. Turns out she didn't have a clue what the house was worth, and she was so desperate to get out of there she was ready to sell it for what she paid twenty years ago. I was the one who suggested $550,000 would be a good deal."

"I thought you said the lower the price the more commission you made."

"Yeah, that's what the buyer thought too. But when you do the math it turns I make the most money at $550,000. Any less than that and my commission starts going back down." Carol Ann paused, waiting for her father to catch up. A slow grin spread across his face.

"I'm thinking I just can't wait to meet our new widow," he said, visions of the BMW 700 series dancing in his head.

3

Maggie looked in the rearview mirror and realized an urgent course correction was needed. The conversational pall that began when they drove into the landscape of rolling hills and picturesque farms of eastern Pennsylvania was now inflating to the point of consuming all the air in the car. Ever since Albie had pointed out Dooleysburg High in a field in the middle of nowhere Mac had remained slumped in the back seat, his eyes half-open and unblinking. They were at the northern end of Dooleysburg now. Maggie jammed on the brakes and took a sudden left. Albie squawked in protest, but Mac maintained his reptilian funk. They drove over a steep hill and onto a narrow street lined with huge old maples.

Mac sat up suddenly. "What is that?" He pointed at the massive concrete building to their right. Its front lawn was big enough to be a park. "It looks like a castle. Or a nuthouse. I bet there are trolls in the woods behind it."

"That," said Maggie, "is Milton's Retreat. It was the home of Milton Dooley, the guy this town is named after."

"Was he looking to hold back invading Goths?" Albie asked.

"He was obsessed with concrete," Maggie answered. "He spent his entire family fortune making stuff out of it. The place is even crazier inside. Everything is made of concrete."

"Anybody still live there?" Albie asked.

"Nope. He never got married or had children."

"Not surprising," Albie said. "Some things probably can't be done very efficiently on a concrete bed."

"*Some* things?" Maggie asked. "Anyway, it's a museum now. They give tours."

"Can we see it?" Mac asked.

"We will," Maggie answered. "Just not today." She slowed down. The streets in this part of town were barely wide enough for two cars to pass each other. The houses were no particular style, but they were all large, each one with its own version of a grand front lawn.

"You never mentioned you grew up around so much money," Albie said.

"This kind of money wasn't here when I was a kid. When I was growing up a lot of these big places had been turned into boarding houses. There were only two rich families in town back then. One was the Bendz family. They owned a bunch of car dealerships. I went to school with their daughter. She was a total . . ." Maggie caught herself, ". . . brat. The other family was the Carters. Their son went to private school, so he didn't exist as far as we were concerned."

"How come you weren't rich?" Mac asked. "Your father was a doctor."

"Not all doctors made a lot of money. My father's practice was mostly sewing up what was left after bar fights and factory accidents. Some patients only paid by buying him a beer."

"He must have been an okay guy if he took care of them anyway. What was he like?"

Maggie took her time answering. "Everybody called him Doc," she finally said. "Even me. He didn't waste a lot of time being friendly, but I guess that made him perfect for around here."

"Do you think anybody still remembers him?"

"We're almost there!" Maggie pointed at a stately brick church up ahead. "That's St. Agnes of the Precious Lambs, where I went to school. When I was little I always tried to make sure I could see the white spire on top so I wouldn't get lost."

"You went to *Catholic* school?" Mac asked in disbelief. Albie snickered.

"What's the big deal?"

"Nothing," Mac answered. "Except you have a pretty bad attitude for someone who went to Catholic school."

"I have the perfect attitude for someone who went to Catholic school," Maggie said. "Bad attitude is one of the things you learn best there. A Catholic school education prepares you to get away with anything."

Maggie followed the street around to the left of the church and the school behind it. A few blocks later she took another left. This street was much wider, and the houses even bigger than those near Milton's Retreat. She parked at the first corner.

"Which one is it?" Mac asked.

"Across the street."

"How can you be sure? You didn't check the address."

"I don't need to," Maggie said. "I still remember this area pretty well."

On the far corner, with a meticulously groomed front lawn, was a stately New Orleans-style house with tall French doors instead of windows and a wraparound porch. "That one with all the lace curtains?" Mac asked.

"Nope," Maggie said. "The older place next door." This house was sturdy rather than elegant. There was an original section made of stone with white trim and black shutters. Behind that were at least two additions, one sided in fishscale shingles and the other in clapboard siding. They were both painted a rich cream color.

"Can we go in?" Mac was already opening his door.

"Not until the real estate lady gets here," Maggie said. "But you can check around outside if you want." He flew out of the car.

In a few minutes a black SUV with tinted windows pulled up in front of the house. "Looks like the Secret Service has arrived," Albie observed. The driver's door opened and one long sleek leg ending in a spike-heeled shoe snaked out, followed very slowly by the rest of a statuesque blonde. "She auditioning for a pantyhose commercial?" Albie asked.

"I can't do this." Maggie's voice trailed off.

Albie shook her head. "You have to. It's too late to back out now."

"I can't go in there."

"You stay out here then," Albie said. "I'll do the final inspection with her."

The real estate lady walked over and Maggie got out of the car. She had the strangest feeling she knew this woman from somewhere, "Mrs. Rifkind?" the woman asked.

Maggie extended her hand. "It's Rifkin. You can call me Maggie."

"Fine." It came out as a kind of bleat, as if someone had leaned on her horn. "Caroline Carter, Carter Realty."

Close up, Caroline's perfection was marred. There were small powdery deposits of foundation in the faint creases at her lips and eyes. Her hair was stiffly perfect, like a helmet. The overly tanned skin of her cleavage had a hide-like texture.

"Same last name as the firm," Maggie said. "Any relationship?"

Caroline took a little long to answer. "Does it make a difference?" she finally asked.

"Not really," Maggie said.

Caroline looked at her watch. "We don't have much time before the closing. We should get started."

"This is my friend Alberta O'Brien," Maggie introduced Albie. "She's going to do the inspection for me."

Caroline's face tightened. "Won't you be coming in?"

Maggie shook her head. "I'll wait here."

"You're going to buy this house without ever seeing it?"

Maggie looked past her. "I've seen enough," she said.

🔥 🔥 🔥

Mac stood on the stone front porch. They were taking forever. Finally Albie and the real estate lady came across the street. "Let's go see inside," Albie said.

"What about Mom?"

"She said for us to go ahead."

The real estate lady went in first. The front door opened straight into the living room. More rocks, a big stone fireplace that took up one whole wall. Whoever built this place was in love with rocks. Mac took his time walking around the room, turning to see it from different angles. Albie waited for him to finish, then they went through the archway across from the fireplace into the other room at the front of the house. The real estate lady followed them like a spy. "Back in colonial times this was probably the bedroom for the whole family," Mac said.

"It would make a good den now," Albie answered.

"We didn't have one in New York. My dad said wolves have dens."

"As do Cub Scouts. You're not going to turn into one of them either just because you and your mother have a place to watch TV together."

Mac walked across the room. The whole back wall was windows. Outside there was a patio made out of the same stone as the front porch and behind that was the addition at the back of the house. The patio and the side yard were enclosed by a tall fence. Mac liked how the whole thing felt safe and private. Albie was right. This would be a good place to hang out.

They went back to the living room and up the stairs to the second floor. A wide hall ran down the middle, with two bedrooms at the front of the house and one big bedroom and a bathroom in the back. "This is mine," Mac said.

"Which, the big room?"

"No," Mac said. "The whole floor." He stopped. The real estate lady was busy texting somebody. He lowered his voice. "You can have the big room if you come with us. I don't mind taking one of the smaller ones."

Albie shook her head. She made a smile that looked even sadder than a sad face.

"I don't get it. You won't even say why you're not coming with us."

"It's best for all concerned. You and your mother need to start building a life of your own."

"That's not the whole truth." Mac didn't know what made him say that.

The real estate lady closed her phone.

"We'll just be a minute," Albie said. She pulled Mac into one of the bedrooms. "You have to believe this isn't because of you."

"Is it because we're moving away from New York? It's this stupid town, isn't it?"

"I need to start building a life of my own too," Albie answered. "But you know any time you need me I'll come. And you can visit me whenever you please."

The real estate lady opened the door, all huffy. Mac wished his dad was here. His dad always knew how to make people feel bad when they acted annoyed so they'd go away. He needed to keep Albie talking. Eventually she'd tell him the truth.

"We have to get going," the real estate lady said.

"Let's see what else is downstairs." Albie switched to her Nanny Language Lab voice.

Mac hated when she did that. He walked past both her and the real estate lady and didn't wait to see if they were following him. At the bottom of the stairs he went right. Behind the living room was a big kitchen. It had two doors. One went to the secret patio. The other went out back.

"What's behind the house?" Albie asked.

"A breezeway and an oversized garage."

The two of them went over to take a look. Mac went the other way, through the narrow archway between the patio door and the refrigerator. He wanted to be alone, but Albie came after him. They were in a short hall with three doors in it. The first door was a closet. The second one went to the basement. Albie flipped on the light. "We should check it out," she said. Mac ignored her and kept walking toward the third door at the end of the hall. "I'll take a look when we're done up here," Albie said, following him.

The third door led to the addition inside the enclosed yard, the one he'd seen from the den. The room was big, with windows on all three outside walls. It had a walk-in closet and a fancy bathroom. "This will make a perfect room for your mother," Albie said. "She can plant a garden outside and have some-place to sit and relax."

"She doesn't relax," Mac said. "I don't even think she knows how to sit."

"That's why she came back here," Albie said. "To learn. I believe she can be quite successful at relaxing if she just works at it hard enough."

Mac was going to tell her that was a dumb joke, but then he saw she wasn't kidding. That's when he realized maybe even Albie couldn't figure out the real reason she didn't think she should move here with them.

𝄃 𝄃 𝄃

Maggie got out of the car and crossed the street as the three of them came out of the house. Caroline Carter was saying something. She paused as Maggie walked up. "I was just telling your son and your friend that this house has a history."

Albie gave Maggie a look. "That's nice," Maggie said. "Maybe you can finish the story some other time, when we're not in a hurry."

"One of the families who lived here suffered a tragedy."

Maggie looked up the street at a little gray-brown sparrow hopping around. It took off in a burst of flight. "Shit happens," she said. Mac looked mildly shocked.

Caroline seemed not to notice. "People around here thought it was a pretty big deal."

"These houses have been around a long time. I'd be surprised to find one that didn't have some sort of unfortunate event in its history."

"Everything looked good inside," Albie interrupted.

"This is going to be your house," Caroline said. "Don't you want to know about it?" There was something almost taunting in her voice. She looked familiar again for an instant.

"I've never been a fan of gossip," Maggie said.

Caroline's eyes scrunched up a little. "There are lots of locals who still remember. Everybody knew the family. You're bound to hear about it sooner or later."

"Later's good." Maggie looked at her watch. "We still have a little time before the closing. Give me your office address and I'll find it with the GPS and meet you there. The three of us can take a drive through town while we're waiting."

"Fine." Caroline reached into her purse and pulled out a business card. As she walked back to her SUV Maggie glanced down. The card had a colorfully overdone crest, but it was the name that caught her attention. "Carol Ann Bendz Carter," it read. Maggie's fingertips went all tingly and cold. Carol Ann Bendz. No wonder she looked familiar. Maggie had to remind herself she was a grown-up now. In a little over an hour, the purchase of this house would be complete and she would never have to see her childhood tormentor again.

She started a little when Mac spoke. "I wish you came in the house with us. We picked out a room for you."

"It was recently added to the house," Albie said quietly. "No ghosts."

Mac looked from one of them to the other. "Mom," he said, "there's something you're not telling me about this place."

Maggie took a breath. "Suppose this wasn't just some random old house. Would you mind?"

Mac gave her a quick embarrassed hug. "We'll be okay," he said.

🖋 🖋 🖋

Now that the closing was done Maggie hurried up the steep hill on Main Street. She was supposed to meet Albie and Mac at the General Store. She wasn't late, she knew they'd be fine, and yet she couldn't shake the anxious ache that made her guts feel like they were the tail of a kite in a stiff wind.

The early dinner crowd was beginning to filter into town. Lots of the restaurants had outdoor seating. Whatever wasn't a restaurant was either a boutique or a salon. She glanced down a side street and finally saw something she recognized, the tiny park with the table that had a chess board painted on its top. At the next corner the old-fashioned marquee of the Artaud Cinema still jutted out over the sidewalk, though now it showed art films. Maggie crossed the street without waiting for the light to turn green and went onto the porch of the General Store.

A sign over the screen door read "Best Coffee in Dooleysburg" and the place had been painted, but otherwise it looked the same as when she was a kid and it was the Grand Hotel. Something made her stop instead of going in. She wandered over to the edge of the porch and ran her finger around a set of curlicues in the iron railing. An image of being very little and running her finger around this railing in exactly the same way, of someone telling her to come along seized her with a scalding yearning.

"Hey." Albie's voice came from behind her and Maggie turned around. "You must see inside. It's so strange it's fascinating." She looked hard at Maggie. "Everything go okay?"

"Everything went fine," Maggie said, coming back to the present, "except for a momentary failure of common sense when I invited the Wicked Witch to join us for dinner."

"Dear lord!" Albie was aghast.

"Don't worry. She said she already ate."

"Earlier this week," Albie said. "A rib of celery dipped in fat free dressing."

"Snakes only need to eat once a week."

Albie moved closer. "What were you up to when I came out here? You looked a million miles away."

"Just remembering when I was little."

"Good memory?"

"The truth is I was so young I couldn't say. We never came here when I was bigger. At least not that I can remember."

Albie's voice was neutral. "Would you like to tell me about it?"

"There's nothing to tell. It was mostly an impression. If you want a story about when I was big enough to make my own trouble, I remember lots of those."

"I imagine you were fairly expert at that."

"Albie." The way Maggie said her name made Albie stop. "Please reconsider. Please." Albie opened her mouth, but Maggie cut her off. "I'm going to mess up. I know I am. You know I am. There's going to be something critical I'm going to forget to teach him or warn him about, and we're all going to end up paying for it."

Albie shook her head. "You're going to do fine. He's going to do fine. Give yourselves some credit."

"I don't know how to be a mother."

"I know," Albie said gently. "That's why you came here, isn't it? To learn before it's too late?"

"We need you."

"This isn't all about you."

Maggie inhaled sharply, as if someone had just doused her with cold water. "I didn't . . ." she began.

"No," Albie said. "You didn't. You never have. And now I'm not giving you a choice, because I deserve a chance to have a life too." She opened the screen door before Maggie could answer. "Come on," she said, not unkindly. "Your son's inside fraternizing with the local riffraff. He's attracted the attention of the sub-compact version of a juvenile delinquent."

"Oh, geez," Maggie said, heading for the door. "I hope I'm not too late."

"Calm down. MacDonald is not going to turn to the dark side in the space of one cup of hot chocolate. But this would be a good opportunity to start your Mother 101 training."

4

Deep down inside, way down where he was sure nobody could see, Carl Bendz wondered if he might be a failure. Sure, he had money out the wazoo and a Dynasty of Dealerships no ordinary man could have put together. But he was never going to realize his dream of a Pangaea of car lots reigning over the north side of town, a dozen brands of luxury, every car with the Bendz name affixed to its trunk in little silver letters. He was one brand short, stuck at eleven brands. He simply didn't have the space to bring in a twelfth line and still maintain his sales numbers on the existing eleven. He obsessed over this like a mathematician with an insoluble equation. It provided him with intellectual stimulation at the dullest cultural events, the most turgid family gatherings and every town meeting where the topic didn't directly affect him. It glowed with a heat none of his human relationships could sustain.

Though he grabbed up every piece of land around his lots as circumstances permitted and was not above helping circumstances along, he had lost the one big parcel that was the key to his success. In the only strategic error he ever made, he waited patiently for the old farmer who owned the desired piece of land to drop dead. He never suspected somebody else was also waiting. A bidding war ensued, Bendz versus some anonymous coward who, he noted with disdain, didn't even have a logo. What Mr. Nobody did have was a bottomless wallet, and he walked off with the land.

Bendz might have drowned in the hopeless gloom of this loss had he not decided that revenge was a passable substitute for victory. The parcel was landlocked, and Bendz owned all the rights of way. When the new owner filed plans to build the North End Plaza, a goddamn strip mall, Bendz wouldn't let him have access for a driveway. A different sort of bidding war ensued, this time to see who could buy off more members of the Zoning Board. After a couple of years the North End Plaza did get built, but it only had one skinny little driveway. Hardly anybody but the people who worked there even knew it existed. Bendz sat back, sure it was only a matter of time before the place went under. He was wrong. It made no sense, but the owner hung on, year after year.

Bendz finally recognized that patience doesn't pay. He had to go after that land, and to do that he needed enough money to drown his unknown adversary. This was the perfect time to take on a partner, someone rich enough to enable him to get away with anything and gullible enough to let him do it. That's where Crossley Carter came in. While Carter had the intelligence and ambition of plankton, he was the sole heir to the real estate fortune his father made when the town got its second wind. He was so goddamn dumb he didn't even know how much money was in all those piles he was tripping over. He was happy to let Bendz be the idea man.

The instant he got a look at Carter's books Bendz learned the painful truth about who the secret owner of the North End Plaza was. The knowledge nearly did him in. How could he continue to let Carter have a piece of the action when the bastard was standing between him and his dream? Worse, now that they were knee-deep in each other's business, how was he going to give Carter the shafting he deserved without getting a length of pole up his own butt? In desperation he flew to Vegas, hoping to find inspiration in losing a pile of Carter's money. At 4 AM on his third night there, sitting at the $500 blackjack table with a dazzling bimbo on each arm, he had his epiphany. Revenge was not the answer. He got the next flight home and arrived, red-eyed and smelly, in his daughter's bedroom. Awakening Carol Ann from her own drunken stupor, he informed her she was going to marry Carter's only son, Wesley.

He was prepared for a loud and strenuous argument. He was mistaken. Always alert to the potential deal, Carol Ann demanded to know was what was in it for her. Bendz handed over the Tiffany pendant he'd been saving for the next time he needed to placate his wife. Carol Ann said he could do better. Bendz scurried to his computer and returned with a list of Carter's investments. He watched, trying not to fidget, while Carol Ann took her time reading it. Then, to his surprise and delight, she demanded to know what was in it for him. Feeling shy for reasons he couldn't explain, Bendz confessed that he wanted her to get title to the North End Plaza and hand it over to him. He would pay her generously for it, of course.

And so, in exchange for her first serious diamond and the chance to develop her natural talent for finding opportunity in the misfortune of others, Carol Ann agreed to marry the richest, dumbest boy in town. Once she was Mrs. Carter it didn't take her long to commandeer the local real estate market or tidy up the Bendz reputation. And she found her new status in the community made it easy to discreetly fill any gaps in her marital satisfaction. The whole plan went so smoothly that Bendz never suspected it was doomed from the start. It turned out he had done such an effective job of forcing the North End Plaza into debt that no bank was willing to back him in taking it over.

Bendz was not a quitter. His dream might be out of reach, but he could still impress people. He decided to build a new showroom, something even the word ostentatious couldn't do justice. When it was done the showroom was nearly half a mile long. It sat on a rise, towering over the surrounding landscape. The building was a classic Greek temple style, with huge columns and a pediment roof. Every surface was made of pale beige marble and the front doors were big enough to accommodate a jumbo jet. Smells of burnished leather and new car were pumped onto the cavernous sales floor like sacred incense. Ornately framed blow-ups of Bendz taken from his ads in *The Daily Intellectual* adorned the walls. Customers sat in overstuffed leather chairs sipping Fair Trade coffee or Italian sodas while they finalized their purchases, served by showroom staff who could have been waiters in a high-end restaurant. No detail except the occasional encounter with Bendz himself ever detracted from the pampered luxury of a Bendz Automotive experience.

It was a given that he would show up at the dealership every day. He always made a grand entrance, trolling around the sales floor to play with the merchandise and harass the staff before retiring to his plush office on the second floor balcony. Occasionally he would step out onto the balcony like he was about to give an audience, but even when he was sequestered he was watching everything. There were security cameras all over the building that fed a wall of video monitors in his office. The staff disliked being under constant scrutiny, but most of them considered it preferable to having him pop into a sales cube and screw up their deals like he did in the old days.

Today the main cameras showed Harry Butts coming in the big front doors. Harry's official title was "Showroom Coordinator", but everyone knew he was Bendz's errand boy. Harry wasn't the shiniest penny in the bank, but he was as faithful as a man could get without crossing over the line to dog. People joked that he and his brother Joe, the cop, made a deal when the genes were being shuffled that Harry could have all the hair if he let Joe have all the brains. Bendz suspected Harry weighed the two piles and went for the better deal.

Harry was not looking happy. As he made his way across the showroom his pace slowed and his shoulders slumped. Bendz steeled himself for the report of a failed mission. He answered the knock on his door with a gruff, "Yeah?"

Harry came in. He kept his head down, but Bendz could see him checking out of the corner of his eye, looking for some indication of how bad Bendz's mood already was. Bendz gave away nothing.

Harry took a deep breath and got directly to the point. "She bought a car." Bendz stared at him. "Not from us," Harry added.

"I know not from us, dammit!" Bendz exploded.

Harry flinched. "I dropped by, like you told me to. Gave her a Welcome Wagon type basket and my card."

"That's it?" Bendz demanded. "You figure some furniture polish and a few pieces of hard candy are gonna sell a luxury vehicle?"

"No, no, boss. No. That was a couple days ago. So I go back yesterday, I ring the doorbell. She comes out, I ask her, can you spare a few minutes, she says sure."

"Yeah?"

"So I start explaining how, being she's already done business with the family, Carol Ann being her realtor and all, we could take care of her needs for a car."

Harry appeared to have followed instructions. But this woman just bought a house for cash. Squeezing a car out of her should have been like falling off a log. "So where'd you drop the ball?"

"That's just it," Harry said. "She invites me in, offers me a cup of coffee which, by the way, was the worst shit I ever drank in my life, and then proceeds to run my ass up the flagpole about why do we only have eleven brands instead of an even dozen. I'm telling you, she was like a dog with a bone."

Bendz tried not to breathe too heavy. "So what did you tell her?"

"I didn't get a chance to tell her anything. She didn't even shut up long enough to take a breath. I swear, she just kept jamming my channels."

"She had to stop sooner or later. You're here aren't you?"

"Yeah well, okay, she finally loses her wind, and I start to pitch her on the kind of car a woman with a teenage kid needs. You know, dependability, great safety ratings, good handling for when the kid gets old enough to drive, but not so hot he feels the urge to race around, yada, yada, yada. And she cuts me off and says, 'If Carl's last name is Bendz, how come he doesn't carry Mercedes?'"

Bendz looked at him in disbelief. "She said something that dumb?" Harry lifted his shoulders and nodded. "So what did you tell her?"

"The truth. You spell your name different. You have a 'd' before the 'z'."

Bendz felt like the top of his head was going to blow off. "That was the best you could do?" he exploded.

"No, no, Carl." Harry waved his hands like he was trying to land a rogue jumbo jet. "That was just for starters. Then I talked about the BMW, the big one, just like you told me to. About how safe it is and how it keeps a great trade-in value and our service plans. I did everything I could."

Bendz calmed down. You can't lose the game, he told himself, to somebody who's playing on a different field. "Well," he said philosophically, "if she had her mind made up on a Mercedes, there isn't much we can do about that."

Harry seemed to shrink down inside his suit. "Well, that's the thing," he began. "I was just walking down State Street, right in front of the Artaud Cinema, and this big green BMW 7 Series pulls up next to me and honks. So I look over, and it's her. She stops right there in the middle of the street, holding up traffic, and rolls down the window and yells, 'Thanks! I was going to buy a Mercedes, but after you talked to me I decided to go for this instead!' And I say, 'So you test driving?' And she goes, 'Nah. I checked around online and got a great deal. Thanks again!' And she drives off and leaves me standing there with my pants down around my ankles for the whole street to see."

Bendz felt surprisingly calm. "Call your brother," he said. "I think it's time we asked Officer Joe for some help welcoming our new neighbor to town."

☙ ☙ ☙

"Don," Principal Babson said, "I appreciate how to some people you seem to be a star. But life is not a democracy, and we are not having a discussion."

Don Dickerman clenched his jaw. He tried to ignore Babson's tone, tried not to imagine how easy it would be for Babson, a few sheets to the wind, to slip and address him as "boy". He knew it was a waste of time to confront Babson. He would do it anyway, sooner or later. But not yet. Classes hadn't even started. "With all due respect, sir . . ." he began.

Babson held up his hand. "Statements that begin like that never end in a satisfactory way." His grin went from slightly ingratiating to predatory. "And you need this to have a satisfactory outcome."

"Satisfactory to whom, sir?" He knew that was a mistake as soon as he heard it come out of his mouth. It felt good, but it was going to cost him. This time it wasn't about being a black man disagreeing with a white superior. Babson was just following orders.

"If you believe there is an ethical issue here," Babson turned red, "put it on the table!"

"Excuse me, sir." He had to back this way down. "I sincerely apologize for offending you." That was a nice touch. Most people, too proud to be smart, apologized by saying, "*if* I offended you" making it obvious they weren't really apologizing at all.

"Apology accepted," Babson said. He lost the wolfish grin.

"Sir, I sincerely do not want to create a bad situation for anyone, least of all the School Board or yourself." Another nice touch. Pompous jerks always preferred 'yourself' to the grammatically correct 'you'.

"Understood." Babson was all business now. "So we don't have an issue."

"Sir, if I may, and my intent here is not to self-aggrandize, but my success with even the most challenging students is largely due to my familiarity with their cultural norms."

"As a matter of fact," Babson leaned way back in his chair, "I've heard complaints that you take familiarity too far."

"Sir?" He was dumbfounded. "Do you have something specific in mind? To help me identify the offending behavior?"

"You encourage your students to address you by your first name."

He shook his head slightly. "They call me 'Mr. Don'."

"What kind of respect do you think I would command if I let students call me Mr. Bill?"

Probably the same kind you get right now, Mr. Don thought, since you'll never figure out respect isn't something you *command*. "Sir," he said, "your last name hardly presents the same kind of challenge mine does. You have to agree Dickerman is an unfortunate last name for a high school teacher."

Babson cleared his throat. "Getting back to the topic at hand, a well-rounded musical education needs to include the classics."

"Barry Manilow is *not* the classics. Especially not for a marching band."

Babson sighed impatiently. "We'll review this one more time. The Chipmunk, whose opinion is above question, considers Barry Manilow to be classic."

"If Mrs. Chipmunk is such a Manilow fan, maybe he should just take her to a show."

"Is that supposed to be funny?"

Mr. Don had the good sense not to answer.

"Because I'm not laughing. Carl Bendz buys all the uniforms for our marching unit. Every dime you make from bake sales and car washes goes to your discretionary fund thanks to that man! How much of a sacrifice is it to play his choice of music at a parade?"

"It's not just the parade, sir. It's the rehearsals. And it's more than just my own personal suffering. The kids have to rehearse even on their days off. If I make them play things they hate, they'll stop showing up."

"We all have our challenges."

"And there is no marching band arrangement of 'I Write the Songs'."

Babson stood up, indicating the meeting was over. "Don, I appreciate the sacrifices a man with your gifts makes to teach in a public school." He emphasized the word *public*. "Just as I know you will appreciate our position once you've had a chance to consider it. Think things over. It's not like The Chipmunk is being unreasonable. He's giving you a whole school year to make this happen, plenty of time to come up with some great tunes. I'm sure you'll figure it out." Babson opened his door and patted Mr. Don on the back, steering him out of the office. Standing next to his assistant's desk, he made a show of pumping Mr. Don's hand and thanking him for his efforts. Then he held the outer office door open until Mr. Don went through, closing it quietly behind him. He turned to his assistant. "Put a red sticker on his file."

The woman's mouth dropped open. "Mr. Don?" she asked.

"Yes Mr. Don," Babson snapped. "The man's a troublemaker."

Out in the hall, Mr. Don played the Trio section of Haydn's Symphony no. 38 in his head. It worked momentarily, but as he walked to his Band Room he started to steam. He was here to teach kids to love music, not to waste his time with local politics. He didn't care if the whole town sucked up to The Chipmunk. The man was not a philanthropist, he was merely using his money to shop at the mall of his twisted fantasies. By the time Mr. Don got to the Band Room, he had worked up a fury. He didn't notice the kid standing there until after he stormed in and slammed the door.

The poor kid almost jumped out of his skin. "I can come back," he stammered.

Mr. Don laughed. "Somebody scared me like that, I sure wouldn't come back."

The kid relaxed a little. "Are you Mr. Dickerman?"

"Everybody calls me Mr. Don. What can I do for you?"

"We just moved here," the kid said. "I'd like to be in the band."

"You have a name?"

"MacDonald Rifkin. Everybody calls me Mac."

"So, Mac, you ever been in marching band before?"

Mac looked amused. "They don't have a marching band at Julliard."

"You're coming here from Julliard?" Mr. Don was amazed.

"Nah. It's just a good line. But they don't have marching bands at any of the schools I did get into."

"So if you got into other schools what made you decide to come here?"

Mac shrugged. "It wasn't up to me."

Mr. Don looked at him a minute, taking his measure. "You want to try out for my marching band?"

"I was thinking about a different kind of band. I don't think what I play is marching band stuff."

"What do you play?"

"My dad and I used to listen to Buddy Rich all the time. When he was alive. My dad, I mean." He paused awkwardly.

Mr. Don felt for him. "So you play the drums."

Mac nodded. "And guitar. But I'm better on drums."

"You willing to play for me now?"

"Sure." Mac pulled a pair of drumsticks out of his backpack. Mr. Don nodded toward the drum set in the corner of the room. Mac walked over, full of self-confidence. He sat down, made some minor adjustments, and then launched straight into a jazz riff. He played with energy and enthusiasm, but he sucked. Mr. Don let him go for as long as he could take. "Okay, I got it," he said loudly.

"So do I get in?"

Mr. Don paused so his answer would appear to bear the weight of thoughtful consideration. "You ever take lessons?" he asked.

"Sometimes," Mac said. "But my dad taught me all the good stuff. Whenever he was home."

"Well, you're right that what you play is not marching band material. But I also have a jazz band. I'll warn you right now that the people in it make it their entire focus. We practice crazy hours. We go to competitions on weekends and holidays when sensible people are having a day off. It's not just a big commitment, it's a big responsibility. You're not ready yet, but if you're willing to work hard and take lessons, I'll let you start out by sitting with us as back up on drums. You want in?"

Mac's eyes popped with excitement. "Yes," he breathed.

"I mean it about taking lessons. Your mother's going to have to agree to that too."

"Okay! I mean, she will!"

"And you're going to have to practice your butt off."

"I will! I promise."

"Good." Mr. Don walked to his desk and found the required forms. "Bring these back after they're signed. If you don't have a teacher you prefer, there are a couple of good ones who give lessons at the music store in town. Don't wait until we're into the school year to get started. The sooner the better."

"Yes, sir," Mac said. He hurried out of the room, turning at the door to yell, "Thanks!" again.

Mr. Don sighed. He should probably start thinking about bribing his current drum chair to give up anything riskier than sleeping. If they ever had to let this new kid play they could kiss the State trophy goodbye. And if Babson ever figured out what he'd just done, the heat would turn up so high even Mr. Don would get a tan. Refusing to make his band march to Barry Manilow was small potatoes compared to Babson's favorite beef. The grievance that never went away was that Mr. Don refused to put in some ringers to bring home that trophy from State. At least once a week Babson snagged him in front of the main lobby display case and he had to put up with that same tired old line of shit about how the empty spot reserved for the State Band Trophy was glaring at them like a missing front tooth. It was not going to be pleasant if Babson figured out his drum chair backup was now a kid who played like a pile-up on the Turnpike.

5

Mac came into the kitchen with a handful of mail. "I got something from the school."

"Let me see," Maggie said.

He ignored her and opened the letter. "It's nothing important." He handed Maggie the paper. It was a list of recommended readings and supplies for the fall term.

Maggie felt that familiar twinge of blossoming panic. Back at private school in New York parents were responsible for making sure tuition bills got paid. That was it. Certain items dictated by fad and fashion were purchased at the beginning of every year, but anything that was actually important was taken care of by somebody who got paid to know how to do it. Now that was her job, and Maggie knew it was only a matter of time until she screwed something up—the location of the bus stop, filling out some critical form, remembering what Mac wanted for lunch. Her expertise was in piecing together severed arteries and stitching up ruptured organs. She should be taking up something that capitalized on her skills, like quilting. She should not be depended on for those things where she had neither experience nor aptitude. She stared at the letter, wondering what to do about it.

"Hey," Mac said, "when you're done freaking out, can you take me into town to buy that stuff?"

⌐ ⌐ ⌐

Maggie looked up Main Street. They were outside Dooley Books, having bought everything on the reading list. Directly across the street was Randolph's Sporting Goods, and Maggie thought they should look at new backpacks even if Mac preferred his old beat-up one. She couldn't see how it made any sense for them to walk all the way uphill to cross at the light. It's not like there was any traffic. "Come on," she said, grabbing Mac's arm.

Though she'd looked both ways for cars, she hadn't thought to check the opposite sidewalk. Waiting for them when they stepped onto the curb was a balding, pot-bellied policeman. "Cheese it," she said under her breath, "the cops." Mac didn't move. He was glued to the sidewalk like he'd just caught a glimpse of Medusa.

"Peace Officer, ma'am." The cop had heard her.

Maggie strained to see the name on his badge. "Afternoon, Officer . . . Butts." Though she really tried hard to stifle it, the tail end of a snicker slipped out. The cop gave her a hard look and reached for something in his back pocket. After years of dealing with New York's finest Maggie knew that a summons pad could hide, like a coiled asp, in the dark recesses of even the snuggest uniform. "You're not serious," she said. "You're going to give me a ticket?"

"Zero tolerance, ma'am."

"For crossing the street?" Maggie's voice rose.

"For jaywalking. There's no jaywalking in Dooleysburg."

"There's no jaywalking in Tokyo," she snapped, "because people in Japan aren't aware it can be done. Everywhere else in the world people believe that the shortest distance between two points is a straight line." She caught herself. "See, we were over there at Dooley Books and then we needed to come to Randolph's because we're buying Supplies and Sundry Necessities." She held out the list that had come in the mail, but Peace Officer Butts did not seem interested. "We just needed to get across the street."

He pulled out a pen and flipped the pad open.

"Okay, Joe, hold on."

Maggie looked around. The guy who had just spoken walked closer. He had the graceful build of somebody who ran, but not often enough to be obsessive. His dark tee shirt and jeans had seen better days, and he needed a shave. Maggie instantly made him for a cop. She always felt them giving off an aura like they were entitled to withhold or dispense grace. No doubt he'd appraised her as well.

"You're the new family that moved into the Morello place, right?"

He scored some points for referring to them as a family, but Maggie was beginning to tire of the small town slant. "We are."

"JD Charles. I'm the Chief of Police." He extended his hand.

Maggie shook it. "Maggie Rifkin. This is my son Mac."

JD shook Mac's hand as well. "Officer, we'll give the Rifkins a warning this time."

Butts' fleshy cheeks turned bright pink. With a sullen shrug, he walked a little way up the street and started chalking tires.

"Thanks," Maggie said. Then she whispered, "Let's go," and nudged Mac toward the store.

"Hang on a minute," JD said. "Officer Butts can be a little zealous, but he was right. Next time, use the crosswalk. Saves us from having to scrape you up later."

Maggie struggled against her natural inclination to react badly to authority and lost. "Consider us appropriately chastised."

JD stiffened. "This is not New York."

Maggie looked him up and down. "I can see that."

The remaining vestiges of his easy-going manner disappeared. "I'm off duty. That doesn't change my responsibility to uphold the law or relieve you from yours to obey it."

"Right," Maggie said. "Got it." She turned to go into Randolph's.

"Hold it." JD's tone stopped her. "Son," he addressed Mac, "go on inside. I need to speak to your mother for a minute."

Mac looked at Maggie. She had a hard time interpreting his expression. "Go ahead," she said. "I'll be right there." Once Mac was inside she turned back to Chief Charles. "Yes?"

"I would ask you to consider setting a more appropriate example for your son."

Maggie stared at him. "My son is my highest priority."

"That being the case, maybe you can prioritize trying not to frighten him."

"Am I free to go?" Maggie tried to ignore the angry pulse in her neck.

"In a minute. You're new here, so let me assure you, we're pretty easy to get along with as long as you keep in mind the expectation that adults will act like adults."

"I won't jaywalk again," she said curtly.

The chief gave her a hard look, then walked away. Maggie marched into Randolph's. Mac was standing in front of one of the displays. "Well," she said, walking up, trying to sound amused, "I just got scolded by the town's dad."

Mac didn't reply. She noticed then that he wasn't really looking at the backpacks, he was just moving them around. She waited for him to acknowledge her, but he didn't. "That didn't upset you, did it?"

Mac walked away. Maggie followed him, getting more rattled. "Want to tell me what's up?" she finally asked.

"Why did you act like that?" There was something in his tone Maggie didn't recognize.

"I don't like bullies."

"Mom," he said, lowering his voice, "that was the cop who arrested the kid from the General Store. The one Albie and I saw on the webcam!"

"Who? The police chief?"

"No! That Butts guy!"

"Then he's got an appropriate name."

Mac didn't laugh. "Nobody here knows me. Do you have to make such a big deal out of everything?"

Now Maggie had a name for the unknown quantity in his voice. Exasperation. "I'm sorry. I thought the whole thing was pretty silly."

"How come you never care how other people feel?" Mac walked away again.

Maggie was stunned. She followed him to the next rack, a selection of messenger bags. "I didn't realize . . ."

"You can't do stuff like that. We're not in New York anymore." Mac moved on.

This time Maggie didn't follow. He'd never acted like this before. What did that police chief, a total stranger, see that she missed? If the way she saw things was wrong, how would she ever figure out what right was? She waited for Mac to decide on a pack, then walked up to the register behind him and paid without saying anything. She wanted to fix things so badly her throat ached, but she had no idea where to begin.

Mac took his package and they went outside. "Want to get something from the General Store?" he asked.

"Sure." Maggie kept her answer to one word, afraid that something she'd say would just mess things up further. They went up the hill and into the General Store's big main room. The same undersized kid Albie warned her about a few weeks ago was behind the counter.

"Ay," he greeted Mac.

"Hi," Mac answered.

Nobody acknowledged Maggie. Mac ordered a decaf cappuccino. Maggie got a double espresso. The kid behind the counter reached over and took their money, then motioned for them to move down the line. When their coffees were ready they found a couple of chairs.

Mac took the lid off his decaf and stirred in two packets of raw sugar. Maggie took a sip of her espresso. It was bitter, which seemed fitting. "So," she began tentatively, "are you friends with him?"

"Who?" Mac asked. "Morsel?"

Maggie shot him a look. "It's not very nice to call him that. Doesn't he have a real name?"

Mac waited long enough before answering to make it clear his goodwill had still not recovered. "That's what he told me to call him."

"So you know him pretty well?"

Mac shrugged. "Everybody knows Morsel."

Considering the kid worked at the local hangout, that seemed reasonable. Still, Maggie felt wary about him.

Morsel came out from behind the counter and began wiping down tables with a stained white rag. He turned to Mac. "You going to the parade tomorrow?"

"I guess," Mac said.

"Cool," Morsel said. "Maybe I'll see you there."

"Is the Labor Day Parade a big deal around here?" Maggie asked. Her heart was pounding. She hoped talking to Morsel wouldn't violate some unspoken rule.

Morsel looked like he really wanted to let her squirm, but his natural loquaciousness got the better of him. "People get pretty excited about it. Especially The Chipmunk."

"There's a chipmunk?" Maggie asked. "On a leash or something?"

Morsel snorted. "Nah. It's that old fart who owns all the car dealerships."

"Carl Bendz? He didn't look like a chipmunk when I saw him."

Mac looked pained, but Morsel said, "I like that. That's pretty funny."

"So he dresses up like a chipmunk?" Maggie asked.

"Yeah."

"And the little kids get excited about it?"

"Not the kids." Morsel shook his head. "That's what I'm telling you. The townies get all worked up."

"The adults? That's kind of odd, isn't it?"

Morsel looked at her. "I guess that depends what else you got going on to be excited about, don't it?"

🪶 🪶 🪶

The next morning, Mac slept until almost eleven, another sign of his metamorphosis. At least when he came downstairs he seemed more like his old self. "You still want to go to the parade?" Maggie asked.

"Kind of."

"Well, it starts in about an hour, so if we're going we'll need to leave soon."

"It only takes five minutes to drive to town."

"We have to walk. All the streets will be closed."

"Okay," Mac said. "I just have to put my shoes on."

He was back in a few minutes, and they set off. They went through the oldest part of town, the neighborhood surrounding the Courthouse. The streets here were too narrow for sidewalks, almost alleyways. The houses looked like they'd been taken from a Victorian Christmas card, tall and narrow, with fancy picket fences and miniature cottage gardens. Many of them had ornate gingerbread trim and little wooden plaques that proudly told their histories. When Maggie told Mac that this area was once so full of crime and poverty that people wouldn't even walk here in broad daylight he couldn't believe it. She wondered if that other Dooleysburg had somehow darkened and become more menacing in her memory.

As they got to the center of town the sidewalks became so crowded they had to walk in the street. They went all the way to the sawhorse barrier at the end of the parade route without finding an open spot. Maggie was about to suggest they double back when Mac yelled, "Hey!" He'd spotted Morsel, waving energetically from the second row of the viewing stand on the corner. Morsel looked like he needed a shower, or at least a change of clothes. Maggie imagined when they got closer they'd be able to tell exactly what the breakfast specials had been at the General Store that morning. The upside of Morsel's deficient hygiene was that despite the crowds on the bleachers, nobody was within sniffing distance on either side of him.

"Dude!" Morsel called. "I saved some space for you!"

"Do you really think he saved it for us?" Maggie asked.

"At this point, do you care?"

They struggled through the jostling, annoyed crowd. When they finally sat down, all they could see were the backs of the people on the sidewalk. "Good seats," Maggie said.

"Have some faith here, Mrs. R," Morsel said.

"Moses going to come along?"

Morsel looked confused. "Moses who?"

"Never mind," she said.

There was a blast of sound, followed by a low-pitched hum of anticipation from the crowd. "What's going on?" Mac asked.

"Somebody must've spotted The Chipmunk," Morsel answered.

"I'm really curious," Maggie said. "I wish we could see."

Morsel gave Mac a look that might have been sympathy. "You want to see," he said, "get up." As he said it, people around them began standing up on the bleachers.

Maggie did the same. She could see over the crowd now. The sound of the marching band was getting closer, but the first group to come into view was a bunch of kids so little that bystanders would periodically have to round up the strays and point them back in the right direction.

"Those are the Pee Wee Explorers," Morsel said.

"They must have some interesting expeditions," Maggie said.

"They don't explore nothing," he replied. "It's like a club. They start out with the little kids, but they got all ages."

"Do you belong?" Maggie asked.

Morsel rolled his eyes. "Sure," he said. "But I only go on the nights I don't have ballet."

"It wasn't such a stupid question. You said they have all ages."

"Well, see that guy who can't even get them lined up straight? He's a cop." Morsel stopped suddenly.

Maggie suppressed the urge to say, yeah, I guess you already get to spend enough time with the cops. She turned back to the parade. An odd assortment of participants marched past over the next several minutes, from Boy Scouts and acrobats to clutches of pigeon-shaped women in colonial garb. Her favorite was a bunch of elderly gentlemen in garishly sequined and feathered costumes. They marched to their own rhythm, with great dignity like a defeated army. "Excommunicated Mummers?" Maggie asked.

"They used to be the mascots," the woman next to her answered.

"They look perfect for the job," Maggie said. "What happened?"

The woman sized her up. "Bendz," she said, without appearing to move her lips. "Nobody will say it was him, but who else would've cared?"

"What'd he do?"

"He got Town Council to hire a *consultant*." She said the word like it was a smelly dead thing. "Did a study and said Council needed to appoint a new mascot."

"And what did the old mascots say about that?"

The woman made a noise. "Most of them were smart enough not to say anything."

"Why?" Maggie was amused. "What happened if they did?"

"Took them out and shot them," the woman said.

Maggie took a sharp breath. "Seriously?"

The woman looked at her with open contempt. "You need to borrow my swipchisel?"

It took Maggie a second to figure this out. "Does that mean you're pulling my leg?"

"Yeah," the woman said. "Pretty much."

"So what really happened?"

The woman sighed, no longer interested. "Bendz wanted to be mascot. He paid for the consultant, put out the money for his own costume, bought his own float. Who cares if a bunch of old farts piss and moan about it?"

"Why would he do that?"

"How do I know? Maybe he woke up in a sweat one night worrying that somebody would come along that us idiots like better." She looked at Maggie again. "You're new around here, aren't you?"

"Kind of," Maggie said. It was easier than getting into the details.

"Well, get ready," she said cryptically, "because things are going to get wild." She turned her attention back to the parade.

For a while Maggie paid attention too, but the heat was making her wilt. "How much longer till something interesting happens?" she asked the woman.

"Trust me, you'll know The Chipmunk's coming long before he gets here."

"You think I've got time to go get a drink?" The woman shrugged. "You want anything?"

"Not unless somebody's mixing Margaritas."

Maggie turned to Mac. "I'll be back," she said. "I need to get some water."

"Don't take too long," Mac said. "I'd hate for you to miss it if things finally get good."

Maggie climbed off the viewing stand and cut through the parking lot behind it to the back entrance of Dooley Books. She took her time walking to the refrigerated cases near the registers, basking in the air conditioning. As she grabbed a few bottles of water she noticed a poster on the wall. "Women of a Certain Age," it said in red block letters, "Come join together in an empowering Book Group." In smaller font it gave the details. The bookstore was going to sponsor a monthly meeting. Maggie wasn't sure what 'a certain age' might be, but it didn't sound very appealing.

Mac was beginning to worry by the time she got back to the viewing stand. "I was afraid you were going to miss it!" he said, his voice cracking slightly.

"You really think The Chipmunk is going to be worth all this excitement?"

"Look!" He pointed, a hint of little boy in his gesture.

Because of the way the street curved, at first all Maggie could see was the marching band. It took her a minute to notice what looked like swaying treetops towering over their last row. The crowd was jostling around now, small manic squeals breaking out here and there. Then the float came into view. It was a forest scene of impressive scale. The tree trunks were as big around as outhouses. The forest floor was littered with chair-sized red and yellow toadstools where scantily clad elves sat, waving to the crowd. In the center of the float, roosting on a nest of oversized evergreen branches, was a man-sized Chipmunk in a worn costume. The Chipmunk head bore an innocent grin, but the man inside leaned toward the closest elf in a predatory way. The tractor pulling the float ground to a halt in front of the viewing stand and shouts of "Carl!" exploded from the crowd amid thunderous applause.

Maggie turned to the woman who'd spoken to her earlier. "This is it?" she asked. "Everybody's going apeshit over a guy in a chipmunk suit?"

"Hang on," the woman said. "The fun is just beginning."

As if on cue, the band finished with a huge crashing of cymbals and the largest tree on the float belched. Its top flew up and back on a hinge, and small, hard objects blew out, pelting the crowded sidewalks. Stunned, Maggie watched as people in the strike zone hunched over, trying to cover their heads and protect their children. The objects flying out of the tree were Starlight Mints, Jolly Ranchers, Root Beer Barrels, assorted hard candies that bounced off the pavement and the crowd like slingshotted pebbles. The air filled with exclamations of pain. And then, as quickly as it had begun, the hail was over and the fulsome elves were tugging on ropes to raise the treetop back into place. The Chipmunk was still waving, but no one was paying attention. All around, people scrambled madly, hunting in the debris.

"What am I missing?" Maggie asked the woman.

"Every once in a blue moon," she replied sourly, "he puts a car key in there. It's been a few years since somebody found one. That always increases the interest."

"What happens if you find it?"

"You get a year's lease."

"On a car?"

"No, on a house in the Baltics. Of course a car. You want to hop down there and join the fun?"

"No thanks," Maggie said. "How come you're not looking?"

"My neighbor works for him," the woman said contemptuously. "He didn't have to take anything back under the Lemon Law this year. There's not going to be any key."

Maggie looked at Mac. "I swear I didn't know about any of this."

"It's okay, Mom," he replied. "It makes sense that they have a chipmunk for a mascot, cause they're nuts."

6

Maggie completely forgot about the Book Group until she saw the announcement in *The Daily Intellectual*. These days the bulk of her time seemed to be devoted to forgetting. Ever since Mac started school a few weeks ago, she couldn't keep track of anything. She woke up with her mind swirling with lists, so much to get done she couldn't sort it out. As the day wore on, she would force herself to pick one thing, but then couldn't stay with it long enough to make much progress. She couldn't even read. She would pick up a book and find herself going over the same sentences she'd read before, hearing the words sound vaguely familiar in her head without understanding what they meant.

Even if she wasn't having trouble concentrating there was no way she could imagine reading this month's Book Group selection. It was called *Taking Pride in Your Shortened Stride*. Still, she was curious to see who might consider themselves to be "women of a certain age," so she decided to go to the meeting. It was a glorious day out, sunny but cool, and yet it made her feel vaguely sad, as if she was missing something important. She decided it would do her good to walk to town.

She arrived at Dooley Books two minutes after the meeting start time and was proud of herself for doing it. Two minutes late made her slightly anxious, but not enough to ignite the panic she felt when she thought about missing the start of anything. She was convinced that if she was late there would be some key piece of information she'd miss. She had a hard enough time figuring out the rules everyone else seemed to know under the best of circumstances. Being late would only increase the odds against her. But she hated being early too, standing around without enough other people there for her to feel invisible. She wanted to be a rogue electron, caroming around, stopping momentarily when she collided with something, but never remaining part of anything for long.

It took a few minutes to find the group in the reading alcove between Seasonal and Travel. They were sitting in a quietly tense circle, an untouched platter of cubed fruit and cheese on the coffee table in their midst. Only two empty seats were left. One was occupied by a shapeless velvet patchwork sack. The woman sitting next to it, looking like an escapee from a band of well-to-do gypsies, glared at Maggie implying that the sack, like an imaginary childhood friend, was entitled to its own chair. The other open space was half of a loveseat. Everyone had started staring at her, so Maggie walked over and sat there. The other woman on the sofa, busy filling out nametags, didn't look up.

Maggie glanced around, discreetly. It looked like she wasn't the only one who perceived some ambiguity in the phrase "women of a certain age." These women didn't have much in common. The most striking one was whippet thin, well-preserved enough so it was impossible to figure out how old she really was. She wore tastefully casual clothing that murmured "money, money" with the persistence of a gentle breeze. Her jewelry was the real deal, but intentionally designed to look like costume stuff, as if it had gone through a gauche wormhole. Her nametag read, "Lillian B."

The woman to Maggie's immediate left looked disturbingly familiar. Her khakis and oxford cloth shirt could have popped right off the gardening shelves behind her. In fact, given a pair of wellies and a hot glue gun, she could have been Martha Stewart's body double. She even had the trademark artificially unkempt blonde hair. Maggie realized the woman was checking her out as well. She extended her hand. "Maggie Rifkin," she said.

Martha's doppelganger reached over and shook hands. "Martha Stewart," she said. Maggie was at a loss for words. "I know," the woman continued. "Regrettable coincidence. I couldn't wait to get married and change my last name, and look what happened."

"Did you have an unfortunate maiden name?" Maggie asked cautiously.

Martha looked at her a long moment before answering. "Washington." She leaned forward to talk to the other woman on the sofa. "Hey, Cynthia," she said, "how about you make a name tag for Maggie R.?"

"In a moment," Cynthia said, snippy. "I'm not quite done with the tags for the regulars."

Maggie looked at her. "If someone's a regular, doesn't everyone already know their name?"

"Her name," Cynthia corrected, without looking up.

"Cynthia's our leader," Martha stated. "As you can tell from her grammatical authoritarianism."

"And her artisanal tag-making skills," Maggie added.

Martha nodded. "You've just moved to town," she stated, rather than asked.

"That's right," Maggie said. "The old MacDonald place." Martha looked at her, poker-faced. "You didn't think that was funny," Maggie continued.

"Those of us with name issues are rarely amused by that kind of joke."

"My mistake. Sorry."

"No need," Martha said. "I was just firing a warning shot across your bow."

"Do you live around here?"

"My husband and I own a business in town."

"What kind of business?"

"Art gallery and frame shop." Maggie's stomach seized. It was like opening the garage door and finding a stranger standing there. Even if it turned out to be someone innocuous, the initial shock was inevitable. Martha seemed oblivious to her reaction. "Here." She handed Maggie a business card. "Daniel Stewart Shop. Fine art. Custom framing," the card read. "You should stop in and look around. We might have something interesting for your new place."

"Sure," Maggie said. She took the card, her hand shaking slightly, and put it in the back pocket of her jeans.

"Ladies." Cynthia stood up and clapped her hands. "If I could have your attention. Everyone please take a seat."

"Everyone's already seated," Maggie whispered to Martha.

"Sometimes we do the Mad Hatter's tea party thing just to humor her," Martha answered. "You know, everybody moves over one seat."

"You're kidding, right?" Maggie asked.

The corner of Martha's mouth curled slightly. "Be patient. You'll see."

"Shall we begin with introductions?" Cynthia asked.

"Oh, for crying out loud," the gypsy woman said. "Sit down, Cynthia. Let's get started."

Cynthia floated back down onto the loveseat with the deliberateness of a falling blossom. It took her several attempts to get control of the group, but Maggie quickly realized they were better off out of control. Cynthia ran the meeting like a twelve-step program, and some of these women were divulging all kinds of sorry facts about themselves. Maggie suffered the sharp-edged mortification of the voyeur, unable to turn away but deeply embarrassed to be watching. She leaned over to Martha. "Maybe somebody could derail the cathartic freight train?"

"I don't know how."

"Asking what people thought of the book?"

Martha patted her hand. "Relax."

"I hope I never run into some of these women in the supermarket," Maggie whispered.

"Last month we had to listen to Esmerelda," Martha inclined her head at the gypsy woman, "talking about all the things Quasimodo can do with rope." Maggie blanched. "I'm kidding," Martha whispered. "That was a Hunchback of Notre Dame joke."

"Are those big around here?"

"What, literature jokes? Absolutely. Every time one of the classic authors comes out with a new fragrance."

"Well," Cynthia finally said, "perhaps we can tie up some of our loose ends by relating our personal stories to the archetypal themes in this month's selection. I'll go first." She was interrupted by a loud disturbance from the rear of the store. Everyone froze. Cynthia's mouth hung open as if the word she was about to say was wedged in there.

"Cynthia," Lillian said crisply, "you promised."

Cynthia turned red. "I consulted with my management."

"And?" Lillian bristled.

Cynthia backed farther into her corner of the loveseat. "Dr. Hawthorne is a very good customer."

Lillian's stare was icy. "Am I not a good customer?"

"*Of course* you are," Cynthia said. She was so ingratiating Maggie could almost see her words fluttering around like animated butterflies.

Lillian got even stonier. "This will be the last time."

"Now, Lillian," Cynthia said, "I'm sure management will do its best to intervene."

"Can't get this kind of fun at the chain book stores," Martha whispered.

"I'm thinking some of these women need to find a real therapist."

"Forget it," Martha said. "They're only here in the first place because they're either too crazy to figure that out or too cheap to do it."

"I *said*," a melodic voice pounded over the bookracks, "I am *fully* conversant with today's topic and wish to contribute." There were several beats of silence, during which every face in the Book Group turned toward the unseen disturbance like sunflowers straining toward the sun. And then the voice broke forth again. "You best *move* your ass, unless you're looking for me to use it for a red carpet!"

The source of the commotion blew into the alcove, bristling with so much energy paper seemed to flutter in her wake. She was African-American, probably around Maggie's age, and everything about her, from the long extensions in her hair to her boldly colored clothing, was a statement. Though she wasn't really that large, she gave the impression of taking up a lot of space. She didn't seem to notice there were hostiles in the crowd. Maggie felt an immediate affinity for her.

"Dr. Hawthorne," Cynthia said, in a tone of voice she probably kept in reserve for wild animals and sociopathic teenagers, "good of you to join us."

Dr. Hawthorne gave her a withering glance. "Cynthia, your life could be a lot less effort if you just learned to call a spade a spade."

Some of the ladies gasped. Martha smiled grimly. "Vee," she asked, "a little cream and sugar with your provocation?"

Dr. Hawthorne swiveled her head around slowly, as if she were a security device looking for intruders. She fixed on Maggie. "My, my," she said, drawing out her words. "New blood."

Martha gestured impatiently. "For crying out loud, Vee," she said. "Sit down and cut the crap. You're annoying the regulars."

Dr. Hawthorne came over and sat heavily between Maggie and Cynthia. "Please don't interrupt yourselves on my behalf," she drawled.

"Well, then," Cynthia tidily rearranged her flowered skirt, "let's focus on today's topic. I personally found a great deal I could relate to in this book. Maggie, as our newest member, why don't you share your thoughts?"

"To tell the truth," Maggie said, "I just decided to join the group a few hours ago. All I read is the back cover."

"That's wonderful," Cynthia said. "You can share your impressions so far."

Maggie wondered if the best way to do that wouldn't be to just get up and leave. "So far I have no impressions. I haven't read the book." Everyone stared at her. Nobody moved or answered. She succumbed to the pressure. "I guess it's not the most inspiring back cover I've ever read."

"Nonsense!" Lillian fumed. "What about that inspiring quote about losing and loving it! Clearly," she looked pointedly at Dr. Hawthorne, "some people could benefit from learning to love losing."

Dr. Hawthorne appeared to inflate as she opened her mouth to answer. Cynthia cut her off. "Let's remember our rules," she said. "No personal comments. We are here to share ideas inspired by the book."

"Or its cover," Martha muttered.

"She can't get personal on *me*." Dr. Hawthorne said, looking at Lillian. "Before she could do that, she'd have to visit the notion that someone who is black is a *person*."

"Vee, let it go," Martha said. Dr. Hawthorne grumbled something under her breath, but made no further comment.

"Personally," Maggie continued, hearing the word too late, as it came out of her mouth, "I think it's become a real cliché to talk about making the most of loss."

"Why is that?" Cynthia asked.

"Losing is so common." As she said it, she saw Lillian stiffen with disapproval, apparently taking a different meaning for the word 'common'. Maggie rushed on. "Losing is an everyday occurrence. Anyone who believes it won't happen to them just hasn't been in the right place at the right time yet, so to speak."

"You devalue the effort involved," Lillian said, huffy. "Losing is hard work!"

"Did you *read* the damn cover?" Dr. Hawthorne demanded.

Lillian stood up. "Cynthia," she announced, all offended dignity, "I have represented the group's opinion about this kind of conduct before. If you won't put a stop to it, I will have no choice but to terminate my membership."

"She didn't read the cover," Dr. Hawthorne said primly.

"Hey Lillian," Martha said, "I don't remember asking you to represent me." She leaned over to Maggie. "She must have been elected by the silent majority."

Dr. Hawthorne looked at Martha. "That's a good diss for old folks," she said, "since they're the only ones who remember what the silent majority means."

"Ladies!" Cynthia's face matched the poppies on her skirt. "We don't want to have to recess another meeting, do we?"

"She thinks," Dr. Hawthorne gestured toward Lillian, "this book is about *losing weight!*"

Lillian retrieved her purse from under her chair. "In a true intellectual debate there is respect for all opinions. I should not be subjected to unfair criticism because I have a different perspective."

"Honey, this book is intended as a trail guide for *losers*," Dr. Hawthorne replied. "It has nothing to do with eating disorders."

"I have too much self-respect to value your judgment of me," Lillian snapped. She stormed out of the alcove. The other members of the group looked at each other. They reminded Maggie of a flock of geese she had once seen trying to land on a pond that had frozen overnight. They had that same aura of irate disbelief, as if somebody better take responsibility for this nasty turn of events and make it right. She wouldn't have been surprised if the women around her started patting the floor with their feet, checking its solidity.

"Perhaps we could continue?" Cynthia said.

"You all go on without me," Dr. Hawthorne said. "I've had my fun for the day." She stood up and turned to Maggie. "I believe it's feeding time. You hungry?" She headed off toward the front of the bookshop without waiting for an answer.

Maggie followed her, if for nothing more than the pleasant anticipation of her next performance. She caught up at the front counter. Lillian was standing there, breathing deeply and paying for a Natural Elements Diet Green Tea. Dr. Hawthorne leaned close to her as they walked past. "You really didn't read the cover, did you?" she hissed, loud enough for everyone present to hear. Lillian pretended not to notice.

"So what was that really about?" Maggie asked when they were outside on the sidewalk.

Dr. Hawthorne gave her a measuring look. "You're an only child, aren't you?"

"What makes you say that?" Maggie asked.

"Um-hmm," Dr. Hawthorne said. "I knew it."

"Does that mean I'm not invited to lunch anymore?"

"Means you got the survival skills of a lemming," Dr. Hawthorne said. "You don't even know the game 'Last Word'."

"Is that a problem?"

"It impedes your appreciation of the fact that I just won." Dr. Hawthorne started up the hill. She moved fast.

"Doesn't look like you had much fun." Maggie had to work hard to keep up and talk at the same time.

"I was actually enjoying myself immensely. Why else would I bother to play with someone like her?"

Maggie had some ideas, but was wise enough to keep them to herself.

🐾 🐾 🐾

Inside the bookstore, Lillian was using the tip of her carefully manicured thumbnail to speed dial her phone. The call took a moment to connect, and then Lillian put the phone to her ear. "Carol Ann?" she said. "Yes. It's Mother. I've just had the most upsetting encounter." Pause. "Yes, it was that awful woman again." Pause. "Well, I thought we had an agreement as well. She was supposed to be ejected from the Book Group before today." Here she looked pointedly at the college kid behind the counter as if he had something to do with anything. He turned away in discomfort and pretended to be busy.

"Yes," Lillian spoke into her phone again. "I'm just distraught. Can you meet me?" Pause. "Oh, I don't know. Somewhere we can share a salad." Pause. "That will be fine. See you in half an hour."

7

Dr. Hawthorne hadn't even broken a sweat in their slog up the hill to the General Store. She appeared not to notice Maggie was out of breath. "You okay with a salad?" she asked.

"I thought I saw some sandwiches and stuff in the case last time I was here."

Dr. Hawthorne led the way inside. "You can pick something from the case if you want. Just if you do, you have to deal with Lola/Mercedes." A disagreeable looking woman, the dark roots of her hair showing through its unnatural carrot color, glared at them from behind the case. Dr. Hawthorne said, "Salad," and the woman jerked her head to indicate Dr. Hawthorne should move along. Maggie understood now where Morsel got his ideas about customer service.

"What do you recommend?" Maggie asked. The woman stared at her.

Dr. Hawthorne grabbed Maggie by the sleeve. "She'll have a Cuban." She steered Maggie to a table. "Just sit down." She went off to get silverware and napkins. When she came back she asked, "So what brings you to Dooleysburg?"

"The friendly buzz."

"She's a killer cook." Dr. Hawthorne seemed unaware that Maggie's comment might have a broader reference than just the lunch service. "People who think a good meal includes conversation with the chef know better than to come here."

"I suppose this type of work can be very dehumanizing," Maggie began.

"You make one more comment like that and I'm getting mine to go."

"I just meant she might respond to a more personal approach."

"I don't think she'd respond to a tranquilizer dart."

"Maybe it would help if people addressed her by name."

"Can't. Don't know which one she is."

Maggie was confused. "Which one what?"

"There are two of them. People assume they're sisters, but nobody knows for sure. One's named Lola and the other one's Mercedes. Can't tell which one's which."

"You could just ask her."

"You're never going to fit in around here if you keep thinking like that," Dr. Hawthorne said. "In this town people don't go looking for ways to improve on something that works okay."

"I just know I prefer it when people call me by name. I'm Maggie."

Dr. Hawthorne pointed at her nametag. "I can see that."

"Shall I call you Dr. Hawthorne?"

"I'll let you know after we finish lunch. My friends are allowed to call me Vee."

"I didn't get the impression things were all warm and fuzzy between you and Martha Stewart," Maggie pointed out, "and she calls you Vee."

"She takes liberties," Vee said. "You keep an eye out for her. If anything warm and fuzzy ever gets within striking distance, she's likely to unhinge her jaw and eat it."

"What happens if I don't make the cut?" Maggie asked.

"I'll discard you like last year's shoes."

Lola/Mercedes came over with two mugs of coffee they hadn't ordered. She plunked them down, slopping a good deal of the coffee over the rims. "I be back," she said, indicating the mugs, "to feel you up."

"I guess we're having coffee?" Maggie asked.

"Don't have to drink it if you don't want to," Vee said. "Of course, you still have to pay for it." She put sugar in hers. "You married?" she asked, concentrating on stirring.

"Not anymore," Maggie said, then felt odd about answering that way. "What about you?"

"Hell, no." Vee was emphatic.

"Why hell no?"

Vee made a 'huh' sound. "Honey, there is no species on the planet with less reason to get married than a wealthy, successful black American woman." She took a dainty sip of her coffee. "So what are you looking for in Dooleysburg?"

Maggie's tone was bland. "Do I have to be looking for something?"

"No," Vee said sarcastically. "Strangers show up here every day for no reason and plunk down the kind of cash you did on that house."

"Maybe I was just looking to get feeled up."

"Umm," Vee said. "Not likely around here."

Lola/Mercedes came back and delivered their food with the same kind of care she'd shown with the coffee, which she did not refill.

"So is it common knowledge?" Maggie asked. "What I paid for the house?"

"Yeah. It gets published in the *Intellectual*."

"That I paid cash?"

"No. That piece of information I had to find out the hard way."

"Which is?"

"Same way as everybody else," Vee said.

"Never mind." Maggie realized she would have to figure out the secret password before she got into the club. She changed the subject. "I wasn't looking for anything out of the ordinary when I moved here. I'm recently widowed. This seemed like a good place for a single mother to raise a kid."

"What'd he die of? Your husband?"

"Lack of good sense, mostly. He tried to cross the street in front of a bus. The bus was moving at the time."

"He must have taken good care of you if you're living here and you never worked."

"Oh, I worked," Maggie said, catching herself too late. "I'm retired now."

"You're awfully young to be retired."

"Maybe retired is too permanent. I'll go back to work eventually. But for now I just want to concentrate on raising my son."

The volume suddenly increased as an elderly couple at the table behind Vee launched into an argument. Lola/Mercedes stalked over and slapped plates of food down in front of them. "How many times I tell jou," she demanded, "jou want to fight, take it outside."

"He's just so stubborn," the woman said sharply. Then she looked at the plate in front of her. "I didn't ask for this," she said, her voice cranky now.

"I didn't ask jou to come for lunch neither." Lola/Mercedes walked away. The woman began to grumble in a tone that carried across the room. Lola/Mercedes glanced back at her. The woman picked up her fork and began eating.

Vee tapped her fingernails on the table to get Maggie's attention. "What about your son?"

"Mac is fourteen."

"That's his name?" Vee asked incredulously. "Mac Rifkin? Sounds like a fifty year old furniture salesman. Why would you do that to a child?"

"His real first name is MacDonald."

"Good lord." Vee shook out her napkin. "MacDonald Rifkin. Why didn't you just name him 'kick my ass?'"

"He's named after my father."

"Who was that, Old MacDonald?"

"I already used that joke today. It wasn't funny then either. MacDonald was my father's last name."

"He didn't have a first name?"

"Haimish," Maggie said.

Vee shook her head. "What is it with folks and names? People are always so full of whatever stupid idea inspired them they don't even stop to think about the poor innocent baby. Stick some stupid tag on it like the kid's some cut of meat to be put out to pasture."

"I think you mixed your metaphors."

"Eat your lunch," Vee ordered. "Before you get stale."

Maggie noticed Vee ate with great delicacy, using far better manners than she did herself. "So," she said, between bites, "what is Vee short for?"

"None of your damn business," Vee snapped.

Lola/Mercedes came by to see if they wanted dessert. It was the first attempt at customer relations Maggie had seen her try. Vee shooed her away.

"You should try harder to reinforce her when she's nice," Maggie said.

"Wasted effort," Vee said. "Besides, I got something else in mind for dessert."

"So what kind of doctor are you?"

"Ph.D."

"In what?"

"Comparative anthropology." Vee looked at Maggie as if throwing out a challenge. "And now you're thinking, what a pompous ass. She makes people call her doctor when all she has is a Ph.D."

"Actually, I wasn't thinking that," Maggie replied. "A Ph.D.'s a lot of work. It's okay with me if you want to flash it around."

"So you're a Ph.D." It was not a question, so Maggie didn't answer.

The door opened. Lillian and Carol Ann stepped inside. Maggie figured they had mere seconds to consider their options. "Double whammy," she said. "One whammy for you, one for me."

"Yoo hooo!" Vee called, waving enthusiastically. "Ladies! Would you care to join us?"

Every head in the place turned either to their table or the door. Carol Ann whispered something to her mother and they turned and left with a great show of disdain.

"Your name will be shit in this town now," Vee said.

"It's like Chutes and Ladders," Maggie replied. "You just took me on a short-cut to where I was already going anyway."

"Yeah, but was it a chute or a ladder?"

"Depends on who controls the board."

Vee leaned back in her chair. "It strikes me that you brought your child to this town from New York City because you were looking to fit in somewhere." She paused when she saw the expression on Maggie's face. "Don't look so surprised that I already know something about you. First, I am trained in studying people. And second, there are no secrets in a small town. You fart in one end, the dishes rattle in the other. Choose sides carefully, because there's no going back."

Maggie took a final sip of coffee. "If the rules are that tough, why are you here?"

"I teach in Philly. A former student of mine lives here. He sold me on how great it is."

"You're not here because someone else thinks it's great. I've known you thirty seconds and I'm already sure if there wasn't something you like here, you'd be gone."

Vee stood up. "Let's go get some dessert."

"Actually," Maggie said, "I should get going. My son will be home from school soon."

"Why don't you give the boy a key?"

"I did."

"Then stick with me a little longer. I want to show you something." They paid and went out into the beautiful afternoon sunshine. "You got a car here?" Vee asked. Maggie shook her head. "Good. I'll drive." They walked to Vee's car. It was parked illegally.

"You're lucky you didn't get a ticket," Maggie said. "Dooleysburg's finest are a pretty big lot of assholes."

"Luck had nothing to do with it."

Maggie wasn't sure what to make of that, but since the answers in Dooleysburg, like in Wonderland, were often more confusing than the questions she didn't bother to ask. Vee drove north, away from the center of town. After a few blocks, she turned into the parking lot of a place with a glowing sign that read 'Cremee Freeze'. There was an outdoor patio with tables made of fat ice cream sandwiches, and gnome-sized light-up ice cream cones rotated on either side of the driveway.

"You craving a little soft serve?" Maggie asked.

"Nope." Vee pulled into a parking spot and turned off the car.

"We just going to sit here?"

"For a while."

Maggie opened her door. "I'm getting some ice cream. You want anything?"

"Sure," Vee said. "Get me a black and white."

Maggie looked at her. "You're setting me up, aren't you?"

Vee gave a throaty laugh. "You might make the cut after all. Get me whatever you're having."

Maggie got two small vanilla cones and headed back to the car. She handed Vee's through the window and stood outside eating her own.

As if someone had opened the door of a pen, a herd of teenagers appeared. "Ah," Vee said, "school's out."

Maggie looked at her watch. "It's later than I thought. I better get home."

"Indulge me a little longer," Vee said. "I'll give you a ride."

The Cremee Freeze was overrun with kids swarming around like mosquitoes on a plump thigh. Some got ice cream, but most just engaged in the rites of hanging out. As Maggie finished her cone a group of boys came thundering around the corner of the brick house next door, startling her. She looked at the place more carefully. It was old, rundown and nondescript but there was nothing specifically peeling, crumbling or falling apart. It was almost like someone was intentionally trying to make it look unremarkable. "Is that house what you wanted me to see?" Maggie pointed.

"Something strike you about that house?"

"I can't put my finger on what it is, but the old guy sitting on the side porch is odd. He's holding that broom across his lap like one of those pictures of a moonshiner with a shotgun."

"You got an interesting observation technique. But that's not what I brought you here to see. Stop focusing on the details."

Maggie was baffled. "It's not the house? The only other thing going on here is a bunch of kids taking over a public place. That happens everywhere."

"Look harder," Vee said.

With a sudden flash of insight Maggie realized things were different from Vee's point of view. "Are you referring to the fact that some of the kids are black?"

"You didn't notice until I made you look for it," Vee said.

"Not really, no."

"And why was that?"

"Because race doesn't make any difference to me?"

"Yeah, right," Vee said derisively.

"Okay," Maggie said. "I give up. Why?"

"Because there's no segregation. The kids are in groups that mix and reform organically. There are no clear affiliation lines, which means everybody's more or less desirable based only on personal distinctions. The black kids aren't different just because they're black. And they're not uncomfortable with that because they've grown up with it as their norm."

"I doubt it," Maggie said.

"No, really," Vee insisted. "This town's like the integrated version of *Brigadoon*."

"I think you're fooling yourself," Maggie said. "But if that's really true, then this town is doing them a big disservice."

"Maybe," Vee agreed. "Or maybe the best way to prepare them for the reality of prejudice is to make them so strong and sure of themselves that they're shitproof by the time they leave here."

"So is that why you stay here?" Maggie asked. "Because you don't get judged on the basis of anything except who you are?"

Vee looked at her like she was an imbecile. "You mean being disliked purely and simply because I'm me and not just because I'm black is an advantage I can't find just anywhere?"

8

Vee was coming to dinner. In between spikes of nervous anticipation Maggie was annoyed. She'd been duped. Everything appeared to start innocently enough when Vee commented that they should get together for dinner some time, but somehow that morphed into dinner at Maggie's. Maggie realized now she'd underestimated the serious curiosity her presence created. She wondered if she should demand a cut of whatever reward Vee was going to get for sharing intelligence about the inside of her house.

This was the first dinner party Maggie had ever hosted without benefit of a caterer. She couldn't remember the last time she'd tried to cook anything that didn't have instructions printed on the side. She wasn't worried about impressing Vee, whose natural disinclination to be pleased let Maggie off that hook. But Vee was bringing the guy who convinced her to move to Dooleysburg. She got him included by letting Maggie believe they were involved. And then, over the last few days, with a little slip here and there Vee let her figure out there was actually nothing going on between them. So on top of everything else, tonight might be Vee's feeble attempt to set her up with Mystery guy.

In her saner moments Maggie realized getting worked up about all of this might just be her way of not dealing with the real problem, her inability to cook. Early in adulthood she had had a liberating insight about cooking. Nobody expected a dog, no matter how smart it was, to use a keyboard because nature didn't intend for dogs to type. That was how it was with her and cooking. Without Albie around they'd done okay alternating between take-out and her favorite meal, chicken nuggets with a side of macaroni and cheese and something green. But she couldn't get away with that when there would be witnesses. A trip to the library and a kindly reference librarian had resulted in some recipes she thought she would be able to manage.

She was still calm when she went to the grocery store around lunchtime, but that was only because she was unprepared for the effort required to find the things on a shopping list. She stuck with it for as long as she could before giving up and settling for things she recognized. Then she saw a display of baby vegetables. She had no idea what to do with them, but they were irresistible, tiny little zucchini and pattypan squash, eggplants the size of uninflated balloons, teensy grape tomatoes. They were so cute she figured they could always serve as decoration.

By the time Mac came in from school she was in the kitchen, working up a sweat trying to sort things out. Ingredients were piled all over the place. Mac rapidly got himself thrown out of the room by saying her new friends wouldn't die from one lousy meal. Then Vee arrived ridiculously early. She walked in without even knocking, and after a perfunctory greeting loomed over the stove like she was entitled to act in a supervisory capacity. Maggie couldn't take the pressure. She began whipping around like a terrier on speed.

"Slow down." Vee used her public voice. "You're creating a tail wind." Mac stuck his head around the door cautiously. "You must be MacDonald," Vee said. "I'm your mother's new friend. I think we need to get her some medication."

Mac looked confused. "Sorry?"

"What's your preference?" Vee asked Maggie. "White or red?"

"White. Dry. Very cold."

"Oh," Mac said, "wine. Why do you need me for that?"

"Ask her if she remembered to buy anything else to drink," Vee replied.

"Crap!" Maggie felt stupid. "We can drink water."

"You remember to buy water?"

"I have indoor plumbing."

"Y'all don't serve a guest *tap* water. You planning to put out a bucket with a hose in it?"

"Sorry," Maggie said. "I'll get you some cash." She disappeared into her room.

"What's eating her?" Vee asked Mac.

"She's afraid of screwing up."

"What's she going to make? Homemade mayonnaise? Soufflés?"

Mac looked uncomfortable. "I don't think I'm supposed to tell. But she's going to try breaded chicken tenders and homemade macaroni and cheese. Those are her favorites."

Vee guffawed. "Glad to hear she had a good reason."

Maggie came back into the kitchen and held out a twenty. Vee shook her head. "This is on me. Consider it my contribution. And what is that delectable aroma?"

Maggie looked at the various piles on the counter. They didn't smell like much of anything yet. "What aroma?" she asked.

"I'm thinking it could be cheese sauce," Vee replied.

Maggie gave Mac a dirty look. He avoided her gaze.

"We'll just be a few minutes," Vee said. "You get started on that cheese sauce and I'll give you a hand with the other stuff when we get back."

"I'd appreciate it," Maggie said. "If you pull around behind the house to my driveway when you get back you can bring stuff straight into the kitchen."

After they left Maggie finally started feeling in control. Cooking, she realized, was like surgery. There would be a few tense moments, some predictable and some not, but otherwise you just needed to stick with the plan. Paying attention and having everything within reach was key. She organized the ingredients, measuring, creating order. Then she read the first step in the macaroni and cheese recipe again. "Melt four tablespoons of butter in a heavy saucepan," it said. She felt like she should have a pang of guilt about using butter, but after all the prepared foods they'd eaten in the last few months four tablespoons of it wasn't going to make enough of a difference to risk changing the recipe. "Add four tablespoons of flour to the melted butter, stirring constantly just until the flour is cooked through."

"Don't let the flour brown," the librarian had written in the margin. If you did, she explained, your white sauce wouldn't be white. Maggie wondered, with irritation, how she was supposed to know the flour was cooked through if she didn't let it brown. She made herself take a deep breath. Getting pissed off wasn't going to help. Then she realized no one would ever know what color the flour was once she added the orange cheese to it.

"Gradually add four cups of milk, whisking constantly." She only had to try to realize that was never going to happen. It was harder than rubbing her stomach and patting her head at the same time. Trusting her newfound instincts, she added a little milk, stirred until it was fully incorporated, and then added a little more. She stuck with it until it became clear that at this rate she'd still be dribbling milk into the pot at bedtime. So she dumped the rest in all at once. The sauce turned into a pot of milk with oily blobs in it.

The recipe said the sauce would be thin and to stir constantly until thickened. Hoping for the best, she stirred. Maybe it was just wishful thinking, but after a long while she began to feel a little resistance on the bottom of the pot. She kept stirring. Lost in the Zen of her sauce, she only gradually became aware of a commotion behind her garage. A horn blasted, car doors slammed. A voice she didn't recognize was shouting. Vee's unmistakable contralto answered. She was torn between needing to find out what was going on, or stirring. Leaving her sauce at this critical stage might cause irreparable harm.

The back door flew open and Mac ran in. She could hear Vee clearly now shouting, "Shoo! Scram! Get away from here!"

Scram? Maggie thought. The only time she ever heard anyone use that word was on reruns of the old Batman TV show. "What's going on?" she demanded.

"Vee needs a broom!" Mac yelled, heading for the basement door. In a moment he ran back out, broom in hand.

"What is it?" Maggie called at his back. He didn't stop to answer.

She was stuck, trapped at a hot stove by a pan of temperamental milk. She was not fond of animals, and she dreaded to think what might be out there, hoping Vee would take care of Mac. Things suddenly went silent. Maggie stirred a few moments longer, her anxiety thickening along with the perfectly smooth white sauce.

Finally Mac and Vee came through the back door, each carrying a grocery bag. "Sorry we took so long," Vee said.

"What happened?" Maggie asked, relieved they were okay.

"We had to stop at the State Store for the wine. It's a real pain. Back in Carolina you could buy everything at the Piggly Wiggly. No need to make six stops for one errand."

"Is that where you're from?" Mac asked. "Carolina? North or South?"

"Hey guys!" Maggie raised her voice. "What happened out there? It sounded like you were trying to chase Godzilla off the property."

"Minor annoyance," Vee said. "Afraid you'll need a new broom though."

"What was it?" Maggie was really concerned now. "Should I call Animal Control?"

Vee found this enormously funny. "Somebody's probably already tried that. I doubt they'd want him either."

"*What* are you talking about?"

Mac looked guilty. "The little man next door. He tried to tell Dr. Hawthorne she's not allowed to park in our driveway because she has to cross his alleyway to get here."

"You finally met the next door neighbor?" Maggie asked.

"What's the big deal?" Vee answered. "If you want to meet him all you have to do is go to his deli and start reading expiration dates. Everything in there is so old he comes running out of the back faster than a cockroach when the lights go on to make you stop."

"He owns a deli?"

"That crummy little place over by the park. How could you miss it? Everybody knows about the Gamey Deli."

"And you chased him away? What kind of an impression is that going to make?"

"Honey," Vee said, "you have windows in this house. He's already got all the impression he needs. Probably has pictures and video too."

"He can't be that bad."

"It'll take you a hell of a lot more than a broom to get rid of him," Vee said.

Maggie had a sudden horrifying realization. "Where's the broom?"

Vee looked unconcerned. "I'll get you another broom."

"You broke the broom?" Maggie was aghast. "You *hit* him?"

"No." Vee was all prim indignation. "I did *not* hit him. I would have, but I couldn't get the broom back. He was hanging on like a mud crab on a toe."

Mac snickered. "It was pretty funny when you let go."

"Oh my god," Maggie said. "Did he fall? Did he get hurt?"

"Only his dignity. And before you go feeling all bad for him, remember he took your broom."

"I don't blame him."

"He said it was evidence for his assault complaint," Vee added calmly.

Maggie's cheeks flushed. "You think the police are going to find this frivolous? This is the same police force that wanted to send me to the big house for jaywalking. You think they're going to be amused about you beating some midget in my driveway with a broom?"

"You worry too much," Vee said. She put the soda in the refrigerator. "You are up to date with your homeowner's, right?"

"Mom?" Mac asked. "Why is there smoke coming out of that pot?"

Maggie turned back to the stove just in time to watch the white sauce boil over. This was the last straw. Vee needed to understand who was in charge. Maggie opened her mouth. The doorbell rang.

"Oh," Vee sounded pleased. "I bet that's our mystery guest."

"Does nobody in this town respect the convention of arriving for dinner at the time they were invited?" Maggie snapped.

"What do you care?" Vee asked. "It isn't like there's going to be any dinner."

"I'll get it," Mac said loudly, and hustled out of the kitchen. His relief at escaping evaporated when he opened the front door. "Uh, hi," he said, holding the door mostly closed with his foot.

"Hey." It was the police chief, JD Charles. "Okay if I come in?" Mac looked at the floor and stepped back. "Dr. Hawthorne here?" the chief asked.

"She didn't mean to do anything." Mac stumbled over the words.

"That's unusual," the chief replied. "She usually means to do exactly what she does." Mac froze like a bunny facing a hound. "Hey," the chief said. "That was humor."

"Okay," Mac said, still not looking up.

"So what did she do this time?"

"It wasn't her fault!" Mac blurted. "We just wanted to get to our driveway. My mom's and mine, I mean. We have a right to let company use our driveway! But that guy next door got in front of her car and she told him to move and he got right up in her face and yelled at her." Mac thought about this a moment. "Well, almost in her face," he amended. "As close as he could reach."

The chief remained calm. "Did she hit him?"

"Not really. She just pushed him a little."

"Hard enough to mark the car?"

"Not with the car. She got out of the car."

"How'd she push him?" the chief asked. "With the flat of her hand, or with a fist?"

"With a broom. But he pushed back," Mac added defensively.

"Ah. Can I see the weapon?"

"It wasn't a weapon!" Mac was scared. "It was just a broom!"

The chief put a hand on Mac's shoulder. "It's okay," he said, obviously amused with himself. "I was just busting you."

Mac rushed on. "He wouldn't give it back. He said it was evidence."

"Okay," the chief began slowly, "let me bring a few things to your attention. Number one, I'm wearing khakis, which would indicate I am off duty. And I don't show up at crime scenes when I'm off duty unless they involve something a little more serious than a broom. Number *two*, said khakis, if you knew me better, would indicate that I am here in a social capacity or at least hoping to impress somebody. Number three, I am carrying a nice assortment of flowers, which is definitely not a reasonable thing to bring to a crime scene, and could be taken as confirmation of item number two."

"You're not here to arrest someone?"

"Not unless I see evidence of a crime."

"Stop tormenting the child, JD." Vee was standing in the kitchen doorway.

"How are you darlin'?" JD walked over and kissed her cheek.

Maggie walked up behind Vee and stopped. "This is your special friend?"

"You've met?" Vee stepped to the side.

"Mrs. Rifkin." JD offered her the flowers.

"Thanks," Maggie said, taking them. "Welcome to my home." She didn't put a lot of cordiality into it. "I'm afraid there's not going to be any dinner. We've had a kitchen disaster."

"Nothing involving a broom, I hope."

"MacDonald!" Vee exclaimed. "I cannot believe you gave me up!"

JD took pity on Mac. "I didn't give him a choice."

"I haven't even met my next door neighbor yet," Maggie said, "and now he thinks I'm looking to engage in hostilities."

"Hey," Vee said, "on the seventh day God rested. On the eighth he squeezed out a little fart and named it Gamey. The guy is nasty."

"Perhaps you inspire him," JD said.

Maggie looked from one to the other. "Somebody want to clue me in?"

"Tell you what," JD said. "After dinner I'll introduce you to him."

"I already told you. There is no dinner."

JD sniffed. He looked at Vee. "How bad is it?"

"Just the side dish," she said. "But it's beyond repair, even for you."

"You can make light of this if you want," Maggie said. "But first you should consider what I'm capable of doing to the main course."

"What is the main course?" JD asked.

"Chicken nuggets," Mac said, before Maggie could answer.

"From a box?" JD stared at her. "You were going to feed dinner guests from a box?"

"No, not from a box." Maggie was out of patience. "I bought real chicken and bread crumbs and olive oil to make them from scratch."

"Okay," JD said. "This isn't so bad. We've got chicken and olive oil. What else?"

"Baby vegetables. And macaroni. And the cheese. That didn't go into the sauce yet."

"Chicken stock?" he asked. Maggie made a pfft noise. "Tomato paste?" She shook her head. "Salt and pepper?" She finally nodded. "Good. Gamey's got an herb garden. I'll get some stuff from him."

"You expect him to give you herbs after what just happened?"

"Nah," JD said. "I'll help myself."

ℙ ℙ ℙ

It only took minutes for JD to make himself at home in the kitchen. He put Mac to work grating cheese, and had Vee wash the baby vegetables.

"Something I can do?" Maggie asked pointedly.

"You want another go at making sauce?" JD asked. She made a wry face. "How about prepping the chicken?"

"Do I have to touch it?"

He raised an eyebrow. "Hard to cut it up any other way."

"I don't touch raw meat."

"Without gloves on," Mac said without turning around.

JD gave Maggie a curious look, which she ignored. "Tell you what," he said. "You can be in charge of setting the table."

"Sure," Maggie said sarcastically. "Why not?" She grabbed a handful of silverware and napkins and went out to the patio.

Vee came out in a few minutes with glasses and wine. "And to what do we owe your current foul humor?" she asked.

"Why didn't you bother to tell me your special friend was the cop who messed with me and scared my kid our first week in town?" Maggie didn't lower her voice. She didn't care if JD heard her.

"You expect me to answer a question that dumb?" Vee opened the wine and gave Maggie a glass. "Drink this," she said. "Maybe it'll dilute some of your piss and vinegar."

When the food came out Maggie's mood brightened. JD had browned the chicken without breading it, a culinary option Maggie didn't know existed, and then made some sort of sauce with the baby vegetables and the cheese. It was all served over the macaroni. "My personal take on ratatouille," he said, presenting the dish with a flourish.

"It smells amazing," Maggie said, taking a good whiff.

"My secret ingredient. Caramelized onion. But not just any onion . . ."

Vee's face got stern. "Let it go," she said. JD grinned at her wickedly.

"I bought a Vidalia onion," Maggie said helpfully.

"A Vidalia," JD crooned. "The sweetest onion of all." Vee made a contemptuous noise.

"Wait a minute." Mac turned to her. "Your real name is Vidalia?"

Vee narrowed her eyes at JD. "You are a shit."

"I can't believe your name is Vidalia and you gave me a hard time because my name is MacDonald," Mac said accusingly. Vee patted his hand.

Maggie took a long sip of wine. "That would explain why you're so wired up about the whole name thing."

"If you know anything at all about culinary history," Vee said with immense dignity, "you are well aware that I preceded the famous onion. My mother never imagined she would be rendering me a disservice with such a sweet-sounding name."

"Not being able to foresee, one assumes, your eventual temperament," JD pointed out.

"Ask him what JD stands for," Vee said to Maggie.

"What does JD stand for?" Maggie asked.

"JD," he replied.

"Bull pizzle," Vee said.

"So why did you tell him your name if you didn't want him to know it?" Maggie asked.

"She didn't have a choice," JD replied. "Traffic stop."

"Wait a minute," Maggie said, "you pulled her over? What was she doing, driving a stolen car?"

"Failed to yield at the four way stop on North Street," he said. "Can't overlook the potential for harm in that kind of behavior."

"You waved me on!" Vee exploded. "Like you were telling me to go first!"

"Friendly greeting," JD said. "You remain responsible for your actions."

"You were just looking for an excuse to see my license!"

"Tell me you didn't give her a ticket," Maggie demanded.

"Why didn't you just look her up in the computer?" Mac asked. The adults looked at each other.

"Well," JD said. "Shall we eat before it gets cold?"

The food and wine had a welcome sedative effect. Maggie was on the verge of deciding she was having a nice evening when Mac announced, as they finished up, that he wanted to join the Explorers. He liked that the kids his age met at the Rescue Squad.

Maggie tried not to show her annoyance that he was bringing this up for the first time in public. "We'll discuss it later."

"I think it's a good idea," JD said.

"Thanks," Maggie replied. "I'll take that into consideration."

"Your husband was a doctor, wasn't he?"

Maggie stood up and began stacking the dishes. "Doesn't anybody around here ever feel uncomfortable poking into other people's business?"

"Small towns run on other people's business," JD said. "Plus, poking into other people's business is what I do for a living."

"It's okay," Mac volunteered. "I told him about Dad."

Vee continued daintily chewing her dinner. Maggie picked up some plates and went into the kitchen. JD followed her, putting a handful of dirty glasses on the counter. "I'd appreciate it if you'd let us work our way into things around here at our own pace," she said.

"I understand," he answered. "After I lost my wife, there was a time when I couldn't even say her name because it felt like I would lose another piece of her if I did. I apologize for invading your privacy."

Maggie nodded without answering. They walked back out to the patio. She leaned down and whispered to Vee, "Next time you decide to invite Opie to dinner, give me a heads up first."

"Opie?" Vee said out loud. "He was the kid, wasn't he?"

Maggie glared at her. "You are the most uncool friend I have ever had."

"That would be more impressive if I had some worthy competition." Vee continued eating at a leisurely pace.

The doorbell rang. "I'll get it!" Mac jumped up a little too quickly. When he came back Morsel was with him. Morsel saw everybody out on the patio and froze at the kitchen door.

"We've got plenty of food here," Maggie called. "You want some dinner?"

He shook his head. "I'm good."

Vee snorted. "That's likely."

"How's work?" Maggie asked.

"Go ahead, sugar," Vee drawled. "Tell her how work is." Morsel gave her a hostile stare. "He got fired," Vee said.

"Me and Mac were going to hang out down the Rescue," Morsel said.

Mac looked at Maggie. She was caught between being pissed off to find herself on the receiving end of a secret plan, and knowing this was how kids operated whenever you let two or more of them get near each other. "It'll be dark soon," she said, mortified that she couldn't come up with anything better than that on the fly.

"If we leave now we'll make it before dark," Mac said.

"I'll have to come pick you up and give you a ride home."

"That's okay," Morsel said. His tone made it clear he was in charge. "I got a car."

"Does the owner know?" Vee asked. Morsel ignored her.

Maggie exhaled loudly. "All right," she said. "You can go, but be home by ten. One minute late and you can forget about going out for a month."

"Thanks, Mom!" They took off, Morsel saying something under his breath to Mac.

"I think he just called your son a wuss," Vee said helpfully.

"I didn't think Morsel was old enough to drive," Maggie said. "Isn't he in the same grade as Mac?"

"I believe he is," Vee said. "And has been for the past two years."

"Does he have a learning disability?"

"It's more complicated than that," JD said. "The parents are divorced and he lives with the father and stepmother. Something's going on, but we haven't been able to nail it yet."

Vee turned to Maggie. "You're looking to worry, forget the Rescue Squad. You let your son fraternize with that boy, you'll have more worry than you can handle."

"You made it pretty clear you're not especially fond of him."

"You don't have to take my word for it." Vee put her silverware on her plate. "But you just let your son go out on the wire without a net."

"That kid is not capable of turning Mac into a juvenile delinquent."

"That kid is a lying, thieving, obstreperous little fraud. You're going to be sorry if whatever's going on with him is catching."

Maggie acted like Vee was making too much of the whole thing, but her stomach churned. What did parents have at their command that was stronger than the appeal of a loser? Schools put so much effort into trying to convince kids not to catch STDs or use drugs, but completely overlooked how contagious plain old trouble could be. "How come he got fired from the General Store?" she asked.

"The official word is that he didn't work out," Vee replied. "Unofficially, Lola/Mercedes wasn't willing to put on an addition to make the place big enough for both of their attitudes."

"Does he have a real name?" Maggie asked.

"If he does, he's never told it to anybody. But remember, you don't want to get me started on names," Vee said sharply.

JD changed the subject. "I'm not sure what's up with this whole Rescue Squad thing."

"You just encouraged Mac to join," Maggie said. "I thought you helped run the group."

"I do," he answered. "That's why I have this feeling something's going on. All of a sudden everybody wants to join, but only that one chapter, at the Squad. Nothing's changed about what the kids do there, and yet there's this surge of interest."

"You think Morsel's got something to do with it?" Vee asked.

"That's an even bigger reason to discourage Mac from joining," Maggie said. She picked up another load of dishes, too anxious to sit still.

This time Vee got up. "If we're going to introduce her to Gamey," she said to JD, "let's get it over with."

"Sure." JD took out his cell phone. When Vee and Maggie came back from the kitchen he told them they were meeting Gamey at the Cremee Freeze.

"Why didn't he just come over here?" Maggie asked.

"Said he'd feel safer in a public place," JD said. "I told him to give us half an hour to finish cleaning up."

☙ ☙ ☙

JD had walked to Maggie's, and Maggie being a New Yorker, nobody was willing to ride with her. So Vee ended up driving them to the Cremee Freeze. They pulled in and a guy at one of the ice cream sandwich tables jumped up faster than a Chihuahua with an adrenal condition. Maggie was unprepared for the reality of him. He was not small so much as truncated, as if whoever built him started out with a full-sized model but ran out of funding somewhere between his hips and his ankles. "You have to feel bad for him," Maggie whispered to Vee.

"You go ahead and hold on to that as long as you can," Vee replied.

"Roland Gamey," he said, charging forward with his hand outstretched. Up close, his lurid stare gave Maggie the willies, but she reached out anyway. Gamey took her hand in both of his with a touch that was mostly caress. He lifted it to his lips and gave it a lingering kiss, then held on tightly, making her jerk her hand free. He grinned at her. She moved to the far side of the table. "Pleased to meet you, neighbor," he said. His voice implied he was interested in more than just meeting her.

"Can I have my broom back?" It wasn't what she planned to say, but now it felt right.

"Depends," Gamey said.

"On what?"

"On what you propose to do with it. I don't believe I'm obligated to return it if you're planning to assault me again." He looked innocently at JD. "Right, Chief?"

"Keep the damn thing," she muttered.

"Told you I'd buy you a new one," Vee said.

"You really need a broom?" JD asked.

"What's that supposed to mean?"

"You don't strike me as someone whose focus is housekeeping."

Vee looked at JD. "It could be time for you to go get us some ice cream."

"Sure," he said amiably. "What'll it be?"

"Vanilla cone," Vee said.

"Same for me," Maggie added. JD and Gamey went into the building. "I should've said two dips," Maggie added.

Vee nodded. "They are, aren't they?"

There was a sudden burst of activity at the brick building next door. The old man with the broom across his lap was still sitting on the side porch, but now a noisy group of teenage boys was shouting things and trying to push each other onto the property. A man's head was briefly visible inside as he hurried past a window. "Hey, Dad!" one of the boys yelled. "Come on out! Your son's here!" The old man raised the broom in one hand and shook it at them. They laughed rudely.

Maggie stood up. "Where are you going?" Vee asked.

"I'm not going to sit here and watch them torment that old man."

Vee motioned for her to sit down. "He can take care of himself," she said.

Maggie was about to argue, but since JD and Gamey were coming back with the ice cream she decided to delegate. "Did you notice what's going on at that house?" she asked JD.

"Hmm?" he responded absently.

"The brick house next door," she said. "Those kids are bothering that old man."

"It's okay," Gamey interjected. "That's what he gets paid for."

Maggie looked at him. "He gets paid to take abuse from a bunch of nasty kids?"

"He gets paid to run interference. To protect the privacy of the occupants, as it were."

Maggie was bewildered. "What exactly goes on over there?"

"Got me," Gamey said. Vee made a small choking sound, but when Maggie looked at her, her face was completely blank.

Maggie turned to JD. "You want to tell me what's going on?"

"Got me," he said, as if he hadn't just heard Gamey say it.

"You're not serious."

"Hmm?" He poked intently at his sundae, fishing deep into the plastic saucer and then making a small satisfied noise as he came up with a walnut.

"Some police chief you are."

"Truer words than you might imagine," he said.

9

Maggie was about to leave for Back to School Night when Mac brought up the Explorers again. She was beginning to suspect he purposely saved this topic for times when he was sure there would be no chance to discuss it. "You know I don't like the idea," she said, trying for that note of finality that came to other adults automatically.

"Why not?" Mac asked, trying for that note of innocence other teenagers used, and also failing. "Volunteering will make me a better citizen and introduce me to desirable influences."

"You sound like a bad parody of a guidance counselor."

He held up an Explorers' pamphlet, crumpled from long habitation in his pocket. "I'm quoting. It's all right in here."

"Honey," she said, zipping her hoodie, "I don't like the idea of you hanging around at the Rescue Squad, even if it is a supervised program."

"Come on, Mom," he pleaded, following her as she grabbed her keys. "It's not like they let you *do* anything. You just get to roll bandages and stuff."

"*Roll bandages?*" Maggie repeated. "Who directs their program, Florence Nightingale? The last time anybody rolled bandages was the Crimean War."

"I made that part up."

"Making things up is a new skill for you. Was that inspired by your little friend?"

"Mom!" Mac stage whispered. "Be careful what you say about him!"

"Unless he has this place bugged, which wouldn't surprise me, he'll never know what I say about him."

"Almost never," Mac said. Maggie was horrified. "Don't worry," he continued. "I only repeat the funny stuff."

"No wonder he doesn't like me!"

"He likes you fine," Mac said.

"And if I let you do whatever he wants, he'll like me even better, right?"

"If you let me do stuff normal people do, maybe I'd make more friends."

Maggie wished she could ignore how this made her feel. "I just worry about you."

"Poor Mom." He gave her an embarrassed hug. "You don't need to worry so much."

Yes I do, Maggie thought. I need to worry every second. I just need to hold that worry where you can't see it, so you won't know it's the only way I have to protect you. "What kinds of stuff do they really let the kids do there?" she capitulated. "If I knew it would help me decide."

"What if it's stuff I want to do, but you don't think it's okay?"

"Like what? Starting IVs? Giving drug tests?"

Mac rolled his eyes. "Sweeping floors. Doing the dishes when the squad guys cook. Washing vehicles. Stuff like that."

"Janitorial duties."

He looked disappointed. "See? I knew you would think it's not good enough for me."

"What about drinking?" she asked. "When I was growing up the squads were nothing but clubhouses, places the men hung out and drank beer without getting in trouble with their wives."

"If they're doing that now, we don't know about it."

"So you're already going there." She was aggravated, but somehow not surprised.

"You let me go once, remember?" Maggie stared at him like she was flushing quail. "A couple of times," he admitted.

"So why bother to ask my permission now?"

Mac looked her square in the eye. "I don't like lying to you." He paused. "But I really want you to be okay with it."

"Honey," she said, "helping people isn't all it's cracked up to be."

"You just think that now because of all the stuff that happened," he said. "But you didn't always think that way. And some day you won't be mad at the world anymore."

Maggie sighed. "All right. You can try it for a month and we'll see how it goes. No going to fires or accidents, no touching blood products or body fluids, and if anybody brings so much as a can of beer into the place all bets are off."

"Thanks Mom!"

"And you have to keep your grades up."

"I know," he replied. "Otherwise, how will I get into medical school?"

She didn't answer. As far as she was concerned, this family had already wasted enough of their lives trying to save humanity one weak creature at a time. But she realized there was no point trying to explain how she could believe that to her fourteen-year-old son.

🐦 🐦 🐦

Maggie drove around the parking lot to the back of the school. She wanted to avoid the front entrance and everyone else coming in, with their insider language based on years of Back to School Nights and Winter Carnivals and PTA Field Days. Mac's old school had Sponsor Teas and Seasonal Receptions, tastefully elegant events that didn't require parents to bond. She loitered in the hall, one of the few adults interested in more than just her own child's projects. When she couldn't stall any longer she went into the auditorium. It was nearly full. She chose an empty seat in the center of the room.

Principal Babson, a florid, loose-fleshed man, kept walking on and off the stage, each time coming a little closer to the podium until he finally touched it and stayed. The loudspeakers screeched a few times and then he began talking. Despite her good intentions, Maggie's mind wandered. She focused just in time to hear Babson's instructions for parents to follow their students' class schedules when the bell rang.

"Before we begin our model school day," he said, making it sound like an afterthought, "I'm sure some of you would like to hear a little music from Mr. Dickerman's Jazz Originals."

A large black man in a crisply tailored suit strode onstage and the energy level in the room ramped up as if people had money riding on this event. He waved like he'd spotted some old friends, and the crowed cheered and clapped. Then he made a gesture and they instantly got quiet, as if they'd been trained.

"Good evening, parents. Partners." His voice was cultured and warm. "We have much to be proud of tonight. With only weeks of rehearsal your students, both those who have done me the honor of returning and our most welcome new members, are going to astonish you. Please join me in welcoming the Dooleysburg High Jazz Originals!" The gold-trimmed maroon curtains behind him opened a foot or so, stopped with a jerk and then hiccupped the rest of the way across the stage. The jazz band looked incredibly composed. There was not even a nervous twitch up on stage. The crowd applauded again, but with a bit more restraint.

Mr. Don stepped in front of the kids. His used his baton like a magic wand. The band and the audience seemed equally immersed in the music, though it was no secret that Mr. Don's popularity among the parents was partly thanks to the satisfaction they got from finally seeing a payoff on all those years of instrument rentals and music lessons.

After a few numbers Mr. Don invited this year's new band members onstage. He said that in his band every student who demonstrated commitment got a chance to perform. Maggie got a feeling of achy apprehension about why Mac wasn't up there. She told herself not to make it into a big deal. It was probably just a misunderstanding she could straighten out with the teacher and Mac would get to play in the next concert.

At the end of the number, the band stood and took a bow. The crowd went wild one last time. Mr. Don smiled and waved, exiting the stage with his students and leaving Principal Babson to try to get things under control. Babson made two or three half-hearted attempts, then gestured to someone offstage. The dismissal bell rang and parents got up and rushed from the room as if they'd heard a starter's pistol.

☞   ☞   ☞

Maggie struggled to get through the crowd to Physics, Mac's first class. Parents muscled each other like linebackers. Their impatience was a symptom of the competitiveness that flowed through Dooleysburg High like an underground spring. In the Back to School Night event, where they were specifically forbidden to brag about their individual students, being first to class might be the only way to get special attention.

Maggie located Mac's desk from the chart near the classroom door and sat down. She spent the next fifteen minutes trying to like Mac's teacher. He couldn't help that he was a bean counter. She just wished, for once, that Mac could get a science teacher who didn't think the magic behind reality needed to be reduced to things that could be memorized or demonstrated with an equation. The bell finally rang and she rushed for the door.

"Mrs. Rifkin?" The teacher stopped her as she whizzed past his desk. Surrounding parents quickly looked away. No good was likely to come from being singled out on Back to School Night. "You are Mrs. Rifkin, right? You were sitting in MacDonald's seat." Maggie nodded. "Can you stay for a minute? I'd like to talk to you."

"Sure." They waited awkwardly for the room to clear. Maggie wished she knew some physics small talk. Though it was unlikely, she clung to the hope the teacher just wanted to tell her wonderful things about Mac and his physics brilliance. Physics facts were one of the ways Mac used to hold Gary's interest. "Is everything okay?" Maggie started. "Mac really likes physics. He's been studying it on his own for years."

The teacher waited for the door to click shut behind the last parent. "Maybe that's the problem," he said thoughtfully. "MacDonald seems to be experiencing motivational difficulties. Maybe it's because he already knows the material."

"It's possible," Maggie said. "What's he doing?" This was hard. She wanted to come across as open-minded and engaged, but it was not okay for some stranger to have authority not just over her child, but over her as well. In Mac's old school unless a situation involved criminal intent it was quietly resolved without causing parents unnecessary distress.

"For starters, he's not completing his assignments."

"For starters?" Mac not doing his homework was unbelievable enough all by itself. How could it only be a starter?

"And he's disruptive."

"Excuse me?" Maggie could not have been more shocked if he'd just said he'd caught Mac swinging cats around by their tails.

"Well, not in any ordinary way, I'll give him that. The first time I had to ask him where his homework was, he said his dog ate it. That got a big laugh, which no doubt encouraged him. The next time, I was walking around the classroom collecting homework and when I got to his desk, he tried to use the Jedi mind trick."

"He did *what*?"

"He held up his hand and wiggled his fingers and said, 'you don't need to see my homework'."

Maggie grinned, despite her best intentions. "I'm sorry," she gulped.

"Mrs. Rifkin, this is no laughing matter."

Maggie burst out laughing. What the hell was it with teachers? Why were they always so clueless about making people get themselves in trouble?

The teacher stood there watching, arms akimbo. Akimbo. The only time she'd ever seen that word was on one of her own high school vocabulary lists and now it came after her like a dog on a squirrel. The harder she tried to stop thinking about it, the sillier it sounded. She laughed until her eyes started to tear.

"Mrs. Rifkin," the teacher's face was expressionless, "if you don't take this seriously, how can I hope for MacDonald to understand his behavior is inappropriate?"

"I'm sorry," she guffawed. "I know how wrong this looks." She laughed so hard she made a snorting noise when she tried to catch her breath.

Every so often one of the parents waiting in the next group outside would pull the door open, hear her laughing, and let it slam closed. Maggie knew there would be no recovery if she made the teacher look bad in front of his second period parents, but she couldn't stop. If there was ever a time to play the dead dad card, this was it. "I'm sorry to take this all out on you. We've been under so much stress lately, you know, moving here right after my husband died. Mac's father. Just give me a minute to get under control. I give you my word I'll handle this the right way." She wiped her eyes with the back of her hand.

Tears came in handy, even when made under false pretenses. The teacher softened. "Okay. Sure. Fine."

Maggie left the room quietly, eyes on the ground. Mac's second period class was Band. By the time she got to the Band Room things didn't seem quite so funny anymore. She was late and if she went in now she'd be disrupting an ongoing class. But if she skipped Band she wouldn't be able to find out why Mac didn't play in tonight's concert.

Maggie tried to open one of the metal doors to the Band Room. It was so heavy it could have withstood the possibility of the tuba going supernova one day and trying to blow the rest of the band out of the room. She pulled with all her weight and the door screeched open slowly. When she finally got into the room, Mr. Don and everyone else was staring at her. She tried to say 'sorry,' but her voice disappeared into the back of her throat.

Mr. Don turned back to the parents and resumed speaking. The room was huge, shaped like a big slice of pie. Mr. Don was standing on a low stage in the pointy part with the parents facing him on folding chairs. The walls behind them were lined with closed bleachers. There was another set of double doors across the room that Maggie guessed went outside to the sports fields. She barely finished looking around when the dismissal bell rang. Parents stood up and began shuffling toward the hall, finally tired enough to act their age.

Maggie sidestepped through the crowd to Mr. Don. "Hi," she said, cringing at how dopey that sounded.

"Hi." Mr. Don made his sound like a question.

"I'm Maggie Rifkin. MacDonald's mother."

"Nice to meet you."

His tone made Maggie want to say, really? Where was all that charm the guy had up on stage? "Mac's having a good time in band." Mr. Don nodded, still saying nothing. In truth, Maggie had no idea what Mac thought of band, but Mr. Don's lack of encouragement was bringing out her inner moron. The next group of parents was starting to come in, taking their seats. "I was just wondering. He wasn't supposed to be playing tonight, was he?" She kept babbling. "I would hate it if he was supposed to be here and let anyone down."

Mr. Don's voice stayed even. "MacDonald has a unique opportunity as backup drum chair. But before he can move up to a bigger role, he needs to show some improvement."

"He does?" Maggie hoped her face didn't finish the thought for her.

"How is he coming with his lessons?"

"His lessons?"

Mr. Don looked at her oddly now. "He hasn't started his lessons yet? When you signed the band form, you agreed to start lessons within two weeks."

"Oh," she said, making a dismissive noise. "Of course. His lessons." What lessons?

"You do remember signing the band form, don't you?"

Maggie felt panicky. "Of course."

"I would like to give MacDonald more exposure in the Jazz Originals," Mr. Don said. "But first he has to show me he's serious about learning to play the drums."

Maggie could feel her eyes narrowing, but she gave a neutral nod. Learning to play? This small-town impresario couldn't even be bothered to figure out which kid they were talking about. "Sure," she said politely. "Thanks for your time." She walked out of the room. She'd had enough crap for one night. How was it that her son, the perceptive, funny, smart boy who left the house every morning, didn't seem to be the same kid who showed up at this school? What entitled these strangers to form opinions about him? She was sorry she had come. The bell rang for third period. The hell with this, she thought, and walked out to her car.

On the drive home the mutually exclusive facts of the situation kept gnawing at her. Everything she knew about her son said he was a perfect kid. So why was she hearing about bad things he did from people who had no obvious reason to lie? By the time she got home, she was steamed. She blew in from the garage. Mac was sitting at the kitchen table, a textbook open in front of him. "What are you doing?" she snapped.

"Homework?" he said tentatively.

"Ah." She pulled out a chair and sat down. She spun the book around so it faced her. It appeared to be algebra. "We do homework now?" she demanded. To his credit, he did not feign surprise. "The Jedi mind trick?" she continued caustically.

"It could have worked. What if it worked? I would never know if I didn't try."

"Mac," she sighed, "how are you going to succeed if you won't play by their rules?"

"I do."

"You don't. You cruise below the radar, not even paying attention until you get caught."

"You don't play by their rules," he said.

"That's different," Maggie said. "I'm working out of another section of the play book."

"Me too," he said.

"You have to earn your way there first. And what's the deal with Band?"

"Oh yeah," he said. "I need to get some papers signed."

"Really?" she asked. "From what I heard they've already been signed, haven't they?"

He looked at the table. "I'm sorry. They wanted me to take lessons from a local teacher. You should hear what they expect the kids to do. They'd never appreciate me. I don't want lessons from some jerk who thinks he needs to teach me to sound like everybody else."

"Even if you're right, that doesn't make it okay to have someone forge my signature."

"I know." He looked directly at her now. "I've been feeling bad ever since I did it."

"You were just worried about getting caught."

"No." He shook his head. "I'm kind of glad you finally found out."

"Promise me you'll cut the crap."

"I promise."

"No. *Really* promise me."

"I mean it. I swear."

She realized there was nothing he could say that would sound convincing. "You know I can't watch you all the time. So once in a while it might look like you're going to get away with something. But trust me, what goes around comes around. I will *always* find out. And until I do, you'll hate how you feel for lying to me. But don't kid yourself. I *will* always find out."

He raised his hand in front of her face and slowly moved it back and forth, wiggling his fingers. "The boy is lonely," he said in a deep hypnotic tone. "He needs a dog."

"Oh, for crying out loud," Maggie said, getting up.

"Come on," he said. "Admit it. You thought that Jedi mind trick stuff was pretty funny, didn't you?"

10

"Daniel!" Martha called. "Come on! This one's a timekeeper. *Please* don't make us late." She picked up and slammed down some stuff on the counter for emphasis. If Daniel made her choose between indulging him or annoying a potential customer he was going to lose. "Get a move on," she said. "We can't afford to get off on the wrong foot with her."

"I'm an artist," Daniel answered. "She'll find me eminently forgivable."

"Or incredibly pompous," Libertine said.

"What's that?" Daniel raised his voice. Libertine was a new hire, one of those career art students. But her qualifications for the job had nothing to do with her knowledge of art. She had a Marilyn Monroe whisper of a voice that turned male customers to putty. Unfortunately, it also threatened to beat Daniel at his own game. "Speak up," he said gruffly. "You're talking to my bad ear."

"No shit," Libertine said, throwing him a flirty little wave.

"Someday he's going to hear you," Martha warned her.

"Then he'll get to fire me and put me out of my misery."

"You don't have to stay if you're miserable."

Libertine blinked, as if this option hadn't occurred to her. "For sure I'll quit some day."

Martha wasn't worried. The idea was likely to slip through the screen door of Libertine's memory without leaving a trace, just like everything else they tried to tell her. Martha was in no hurry for her to go anywhere as long as she remained good for business. The only downside about employing her was she expected to get paid. That's where Maggie Rifkin would come in so handy. A painter needed patrons. Maggie Rifkin was rumored to be painfully wealthy. All they had to do was snag her before anyone else in town got a chance to cozy up. "Daniel!" Martha yelled irritably, "move it!"

❧ ❧ ❧

Maggie pulled into the lot behind Dooley Books. It was not the most convenient place to park, but at least she didn't have to feed a meter here. She found a shady spot and left the car open while she went to buy a parking tag. She almost looked at her watch, then caught herself. She was making progress with the habit, but it took constant vigilance. She'd finally managed to forget sometimes about the sweep of the second hand, but she wasn't able yet to stop worrying about the minutes. She was pretty sure she still had a few left before she was supposed to meet Martha. It took everything she had not to check. She knew it wouldn't matter if she was a few minutes late. What difference would a few minutes make? She fed some quarters into the slot of the parking machine and it spit out her receipt. She walked back to her car and opened the door. Reaching in to place the receipt on the dashboard, she glanced at the time stamped on it. 09:57. No sweat. She could make it take exactly three minutes to get to the General Store.

⁊ ⁊ ⁊

Martha sat on the wooden stool she kept strategically placed inside the front door so she could see up and down State Street without being detected. "There she is," she called toward the studio area at the back of the shop. Maggie was walking purposefully, looking as if she was deep in concentration. "Daniel," Martha said, "This one is definitely odd."

"They're all odd."

"She's not the kind of odd we usually have to deal with. It's like there's some unfinished business about her."

"We're not going to have to play amateur psychologist again, are we?"

"I just want you to be prepared." Martha stopped. There was no point asking him to treat the new customer with some extra care. The request had never worked before.

"Tell you what. If you get her to buy a portrait, I promise to make her look normal."

"It's not the way she looks that isn't normal. You ready to go meet her?"

"Not yet."

"Daniel!" Martha exploded. "I asked you to get ready half an hour ago!"

"I'm painting here. I can't just put the brush down at someone else's convenience."

"How much longer do you need?"

"You go on over there and soften her up. I won't be long."

Martha didn't feel like arguing. And since Maggie didn't know she was planning to introduce Daniel, there was no harm in going over alone first.

⁊ ⁊ ⁊

Maggie walked into the General Store. Mid-morning on a weekday and she still had to wait in line. She got a mocha and went out to sit on the porch. The unseasonably soft weather had filled the streets with people, mostly women. They were carrying packages, pushing strollers, rushing around with a deliberateness that implied they were working on burning a target number of calories.

Martha came out of the Art Shop and across the street. She said hello before going inside to get an espresso. Maggie was a little puzzled why Martha seemed so determined to meet for coffee. There wasn't the kind of easy friendship she had with Vee, where they hung around together whenever they felt like it. Martha always had an edge. Being with her was work.

"So how's it going?" Martha asked, putting her coffee on the table and sitting down.

"Better than a few minutes ago," Maggie said. "I was pretty cranky until I got my caffeine. I think I'm addicted."

"I thought they called the caffeine thing a dependency."

"That figures. If you have to depend on anything, you're screwed." Watching Martha's face, Maggie realized how odd that comment sounded. She looked for a safer topic. "Looks like there are a lot of stay at home mothers in this town."

"Yeah," Martha answered. "They like to start young and have their kids close together so they can get it over with."

"If they want to get it over with, why do it in the first place?"

"A question more people should have asked themselves when they had the chance." This time Maggie was the one who didn't answer, so Martha changed the subject. "I'm glad they finally got rid of Morsel. That kid is trouble."

"Vee Hawthorne said that too." Maggie started tearing tiny pieces off her napkin. "My son spends a lot of time with him."

Martha made a brittle smile. "So how's your son adjusting to school?"

"Is his reputation really that bad?" Maggie asked.

Martha looked confused. "Who? Your son?"

"No," Maggie replied, "Morsel."

Martha made a dismissive gesture. She toyed with the lid on her coffee and then, with a sigh of relief, looked over Maggie's shoulder. Maggie turned to follow her gaze. Daniel Stewart was coming up the porch stairs. Maggie's expression went utterly blank. Daniel stared at her, speechless, for several seconds. "Margaret?" he said. "It is you, isn't it?"

Maggie did not move or speak. Martha looked from one to the other. "You two know each other?" she finally asked.

"I should say," Daniel replied, walking over, staring at Maggie the whole time. "How have you been?" he asked, taking her hand.

Maggie fought the urge to pull her hand away. She was a child again, filled with discomfort at Daniel's delicate touch, so unlike the hammy firmness of her father's hands. She used to pretend her father's hands had magic powers. If she could only hold his hands she would be safe from everything that scared her. But it never worked out that way. When she needed somebody he always sent Daniel, with his small unsatisfactory hands.

Daniel pulled a chair around and sat facing Maggie. When he spoke, the customary gruffness was missing from his voice. "This just goes to show what a blockhead I am. All this noise about a new woman from New York and I never considered it might be you." He paused. "I've been wondering about you for a long time, hoping you were happy. I didn't know you were widowed." He stopped talking.

"Daniel, don't."

"I'm sorry." He took a breath. "I tried to reach you after your mother and Doc . . ." Maggie continued to stare at him. "You never answered my letters. I was afraid you didn't find out in time to come to the funeral."

Maggie blinked. "I knew."

Daniel sat back in his chair. "I guess I shouldn't be surprised you didn't want anything to do with all of it. But they never changed the will. I was still the executor."

"You did a fine job," Maggie said. "I have no complaints."

"That's not the point." The harsh ring of impatience was returning to his voice. "I got a cut of the money. I wanted to give it back to you."

"I don't need it. I've got enough."

"Well take it for your son then!"

"He doesn't need it either. His father took care of him." In a sense that was the truth.

"Well dammit, I don't want it! It's yours."

"Daniel," one corner of Maggie's mouth began to lift in an arch smile, "it was decent money then, and unless you've been keeping it under your mattress, it's a whole lot more now. You know you want that money."

"You're wrong!" Daniel exploded, standing up so abruptly he knocked over his chair. The other customers on the porch were startled, but quickly looked away. "I saved it for you! And your little boy!"

"He's not little."

"He was! He was little when they died!" Daniel turned and stormed off the porch too fast to see that he had finally gotten a reaction.

"How do you know that?" she called after him. She turned to Martha. "How does he know how old Mac was when my father died?"

"Tell you what," Martha said, righting Daniel's vacated chair. "You explain to me what the hell just happened here and I'll see if I can find out an answer for you. Of course, I'll need to wait until he cools down. You did an impressive job of pissing him off."

"How much money is it?" Maggie asked.

"Damned if I know," Martha replied. "We've been married a long time and he never mentioned it before."

Maggie looked across the street. "Some day I would like to meet a man who doesn't keep secrets."

"Hey," Martha snapped, "stay with me here. What's the story between you and my husband? Or more accurately, what's the history?"

Maggie's face hardened. "He took care of things for my father."

"You make him sound like a hit man. What kind of things?"

"Me. He carried out orders with regard to me." Maggie stood up.

"Wait a minute." Martha grabbed her arm. "There's unfinished business here. You can't just get up and leave."

"I said keep the money. I meant it."

Martha looked at her incredulously. "This isn't about the money. Did you *hear* him? His heart is breaking. You think it's okay for you to walk away from that?"

Maggie looked at Martha's hand on her arm and Martha let go. "He has no obligation to care about me."

"Calm down," Martha said. "You don't have to be hard-nosed about this. You've got no parents, Daniel has no children. Maybe there's room for him in your life. Maybe your son could use a little extra family." Maggie started to walk away. Martha continued. "Maybe you can lighten some of your own load by forgiving him for whatever it was he did."

Maggie turned around. "If you think that's what he's looking for, tell him to take a number."

r   r   r

Maggie stayed away from town for several days, but it didn't help. Her meeting with Daniel lingered with her like the afterimage of a nightmare, leaking into her thoughts until it took up all the space in her head. She decided there was no benefit in avoiding town and went to the General Store for a coffee. But when she got there, she had trouble choosing a blend. She finally picked something, and then she had trouble deciding where to drink it. Take it home? Find a place to sit where she wouldn't be seen? Throw it out?

Eventually she sat down inside the front window of the General Store and stayed there, making her coffee last as long as possible. She stared across the street at the Art Shop, certain somebody over there was staring back. She got up to go to the bathroom. When she came out, Martha was standing there waiting for her. "You look like you just got caught," Martha said.

"I wasn't expecting to find you guarding the crapper like it was a Troll Bridge."

"I got tired of waiting for you to come across the street."

"You were watching me?"

"Don't act so indignant. You were staring right back at me."

"This is beginning to sound stupid."

Martha handed Maggie her coffee. "Just go over and talk to him."

Maggie was having a hard time getting words out. "I don't know where to begin."

"You need to lighten up. Not every conversation has to be meaningful. Some people actually talk about nothing at great length."

"Not Daniel."

"No, Daniel *complains* about nothing at great length. So do me a favor. Go over and listen to him for a while."

Maggie walked outside. She had to force herself to take every step toward the Art Shop. Details took on a crystalline sharpness, and she was out of breath even though she was walking downhill. At the door of the Art Shop, she stopped. She stood there, staring at a framed pastel in the window, one of Daniel's dancers.

Back when she was in high school, before Martha's reign, Daniel had done a series of ballerinas. Maggie showed up here almost every day to watch, fascinated by the slender, delicate girls who came to pose for him, the way they held their backs and fixed the positions of their arms with utter precision. The shop was a real studio then, littered with half-finished canvasses, dirty coffee cups and rags smelling of turpentine and linseed oil. There were dark corners where Daniel let misfit kids sit around and watch him work while they hid from the attendance officer from school. The faint tang of pot and beer and fast food hung off the walls like mold. Daniel barely acknowledged any of them, though he tolerated them all.

Maggie opened the door and walked in. Except for some of Daniel's favorite oils and pastels, there was nothing in the shop she recognized. Martha had turned the long narrow space into a gallery, leaving only a small area in the back for Daniel. There was no way he did his real work in such a tidy space. And he would never paint where bystanders could watch, like he was some sideshow act. But he was back there now, pretending to push paint around on a small canvas.

Libertine was standing at the counter. "Can I help you?"

"Where are all the losers?" Maggie asked.

Libertine was annoyed. "The *what*?"

"The kids who used to cut school and hang out here. Remember, Daniel?"

Daniel pretended to be engrossed in his painting. "Speak up," he commanded. "You're talking to my bad ear."

"The losers," Maggie repeated loudly.

He turned halfway around. If he was surprised to see her, he didn't show it. "They don't need me now that they're allowed off campus during school hours."

Maggie walked toward the back of the shop, ignoring Libertine and her displeasure. "Mac tried to convince me he could leave school during the day if I wrote him a note."

"Is that your son's name? Mac?"

"Turn around so I can talk to your good ear. I don't like shouting," Maggie said.

"Named him after the old man, huh?" Maggie didn't answer. Daniel finally turned to face her. "So did you write your son the note?"

"No."

"Bad decision," Daniel said. "All he's going to do is get some girl to write it for him."

"He's not that kind of kid." Maggie felt entitled to protest, though she was no longer as righteous about it as before.

Daniel snorted. "He's a teenage boy, isn't he?"

"You still believe you know so much about teenagers?" Maggie asked.

"I know they're pretty unforgiving," he answered.

Maggie made an effort to control her sudden fury.

Daniel turned back toward his easel. When he spoke, his voice was low. "Over the years I've come to regret a lot of things."

"I feel sorry for you then. Regret is pointless. It's like being trapped in a locked crate. All it lets you do is punish yourself without offering an option to make amends. Unless, of course, that's what you're looking for."

"What was that?" Daniel asked. "I didn't catch all of it."

Maggie walked closer to him. "Is that your game now?" she asked softly. "Pretending to be deaf? Shame on you."

He shrugged. "What the hell. It was getting damn boring around here once Martha made me clean up my act. This way, I hear all kinds of stuff. Amazing what people will say when they think nobody can hear them."

Maggie looked up. Libertine was watching them with a mixture of disbelief and incipient horror. She was too far away to hear what they were saying, but obviously she knew nobody was shouting. "Didn't you know he could read lips?" Maggie called across the room. "If I were you I'd be careful around mirrors." Libertine flushed and checked nervously around the shop.

Daniel continued painting. "You've just ruined a good bit of my fun."

"I'm sorry, Daniel. I was hard on you the other day for stuff that wasn't your fault."

He didn't look up. "One of the things I regret most is that I never made him tell me why. Sometimes the stuff he asked me to do made no sense to me, and I did it anyway."

"Maybe you already knew he would never tell you," Maggie responded. "He would have just cut you off for asking."

"I still wonder if I could have changed things if I stood up to him."

This was the wrong thing for him to say. "Like what? Ditching a fifteen-year-old kid alone in New York City?" Maggie's voice cut the air like a razor. Neither of them noticed Martha coming in the front door.

"He told me someone from a school would be picking you up. I should have at least waited with you to make sure that happened."

"And you had no clue why he was sending me away."

"I knew whatever his reasons were, in his mind even being left alone in New York was better for you than staying here."

"My son's almost the same age now I was then. He was supposed to go away to prep school this year. That was the plan. But I couldn't imagine being cruel enough to send him away from everything he knew, no matter how 'good for him' it was supposed to be. At least he would have known somebody cared about him, which was more than I had. But it's an inhuman thing to do to a kid."

Daniel stood up, helpless in the face of Maggie's anger. "I'm sorry," he said. "Your father made it clear I was to drop you off and not contact you again. I never stopped being sorry I listened to him."

Martha came over. "Can I do something to help here?" she asked.

"No." Maggie turned away. "I was just leaving."

"Wait," Daniel said. It was not a request. "Stay here. I have something to give you."

"I already told you, I don't want their money."

Daniel gestured at her impatiently and headed into the back room.

"What is it with you and the money?" Martha snapped. "You think he keeps it in a shoe box?" She shook her head. "Why didn't you tell me you knew him?"

"What difference would it have made?" Maggie's voice was flat.

"None at all," Martha answered coldly, "if he wasn't trying to waste a chunk of his heart on you."

Maggie walked toward the door.

"Don't leave," Martha ordered her. "He asked you to wait."

Maggie stood by the front window, staring outside. When Daniel walked up behind her she turned so abruptly she nearly banged into him.

"Here." He held out a yellowed envelope. It was in pretty bad shape. "It's not really that old," he said. "Paper usually holds up better than this. But it wasn't taken care of until I got it." Maggie made no move to take it from him. "There's no money in it," he said, annoyed.

"I'm sorry." It was reflexive. Maggie had no idea why she was apologizing.

Daniel softened. "Take a look. I think it's something you need to know."

Inside the envelope was a photo, a wallet size headshot of a young couple, stiffly formal. The woman had on too much dark lipstick and a small orchid pinned to the lapel of her jacket. The man looked vaguely miserable. "My mother and Doc," Maggie said. "Is this their wedding photo?" Daniel nodded. "I've never seen it before."

"Take out the rest," Daniel said.

The paper behind the snapshot was thin and slick, old photocopy paper. The type was badly faded. It was her parents' marriage license. It took a minute to for her to notice what she was supposed to see. She looked at the date again and laughed, more startled than amused. "They got married six months before I was born," she said.

"I know," Daniel replied.

"That's their big secret?" Maggie asked. "They messed up their lives because she got knocked up? If only they'd waited a few years they could have gotten rid of me and each other without so much fuss."

"Margaret," Daniel said somberly, "if that's what they wanted to do, they didn't need to wait for a Supreme Court decision. He was a doctor."

Maggie was suddenly finding it impossible to get enough air. "I don't understand."

Daniel grabbed Martha's hiding stool and made her sit down. "Martha," he said, "get some water." Martha gave him a look before walking away. "I'm sorry," he said. "I didn't imagine it would have this kind of effect on you."

"Me either," she managed to answer.

"I mean, I thought, when you didn't come home . . . Not that I blame you."

Maggie held up her hand to stop him. "It's not that." Martha returned and held out a cup of water. Maggie's hand trembled as she took it. "What did I do?" Her voice caught. "They wanted me before I was born. What did I do to mess it up?"

"It had nothing to do with anything you did or didn't do," Daniel said.

The light went off in Maggie's head. "That makes it even worse. They had me because they didn't believe in abortion?"

"That's not what I'm saying at all. It wasn't some abstract political issue for him. You're here because he wanted you."

"But she didn't."

Daniel put his arm around her. "Libertine is standing behind the counter with her mouth hanging open like a dead fish. Let's go across the street where we can talk in private."

Maggie was exhausted. She let him lead the way. Neither of them noticed Martha, standing there watching as they walked out the door.

☙ ☙ ☙

Daniel brought over two cups from the counter. "Hot cocoa?" Maggie was amused despite herself.

"Used to work wonders when you were a kid."

"Stop trying to pretend you can make this all better," she said.

Daniel struggled to find the right words. "That's what's wrong with us. We believe saying what we think is a privilege. Some people take it as their right."

Maggie took a sip of her cocoa. "Like Martha. But she comes from a different universe than you and me."

"I'm sorry I was a coward."

"You can stop apologizing. We both know it wasn't your responsibility, no matter what I say when I'm angry."

"But I wanted it to be my responsibility. I just didn't do a very good job of it. I was afraid you wouldn't have anybody."

Maggie looked away. There was a funny feeling at the back of her nose.

"Please don't cry," Daniel said.

She looked at him. "I'm not crying," she said. "I never cry."

"I should have realized how bad it was before he had me take you away. Maybe I didn't want to see."

"Stop blaming yourself." She said it without sympathy, but without any meanness either.

"That's what Martha said. The worst of it was over by the time I met her. She wanted to help, but there was nothing she could do to let me off the hook. There is no such thing as not being responsible when you're faced with a situation like that."

Maggie sighed. "That's a romantic notion. There's nothing you could have done. They were both damaged people."

"Who isn't?" he said almost angrily.

Maggie looked out the window. When she spoke, her voice was low. "He wanted me to come home. He sent me a letter. After I read it I threw it away."

"When you were at school?"

"After I graduated."

"He asked you to come home instead of going to college?"

"She was too much for him. He sent me away so he could focus everything on her, and she still overwhelmed him."

"He should have put her away," Daniel said forcefully.

"You know the choice wasn't that simple. Institutions back then had nothing for her."

"I was thinking of the two of you."

"Oh, Daniel," she said, and the pain behind her nose spread to her throat and behind her eyes now. "What if he wanted me to come home so he could tell me he was sorry? I stayed away because I figured he wanted to dump her on me. But what if all he wanted was to see me again before it was too late?"

"You can't think about that," Daniel said, taking her hand again.

11

"Come on, Mom. Please." Mac was pulling out all the stops.

"Nice try with the puppy eyes," Maggie said.

"Good one," Mac grinned. "Puppy eyes." He batted his lashes dramatically.

"No. No means no. The last thing I need is a dog."

"It won't be *your* dog."

"Spare me. I will pay for it and everything it needs. I will end up walking it, feeding it, cleaning up after it, and, once the novelty wears off, being emotionally responsible for it. No."

"But I'm an only child. I need a companion."

"What happened to Morsel?"

"What am I supposed to do for a positive influence?"

"Watch public television."

Mac lowered his voice. "We have a very narrow window of opportunity here. Before you know it, I'll grow up and go away to college."

"My point exactly. You'll go off and live your life and I'll be stuck with your smelly, hairy dog."

"Mom," Mac pleaded, "the whole time we were moving here, I kept thinking how we were finally going to have a chance to be normal."

The dam holding back the reservoir of guilt that fed Maggie's engine took a direct hit from that one. She searched for something to say. "I don't even know how to get a dog."

"Easy." Mac whipped out a copy of *The Daily Intellectual* he'd stuck between his books. "Look. Right here, in the classifieds. 'Female Lhasa seeks loving home'."

"That sounds like a personal from the back of some sleazy magazine."

"Listen, Mom! 'Time is of the essence'."

Maggie was instantly suspicious. "Why?"

"It doesn't say. But there's a phone number. Can I just call and find out? Please?"

"You can call and find out. But that's it. Don't make any commitments."

"Thanks!" He raced out of the room. Within minutes he was back. "It's really sad, Mom. I talked to the guy, and his aunt is going into a nursing home and she can't take her dog with her, and he can't keep it because he already has too many of his own. If nobody adopts her, he's going to have to take her to the pound."

Maggie's eyes narrowed. "How much does he want for her?"

"He's not asking for any money. He'll even give us her crate and all her food and stuff. He just wants her to have a good home."

"Something's fishy."

"He said we could come and meet her right now if we wanted. Can we? Please? I wrote down where he lives, just in case you said yes."

"Mac, we have no idea what's going on with this dog. What if she's one of those psychotic yappy little things?"

"I only want to go see her. I'm not getting my hopes up or anything."

"Okay." Maggie resigned herself to the fact that she was outmaneuvered. She did realize her current difficulty saying no was only going to get exponentially more difficult once they met the dog. But she was determined to take a firm stand on the dog issue. She took her time following Mac out to the car.

They had to inch out of the garage. Every so often Gamey planted some obstacle in the alley. The most recent one was an LED speed display. Nothing moved fast enough to trigger it except the occasional terrified squirrel. After a few days it went away as mysteriously as it had come, right before a story in the *Intellectual* about a similar device that recently reappeared on a distant highway after an unexplained absence.

They drove several miles north on 616, the main route out of town, without finding where they were supposed to turn. "Are you sure you got this right?" Maggie asked. "We're pretty far out in the country."

"I'm sure," Mac said. "He lives on a farm."

Mac!" Maggie yelped, "why didn't you tell me that before we left?"

"What difference does it make?"

"What *difference* does it make? A woman and a teenage boy lured out into the middle of nowhere by some stranger. Doesn't that sound like the beginning of a horror movie to you?"

Mac leaned forward. "Slow down! You're going to miss it!" Maggie braked hard. "This is it," he said. "Go left." The tires screeched as she turned the corner. "Sounds like you need to get some air," Mac said.

"What I need is someone who can give me decent directions. To someplace it makes sense to go."

"Over there," he pointed. "That gray house."

The house was big and set way back from the road. It had an aura of genteel dilapidation, something the Beverly Hillbillies might have liked if they'd stayed in the hills of Tennessee. There was a long gravel driveway. They crunched slowly along, kicking up clouds of dust and small stones. They were most of the way to the house when Maggie realized the noise she heard over the car's engine was a whole lot of baying dogs. She stopped short.

"That's it," she said, putting the car in reverse. "We're out of here."

"Wait!" Mac pleaded. "Somebody's coming out of the house."

"Duck down," Maggie said. "Maybe he won't notice us."

"Look!" Mac exclaimed. "He's got her with him!"

Indeed, the grizzled apparition was carrying a small, furry white bundle. Like his house, he was large and mostly gray. Only his buffalo check hunting cap added a touch of color.

"Don't get out of the car," Maggie ordered.

Mac flung open his door and jumped out. The noise of the hounds, as well as their skunky odor, grew noticeably stronger. Despite her misgivings Maggie got out too.

"Stay there," the man called. "I'm bringing her to you." He pronounced it "branging her to ya." He stopped a few feet away from them.

"We're the ones who called about the dog," Maggie said.

"That so?" he asked. "I thought maybe you was selling Avon."

Maggie smiled unconvincingly. "You from around here?" She wondered if her friendly conversational tone was fooling anybody.

"Born and raised," he responded. "But you ain't. I can tell from your accent."

"Born and raised," she replied and they stood for a moment in respectful animosity. If he was grateful to her kind and their romantic notions about country living for making him very wealthy just because of his tenacious unwillingness to move somewhere else, he wasn't showing it. "Sounds like you have a lot of dogs," Maggie said.

"Them's my hunting dogs. That's one reason I got to get ridda her. They'll take her for a rabbit, eat her in two bites."

Mac shuddered. The old guy, instinctively wily, plopped the dog into Mac's arms. "Mom," Mac said, "she's shaking."

I'd be shaking too, Maggie thought. "So your hounds are one reason you need to get rid of her. What are the others?" She'd be damned if this guy was going to unload some neurotic dog crisis onto her.

"Only one other," he replied.

"And that is?"

He pointed to the quivering ball of fluff. "That there's a lady's dog." He said it with all the disdain deserved by ladies *and* their little dogs.

"Mac," she asked, imitating the old guy's intonation, "you want a *lady's* dog?"

He shrugged. "Sure."

"What's her name?"

"Call her whatever the hell you want. Ain't like she's smart enough to answer to anything."

Maggie wondered if this was the same reason he hadn't bothered to introduce himself. "Do you know anything at all about her?"

This offended him. "I ain't neglectful. She's been fixed, and she's up to date on her shots. She's somewhere around two years old. You want to know exactly, ask the vet. He could prob'ly tell you her name too, if you care."

"Who's her vet?"

"You taking her?"

She looked at Mac. It was a lost cause. She would never be able to justify it to him if she left the poor creature here. "Yeah. We'll take her."

"Open your trunk. I'll bring out her stuff and set it in there."

Now that he had possession of the dog, Mac hurried back to the safety of the car. Maggie waited outside while the farmer loaded the little dog's paraphernalia into her trunk. "You like this BMW model?" he asked as he finished.

The question took her by surprise. "Sure," she said.

"I'm partial to Mercedes myself. The big one. Got two, swap one off every other year so's the mileage don't get too high. Plus it makes Carl Bendz stroke out every time I drive by with a brand new car that's not one of his. Worth a couple grand for that pleasure alone."

Maggie couldn't help smiling. "Maybe we have more in common than you think."

"Some day I'd like to get my hands on that chipmunk head of his and do something real nasty to it."

"Okay," she said brightly. Maybe they didn't have quite as much in common as she'd imagined. "You sure your aunt isn't going to mind you giving away her dog?"

"Naw. She's dead. Just didn't want to upset the boy."

"Oh. Thanks." Maggie walked briskly around the car and got inside, turning the key in the ignition before she even closed her door. She looked at Mac holding the dog, which was clearly already his. "Your magic powers must have led you to that poor dog."

Mac buried his face in her fur, but immediately sat up again. "I think she needs a bath."

"Welcome to the joys of pet ownership. She's all yours, remember?"

"You don't have to keep saying that. I'm not going to lose interest, like she's a new toy or something. Her name is Penelope."

"Penelope?" Maggie asked. "What kind of a name is that for a cute little dog?"

"Penelope was Ulysses' wife," Mac informed her. "She waited twenty years for him to return home, and never once gave up hope. She refused every other suitor because she never believed Ulysses was dead."

"That's sweet," Maggie said, but something about it gave her a chill.

🖑 🖑 🖑

"May I help you?" The flamboyantly dressed host didn't look like he especially wanted to help anyone.

"Reservation for Bendz," Lillian said.

Carl leaned over and whispered in her ear. "This is the guy who called me a nouveau beastie last time we were here. I thought you were going to get him canned."

"It didn't work out," Lillian said, moving away ever so slightly. "Table for four at 7 PM," she said to the host.

He glanced at her from under his eyebrows and continued running his finger slowly down the list on his podium. "Nope," he mumbled to himself, but loud enough to be heard. Then he paused dramatically, and looked up at Bendz. "Stop stamping your hooves, darling," he said. "I've found it." He picked up four menus and walked lightly up the stairs against the front wall without bothering to tell them to follow him.

Lillian hurried after him. She turned at the bottom stair. "Come along."

Bendz, irate, turned to his daughter and her bulb-headed husband, Wesley. "Why do we always have to come here?" he snapped.

"Now, Daddy," Carol Ann slipped her hand under his arm, "the view of the river is charming, and the food is very good."

"How the hell would you know? You and your mother going to share another bowl of water with lemon?" Carol Ann dropped his arm.

"Carl, Carl, Carl." Wesley shook his head with amusement.

Bendz glared at him. "Why don't you get a rug? Your head looks like a honeydew melon sitting on top of your shoulders." Wesley chuckled. Bendz couldn't stand that he was so dumb he didn't even care he was being insulted.

"Are you *coming*?" the host called, halfway up the stairs.

"Later, sweetheart," Bendz muttered under his breath. "After I ditch this crew."

The small room at the top of the stairs was hot and noisy. They followed the host across it, sucking in stomachs and raising arms to fit between the tables. "Look at all these fools," Bendz muttered. "I can't believe the kind of money people waste for the pleasure of showing off for their friends."

Lillian gave him a withering glance. "Odd sentiment coming from you."

"Cars are different," he snapped. "People need cars."

"Yes, you're such a charitable man, Carl. Always thinking about what people need. At least Rockefeller threw dimes, not hard candy."

The host picked up speed. At the far side of the room, he flung open a door and led them out onto a rooftop deck. "Table for four," he said, pulling out one of the chairs.

"You take that one," Bendz commanded his son-in-law. "I don't want the sun in my eyes." He sat down and resumed complaining. "You sit up here with the stink of citronella to get a view of the Delaware and all you see are a bunch of crummy rooftops."

Carol Ann looked at her mother. "You didn't premedicate him," she said accusingly.

"He was late. We didn't have time for a cocktail."

"Mother!" she exploded, "what is *wrong* with you? Don't I take enough responsibility for managing him? Do I have to remind you to do every little thing?"

Lillian picked up her menu. "I'm not all that hungry tonight," she said. "Carol Ann, shall we ask them to split a salad for us, with microgreens and those yellow teardrop tomatoes?"

"Ah, they've got the Kobe beef burger special again," Wesley beamed at no one in particular. "These Friday night family dinners are such a treat."

r r r

Gamey pulled into the parking lot behind the police station. He was peeved about doing this delivery, but he had to put a good face on it. It was important to make happy with the boys. No point going to the trouble of donating their dinner every Friday if you were going to throw away the goodwill by being a sourpuss.

He opened the door of his van and climbed out. It was one of those real old-time vans, not some soccer mom job. It handled like a truck and towered over him when he stood next to it. He never let anybody else drive it. It wasn't only that he loved the thing. It was also nobody's business about those blocks he installed on the pedals so he could reach them.

He hefted the insulated sack onto his shoulder. Then he grabbed the oily white loaf bag off the floor and walked across the parking lot. In a misguided fit of civic improvement some earlier town council had ordered up a new police headquarters in the style of a Spanish hacienda. Gamey went in through the employee entrance on the side. To his left were the public areas of the rancho—the squad room, the chief's office, and at the front, right off the street,

"Reception". On his right, partially hidden by a wall, were the cells. These were mostly used for storage, though occasionally somebody was obstinately foolish enough to get locked up for a little while.

Gamey turned left and went into the squad room. "Dinner time!" he sang, still annoyed that nobody thought it was funny when he yelled, "Soo-ey!" Bunch of sticks. Joe Butts, Walter and Officer Mike sauntered into the room. "Cheez-steaks all around," Gamey announced, taking the foil-wrapped packages out of the insulated sack and passing them out. "Where's Miss Priss?" he demanded.

"Chief's watching the Henhouse," Walter said, his mouth already full. "Said to tell you to come by when you finish here."

"Dammit!" Gamey said. "It ain't bad enough I got to make a special stop at the Hoagie Hole to get him an eye-talian because he can't eat a good old cheez-steak like a normal human. I got to deliver it too?"

"You delivered our dinners," Walter answered amicably.

"Guy's a pain in my ass." Gamey slammed out of the room, long white oily bag in tow.

"Bet you could throw your back out being a pain in his ass," Officer Mike said. "Got to bend down so low to find it."

r　r　r

"I don't know why we go out to dinner with them every week," Bendz said tightly.

"Because they're family," Lillian replied.

"Families do other things besides eat. Or not eat, at forty-five bucks a head!"

"Oh, Carl," she said, "don't be such a skinflint. You can afford it."

Lillian wasn't really paying attention to him, he knew. She was busy doing her yoga. She had that yellow crap all over her face again. It was supposed to preserve her beauty. In fact, the only effect he could see was to make him not give a damn that she could twist her legs up around herself like something out of the Kama Sutra. He hovered nearby, frustrated that he couldn't find a way to get her attention. Finally, in desperation, he said, "You look like a classic Philly treat. Pretzel with mustard."

"Carl," she said archly, "is it not important to you that I maintain my appearance? I know how proud you are when we attend public events and people notice how good I look. A man in your position needs a wife with equivalent status."

"Hey, don't try to tell me you're doing this for me," he snarled. "In the story of our life together, I'm fucking Sara Crewe and you are nothing but hot cross buns."

🐚 🐚 🐚

"Mom," Mac said, "don't do that."

Maggie drew her hand back toward her plate. "Come on, Mac. A little bit won't hurt." The dog looked at her sadly, or at least Maggie thought it could be sadly. It was actually pretty difficult to tell if the dog even had eyes behind all that hair.

"If you feed her from the table, you'll spoil her."

"It didn't spoil you. It's just a little piece of chicken tender. I want her to feel welcome."

"You want her to feel welcome," Vee muttered from her side of the table, "you should try offering her something besides chicken tenders once in a while."

🐚 🐚 🐚

Bendz punched the large button that raised the farthest garage door. He liked to use the silver Lexus SUV when he wanted to feel inconspicuous. Any number of middle-aged Dooleysburg males drove a silver Lexus SUV, more often than not purchased from him. Some of those men were likely to be at the destination where he was headed tonight.

He got into the SUV and started it up. "Madame," he said, in the direction of his sun visor. He could hear the phone dialing. Ah, Blue Tooth.

The phone rang twice. "Hey sugar," she answered, in that deep masculine-sounding voice with the thick Russian accent.

God he loved her. He loved her fake hair, he loved her fake nails, he loved her fake tits. But most of all, he loved her fake adoration of him.

"Coming in for a landing," he said. "I'm in an early autumn sort of mood. What would you suggest?"

"Vell," she strung out her words, "if you vant something different, ve could start vif Cranberry Fool."

Bendz considered this. "Nope," he finally said.

"Maybe Apple Crisp?"

"Apple Crisp," he repeated thoughtfully. "She back to work already?"

"Is good as new. First night back. I save special for you."

"Sure you did," he said sarcastically.

Madame Yaskagya waited. She didn't want to run through the whole menu too quickly, since he always refused anything she suggested in the first few minutes. It had nothing to do with her girls. They were as luscious as the desserts Madame named them after. But a big shot like Chipmunk Carl needed to feel picky. He would take his time, but Madame knew in the end he could not resist her marketing strategy of combining a food theme with sex. "Maybe a little Peaches Cobbler?"

"I don't know what I feel like tonight."

"You like to eat some Strawberry Shortcake?"

"Nah." He sounded glum.

"Vif Lemon Meringue?"

He brightened. "I might feel like a dessert buffet."

"Girls vould be delighted." Madame Yaskagya turned on the sincere false enthusiasm.

"Good. Tell them to surprise me."

Madame hung up and blew a smoke ring. "Chipmunk Carl is coming," she said, her tone managerial now.

"Shit!" Lemon Meringue shot off the couch, her long blond topknot bouncing madly as she moved. She waved her hands around, her extraordinary red nails flashing like talons. "I'm not dry yet! And I think somebody's already using his Jimmy Choos!"

"Not to vorry," Madame said. "He vants play double-header tonight."

"Great," one of the girls said. "His bat ain't even got enough wood in it to hit a single."

"Yeah," Lemon Meringue said, "but it still takes him half the night to strike out."

"No complaining," Madame rasped. "I always miss best part Letterman vhen comes time to make him go home."

"Hey," Strawberry Shortcake said, "I thought he offered a special bonus to the first girl to take him all the way to the moon."

"My ass," Lemon Meringue answered. "Last time I fell for something like that, I got stuck with a hummer. And I'm not talking about something I could drive."

12

Vee was redoing her bathroom yet again. Other customers of her contractor always had to hear how that bathroom was her substitute for having a husband to drive insane. This time around she was replacing some fixtures. She had ordered a custom brass faucet from the shop on Main Street the local handymen affectionately called Plumb Whine. She had classes all week and asked Maggie to do her a favor and pick the faucet up so it could be installed.

Maggie didn't mind. It wasn't like she had a whole lot to keep her occupied. Shortly after eleven she showered and dressed, then went into town. She parked behind the shop and went in the back door. On her way up front she stopped to look at thousand dollar sinks and tubs that cost as much as trailer homes. Two saleswomen were eagerly waiting for her at the counter. "Don't swoon," she said coolly. "I'm only here to pick up Dr. Hawthorne's faucet."

The women looked at each other. "It's not in yet," one of them finally said.

"What do you mean?" Maggie said. "She specifically asked me to pick it up today."

"I'm sorry," the woman said, "but we told her when she ordered it that it could take up to two months to get here. It's only been a few weeks."

"She must have had some reason to think it was here. Why else would she ask me to pick it up?"

"I don't know. I didn't call her." The saleswoman turned to her colleague with an odd look. "Did you call her?" The other woman just shook her head, eyes wide. "I'm sorry," the saleswoman said again. "Sometimes we have communication challenges with Dr. Hawthorne."

"You need to call her and let her know it's not here," Maggie said.

"I don't think so," the saleswoman said.

"Is there any chance . . ." Maggie started.

The saleswoman shook her head emphatically.

"She's a good customer," Maggie insisted. "This could cost you her business."

"Oh," the saleswoman said. "Okay."

Maggie looked at her with dismay. "Come on," she said. "You know she's not going to take this quietly."

"Hey," the second saleswoman finally spoke. "Better you than us."

Maggie turned and stalked out the front door. Maybe she could soften Vee up with a little gift before she mentioned the faucet. She walked to the corner and repeatedly punched the button to make the light turn green. Nothing happened. There wasn't a car moving on the street, so she decided to go for it. She was most of the way across when she saw JD coming up the hill toward her. It was too late to turn back. "Bring it on," she said when he got there. "I'm already cranky and I really don't give a damn."

"Excuse me?" he asked.

"Just get it over with, okay?"

"Ah," he said. "Nice to see we've progressed to crossing at the corner. Is it in your development plan to work on waiting for a green light?"

"Thanks," she said. "That's funny. Do I get a summons this time?"

"Nope," he said. "It's Chivalry Day."

"I'm free to go?"

He made a sweeping gesture with his arm. "Mosey on."

"Mosey?" She cracked up.

"Amble," he said. "Saunter. Stroll."

"Is this your way of trying to discipline me?"

"When things are slow, I work on building my vocabulary."

"That is really sad," Maggie replied. "But since I'm going to have to listen to Vee piss and moan because her faucet isn't here, I can't spare you any sympathy right now."

"Sorry to hear that," JD said. "Want to get some lunch?"

"That was smooth," Maggie said. "What did you have in mind?"

"I'm partial to the Chinese place if you're interested." They walked down the block and went in. The restaurant was small, dark and empty. Maggie sniffed. "What?" JD asked.

"Doesn't smell like New York Chinese."

"Nope," he said. "But it doesn't smell like Alabama Chinese either, so count your blessings." He grabbed some menus and they sat down.

"You serve the food too?" Maggie asked.

"When it's slow like this, sometimes I even go in the back and cook."

Maggie was about to ask if he was kidding, but the waitress startled her by coming out of nowhere. She plunked down two glasses of water. "You ready order?"

"You an adventurous eater?" JD asked. Maggie made an ambiguous gesture. "Two hot and sour soups," he told the waitress. "And tell the chef to make whatever else he feels like." The waitress nodded and walked away.

"Why do the eateries in this town treat customers like nobody cares if they don't ever come back?" Maggie asked.

JD thought about this. "It probably has something to do with avoiding commitment."

"I'm not touching that with a ten foot pole."

"Did Vee ever tell you how we met?" JD asked.

"She mentioned you were one of her students. You still in school?"

"Not anymore. I was working on my Ph.D."

"Some kind of law enforcement specialty?"

"No. Psychology, actually."

"I should have guessed. No wonder you're so annoying. You're a cop *and* a shrink."

"Nope." He took a sip of his water. "I'm a cop and a drop-out."

"You gave up?"

"They gave up on me. Said they couldn't turn me loose on an unsuspecting public until I was able to overcome my need to always be right."

"Funny," Maggie said. "That sounds like the perfect description of a shrink to me."

The waitress put two small plates between them. One held limp slices of pickled cucumber. The other was filled with seasoned peanuts. "Chopsticks?" JD asked. The waitress smacked down two paper packages of bamboo chopsticks and shuffled away.

"So what class did you take with Vee?" Maggie asked as she pulled her chopsticks apart.

"The Politics of Aboriginal Matriarchal Societies." JD picked up a slice of cucumber with his chopsticks and ate it. He had to wipe a little pickling liquid off his chin.

Maggie picked up a slice of cucumber with her chopsticks, gently tapped off the excess liquid against the edge of the plate, and placed it in her mouth. "So what was the course like?"

JD reached into the saucer of peanuts with his chopsticks, fished around until he managed to trap one, and then awkwardly ate it. "It was me and eleven energetically belligerent, extremely politically engaged women of color."

Maggie picked a peanut off the top of the pile with surgical precision and popped it into her mouth. "What made you take that class?"

"Believe it or not," he said, "I was interested in the subject."

"Not," Maggie said.

JD put his chopsticks down. "I also needed to fulfill a humanities requirement." He picked a peanut out of the dish with his fingers. "And it fit my schedule."

"So did you like it?" Maggie switched the chopsticks to her left hand and selected another peanut without even looking.

"I'm glad I met Vee."

The waitress delivered their soup. "What was the most interesting thing you learned?"

"That after one hostile classmate totally eviscerated me, Vee would protect me from the other ten. But not until." He picked up his spoon.

"You're not going to eat your soup with chopsticks?"

"You're pretty competitive, aren't you?" JD asked.

"Yeah," Maggie said. "But only with guys. Most guys get it. They realize it's just a game, that it doesn't matter who wins."

"Would you feel like that if you didn't win all the time?"

"Don't know," Maggie said. "I haven't lost yet."

JD ate some soup. "So why do you only compete with guys?"

"Because if you compete with other women, you're likely to end up with a chopstick in the eye."

They finished and the waitress brought over clean plates and forks. "You said most men get it," JD continued. "What about the ones who don't?"

"They fall into two groups. First there are the guys who are so insecure you would never compete with them to begin with."

"Too easy to win?"

"No," Maggie said. "No fun stomping on something that's already flat."

"And the second group?"

"They're the dangerous ones. They act like they're having fun. But whether they win or not is immaterial, because you became a target as soon as they noticed you could compete in the first place. You don't even need to be competing with *them*."

"So how do you protect yourself? How do you know which ones they are?"

"You don't, until you find yourself in a dark parking lot with a chopstick through your heart."

r r r

Vee grabbed a shopping cart outside Gallardo's and pushed it into the store. She was one of those shoppers nobody liked. She drove her cart aggressively, tossed things into it as if she was punishing them and was belligerent to others. She only did it because it amused her that white folks would take so much more shit from her than they would from each other. But today was different. Today she was planning a dinner for her special friends. She'd spent a lot of years at peace with the slim chances of finding anyone who would respect her uniqueness as much as she did herself. This was not a sacrifice, since it was always better to be alone with your own deep thoughts than at the constant mercy of someone else's shallow ones. She was happy with her fine life. So when she and JD became friends it was icing on the cake.

JD was nice. Nice manners, knew the rules about how to treat a lady. Even without the accent there was no question he was a southern boy. She couldn't understand why he kept it a secret. Still, in many ways he filled the gap where a man of her own might have been. Not her type, but quite passable in almost every other way.

Except where cooking was concerned. Where cooking was concerned, he was a pompous pain in the butt. Sure, he was good. Great even. But he loved to rub people's noses in it. Make a tasty dish? He'd make it better. Cook a special family recipe? The next thing you knew, he'd be serving it to you in front of company, except he'd add some ingredient that made your version taste like the flabby imitation. And when everybody made a big deal about his dish, he'd pretend to be humble, the whole time looking at you with that shit-eating grin. This particular dinner, she was going to whup his ass. Maggie was coming too, and there was no way Vee was going to let him show her up in front of her new friend. She started in the produce section, picking each and every ingredient with exquisite care.

☞ ☞ ☞

Maggie arrived for dinner carrying a cute gift bag with Vee's favorite soap and a really touching card about friendship. She was already a little sweaty from nerves when she rang the bell. She had a bad feeling this wasn't going to work. Sure enough, the minute Vee opened the door she pinned Maggie with a look.

"Klaatu verada nikto," Maggie said.

"The hell you say?"

"It's from *The Day the Earth Stood Still*, an old sci-fi movie. This galactic policeman comes to Earth to warn us that if we develop nuclear weapons, his robot will pulverize the planet with his death-ray eyes. So what do the earthlings do? They kill the policeman. But he figured they'd do something stupid, so he tells this single mother the secret words to turn off the robot. Klaatu verada nikto."

"Where's my faucet?"

"They didn't *have* your faucet. Did you even check to see if it was in?"

Vee looked slightly abashed. "Come on in," she said.

"You knew the faucet wasn't there, didn't you?" Maggie asked with irritation as Vee closed the door behind her.

"Not exactly." She led Maggie into the kitchen. "What would you like to drink?"

"Hemlock?"

"Sorry," Vee said, slamming the cover down on the pot she'd been stirring. "I didn't think it would be such a big deal."

"You could let me know instead of setting me up."

"I'm sorry." Vee actually sounded contrite this time. "It's just, when I call they're always so patronizing. I wondered if maybe I was getting a little special treatment, if you know what I mean. So I figured I'd send you in and see if you got anywhere. But if I told you what I was up to, you'd blow it. You can't keep up a lie to save your life. The minute it starts forming in your head, you're already looking like you see the nun with the ruler heading your way. I'm sorry I set you up."

"Oh," Maggie said.

"That's it?" Vee demanded. "I make the most abject apology I've made in a decade, and all you can say is, 'Oh'?"

"I'm sorry," Maggie said, lifting the lid to get a whiff of what was in the pot.

"Look at you!" Vee started jabbing a finger in Maggie's direction. "That's not what you were all fired up about at all! Your mouth is opening and closing like a goldfish. You're thinking about trying to lie."

"Fine!" Maggie banged the pot cover back down. "I ran into JD and we had lunch together. I thought you set it up."

Vee had a good laugh while she went to the refrigerator and took out the bottle of cranberry juice she always kept in there. "Where's my boy?" she asked. "He decide against joining us tonight?"

"He's out with the Explorers. I'm still not sure about them, you know? I can't shake the feeling they're up to something. Why would a bunch of teenage kids want to hang out at a Rescue Squad all the time?"

"Hanging out is what kids do."

"Yeah, in dark corners of each other's basements. Not at some supervised venue."

"You know," Vee poured herself some juice, "kids hang out for reasons besides sex."

"That's what makes me nervous."

"Don't worry so much. It's only easy to corrupt an empty child." Maggie looked unconvinced. "You really were an outsider, weren't you? How do you think they pass on the information they need for social survival? Through hanging out. Sociobiology. You do stuff to give your own kind an advantage. If you're not in the right place at the right time to observe the rituals, you'll do stuff that marks you as different." Vee put some vodka in her juice. "So how was your lunch with JD?"

"We ate at the Chinese place. It was very nice."

"And then?"

"And then I got in the back of his squad car and gave him a blow-job. What do you mean, and then?"

"You wouldn't be the first."

Maggie cracked up. "If that day ever comes, I promise you I will be the last."

"Did he ask you for another date?"

"This was not a date."

"I bet you wouldn't even know if it was."

"You're probably right," Maggie said. "I don't know that I'm ever going to date again."

"It's not time yet for you to decide whether you want to spend the rest of your life alone."

"You're spending yours alone."

"What you see is misdirection," Vee answered. "I'm just waiting for the right victim."

Maggie laughed. "There are worse things than spending your life alone."

"Like what?" Vee demanded.

"Like spending it with someone you can't trust."

Vee busied herself setting the table. There was a hint of jumpiness in her motions. "What about JD?" she finally asked. "You can trust him."

"Get real," Maggie said. "The man is a player."

"He is not a player. He's just a harmless flirt."

"He is not harmless," Maggie said. "He wants some heart in there. And when he gets it, he sticks it in his back pocket along with all the other junk and he forgets about it."

"That's a pretty final judgment considering you hardly know him."

"I don't need to know him," Maggie insisted. "I know the type."

Vee thought about this. "Even a player deserves a chance now and then."

Maggie looked at her a long moment. "From my perspective it's not worth the risk. You don't even need to be the wife or the girlfriend to get hurt, you just need to be in range. They cause a full 360 degrees of damage."

The doorbell rang. Vee looked like she'd just been caught picking someone's pocket. "I'll get it," she said, a little too enthusiastically.

Maggie was confused. "Of course you'll get it," she said. "This is your house." Vee smiled uncomfortably, and the light bulb finally went off in Maggie's head. "Oh, for chrissake," she said. "You invited him for dinner, didn't you?"

"He's my friend too," Vee protested.

"So if this was all so innocent, how come you neglected to mention he was coming? You *were* trying to set us up, weren't you?" She did not sound happy.

"It won't happen again," Vee said. "I promise."

13

Growing up, Maggie never liked the fall. The change in the quality of light from summer always made her feel like something dangerous was getting ready to strike. Maybe because Dooleysburg was so different from what she remembered, this fall she didn't get that feeling of menace. The house itself held few memories, and she was doubly glad for the garage, since it completely covered the back of the yard where her father had made his vegetable garden. Thinking about that garden filled her with regret. In the spring her father would hire one of the out of work "boys" to dig it up. His idea of planting was to toss seeds into open rows. He gave Maggie the job of burying the roots of tender young tomato plants he hadn't bothered to harden. Then he would insist things had to manage with whatever water nature provided. Weeks into the spring, chastened by his stunted, withering results, he would put out a couple of barrels. Maggie would dispense the rainwater that collected in them. In a good summer they might get some tough, woody beans and a handful of cucumbers the size of gherkins. At the end of each season he would throw away his seed catalogs, ranting about companies that sold such inferior products, and vow he was done wasting good money this way. Like most of his vows, this one was subject to whim and inattention, so most years the cycle was repeated.

Maybe another reason Maggie enjoyed this autumn was her daily walks with Penelope. They had come to a watchful understanding. Penelope gave the impression she was still considering whether Maggie might deserve a good bite sooner or later. Maggie believed the dog, though basically trustworthy, was still capable of causing trouble. They were both amenable to aggravating each other.

"Let's go, Penelope." Maggie snapped on the dog's leash, determined to stay in charge today. She didn't mind if Penelope wanted to pee or sniff, but the dog had a peculiar habit of simply stopping dead in her tracks for no apparent reason. She would trot obediently at Maggie's heel until whatever it was struck her, and then come to a standstill so suddenly she pulled Maggie off balance.

Maggie couldn't afford for Penelope to get an attack today. They had to go to Gamey's Deli, and the stop needed to be as brief as possible. The deli was in a small clapboard Cape on a residential street. The place looked like the other houses except for the weedy stone patio out front with picnic tables and racks of junk food. The neighbors complained about this eyesore on a regular basis, so Town Council made Gamey put everything away each night. Then he had to put it all back the next morning. He lost any sympathy votes by doing this with the same ill humor he applied to everything else.

Despite only seeing him infrequently, Maggie felt Gamey was barely tolerable. She had her own special game of figuring out how to avoid him. She imagined every angle he might use to watch her over his privacy fence and took pains to conceal herself. If he was home, she only left her house by car or with someone else.

She didn't think her behavior was any big deal, but Vee started making fun of her for being afraid of Gamey. To prove that wasn't true, this morning she was going to walk the dog right in front of his deli. She had her camera so she could get proof. After school Mac was going to e-mail the photo to Vee. The bet was that if she got a picture Vee had to bring home ribs for dinner. Real ones, from the Rib Pit.

As if she felt there was something in it for her, Penelope trotted along like a show dog. When they got to the deli and Maggie told her to sit, she posed right on the front walk. Maggie aimed her camera. That's when she saw Gamey in the top corner of the shot, coming out his front door with a load of junk food. "Come, Penelope," she said. The dog collapsed into a fur-covered block of concrete. "Come *on.*" She tugged furiously on the leash.

"Well, howdy, neighbor," Gamey leered.

"Gamey," she replied.

"How are you this fine morning?" The way he said it made Maggie want to check and make sure her shirt was still buttoned.

"Fine, thanks. We were just going." She tugged on Penelope's leash again. The dog responded by somehow, mystically, increasing her weight until it felt like the leash was attached to a boulder.

Gamey smirked at them. "I see someone did a good job of training your new dog."

"She's still adjusting."

"What kind is it?" he asked.

"The guy we got her from told us she's mostly Lhasa."

"Looks like a throw rug to me."

Maggie kept pulling ineffectually on Penelope's leash. "I just need a chance to work with her."

He looked up at Maggie with pure derision. "I can see you're very experienced training dogs."

"What makes you the expert?"

"I've had dogs my whole life."

"You don't have one now."

"Sure I do. He mostly stays here, like a watchdog. I bet they'd enjoy making each other's acquaintance."

"Some other time," Maggie said. She pulled on the leash harder. "Come *on*," she hissed.

"Oscar!" Gamey yelled. "Come on out here! We got company!" A deep baying came from inside the deli.

"Great," Maggie said. "Your dog is going to eat mine." Penelope, perhaps remembering her brief stay at the farm, began to howl. Maggie looked at her. "You could run, you know."

"Nah," Gamey said, raising his voice to be heard, "Oscar's a lover boy. Only thing he ever hurt was a hunk of Genoa salami accidentally rolled out of the meat case one time. Hey, boy!" he yelled. "Come on out!"

The baying subsided as the creature appeared at the door. His head came first, giving the initial impression he was a dachshund. But as the rest of him came into sight he looked more platypus than dog. His body was so fat it appeared as if his legs weren't touching the ground. He got halfway out the door and then his huge belly got hung up on the sill. He balanced there precariously, teetering back and forth on the fulcrum of his gut, his legs waving in synchronization like he was trying to row himself free. "Mrs. Rifkin, Throw Rug, meet Oscar Mayer the wiener dog," Gamey said proudly.

"Holy shit." Maggie's voice was a mixture of horror and wonder. "What the hell is that?"

"Well," Gamey said, "he's not pure wiener dog. He's part basset hound. That's what gives him that nice, deep bark."

"Gamey, he's stuck. Go help him!"

Gamey obligingly walked around behind the dog and lifted its back end with his foot, giving it just enough leverage to get over the sill. "Come on, boy," he said. "Come meet the nice ladies."

"Hey!" Maggie suddenly remembered her mission. "Take some pictures of Penelope and me." She handed Gamey her camera.

"You want pictures? Why?"

"Come on," Maggie said. "Go over there by the street and get some shots of us in front of your store."

"What are you going to do?"

"Nothing. Don't be so paranoid."

Just then a patrol car pulled up. Officer Mike stepped out. "Morning," he said.

"Hey, Mikey," Gamey said. "Get a picture of me and her with the dogs."

"That's okay." Maggie tried to head this off. "Just me and my dog is fine."

"Nah, come on," Gamey insisted. "You give me a copy, I'll put you up inside on the wall of fame." He walked over and stood next to Maggie. His dismal little head came right to the level of her breasts. He grinned wickedly as he put his arm around her. "Okay, Mikey, this is a good one." There was a brief whirring noise, and then Maggie shook him off. "That'll do."

"No, no," Gamey persisted. "Let's get one with the dogs."

"You probably want to straighten them out first," Officer Mike said.

They looked down. Oscar Mayer had waddled over to sniff at Penelope. "That's interesting," Gamey said.

"What?" Maggie demanded.

"Didn't know old Oscar here was into necrophilia."

"That's funny," Maggie said trying again to yank her dog back to life. Oscar Mayer seemed unable to discriminate between Penelope's rear and front ends, and was attempting to become intimate with her head. "Gamey!" Maggie yelled, "get your pervert dog off her!"

"What a smart little boy," Gamey beamed.

"Gamey! He's too fat! He's going to break her neck!"

Suddenly Oscar Mayer gave a high yelp of pain. Officer Mike pulled him off while Maggie grabbed Penelope.

"She bit him!" Gamey screamed.

"Good," Maggie said. "He deserved it."

"Mikey, you're a witness. I'm gonna sue!"

"Gamey," Maggie said furiously, "you have absolutely no redeeming qualities."

"Would you like a ride home?" Officer Mike asked awkwardly.

"Sure," Maggie snapped. "Fine." She loaded Penelope into the back of the patrol car and climbed in after her, not waiting to be invited into the front seat. When they pulled up in front of her house, Officer Mike popped out to open her door. "Don't forget your camera," he said, handing it to her. "I'm guessing you wouldn't want to have to take that picture twice."

🐔 🐔 🐔

Vee showed up around 5:30. Maggie had taken refuge on the patio while Mac practiced his drums in the basement. Vee poked her head out the kitchen door. "There you are," she said with false heartiness.

Maggie did not look up from her book. "I hope you enjoyed your goddamn picture."

"Well, honey," Vee replied, "just come on in here and smell these ribs."

"I can't believe you made me demean myself just to get some ribs. And what about my poor little dog? She can't even eat ribs!"

"I think you may be overplaying your hand," Vee said. "You don't even like that dog."

"Even so," Maggie said. "There should be something in it for her after what Gamey's oversized excuse for a pet tried to do. How did I end up with such a jerk for a neighbor?"

"I hear he bought his place when the old doctor and his wife still lived here and that they were an even match for him. According to Carol Carter, nobody normal was willing to live next door to them."

Maggie stood up abruptly. "Let's eat."

"It's something to think about though," Vee continued as they went into the house. "Most cultures with any kind of mythology have some pretty strong beliefs about place. Like, what goes around comes around, that sort of thing."

"People bring their own destinies with them," Maggie said. "That's why you can't ever get away from your problems. We're doomed to keep screwing everything up exactly the same way over and over again until the day we finally turn the spotlight on ourselves."

"I'm just saying there's no benefit in refusing to consider things beyond your immediate perception."

"Hey," Maggie said, opening the bag on her kitchen table, "these ribs *do* smell good." Even Penelope was showing interest. The smell must have made its way to the basement as well, because Mac came crashing up the stairs.

"Take it easy," Maggie ordered. "We've got plenty."

"Poor child," Vee said. "Willing to risk his neck for some real food."

"You guys want to see the new trick I taught Penelope?"

"Sure, honey," Vee said.

"Penelope," Mac called, "let's see your trick." The little dog trotted over.

"That's good," Vee said, pretending to be impressed.

"That's not the trick," Mac said. "Watch." He held his forefinger in front of her short snout and said, "Pull my finger." The dog gently took his finger between her teeth and tugged on it. Maggie and Vee watched in horror as Mac's stomach rippled like an animated earthquake. And then he belched.

"MacDonald," Maggie said, "that is just gross."

"You didn't get it right," Vee said. "After she pulls your finger you're supposed to pass gas."

"People are more likely to laugh at something that ends in a burp," Mac insisted.

"Actually," Maggie said, "she used that behavior in a very adaptive way this morning."

"I think you need to stick to your drumming," Vee said. She reached into the bag and pulled out three Styrofoam boxes, a large rectangular block covered in foil, and two tiny plastic containers. "These," Vee indicated the containers, "are our sides. Potato salad and cole slaw."

"You're kidding," Maggie said. "What's in there, about a tablespoon of each?"

"Probably," Vee said. "Bear in mind, these ribs did not come from a neighborhood where vegetables are a food group. This here," she opened a flap on the foil-wrapped rectangle, "is our utensils."

"That looks like white bread," Maggie said.

"Not just any white bread. Wonder bread."

"I can't wait to see the ribs." Maggie popped open a Styrofoam box. The contents were a big messy blob of meat and sauce, with butt ends of bone poking up haphazardly from the goo. "I'll get some forks. Doesn't look like we'll need knives."

"You are *supposed* to use the bread. And your hands," Vee admonished her.

The meat was incredibly tender, permeated all the way through with the sort of addictive smokiness that must have tempted cavemen to take the risk of getting meat into and out of a fire. The sauce was very slightly sweet, and started with the merest hint of a bite yet somehow ended up with a sharp tang on the lips and tongue. They ate with the sort of primal pleasure usually only seen among hunters and bulimics. Vee gave up first. "I'm gonna bust," she moaned.

Maggie peered into Vee's Styrofoam container. "You missed some," she said. "But not much."

Vee folded back Maggie's lid so she could check the competition. "Damn, girl," she said. "Being squeamish about touching meat doesn't seem to have gotten in your way."

Mac licked his fingers. He tore off a piece of bread and mopped up the remains of the sauce from his carton, then got up and dropped the bread in Penelope's dish.

"Hey," Maggie said. "I thought no feeding her from the table!"

"I'm not," he said. "I put it in her bowl." He gathered up all the trash and stuffed it back into the stained bag. "There," he said. "I just did the dinner dishes. Is it okay if I take off for the Squad now?"

"Home by ten," Maggie said.

"Yup," he agreed, taking the bag out the back door with him to put in the trash.

"You know he's a good kid, right?" Vee asked.

Maggie rolled her eyes. "Hey," she said suddenly. "What would've happened if I lost the bet?"

Vee looked at her. "No ribs."

"Bull. There's no way you weren't going to bring those ribs home once they got in your head."

"Nobody said I would share them."

"Sure you would. As a matter of fact, I'll bet you were counting on me not getting that picture because there was something else you had in mind the whole time. You were going to come in here and wave those ribs under my nose," she mimed the gesture with her sauce-stained hand, "until I was a drooling, slobbery mess, and then you were going to blackmail me into doing whatever stupid idea you thought up now."

Vee laughed delightedly. "You are getting *good.*"

"So what was it you wanted me to do so bad you were willing sacrifice your dignity?"

Vee looked like she was about to speak, then waved her hand. "You don't want to know."

"You know what?" Maggie stood up and started clearing what was left on the table, "you're right. I don't want to know."

"Okay," Vee said. "You want to go get water ice for dessert?"

"I thought you were full."

"That was *minutes* ago."

"Fine," Maggie said shortly. "Don't tell me."

"I thought you didn't want to know."

"What do you want me to do, beg? Because I don't do begging."

"That's good," Vee said. "I wouldn't want you to demean yourself."

"Besides," Maggie turned to put their glasses in the sink, "what could you have in mind for me that would be worse than getting assaulted by Gamey and his dog?"

"Going on a date."

"*Excuse me?*" Maggie turned back toward Vee. "Did you say a date?"

"My god," Vee said. "Would you listen to that righteous indignation? It's not like I suggested you should rob a bank."

"I don't need to rob a bank. Just like I don't need a man."

"Honey," Vee said, "everybody needs a man. At least every now and then."

Maggie was about to answer when they heard the sirens, multiple sirens coming from multiple directions. "Police, fire and rescue," Vee said. "Both fire stations."

"Do they usually all come out to answer an alarm like this?" Maggie asked anxiously.

Vee shrugged. "If it's a bad enough fire. Or car accident."

"I hope Mac is okay. I hope he has enough sense to stay out of the way."

"I don't think you need to worry about him. They let the kids feel important, but they don't let them get near anything."

"Do you think I should go down to the Rescue Squad?"

"I think you should stay exactly where you are and depend on people to do their jobs. I also think you should have more faith in your son's good sense. And if you really can't stop yourself from being so neurotic, you should break down and get the boy a cell phone or tag him like a porpoise."

The phone rang and Maggie jumped for it. It was Mac. "Are you all right?"

"Why are you yelling?"

"Sorry." She forced herself to calm down. "Where are you?"

"At the Squad. We're going over to the fire soon. That's why I'm calling."

"What fire? Where?"

"At the Henhouse."

"The what? What is the Henhouse?"

Vee popped out of her chair. "The Henhouse is on fire?" she yelled. "Grab your shoes, woman. We're not missing this!"

"Mom, can I go? They won't let us near anything. I promise I'll stay back. Please?"

"I'm lea-ving," Vee called.

Maggie couldn't take the pressure. "Fine!" she yelled into the phone. "Vee and I will meet you there." She ran out the back door after Vee. "What is the Henhouse?"

🄫 🄫 🄫

Vee drove maddeningly slowly, braking as they approached every intersection.

"Would you cut it out?" Maggie finally bellowed.

"Calm down," Vee said easily. "It sounds like a nice big fire. We won't miss anything."

"How can I worry about missing anything? You won't even tell me what's going on."

"Everybody keeps secrets," Vee said.

Maggie looked at her, but Vee continued to stare ahead at the road. She liked Vee, but that didn't make it easy to figure out whether to trust her. "So what is the Henhouse?"

"Remember our first date, when we went to the Cremee Freeze? And the red brick house next door?"

"The one where the old guy was guarding the porch with a broom? That's on fire?"

"Yup."

"Do you think he's okay?"

"Honey," Vee chuckled, "that tough old bird's survived worse than fire."

"So why's it called the Henhouse?"

Vee braked and looked at Maggie. "You seriously don't know?" This gave her a good laugh. "You're a little old to be such a lamb."

"Just tell me!" Maggie demanded.

"Nuh-uh," Vee replied. "I'm not giving up the fun now. You'll see for yourself soon enough." They pulled up behind a short line of cars. Joe Butts was at the front of it, waving a flashlight where the street was closed. "Might as well park here," Vee said.

They got out of the car. The air was cool and full of the vivid smell of burning wood. To their left, rooftops shone brightly in the light of a moon that looked possessed. On their other side the sky above the treetops glowed a sickly neon red-orange, one of those colors that never occurs naturally. It evoked something primeval in Maggie, as if her brain knew a night sky that color meant danger.

"You missed the good stuff," Joe Butts said as they walked past him. "You should have seen them coming out of there. Like termites running from the anteater's tongue."

"The man's a poet," Vee muttered, as she led the way around the corner and up Main Street. They got about two blocks from the frenzy before they were halted by a small but growing crowd. "I'm never going to find Mac," Maggie said somewhat frantically.

"Why don't you just put him under house arrest?"

"You don't understand," Maggie snapped.

"Oh, I do," Vee assured her. "But you better learn to keep your neurotic fear about losing him to yourself before you accidentally crush him."

The crowd shuffled a little and they got a clear view of the blaze through the blackened skeleton of the building. Spires of flame snapped and licked at the sky, occasionally gathering enough energy to break loose and flare off like rockets. Wraiths of vaporous light made the images behind them look like ripples in a pond.

"It's remarkable that something so transient can be so compelling," Maggie said, mostly to herself.

"Most dangerously beautiful things are." Maggie turned around at the sound of JD's voice. "You ladies care to move back?" he said.

"JD," Vee interrupted, "she's acting like a lunatic. She thinks her kid's in there."

JD took this seriously. "Do you have reason to believe your son was in that building?"

"Of course not," Vee answered. "He called her from the Rescue less than half an hour ago and said he was coming over. She's just being ridiculous."

"Have you seen him?" Maggie asked.

"I haven't, but I can assure you, if he came over with the Squad, he's being kept out of danger. Unless he's as blockheaded as you two and won't comply with directions."

"Was anybody hurt?"

JD motioned toward a group huddled behind a barricade. Though it was hard to see details, they looked like they might be celebrating Halloween a little early. They were wearing sequined clothing, feather boas, stiletto sandals and various other things not usually seen on the street. "The girls all made it out okay. One of the customers was reluctant to vacate the premises in a timely manner. He was trying to find something more appropriate to wear and was overcome by smoke."

"You gonna say who he was?" Vee asked eagerly.

"You know I can't do that," JD said.

"How about a clue?"

"There were charred hot pink feathers all over the stretcher when they brought him out."

"You gotta give me more than that."

"The Squad took him over to the hospital. That means the *Intellectual* will pick it up."

"You seriously intend to make me wait for tomorrow's paper?"

"I intend to bust you for disorderly conduct if you don't move back twenty feet."

"Is he okay?" Maggie's voice was so strained they barely heard her.

"Honey," Vee put a hand on her arm, "MacDonald will be fine."

"Not him," she said. "The guy who was in the fire. Did he get appropriate care? Do you have sufficient medical expertise on hand?"

"He'll get whatever he needs at the ER, and everyone here is fine." JD looked quizzically at Vee.

"I'm working on it," Vee said. "She's wound up tighter than the string on a new yo-yo."

"Why don't you get her home?" JD said. "I'll make sure somebody brings her kid along once things quiet down here."

Vee nodded and began to steer Maggie away. "I know I sound crazy," Maggie said. "I promise I'm not. I've just been through a lot."

"I know, honey," Vee said. "You're such a big old bundle of mystery you're becoming something of an obsession for folks around here."

"That's good," Maggie said distractedly.

"Yeah," Vee said. "Give them something to keep tabs on now that the whorehouse burned down."

14

Maggie was hoping to get some details about the fire from Mac, but thanks to the fuss she made, the Squad guys brought him home before he got to hear any gossip. As soon as he left for school the next morning, she called Daniel. "Any scoop?" she asked.

"About what?" he demanded, cranky.

"The *fire*. The Henhouse burned down last night!"

He was astonished. "Are you sure?"

"Of course I'm sure. I was there."

"Didn't start it, did you?"

Maggie laughed. "I don't care enough about what goes on between consenting adults to cause that kind of trouble. But how could you guys not have noticed? The flames must have been four stories high."

"Everybody make it out okay?"

"Except for one of the customers who had a hard time pulling himself out of there."

"Lousy puns are never appreciated, but especially not at this hour." Daniel yawned. "Who was he?"

"Nobody would say."

"You must've asked the wrong people. Did you check today's paper?"

"I don't *have* today's paper. That's why I called you. Does it say who he was?"

"Don't know. Haven't opened it yet."

"Well, can you just read it to me?"

"Sure," he said. "Meet me at the General Store at ten." He hung up before she had a chance to protest.

ɼ   ɼ   ɼ

Maggie pulled the lid off her mocha and blew on it. She took her first tentative sip just as Daniel showed up. He had the paper like he'd promised, but JD was with him as well. "Don't you ever go to work?" Maggie asked.

"I'm on afternoons this week."

"And you have nothing more interesting to do on your morning off than come here?"

"I wanted to see what the *Intellectual* had to say about the fire," he answered. "Except Daniel won't let me have his copy." Maggie reached across the table and took the paper. "If you're not going to share," JD said, "read it out loud."

She gave him a look, then began. "'Last night's fire in the Henhouse prematurely halted the debate in Town Council on the Zoning Board's authority over illicit enterprises. Given that the facility is no longer operational, evaluation of its compliance with the Americans with Disabilities Act will remain incomplete until such time as illegal activities resume.'" Maggie looked up. "If one of you was reading this to me, I'd accuse you of making it up."

"Read on," JD said. "Maybe it gets better."

Maggie scanned the page. "They quote you here. 'When asked for his reaction to the discovery that one of the 'Burg's leading citizens was patronizing the house of ill repute at the time of the blaze, Chief of Police JD Charles responded, 'Nobody should expect special treatment. We can't go all soft on these kinds of issues.' Did you really say that?"

"It was hard, but somebody had to drive home the point."

🐓 🐓 🐓

Lillian Bendz stared numbly at her reflection in her dressing table mirror. If he didn't make things right somehow, this time she would leave him. There was only so much a woman could endure for the sake of maintaining a lifestyle, and she had reached her limit. If she could not walk through this town with her head held high, she would find somewhere else to walk. Someplace her taste and reputation were not sullied by his antics. Damn him. Damn them all.

The Daily Intellectual lay next to her hand, opened to the front-page article about the fire. It didn't mention Carl by name. It merely alluded to the presence of a prominent Dooleysburg businessman. At least the annual executive lease Hyundai that quietly showed up each fall in the editor's parking space had paid off. But damn it, what was wrong with that Rescue Squad? They'd taken him to the ER at Dooleysburg General. What the hell were they thinking? Half the town either worked there or knew someone who did. It would only be a matter of days before the sordid details were all over the place.

She'd gone to see him last night with the misguided expectation that this time he would finally be contrite. He'd suffered mild smoke inhalation, but his more uncomfortable injuries were the burns from the hardware on his garter belt. It had superheated in the flash flame caused by his feather boa dangling too close to an aromatherapy candle. That's what started the whole thing. And some fool, claiming the candle might be evidence, had actually turned it in to that jack-off of a police chief. He'd had the lack of class to tell Lillian it was from the Herbal Tranquility series. "Well, of course, Chief Charles," she had responded with total aplomb. "Carl was at the temple of the flesh to align his chakra."

It was painfully clear now that Charles was the wrong choice for the chief's job. He was charming and intelligent, but his pretensions of moral complexity were counterproductive. They put Lillian in the unacceptable position of being unable to ensure there would be no legal fall-out from the fire. She couldn't bear to imagine her pain if Carl had to describe the incident in court.

None of this, of course, addressed the distasteful problem at hand. Here she was, dressing as if this were just another ordinary day of errands and appointments, when what she had to do was bring her jackass of a husband home from the hospital. They'd kept him overnight for observation. Since getting up this morning she'd nurtured a faint hope someone would call to tell her unforeseen circumstances necessitated keeping him. For the rest of his life would have suited her fine.

She stood up and dumped the newspaper into the trashcan. Then she strode resolutely through the house and out to the garage. She failed to notice that she left the door from the house to the garage unlocked. And she was so absorbed in her problems that she completely forgot to hit the remote as she backed out and pulled away leaving the garage door wide open.

ꝑ　ꝑ　ꝑ

Penelope suddenly started barking and scampering around. Maggie came downstairs to see what was going on, since Penelope rarely moved at all until Mac got home from school and the bus wasn't due for almost half an hour. She walked into the kitchen just as Mac and Morsel blew in through the door.

"What are you doing home so early?" Maggie asked.

Mac was as excited as the dog. "Morsel drove. He got his own car!"

"Really," Maggie said, with that unmistakable tone of voice. "Congratulations." Morsel looked at her. He made direct eye contact, and yet there was something utterly shifty going on. Maggie finally understood why none of the other adults trusted him. "What did you get?"

"My mom's car. She gave it to me."

"What's she driving?"

"She don't really need a car for much. She lives in Northeast, so she can take the bus."

This distracted Maggie. "She doesn't live around here?"

"Her and my dad are divorced. I live with him and his wife and kids."

"Hey, Mom," Mac interrupted, "can I have some money so we can go hang out at Cremee Freeze?"

Maggie hesitated. She'd let Mac ride with Morsel a few times before when he had his mother's car, but that didn't mean she liked the idea. "I'm concerned about you guys driving around."

"Mrs. R," Morsel said, the poster child for sincerity, "I promise you, I am the safest driver in all Dooleysburg. I don't speed, I stop at yellow lights, I don't do nothing I'm not supposed to, like eating or texting while I'm driving."

"Just to the Cremee Freeze and back," she capitulated. "No other stops."

"Course not," Morsel said. "Where else would we go?"

She looked at him. "Don't oversell your hand. A good poker player knows when to walk away."

"Huh?" he said.

She had to hand it to him. The kid knew how to walk right along the edge. "Never mind." She got a ten from her purse. "You have to put down fertilizer before Sunday," she said.

"Sure. Thanks." Mac and Morsel nearly collided in their rush for the door.

At Morsel's insistence, they had parked around the corner. They hurried to the car, an old maroon Bonneville that looked lovingly cared for. "See?" Mac said. "You didn't need to hide the car."

"You're a real wimp, you know that?" Morsel replied sourly.

"What's your problem?"

"Sure, Mom," Morsel said in a mimicking tone, "I'll scrub your toilets and wash your undies for a buck. Whyn't you just tell her to give you the money?"

"Shut up." Mac punched his arm.

"Ow! Cut it!"

"You're the wuss. What's the big deal about doing some yard work? You have chores at your dad's, don't you?"

"Oh, I got chores all right. But they know I'm not their slave. I ain't picking up his frickin' butts and beer cans, cleaning up after him like his old lady."

"I don't mind helping out," Mac said.

"That's cause you're a wimp, like I said."

🦢   🦢   🦢

Lillian pulled onto the driveway, intentionally going way too wide on the turn. Carl didn't make a sound, though she knew this drove him crazy. Just like the fact that she recently had the whole driveway torn up and replaced with ridiculously expensive pavers. The driveway cost more money than some people paid for a house. But since it was retribution for one of his larger indiscretions, he had to watch without so much as a whimper. Lillian firmly believed exorbitant vengeance was worth every penny. Now she was doubly glad she'd done it, because it meant his penance for this latest transgression, which included the ultimate crime of publicly humiliating her, would require an even grander and more expensive gesture. She was certain he would find one. She knew the only weakness for which he had no defense. He actually loved her.

She hadn't spoken a word since signing the discharge papers at the hospital, where they handed Carl over faster than a load of tainted meat. As they crested the rise of the lawn Lillian aimed the car away from the front portico toward the side-entry garage. The custom door of the third bay, the one where Lillian kept her car, was open. "You do that?" Carl asked.

"I have no idea," Lillian said. "I wasn't exactly myself when I left."

They pulled in. Nothing seemed amiss. Lillian turned off the car. It was low to the ground, and Carl struggled to get out, more because of the excess weight he carried around his midsection than because of the burns on his thighs. Lillian fully expected this. It happened every time he rode in her car. It was why he always insisted that they ride in the SUV, which she could have brought today. But she didn't. This was just the beginning of his punishment. He grunted with the effort of extricating himself from the car, but otherwise held his tongue.

Lillian walked up the short flight of stairs to the interior door. She touched the knob and the door opened. "Why is this unlocked?" she asked.

"Don't go in there!" Carl shouted.

"*What* is your problem?" She turned to face him.

"What if someone's in there? What if the place is wired with explosives?"

"Carl," she said, "don't be a horse's ass. You set fire to a whorehouse. That's not exactly the kind of thing that inspires hate crimes." He cringed as she stepped inside and then, when nothing happened, rushed in behind her.

"Hello?" she called. "Is anybody in here?"

"Oh, good idea," he hissed. "Mr. Robber," he continued in a singsong voice, "it's me. I'm home. Come get our Rolexes and my big ugly diamond ring."

"Shut up a minute, would you?" Lillian demanded. Carl mimicked her silently. "I think I hear something."

Carl concentrated. "That ain't nothing but the sound of time, honey, passing you by."

She looked intently around the room. "Nothing's missing, nothing's out of place, and yet I have this disturbing sense that something's not quite right."

"You want to check room by room?"

"No," she sighed. She punched in a code on the security pad. "Nothing's been opened but this door. I suppose I'm just edgy thanks to what you've done. I'm going to take a nap."

"Wait," he said. "I'll come with you." She gave him an evil look. He raised his hands in the universal gesture of surrender. "Just to be sure everything's okay."

"Fine," she snapped. "But lock up first and turn on the alarm." She huffed impatiently while he armed the system. Then they walked through the marble-floored foyer and up the curving staircase. They could have taken the back stairs from the kitchen, but Lillian's room was in the front of the house. They paused on the upper landing. Everything looked fine up here too. "This is silly," Lillian said, and stalked off to her bedroom.

Carl hustled to keep up. "Just let me check first," he said.

"What are you going to do if someone's in there, Carl? Sit on him?"

"Please," he coaxed her.

She made a face. "Whatever you want."

Carl stepped ahead of her and gingerly peeked around the doorjamb. Her room was empty and as perfectly arranged as always. He proceeded to her dressing room and then her bathroom. Everything was in order. He turned around to call her and jumped, startled that she was right behind him. "You want to check your jewelry?"

"All the valuable stuff is in the vault at the bank."

"If you say so."

"Fine!" She moved aside a false front on the built-in mahogany cabinets in her dressing room and opened her personal safe. "Nothing's missing," she said. "Get out."

"Lillian," he began in his most respectfully submissive tone, "I am truly sorry."

"I'm sure you are," she said. "Sorry you got caught."

"Sorry that I've hurt and disappointed you."

"You forgot mortified, demeaned, belittled . . ."

"Okay! Okay, I get it."

"You always *get* it, Carl," she said disgustedly. "You're just never willing to *do* anything about it. We've had this conversation so many times I know all your lines. If you'll just get the hell out of my room, I can finish up by myself."

"Lillian. Sweetheart. Please just let me make this up to you. Let me try."

"Not this time," she said. "This time you've gone too far. Making it up to me would be too easy for you. You need to feel some pain."

"Please," he begged. "You name it and it's yours."

"Fuck off, Carl. There is nothing you can buy me that will make me forgive you. You hear me? Nothing." She knew he was stymied. He would have no idea where to go from here. Bribery was not only his weapon of choice, it was the only thing he had in his emotional arsenal. She was about to deliver the coup de grace when she was interrupted by the brain-searing screech of the security alarm. They looked at each other a moment in stunned silence, then rushed to the control panel on Lillian's bedroom wall. "BASEMENT EGRESS" it read.

"Somebody was in the basement," Carl said faintly. "I think I feel sick."

"That door's on the blind side of the house," Lillian said calmly. "No windows to get a look at whoever it was. By the time we get downstairs, they'll be in the woods."

"I suppose we should call the cops?" he asked shakily.

"Don't bother. The system is hardwired. They're already on the way."

15

JD brought two cups of coffee to the table. His was the regular stuff, but Martha always had to have the special. Today it was cinnamon pumpkin spice. Or at least that's what the sign said. He suspected the only thing special about it was the fancy name Lola/Mercedes made up every day and the extra fifty cents she charged. She still poured everything out of the same pot.

"Nice of you to move things around to make it this early," he said, putting the cups on the small table between them.

"Shut up until I've had some coffee," she answered.

JD liked to watch Martha's coffee ritual. She used her fingernails like forceps to remove the plastic lid. This week each nail was squared off and purple with a pink corner. There was a small crystal on her left pinkie. "I like the manicure," JD said. "It's a smart look for you."

"Anybody ever tell you it's dangerous to be a wiseass?"

JD looked at his watch. "I don't want to rush you, but if we could get to whatever you wanted to talk about, I do have another appointment this morning."

"I'm aware of that."

"You're aware of everything. Dooleysburg's very own Jeane Dixon."

"Diane de Poitiers," she corrected him. "Everything's a plot, and everyone's a potential enemy. Or victim."

"So what's on our agenda today?"

"I'm concerned about you."

"Who is it this time?"

"What's that supposed to mean?"

"Come on, sweetie. You warn me off everyone sooner or later."

"Hasn't worked yet, has it?"

JD grinned. "A man's gotta do what a man's gotta do."

"Believe it or not, I really don't care about your sex life."

JD raised an eyebrow. "What's left to worry about, my immortal soul?"

"Go ahead and make jokes," Martha said. "But you have no idea what you're getting yourself into."

"Martha," he said kindly, "you are a good friend. I'm touched that you care about me. But I'm a big boy. If I want to run with a bad crowd, I promise to keep an eye on myself."

"You don't pay attention to your reputation."

"My reputation's fine."

"It's not going to stay that way if you keep hanging out with that woman."

JD tried not to smile. "Which one did you have in mind? I can think of a few."

"Your professor friend."

"Vee?" he said, incredulous. "She wasn't even on my list."

"She's a sham. You know she is. She's got all that education, she's lived all over the world, and look how she acts. She pretends like she's right off the farm."

JD took his time answering. He was between the proverbial rock and a hard place. To him Vee's idiosyncrasies were endearing, but he knew they weren't really what Martha was complaining about. He hated taking sides in these skirmishes, but couldn't risk staying silent in case Martha saw that as agreement. "I think she's proud of who she is," he began carefully. "I admire how she doesn't feel like she has to whiten up her presentation to validate herself."

Martha waited a long moment before answering him. "If you weren't the Chief of Police," she finally said, "I might tell you what a horse's ass you sound like."

JD could see Martha was pissed off about something bigger than her usual snit over Vee. "You're my first and best girlfriend," he assured her. "But don't forget men are dogs. Is there some other wish I can grant you instead of joining your vendetta?"

"Yeah," she replied immediately. "Stay away from that other one too." She took a last swig of her coffee and stood up to leave. "You know. Dr. Hawthorne's new best friend."

"Hey," he said, "can I bring you back some apples from the orchard?"

"Go ahead and treat this like a joke," she said brusquely. "But if you believe nothing else, trust me that you will not go near that inferno without getting burned."

᛭ ᛭ ᛭

Maggie was waiting out front when JD pulled up. She considered it prudent to keep everything out of doors. She wasn't convinced she should be doing this at all, but she would lose face if she backed out now, after publicly accepting his invitation to go apple picking. She tried pressuring Vee into coming along until Vee finally said, "Honey, I did not get my Ph.D. to do *that* kind of field work." And now, because real life could always be worse than you imagined, JD was coming down the street in a police car. He pulled up next to her and got out. "Just a minute," he said. "I'll get your door."

Maggie stared at him. "You brought a patrol car?"

"My car's in the shop."

"You're taking me on a date in a police car?" She couldn't get beyond this.

"It's not a date," he said. "We're going to pick apples."

"Are you going to make me sit in the back, behind the cage?"

"I wasn't planning on it. But I can cuff you if you like."

Maggie backed away. "I think this is turning out to be a bad idea."

"Okay," he said. "I'm sorry. I won't make any more hardware jokes. Would you rather take your car?"

"This is like the lady and the tiger. I can either choose to mortify myself by riding in this, or I can choose to mortify myself by leaving it sitting in front of my house for a few hours."

"Empty," he pointed out. "So the harpies can all conjecture on the whereabouts of the driver."

"Great," she said, and got in the front seat.

They didn't talk much as they drove to the orchard. Maggie admired the countryside, and JD took perverse pleasure in startling other drivers by gradually pulling up behind them with the cruiser. "So what's new with Gamey?" he asked out of the blue.

"I have no clue. I do my best to pretend he doesn't exist."

"How come none of you are willing to give the guy a break?"

"None of who? My class of people? My gender?"

"Hey, I'm just asking, okay? I mean, since you're new in town, I'd hate to see you basing your judgment on someone else's opinion."

Maggie looked at him without answering.

"I don't mean to offend you. I just thought you might give the guy a chance, that's all."

"A chance to do what? He's creepy."

"A man is more than the measure of his characteristics."

"You really think I'm that shallow? My distaste for him is totally earned."

"What has he done?"

"Nothing overt. It's all insinuation." JD didn't answer. "*Don't* even think about telling me it's my imagination," Maggie warned.

"I wouldn't do that. But how about the incredible number of charitable things he does for the community? Without ever asking for recognition."

"He breathes air too. Occasionally he's going to do some of the same things decent humans do. That doesn't qualify him for membership in the club."

The parking lot was crowded for a midweek morning and they just managed to get the last two seats on the wagon out to the orchard. At the end of the ride they had to wait an eternity while the driver went through a litany of rules. It began to look like the apples would rot off the trees before they got to pick any. When the driver finally came around and unlocked the gate the wagonload of visitors scattered like buckshot.

Maggie and JD walked by a group of little kids waiting for the wagon ride back to the weighing shed. A small boy with Down syndrome started jumping around, shouting, "Chief Charles! Chief Charles!"

"Hey, David," JD said, walking over. "What are you doing here?"

"I'm picking apples. Hey lady," the kid turned to Maggie, "this is Chief Charles!"

"He a friend of yours?" Maggie asked.

"No," the little boy said seriously. "He is my coach."

"Your coach? What do you play?"

"Goal-ie! Goal-ie!" He started jumping up and down with escalating excitement.

"Okay buddy," JD said calmly. "High five." David jumped up and slapped JD's hand. "Time to go back to your apple picking team."

"They are a good team," he said. "They help each other to find the biggest apple. Want to see it?"

Maggie followed JD over to check out the apple, and then they helped load the baskets onto the wagon. After it lurched away Maggie looked at JD. "You coach his soccer team?"

"Yeah." He took an empty basket from the stack at the end of a nearby row.

"And you take stray kids camping. And chaperone a youth group."

"Does this present a problem for you?"

"I hope it doesn't get too windy out here. Your halo might blow off."

JD stopped walking and looked at her. "Is there anything I could do that you wouldn't find to be cause for derision?"

"Probably not," Maggie replied.

He started walking again. "So where did you get this problem with authority?"

"From having to deal with it."

JD didn't answer. They turned down a row. All the fruit within reach was either shriveled or unripe. Maggie slipped through the trees to one of the forbidden rows where the ripe fruit pulled the branches almost to the ground. JD followed her. She picked an apple. "I don't have a basket."

"Better use mine," JD told her. "If you go back to the main path to get your own, somebody might notice you and make us move." Maggie gathered a few more apples, placing them in the basket.

"So how'd you meet your husband?" JD asked.

Maggie hated talking about herself. "I was in school," she finally answered. She braced herself to head off the interrogation she assumed was coming.

"I knew Rebekah since we were kids," JD replied. "My wife." Maggie looked at him with veiled surprise. He continued picking apples. "Her family took me in as a foster child and decided to keep me. I worshipped her from behind doors and around corners. She was my unattainable dream. And then I tried to make her miserable whenever she got close."

Maggie choked slightly. JD looked at her. "What?"

She cracked up. "You married your sister?"

"You think you're pretty funny, don't you?"

"No," she said. "I think *you're* pretty funny."

"Rebekah used to love to pick apples," JD said.

"Here?" The thought made Maggie feel a little icky.

"Nope," he said. "We never lived here. I wouldn't go with her."

"So you guys were inseparable, except for the apple orchard?"

"You're a hard nut, you know that?"

"You don't even realize."

JD plucked a few more apples off a high branch. "When we were kids, she always had the upper hand, even though I don't think she was really trying. She just always did the right thing. She didn't seem to notice if anybody else got screwed in the process."

"Literally?" Maggie asked.

"Please," he said. "We're talking about the preacher's daughter."

"Okay," Maggie said. "I'm going to stop now, before I say something you'll regret."

"I appreciate that."

"What did she die of?"

"Breast cancer. Less than two years after it was diagnosed."

"I'm sorry." She meant it. Still, she wished there was some way she could gracefully turn off the spigot of confidences. She wasn't sure what to do with them.

"When we got married, she was my idea of the perfect wife," JD continued, oblivious to Maggie's discomfort. "She was an excellent cook and a perfect housekeeper. That was her vision for herself."

"And did she have a vision for you?"

"It was her idea for me to become a police officer."

"I always wondered about that," Maggie said, "about what makes someone become a cop. I thought maybe it was to prove something."

"In my case," he replied, "it proves why a man shouldn't get married when he's nineteen years old."

"So you regret the decision?"

"Not sure which decision you're asking about," he said, "but I don't regret any of them."

"How did you end up a foster child?"

"I had a bad case of measles when I was thirteen. They needed to put me someplace where I'd get adequate care."

Maggie squinted at him. "You don't look old enough to have gotten all the way through school before immunizations were required."

"They were required," he said. "I just didn't get them. Sloppy bookkeeping."

"So what happened? I mean, with your perfect marriage? Because it sounds like maybe there was some disillusionment at the end. Before she got sick, of course."

"As time went on," he said, without rancor, "I started to feel like I could do more, like maybe I was smarter than I gave myself credit for. So I went back to school to get my degree."

"And she didn't like that?"

"She never said. College was tidier than building stock cars or shooting small animals, so I'm guessing it was fine with her. The problem was, the more I learned, the more I wanted to talk to somebody about it all and Rebekah just didn't care. She wasn't being mean, it just didn't matter to her. Gradually I figured out that nothing much did. Other than getting fussy occasionally if I left a mess somewhere, the only feeling I was ever sure I saw was indifference. She always listened politely for a reasonable amount of time, but she wasn't interested in anything unless it was her idea. It took years to hit me, but in the end it was like a root that takes hold in a rock wall and gradually pushes the stones apart. You don't notice the damage until it's pretty bad."

"And then she got sick."

"Not right away. But I think even if she lived neither of us would have ever figured out how to fix things. We just went on that way, growing farther and farther apart. I kept going for more degrees, and she kept perfecting her Windex shine."

"That's not very generous."

He shrugged. "It is what it is. She never gave up the pursuit of perfection, even when she was really sick. Right up to the end she figured out how not to need me. We lived totally parallel lives." He paused. "And there are still times when I miss her so much I feel like my heart is trying to punch its way out of my chest."

"I'm sorry," Maggie said, surprised at the intensity of her feelings.

JD simply said, "Thanks." He put a couple of apples into the basket. "So what about you and your bad attitude? Guess your husband appreciated that?"

"Our relationship," Maggie said, "wasn't consistent. Actually, Gary wasn't consistent. When he wanted to be, he was the wisest, funniest person you can imagine. But marrying him invoked some rule I didn't know existed and I became this wife thing instead of me."

"Maybe he just changed."

"I don't think so," she said slowly. "He was still wise and funny with Mac."

"Once you seriously grow apart," JD said, "I'm not sure you can find your way back."

"My case was, unfortunately, more straightforward than that. Gary's mother set up her will so that he couldn't get his inheritance until he had a child. Around the time he found that out, I was handy. I suspect in the heat of anger I looked like a good choice because his mother would've dropped dead all over again if she knew he got her money by marrying someone like me. Once he got over being pissed off, I think he regretted his choice. I was too different. I got the feeling that every time he looked at me, all he could think was how badly he'd screwed up. If he left me, he lost Mac. And I always wondered if somewhere in the back of his mind he wasn't also scared that marrying a shiksa doomed him to hell."

"I'm not sure that's a Jewish concept."

Maggie shrugged. "It's probably a universal concept, don't you think? Designing your own version of hell based on what makes you miserable in life?"

"Why didn't you divorce him?"

"Us Catholics don't believe in divorce, remember?"

JD looked at her skeptically. "That's not really the reason, is it?"

"I guess I never stopped to consider that option," she said thoughtfully. "I just assumed that's what marriage was supposed to be like."

JD picked a few more apples. "Something sure gave you some unique expectations." He looked into the basket. "It's pretty full."

Maggie was surprised. She didn't realize they'd picked so many. "Want to head back?"

"I don't hear the tractor," JD said. "Could be a while before we get a ride."

"We can carry this."

"You ever try to lift one?"

Maggie made a dismissive noise and began dragging the basket by one handle. JD let her get a few feet before coming up behind her and lifting it up. "You don't have to do that," she said. "I can manage."

"How about we each get one side?" He put the basket on the ground, and they each took a handle. Since JD was taller his side was higher. Maggie made no effort to accommodate the difference and he had to lower his side so the apples wouldn't fall out.

At the weighing shed JD lifted the basket onto the counter. The girl behind the register dumped the apples into a bag and put them on the scale. "Fourteen dollars," she said.

"Fourteen dollars?" Maggie repeated. "For apples?"

JD pulled out a twenty. "My treat."

"No thanks." She turned to the girl. "Do you have another bag? So we can split these?"

"Sure," the girl said, looking from one of them to the other.

"You can have them all if you'd like," JD offered.

"What would I need them all for?"

"I don't know." He smiled puckishly. "What do you need half of them for?"

Maggie pulled her money out of her jeans pocket. She counted off seven dollars and threw it on the counter. "Here," she said. "Work it out." She walked outside.

JD came out a few minutes later carrying two approximately equal bags of apples. He popped the trunk on the cruiser and swung the bags down inside. Then he closed the trunk, using more force than necessary.

"Are you pissed?" Maggie asked.

"Would that make you happy?"

"You are, aren't you?"

"You behaved pretty rudely in there."

"Did I embarrass you?" she asked.

His expression was hard. "I would think you embarrassed yourself."

"Nope," she said. "New York attitude."

JD opened his door. "You ready to go?"

"Yeah," Maggie said, and got in the passenger side.

JD drove carefully down the narrow dirt driveway toward the street. Maggie felt the tension in the car, but it didn't bother her. It wasn't anything she wasn't accustomed to. Maybe JD sensed that, because he cooled off quickly. "So what are you going to do with all those apples?" he asked.

"I don't know," Maggie said. "Eat them?"

"Hell of a lot of apples. Probably enough to keep you till next spring."

"You sound as if you have something in mind."

"How about baking some apple pies?"

"Sure," she said sarcastically. "Baking was one of my best grades in school."

"So you don't know how to make a pie?"

"No, Billy Boy."

"If you feel like coming back to my place," he offered, "I'll show you."

She looked out the window. "And he bakes too," she said to the scenery.

"Is that a yes?"

"What am I going to do with pies?" she asked.

"I don't know," he replied. "Feed your son?"

Maggie looked at him sharply. "You're real touchy about me judging you. How about you stop judging me?"

He nodded. "Fair enough." He slowed down and signaled a right turn. "He's a good kid, you know."

"Of course I know. How can you think I would not know?"

"I'm sorry," he said. "This is coming out wrong. I meant to indicate I like him." Maggie did not reply. "If you wanted to say thanks here it would be appropriate."

"I'm supposed to thank you for liking my son?"

"There may have been a compliment embedded in there somewhere."

Maggie's voice was tight. "I don't deserve any credit."

"Bullshit," JD startled her. "You do my job, it's easy to pick out the kids who know they're loved."

"That's really why you do it, isn't it?" she asked, surprised by this insight. "It wasn't because your wife told you to. It's because you like kids."

JD glanced at her. "Partly."

"So why didn't you have any kids of your own? Was it because your wife got sick?"

"Nope." He took a left this time. "We tried for a while and when nothing happened we did the usual tests. Turns out I'm shooting blanks. Measles at puberty, remember?"

"Oh," Maggie said. "So why didn't you adopt?"

"I might have," JD said, "but Rebekah wasn't all that disappointed things worked out the way they did. I think for a while she liked the idea of having kids because it was part of the fiction, the life she imagined. When it turned out she was off the hook, I think she was relieved. Deep down inside, she must have known the reality would drive her crazy. I can't imagine how she would have dealt with things like messy, noisy and disobedient."

"It sounds like she would have been the kind of mother to keep it all under control."

"She would have done okay as the controller, but who knows what she might have gotten for a controlee? Can't predict where the ball's going to drop in the game of genetic roulette."

Maggie didn't answer. It was a good metaphor, but she had reached the point of being exhausted.

16

Gamey pulled up to the back door of the Golf and Cricket Club. He usually took great pleasure in driving his big old van right up to the fancy front entrance, leaking smelly exhaust all over the helmet-haired ladies who came here to lunch. He also liked to watch their faces as they realized all the dreamy hardbodies working in the spa were going to eat cheez-steaks and fries while they nibbled at their frisée like hungry bunnies. But today was Thursday. Thursdays the receptionist at the spa had a lunchtime rendezvous in the back of the Multiplex out on 616. It pained Gamey to have to choose between the certain joys of an unguarded spa delivery or trying to catch the lovers in action at the movies, but in the end, certainty always won out.

Whenever the receptionist was out Ionnis answered the back door. Good old Ionnis, the knucklehead masseur with a taste for free cheez-steaks. Gamey banged on the door and it opened a crack. "Lemme in," he demanded. Ionnis held out his hand. Gamey slapped on a hot, foil-wrapped cheez-steak. "Where are the good tights today?" Ionnis pretended not to hear, or maybe he just didn't understand. Gamey pushed past him and walked over to the window that looked into the gym. "Oh, mama," he said, in a voice that belonged in an X-rated flick.

"You be quiet," Ionnis ordered in his thick Eastern European accent. "They hear you, be trouble."

Gamey stood, transfixed, watching today's batch of yoga queens. Lunch hour class was the best. Morning classes were full of the old dollies. No point in burning your retinas with those images. Midday classes, on the other hand, drew the legal secretaries, the prowling divorcees, the trophy wives and their sycophants. Gamey watched like he was burying his face in a big bowl of whipped cream. He was so engrossed it took him a few minutes to realize he didn't hear the usual snuffling sounds of the goon eating his lunch. He turned ever so slightly, checking out of the corner of his eye. He was alone. A dream come true. He scurried toward the locker room. The class would be ending any minute. If he could get himself positioned just right, he'd be able to see all the way to heaven.

Racing into the shower area he threw himself over the edge of the towel cart, burrowing furiously into the pile of dirty towels. He was mere seconds from success when a giant hand grabbed the back of his collar and lifted him into the air. "Come from there," Ionnis rumbled.

"Let go of me, you big dumb Polack," Gamey demanded, trying to wriggle free.

Ionnis shook him slightly and gave him the bum's rush out of the locker room. "No good they see you," he said.

"What are you talking about?" Gamey protested. "What do you think they do this for? They're all dying for somebody to admire their investments."

"Investments?" Ionnis was confused.

"Sure, investments," Gamey continued. "Some of these babes paid as much for their tits as a smart man spends on a car."

"Which?" Ionnis challenged.

Gamey, still in Ionnis' iron grip, strained toward the workout room window. "Lookit that one over there." He pointed to a woman who was so slender she might have vanished when she turned sideways were it not for her breasts, which made her look like the prow on a schooner. "Those are easily a year-end bonus pair."

"Not to be so," Ionnis said firmly. "I give her massage."

"She lets you massage her titties?" If Ionnis hadn't been holding him by the scruff of his neck Gamey's knees would have buckled under him.

"No touch," Ionnis said.

"So how the hell would *you* know?" Gamey demanded.

"Am man," Ionnis said.

"Huh," Gamey dismissed him. "*I'm* the expert. I was evaluating tits back when they were the only way you could tell your mother from your father."

"Huh," Ionnis echoed back. "I no touch at work. But *you* never touch. Woman let for you to touch only have titties like little boy."

"Hey, screw you!" Gamey said, shaking himself loose and straightening his shirt. "I get to touch titties whenever I feel like it. Real ones!"

"Yeah, sure," Ionnis said. "Soon my brother come from Bulgaria. He look for you."

Gamey straightened up to his full height and walked out the door with dignity. He was sick and tired of not getting treated like an equal. He could so get his share of feel. He just needed some time to figure out how.

☙   ☙   ☙

JD's house was less than a mile from Maggie's, but it was from a different era, a tall red brick Federal style with white trim and black shutters. The front yard was enclosed by an ancient evergreen hedge nearly two stories tall. The narrow driveway along the side of the house led to a detached garage in the back yard. JD pulled up to the garage and turned off the car. He popped the trunk and, grabbing both bags of apples, led the way to the house's rear door, which faced the driveway. This door opened into a mudroom where the bottom half of the walls were wood and the top small panes of glass. JD unlocked the inside door and they went into his kitchen. It was large, with modern appliances, decorated very sparely. He put the bags of apples on the table. "Make yourself at home," he said. "I have to go get the pie stuff from the basement."

"Is there some place I can wash my hands?" Maggie asked.

"Sure." JD showed her the powder room off a short hallway between the kitchen and the dining room. Maggie closed the door and turned on the water, sluicing her fingers back and forth until it got nice and warm. Then she started washing her hands, scrubbing around her cuticles, soaping up her forearms, lost in the moment. She was startled when JD called, "Hey, what are you doing in there? We're going to bake, not do surgery." She froze for an instant, then realized he was joking. She turned off the water and dried her hands.

Back in the kitchen, JD was lifting some sort of gadget out of a carton. It had a crank and a short, mean-looking spear. "What do you assault with that?" she asked.

"You've never been to a Cosseted Cook party?"

"Not unless it's something that involved cater waiters. Or adult paraphernalia."

"This," he said, "is the Apple Wizard." He screwed it to the table and impaled an apple on the spear. Then he turned the crank. The apple spun around and popped off, skinned and sliced into a spiral.

"No wonder you think making pies is easy," Maggie said.

"You can have this job," he said. "I'll make the crusts."

"No," Maggie said. "You said you'd show me how to make pies. I want to learn everything."

JD got a mischievous grin. "You want to learn how to make crust from scratch?"

"Yeah. But not like Sissy Spacek in a movie about Appalachia. Like Jacques Pepin, with the latest kitchen equipment."

"You're smarter than you look." He went to the cabinet under the sink and pulled out a food processor. "Man's best friend," he said, placing it on the counter and plugging it in. He opened an upper cabinet and took out two large canisters. "Flour," he held up one and then the other, "and sugar."

"I'm already out of my league," Maggie said. "I thought sugar came in little packets."

JD took out a box of tapioca starch. "My secret ingredient." He also took out a bottle of vanilla. "Here." He handed her the bottle. "Smell this. It's the real stuff. Madagascar."

She opened the bottle and took a sniff. "Smells like vanilla," she said.

"Yeah, but sweeter." He took two sticks of butter from the refrigerator. "Pie-crust recipes call for some kind of shortening. If you use real butter, the crust comes out a lot shorter."

"Isn't the crust always short?"

"It's a pastry term," he said. "It means flaky and buttery."

"Gee," she replied, "I guess that's why butter works well, huh?"

"The spices are in that cabinet." He pointed. "Go pick some out."

"Which ones?"

"Use your head," he replied. "You've probably eaten apple pie at least once in your life. And if that doesn't work, use your nose."

Maggie went over and opened the cabinet. She looked at the contents. Cinnamon clearly went into apple pie. She took out the small rectangular can of pumpkin pie spice and sniffed. It was too strong, like it might smother the apples, so she put it back. She decided nutmeg made the cut without checking how it smelled. Then she picked one more small bottle and brought everything over to JD. "Dried lavender?" he asked.

"Sure," she said. "Why not?"

He considered this. "Okay. Why not?"

"So how do you know how to do all this stuff?" she asked. "Did Rebekah teach you?"

"Nope," he said. "Rev did. Her father. He taught us both at the same time."

"Was her mother alive?"

"Sure," he said. "But her cooking sucked. So Rev never let her near the kitchen. I suspect the real reason he taught us how to do stuff was so he'd have some company."

"Did Rebekah let you cook once you were married?"

"You are disappointingly nosy."

"Did she?"

"I was working or in school most of the time, but when I was home she didn't have a choice. I like to cook. And I was better than she was."

"Did that make her mad?"

"Only if I left a mess," he smiled.

"Show me what to do," Maggie said.

"Okay." He took measuring cups and spoons out of a drawer. "Baking is a lot like chemistry. You need to be precise about measuring and mixing, and then you need to observe. If something isn't working, you have to make an adjustment right there, on the spot, or you're screwed." He measured a cup of flour, showing her his preferred method of leveling it. "We're going to make two double-crust pies," he said. "So you'll need two cups of flour for each pie."

"How do you know?" she asked.

"Experience."

"What if I don't have experience?"

"Buy a cookbook," he said. "It won't kill you to consult an expert once in a while."

They put the flour and butter into the food processor in batches and he showed her how to pulse it. "You have to do this just until the mixture breaks up into pea-sized clumps," he said. "This used to be a bitch to do by hand."

While Maggie finished up, JD made a bowl of ice water. They gradually added it through the chute of the food processor, one tablespoonful at a time, until the dough held together. "Some people like to add sugar to their crust," JD said, "but I only use vanilla." He added a couple of drops.

Maggie shrugged. "I certainly don't have an opinion."

JD took the lump of dough out of the processor, wrapped it tightly in plastic, and stuck it in the freezer. "Twenty minutes exactly," he told her. "Any longer, and it gets too hard and breaks up when you try to roll it. Any less and it'll be too soft."

While they were waiting for the first batch of crust to firm up, JD turned on the oven to preheat and made a second batch of dough. Maggie finished preparing the apples. She divided them into two large bowls. Then she measured in the tapioca flour and the spices. "This is a lot easier than I expected," she said.

"Think so?" JD asked. He switched the new packet of dough for the one that had been chilling. "We didn't get to the hard part yet." He reached into the space between the cabinets and the refrigerator and pulled out a large slab of marble. "Rolling time." He put the slab on the kitchen table and took a rolling pin from the carton he'd brought up from the basement.

Maggie wrinkled her nose. "You want to clean that before we use it?"

"You intimating my basement isn't sanitary?"

"People used to say 'you'll eat a peck of dirt before you die'. That was back when most of them died at forty-two."

"How much dirt is in a peck?"

"Give me that." She reached to take the rolling pin from him.

"I was only joking," he said, amused. "You could stand to lighten up, you know that?"

"Try to remember I'm here to learn how to make pies, okay?"

JD cleaned the rolling pin and the marble slab. "You want to learn how to roll crust the manly way or the easy way?"

"Don't you find it interesting that those two things are mutually exclusive?"

"Fine," he said. "Manly way it is."

"Wait," she replied. "What's the easy way?"

"Between two sheets of waxed paper."

"So what's the manly way, under your truck tires?"

"Watch." He reached into the flour canister and took some out, sprinkling it on the marble slab. "Don't worry," he said, "I boiled my hand earlier today." He spread the flour around, coating the slab. Taking the dough out of the plastic wrap, he tore it in half and put one piece in the middle of the floured area, lightly flouring the dough as well. He began rolling, moving the rolling pin out from the center as if following the spokes of a wheel. The dough obligingly flattened into a uniform circle. At one point it began to stick and he stopped and rubbed some flour on the rolling pin. "You have to be careful not to use too much flour," he said, "or the dough will get tough."

"I heard that somewhere," Maggie replied, "but I'm not sure I get the hazards of tough dough. Are we afraid somebody's going to choke on it? Break a tooth?"

"No ribbons at the county fair," JD said. "Also, it inhibits access to the apples."

"That would explain all the anxiety."

"The really hard part," JD said, "is getting the crust into the pan without messing it up." He lifted the dough from the slab in one continuous motion, rolling it onto the pin and then unrolling it, perfectly centered, into the pie pan.

"Show off," Maggie said.

"Want to try?"

"Sure." She took the rolling pin and repeated everything he'd done. While she worked he put the apples into the pan.

"Okay," he said, watching her. "That's thin enough. You want me to put it on?"

Maggie raised an eyebrow at him as she lifted the crust with the rolling pin and got it perfectly centered over the apples. With a small sharp knife JD trimmed off the excess dough and cut a pattern of slits in the top. Then he showed Maggie how to crimp the edges. He slid the pan onto a cookie sheet and then into the oven. They repeated the process for the second pie, working in comfortable silence. When the second pie was in the oven JD asked, "So what did you do in your former life? Before you became a rich widow."

"Guess."

"Brain surgery."

"You know what makes a good guesser?" Maggie asked.

"What?"

"Most people think it's somebody who picks up clues. But that's only part of it. After they pick up the clues, a good guesser throws them in someone else's path and watches for a reaction. If the person walks by the clue without noticing, the guesser never mentions anything. He just picks up the clue and waits for the next sucker to come along."

"And what if the passerby notices the clue?"

"If they're just curious and stop to examine the clue, the guesser tries to convince them it's nothing so they won't think it's worth mentioning to anyone else. The guesser wants to wait for the person who comes along and reacts to the clue with surprise."

"And what does the guesser do then?"

"If he's a smart guesser, nothing. He just takes note and bides his time until he can use that piece of information to his own advantage."

"That's a unique way of looking at it," JD said. "But you still haven't told me what you used to do."

"No, I haven't," Maggie replied. "The answer isn't all that interesting."

"Probably not. But the commitment to deception is."

"Just stringing you along, honey," she said lightly. "You cop types love that hint of mystery."

"Pies are starting to smell good," JD said.

"Are they done yet?"

"Nope. Apple pie needs to bake over an hour."

Maggie looked at her watch. "I should get going. Mac will be home soon and I didn't leave a note. I didn't think I'd be gone this long."

"I'll give you a ride. I can drop your pie off later."

"I have plenty of time to walk. You don't want to go out and leave the oven on."

JD smiled almost condescendingly. "Do I detect a whiff of neurosis?"

"No," Maggie said. "Common sense."

"It'll only be a few minutes."

"Fine," Maggie said. "You can give me a ride."

They drove most of the way without talking. JD pulled into the alley and stopped in back of her garage. "Thank you," he said. "I had fun."

Maggie smiled as she got out of the car. "Me too, actually," she replied, closing the door gently behind her.

17

Tuohy's Party Shop, according to the sign over the front, was a "purveyor of illusion and costume essentials". Old Mr. Tuohy had moved the business out to the North End Plaza a few years before. It was cheaper than being in town, but more importantly profits had picked up quite a bit once certain people could shop with less risk of running into a neighbor. Nothing, it seemed, was too exotic for him to sell. But the stuff Carl Bendz had special-ordered for his 'wife' wasn't going to be easy to unload. With the Henhouse out of business, there just wasn't the market for those kinds of specialty items, and since the fire Bendz himself had been harder to find than lice on a bald man. Margins were too tight for Tuohy to take the order as a loss. And so, with Halloween coming up, this morning he'd put the whole lot out on the floor.

The store was crowded and noisy today. Nobody paid any attention to two boys who seemed to be having a dispute as they cruised the aisles of the shop. "I don't know," Mac said. "I'd like to dress up in something really nasty and gory."

"That shit's for little kids." Morsel's tone was full of contempt.

"They have adult-size costumes." Mac pointed at the wall. "I never got to do that stuff when I was little. At school we had to make theme masks every year out of creative materials. Then on Halloween, every class took a turn going from room to room trick or treating."

"What about at night?"

"At night there was a show for the parents. We had to wear the masks with our uniforms instead of costumes and do stuff about the theme. Afterwards we'd get cider and cupcakes."

"This is not shit you should be telling anybody," Morsel said.

"One year when Halloween was on a Saturday some kid whose family had a loft in Tribeca had a party. His mother hired a party planner, so we still got stuck with a theme. At least we got to wear costumes."

"Was the theme cool or girly?"

"It was kind of cool at first. *The Legend of Sleepy Hollow.* Everybody showed up as the Headless Horseman, except for a couple of girls. But then they had all this stuff like bobbing for apples and face painting. You know stuff you can't do without a head. So it ended up being pretty boring."

"Hey!" Morsel said. "Look at this." He was standing in front of the Bendz stash. "This stuff is cool."

"That's hooker stuff, man."

"Yeah," Morsel grinned. "Probably get it for a pretty good price now that the market's gone up in smoke."

"What would you do with it?"

"Wear it, you imbecile."

"I don't want to be a *hooker.*"

"You wouldn't *be* a hooker, stupid. It's Halloween."

"You know what I mean."

"Come on," Morsel tried to persuade him. "It'll be fun."

"Look how much this stuff costs," Mac said. "We don't have enough money for all this."

"You buy the makeup," Morsel said. "I'll take care of the rest."

"How?" Mac demanded. "You don't have any money."

"Yeah I do. I just didn't bring it with me."

"You're full of crap."

"No, really. You tell me what you like and I'll go get money and come back and buy it. How about this?" He held a peacock blue boa up to Mac's cheek. "This looks good. Kinda matches your eyes."

"Cut it out." Mac shoved his hand away.

"Come on. Let's go to the drugstore and get some lipstick and stuff."

Mac reluctantly followed Morsel out of the store. They'd only gone a few feet when Morsel stopped so suddenly Mac almost steamrolled over him. "What?" he asked, annoyed.

Morsel did not answer. He was frozen in place. Mac followed the direction of his gaze. Out in the parking lot a mess of cops were swarming all over the old maroon Bonneville. A police cruiser blocked it from behind. Another cop car was in front of that. "Hey!" Mac said. "What are they doing with your mother's car?"

"Shut up!" Morsel hissed.

"We have to find out what's going on!"

"Don't be an asshole. We're going to walk nice and slow to the pizza place at the other end of the shopping plaza, and then you're going to buy us some sodas and then we're going to walk home."

"And just leave the car here?"

"Come on. Just start walking. No, not like that. You go on the outside."

Mac stopped. "Whose car is that?" he demanded.

"It's my mother's!" Morsel's voice squeaked. "You know that."

"So why are the cops so interested in it?"

Morsel shrugged. "I dunno."

"Well, I'm going to find out."

"Suit yourself. But I'm outta here. Don't do anything dumb."

"Like what?"

"Like telling them my name."

Mac began walking toward the car. When he glanced back, Morsel had disappeared. That's when he realized, too late, exactly how stupid this idea was. But a cop had already spotted him. If he turned around now, it would all be over. He felt kind of dizzy, and his fingertips were all tingly. He bent over, afraid he was going to pass out.

"Hey, son," the cop asked, "you all right?"

He straightened up slowly. "Yeah," he said. "I was just looking for my wallet. I thought maybe I lost it around here when my mom dropped me off. Did anybody find a wallet?"

"Not that I heard. Give me your name and phone number. If anything shows up, I'll let you know."

Mac's stomach hurt as he gave the cop the information. Then he said, as if the thought had just struck him, "What's up with that car?"

The cop's eyes narrowed slightly. "What's it to you?"

"Nothing. Just curious."

"It was reported stolen in Northeast Philadelphia."

"Wow," Mac said. "That sucks."

The cop shrugged and walked away.

Mac felt miserable. He was glad it was a long walk home. At least that gave him a chance of feeling kind of normal by the time he got there.

🐾　🐾　🐾

The phone rang. "Mac!" Maggie called from the kitchen, "It's for you!"

"I got it," he called back, picking up the phone in the hall. She was so old-fashioned. One phone in the kitchen, one in the upstairs hall, like when she was growing up. They might as well be living in the Dark Ages. "Hello?" he said.

"Hey, man," Morsel replied. "What are you doing?"

He waited for the click of the downstairs phone being hung up before he answered. "You stole your mother's car!"

"I did not!" Morsel was offended. "I just borrowed it."

"So why'd she think somebody stole it?"

"She told me I could use it any time I wanted. She even let me have my own set of keys. I figured she'd let me know when she wanted it back."

"How? By sending the cops to get it?"

"I don't know. Maybe she got pissed off or something." Morsel changed the subject. "So what're you doing?"

"Are you serious?" Mac was so irritated his voice cracked. "I'm not hanging out with you anymore."

"Fine," Morsel said shortly.

Mac hung up the phone. It rang again in less than thirty seconds. He picked it up.

"Hey," Morsel said, "I got all the stuff for our costumes."

"How'd you do that?"

"I *told* you I had money. My stuff's all black. I got you red."

"I'm not hanging out with you anymore, dude. I mean it."

"That's too bad," Morsel said. "You'd look good in red. I'll drop the stuff by your house and you can see for yourself."

"Forget it. I'm not going out with you on Halloween."

"Whatever," Morsel said. "I'll drop the stuff off and you can decide." Before Mac could protest again, Morsel hung up.

18

Daniel applied more paint to his canvas. The morning light on the lake this time of year ignited his perception. By this late in the fall he usually only got a few hours before lunch to get some painting done. The wind often kicked up at midday, as it was starting to do now. Plus, it wasn't wise to leave Libertine in charge of the shop for too long. Her tendency to forget why she was there could manifest itself in a variety of undesirable ways.

He tried to make the most of these last few minutes, focusing on the texture of his oils as he worked to capture the picturesque lake. There was a light chop on the water that broke the sunlight into glittering shards. With most of the leaves gone, the landscape went much farther into the distance this time of year. But no matter how hard he tried to concentrate, he couldn't block out Martha. She was being antsy. She knew this bothered him, but she didn't stop. It was her damn hair appointment. The way she was stalking around, you'd think she was going to traffic court instead of a new hairdresser. Eventually, to his relief, she walked down to the water's edge.

Daniel lowered the front brim of his geeky straw hat, hoping to make her believe he wasn't watching her. A couple with a golden retriever puppy jogged past and the dog ran over and jumped up on her. The owners called it back, but Martha enticed it to stay by rubbing it behind the ears. The owners had no choice but to walk over and talk to her.

Daniel desperately hoped they had a lot to say. He increased the pace of his painting, feeling the minutes slip away under his brush. Martha finished talking to the joggers and walked back to the car for something, but he knew it was only a temporary reprieve.

"Are you still working?" Her voice startled him as she came up behind him.

The question annoyed him more than anything else she could have possibly said. Is my brush still moving? he wanted to yell. Am I still putting paint on my canvas? Instead, he chose a safer, though far less satisfying route. "Can't you just tell me you're ready to go? Why must you attempt, never successfully, I might add, to manipulate me?" Despite having good intentions, he began to spool up. He could see it happening, but his mood was a rollercoaster and he was strapped in. They were climbing that first hill, he and his aggravation, pulling up against gravity at a dreadful angle. He sort of looked forward to that moment when he could start careening through his tirade, out of control.

"Oh, cut your crap," Martha said, totally interrupting his ride. "You want some help packing up?"

His annoyance mostly evaporated. "I guess that means we're going," he said. That was the thing about Martha. She always got her way, but she usually managed to make you thank her for it. They began loading his painting gear into the granny cart he used to lug it around.

"You got a good bit done today," she noted.

"Probably could have finished if you'd just been patient."

Martha grinned at him. "But then we wouldn't have had an excuse to come back."

He kissed her. "You are a wicked girl."

She looked like an uninvited thought had just possessed her. "I'll tell you who's a wicked girl."

"Hmm?" He was closing cases and wrapping things up, not really paying attention.

"Your friend Maggie."

That got him to look up. "How so?"

"She walks through life leaving a trail of havoc, but since everything she knocks down is behind her, she gets to pretend she doesn't notice."

"That's not fair," Daniel said patiently.

"*Life's* not fair," Martha retorted. "But let me tell you, I have never seen a human being so devoid of emotion."

"Why would you assume that?"

"Please," Martha said. "Have you ever watched her? She's utterly blind to what she or anybody else is feeling."

"That's not true," Daniel said.

"The hell it's not. She's going to do somebody some real damage before she's done."

Daniel looked at her closely. "Martha Stewart," he said, "you are jealous."

"Get bent," Martha said.

"You are. You're jealous of Maggie."

"Why would I be jealous of her, Daniel?" She stared at him accusingly. "You want to think about that?"

He put his arm around her. "There are things about her you don't know. There are things even I don't know, but I know enough."

"So her secrets get to come between us?"

"Not at all," Daniel said. "But if I tell you, that means you share the burden of protecting her. Are you sure that's what you want?"

Martha took her time answering. "Is it that bad?"

"Maybe," Daniel said. "Maybe not. Only she can ever really say. But once you know, you know. No looking at her funny, no asking leading questions. And no going back."

"Just tell me," Martha said.

🐓 🐓 🐓

Lillian pulled up outside the high school wing of St. Agnes of the Precious Lambs. She was driving the Navigator today. She generally didn't like taking something this big to town, but it was a comfortable vehicle and more importantly, it made Chrissie happy. Lillian liked to make her granddaughter happy. Chrissie looked astonishingly like her mother had as a teenager, but where Carol Ann had already been a wicked bitch at this age, Chrissie adored her grandmother. They were buddies in the most unexpected ways. She hung on Lillian's every word, respected her judgment, admired her taste. Lillian often picked her up on Wednesdays, when school let out early to accommodate catechism classes for the public school children. Today they had an appointment at the salon. They went together once a month, as they had been doing since Chrissie was old enough for it to matter.

Kids began pouring out of the school. In a moment, Lillian spotted Chrissie, surrounded by her cheerleader friends. Lillian firmly believed that if pride goeth before a fall, it was only because some slack-jawed fool was likely to trip while staring at the women in her family. Chrissie was beautiful, nearly perfect in every way, with Lillian's coloring, good bones, and effortless grace. Thank heavens most of Wesley's genes, like the man himself, were submissive, though no doubt Chrissie's one anomalous affliction came from his side of the family. It was only the tiniest bit of fuzz on her upper lip, but their salon technician was such a perfectionist, she had recently insisted it was time to graduate from bleaching to waxing.

As Lillian watched, the boy interrupted Chrissie's progress toward the SUV. She was not pleased that Chrissie stopped and spoke with him. He was tall and well built, and held himself with the cocky ease of a gifted athlete. Lillian gave herself two deep cleansing breaths and then tapped the car's horn insistently. She was irritated that the horn made such a cultured bleat, not intrusive enough to disrupt Chrissie's conversation. Then she realized how good it felt just to express herself and leaned heavily on the little horn symbol on the big steering wheel, momentarily distracted from the pain of not having her way.

Eventually Chrissie resumed her sashay to the car. She opened the passenger door and climbed in, obviously aware of the boy still watching her. She moved in a way designed to maximize what little seductive value there was in her pleated uniform skirt. "Hey, Grams." She leaned across the console and planted a big kiss on Lillian's cheek.

Lillian was unmollified. "You know I detest being late." She edged the big SUV away from the curb.

"We're good," Chrissie said blithely. "We've still got ten minutes."

"I have to find a parking place."

"Make the receptionist park it for you."

"Who was that boy?"

"Nathaniel Jackson."

That was one of the things Lillian admired about the girl. No false coyness. "You seem fond of each other."

"Umm." Chrissie was noncommittal.

"I haven't seen him before."

"He's a ringer. Somebody found him playing quarterback in Norristown. He's from Barbados. They gave him a huge scholarship to come captain here. He has a really cute accent, and the most amazing manners. I think he's pretty hot."

They pulled up to a red light and Lillian looked at her granddaughter sternly. "I think he's pretty black."

"Silly Grams." Chrissie patted her hand. "I'm not going to marry him. I just want to see if what they say about black men is true."

🐦   🐦   🐦

Martha moved around, trying to find a comfortable position on the hard little sofa. She suspected she was being made to wait longer than a regular. Somehow, she had foolishly neglected to book ahead at her own salon. After waiting two weeks for a cancellation, she called around in a panic, desperate for anyone who would tend her hair on an emergency basis. She finally got an appointment here at Picasso's. Although wisdom urged her to suspect anyone who had a same-day opening, her sense of caution, like her hair, had gone to the dogs.

The receptionist popped her head over the tall counter that isolated waiting patrons. "Can I get you a drink?" she asked. "Maybe some wine?"

"Sure," Martha said. "White wine would be nice. Just a little, though."

The girl came back with a large stemmed glass. Martha took a sip. The wine was good. She sipped some more. It was boring sitting here. They didn't have techno playing in the background, or a collection of thumbworn magazines, or even some out-of-date hairstyle books. All they had were shelves of expensive hair products, useless in the hands of anyone but an overpriced stylist. Martha chugged the rest of her wine. To her right, the entry door opened and Lillian Bendz walked in with her granddaughter. Finding themselves in unavoidable proximity, they had no choice but to acknowledge each other.

"Martha," Lillian said, "I didn't know you'd changed salons."

"I forgot to book ahead at Frequency," Martha replied. "Luckily they had an opening here."

"With whom?"

"Randy." Lillian and Chrissie exchanged a look. It wasn't lost on Martha. But there was no subtle way to find out what was up. Everyone within earshot was probably listening.

"Excuse us," Lillian said. "We're running a little late." She walked away as she spoke. "Lovely to see you. Give my regards to David."

Martha knew it would be a waste of time trying to correct her. And somehow, during this exchange her wine glass had been refilled. She knew she'd already had enough. The volume on her internal monologue was threatening to become audible. But she was so bored. What the hell, she thought. Bottoms up.

Randy finally emerged from wherever he'd been hiding, "You *must* be Martha," he said, with exaggerated enthusiasm.

Martha was sloppily furious. "Why?" she demanded. "Because I'm the only one who's been sitting here so long there are cobwebs on my ankles?"

He put a forefinger to his lips in a caricature of 'thinking'. "Well, let's see. Because you look like nobody's updated your style since you finished sewing the stars onto the stripes?"

"That was Betsy Ross, you imbecile."

He came over and grabbed her hand. "This one's special," he said to the receptionist. "I like her."

"If you're going to come near me with scissors, start treating me with respect," Martha said sternly.

"Come on, sweetheart," he said. "Let's give you a look that matches your pizzazz." Despite the two glasses of wine, Martha rose from the bench with dignity, stumbling only slightly as she walked to the sink.

She didn't realize she was so tipsy until Randy shampooed her, giving her head a nice long massage, and she almost slid out of the chair. At some point he asked if it wouldn't be a super idea to brighten up her color, and it sounded like the best suggestion anyone had made in years. When they finally finished at the sink, Randy wrapped a towel around her head and escorted her back to his station. As she sat down, she spied Lillian and her granddaughter in the mirror. She nodded toward their reflection. "You know them?" she asked.

"*Everyone* knows them," Randy hissed. "The old lady throws cash around like a blizzard, but nobody would mind if she took her money somewhere else. Bitch on wheels."

"And the kid?"

"Oh, that's the best part. Grandma's sitting there getting her own puss waxed and the whole time she's insisting the kid got the mustache from the other side of the family. She tried to convince us she only needed a little bleach, but I swear she looked like Magnum PI."

"Are they going to get waxed now?"

"That's what they're here for. Standing appointment."

"Turn me around so I can watch."

"Honey, I'd love to accommodate, but I can't just let you sit here. I've got somebody booked right behind you."

"So cut while I'm watching."

"Whatever you say," he shrugged, and spun her away from the mirror. Martha watched, hoping every pluck of the tweezers hurt like hell, as Lillian got her chin and upper lip weeded. She was barely aware of Randy snipping happily around her head. At one point, she did notice that her ears were feeling chilly, but Randy told her not to worry, she was going to love how this new look brought out her eyes. Across the room, Lillian and her granddaughter were now getting their faces varnished with brownish-green slime.

"You look astonishing!" Randy exclaimed loudly. The sound of his voice startled Martha out of her mellow alcohol-induced reverie. It also caught Lillian's attention. Her mud-caked face contorted into a grimace. She nudged her granddaughter, and the girl made an equally pained expression.

"Take a look!" Randy spun the chair around. Martha was too shocked at first to even breathe. Her hair had been dyed a shade somewhere between magenta and cherry cola. Randy had razored the back and sides short enough to qualify for boot camp. But there was plenty of hair left on the top of her head, and Randy had moussed that into thick fronds. She looked like a palm tree. Martha struggled to retain some semblance of dignity and lost. "This is the worst fucking haircut I have ever seen on anyone in my entire life."

"You don't like it," Randy said, offended.

"I've seen better looks on people recovering from neurosurgery," she snarled.

"Just give it a chance," he said. "Walk around with it for a few days. See if you don't get some positive reactions."

Martha picked up her purse and stormed out of the salon. She would have to do something about her hair, but she had no idea what. Maybe Daniel could think of something. She walked around the corner to the Art Shop, praying she wouldn't run into anyone she knew, but from the door she could see that the shop was full. She turned around to leave, and as if on cue, Libertine called out, "Hey, Martha, cool!" Everyone turned to look. "The hair," Libertine continued loudly. "You've got some balls! You'll have the best costume in town."

"What are you talking about?" Martha snapped.

Libertine looked at the customer she was waiting on. "Doesn't she look just like Sideshow Bob from *The Simpsons*?" she asked.

Martha stormed into the back room, slamming the door behind her.

19

The weather turned cold with a sudden fierceness. People went to sleep one night with their windows open and woke the next morning marooned in their beds by floors as cold as skating ponds. There were a few cheery diehards who used words like brisk and refreshing, but most of Dooleysburg disappeared off the streets like migratory birds. To get them to come back out, Town Council approached each seasonal holiday as a major marketing campaign.

Halloween kicked off the fall schedule. Decorating was left to individual shop owners, which instantly made it a competitive event. On the first Saturday in October every business on Main Street filled its windows with corpulent ghosts, tumbling piles of gourds and high tech jack-o-lanterns. Doorways had floor mats that cackled and moaned. Automated creatures tried to engage passersby in conversation.

It all made Maggie feel a little betrayed. This Dooleysburg was the cartoon version of the fairy tale, while she remembered the Brothers Grimm. She tried, without success, to disguise her feelings. In typical Dooleysburg fashion, people felt compelled to cheer her up. "Remind me why we come here," she asked Vee after a particularly trying encounter where she had to deal with Lola/Mercedes demanding a smile in exchange for coffee.

"Better food than your place," Vee said. "Better service than mine."

"It is seriously cold out." Maggie warmed her hands on her coffee cup. "Hard to believe that a few days ago I was out picking apples."

"How did that go?"

"It was fine."

"Fine?" Vee repeated. "*Fine* is how you describe a boring job interview."

"We had fun. We baked pies."

"You *what*?"

"After we picked apples. We went back to his place and baked pies."

"I knew it!" Vee slammed the table hard enough to make Maggie jump. "I knew he was a southern boy!"

"Because he knows how to make pie?"

"What was his crust like?"

"It seemed okay to me, but I'm not exactly a connoisseur."

"Well, I might be able to say if you were thoughtful enough to offer me some."

"You're not going to start whining about a piece of pie, are you?"

"I am if you don't give me some."

Maggie sat back and looked at her. "You know what? I think you're telling the truth. That piece of pie matters enough to you that it's worth making a fuss over if you don't get it, and if you do that's all it will take to make you happy."

"That's what I just said." Vee shook her head. "Is there something remarkable about people knowing what they want?"

Maggie nodded. "In my world there is. You're like that toy they used to make, the one that looked like a little person shaped like an egg. Remember how when you pushed it over it always kept its balance and popped back up again?"

"Weebles?"

"That was it! Weebles. You're perfectly centered, like a Weeble."

"I had them when I was a kid too. I was playing with a friend one time and I started singing the commercial, about how Weebles wobble but they don't fall down. So he takes all the Weebles and lines them up on the edge of the table and then knocks them all off. And I said, what are you doing? And he looks at me and says, 'They fell down'."

Maggie laughed. "And the moral of the story is?"

"Beware of the person who sees things in ways you don't expect."

🐓 🐓 🐓

Maggie and Vee came in from the breezeway. "Don't get your hopes up," Maggie said. "There wasn't that much pie left this morning. If it's gone, you'll need to go bother your buddy for some of his."

"Forget that," Vee said. "The guys at the station were lining up as soon as they heard he was going apple picking."

"I think he cooks to show off."

"Honey, I'm telling you, he cooks because good food is in his genes."

"If it matters so much to you where he's from, why don't you just ask him?"

"I did. He gets all cryptic about it. Probably waiting for me to bribe it out of him."

"So what's stopping you?"

"I just haven't figured out the right bribe yet." Vee sniffed the air. "There's still some pie around here somewhere."

"Hey Mac!" Maggie called. "I'm home. Vee's here too. She wants some pie."

"I'm in here!" Mac called from the den. "Bring a fork."

"Not a plate?" Vee asked. "He's only going to give me a fork's worth?"

"I've got more apples," Maggie said. "I'll make you your own pie."

"Finally," Vee said. "It sure took you long enough to offer."

"If you wanted me to make you a pie, why didn't you just ask?"

"Wouldn't have been polite." Vee took a fork from the drawer and walked off to the den.

When Maggie came in a few minutes later, Vee and Mac were busy scraping the pie tin, getting up the last of the goo. "Good pie," Vee said. "We're very proud of you."

Mac stood up. "Is it okay if I practice now?"

"I don't mind," Vee said.

"Try not to get too loud," Maggie told him as he left the room.

"You know how good he is on those drums, don't you?" Vee asked. "Seems kind of a pity to keep him hidden in the basement."

Maggie smiled sadly. "That's how he wants it. The drumming was something really special between him and his father." She paused a moment. "You know, a funny thing happened at Back to School Night. The music teacher gave me some tough love about Mac needing to take lessons."

Vee shrugged. "It's probably a standard requirement."

"Yeah, that's what I thought too. So I went looking for a teacher, and we ended up at the Music Scene. You know the sweet old guy who owns the place? He gave Mac a drum pad and told him to play something. The next thing I know Mac's doing stuff that's more difficult than I ever heard him play before. The old guy said Mac's well beyond anything he can learn around here. I told him Mac is required to take lessons for Jazz Band and he said I'd just be wasting his time, unless I feel like taking him to Philly."

"So what are you going to do?" Vee asked.

"This is where things get a little suspect. I said I was going to call the school to talk to the band teacher, and Mac got almost panicky. He said he wanted to talk to the teacher himself."

"And?"

"And nothing. I never heard another word. He's still in the Jazz Band, so I guess everything worked out."

"If you're not convinced you should look into it further."

Maggie thought about this. "It's just that when you have a kid this talented, you learn to expect people will notice. I guess I'm surprised the band teacher hasn't mentioned it."

"Your problem is, you fail to appreciate the importance of being average. That teacher spends his life with kids Mac's age. He knows how they hate to be singled out."

"You think?"

Vee raised her voice to be heard above the drums. "You need to see that this glass is half full. Don't forget you brought MacDonald here because you wanted him to have a chance at being normal."

🐾 🐾 🐾

As Halloween approached Vee became insistent that Maggie had to spend it with her. Maggie had no intention of going anywhere on Halloween. But Mac had plans and he agreed with Vee that only a loser would spend Halloween alone if they had a choice. Eventually Maggie gave in. As usual, the moment she did, she discovered there was a hidden agenda.

Vee was Chairperson for this year's Halloween Patrol, a group of poor souls with the mission of ensuring Dooleysburg's trick-or-treaters stayed safe and happy. Safe, Maggie thought, might be possible. But she couldn't imagine what sort of innocent believed there was something they could do to make tired, sugared-up, overheated children happy. In the end she agreed to participate because it was the only way to get Vee to stop nagging her.

When Vee answered her door on Halloween night Maggie was overcome by a mix of savory smells. "What is that?" she asked.

"Home cooking," Vee said. "Would you like to try some?"

Rays of suspicion dawned on the horizon. "Why?"

"Because you're hungry?"

"You already got me to volunteer. There's got to be something else you want. I'm not coming in unless you tell me."

"We need to dress up for Halloween Patrol."

"Forget it," Maggie said. "You never mentioned costumes."

"We're doing this for the children. What fun will it be for them if we're not in costume?"

"Vee, I can't figure out a costume now."

"Relax. I took care of everything."

Maggie's eyes narrowed. "You got me something demeaning, didn't you? That's really why you're trying to bribe me with food."

"I got you exactly the same thing I got me. We'll be like twins."

Maggie snorted. "There are one or two rather salient differences."

"I took that into account." Vee opened the box on her couch. "California Raisins."

"The California Raisins are black."

"Are not. They're purplish brown."

"Whatever. I am not the appropriate shade." As soon as she said it, she flinched. It was astonishing how the mind, left unguarded, had a gift for offering up the absolute wrong words.

To her relief, Vee let it slide. "Not to worry," she said, pulling out the second costume. "You're the token white raisin."

☙   ☙   ☙

Though their shift was only two hours long, Maggie felt physically and spiritually wilted. The California Raisins were so dated only a few adults recognized Vee's costume, and not a single person got the white raisin joke. The closest anyone came was some guy who guessed they were raisin bran and Maggie was a soggy, milk-bloated flake. They only came across one unaccompanied child the whole time, a teenage boy whose purple hair, leather clothing and tattoos were probably not a Halloween costume. He took the cigarette out of his mouth just long enough to offer to take them across the street, pointing out that their juicy plumpness limited their ability to see the curbs. By 8:30, Maggie had become the voice of the sour grape. "Are we done yet?" she demanded.

"Show me some Halloween spirit," Vee said.

"Get real. I have never been so humiliated in my life."

"That can't possibly be true."

"Of course not," Maggie huffed. "I'm trying to make a point. I've had enough."

"Tell you what," Vee perked up. "Let's go over to the Art Shop and see what kind of homemade goodies scary old Martha cooked up." They slogged down the block in clumsy unison. With an ill-timed burst of energy, they both tried to get into the Art Shop at the same time and managed to wedge themselves in the doorway, where they flailed around helplessly.

Martha came from the back of the shop to watch. Yielding to the inevitable, she had dressed as Sideshow Bob. "And I thought *I* looked like an asshole," she said.

"This was not my idea," Maggie replied.

"You would think with all the sweat I got worked up in here, I'd slide right past you," Vee said.

Daniel appeared from wherever he had been hiding. "You two look pitiful," he said. "A cup of coffee for whoever gets through first."

Maggie struggled to free herself. "I need it more," she said. "Start fixing it. I'll have this figured out by the time you finish."

Daniel made a show of cleaning out a mug. He arranged the sugar, powdered creamer and a spoon on the counter. Then he lifted the glass coffee pot from its warming tray. The bottom of it was an archaeological treasure of burned on coffee.

"You going to drink something that comes out of there?" Vee asked.

"Further proof of my superior courage," Maggie said.

"Not hardly," Vee replied. "I already know you're just plain foolish."

"Pour the coffee," Maggie said to Daniel. "Here I come." With a flourish, he dribbled a few tablespoons of coffee into the mug. All three women stared at him in disbelief. "You leave bigger spills than that on the counter," Maggie said.

"You better figure out how to get out of the way," Martha said. "You're blocking the door in the event someone else wants to come in."

"In the *unlikely* event," Maggie answered.

"Not as unlikely as you might think." Martha gestured behind them. Maggie managed to free herself and turned around. She was startled to see Joe Butts standing there.

"Officer," she said, her tone polite.

"Evening, Mrs. Rifkin," he replied. "I'll need you to come with me."

"Excuse me?" An unmistakable note of authority crept into her voice.

"Your son needs to see you. He claims you don't have a cell phone so he had no way to reach you. The taxpayers are already footing the bill for the time required for me to track you down. You better come along pronto."

"What happed to Mac? Is he okay?" Maggie's annoyance became panic.

"He's in custody."

"You mean he's been arrested?" Now her tone shifted to outrage. "For what?"

"Malicious mischief."

"Malicious mischief." Maggie turned to Vee. "Malicious mischief?"

"He bite you?" Vee asked.

"This is serious," Butts said, his voice stern.

"What happened?" Maggie demanded.

"You need to come over to the station. The Chief will give you the details."

"Did anyone get hurt?"

"Luckily, no."

Vee took her arm. "You okay? You look all white."

"Pale," Martha corrected. "She looks pale."

"I'm okay," Maggie said, but her voice was shaky.

"Hang on a minute and Daniel will get the car," Martha offered.

"The station is only a block away," Vee said. "I'll go with her." They went out the door, taking care not to get stuck this time. They kept far enough behind Butts to stay outside his radar. "I like how you said that," Vee whispered.

"Said what?"

"You said, 'what happened?' Not 'what did he do?' No admission of guilt. Good thinking."

"Not thinking," Maggie said. "Just years of training."

Vee did a restrained double-take. "Training at what?"

"It's not important," Maggie said. She picked up her pace and tried to catch up with Butts as he went up the short flight of brightly lit front stairs. Once they got inside he slowed down maddeningly, taking his time leading them into the squad room. Then he took off his jacket and draped it fastidiously over the back of his chair, finally sitting down.

"Where's my son?" Maggie demanded.

"In the holding cell."

"In a cell! You busted him for mischief and you put him a cell? Get him out here!"

"We have procedures that need to be followed." He was not having fun anymore.

"Butts," Maggie straightened up to her full height and leaned on his desk, her raisin suit towering over him in plump menace, "I don't know why, but you have it in for me. Don't take it out on my kid. If you want a face-off with me, I am ready, willing and incredibly able. But either leave my kid out of it or prepare to meet your doom."

"Prepare to meet your doom?" Maggie looked up. JD was standing there. "You were doing good until you said that."

"Doing well." She corrected him without thinking. "Why are you detaining my son?"

"Let's go to my office." He turned to Vee. "You'll have to wait here." They went down a short hall to his office and he closed the door. "You wearing anything under that?" he asked.

"What kind of a question is that?" she demanded. "What did you bring me in here for?"

"I brought you in here to discuss the dangerous and illegal behavior that landed your son in jail tonight. But your face is all red and sweaty. I thought if you take off that ridiculous costume it might save me from having to inconvenience the Rescue Squad again tonight."

"Fine." She had on a tee shirt and sweat pants. She wriggled out of the costume and felt immediate relief. "*Please* just tell me what happened."

"Your son created havoc at the intersection of Route 616 and Bog Road."

"How? Why?" She envisioned Mac running in front of speeding cars and shuddered.

"Why is most likely because he's a kid, and he had a stupid idea he thought was funny. How is slightly more interesting. There is a device Rescue Squads use to remotely control traffic lights. When an ambulance gets near an intersection, this device turns the lights red in all directions, halting traffic long enough for the emergency vehicles to get through without anybody getting in the way. When they release the control everything goes back to normal. Except if someone turns the control on again as soon as the cars start to move.

Which is what occurred at said intersection tonight. Repeatedly. And one of these devices was reported missing from the Squad a few days ago."

"And you think Mac was involved?"

"The missing device was found in his possession when the police removed him from the shrubbery at said intersection."

Maggie was speechless. "I don't understand," she said, mostly to herself. She sat down hard on the chair in front of JD's desk.

"Stay here," JD said. "I'll go get him."

20

Mac sat hunched over, staring at his feet. He hadn't moved since they'd been put in here. Morsel was next to him on the metal bunk suspended from the wall, fidgeting. He suddenly jumped off and stood in front of Mac, his chin thrust forward. "You can blame me," he said. "It was my idea."

Mac answered without looking up. "It doesn't matter."

"What do you think your old lady's gonna do to you? I mean, what's the worst she can do? Ground you? Take away your drums?"

Mac hadn't considered the punishment aspect of things yet. "I don't know," he said. "I've never been in trouble like this before."

"My old man's gonna beat the crap outta me." This made Mac look up. "It don't really matter though. What I hate is when they yak in your face. They just go on and on about what a screw up you are until you can't wait for them to belt you and get it over with."

"Does he really hit you?"

"Is there such a thing as fakely hit you?"

"I mean, a lot?"

"Depends. If he's only kinda drunk, he stops after he feels like he taught me a lesson. If he's really drunk, he stops even quicker, cause it's too much work. It's when he's medium drunk I'm in trouble. He's like the friggin' Energizer Bunny. He just keeps going and going."

"Doesn't your stepmother do anything?"

"Yeah. She stays out of the way. She's thinking better me than her."

Mac did not say anything. Morsel began to pace, getting more antsy with each turn. "It was a dumb thing to do," Mac finally muttered.

"Come on," Morsel said, a little too eagerly. "You had fun, didn't you?"

"Not really."

"So why'd you do it? I didn't make you."

"Nobody's blaming you."

"They will. Everybody'll blame me. You're the rich kid with the good grades. You never get in trouble. They'll all think it was cause you were hanging out with me."

"I won't blame you." The boys were unaware that JD had paused a few feet from the cell and was listening to them. "Everything's different for me now," Mac continued. "Since we moved here. Since my dad died."

"I wish my dad would die," Morsel said wistfully.

"I wish mine was still alive. Sometimes? It's strange, but sometimes I kind of forget he's dead. He used to go on these trips all the time, and he'd call once in a while, but mostly it was like he forgot about us and we forgot about him. Then he'd show up home again and it would be like before he left until he got the next jerked off idea and left again. Sometimes I feel like he's just on one of his trips and he'll be back sooner or later."

Morsel stared at him. "I don't get it," he said. "What's the big deal if one of your parents disappears?"

JD appeared noiselessly in front of the cell. Morsel jumped. "Jesus!" he exclaimed. "You have to sneak up like you're a cheetah or something?"

"You are in jail," JD replied. "We're not going to call first to see if it's convenient for us to drop by."

"Did you get a hold of my old man?"

"Not yet." JD motioned to Mac. "Come on. Your mother's here."

Mac stood up. "What'd she say?"

"She's finding it difficult to believe you would do something so stupid." He opened the door and Mac walked out, still looking at the floor. JD closed the door again.

"How long you gonna leave me here?" Morsel demanded.

"Don't know yet," JD replied.

"I have rights!" Morsel declared. "I could get a writ of habeas corpus."

"Okay," JD said. "You need something to write with?"

"You think you're funny, but I know my rights."

"You have the right to remain silent," JD said, and motioned for Mac to go ahead of him down the hall.

When they were out of sight of the cell, Mac said quietly, "He's scared."

"Could've fooled me."

"His dad's going to beat him."

JD was unimpressed. "Somewhat old-fashioned, but not totally inappropriate, given the circumstances."

Mac stopped walking. "No, you don't get it. I think his father beats him up a lot."

When JD answered, his tone was short on patience. "How about you worry about your own situation? If you did as good a job of taking care of yourself as Morsel does, you might not have landed here tonight. Now, go on to my office."

Mac didn't move. "Will you help him?"

"I just told you to move."

"Okay, but will you help him?"

"I'll talk to him," JD capitulated. "Now, get going." Mac finally obeyed. Behind him, JD shook his head.

🐾　🐾　🐾

Mac walked into JD's office. The red rouge spots on his cheeks were still intact, but the remainder of his costume was a shambles. Remnants of crimson feather boa clung to his sweatshirt and his wig was askew. One chandelier-style earring hung doggedly from the bottom of his right earlobe. Maggie stood up, torn by her feelings. She wanted to comfort him at the same time she was hugely pissed off. In the few seconds she tried to sort everything out she lost the chance to give him a hug.

"Have a seat." Maggie and Mac both obediently sat down facing JD's desk. He sat across from them.

"I'm sorry, Mom," Mac said without looking up.

"I know, honey." She patted his hand. She was grateful for the excuse to touch him.

JD started off solemnly. "MacDonald, you realize what you did, although you say you didn't intend any harm, was quite dangerous. And against the law."

"Yes," Mac whispered at the floor.

"And it was only luck that there was no property damage and nobody got hurt."

"Yes."

"The law permits significant penalties for this kind of offense. If you get charged, you'll have to go to juvenile court. Based on the fact that you were caught red-handed, I feel confident you would be found guilty. You might even get sentenced to juvenile detention."

One solitary tear slid down Mac's cheek. Stop! Maggie wanted to shout. You don't need to scare him like this! But she knew the rituals of authority. JD would torment her kid until he believed they had learned some kind of lesson. She focused her attention on the woven pattern in the carpet. Hurry up, she thought.

"It was a really dumb idea," Mac said, his voice just a whisper.

"We've established that."

"And I promise I'll never do anything like that again."

"Well, I appreciate that," JD said. "But you're not a little kid anymore. You're old enough to be held responsible for your actions. Officer Butts thinks we should press charges."

"No!" Maggie said, before she could stop herself. She quickly backtracked. "I mean, what's the value of throwing him into the system? You know he gets adequate supervision at home."

"How would I know that?"

Maggie felt her face turn red. Do not take the bait, she told herself.

"I've discussed the options with Officer Butts," JD continued. "I agree with you that MacDonald's not likely to benefit from being put into the system."

"Thank you." Maggie relaxed a little. It looked like JD just wanted to mess with her.

"However, I also agree with Officer Butts that your son needs more structure. It looks like he'd also benefit from exposure to influences with less animosity toward authority."

"I beg your pardon?"

JD stared at her. "Let me be clear. Your son is a good kid. We want him to get a fair chance at staying that way. He needs some more positive role models."

Maggie breathed deeply and gripped the arms of her chair to keep from showing her anger. "You want him to join one of your sports teams?"

"Mom," Mac said, "I suck at sports."

"You can learn sports."

"Obviously sports is not the only solution," JD said. "He can get the same benefits from participating in other kinds of structured activity."

"Like Rescue Squad volunteer?" Maggie asked. Mac glanced at her, his eyes pleading, then looked away.

"You see?" JD said. "That's the kind of thing that concerns us. He needs to get a more balanced perspective about how people feel toward authority."

Maggie felt cold panic. "You're not going to take him away from me, are you?"

"No." JD backed off. "I don't think that's called for. And we will not press charges if you agree he should spend some of his free time in a structured setting."

"What sort of structured setting?"

"Roland Gamey offers jobs to several kids every year."

"Wait a minute." Maggie's fury turned cold. "Roland Gamey, my creepy next door neighbor? You figure that slicing bologna for a pervert will turn my son into a fine upstanding citizen? That's ludicrous."

"Gamey is good with kids. He teaches them respect and discipline. He provides a variety of ways for them to serve the community. He's highly respected."

"He's a sick little weasel, and you justify what he does by turning a blind eye to it. I can't believe you think he'd do a better job of raising my kid than I would!"

JD appeared not to have heard anything Maggie said. "He pays the kids very well."

"Forget it."

"Fine. Have it your way." JD reached into a file folder and pulled out a form. "Let's get some fingerprints."

"Mom!" Mac's voice cracked with fear.

Maggie stood up, trying to master her indignation. "This is blackmail. And it is also just plain insulting. What right do you have to force your decision on me?"

"Absolutely none. This is completely your choice."

Maggie finally saw the elegance of his trap. "Fine," she snapped. "You win."

"No," JD said. "It is my hope that your son wins."

ſ ſ ſ

Hours later on Halloween night JD got a call from the hospital. He usually didn't mind responding when they called him directly, but tonight he was bushed. He tried to protest, but Shirley, the ER charge nurse, said, "Do me a favor on this one," and hung up.

He thought about calling back for more detail, but decided it was probably just easier to go over. Shirley met him right inside the entrance. "Okay," he said, "what's so important you needed me in person?"

"It's the Bazewski kid," she said. "Came in a while ago. He has some decent bruises, a few minor lacerations. Nothing broken."

"How'd it happen?" JD asked.

"That's why he said we should call you. Said you'd know how it happened."

"Who brought him in?" JD asked.

"He brought himself," Shirley said. "He isn't hurt that bad."

"You figure he came here looking for somebody to make his old man stop?"

Shirley weighed the question. "I think he was scared but he's too proud to say so."

"There's nothing I can do," JD said. "You need to get Youth Services involved."

Shirley looked at him. "I did an informal poll. Everybody agrees what the kid needs is somebody to give a damn. Maybe that's why he asked specifically for you. It's not likely the stepmother is going to stop his father from beating the crap out of him. She's probably pissed he won't take the hint and go back to his real mother."

"Where is his real mother?"

"He won't say."

"Any idea why?"

"I would think because he doesn't want to get sent there either."

JD shook his head. "If we call Youth Services, they'll ship him off to juvie. He's not going to make out any better there."

"Except that nobody will beat him."

JD made a face. "No *adults* will beat him."

"Yeah," she said. "It's going to be tough to find anybody who'd put up with the mouth on him for long."

"Okay," JD relented. "Let me go talk to him."

Shirley took him to the examining room. Morsel was sitting on a stretcher, engrossed in whatever was on the TV. He looked up when JD came in. "Told you," he said sullenly.

"Your father did this to you?"

"No," Morsel snapped. "I walked into a door. Couple of times. I'm dumb, remember?"

"You don't want to tell us it was him, we've got to take you back there."

Morsel didn't even flinch. "Let me finish my show. Then I'll get out of here."

"Where you planning to go?"

"I can take care of myself. I'm eighteen."

"You have a couple of birthdays while you were sitting here?"

"I'm almost eighteen." Morsel changed his story without missing a beat. JD reached over and snapped off the TV. "Hey!" Morsel protested. "I'm not done yet!"

"You are unless you feel like talking to me," JD said. "People around here care about you. What can we do to help?"

"Put me down and give me a chance to be born as somebody else."

JD shook his head and turned the TV back on. "You hungry?" he asked.

"Yeah, but I can't eat the shit they make around here. Get me one of them cheez-steaks from the Gamey Deli."

"That stuff's not real cheese," JD said. "It's probably not even real meat. Why don't I just get you a tub of Crisco?"

"Hey, after I'm done here, who knows when I'm gonna eat again? This is like my last meal. I should get whatever I want."

"Fine," JD said. "He's closed, but I'll see what I can do."

"And some fries too."

"Don't leave. If I come back and you're not here, I'll make you sorry."

"Hey," Morsel called as JD walked out the door, "get me a vanilla shake to go with that."

🐾 🐾 🐾

JD stood at the triage desk wondering how he was going to get the kid off his hands. He'd talked Gamey into making the food for him, but that was the easy part. The ER attending happened to stick his head out of the small office behind the nurses' station and spotted JD. He motioned for JD to come in, then closed the door.

"Take a look at this," he said. He flipped the switch on the x-ray lightbox. He used the back end of a pen to trace the arc of bones on the film. It took JD a minute to realize what he was looking at. It was a spinal x-ray, but the spine was deformed by side-to-side curvature.

"This the Bazewski kid?" JD squinted at the film.

"Yeah," the doctor said. "Something was clearly wrong when I examined him, so I ordered some films. It's even worse than I suspected from the physical exam. Might be the worst case of scoliosis I've ever seen. That's actually not a short kid, that's an averaged-sized kid with a badly deformed spine."

"Can anything be done for him?"

The doctor exhaled. "He's essentially done growing now. It would take some pretty invasive surgery, plus a whole lot of commitment from somebody to oversee his recovery."

"The father's the custodial parent. You planning on talking to him? From what I understand the mother is MIA."

"Here's the problem," the doctor said. "In this school system, they get checked for scoliosis every year starting in grade school. A case like this wouldn't get missed, and they would have required further evaluation. So I requested any studies we had on file, and sure enough, there's a set every year starting when he was eleven. There's also a copy of the letter sent to the father each year telling him how serious this was and how it was critical to seek appropriate treatment right away."

"But he never did."

"Apparently."

"And whose job should it have been to make sure that happened?"

"You tell me. Kids fall through the cracks all the time."

JD looked at the x-ray again. "Got any ideas what we can do?"

"Off the record?"

"However you want it."

"He says the old man beat him for taking his stepmother's credit card to pay for his Halloween costume. Maybe that's true. Or maybe the father was mad he had to miss his favorite TV show because the kid got in trouble. Or maybe he beat him because it's Thursday. The nurses tell me the father's a beefy guy. The kid's not hurt that bad this time, but who knows what might happen next time? My guess is the kid came here hoping somebody would notice him before it's too late. If you can figure out a way to get him out of there without messing up his life even further, do it."

"I'm a police chief," JD said with resignation. "Not a wizard."

"You know what the odds are this will continue to happen until he doesn't have anything left to start a life with?" the doctor asked. "This could be his last chance."

JD walked out of the office. Shirley spotted him. She held her finger up to her lips and led him back to Morsel's room. Gamey was in there, sitting on the stretcher with the kid. They were both eating cheez-steaks, their eyes glued to the TV. Now and then, one would snicker and nudge the other with his elbow. Without warning, the nudging got enthusiastic and soon Gamey was wearing a huge smear of cheez on his sleeve and Morsel was laughing like a jackass.

"Do me a favor and go shake Gamey loose," JD said to Shirley.

Gamey came out into the hall and he held out his hand. "Fifteen-fifty," he said.

"Pretty expensive for fake food," JD said.

"Better living through chemistry."

"For one sandwich?"

"French fries, vanilla shake and two sandwiches," Gamey replied.

"You ate one sandwich yourself."

"Fine," Gamey said. "I was giving you a discount on the second sandwich, but you want to be that way, ten-fifty for the food and five bucks delivery charge."

"Or you could consider it an investment in your future," JD said.

"I knew it! You're always looking for something. Whatever it is, forget it."

"You and the kid seem to get along pretty well."

"The hell you say. You want me to take the kid?"

JD clapped him on the back. "I always knew you were sharp, but that's impressive. You just named that tune in two notes."

"Stuff it," Gamey said. "I don't need no strays. If he ain't got a home to go to, send him to the pound."

"He's got a home," JD said. "He's just not safe there."

"Not my problem," Gamey said.

"Just take him in for a while."

"What's a while?" Gamey demanded. JD did not answer. "Don't be telling me till he graduates school, cause that'll be half a lifetime."

"Roland," JD said, all sincere, "the boy needs a chance."

"And don't ever call me that!" Gamey hissed.

"Fine," JD said, turning away.

"Wait a minute!" Gamey commanded. "Why isn't he safe at home? Is it cause he's a royal pain in the ass?"

JD was tempted to say, takes one to know one, but that wouldn't help his case. "I'm not trying to get one over on you. The kid's a challenge, for sure. But maybe with the right kind of influence he could pull out of his nosedive."

Gamey's natural suspicion asserted itself. "I don't want this turning into one of them deals where the old man gets a bee up his butt and sics some social worker type on me. Next thing I know I answer the door and there's orthopedic shoes and a clipboard pointed at my head. Plus I hear he's pretty big. I got no interest in taking a ride on the Jolly Green Giant's boot."

"I can't make any promises," JD said. "But chances are he'll be only too happy to wash his hands of the kid. I'll pay him a social call, see if I can't help him feel agreeable."

Gamey paused and looked at JD. "If you think this is such a good idea, why ain't you taking him yourself?"

"I can't be around all the time to keep an eye on him. And I also can't give him a job in the family business."

"You figure I'm gonna be a sucker here because he's short, don't you?" Gamey poked a finger into JD's chest. "If I regret this, you're going to regret this."

JD held out his hand. "We got a deal?"

Gamey shook hands reluctantly. JD turned and walked toward the exit. "You still owe me fifteen-fifty," Gamey muttered at his back.

ɾ   ɾ   ɾ

Maggie paced around the den. She couldn't sit still. Mac had gone straight to bed when they got home. It was just as well, since she couldn't figure out what she should say to him. It was a huge mistake moving him here, away from the only source of consistency and discipline he had ever known. She made one more circuit around the room, then went to the kitchen. Grabbing the phone, she dialed. Albie answered on the second ring. "Everything okay?" she asked immediately. "Why are you calling so late?" Albie didn't need to ask who it was. She wasn't stubborn about things like cell phones and caller ID.

"No," Maggie said. "Everything is not okay. I screwed up. And I'm going to continue to screw up. I don't know how to do anything right."

"I don't know," Albie said. "You're not half bad at taking people apart and putting them back together again."

"I went to school for that," Maggie replied. "I got to watch other people do it first. And it took me years and years to learn."

"Just like being a parent."

"Nobody teaches you how to be a parent."

"Hello," Albie said. "There's an original thought."

"Please come stay with us," Maggie begged her. "Please. Before I make a really big mistake. I'm not giving up until you say yes."

21

Maggie drummed her fingers on the steering wheel. She was parked at the train station, waiting for Albie's bus. Here was yet another idiosyncrasy of this town. Why did the long distance bus stop at the train station? Why not the courthouse, or the shopping plaza, or some other place people might want to go? What were the chances someone would take a bus all the way here so they could turn around and hop on a train to go somewhere else?

She hadn't paid the fifty-cent fee to park in this spot. When she arrived, she should have gone over to the rack of ancient metal boxes and dropped two quarters into the slot. But she didn't think she'd be here that long, and besides, she wasn't really parking if she stayed in the car. Now Albie's bus was late and Maggie was increasingly anxious that someone was going to come along and give her a hard time or a ticket. She drummed her fingers on the steering wheel again and sighed deeply. It didn't help her decide what to do.

ꞇ   ꞇ   ꞇ

"Now this," Gamey lovingly patted the brutal-looking steel machine, "is the slicer. You don't touch the slicer. *Nobody* under eighteen touches the slicer. You need sandwich meat, you need cheese, you tell me. You see anybody under eighteen so much as lay a finger on the slicer," he delicately placed a finger on the casing to demonstrate, "you tell me. Capisce?"

"What does 'capisce' mean?" Mac asked.

"It means 'understand,' stupid," Morsel said.

"And you." Gamey whipped around and pointed at Morsel, "don't you be calling names. Any verbal abuse to be done around here will be done by me. You got that?"

"Yeah."

"Yes, *sir*," Gamey said and stared up, if only slightly, into Morsel's eyes. He held the stare until Morsel deflated.

"Yes, *sir*," he said sullenly.

"Over here is the grill." Gamey led them to the blackened, greasy metal slab. "This is hot, as in be careful. You don't want to take my word for it, go ahead and burn yourself. Anybody who's stupid enough to do that gets on the wall of fame." He gestured to a collection of dog-eared photos tacked up over the grill. The central figure in each had a bandaged hand.

"Here's your spatulas and rags. You finish cooking, you scrape down the grill with your spatula. You get a little break between orders, you wipe it down, hard, with a damp rag. You walk away and leave the grill dirty, you clean it with your paycheck. And above all, remember the grill is for *grilled* items only. Grilled cheez-steaks, *grilled* burgers."

"What do you think we're gonna make on there?" Morsel asked. "Ice cream sundaes?"

"That's funny," Gamey said, not amused.

"So what are we *not* supposed to grill?"

"Nothing with cheese. We don't make cheeseburgers."

"You got cheese right here. Why can't you make cheeseburgers?"

"It ain't that we can't. We choose not to. We're kosher style."

"But you make cheesesteaks," Mac pointed out.

"They told me you were a smart boy," Gamey said. "Read the menu." Mac looked at the plaque on the wall, grossly discolored by years of accumulated grease particles. "It says Cheez-steak," Gamey said, "Cheez."

"Cheez isn't cheese?" Mac asked.

"It's processed cheese food product, no dairy. Keeps certain premium clients happy. Plus, it melts better."

"But you cut meat and cheese on the same slicer."

"What's it to you?" Gamey demanded.

"In New York, the kosher delis always had separate slicers for meat and cheese."

"Congratulations to them," Gamey snapped. "I said kosher *style*."

"Gotcha," Morsel said. "What they don't know can't hurt 'em."

"You want to be a smart boy too?" Gamey turned on him. "Try to remember that a smart boy knows when to shut his mouth." He walked over behind the register. When the boys did not immediately follow, he turned around and snarled, "Come on." Then he pointed at Morsel. "You," he said.

Morsel looked over his shoulder, then pointed to himself. "Me?"

"Yeah, wiseass, you. You drive, right?" Morsel just barely nodded. "Good. You're my new delivery boy."

Morsel's whole attitude changed. "Cool," he said.

"But you gotta be dependable," Gamey added. "We're talking perfect. Every single day. The old folks panic if you start screwing around with the delivery times."

"What's the big deal?" Morsel asked.

"The big deal is, you're bringing them their dinner and whatever else they need." He pointed to a list on the wall. "We got a schedule. You start at 3:30 and you get to the last place no later than 5:00. Same route every day, everybody gets chatted up five minutes when they open the door, no more, no less. You think you can flap your yap for exactly five minutes?"

"I guess so."

"Well, make sure. Otherwise you mess up the schedule. If somebody doesn't come to the door, you call me right away. You got it?"

"I could ride with him," Mac offered.

"What for?" Gamey demanded. "So you can get out of doing real work around here?"

"I could make change and run charge slips while he's talking. Stuff like that."

"Forget it," Gamey said. "You two ain't going nowhere together. Besides, my special dinner delivery is on the house." He pointed up at the menu on the wall without waiting for questions. "Now this here is gospel. We don't make substitutions, we got no daily specials. Somebody comes in, they want to know what we have, this is it. Somebody calls, they want to know what we make, this is it. Anybody got a problem with it, they can go someplace else."

Morsel gave him a look. "What's the big deal?"

"The big deal is," Gamey said, out of patience, "everybody and their brother wants a cheeseburger."

"Mr. Gamey?" Mac began.

"What?" Gamey snarled.

"Are you Jewish?"

"Go mop the floor in the back!" Gamey exploded. Mac scurried off.

"Hey," Morsel said, "be nice to the kid. He just catches on a little slow."

"What's he doing asking me am I a Jew?" Gamey huffed.

"Probably cause he's a Jew," Morsel said. "You know all that crap the Chief said about role models and stuff? Maybe he's looking for another Jew to make friends with."

"You think that's why his old lady's such a hard-on?" Gamey asked, his voice leaking eagerness. "Cause she's looking to hook up with a nice Jewish guy?"

"Could be," Morsel said. "You never know."

ɾ   ɾ   ɾ

"I don't understand," Vee said.

"What's not to understand?" Daniel asked. He continued to push paint around on his canvas, mostly for the joy of feeling the squishy texture. This was the real beauty of being an artist. Even Martha would never know how much of his painting time was pure play. If he could only get away with it he would slop the oils around with his bare hands.

"What does she believe this Melba woman can do that I can't?" Vee demanded.

"Albie," Daniel said, only half listening. "Not Melba. Albie."

"What kind of a name is that? Albie."

Daniel turned on his mental filter and blocked out the noise of Vee's name tirade. Here was the downside of being an artist. You were always *there* if you were there, stuck at your easel, at the mercy of every crabby bore who stopped in to bother you. I should have been a dentist, he thought. Dentists get to play with stuff too, but they're in charge of who gets to talk. He imagined Vee with a mouth full of dental instruments. The image made him shudder.

"What's wrong?" Vee asked, interrupting herself.

"Just envisioning a career change."

"What else could you be?' she said.

"Doesn't matter," Daniel said. "Not going to happen. Just like you're not going to erase fourteen years of friendship, no matter how much Maggie likes you."

"You think that's what this is all about?" Vee snapped.

"Yup."

"What the hell do you know?" She picked up her purse and stormed out of the shop.

"I know how to get rid of a pain in the ass," he said to the closing door.

🎔 🎔 🎔

Albie followed Maggie upstairs to the bedroom across the hall from Mac's. "This is the official guest room," Maggie said, "although you're the first guest to use it."

"Smells a bit musty," Albie said.

"Pretend it's a castle."

"Pretend you're a real hostess and air the place out before a guest arrives."

Maggie slung one of Albie's suitcases onto the bed. "Thank you for coming."

"You can stop saying that. And get the suitcase off the bed. It's no wonder the boy got into trouble if you've started messing around with the rules."

Maggie ignored her and sat on the bed. "Why do you think he did it?"

"Because he's a kid. Because he and his friends were joking around about it and that made it sound like a great idea. He's not turning bad, if that's what you're worried about."

"He never got into trouble in New York."

"How would you know? You only find out they're in trouble if they get caught. What kinds of things did you do that your mother didn't know about?"

"Eat. Sleep. Breathe."

"Rhetorical question," Albie said. "No response required."

"So you think he was just being a normal kid?"

"He's never been a normal kid. He's never going to be a normal kid. He's brilliant. He's musically gifted. He knows he's different, so he's going to try doubly hard to fit in. It's every adolescent's heartbreaking fantasy, to be just like everybody else. It's so out of his reach you need to expect him to make mistakes now and then trying to get there."

"So what am I supposed to do for him?" Maggie asked.

"Same as any other good parent," Albie answered. "Hope you put enough moss on the ground to cushion a fall and pray he doesn't decide to leave the nest when the falcon is hungry."

"That gives me absolutely no comfort."

"Probably for the best," Albie said.

ᚱ ᚱ ᚱ

Mac was on his best behavior with Albie there. Vee was on her worst. She hung around every minute she possibly could. She even cancelled a few classes with the excuse that her students needed time to prepare for the holidays. Albie did nothing to help matters, stretching her territorial imperative into every nook and cranny of Maggie's life. She cooked, she cleaned, she organized. If she was not in the same room as Maggie and Vee, she hummed some enthusiastic Gaelic tune as a counterpoint to their conversation.

In an attempt to provide distraction, Maggie planned a hectic schedule of field trips. They spent a day at Gorge Park, the "Grand Canyon" of Bucks County. They did a winery tour, starting at Washington's Crossing and sloppily ending up, six wineries later, at Sand Castle. They went bargain hunting at every flea market within half a day's drive. Maggie spent each trip wary as a sentinel, watching for the signs that this would be the day she got stuck in the middle when Vee and Albie finally got down to the business of annihilating each other.

Toward the end of their second week together, Maggie took an unplanned turn to avoid getting stuck behind a garbage truck and they passed Milton's Retreat. "The castle!" Albie exclaimed. "I entirely forgot about it."

"It's just a tourist attraction," Vee said from the back seat.

"Have you been in it?" Albie asked.

"I'm not interested," Vee said. "The guy was an evolutionary dead end."

"Let's go see it," Albie said.

"No thank you," Maggie replied. "I did enough school trips there to last a lifetime." She heard herself too late.

Vee caught the slip immediately. "You grew up around here?"

"Yup," Maggie said, staring straight ahead.

"What's the big secret?" Vee demanded. Maggie didn't answer. "You got something you don't think you can share with me, that's fine." She subsided into a grim silence that turned the air in the car into a plasma of tension.

When they got to Maggie's she pulled into the garage. "Anybody for coffee?" she asked.

"You sure you want to share your coffee with me?" Vee asked sarcastically.

"I'm sure," Maggie said. "Come on."

She let Vee into the house, but stopped Albie at the door. "Please don't judge her," she said. "I know she's tough. But she honestly cares about us. I didn't mean to hurt her feelings."

"You didn't hurt her feelings," Albie said. "She's just jealous that I know more about you than she does."

Maggie looked at her. "Can you please make a little bit more of an effort? This is where I live now, and I'm not going to leave. You will always be welcome here, for as long as you want to stay. And the invitation still stands for you to live with us. But since you won't, please don't begrudge me the people who are part of my life now."

"Ahh, happy horseshit," Albie said. "Maybe we'd all benefit from some new friends." She stalked into the house.

ᚱ ᚱ ᚱ

"Let's go!" Albie called. "You dasn't be late, from what I hear."

Mac came into the kitchen. "You don't need to walk me to work. I don't need a babysitter."

"Nonsense," she informed him briskly. For the first time since she laid eyes on him as a newborn, Mac was sullen. "You had lots of freedom and you screwed up. Now we're going to hand you off to each other like a hot potato until we're good and ready to trust you again. I'll bring your doggie along for her walk so you have a reasonable excuse for me to be there."

She held the door open. Mac went out to the alley and around the corner, moving quickly. By the end of the first block it was clear he was trying to outpace them. Penelope was having trouble keeping up, and then she decided to stop and sniff a mailbox. "Come along, Penelope," Albie commanded. The dog instantly flopped down on the ground like a beanbag. Albie and Mac looked at each other. "Come!" Albie pulled on her leash. Penelope held tight like a hubcap on an electromagnet. "You go on," Albie said. "I'll figure this out."

"Hold on," Mac said. "I have an idea." He started walking slowly. "Stay, Penelope," he commanded. The dog stood up and scampered over to him. "I knew it!" he exclaimed. "Some dipshit purposely screwed her up." Albie looked at him quizzically. "Watch. Come Penelope," he said, and the dog went limp on the ground again. "Stay," he said, and she began following him. "See? They reversed the commands."

Albie exhaled loudly. "Life around here must really be dull if people have to amuse themselves by messing with a dog's head."

"Tell me about it," Mac replied. They walked the rest of the way in companionable silence. When they got to the deli, Mac held the door open for them.

"What a dump," Albie exclaimed as she stepped inside.

"It's not that bad," Mac said.

"It needs a paint job and a good scrub. And the shelves look like they were stocked by monkeys."

Morsel burst out of the back room. "Hey!" he said, putting a finger on the slicer as he raced past it, "am I glad you're here! We screwed up the back room and Gamey's gonna be here any minute. He's gonna send our asses to juvie when he finds out!"

"Perhaps he will send your ass to juvie," Albie said, "but MacDonald was not a party to anything, as he has just arrived with me."

Morsel ignored her. "Dude, somebody accidentally spilled some grease and slipped in it? And then somebody else tried it, and it was just like boogie boarding. So we figured if we greased up more floor we could go farther, you know? So I got a bottle of Mazola, and we put some all over the floor, and if you run in from way out here you can slide all the way to the back door. And we figured we'd wipe it up before Gamey got back, but that shit don't wipe up. We already used up two rolls of paper towels, and all it does is spread around. When Gamey gets here we're screwed!"

"MacDonald," Albie said, "I believe I hear your mother calling."

"Albie," Mac pleaded, "I can't ditch my friends."

Albie considered this for several painful seconds. "Very well," she finally said. "You, Crumb, or whatever your name is, go find a bottle of Mr. Clean. You," she turned to Mac, "find some rags. And tell whatever wretches are in the back to fill a few buckets with hot, hot water."

"Thanks, Albie." Mac hugged her and sprinted off.

"Be careful on that floor!" she yelled.

Morsel appeared from behind a display, bottle of cleanser in hand. "Hey, thanks for being cool," he said.

"Wait a minute." She held him by the arm. Her eyes were hard. "This is all a game for you. You imagine you have nothing to lose. You are wrong. But because you believe that, you go on courting greater or lesser chunks of disaster without ever considering what you're putting at risk. Try to remember you're not traveling alone."

He pulled away. "You're whacked, lady. I got no idea what you're talking about."

"Then start figuring it out. There are people who care about you now. Just because that's a new state of affairs for you doesn't mean you shouldn't treat it with respect. If you don't, sooner or later you *will* do them harm, and trust me, that's a whole lot harder to live with than the rules." Morsel shot her a furious glance and stormed into the back room.

Within moments the front door opened and Gamey walked in. "Help you?" he asked, starting past Albie to the register. He made no effort to keep the foul mood from his tone. Then he noticed Penelope. "Get the mutt outta here."

"Mr. Gamey," Albie said, all charm, "a pleasure to finally meet you. I've heard such lovely things about you." She extended her hand.

"From who?" Gamey asked. He looked at her hand, but did not take it.

"Shake my hand, dear. You're exhibiting poor form." He reluctantly obeyed. "Alberta O'Brien," she said. "My friends call me Albie."

"You can't bring that dog in my store."

"I thought dogs were welcome here. I believe you have a dog of your own?"

Morsel walked out from the back room. "Hey, Gamey," he said. He was good. Albie had to give him that. If she didn't know he had reason to be scared, she wouldn't even have noticed the slight quiver in his voice.

"You got tonight's dinner order ready?" Gamey asked, still surly.

"Uh, yeah," Morsel said.

"Lemme see." Gamey began to walk toward the back of the deli.

"Mr. Gamey," Albie interrupted, "I was just about to walk the dog. I was so hoping you might join us. I've been told you're quite the expert on local points of interest. The boys say you're a pretty good storyteller as well."

"Absolutely," Morsel said. "You're the best."

Albie stepped over and took Gamey's arm. She nodded at Morsel behind Gamey's back. "Shall we go then?" she asked. Gamey and Penelope both happened to look up at her at the same moment, and the expressions on their faces were remarkably similar. Albie steered them out of the store.

22

Lemon Meringue sashayed into Gallardo's. She was wearing platform shoes, something a little practical for the daytime. But her heels were still so high she teetered slightly as she walked, creating a distraction. Luckily, she was used to being the center of attention. Besides, with money so tight since the Henhouse burned down, she was not about to invest in a new career wardrobe until she knew what her next line of work would be. She took the long way, through the produce section and past the cereal aisle, to Customer Service.

"Can I help you?" The woman behind the counter sounded pleasant enough, but there was that look.

You spot an alien? Lemon wanted to ask. Instead she said, "The sign says you're hiring."

"Well, sort of."

"What do you mean, sort of? You hiring or not?"

"What kind of position are you looking for?"

Something easy, like missionary, Lemon wanted to say. Instead she said, "What have you got?"

"Well," the woman stalled, "I'm not really sure."

"Who is sure?" Lemon demanded.

"Let me check with the manager." The woman disappeared through an unmarked door.

Lemon tapped her foot and sighed noisily. This was such a pain in the ass. First they tried to reject her unemployment claim, but she had all her paperwork. Then they made her prove it wasn't her fault she was unemployed. She was finally collecting, but now she had to go look for a new job. Somebody, she didn't remember who, told her she only had to apply for things in her former line of work, but even Lemon thought that might be pushing things. Plus, if one of these places offered her a job, she'd be willing to try something new. How hard could this stuff be, compared to what she used to do?

While Lemon idled out front, the woman from Customer Service stood in the store manager's office. There was a one-way mirror that looked out front, but the manager's attention was focused on his computer screen. "Just give her an application, Helen," he said wearily. "We can keep it on file."

"Would you take a look at her?" Helen insisted. "She looks like the Grinch."

The manager finally craned his neck to see out the window. "Holy crap!" he exclaimed. The woman waiting at the counter really did look like somebody from Dr. Seuss. Her hair, if it was hers, was polar bear white. It was in a ponytail that sprouted from the top of her head like a fountain before falling straight down to somewhere below her butt. Her vibrantly colored makeup was painted on in heavy layers. She had on false eyelashes that could have come from a Greek man's chest and bright crimson fingernails easily two inches long. The manager turned back to his desk. "You know company policy on discrimination. Give her an application."

"Okay," Helen sighed. She began to leave the room.

"Oh, and Helen?" the manager said. "Use the courtesy card camera to get a picture. Attach it to her application."

"Yes, sir." Helen's face brightened.

"That took you long enough," Lemon said when the woman returned.

"Sorry about that." The woman sounded way too cheerful to be sorry about anything. She handed Lemon an application and a pen.

Lemon moved to the far end of the counter and started to fill out the form. Things were pretty straightforward until she got to the part about employment history. There was space for up to four previous jobs, but she only had one. 'Whore,' she wrote. For employer she had a harder time. Officially it was the johns who paid her. 'Various,' she wrote.

Following the directions, she turned the application over. List significant achievements, it said. She considered her options. If she padded things a little, they'd never be able to check. 'Managed the costume collection,' she wrote.

The last item was an essay-type question. State briefly why you want this job, it said. 'If I ran the Customer Service Counter,' she wrote, 'no one would ever leave my booth unsatisfied.' When she finished, she walked over and slapped the application down.

The woman looked at it like it had cooties. Lemon stared at her until she reached out and took it. "Just a minute," she said. "I have to take your picture."

Lemon posed for the camera. "You gonna call me?" she asked when they were done.

"Maybe," the woman said, and Lemon could see she meant maybe when hell freezes over. "We'll review all the applicants and call the most qualified ones back for an interview."

"Great," Lemon said. "Thanks." She began to totter away.

"Uhh, my pen?" the woman said.

"Oh," Lemon said. "Sorry." She looked at the pen in her hand. It was a cheap Bic Clic. Probably had a carton of them behind the counter. The woman must've wanted to make a point. Lemon held the pen up and gave it the most amazing tongue she'd given anything since the Henhouse burned down. She was pleased she wasn't out of practice after all these weeks. "Here you go," she said, and laid it, glistening, on the counter. She walked away with great dignity.

She was almost out the door when her cell phone rang. She flipped it open. "Yeah?"

"Hey, gorgeous, how are you?"

She recognized his voice immediately. "Closed for repairs."

He sounded distraught. "What's broken?"

"My heart. From not seeing you."

"That's my girl," he said gleefully. "You busy?"

"Yeah. I just applied for a job in Customer Service at Gallardo's." He laughed. "What?" she demanded. "You don't think I can do it?"

"As I recall, courtesy was not your strongest talent."

"I was always nice enough to you."

"You know," he said, putting on his version of seductive, "I'm kind of in the mood for something sweet and sour."

"Order in Chinese."

"Come on," he pleaded. "I was dreaming about a nice juicy piece of pie."

"Nothing kinky," Lemon said. "I don't have time to get in the zone."

"You can take your time getting over here if that helps," he offered.

"Nope." She looked at her watch. "I got knitting class today."

"Whatever suits your busy schedule."

"Damn right," she said, and flipped her phone closed. Then she opened it again and used speed dial. She got an instant answer. "He just called me," she said. "I'm on my way over there now." She listened for a moment. "I can give you ten minutes. That's it. If you can't make it happen by then, better luck next time."

ɾ　ɾ　ɾ

Bendz watched the monitors on the wall. Yet another nice-looking couple was checking out the Hummers. Hot damn, it was pure genius bringing those into the showroom. Everybody knew they were a curiosity draw, but common wisdom said they were a waste of floor space, too exotic to impact sales. Bendz disagreed. He had a hunch that letting the customers climb into the big toy and fiddle with the knobs and switches would give them an appetite they could only satisfy with an expensive substitute. The sales stats backed him up.

The average price on his turnover had gone through the roof ever since he brought those ugly monsters inside.

His reverie was interrupted by the sight of her coming through the front door. She was a vision, her long blonde hair swinging as she moved. People stared as she made her way through the showroom, and she knew it. She started up the stairs, and he watched until she was out of camera range.

The office door opened and she burst in. "Hi, Pop-pop!" Chrissie yelled. She ran over and threw herself toward his lap.

"Hey, hey!" he yelled, cringing in anticipation of her landing. She planted kisses all over his face. "Stop that!" he finally commanded. She giggled and jumped up. "How are you, kiddo?" he asked.

"Very cool," she said, walking over to the bank of monitors. "Someone told me," she looked at him over her shoulder, "that you have a special surprise planned for my birthday."

"Indeed I do," he beamed.

"Should I guess?"

"What? And ruin it?"

Chrissie stood in front of the monitor that was aimed at the heart of the sales floor. "I know what I'd like it to be," she said, her voice pure and sweet.

"Well, let see," he said. "Pop-pop owns a car dealership . . ."

"And I get my license . . ."

"You're ruining it!" He slammed his hand on the arm of his chair, but he was beaming.

"I like that one," she said, pointing to a fire engine red Humvee.

"Aw, Chrissie," Bendz said, "come on now."

"What? That one would make me *so* happy."

"Well, of course it would, honey, but it would bite Pop-pop in the wallet big time."

"You know how sad it makes me that my birthday is on Christmas," she pouted. "It's like I'm not even special."

"Now, that's not true. You know how special you are to me and your grandmother."

She walked over and sat on the corner of his desk. "You don't want me driving around in just any old thing, do you?"

"Sweetheart," he started, "I love to make you happy, but . . ."

"What's that?" she interrupted, her voice incredulous.

"What?"

"That *woman*. At least I think it's a woman. She's *weird*."

Bendz looked at the monitor covering the front entrance. There was Lemon Meringue, adjusting one of her bra cups. Bendz lost it for no more than a second, just a flash of panic, but it was enough. Chrissie didn't miss a thing. Under normal circumstances that was one of the things he liked best about her.

"Friend of yours?" she asked. Bendz shrugged. Chrissie changed the subject. "Grams is picking me up in a few minutes. I told her to meet me up here so you could say hello to her."

"No need," he said, working up a little sweat. "I say hello to her all the time."

"I know." Chrissie looked at him. "But she's usually not all that interested. Not like she'd be if she walked into the showroom right now." Bendz shook his head. "Of course," Chrissie continued, "I could call her and ask her to meet me out on the lot. That might avoid some . . . *confusion*."

Bendz stared at the monitor helplessly, watching Lemon walk toward the stairs. He could feel the hard buzz of his blood pressure rising in his neck. "It's too late." He loosened his tie. "If you did that now, she'd just get suspicious and come barreling up here."

"Not if there was a reason for her to meet me out there," Chrissie said. "Like if I needed her help to pick out my Hummer."

Bendz turned slowly toward her. "You are wicked child," he said.

"Thank you, Pop-pop!" she squealed. She raced around the desk and planted a kiss on his forehead. "I promise, I've got you covered!"

"How about a nice little H3?" he asked forlornly, seeing all those lovely dollars flying out of his grasp. "It's cute, like you."

"And cheaper too."

Bendz tried to look sad enough to make her relent. Then he saw Lemon disappear from the monitor. "You better get going," he said.

Chrissie raced for the door. Once she was outside the office, she waited until she saw the ponytail on the top of Lemon's head bouncing up the stairs before starting down. She needed to time this just right, so they'd pass each other in the 'dead' spot, the one place on the stairs where no cameras would pick them up. As they came abreast of each other, Chrissie avoided eye contact. For the briefest instant, she held out her hand, and Lemon bagged the folded hundred-dollar bill from it. "Thanks," Chrissie said. "Perfect timing."

"Whatever," Lemon said, and continued on to her appointment.

23

Maggie stood over the half-price case at the Czar's Cave, mesmerized by all the shiny jewelry though she couldn't figure out why. Jewelry had never interested her before. There was a time when she used to think if Gary bought her something that hinted at romantic feelings she would have worn it, even if she hated it. But he never did. She didn't understand why she was suddenly feeling sad about that now. But she awoke on this rainy November day with a craving for something that glittered, almost like she was driven by a forgotten dream. When the afternoon's gloomy dampness got to be too much for her, she gave up and came here.

She sighed and looked at an opal pendant in the case. The stone was easily the size of a thyroid gland. She vaguely recalled someone telling her, years ago, that opals were bad luck. She wondered why anyone would buy one this big, unless it was a gift for somebody they *really* disliked. A lovely curse.

The bell on the door behind her jingled and Mac walked in. "Hey, Mom," he said. "I got my books. You almost done?"

"Sure." He took a step, and Maggie saw he was limping. "What happened?"

"Nothing," he said. "Just a splinter."

"Let me have a look at it."

"No!" He moved out of reach.

"Come on. I won't hurt you."

"Oh, sure," he said. "You haven't cut anything but chicken in months. You're probably dying to get your hands on real flesh."

"MacDonald," she said, "I am capable of behaving like a standard mother. I won't use anything sharper than tweezers to take out your splinter."

"That's okay." He backed toward the door.

"Okay. I promise I won't touch you."

"Good," he said. "I feel like getting a cheesesteak."

"How can you even consider eating one of those after working in Gamey's grease pit all week?"

"Not from the deli," he said. "I won't even eat the stuff he gets pre-packaged from somewhere else. I want one from the Hoagie Hole. They use real cheese and real meat."

They went outside. The heavy mist hanging in the air earlier had turned into full-fledged rain. Maggie opened her umbrella. They only got a few feet before Mac's limp became a serious hobble. "Come on," she said. "Let me see your foot."

"I'm okay," he insisted.

"Then hurry up," she said, purposely speeding up. "I'm getting wet."

"Wait!" Mac said. "I need to stop a minute." They were in front of the General Store, where the porch awning had kept everything dry. "I can take the splinter out myself." He limped over to a chair and took off his sneaker and sock. Then he tried to twist his foot around to see the bottom. Maggie inched a little closer. He spotted her. "Don't even think about it!"

As she stepped away something in the primitive core of her brain made her look up. Back down the street, partially obscured in the doorway of the Czar's Cave, a wild-haired man was watching them through a telephoto lens. Maggie stared at him intently until he put the lens down.

Mac yelped and she turned around to see if he was okay. When she looked up again the man was standing on the sidewalk in front of them, seeming not to notice the rain pelting his head. "I'm with the press," he said. "*The Daily Intellectual.*" He held up the badge hanging from a chain around his neck. "I might be doing a piece on the rainy weather."

"You afraid someone won't notice it on their own?" Maggie asked.

"I just need to get some information." He turned to Mac, who was still engrossed in his foot. "What's your name, son?"

"MacDonald."

"And your first name?"

"That is my first name."

"Oh." There was no change to his slightly stunned expression.

"MacDonald Rifkin," Mac said helpfully.

"Oh." He pulled an envelope and a pencil stub from his pocket. "Can you spell that?"

Mac looked at Maggie. This was one of their favorite stupid questions. "Go ahead," she said. "Do the man a favor."

When Mac finished, the photographer asked, "What are you doing?"

"I have a splinter in my foot," Mac said.

The photographer turned to Maggie. "And your name?"

"Margaret."

"Margaret what?"

"Rifkin," she said. "Like him. I'm his mother."

"Okay," he said. "Your picture might be in tomorrow's paper." Without another word, he walked away.

"If we had a cell phone," Mac said, "we could call all our friends and tell them how we're going to be famous."

"I'm pretty sure it wouldn't make the slightest difference to any of them," Maggie answered. "Now let me do something about that splinter before your foot falls off."

꙰ ꙰ ꙰

The next morning, way too early, Martha called. "You made the paper!" she said, not waiting for Maggie to say hello. "You and Mac. Your picture's in today's *Intellectual*."

Maggie was a little dismayed that she felt so excited. "Can you grab a few extra copies? I'll be over later, at a time when normal humans are up and around."

When she arrived at the Art Shop, Martha handed her the *Intellectual*. There they were on the front page of the Living Section, three columns wide. Mac looked like a grooming ape, enraptured with his foot. Thanks to the angle of the shot, Maggie's chin appeared to have vanished into her neck. She wasn't making the slightest effort to suck in her stomach. The caption read, "Rainy Day Enterprise. MacDonald Rifkin attempts to pick something out of his foot while his mother, Margery, shelters herself from the rain."

"You're famous," Daniel said helpfully.

"Nah," Martha said. "She won't be famous until somebody draws a mustache on her picture and hangs it up at the General Store."

"Thanks," Maggie said. "That makes me feel much better."

꙰ ꙰ ꙰

Vee steered her car up the long drive to Milton's Retreat, her face set and grim. Albie sat in the passenger seat, staring straight ahead. "You want to tell me," Vee demanded, "how the hell it became *my* job to take you sight-seeing?"

"No," Albie said. Vee exhaled audibly through her nose. "You sound like you're about to begin pawing the ground with your hooves," Albie observed.

"Does your friend Maggie know what a bitch you are?" Vee asked.

"No," Albie said. "But if you really want to make yourself look insecure and foolish, you can try to tell her."

Vee turned sharply into the parking area, throwing up a cloud of dust. "Get out," she ordered.

"You know, I can find my way home from here."

"Oh, honey," Vee said, "don't you worry about that. I'll deliver you back, safe and sound. I won't be getting rid of you until I get the chance to fill your pockets with cannon balls and throw your ass off a nice high bridge."

Albie looked up at the castle, her face serene. "Shall we?"

Vee got out of the car, slammed her door and stalked off. Albie made no attempt to keep up, but as they came to where the driveway turned into the castle forecourt a car passed and they were forced to stand together on the side of road. "Do you suppose this is what they call companionable silence?" Albie asked.

"You believe you're pretty funny, don't you?"

"Maggie seems to think so," Albie said.

"Maybe she's just after your Lucky Charms."

"Is that the best you can do?"

"Saw you making time with Gamey the other day," Vee said. "I know you Irish got a thing for little people, but I didn't think you'd cross species lines."

"He's a lovely man. He's just not well understood."

Vee looked pointedly at Albie's miniscule chest. "Some of us understand him just fine." Albie ignored her and opened the heavy oak door of the castle. They walked into a small foyer. The floor was covered in muted multi-colored tiles, but everything else, including the furniture, was concrete. It was a dark, mud-colored blend that gave the place an air of doom.

"Hello!" A woman greeted them from behind the concrete desk that dominated the room, her chirpy voice incompatible with the setting.

"You giving tours?" Vee asked.

"I'm on greeter duty," she answered, "but one of our other docents will be along shortly."

Albie had gone over to examine some items on the wall. "Look at this!" she exclaimed. "Are these real?"

"I should hope so," the docent said.

Vee walked over. "Holy crap!" she said. "These are cuneiform!"

"Mr. Dooley was quite a collector. Anything clay or molded greatly appealed to him."

"But look at this," Vee said, fuming. "He plastered them into the wall!"

"Cemented them in," the docent corrected her.

"Isn't that illegal? To do something like that to antiquities?"

The docent shrugged. "Not much they can do to him now."

"That's the spirit," Albie said.

"He was a great believer in the preservative power of concrete," the docent continued. "He ordered that his own remains were to be set in it when the time came."

"Wait a minute," Vee said, her eyes wide. "You telling me he's still around here?"

"Well, of course," the docent said. "This is his home."

"*Was* his home," Vee said. "I have a home too. But I'm not planning on spending eternity stuffed in one of the walls."

The docent clucked her tongue. "He's not in the *walls*. He's in the basement."

"That's it," Vee said. "I'm out of here."

"Oh, don't be such a spook," Albie said. Silence fell with a palpable weight.

"*What* is the matter with you?" Vee finally demanded. "You can't say something like that to a black person!"

Albie looked confused. "Why not?"

"You trying to tell me you don't know 'spook' is an ignorant racial slur?"

"Don't be silly. Spook means ghost."

"It is a demeaning epithet for black people."

"Not when I use it," Albie stated. "As a matter of fact, I'm part black Irish myself."

Vee looked her up and down. "Sorry to hear that," she said. "On behalf of the race." She turned to the docent. "Now would be a really good time for you to go find us a guide."

"I can take you myself," she said, with a nervous little giggle.

Vee looked at Albie. "This is going to be one hell of a tour."

"I just have to gather some other guests who are also waiting." The docent nodded her way out of the lobby. She returned a few minutes later with six other people. She motioned the group through a door behind the desk. Vee marched to the head of the line. Albie fiddled around, lagging behind.

The tour of the castle was just plain confusing. The place was more like a Civil War safe house than a fortress. Its concrete rooms were connected by twisting staircases, steep tunnels, and passageways that ended abruptly in dead ends. Windows had views of blank concrete walls or other windows. They stopped at random, whenever something inspired the docent to launch into whimsical commentary. She would become enchanted with an empty key rack or a hanging net full of skulls, and begin rambling some completely irrelevant tale.

Hoping to get away, Vee slipped back into the crowd. She ended up next to Albie. "I don't suppose you'd be willing to give me the car keys?" Albie whispered.

"You'd never find your way out of here," Vee said. "You're welcome to them if you'd like to die trying, though."

"It's tempting," Albie said.

The group made its way painfully from floor to floor. At one point they stepped out onto a balcony. The ground was several stories below. "Damn," Vee muttered. "Too high to survive the fall."

On the very top floor they went around a corner and came face to face with a guillotine. "This was one of Mr. Dooley's found objects," the docent said.

Albie turned to Vee. "Where does one find this sort of thing?"

"I was more curious," Vee said, "about what kind of person says, hey, I have just the spot for that."

"When you look at the room as a whole," the docent said, "you'll notice there's a theme." She opened the doors of a cabinet protruding from the wall to reveal a display of large tiles.

"There's pictures on them," one of the other guests said. "What are they?"

"It's the story of Blue Beard. The fairy tale," the docent replied. "Not the pirate."

"Hold on." Albie pointed to a tile near the bottom. "The guy with the Blue Beard is holding a woman's head. But there's no sign of the rest of her."

"That's right," the docent said, sounding like a teacher pleased by a sharp pupil. "Blue Beard cut off his wives' heads. We have a book about him in the gift shop," she added.

"Does it have instructions?" Albie asked.

The docent straightened up, as if someone had given the knob that held her together half a twist. "It's a *fairy tale*," she said.

"Odd theme for a kid's book," Vee said.

"It's clearly not a children's book. In fact, it might be the sort of thing that interests someone like you." The docent paused. "People tell me it's quite lascivious."

Vee turned to Albie. "Now what do you suppose she means by that?"

Albie appeared to give the question serious consideration. "I think she's suggesting you would find the book very exciting. In a socially unacceptable sort of way."

"Shall we move on?" the docent asked.

"Don't you want to tell us more about the exciting book?" Albie asked.

"No," the docent replied. "I don't think so."

"Because we'd be happy to hear more about it."

"Speak for yourself," Vee said.

"Imagine that," Albie continued. "My friend here, it turns out, doesn't want to hear more about your exciting book. She's actually rather modest, you see, despite the color of her skin." The room grew uncomfortably quiet. "That is what you were hinting at, isn't it?"

The docent glared at them and stalked from the room. The other guests hurried to follow.

"That was interesting," Vee said, "watching my game played by someone else. You think she really intended to insult me?"

"I think she calls her dildo Milton."

"I think you've been single too long." Vee held the door open for Albie.

In the next room, the docent had already finished her spiel. She barely acknowledged them, saying, "You have to keep up. We're taking a different route back to the lobby and if you fall behind you'll get lost." Then she disappeared through the door at the far end of the room.

"Do you think people wonder about us?" Albie asked when they were out in the hallway.

Vee gave her a look. "Nobody has cause to wonder about me. All I lack is a suitable companion."

"What about your friend JD?" Albie asked.

Vee snorted. "JD? What would I want with a scrawny boy like him?"

"Most women wouldn't call him scrawny," Albie said. "By general standards he's built."

"That kind of built doesn't do it for me," Vee replied. "I like a man with some heft to him. Somebody I don't have to worry about suffocating if I roll over in my sleep."

They arrived back in the lobby. Another volunteer was at the desk. Even from behind she was instantly recognizable. Carol Ann Carter. The docent was whispering to her, shooting furtive glances at them. Vee and Albie headed for the far end of the lobby, but a quirk in the acoustics made the conversation at the desk sound like it was taking place right next to them. "That's who she is?" the docent was saying.

"Exactly," Carol Ann said. "So what can you expect if those two are her friends? I never would've figured it out except for her picture in the paper. I thought she looked familiar when I sold her the house, but it wasn't worth worrying about. And then there's the picture of her watching her kid pick his toes, right on the street. And I read the caption and bingo! Margery from St. Agnes! Remember how strange she was?"

"If I was her I'd never come back here," the docent added.

"I know," Carol Ann said. "She shows up with her mongrel kid, acting like nobody's going to remember she just disappeared one day in the middle of high school. Right after that was when the mother started showing up all over the place drunk. Who knows? Maybe that's why mama went off the deep end. There were other stories too, about her and her old man."

"You don't believe all that, do you?" the docent asked.

"Don't you remember what happened?"

"Who could forget?" the docent asked. "I had nightmares about it forever. My father used to go to Doc MacDonald, and I thought, what if he got sick that day? If he was there, would she have killed him too before she shot her husband and herself? Remember how she threatened those women before she went to his office?"

Carol Ann made a derisive noise. "Unless your father was also blowing him, I don't think you had much to worry about."

Albie looked at Vee. "I wouldn't believe it if I wasn't seeing it with my own eyes," she said. "Your face is turning red."

"Excuse me," Vee said. "I need to go break that bitch's neck."

"No you don't," Albie said.

"Figure of speech," Vee said. "I merely intend to shut her up."

"You really don't," Albie said gently. "She only demeans herself by repeating gossip."

"You would believe that happy horseshit," Vee said. "You're a nanny."

"You're right about it being horseshit," Albie agreed. "But you don't need to defend Maggie from the likes of them. They can't hurt her any worse than she already hurts herself." She opened the door and nudged Vee outside.

"You expect me to just walk away?" Vee demanded.

"Is there someplace private we can talk?" Albie asked. "Despite the unequivocal pleasure of tormenting you, I'm really not going to stay here forever. Sooner or later, she's going to need somebody who can help her deal with things. It appears you may be equal to the task. But that means there are some things you need to know."

Vee was still breathing heavy with rage. "We can go to my place," she said, opening the castle's front door again just so she could slam it shut behind her.

24

Thanksgiving dawned gray and overcast. Martha was not overly disappointed by the foul weather. It went well with the tempers that bristled like porcupine quills all over town as people stressed out over the holidays. She took a quick shower and toweled off her hair, grateful now for her freak encounter with Randy the Stylist. To everyone's surprise, she'd made Picasso's her regular salon, and got what remained of her hair cut shorter with each visit.

She was having a crowd for dinner. She'd been preparing all week from a carefully organized list. Everyone had offered to contribute something, and Martha had carefully planned it so each guest got to do or bring what would make them happiest. Except JD. He would be wiping china, watching while somebody else got to stir and season and taste. Martha suspected her other guests would get as much satisfaction as she would from watching JD suffer his thwarted culinary ego.

He was the first to arrive. Martha was surprised he was only half an hour early. He came in balancing a platter in each hand. "You said it was okay to bring dessert," he told her.

"That's fine," she said. "What have you got?"

"This one," he held up his right hand, "is pumpkin mousse cheesecake. And this," he extended his left hand slightly, "is apricot pecan zucchini bread with cream cheese frosting."

"Sounds like you had a bit of a cheese theme going."

He looked crestfallen. "You're disappointed."

"I am *not* disappointed. They sound delicious."

"I should have made pie."

"No you shouldn't have. I made pumpkin and someone else is making apple."

"Who?" he demanded.

"Maggie." She took the cheesecake from him and walked toward the dining room.

JD followed her. "That's my recipe! I taught her to make apple pie."

"Well, that's wonderful," Martha said. She placed his desserts on the sideboard. "I bet you're dying to give me a hand. I thought I'd do traditional southern. Okra, hoppin' John with ham, greens with fatback, cheese grits, bourbon sweet potatoes and cornbread stuffing."

His face brightened. "It sounds too good to be true."

Martha noted that he was awfully excited about the southern menu. She wondered what Vee might be willing to trade for this information.

"What would you like me to help with first?"

"I've got a special job for you," Martha said.

The next guests to arrive were Maggie and Albie. The moment Martha opened the door, the tension between them was obvious. "Okay," she said, "let's get this over with before you ruin dinner. What's going on?"

"She," Maggie looked at Albie, "invited Gamey and Morsel to dinner."

"My god," Martha said, "what were you thinking?"

"Is there a problem with extending hospitality on this most friendly of holidays?" Albie asked. "Surely there's enough food."

"Food's not the problem," Martha said. "You happen to have a package of Peaceable Kingdom napkins in your purse?"

"That is what Thanksgiving is supposed to be all about, isn't it?"

"Honey, no turkey in the world has enough tryptophan in it to sedate those two."

"Come on. It's in the spirit of the settlers and the natives sitting down to break bread together on that first Thanksgiving."

"As I recall," Martha pointed out, "shortly after that they tried to wipe each other off the face of the planet."

The doorbell rang furiously. Before anyone could answer it, Vee walked in. "Happy Turkey Day!" she said.

"Not around here." Maggie pointed accusingly at Albie. "She invited Gamey and the chimp."

"Well, isn't that nice?" Vee asked. "That's the holiday spirit."

Maggie looked from Vee to Albie. "You were both in on this, weren't you?" Vee gave her an outrageous look of innocence. Albie said nothing. "Screw you both," Maggie said.

"What a lovely way to start our celebration," Martha said. "Margaret, why don't you go into the kitchen and see if you can't help JD prepare the tableware?"

"I'm sure he can manage just fine by himself," Maggie snapped.

"I don't know," Martha said. "It's taking him longer than I expected to wipe down the plates. He could probably use a hand with the glasses."

"You've got JD wiping plates?" Vee asked, trying not to laugh.

"Yes," Martha said. "I figured it was time to give him a little tough love."

"Oh, this is too good," Vee said. "You all stay out here a minute. I got to have a little alone time with this." She handed Martha her jacket and bustled off to the kitchen. "Happy Turkey Day!" she chirped, bustling through the kitchen door.

JD had his hand in a cabinet. "Did she tell you what she's got me doing?" he asked without humor.

"I won't get in your way, honey," Vee said. "Martha just asked me to baste the bird."

"Dammit!" he exploded. "Why'd she give you that job? I'm right here! You know how many interesting things there are to do for Thanksgiving dinner? And she has me dusting off the china. You think she could have taken care of that ahead of time?"

Vee finished basting the turkey and closed the oven door. "I guess it's cause you're tall enough to reach," she said.

"You ever heard of kitchen chairs? Anybody could climb on a chair and do this."

She patted him on the back. "Safety first."

He ignored her. "I'm the best cook here. I'm the best cook in this entire town, after Lola/Mercedes. Why the hell did she invite me if she's not going to let me cook?"

"That's the Thanksgiving spirit," Vee said, walking out of the room. As soon as the door swung closed behind her, JD raced over to the stove. He started lifting lids off pots and tasting. He was pleased to see that his earlier interventions had their desired effects. He was nearly as proud of his ability to save dinner without taking credit as he was of his cooking. He went back to the cabinet and took down another plate.

When he heard the door swing open again he didn't turn around. He didn't need to. He knew it was her as soon as she walked in. It was her perfume, completely different from the buck lure he usually smelled around town. After their first encounter he spent almost an entire afternoon in the mall tracking it down, just so he could know its name.

"Happy Thanksgiving," he said.

"Same here," Maggie replied.

That made him grin at her. "Feeling effusive today, are we?"

She did not return the smile. "Yeah."

JD went back to his task. He was startled when Maggie reached into the cabinet. She took out some stemmed goblets. "Martha wants me to polish these. She says there are water spots on them. Like anybody cares. Half an hour from now, these'll be covered with fingerprints and DNA. Nobody's going to notice a water spot."

She finished polishing the glasses and put them on the table. They both reached into the cabinet at the same time, and that was when he felt it, the bolt of lighting in his gut, something powerful emanating from her. Maggie was oblivious. She turned away, and JD felt helpless, like his insides would implode if she left. This was not fair. He hadn't asked to feel this, not for somebody who didn't even like him very much.

"Hey," he said. Maggie turned back. "Can I ask you something?" She sort of nodded. "I thought, after that day we went apple picking we might be friends."

"That's not a question."

"Let me rephrase. Did you think we might potentially become friends after our trip to the orchard?"

"Yes," she replied. "At the time, I did."

"But it seems we haven't."

She moved back a step. "And this surprises you?"

"Yeah," he said. "Somewhat."

"I suppose that might seem reasonable," she said, "if you're blessed with a very selective memory."

He was puzzled. "I'm not sure I follow you."

She looked at him and her cheeks flushed. "Okay," she said, "let's review. I have a kid. A great kid. Good student, good-hearted, good musician. Good you name it. And he screws up." She raised her forefinger. "*One* time. The first time ever. Bad screw up? Yes, sure. Excusable? No. Kids shouldn't get out from under the consequences of their actions just because they're kids. But did he deserve a break? Maybe because his father just died and he got moved away from everything familiar? And as luck would have it, the first kid who befriends him happens to be the town's criminal mastermind? So maybe in an effort to prove to everybody he's one of them, he does something foolish. Okay, beyond foolish. He exercises really bad judgment. But nobody gets hurt. No property gets damaged. Was he lucky? Absolutely." She paused to catch her breath. "But did he deserve what you gave him? Did he?"

"What did I do that you consider out of proportion?" he asked curtly.

"You arrested him! You threw him in a jail cell!"

"Joe Butts arrested him, not me," he said. "And jail cells are where people go when they're under arrest. For many people, and I count your son in this category, one visit is a pretty effective deterrent to future crime. *And* I got him out as fast as I could and dropped the charges."

"That's right," she said. "Judge and jury. Chief Charles delivers his idea of suitable punishment."

"Wait a minute. You are way off base if you think there's anything harsh about making a kid hold a part-time job."

"Working for Roland Gamey."

"Yeah, working for Gamey. We already covered this ground. Your son needed a positive role model."

"Your positive role model is a lecherous, demeaning, sexist prick."

JD was incredulous. "What are you talking about? I've never seen him treat women with anything but respect."

"And just because he's bearable to women when you're around, you assume he never behaves any other way?"

"No one has ever complained about anything like this before. Ever."

"Maybe that's because after being mortified and degraded by him, they couldn't bear the thought of someone accusing them of exaggerating or imagining things."

JD turned back to the cabinet. "If he's so awful, how come your friend invited him to dinner today?"

Maggie picked up the glasses she'd cleaned and started for the dining room. "Grow some breasts," she said. "Nice big ones. Then maybe we'll be able to talk about this like equals."

☙ ☙ ☙

Martha looked around the dining room and allowed herself a tiny self-congratulatory smile. Dinner was going off without a hitch. Well, almost without a hitch. There was definitely some tension between Maggie and JD, but they had the good sense not to bring it to the table.

She also noticed that JD was surreptitiously watching Gamey. Gamey and his charge were both on their good behavior, which still left something to be desired even by generous standards. But Martha decided to give them points for effort. So far she hadn't discovered Albie's ulterior motive for inviting them, but she was sure there was one.

She got up and started collecting plates. "Why don't we clean up a little before dessert?"

"Me and Mac got a special dessert," Morsel said. "We made it from scratch. We just need to put on the finishing touches."

"Maybe we shouldn't," Mac said uneasily.

"You should be proud of yourselves," Daniel said, with great enthusiasm. "I'm very impressed that you two made a dessert."

"I don't know if anybody's going to want to eat it after they see it," Mac said.

"I'm here for you," Daniel assured him. "I'll eat some no matter how bad it looks."

"Come on," Morsel said, giving Mac a light shove. "It's out in the van," he explained. Mac followed him reluctantly.

"Damn," Maggie said. "They were doing so well."

"Have some faith," Gamey said. "Like me. I leave boys like them in charge at the deli all the time. There's never been a single incident."

"That you know about," Albie said. Gamey looked at her, eyes wide. She ignored him. "Let's clear away and see what we've earned for dessert." Everyone except Daniel grabbed something and started for the kitchen. "Are your legs broken?" Albie confronted him.

"I'm here in a supervisory capacity."

"Clear your place or no dessert," Albie said.

Daniel glared at Maggie. "You going to let Mary Poppins boss me around?"

"I'm pretty sure she means it," Maggie said.

JD stayed with Daniel while everyone else left the room. "You really going to make an issue out of this?" he asked.

"This is my house," Daniel said. "Once a year, I should be in charge of something. Besides, you haven't cleared your place."

"Sorry, guy." JD picked up his silverware and plate. "A wise man knows when to fold."

Daniel sighed and picked up his plate. When everyone reassembled in the dining room, Martha started dishing out desserts. JD was openly disgruntled that Maggie's apple pie had more takers than either of his desserts. "What did you expect?" she asked. "I went traditional."

"With my pie recipe."

She handed him a piece. "Actually I began with your pie recipe. But then I improved it."

JD took a forkful and chewed slowly. "It tastes different. What did you do?"

"It's definitely in the filling," Vee said. "But you added vanilla to the crust."

"Vanilla sugar," Maggie corrected. "Plain vanilla is so trite." She avoided looking at JD.

"So what's new in the filling?" Martha asked.

"Did anyone happen to notice," Daniel asked sharply, "that I don't *have* any pie?"

"The filling tastes richer," Vee said. "Creamy almost."

"Did you add extra butter?" Martha asked.

"Nope," Maggie said smugly.

"I know!" Albie said. "Evaporated milk!"

"You used evaporated milk in my American as apple pie recipe?" JD was aghast.

Maggie shook her head. "No."

"What do you mean, no? She just said you did." He pointed at Albie.

"What makes you think she'd know?"

He turned to Albie for confirmation. "You do know, right?"

"Red herring, dear." Albie smiled at him sweetly.

"Nobody gives a damn!" Daniel pounded his hand on the table.

"Oh," Maggie said. "Okay." JD signaled her from across the table. Unsweetened coconut milk, she mouthed. And Jack Daniels. He looked horrified, but said nothing.

No one made a sound. "Now look what you've done," Martha scolded Daniel.

"Nobody gave me any dessert," he pointed out, contrite.

"Hey, we got something for you!" Morsel piped up. He held up the foil-covered platter he and Mac had retrieved from Gamey's van. Mac caught Maggie's eye and very subtly shook his head no.

"We need to get Daniel's vote on the apple pie," Maggie said.

"The boys made something special," Gamey insisted. "The least we can do is try it."

Morsel pulled off the tinfoil with a flourish. There was a collective gasp. "It's brownies," Morsel said. "We mixed 'em a little thick so we could mold 'em, then we decorated them special." The brownies had been shaped into irregular logs and covered in thick dark frosting. They were studded here and there with candy corn. They looked like an artful arrangement of turds. "Here." He held the dish out toward Daniel. "You can be first."

"Pass," Daniel said.

"Come on," Gamey chided. "The kids went to a lot of trouble. Somebody should at least try one." All eyes turned to him.

"Looks like you're our man," JD said.

⌐   ⌐   ⌐

Maggie went into her kitchen and poured herself some white wine. Mac was already upstairs, but she and Albie were going to have a last drink before bed. She made Albie a gin and tonic, not quite accidentally mixing it stiffer than usual. Albie was sitting on the couch in the den, staring at the muted TV. Her eyes weren't following the action. That's how she'd been most of the day, present but distant. Maggie put the drinks down. "Are you going to tell me what's going on?" she asked.

"Yes," Albie said. "Eventually."

Maggie laughed. "We know each other too well."

"Like sisters."

"Never having had one," Maggie said, "I wouldn't know. But I think of us more like a sitcom couple." She sat down next to Albie.

"I believe I'm in love."

"Please don't tell me it's Gamey."

That got a full-blown laugh. Albie took a sip of her drink. "Good lord! What did you do to this?"

"You looked like you could use some extra help lightening up."

"So you decided to poison me?"

"I can add more tonic if you like."

"No, screw it." Albie downed a big gulp.

"This is good news, right?"

"Partially."

"Albie, he's not married, is he?"

"Nope. Not married."

"Terminally ill?"

Albie shook her head.

"A lawyer? Boring?"

"Was that two questions or one? Anyway, no. Sakura is a fiber artist."

"That sounds pretty cool. Likely to lead to a life of noble poverty, but cool nonetheless. So is it serious?"

"Yes," Albie answered, without embellishment.

"Are you going to get married?"

Albie paused, as if considering how to answer this. "I don't think so," she finally said. Her tone, which Maggie had been reading for years, indicated that the subject was closed.

"What is it you're not telling me?"

"Sakura's Japanese."

"And the problem is?"

"From Japan."

Maggie felt like she'd been smacked in the gut with a big dead fish. "Albie, please tell me you're not moving to Japan."

"I'm going to try it."

Maggie worked at sounding reasonable. "You won't like it. Outside of Tokyo they *hate* Americans. Inside Tokyo they tolerate them, but only barely."

"I'm not American."

"Doesn't matter. You're obviously not Japanese. The prejudice over there is ghastly. Against women, against anything not Japanese."

"And how do you know all this?"

"I don't. I'm making it up. I just don't want you to go." They were silent for a while. "That's not my strongest argument," Maggie began again. "I have others."

"No need. There is no strongest argument if you're hoping to change my mind."

"Yes there is. I respect what you want," Maggie persisted. "I really do. But you're asking me to do the impossible. I can't raise Mac without you."

"Bullfeathers," Albie retorted. "You're doing just fine without me."

"Sure," Maggie said. "That's why he got arrested."

"He's bound to screw up now and then. The only difference when I was around was I helped him hide it from you."

Maggie chewed on this unwelcome bit of information. "I don't know how to be a normal human," she finally said.

"I never understood the big deal about being normal," Albie replied.

"There's going to be something critical I'll overlook." Maggie believed with all her heart this was true.

"So he'll figure it out for himself."

Maggie looked around, staving off panic. "Please don't leave us," she said softly. She had never asked anything like this of anyone before. Doing it opened a cut in her somewhere.

"That's nice. You don't want me to go. Didn't mean a rat's ass to you when I didn't want you to leave New York, did it?"

"That was totally different. I had to move somewhere. I only moved an hour away."

"Two hours."

"Whatever. You don't need to cross an ocean to get here. *And* I begged you to come along with us."

"So you come along with me."

"That's good. That's funny," Maggie said. "You going to have room for four in your tube? You're going to have to live in a tube, you know."

"You're asking me to choose between you and myself." Albie's voice was hard. "Do you think you're entitled to win?"

"This is why you wouldn't leave New York, isn't it?" Maggie asked, finally putting two and two together. "You were already involved with him. Why didn't you just tell me?" Albie didn't answer, and they sat on the couch, light-years apart in a shared universe of grief.

"I know what you're doing," Maggie finally said, her voice weary. "If you distract us with a stupid fight, we won't talk about the real issue."

"Which is?"

"You don't want to leave any more than I want you to. So now you've got this awful choice to make, and if we part ways in anger you get to feel like you dodged a bullet. You know what? If I was capable of loving you as much as you love us, I would make that choice for you. I would say, Albie, Mac is growing up. In a few years, he'll be off on his own with nothing but some random glances back at us now and then. And I'll most likely resume my career, and who knows? Maybe find somebody new some day. You just found your somebody first. So you go, get on with your life."

"Thank . . ." Albie started to say.

Maggie interrupted her. "But that's not me. I still don't believe I can raise my child without you. You're not just my backup, you're my failsafe. If you're not around to catch what I miss, we're all going to regret it. So you want to go? Go. But I will *not* make that decision for you. That burden is all yours." She stood up, took her wine, and went off to bed.

25

Lillian walked down the stairs. The finished area of the basement seemed darker than it used to. The new security bars on the windows didn't really block the light, but ever since the break-in the whole house felt different. She'd read an article in *Good Housekeeping*, while waiting at the dentist's, about the post-traumatic stress that resulted from violative crimes. It was small solace that break-ins were among the least invasive.

Despite the distressing nature of the burglary, at least nothing was missing. The police theorized that Lillian and Carl's return had interrupted the thief. Lillian wasn't buying it. Whoever breached the sanctity of her home could have easily stayed hidden in the basement waiting for an opportunity to leave undetected. Instead, he (for burglary, according to the magazine, was a male crime) had deliberately created a disturbance. Lillian felt certain about this. There was an alarm control panel right by the walk-out door. When she and Carl armed the system upon arriving home an orange light would have started flashing "activated," just as it was doing now. With each day she grew more convinced their burglar's sole motive had been to inflict psychological torment. With the special logic she reserved for her marriage, she added this to the growing list of resentments for which she held Carl accountable.

She walked past the big screen TV, the bar and the billiard table, then through the home theater. The door to the storage area was on the far wall. She used her key to unlock it. Reaching gingerly around the doorjamb, she snapped on the light. Then she slowly pushed the door all the way open. It would be just like Carl to set a booby-trap without mentioning it to her. This was his sanctum sanctorum after all, the off-season resting place of his beloved Chipmunk. He was still incensed that Lillian used part of the shrine for storage. He was so unreasonable about it that if she needed something when he was home he would make his dopey sidekick, Harry Butts, come down here with her to get it. Since she was on her own today she had the luxury of getting the Christmas decorations by herself.

She went over to the corner reserved for her holiday things. The Chipmunk's box, highly polished mahogany with ornate brass hardware, was in her space. Carl was nearly as proud of that damn box as he was of the costume, but it reminded Lillian of a miniature coffin. She walked around it and picked up her carton of fragile glass balls. On the way out she nudged the door with her foot. It closed and locked behind her. She was almost to the stairs when she realized she'd left the light on. She put her balls down on the bar and went back.

When she unlocked the door again, the significance of the out-of-place Chipmunk casket finally registered. How very like Carl. Knowing she would come down here sooner or later to get her Christmas things, he had set a trap after all. Even if he unintentionally left the box out of place, he would still hold her to blame for his own lazy mistake. Exasperated, she strode over and picked it up. She almost tumbled backward. The box was much lighter than it should have been. She would have opened it to check why, but of course it was locked and Carl had not entrusted her with a key.

Utterly annoyed, she put the little coffin back where it belonged. She considered whether it was worth the aggravation of telling Carl she'd noticed something odd, but given his tendency toward paranoia, decided against it. Knowing him, he'd probably taken the costume someplace he felt was safer. She preferred believing that to the other scenario that presented itself, a horrid vision of Carl wearing the head while in hot pursuit of his favorite kind of entertainment.

🐿 🐿 🐿

Maggie huffed around Mac's room, trying to keep a lid on her tirade.

"I don't understand why you're so upset," Mac said from the safety of the doorway.

She stopped long enough to give him a withering look. "You don't? There's a great big band adjudication tonight and for days you tell me you don't want to go, and I ask you and ask you if you have a choice, and you're like, of course I have a choice. And then you pop in here after school today, the *day* of the event and tell me not only do you have to go, you have to wear all these . . ." she paused, "*unusual* clothes."

Mac played innocent. "If they're unusual, why bother looking in my closet?"

She waved the sheet of paper he had just handed her. "Black shoes!"

"I had black shoes. You know, for Dad."

She reached into the back of his closet and pulled them out. "You still have black shoes. Except they're way too small. Maybe I should stop feeding you."

"Try to stay focused," he advised.

She looked despondently at the paper. "White shirt, black pants." Then her eyes grew big and round. Mac cringed in anticipation. "Red bow tie!" she exploded. "Where the hell would we get a red bow tie even if we had time to look for one?" Even though it was pointless, she went on, "How long have you known you needed all this stuff?"

"Mom," he said, "you need to stop blaming the victim. The guilty party here is all the band teachers across America who depend on teenage boys to handle communications."

"Get your jacket," she snapped. "We need to go see what we can find before the concert."

☙ ☙ ☙

When they got to Goodwright's in the North End Plaza, the parking lot was nearly full. "See," Mac said imprudently, "we're not the only ones who screwed up." Maggie parked without answering and marched ahead of him into the store. The picked over racks saved them having to fight about trying stuff on. They took the only white dress shirt and black pants that were anywhere close to Mac's size. Maggie held on to them tightly, wary about the possibility of running into an even more desperate mother. It turned out there were plenty of red bow ties, perhaps in response to sales staff being traumatized by frantic parents in past concert seasons.

The final challenge was the shoes. The store had an old-fashioned shoe department, and the lone elderly saleswoman moved with the speed of a cosmic event. The third time she returned from the stockroom empty-handed because the details of size and style had slipped her mind during her prolonged journey, Mac whispered to Maggie, "You're not allowed to hurt her. She's like one of those giant tortoises. They live so long because of how slow they move."

"You know what really sucks?" Maggie asked. "No matter what I do, some day, if I'm very lucky, I'll end up like her."

"At least you'll always have a choice about the perfume," Mac said. "Though I'm not sure I can see you in a customer service role."

"How about we just grab a pair of black sneakers and get out of here?"

Mac leaned over and gave her a hug. After they found the sneakers he decided he was hungry. Maggie checked the time and realized, with a start, that she'd forgotten to put her watch on. She hadn't gone anywhere without a watch since she started medical school. It wasn't quite dark out yet, and Mac didn't have to be at school until 6 PM, so she figured they were okay. They walked to the pizza place and had a couple of slices. When Maggie got up to throw out their trash she noticed a clock on the wall behind the register. It was 5:40.

She hurried back to their table. "It's later than I thought. Take your stuff into the men's room and change. I've got to get you straight over to school or you'll be late." Mac stood up and stretched. "Hurry up," she said, handing him the bags.

"Calm down," he answered. "I'll be fine."

It felt like forever until he returned. "Come on," Maggie said, bolting from her chair.

"Mom," he protested, "it's only been like three minutes."

"Like hell it has," she said. She rushed him toward the door. On their way past the register he pointed up at the clock. It read 5:45. She took a deep breath. "Okay," she said. "I'm going to chill now."

"About time," Mac said.

"Not punny," she said, and they both snickered. "But really, the next time you pull anything like this, you are out of luck. I mean it. There better not be a next time. If this ever happens again, you'll be sorry."

"Mom?" he said, "you might sound scarier if you picked one threat and stuck with it. Besides, I'll already have this stuff next time."

"You'll lose something," Maggie said. "Or stain it."

"Don't forget about tearing it."

"I can handle that," she said. "I've sewed all kinds of things."

"Do you ever miss it?" Mac asked.

"Sewing?" she smiled. "Not yet."

"Don't you worry you'll forget how?"

"It's like riding a bike, buddy. I'll need to take some refresher courses, but it'll be there when I need it."

During the ride to school Mac made a dedicated effort to convince Maggie she didn't need to attend the competition. "I'm kind of like an extra," he insisted. "I won't even get to go on stage. I'm just supposed to be in the audience to show team spirit."

"I should show support too," Maggie countered. "I really want to."

"No you don't," he said. "You don't even like jazz."

"Okay," Maggie admitted. "I'm lying. But it's important for me to be there."

"No offense, Mom," Mac said, "but nobody even knows you exist. They're not going to come looking for a hug from you if we lose."

Maggie turned into the school parking lot. She had expected it to be crowded, but it was far worse than she'd imagined. "I think this is more important than you're letting on," she said.

"Well, it is the final regional competition. Whoever wins goes to State."

"And you're sure I shouldn't stay and watch?"

"Mom, I'm not playing, remember?"

"Yeah, okay, fine," she gave in. "I probably wouldn't be able to find a parking spot anyway." She drove up to the front door of the school. "What time should I pick you up?"

"Gee," Mac said, "if I had a cell phone, I could just call when I was done, couldn't I?"

"Yes," she replied. "But you don't. So either tell me what time to come back or find a good old-fashioned pay phone when you're done and call me."

"I'll call," he said, getting out of the car.

Maggie pulled away, wondering what to do with herself. She finally decided to go home and trim Penelope's nails. If she survived the excitement of that, maybe she would start looking up recipes for Christmas dinner.

The phone was ringing as she came in from the breezeway. It was Mac. "Hey," she said. "What's up?"

"This is why I need a cell phone."

"That's what you called to tell me?"

"No, but it's an emergency. What if you didn't go home?"

"What's the emergency?" She tried to stay calm.

"Tim Guthrie is sick."

Maggie waited for further clarification. It didn't seem to be forthcoming. "Maybe you should try calling Tim Guthrie's mother?"

"Not sick here. Sick at home."

"And . . ."

"And Mr. Don wants me to fill in for him."

"Mac!" she yelled. "That's great!" He didn't answer. "It is great, isn't it?"

"I guess."

"What's the matter? You've been to all the rehearsals, right?"

"Can you bring my drumsticks? Right away?"

"Sure." She thought a minute. "Is something wrong? Would you rather not do this?

"Just bring my drumsticks, okay? And hurry. Warm-ups are almost over. The real concert starts at seven o'clock."

"Doesn't anybody have a pair of drumsticks you can borrow?"

"I need my own."

"Okay. I'll be right there." She ran down to the basement for his drumsticks. It didn't look like there was anything special about them. Maybe he thought they were lucky.

Back at the school, the parking lot looked even less promising than before. She was on her final circuit of the outer lanes, ready to leave the car idling out front while she ran inside, when she saw the space. It was a tight fit, next to the most beat-up vehicle she'd ever seen. When she got out, she accidentally dinged it with her door. Even though it was a rusted old heap, she felt bad. She leaned down to check if she'd made a mark and was repulsed by what she saw. On the door—in fact, all over the vehicle—were stickers. In the winter dark, she hadn't noticed them until she bent closer. They were a collection of extremely offensive racial and ethnic insults, complete with vile illustrations. Maggie shuddered involuntarily. As she walked away, she noticed without thinking about it that the vehicle was an old Chevy Blazer.

🐓 🐓 🐓

Maggie walked through the doors that led backstage. It was dark and there were kids all over the place. She waited for her eyes to adjust. "Excuse me," she asked a passing body, "have you seen Mac Rifkin?" There was no response.

She had no idea how she was going to find him. She'd just assumed he'd be waiting somewhere obvious. She stumbled on a little. "Hey," she accosted the next kid she could catch, "where's Mr. Don?" He pointed over his shoulder toward the lighted area onstage where everything was set up. Maggie was most of the way there before she heard the disagreement going on behind the risers.

"I won't tolerate this, Dickerman," an irate voice said. "What exactly do you think is the goal of your job?"

"Let's see," Mr. Don answered, "teaching music? Helping children build self-esteem? Nurturing a lifelong appreciation for the arts?"

"How many more times do you expect me to go over this?" the voice answered.

"Got me," Mr. Don said. "This is *your* mission."

"Dickerman, we are all measured by our achievements." The voice sounded pedantic now. "And what is the proof of those achievements? Trophies. Where are your trophies, Dickerman?" The voice paused. "In somebody else's trophy case. And why is that?"

"Because somebody else has a more talented population?"

"Absolutely not!" the other voice exploded.

"Okay, okay," Mr. Don said. "I was joking."

"That's your problem, Dickerman!" the voice said, unmollified. "You think there's something funny about this."

"I take this very seriously, sir," Mr. Don said firmly. "My students are hard-working and gifted. They deserve to be recognized. I just don't agree that recognition has to come in the form of a trophy. I would even venture to say it could come as acknowledgement from a relevant authority figure."

The point was lost on the other party. "Then why compete at all?"

"Because you make me?"

Maggie felt awkward standing there listening. But she couldn't leave without giving Mac's drumsticks to somebody who would make sure he got them. She decided to walk around the risers as if she'd just arrived. When she got behind them she saw that the other voice belonged to Principal Babson.

"Mrs. Rifkin." Mr. Don looked a little uncomfortable. Maggie didn't blame him.

Principal Babson turned to her. "Here, Dickerman," he said. "You don't have to take my word. Let's ask the customer. You have a child in the band?"

"Um-hmm," Maggie said proudly. "My son. He plays . . ."

Babson interrupted. "Would you or would you not like to see this band win a trophy?"

"It would be nice."

"My point exactly."

"But it would not be the most important thing my son got from this experience."

"Suppose, though," Babson said, "there was a sub-par performer who jeopardized the band's chance of success? Wouldn't you expect someone to ask them to step aside for the greater good?"

Maggie didn't appreciate being put on the spot. "I don't feel it would be right for me to pass judgment without knowing the specifics."

"Suppose that performer had been given a fair chance and showed no desire to improve?"

"Sir . . ." Mr. Don began.

"No, Dickerman!" Babson spooled up on his own eloquence. "Let the woman speak!"

Maggie sighed. "I suppose if someone was clearly showing no motivation then it might be appropriate to replace them."

"See?" Babson said righteously. "Just like I told you. Do something about the drummer before I do." He walked away.

Maggie looked at Mr. Don, momentarily speechless. "We're not talking about the drummer I think we are, are we?"

"I apologize," Mr. Don said. "Principal Babson was out of line."

"But Mac?" Maggie was dumbfounded. "Mac hasn't been . . ." she searched for the right word, "satisfactory?"

"It is my policy that every child who demonstrates commitment, regardless of, shall we say, natural inclination, gets to perform."

"Regardless of 'natural inclination'? Like, talent?" Maggie was beginning to get the picture.

"Much as I wish it were otherwise, life is very much a competitive sport. I believe music should be one place kids can enjoy themselves without worrying about that."

"It's a nice sentiment," Maggie said. "But it's looking like it could cost you your job."

"Nah," Mr. Don said. "I'm tenured."

"Still," Maggie said, "it would be nice to win."

He gestured philosophically. "It will be what it will be. My first priority is for the children to get something meaningful out of the experience in return for all their hard work."

"Even the drummer."

Mr. Don smiled. "Even the drummer."

"Where is he?" Maggie asked. "He called me to bring these." She held up his drumsticks.

"I can give them to him."

"Thanks," Maggie said. "But I need to talk to him."

"Not about this, I hope."

"Don't worry," Maggie assured him. "I'm an expert at not repeating nasty stuff."

"He usually hangs out in the Band Room."

"Thanks," she said. She walked to the Band Room and motioned for Mac to come out.

"Hey," he said, "thanks for bringing my stuff." He reached for the drumsticks.

"Not so fast," Maggie said, holding them away from him. "Why do you suppose your band teacher thinks you're a charity case?"

Mac feigned innocence. "He does?"

"Never mind," she said, starting to walk away.

"You forgot to give me my drumsticks," Mac said. Maggie kept walking. "Mom," Mac sounded worried now, "come on. This isn't funny."

She stopped and faced him. "No, you come on. You're messing with people, and I want to know why." His face colored. Maggie didn't care. "You're one of the finest drummers this school has ever seen." He rolled his eyes. "Do you remember how proud your father was about how you could play?" Mac stared at the floor. "Is that the problem?" Maggie asked softly.

Mac shook his head. "It was a little, in the beginning," he said miserably. "But mostly I just wanted people to think I was like everybody else."

"Oh, honey." Maggie felt bad for him, but she wasn't sure if this was the place to hug him. "That might be a good plan if the thing that made you different was a persistent sinus infection." Mac smiled despite himself. "But your difference is something people value. If you let people see it they'll only be more interested in you."

"If you believe that how come you hide what you are?"

"I'm not doing it because of what people might think. I'm just tired of being that for now, and until I figure out what to do about it, I don't feel like having to explain. But you're not tired of drumming. You can't let someone's potential opinion determine your path through life."

Mac made a face. "That's deep," he said.

"Fine," Maggie answered. "But people are depending on you. Mr. Don just got a load of crap from your gasbag of a principal about how he better win a trophy tonight."

"You think he's in trouble because of me?" Mac's concern was genuine.

"I think you should at least try to help him get out of trouble," Maggie answered. "Babson believes the band hasn't won in years because Mr. Don lets everyone get a chance to play, whether they're good or not. If you do your best tonight, there's no guarantee you'll win. But if you *don't* do your best, that pretty well guarantees you'll lose, right?"

Mac nodded. "Okay. If you think it will make a difference."

"It will make a difference to me," she said. She looked around carefully, and seeing all was clear, gave him a hug.

26

The rules of the band adjudication were simple. There were multiple elimination rounds until two finalists remained. The Dooleysburg Jazz Originals survived all the early rounds, playing with the enthusiasm of kids who believed they might end up the winners. Each round they survived made them more focused. Even Mr. Don appeared to be developing a glow, though it may have only been the sheen of sweat.

At preliminary competitions people often slipped out once their school had lost. But this was the finals. There were hardly any empty chairs as the night wore on. When Dooleysburg, with their home court advantage, made it to the final round the crowd went wild. Mr. Don and the band took their bow to extended applause laced with whistling and shouting. When the audience finally quieted down, a lone voice thundered out. "No prize for the jiggaboo!"

The auditorium fell deadly quiet, as if all the air had been sucked out of it. Mr. Don walked to the front of the stage, his face showing nothing. "House lights, please," he said. As the lights came up, he shaded his eyes and scanned from left to right and back again over the crowd, taking his time. When he spoke, his voice rolled across the audience like a tidal wave.

"Ladies and gentlemen, esteemed judges, it is regrettable that anyone would show such contempt for these proceedings and the effort they represent. I cannot guess what that person hoped to achieve, but I can guarantee you his lack of respect, for himself as well as others, does not represent the spirit here tonight. I would ask that we treat this interruption as it deserves, by ignoring it. Let's focus on what we came here for, our local talent." He bowed low, and the audience applauded with uncomfortable restraint. He motioned for the house lights to go down. People began shifting in their seats, coughing and rattling their papers again. Under the cover of this background noise, Mr. Don spoke quietly to his first chairs. "Somebody out there is asking to be taught a lesson. Let's finish off whoever's still standing."

The kids played with everything they had. It was the only way they could show Mr. Don how they felt, trying to cleanse the air with music and distance themselves from the taint of ignorance that contaminated everyone. For his part, Mr. Don conducted with extraordinary grace. After he made his final delicate gesture, the room was exquisitely silent. It was not until he motioned for the band to take a bow that the wave of applause swept through the crowd.

The Dooleysburg Jazz Originals stayed onstage until the crowd calmed down. The remaining competitor, the Mammon Slammin' Jammers, came from the wings and took their places. Though it would never be possible to identify the source of the offensive comment, the nature of the situation certainly implicated Mammon. Now they would have to work doubly hard to prove they didn't need to resort to dirty tactics. They were good to begin with, but this made them drive for perfection.

They were absolutely coordinated, crisp and sharp. Still, overall Dooleysburg was better. Except that Mammon had a killer drummer. Years ago someone in the Mammon District had stumbled on the realization that hyperactive kids and drums were made for each other. The district now provided a percussion curriculum that started in their preschool enrichment program. People looking to buy a house in Mammon didn't ask about average SAT scores or percentage of high school graduates going on to college, they wanted a soundproof room in the basement.

Mammon's drummer was a tall, thin boy. His arms and legs were so long he might have been called gangly if he hadn't moved with an athlete's grace and speed. His fans cheered him on loudly after each solo, but he didn't stop long enough to acknowledge them. It was remarkable how nothing broke his intense concentration. Only Mammon's band director was close enough to recognize the kid's medicated reptilian stare.

But Mammon's band director wasn't thinking about his drummer, he was measuring the audience's response. As long as he detected enthusiasm, he let the drummer go on. When the set finally finished, Mr. Don came to the front of the stage. "Judges," he began, "I regret to say it appears we have a violation of the rules." There was a collective groan from the audience. It had been a long night, and at this point what people were most interested in was the prospect of finally being able to go home.

A disembodied voice from the first row replied. "You are correct, Mr. Dickerman. The rules clearly prohibit solos. The Mammon Slammin' Jammers are disqualified."

"Wait! Wait, wait!" Mr. Don held up his hand as if he could stave off the noise from the crowd, which was beginning to sound ugly. "I do *not* want Mammon disqualified!"

The judge walked up to the stage. He and the band directors conferred and then the judge took the mike. "Ladies and gentlemen," he said, "at the request of Dooleysburg, they will now have the opportunity to perform solos, after which the judges will select tonight's winner." The crowd applauded listlessly.

Mr. Don gestured toward the wings, and four kids came out on stage. Mac was one of them. The opening number was an intense kid on flamenco guitar. He was followed by a boy who did a pretty decent imitation of Wynton Marsalis. The third performer was a petite blonde on the flute. Her "Flight of the Bumblebee" got a standing ovation.

And then the spotlight turned on Mac. Maggie suddenly understood why he wanted that big mirror on the basement wall. He'd been rehearsing for this moment for a long time. He held his drumsticks above his head for just a moment too long, waiting for the crowd to become totally hushed. With a sudden flourish he brought them down so hard the sound hit the walls and reverberated back. Then he threw them into the air. Catching them in mid-flight, he flipped them back and forth between his hands so rapidly they appeared to be one piece of wood in continuous motion. They flashed through the air, circled like a halo around his head, and vanished momentarily, only to snap back into his grip. A bare instant before his movements became predictable, he threw the drumsticks up so high they disappeared into the flies. As they careened back down, end over end, he snatched them, and launched into his solo with a thunderous crack. His performance was flawless, primal and hypnotic. Maggie glanced around. Nobody was moving.

Without warning a disharmonious rhythm laid over Mac's rapid-fire beat. Mammon's drummer had come back on stage and was playing, crashing into his drums with the fierceness of a wild animal trapped on a screen porch. The two boys ramped up their energy, trying to outdo each other with pure power. And then, almost too subtle to notice at first, they began listening. A glimmer of communication unfolded, then blossomed into a call and repeat that swelled and grew. They were feeding off each other, pistons of the same engine in coordinated motion until, like a glorious sunset, the performance burst to its peak and rapidly dissipated. With a final riff, they both stopped, dripping with sweat. Members of their respective bands rushed onstage.

Mr. Don and the band director from Mammon walked to center stage. The noise of the applause covered their conversation. With a brittle smile, Mammon's director extended his hand. "No hard feelings," he said.

Mr. Don took his hand and pumped it forcefully. "Glad to hear it," he replied.

Mammon's director leaned in so he could speak even lower. "I meant as in, 'you have no hard feelings toward us'."

"Ah," Mr. Don said. "I may look like the cocoa version of Poppin' Fresh, but as it happens, I am a fairly mean mother. You can have whatever kind of feelings you like. But I already gave you one chance, which is a whole lot more than you deserved." He smiled and waved at the audience. "And now I'm going to call my kids back for one more number and take you down so hard the top of your pointy little head won't even show above the floorboards when I'm done."

Mammon's director broke off the handshake. He stepped to the front of the stage and raised his hands until the auditorium was graveyard quiet, and then he made everyone wait a few seconds longer. "Judges," he finally intoned, "despite the clear superiority of our performance, Mammon forfeits."

ſ   ſ   ſ

Some of the Dooleysburg seniors felt the forfeit deprived them of the win they clearly earned, but overall backstage was one big celebration. Mr. Babson was ecstatic that they not only won a trophy, but did it on their home turf. In his typical classy way, Mr. Don let everyone know how proud he was. Then Mr. Babson put a damper on things by requiring the whole band to shake hands with him. By the time they were done, especially since he kept furtively wiping his hand on his jacket every few people, the festivities kind of petered out.

Most of the kids packed up quickly after that, putting on jackets and gloves and clogging up the exits as they waited for parents or rides. Mac, who was used to being alone whenever Morsel wasn't around, was surprised to find himself the center of a small group. They were totally impressed by his secret talent. He acted like it was no big deal. Gradually these kids peeled off too. Mac could have walked out with them, but he wasted time until everyone was gone. Just because people wanted to be friends now didn't mean he was sure he was interested. He didn't have a problem being an outsider.

He thought it was all cleared out backstage, so he was surprised when Jayme Campbell, the flute player, appeared. He didn't want to dislike her, but it was hard not to notice the differences between them. She was little and blonde and cute. People always wanted to be around her, and as far as Mac could tell, she didn't do anything to deserve it. And the way she spelled her name annoyed him, even though he knew that wasn't her fault. It was like a surgeon general's warning that she was trendy.

She walked straight up to him and said, "Hi." Just like that. Like it was normal.

He knew it was dumb, but he involuntarily looked around to see if she was talking to somebody else. Nobody was there. "Hi," he said back.

"You're an incredible drummer," she said. "I had no idea."

Mac shrugged. "You're good on the flute, too." He could tell she wasn't feeling squirmy like he was. He wished he could make her go away. He couldn't think of anything to say. Then he realized he didn't need to worry about it. She just started talking, and pretty soon he knew everything about her best friends, her favorite bands, what she planned to do that weekend. A couple of times she stopped to take a breath and he thought, who cares? and then was surprised to notice he did. He wanted her to keep talking. He liked to just stand there, looking at her. Finally she stopped, not just for a breath. In the silence, he could hear a buzzing in his ears.

Jayme waited a while for him to say something. "Do you have a ride home?" she eventually asked.

"My mom's waiting for me out there somewhere. How about you?"

"Oh, yeah," she said. "The Secret Service is probably right outside the door."

Mac was surprised. "Really? Is your dad in politics?"

"No, doofus," Jayme giggled. "I meant my brothers. My older brother just got his license. My dad doesn't know who to trust less, him or me, so he sends my little brother everywhere with us. He's supposed to rat us out if we actually do anything."

"That must be cool, to have two brothers," Mac said.

"It sucks."

"I'm an only child."

"What's that like?"

"Except for having to do stuff alone when you don't feel like it, it's okay. I never have to take turns, and I always get to pick the flavor and what movies and things like that. Plus, I get all kinds of stuff out of my mom because there's nobody else." Mac stopped suddenly. His face and neck felt weird, like he just took a drink of warm tea. He tried to cover up. "You probably don't want to hear this stuff."

"I think it's pretty cool." She smiled like she meant it. "I don't get to be alone much."

"I'm not really alone that much."

"You hang out with Morsel."

Mac looked down at her. He liked the feeling of being taller than she was. "He's okay."

"I better get out there before the goon squad starts looking for me," Jayme said.

"Yeah. Me too." As they turned to go, he was struck with sudden inspiration. "You need me to carry your flute?"

Jayme cracked up. "I like you," she said. "You're funny."

Mac felt lightheaded. He made a goofy face because he was thinking too hard. What would his dad say in a situation like this? "You interested in physics?" he asked.

"No." They walked a little farther without talking.

"You like weirdos?" he asked. "Geeks?"

"You're not a geek," she said. "You don't even have zits."

"I'm just on the borderline of puberty. Give me time."

Jayme leaned up on her tiptoes and kissed his cheek. "Ugh," she said. "You're all sweaty."

"You think anybody ever said that to Ginger Baker?"

"What?" she asked, scrunching up her nose.

"Never mind," he said. "It's an old people reference."

"This would be good time to ask me out," she said.

"See? I didn't know that. I told you I'm a geek."

"Just hurry up, before I change my mind."

"Okay. You want to go out?"

"Sure," she said, walking rapidly toward the exit. "Call me."

He waited a second. "Jayme!" he yelled after her.

She turned around, annoyed at being startled. "What?"

He played dumb. "You said to call you."

"Oh god," she said. "That was totally lame."

"Still want to go out with me?"

"I don't know," she said. "I'll think about it. Call me. On the *phone*."

Mac walked out to the parking lot. He was feeling pretty good. The air was cold and hard, as if it had surfaces he was walking into. It was weird that *late* November was *early* winter. Not even winter at all, officially. He wondered why the start of winter wasn't until December 21. If real people got to decide things like that, he bet winter would begin a lot earlier, as soon as it started to feel cold. Maybe they decided not to do it that way because winter would last longer and people would complain. Or maybe it was because it started feeling cold different times in different places. People in Michigan would get pissed off that people in Pennsylvania didn't agree it was winter even when the people in Michigan had to wear hats and gloves. And the people in Florida, especially the ones who lived in Miami, would disagree with everybody up north.

Something hit him from behind, hard. He stumbled from the force, but kept his footing. It didn't hurt that bad, but the shock brought tears to his eyes. Needle-footed spiders of adrenaline raced up his arms. Like the victim of a shark attack, he had been totally oblivious to the possibility of danger. He wasn't prepared to defend himself.

"Hey, drummer boy," a taunting voice said, "beat on this!" He got shoved again.

This time he went down on one knee. That seemed to momentarily satisfy his attacker. Mac looked up. It was the drummer from Mammon. There were other kids with him, though Mac couldn't see how many in the dark. Mac wanted to jump them like some killer dog, but he didn't even know how to fight. His impotence made him even angrier.

"Get up," the drummer ordered. Mac stood up, willing himself not to shake. What was the point of being this mad if all it was good for was making you shake?

"Kick his ass!" a scrawny kid behind the drummer said.

"Shut up, Eric." The drummer never turned his face away as he talked. Mac couldn't really see him, but he still felt like the kid was staring through him. "You like to show off?" he asked. Mac didn't answer. "Maybe we'll fix your arms so you can twirl them around too."

Mac tried to think. It was not one of the things that happened automatically when you were this scared. It was so dark. There was nobody around. He could see at least three of them. If he tried to run, they would get him. If he tried to defend himself, they would get him. The buzzing in his head was so loud it took all his attention.

The drummer pushed him, hard, but not hard enough to knock him down. "So where'd you learn that girly twirly crap, huh?"

"Martial arts training." It was his mom's voice, not her normal voice that made guys look at her like she was an exotic flavor of ice cream, but her manly voice, the one she used with homeless people on the subway. "Mac," she continued, "you know the consequences if you touch any of these boys."

"She's bullshitting," the scrawny drummer said.

"You want to find out, go ahead," she said calmly. "If it's self-defense, he isn't obligated to exercise any restraint. If he can't prove you made the first move, he's not officially allowed to break any bones, but you know how that goes. Accidents happen." Everyone stood in frozen silence. For no reason Mac suddenly began imagining molecule shapes made out of Tinkertoys. That made him feel even stupider. Finally his mom spoke again. "What do you say, Mac? You want me to go back to the car and pretend I didn't see anything? Your call."

He turned around, zombie-like, and walked toward her shape in the dark. The hairs on the back of his neck stood up. Just like in a bad dream, he thought his legs might freeze up and quit moving. His mom grabbed his arm and pulled him to their car. She shoved him in and raced around to her door, flipping the locks the instant she was inside.

Mac looked back toward the school. "They're gone," he said shakily.

"You okay?" his mom asked.

"I want to go home," he said.

"Sure." She started the car. "But I think we should report this to somebody."

"No!" He could just see the cops' faces when they heard what a wuss he was.

"Mac, what they did was wrong. They need to know they can't get away with it. Their parents need to be involved."

"Come on, Mom. Please? I'll never see them again. They were just being jerks. This kind of stuff never means anything until adults get involved and make a big deal out of it."

His mom sighed. "I have this feeling I'm going to regret letting you have your way on this one."

"That's what you always say." He laughed, though it came out sounding more like a hiccup. "It hasn't happened yet, has it?" He knew she was probably thinking, there's a first time for everything. But at least she didn't say it.

27

Dooleysburg in December was the town Dickens would have imagined if he'd only had a perky side. Its architecture was perfectly suited to a Victorian holiday motif. The few buildings that resisted, like the Courthouse, sat like toads in an enchanted garden. Every vertical surface bore a wreath or something glittery or plaid. Shopkeepers wore ill-considered elf costumes and Santa took up residence in a red shack which occasionally, and without explanation, moved from one downtown parking lot to another.

Despite, or perhaps because of all this enforced gaiety, hard feelings sprang up in unanticipated places. Things cascaded out of control as a result of the most insignificant events. Alliances were made and broken for reasons that no one would have been able to predict. Pebbles whose ripples would one day grow to waves were dropped into seemingly trivial ponds.

✻　✻　✻

"Come on," Jayme said. "Would you please just do it?"

"You're not begging," Robbie said.

"I'm beseeching," she told her older brother. "Beseeching is much more classy."

"I don't understand what the big deal is," he replied. "If you have a thing for Christopher Robin, just tell him to ditch his strange little friend."

"First of all," Jayme said hotly, "he can't help it that his mother gave him a name from a nursery rhyme. And second of all, he's not the kind of person to just dump somebody. If I tell him to dump his best friend, he won't like me. You have to do it for me."

"I don't get why you would even look at somebody who hangs out with the little weirdo."

"Morsel went after him when he just moved here. He didn't know any better."

"He's so *cool*," Robbie did a girly voice. "I bet when nobody's looking he plays the drums with his magic wand."

209

Jayme punched him in the arm. "Stop being a jerk," she ordered. "I just need you to make him understand about Morsel. He'll get it with a little help."

"Why don't you just tell him he's not going to get any until he loses the little creep?"

"Forget it." Jayme turned to leave.

"Come on," Robbie said. "He's a guy. He'd sell out his own mother if he thought it meant he was going to get some." When Jayme did not turn back, he capitulated. "Okay. I'll see what I can do. But if he likes the shrimp more than he likes you, sucks to be you."

🐦 🐦 🐦

Mac opened the Band Room door to leave. He was glad he had band last period. He could hang around afterwards as long as he wanted and nobody cared. Being alone in the Band Room was almost as good as being in his old basement. Plus, Morsel wasn't into band stuff, so Mac got a break from him. Morsel was okay, but he was always mad about something.

He walked out into the hall and was surprised to see Jayme's brother Robbie standing there. "Hey," Mac said. "What's up?"

"You want a ride?" Robbie asked.

"Sure," Mac answered. He made sure to act like it was no big deal, grateful that his voice didn't crack. "That would be cool." He'd be in a world of trouble if his mom found out he got in somebody's car without permission. "Is Jayme around?" he asked as they walked out to the parking lot.

"She's in town," Robbie said. "If you want, I can drop you off and you can find her."

"That sounds good."

"Yeah," Robbie said. "That way, neither of us gets bagged for you riding in my car."

Mac got in the passenger seat and looked out his window. Not having a brother of his own, he wasn't sure how to act. Robbie joked around a lot, and sometimes he was sarcastic, but he seemed to mostly like Jayme and her friends. At least he didn't act like he minded when they were around. And he didn't make a big deal about having to follow rules.

Robbie was cautious about pulling out of the parking lot, waiting until the road was totally clear. "You think Morsel's going to be in town?" he asked as he took his left.

"I guess so," Mac said. He really had no idea.

"Seems like he turns up a lot around you."

"Yeah. We hang out."

"I don't know much about him." Robbie drove slower than the speed limit.

"He's okay," Mac answered. "He was the first person I met when we moved here."

Robbie took a right onto Bog Road. "I talked to him a couple of times, and he seemed okay." They went through the light and turned onto North Main Street. "Except, did you ever notice that something always goes wrong when he's around? I never hung out with him, but I heard stuff. It's almost like it can't all be bad luck, you know?"

Mac didn't answer. This bothered him too. Morsel made a lot of noise about not caring if he got in trouble, but if that was true how come he never stuck around after he did something dumb? How come he didn't care if everybody else was okay?

"Hey, cool!" Robbie said. He pointed out his car window. "Randolphs' is having a sale on ski equipment. You ski?"

"I always wanted to learn how," Mac said, thinking fast. "But I never got a chance in New York."

"We go up to Bear Mountain sometimes on the weekends," Robbie said. "If my dad lets me take the van, we have room for one more person. You want to come?"

"Sure," Mac said.

"Okay," Robbie answered, taking a left onto Oak Street and stopping to let Mac out. "When you see Jayme, tell her I said it would be okay if you want to come skiing with us."

"Thanks," Mac said, keeping his voice normal. "And thanks for the ride." He closed the door and Robbie pulled away. Then he stood still on the corner. He was so excited he was afraid he'd flop around like a jerk if he tried to move. Going skiing with Jayme and her brother! Albie would be pretty happy when he told her. Maybe she'd finally stop giving him a hard time about needing to make friends. Thinking about Albie made him realize he better move his butt if he wanted to get home in time to make it look like he'd taken the late bus.

Mac didn't do it on purpose, but after that his life got different. He spent a lot more time with Jayme and her friends. They always had stuff to do and they liked it when he came along. They thought it was awesome that he grew up in New York. Most of the time other guys were there too. He was a lot busier than he used to be. He still made all his shifts at the deli and practiced the drums every day, but he didn't have time for much else. His mom let him get away with missing most of his chores, and Albie took care of Penelope for him. She said since she was leaving after Christmas, she would put in her time with the dog now and he could consider it part of his Christmas present. There was probably other stuff he was forgetting, but he was too busy to worry about it. Besides, if he could forget about it, it couldn't be that important anyway.

Robbie pulled up in front of the Gamey Deli. "You sure you want to go in there? You might never get back out again."

"I'll be fine," Jayme said, "as long as I don't eat anything."

Robbie snorted. "You're going in there to buy food."

"I'm not the one who's hungry." They both turned around and looked at their little brother in the back seat. He was engrossed in his Game Boy and didn't look up.

"We could get him real fake food at the drive-thru," Robbie pointed out.

"Mac doesn't work at the drive-thru. Besides, he'll eat anything we toss back there." She opened her door. "I won't stay long." She walked to the deli, head down to keep her face out of the wind. Inside, Morsel was behind the counter. Her nose wrinkled with distaste.

"What do you want?" he demanded.

"Where's Mac?"

"In the back room."

"Can you tell him I'm here?" she asked.

"No," Morsel said.

"Why not?" Jayme demanded.

"I can get you whatever you need."

"I need to talk to Mac."

"He ain't supposed to socialize on his shift."

"Who put you in charge?"

"I'm shift manager," Morsel said, his voice hostile. "You don't like it, take your business elsewhere."

Jayme glared at him. "He's not a slave!"

Morsel glared back. "He's busy."

"Hey Mac!" Jayme called defiantly.

Mac stuck his head around the door. He saw Jayme and blushed slightly. A grin spread over his face. "Hey," he said.

"Hi," she replied. "Can you make me a cheese sandwich?"

"I could've helped you," Morsel said. Nobody looked at him.

"American cheese," Jayme said.

"No problem." Mac leaned into the refrigerated case to get the big block of cheese.

"Hold on," Morsel warned him. "You need somebody to run the slicer."

"I got it," Mac said.

"You know the rules," Morsel hissed.

Mac shrugged. "Screw the rules. Gamey's not around. I can take care of this." He peeled the plastic wrapper off the cheese and put it on the slicer.

Morsel busied himself moving stock around on the shelves until Jayme got her sandwich and left. Then he stormed back behind the counter. "What the hell you think you're doing?" he demanded. Mac just looked at him. "Mr. Perfect breaks the slicer rule for a chick?"

"It's no big deal," Mac said.

"Will be when I tell Gamey," Morsel snapped.

Mac looked at him so hard Morsel stepped backwards. "You know what?" Mac said, his voice flat, "ever since I moved here, I've been going along with your stupid ideas. I always cover your mistakes. I knew about you doing all kinds of crap, and I never once gave you up. You want to tell Gamey I used the slicer? Go ahead."

Morsel was quiet for a long minute. "Maybe I will," he finally said.

Mac's eyes narrowed. "Go ahead." He took off his apron and threw it on the counter.

"Wait a minute!" Morsel said. "What do you think you're doing? You can't just leave. Your shift isn't over yet."

"You want to screw with me?" Mac asked. "Everybody kept telling me how fucked up you were. I should've believed them."

"I'm not gonna say nothing to Gamey," Morsel said.

Mac grabbed his jacket and walked out the front door. He let it slam behind him.

It was two days before they were both on the schedule again. When Mac clocked in Morsel was already there. Gamey was too. Nothing was said about the slicer. The boys made a point of staying out of each other's way. About an hour into the shift there was a sound on the roof like somebody was throwing pebbles at it. Gamey stuck his head out the back door. "I'll be damned," he said. "It's hailing." Sure enough, a flurry of rice-sized hailstones was bouncing off everything. "I left Oscar Mayer out at home," Gamey said. "You two hold down the fort while I go save him."

Gamey had only been gone a few minutes when the phone rang. Morsel took the call.

"Everything okay?" Mac asked.

"Yeah," Morsel said. "The President of the Sisterhood wants her delivery."

"You tell her to forget it?" Mac asked.

"What do you mean, forget it? They're Gamey's best customers."

"You can't make a delivery in this. Look." Mac walked over to the back window. The small parking lot behind the deli was coated in ice.

"It's Tuesday night," Morsel said, as if this explained everything. "They want their tuna and cheese grinders."

"They'll survive one night without sandwiches."

"Don't tell me what to do." Morsel was suddenly furious.

Mac made a face and went out to the front room, even though there was nothing for him to do. Nobody with any sense was out tonight. He pulled a tabloid off the rack and began flipping through it while he listened to Morsel bang around in back preparing the Sisterhood's order. Finally he heard Morsel tearing off sheets of foil to wrap the order. He walked back. "You need any help?" he asked.

"Now's a good time to ask."

"I meant with the delivery."

"What are you going to do, reach the pedals for me?"

Mac looked at him. "Huh?"

"You think I don't know you and your friends make fun of me?"

"We don't make fun of you," Mac protested.

"Whatever," Morsel said. He threw the grinders into a bag, along with some cans of diet soda, which he shook up first. Then he headed for the door.

"Hey," Mac said, "I'm coming with you."

"I don't need you."

"You shouldn't even go out in this. You definitely shouldn't go out alone."

"We're the only ones here, dipshit. You can't leave the deli with nobody to watch it."

"Who do you think is going to come here while we're gone? Plus, nobody would want anything from this hole bad enough to steal it."

"You got a point there," Morsel said. Mac followed him out the back door. They pretty much slid all the way to the huge old van. Morsel tried to open the driver's door, but it was frozen shut, the handle caked with ice. They had to climb in through the passenger side. It took Morsel several tries to get the van started.

"Are you sure we need to do this?" Mac asked.

"If you're going to be a chickenshit, just get out," Morsel replied. He put the van in gear and they skidded down the driveway. Mac grabbed onto his seat and closed his eyes. He didn't open them again until they came to a stop in the parking lot of the synagogue, despite the pure terror he felt every time the van started to skid. He was more than happy when Morsel told him to just stay in the van and keep it running. He thought he might even be willing to spend the night here if it meant he could avoid the ride back to the deli.

It was only a few minutes before Morsel came sprinting out of the synagogue. He was followed by a herd of Sisterhood ladies. They were yelling. He just kept running without turning around to listen. Despite their fashionable shoes, several of the ladies picked up speed. Morsel scrambled over Mac into the driver's seat. "We gotta get out of here!" he shouted.

"What happened?" Mac realized he was screaming too.

Morsel started laughing maniacally. "I brought them cheeseburgers!"

"With real cheese?" Mac asked.

"Yeah," Morsel shouted, throwing the van into gear. The tires screamed on the ice. "And just to make sure they figured it out, I put bacon on too."

"That stuff's not kosher."

"No shit," Morsel cackled. "Pretty good joke, huh?"

"No," Mac said angrily. "It's a pretty good insult."

Morsel leaned forward, trying to see as he stepped on the gas. The hail was still coming down, and the windshield was coated with ice. He pulled the steering wheel so hard to the left the van felt like it might fall onto its side.

"Watch out!" Mac yelled.

Morsel looked around. "They're faster than I expected for a bunch of fat old broads." Like a hunting party flushing quail, the ladies of the Sisterhood had spread out into a walking line formation and were closing in on the van. Morsel pulled the wheel again and yelled, "Help your captain out here!"

The van skidded wildly. Mac hollered, "You're not my, Captain! Look out!"

"Port or starboard?" Morsel shouted.

"Left!" Mac yelled. "Go left!" Morsel pulled the wheel hard to his right. "No! The other way!" Mac yelled.

Morsel tried to yank the wheel in the opposite direction. The van went into a 360. As it swung around, the President of the Sisterhood came into view, her mouth and eyes and arms all moving in panic. She couldn't get her footing on the ice as she scrambled to get out of the way of the careening van. Morsel jammed on the brakes. With a shattering jolt, the van slammed broadside into the rabbi's Escalade.

When Mac looked up, what he saw upset him a lot worse than the accident. Morsel was glowering at him like a mad dog. "This is all your fault!" he screamed. He threw his weight against the driver's door, forcing it open, and disappeared. Within seconds, the van was invaded by irate Sisterhood ladies. Mac felt like a germ that had made a wrong turn into a herd of white blood cells. Nobody cared that he hadn't been driving. They were screaming at him, trying to pull him out of his seat. Once again, Morsel had left him holding the bag.

ɾ   ɾ   ɾ

Carl stood behind Lillian as she sat at her dressing table. There were enough bottles and tubs and jars in front of her to embalm a small village. He desperately wanted to tell her none of them helped, just for the pure joy of saying it. Instead, he sighed. Two months ago, he would have scattered acid words around her like toxic rose petals. Now he mostly had to be content with directing malevolent thoughts at her back. "Dressing tables," he finally said. "I thought those went out with has-been movie stars."

Lillian did not respond. She never responded now. He remembered forlornly the way she used to rise to the bait. "Alright," he finally said, his voice cross, "what's it going to take?"

"You know what I want."

He had to give her credit. She said it without giving the smallest hint of the powerless desire that was driving her crazy. "I don't know if you're worth it," he answered snidely.

"Fine." She didn't even blink. She just went back to smearing that $200-an-ounce essence of civet pussy on her face, or whatever rare animal discharge she was into this month.

"Pick a car!" He threw his hands up in the air. "Any car! Go pick a diamond from the Czar's Cave! Any piece of jewelry they sell, I'll buy it for you!"

To his surprise, Lillian turned around to look at him. Her face was ugly with rage. "Expensive is easy for you, Carl. Oh, you bitch and whine about how much this or that will cost, but we both know that's only a form of bragging. This isn't just about the money, is it?" Carl didn't answer. "It's about the fact that your precious money would go to *him*. And you hate him. We both know why, don't we? You hate him because I love him. That's right, Carl. I would leave you for him in a heartbeat. Which we both know I'll never get the chance to do. But your precious money can buy me a night with him. You want me to stop tormenting you? Make it happen." She got up and left the room.

Carl picked up the jar of cream she'd just been dipping into and threw it against the wall. The glass was so heavy it just bounced off, leaving a slight dent in the sheetrock. Not one bit of the thick cream inside splattered out as the jar landed on the plush carpet with an impotent thud. She had won. He didn't even need to tell her. She knew. She knew because she always won.

28

JD pulled a sheet of pre-cut foil out of the box and laid it on the table. He measured a cup of stuffing out of the big bowl and plopped it in the middle of the sheet, then twisted the foil into a tight bundle.

"Hey," Martha said, "you're not required to compact it, you know."

"Yeah," JD said, morosely.

"Where's your Christmas spirit?" she demanded.

JD looked around. "What further proof of my spirit do you require? I'm spending Christmas Eve at a . . ." he paused, trying to remember the denomination, ". . . at a church, preparing tomorrow's dinner for a soup kitchen in Philadelphia."

"You don't look very happy about it."

He snorted. "I should be in the kitchen doing the cooking."

"They also serve who stand and wrap."

"They're letting Gamey cook, for crying out loud."

"I have never seen anyone be such a bad sport about letting somebody else cook."

"I'm better at it than everybody else."

"Hungry people in Philadelphia don't care."

"They would if they got a chance to taste my cooking."

"So go in there and shove Gamey out of your way."

"I can't do that. It would be disrespectful."

"You're worried about being disrespectful to Gamey?" Martha asked. "He'd never notice. The man's a pig."

"You sound like Maggie."

"No need to insult me," Martha said.

JD made a hissing sound. "Nice. Where is she, by the way?"

"Home with her kid," Martha said. "Acting like a normal mother for a change."

"She do something to piss you off, or is this just your version of Christmas spirit?"

217

Martha was about to answer when they heard a furious howl from the kitchen. "What's the matter with you?" Gamey was shouting. "You're wasting the beans! I told you, one cup for every gallon of soup! One cup! Who the hell do you think you're feeding here, Emeril? These are poor people! They get three beans in their bowl, they'll believe in freaking Santa Claus!" There was a pause, and then a woman, her face red with fury, stormed out of the kitchen with Gamey right behind her. "Don't you tell me how to make soup!" he shouted. "Not until it's your beans!"

Martha looked victoriously at JD. "A misanthropic philanthrope."

JD was not ready to admit defeat. "Measure the man by the size of his heart, not the size of his mouth."

"It's an interesting philosophical dilemma," she said thoughtfully. "If one does good works with bad intent, they obviously don't count. But what if the intent is good but you're an asshole? Do you still go to heaven?"

They were distracted by a new noise from the kitchen. This time it sounded like heavy objects might be involved. "I better go check this out," JD said.

"You want your badge or your hat or something?" Martha asked. JD made a wry face, but Martha noticed, as he turned away, that he had a pair of handcuffs not quite concealed in his back pocket. She followed him. Everyone in the kitchen was pressed up against the walls except Vee, who was holding a bone-in ham by the handle of its mesh wrapping and swinging it around like a mace.

"Dr. Hawthorne," JD said, "I'd appreciate it if you'd lower that ham."

"JD," Gamey called, "she's trying to bash my brains out!"

"There's a mission that's doomed to failure," Martha said, mostly to herself.

Vee landed the ham with a startling whump on the counter. "Honey," she said sweetly, "you just told me you'd like to insert a part of your anatomy in my hams. I was trying to make the job easier for you."

"That right?" JD's voice was hard. "You think it's okay to talk to her that way?"

"Aw, JD." Gamey made an effort to look charming. "I was just joking around."

JD got in his face. "A joke is based on humor. There is nothing humorous about degradation, insults or sexual harassment."

"Yeah, yeah," Gamey said, becoming belligerent. "I know all about it."

With no warning, JD reached around behind Gamey and yanked sharply on the back of his custom-made Dickies. With his other hand he snapped the handcuffs out of his back pocket. He put one cuff on the handle of the big steel industrial refrigerator and the other on the back belt loop of Gamey's pants. There was just enough difference between the two heights that Gamey was forced to balance on his toes to keep his weight off the gargantuan wedgie JD had given him. The crew in the kitchen burst into spontaneous applause. "Break time," JD announced. "Everybody take ten."

"Hey!" Gamey raged. "You can't just leave me hanging here!" JD turned to leave the kitchen. "Charles!" Gamey screamed impotently, flailing his arms, "come back here!" JD continued to walk away.

"Dr. Hawthorne," Gamey said bitterly, loud enough for everyone to hear, "please accept my sincere apologies for my inappropriate behavior. I regret that I offended you."

JD turned to Vee. "Okay?"

"Hell, no!" she said.

"Vee," JD said, "if you don't accept his apology, I'm going to have to cuff you to him until the two of you work it out. We've got things to get done, and I can't have volunteers assaulting each other with meat products."

"Fine," she said, in a huff. "Merry Christmas."

JD looked at the assembled crowd. He was sorely tempted to say, move along, folks, nothing to see here, but he was pretty sure nobody would appreciate the joke. So instead he said, "Go ahead and take a break, everybody. Ten minutes."

Gamey barely waited for them to leave the kitchen before he started. "Look at me," he demanded. "You made me all weepy, for chrissake!" JD walked over and unlocked the handcuffs. "How could you embarrass me like this?" Gamey demanded. "I feel mortified!" JD continued to stare at him until Gamey began to squirm. "What?" he said sharply.

"You feel mortified? Not a great feeling, is it? That's how you make women feel when you treat them that way. Ridiculed. Ashamed. Too embarrassed to tell somebody who can make you stop. Every time you pull your crap, it leaves them as helpless and mad as you are right now."

Gamey looked down at the floor. "I'm sorry," he said, without raising his voice.

"What was that?" JD asked unsympathetically. "I don't think I heard you."

"I'm sorry," Gamey snapped. "Okay? I said I'm sorry."

"What are you going to do about it?"

"I'm going to stop, okay?"

"You mean it?" JD asked. "You going to cut it out?"

"I said I would," Gamey replied heatedly. "What else you want from me?"

"Nothing," JD said, putting a hand on his shoulder. "You just make sure you do that."

🐓 🐓 🐓

Bendz family tradition was to open gifts on Christmas Eve at Carl and Lillian's. It started back when Carol Ann and Wesley were newlyweds, on the misguided assumption they would appreciate a romantic Christmas morning alone. That illusion wore off pretty quickly, but then Chrissie came along. It was deprivation enough that she had to share her birthday with Baby Jesus. Her grandparents couldn't see making her share it with them as well, so the Christmas Eve gift exchange continued.

Carl tried the knob on Lillian's door. It turned. Merry Christmas to me, he thought. Around here an unlocked door was almost as good as an engraved invitation. No doubt she'd already be dressed, her makeup impeccably applied, the whiff of expensive perfume sparking around her head like a Star Trek space cloud. But still, the door was unlocked. At the very least, this meant she intended to give him a little private time before the family arrived. Maybe if the Christmas spirit was running strong he'd get to fasten her necklace or, if she was feeling really generous, give an opinion on her shoes.

He tiptoed into her room. "Lillian?" he called softly.

She appeared from her dressing room wearing a pair of fancy silk lounging pajamas. Carl was disappointed, but he worked not to show it. Not that there was much she could wear that would make her bony skeleton look even slightly sexy, but he wished that now and then she'd give it a try. "Yes, Carl?" she asked, making her own best effort at détente.

Carl brought his hand around from behind his back. He held an envelope, which he handed to her. She looked at it, turned it over, turned it back. He was glad he'd gone to the trouble of making Harry Butts pick up some expensive stationery. That scored him a few points. "Carl," Lillian said, modulating her voice, trying, he could hear, to disguise her irritation, "I have nothing to open this with."

For a brief instant, Carl felt like he might succumb to apoplexy. Then he took a deep breath. "It's an envelope, Lillian," he said. "Perhaps you could tear it open?"

She looked at him as if he were an imbecile. "That could damage my manicure."

Carl took the envelope from her hand, exercising great care to remove it in a gentle manner. "Let me open it for you," he said, his voice dripping saccharine. He slipped his finger under the flap and yanked it open. Then he slid the contents out just a bit. "Here you are, my dear," he said, handing it back.

Lillian pulled the piece of paper the rest of the way out and unfolded it. She read it, then read it again. "Is this a joke?" she asked, with that schoolmarm tone.

"No, Lillian," he said. "It is not a joke. It is a galley proof for tomorrow's *Intellectual*."

Lillian's eyes actually got teary. "Thank you, Carl," she said.

From downstairs, they could hear the commotion of Carol Ann's arrival. She was already sniping at Wesley about something. Chrissie was delivering her own litany of complaints, oblivious to the fact that her parents were otherwise engaged.

"Shall we go tend to our guests?" Carl asked.

Lillian pulled a tissue from the box on her dressing table and carefully dabbed at her eyes. Then, with the closest thing to a smile that she'd given him in a dog's age, she took Carl's arm with her crimson claws and led him from the room. She held tight to the piece of paper in her other hand. As they descended the curving staircase to the foyer, their daughter, son-in-law and granddaughter looked up, stunned into silence.

"Your old man must have ponied up something huge," Wesley whispered.

"Shut up," Carol Ann hissed.

"What is it?" Chrissie demanded, rushing to meet Lillian at the bottom of the stairs. "Let me see." She took the paper from her grandmother's hand. As she read it, her nose wrinkled slightly. "Barry Manilow?" she asked.

"Your grandmother *loves* Barry Manilow," Carl said simply.

"What about Barry Manilow?" Carol Ann asked.

"He's coming to Dooleysburg," Chrissie replied.

"No way!" Carol Ann exclaimed, reaching for the paper.

"That's what it says," Chrissie insisted. "He's going to do a benefit concert at the Golf and Cricket Club. On Valentine's Day. Sponsored by Bendz Automotive. Pop-pop says here he's doing it to show his appreciation for his wife and his town."

"Isn't that lovely?" Carol Ann said sarcastically.

"Yes," Lillian said, patting Carl's hand, "it is."

ꖛ   ꖛ   ꖛ

Maggie walked out into the breezeway. The bag of garbage in her hand was only half full, but it gave her an excuse to get outside. Funny, she thought, that she still felt like she needed an excuse to leave Albie and Vee alone. They certainly didn't care. Whatever happened between them a few weeks ago, somehow the result was a truce. Truce wasn't even the right word. Cabal was more like it. They had some secret now that bound them together like sorority sisters. Maggie was being patient about finding out what it was. Sooner or later, one of them would slip. It was inevitable. Between Vee's big mouth and Albie's compulsion to always be in charge, it would come out. For now, she was satisfied to drive them crazy by not asking.

It was getting late. Mac was already in bed, and Vee would be leaving soon. Officially she wasn't even supposed to come over until tomorrow, but she couldn't resist stopping on her way home to tell them about Gamey's little lesson at the church. Albie insisted the only thing Gamey learned from the experience was that he needed pants with more stretch in the fabric.

It had begun snowing about an hour ago, a gentle snow with no wind. Maggie put the bag in the trashcan, stalling. Maybe if she stayed out here long enough Albie would go to bed. Things were still tense between them. She walked down the driveway, thinking it didn't feel very cold out. Ever since she was a little girl, she believed it felt warmer out when a gentle snow was falling. She held out her hand to catch one of the big, fat snowflakes swirling lazily through the beam of light from her garage lamp.

Out in the alley the world looked like it had been covered in mounds of whipped cream. There was no noise, as if the snow had carried all the usual night sounds down from the air and hidden them under its blanket. Maggie understood why people associated this time of year with something holy. A gentle gust swirled a few snowflakes around her. As she turned to go back in, she heard a sound like a deflating tire. She took a few steps and the sound came again.

"Over here!" It was Gamey's disagreeable little hiss. He was standing at his back gate. She made herself wave, but picked up speed.

"Hey!" he called, louder this time. "Hold up a minute!"

"What?" She was not interested in wasting any Christmas spirit.

"C'mere!" He motioned at her. She stopped walking, but made no move to go closer. "Come on!" he urged. "I got something I want to show you."

"Yeah," she said dubiously. "I'm sure."

"No, come on!"

"Send me a picture." She started back toward her house.

"Would you just come on?" he whined.

"Gamey," she said, "no offense, but I really don't give a damn. And frankly, there's a good chance you're just trying to lure me over there so you can offend me in some way."

He actually hung his head. "I am sincerely sorry," he said. "I know I have behaved reprehensibly toward you. If there is anything I can do to make amends, please feel free to let me know."

Maggie hesitated. It felt like poor sportsmanship to refuse to talk to him now. On Christmas Eve, no less. "Okay," she finally said. "What do you want to show me?"

"Would you just come over here?" His characteristically short temper reasserted itself. "I can't stand here yelling about it."

Reluctantly, keeping her head down so she wouldn't get snow in her eyes, Maggie walked toward his gate. When she got there, he was gone. "Come on!" he called. He was standing in his kitchen doorway. "Hurry up!" he yelled. "All the warm air is getting out!"

"This is far enough, Gamey," she said firmly.

"Would you just come on?" he said. "I won't bite."

Against her better judgment, Maggie followed him into his kitchen. She was astonished. Having seen the deli, she would have been pleasantly surprised to find a modicum of cleanliness. Instead his kitchen looked like it had been decorated by elves. The soffits were stenciled with tulips and ribbons. There were ruffled curtains at the windows and cutout wooden shelves filled with bric-a-brac on the walls. Fancy dishtowels hung neatly above the sink. "Gamey," she said wonderingly, "you keep this place really nice."

He made an exaggerated little bow. "Cider?" he asked. "Homemade gingersnaps?"

Maggie laughed. "Are you serious?"

"Never more," Gamey replied gallantly. He pulled out a chair and she sat, with only slight misgivings. Gamey set out delicate china plates and sparkling crystal glasses. Using silver tongs, he placed two gingersnaps on each plate and then filled the goblets with cider.

Maggie took a bite of cookie. It melted as she chewed into a sweet, spicy burst. "This is really good," she said appreciatively. "You make these?"

"Indeed." His face was smug.

"How come you don't make stuff like this at the deli?"

"Have you seen who comes in there?" he demanded. "Pearls before swine."

In the spirit of the holiday, Maggie ignored the chance to point out he might be suffering from some confusion about the cart and the horse. "So Gamey," she helped herself to another cookie, "I heard what happened tonight at the church." He hung his head again, but Maggie was not about to get conned. "Not that I don't believe people can change, but I have to tell you, I'm sitting here waiting for the other shoe to drop."

He put a hand melodramatically to his heart. "I am wounded."

"Yeah," she said, standing up. "You invited me over for cookies and juice. Okay."

"Oh!" he said. "I was so dumbstruck by your presence in my humble abode that I completely forgot what I wanted to show you!"

Great, Maggie thought. Here it comes.

"I'll be right back," he said, clearly excited. "Just wait here."

Maggie thought it prudent to stay on her feet in case a quick escape was called for. Gamey returned, unsuccessfully hiding a skateboard behind his back. "Gamey!" Maggie exclaimed, "let me see!"

He held the skateboard out to her, looking so proud he might have glowed in the dark. "Keep it down," he ordered. "I don't want the kid to hear."

Maggie moved closer and examined it. "Did you have this made for him?" she asked.

"You bet," he said. His eyes gleamed with pride. "Buttons Hawaii Dowling Custom. Found it online. Pretty sweet, huh?"

"Yes, Gamey," Maggie smiled. "Pretty sweet."

To her dismay, Gamey got teary. "Nobody never did nothing for that kid," he said. He wiped his eyes with the back of his hand. "It ain't like he complains. Never has a bad word to say about anybody. Whatever life dishes out, he takes, like he got no choice in the matter."

Maggie thought hard about how to respond. It seemed to her Morsel dished out at least as much as he got, but to be fair, who besides Gamey ever cared how things looked from his point of view? "Maybe nobody ever showed him how to look out for himself," she finally said.

"Exactly!" Gamey said, jabbing his finger in her direction for emphasis. "Nobody ever gave a damn about him. And he deserves better than that. Any kid does, but especially this one. When he cares about somebody, he cares with his whole heart. Just nobody ever cared back, so he's got no clue how to make the connection, you know?"

Maggie was overcome with a sudden, inexplicable sadness. "You're a good man for caring," she said softly. "I'm sorry I underestimated you. It's very decent of you to look beyond the obvious and insist on giving him a good life."

Gamey placed the skateboard carefully on the table and held his arms out to Maggie. Hesitantly, she stepped closer and gave him a hug. It was the fake sniffle that did it. She realized his head was in a very undesirable position and he was going in for a snuggle. She pulled back. Gamey held tight. She gave him a vigorous push. He dug in with his horrid little head. In one swift motion she rammed her knee into his crotch and smacked him hard on the head. He loosened his grip and she shoved him away. She heard him bounce off something as she stormed out of the kitchen, leaving the door open behind her. The sound of his laughter trailed her across the snowy lawn.

ɾ   ɾ   ɾ

A lovely fire was still blazing in the great stone fireplace at Carl and Lillian's, though the adults had begun to deflate a while ago. Like the fire, Chrissie was still glowing and full of energy. Once she got old enough to stay up late she insisted on waiting until midnight to open her gifts. At the stroke of twelve, she dove for the tidy pile under the tree. She opened the smallest one first, tearing at the paper as if it stood between her and salvation. It was a lipstick case. "Oh," she said. "Thanks." Carol Ann rolled her eyes at her mother. The next few gifts were CDs, a pair of Manolo Blahnik shoes, and a Prada purse. Chrissie remained polite but disengaged. The last gift was in an extravagantly wrapped package. There was a tasteful tag on it that said, 'To Chrissie, with love, from Grams'. Chrissie removed the paper without much enthusiasm. The box underneath was from Victoria's Secret.

Carl stood up abruptly. "Come on," he snapped at Wesley. "The kitchen's calling us."

Wesley looked befuddled. "I don't hear anything," he said.

"You really want to watch your daughter open a box of panties?" Carl asked peevishly.

"Oh," Wesley said, getting up.

Chrissie opened the box. It was filled with lingerie. "Take things out and look at them," Lillian said, secure in her history of perfect choices. Chrissie picked an item and held it up.

"Mother," Carol Ann said, brightly, "that's just lovely. Chrissie, don't you want to thank your grandmother?"

"Thanks, Grams," Chrissie said automatically.

"You don't like it." Lillian's voice was filled with disappointment.

"Please, Grams," Chrissie said. "This would be like wearing a nun. Nothing would get past it."

"Chrissie," Carol Ann exclaimed, "what is wrong with you tonight?"

"Bet I know." Carl popped his head out of the kitchen like a jack-in-the-box. As everyone watched, his hand slowly appeared, dangling a set of car keys.

"Grams," Chrissie whispered, "is it my Hummer?"

"Yes, dear," Lillian said. "The fire-engine red one."

"Thank you!" She exploded into motion, laughing delightedly and hugging her grandmother before rushing across the room to Carl.

"When she started nagging about that car," Carol Ann said fiercely, "Daddy and I agreed it was too extravagant. Then all of a sudden out of nowhere he starts saying it's the perfect car for her and how she deserves it. I bet she has something on him."

"Nonsense," Lillian replied. "Where would she have learned to do such a thing?"

🐔 🐔 🐔

JD pulled up in front of Maggie's house. The plows hadn't made it to this part of town yet, and the driving was so bad it would have been smarter to walk. Except somebody might have spotted him. He shook his head. He couldn't believe he was feeling this adolescent.

Nothing but the snowflakes moved. Most of the houses around here still had their front porch lights on. Many had Christmas lights burning as well. He shut off his car and took the envelope off the passenger seat. It was the size of a greeting card, but there was only a plain handwritten note inside. He didn't understand why the fewer words you needed to say something, the longer it took to write. He didn't have a lot of practice apologizing, but he felt genuinely bad he hadn't believed her about Gamey. Worse, she'd been trying to tell him she needed help, and he ignored her because she seemed so able to take care of herself. He'd rewritten the note a bunch of times in his head before putting it on paper. In the final version, he left out all the stuff about why things happened and just made it clear he was sorry he hadn't listened to her.

He closed his car door quietly and walked up to her porch, where he slid the envelope into the old-fashioned brass-covered mail slot. Then he lowered the flap gently so it wouldn't make any noise. Just as he turned to leave, her little dog started barking. JD hurried back to his car, hoping the snow would continue long enough to fill in the footprints he'd left behind.

29

Christmas Day was a private event in Dooleysburg. Everyone was expected to spend the day with family or friends. Even the General Store stayed closed. The snow had stopped some time during the night, but the sky remained gray, as if conserving the winter sunshine for a day when more people would be out to appreciate it.

Gamey was busy making bacon and eggs, muffins, and hot chocolate when Morsel stumbled into the kitchen, still half asleep. The kid made a big deal about how he thought the whole tree thing was stupid, so Gamey left his gift, wrapped now, on the kitchen table. "Hey," Morsel said, "this for me?"

"Yeah," Gamey answered, pretending not to pay attention.

"It's a skateboard," Morsel said.

"Ain't you even going to open it?" Gamey asked.

"I could tell it's a skateboard."

"You don't want it, I could find somebody at the deli who does."

Morsel sat down at the table and tore off the wrapping. "Holy crap!" he exclaimed.

"It ain't just *any* skateboard," Gamey said proudly.

"I got something for you too," Morsel said. "But it ain't as good as this."

"Just hand it over," Gamey said.

Morsel went and got his package. It was a poorly wrapped and even more poorly made cutting board. It had been out of square to begin with, and was already starting to warp. "I did it in Design and Tech Class. I hardly got any help."

Gamey started to talk and his voice caught. "I don't know what to say, kid. This is the first Christmas present anybody ever made me."

"It's pretty cool, ain't it?" Morsel asked.

"Yeah," Gamey said. "It's the best."

✂   ✂   ✂

Vee arrived at Maggie's way too early for anybody's liking but her own. It took her nearly an hour to rouse everybody. The minute she finally got them all up she insisted they had to exchange gifts. Like a clutch of irritable grouse, Maggie, Albie and Mac sat in the living room as far apart from each other and Vee as they could manage. "You hand out first," Vee ordered Maggie. "It's your house."

"Could have fooled me," Maggie grumbled. She held out a small package to Mac.

He took it and his whole face lit up. He tore off the paper. "An iPhone!" he exclaimed.

Vee and Albie both looked in astonishment at Maggie and her self-satisfied smile. "I promise I'll only use it to track you down now and then," she told Mac.

He was already busy downloading a ring tone. Maggie smiled softly when she heard it. "Hugh Masekela," he said, grinning.

"You know his stuff?" Vee asked.

"He was one of my dad's favorites." Mac got up and hugged Maggie, then gave her a small package. It was perfume. "The lady in the store told me it's a very youthful fragrance," he announced. "You should smell it." Maggie opened the box. She lifted out the bottle and started laughing. Mac had covered the label with a piece of paper that said 'Eau'ld Lady'. In smaller letters he'd printed, 'For the elderly saleswoman in you.'

"I kind of ran out of money," he said apologetically to Vee and Albie. "So I baked stuff for everybody else." He handed out boxes. Vee and Albie looked at each other, but neither opened her gift. "What's the matter?" Mac asked.

"We've been scarred by memories of your Thanksgiving treat," Albie said. "The one you made that was inspired by excrement."

"That was Morsel's idea," Mac assured her. "These are just cookies." He opened another small package and pulled out something that looked like a finger. "Here girl," he said to Penelope. "I made you one too."

"Albie or Vee next?" Maggie asked.

"Albie," Vee said. "Save the best for last."

Maggie had two envelopes left. She handed one to Albie, who took it hesitantly. "What?" Maggie asked.

"MacDonald's not the only one who's tight on funds," she said uncomfortably. "I've been saving for a special project."

"Don't be silly," Maggie said. "We haven't spent a Christmas without you since Mac was born. Nobody cares about presents."

Albie blushed, something Maggie could not remember ever seeing her do before. She opened the envelope. It took her a moment to speak. "Thank you," she said quietly.

"What is it?" Mac demanded.

"It's a ticket," Albie said. "To Japan."

"Wow!" Mac exclaimed. "You're going to Japan?"

"Yes," she said. "I believe I am."

Mac looked from Albie to his mother and back. "How come nobody else thinks this is cool?"

"I'm sorry," Albie began. "The special project I've been saving for is that I decided to move to Japan. I figured I'd tell you when I got closer to going."

"You want to move to Japan?" he said in disbelief. He looked at Maggie. "And you gave her the ticket?"

"Mac," Maggie said gently, "Albie has met someone. She would like to go to Japan and be with him. He lives there. It seemed cruel to make her wait." She turned to Albie. "The return ticket is open-ended. You can come back any time you like."

"That will be my Christmas gift to you," Albie said. "I will come back any time *you* like. Just say the word." She looked at Mac. "May I have your blessing?"

"Sure," he said, putting on a bland face. "How about my Christmas gift? Will you come back any time I like too?"

She smiled. "I had something else in mind for you. I was hoping you'd join me in New York for New Year's Eve. Remember how we always talked about going to Times Square?"

Mac's face lit up. "You mean it?"

"This seems like the right time, don't you think?"

"Can I, Mom?" he asked.

Maggie smiled. "Sure." She turned to Vee. "Time for your gift."

"This has been such a touching moment," Vee said. "I can't wait to see how you're going to top it."

Maggie smiled wickedly and handed her the other envelope. Vee opened it, read the paper inside, and just looked at Maggie, her mouth open. "Hot damn," she finally said softly.

"You sit like that much longer we're going to start trying to land pennies in your maw," Albie said. Vee handed her the paper.

"Okay," Albie said after reading it. "You win."

"What is it?" Mac demanded.

"It seems your mother has provided for the high school education of ten children in Kenya in honor of Dr. Hawthorne," Albie replied.

Vee walked over and gave Maggie a hug. "My gift's going to seem a little tacky now," she said, handing Maggie an envelope of her own.

"Wouldn't have it any other way." Maggie opened the envelope. She removed the contents and looked them over.

"Cure for cancer?" Albie asked.

Maggie shook her head. "Gift certificates," she said. "For Erin go Braise." Albie looked confused. "It's a kitchen store," Maggie explained.

"Well it is," Vee said quickly. "But I thought you could use the certificates to take some cooking classes."

"Irish cuisine?" Maggie said. "Isn't that an oxymoron?"

"I figured it was a good place for you to start, since it's all based on stuff you boil," Vee said, "like corned beef and cabbage or potatoes."

Albie cleared her throat noisily. "Mom," Mac stage-whispered, pointing to her, "Irish."

"You had your chance," Vee said firmly to Albie. "It's up to the professionals now."

☞ ☞ ☞

Across town, in one of the ostentatious homes that surrounded the Golf and Cricket Club, the Carter family had finally awakened from their long winter's nap. Christmas morning was always something of a letdown for them, since the really good stuff was always given out at Carl and Lillian's on Christmas Eve. Nonetheless, Carol Ann insisted they had to get out of bed and make the pretense. Chrissie had just opened her gift, a leather coat, and was modeling it for her parents. "I know it's no Humvee," Wesley said. "But I hope you like it."

Chrissie went over and planted a kiss on the top of his bald head. "Thank you, Daddy," she said sweetly. "I love it."

"Nice that you remember your manners now," Carol Ann said. "What was with you last night? You behaved with a total lack of maturity. A gift is a token of someone's love, not an obligation to satisfy you. The least you can do is show gratitude for someone's thoughtfulness whether you like the gift or not."

Chrissie looked down at the floor. She was not up for a fight today, especially not now that she had the Hummer. In honor of a successful Christmas, she decided to let the old lady rag at her. "I'm sorry, Mom," she said. "I'll call Grams after breakfast and apologize."

"It's the least you can do," Carol Ann said, unsatisfied.

Wesley walked over and kissed his wife's cheek. "Merry Christmas," he said heartily, putting a small package in her lap.

Carol Ann tore it open. "What the fuck is this?" she snarled.

"It's an opal," he said, blinking rapidly. "They're supposed to be lucky."

"They're supposed to be unlucky! How could you screw that up?" Carol Ann lifted the necklace out of its box. "This is the ugliest fucking thing I've ever seen!"

"It's big," Wesley offered.

Chrissie looked over at it. If she had to guess she'd say it was about the same size as her father's balls, though one of them dangling from the silver chain probably would have made her mother a whole lot happier. "Oh, Daddy," she said, "stop teasing. Tell her about her real gift."

"What's my real gift?" Carol Ann snapped.

Wesley looked around helplessly.

"Come on," Chrissie said, all coy. "Just tell her."

"I can't," he said.

"It's that Baume and Mercier watch you wanted," Chrissie said. "You know, the one with the diamonds?" She looked at her father. The poor twit nodded. "He ordered it for you, but they screwed up and didn't get it on time."

"I hope they're giving you a discount," Carol Ann said. "Something worth more than this ridiculous pendant." Wesley swallowed and nodded.

Chrissie smiled lovingly at him. She was glad she could be of help. It was nice when everyone was happy. She'd figure out what kind of payback she wanted later.

🐦 🐦 🐦

On the edge of town, out past the North End Plaza, Daniel and Martha were in their back yard. Their old stone farmhouse with fifteen acres of wooded land was worth enough to finance a very posh lifestyle. Except, of course, to get the money they'd have to sell it. Instead, they chose to live a gloriously simple existence and keep their little piece of paradise.

They had just finished a breakfast of pecan waffles with sage breakfast sausage and fried apples. Martha was sweeping the snow off the patio, admiring the Christmas card perfect woods behind the house. Daniel came around the corner carrying an armload of firewood. As if nature appreciated their attention, the clouds parted and a shaft of sunlight fell into their yard. Without speaking, Daniel went inside and got the cross-country skis they'd given each other that morning. He managed to get his on first. He picked up one foot and his other leg started to slide out from under him, slowly at first, and then with rapidly increasing speed. With a loud whoop, he fell. Martha tried to ski past him and slid onto her butt. They spent the rest of the morning flopping around their back yard, laughing wildly.

🐦 🐦 🐦

In the townhouses up the road, Mr. Don had just put the finishing touches on his midday dinner of meatloaf and mashed potatoes with homemade gravy, with a side of his mama's favorite cooked-to-death beans. He heaped his plate outlandishly full and went into his study. That was his little joke, calling this room a study when all he did in here was indulge in various forms of play. Earlier today he had opened the present from his students. It was the Ken Burns *History of Jazz* series. The thrilling anticipation of watching it over the holiday break, uninterrupted from start to finish, was what inspired him to cook his heart out. He sat down in his favorite chair, and with a fine sigh of satisfaction, turned on the television and began the first of what promised to be many delightful dinners.

꧁ ꧁ ꧁

In his red brick Federal on Court Street, JD poured two fingers of Glenlivet into a crystal tumbler. It was tempting to fill the glass higher, but he'd learned better. He preferred drinking it neat, but he'd learned better than that too. He added soda and ice. He went and sat on the couch, not directly in front of the fireplace, but off at an angle, so he'd be able to stare at the fire for as long as he liked without getting a stiff neck. He put his feet up on the coffee table and raised his glass in a silent toast to the empty room. Then he took a slow sip of scotch. He wanted to be careful not to get drunk. Over the years he'd figured out if he allowed himself to get drunk, he would merely fall asleep and wake up hours before the day was over. The only thing he'd have to show for his trouble would be a headache and a horrible taste in his mouth that instantly reminded him he was alone. If he sipped carefully, in a measured way, he could hope to make it through the entire day comfortably numb.

He had no idea how long he'd been sitting on the couch when the phone rang. He was awake, but the sudden noise startled him. He jumped up to grab it, his stomach full of butterflies. He knew he was being stupid. She wasn't going to call. Still, it was the house phone ringing. Somebody calling on official business would have used his cell. When he answered he realized he was out of breath. "Hello?" he said.

"Hey, boss." It was Joe Butts. "Merry Christmas."

"Thanks, Joe," he said. "Merry Christmas to you too." He wasn't disappointed. He knew she wasn't going to call.

"What're you up to?" Joe Butts asked.

"Usual day-off stuff," JD replied. "Shaving my legs, bubble bath, pedicure."

"Oh," Joe Butts said.

"I'm joking," JD said.

"Oh," Joe Butts said. "Okay."

"Everything okay?"

"Yeah. Sure. Look, I'm over here at Harry's. We got a ham. Harry said if you're not doing anything, you're welcome to come over for dinner."

"Thanks," JD said. "Tell him I said thanks for thinking of me." He rubbed his hand over his chin, unconsciously listening for the sandpapery sound.

He'd gotten a Christmas gift after all. Fate had just shown him there were worse things than spending the day alone.

"So you wanna come?" Joe Butts asked.

"I appreciate the invite," JD said, "but I'm waiting for a call." The words came out, and he thought, idiot. What the hell was he going to do next, tell everybody he had a crush on her? He gritted his teeth, waiting for Joe Butts to ask who was supposed to be calling.

"Oh," Joe Butts said. "Okay. Merry Christmas."

"Thanks," JD said. "Same to you. And Harry." He took the scotch and re-filled his glass, this time more than halfway. He realized now he was definitely better off in a stupor.

🔥 🔥 🔥

Maggie was upstairs in Albie's room, sitting on the bed while Albie packed. "You'll write to me, won't you?" she asked.

"Every day, if you figure out how to use e-mail."

"Mom!" Mac shouted up the stairs. Maggie and Albie both rushed to the door. They could tell from his voice that something was wrong.

"What is it?" Maggie called.

"It's Penelope! She's sick."

They hurried down to the kitchen. The little dog was standing next to her wicker bed, panting. "Who would have thought the little beast could hold that much throw up?" Albie asked.

"I told you guys to stop giving her stuff from the table," Mac said.

Maggie's nose wrinkled. "I knew this would happen if we got a dog."

"You've been waiting months to say that, haven't you?" Mac asked accus-ingly.

"Yeah," she answered. "Pretty much." She went to the cabinet under the sink and pulled out some rubber gloves. "You guys take her downstairs to the laundry sink and give her a bath. I'll clean up her bed." Mac and Albie took some gloves and went off with the dog. Maggie got a plastic bag for the soiled bedding. As she lifted it up, she noticed something underneath. "What's this?" she said, though no one was around to hear her.

🔥 🔥 🔥

The damn alarm. The bell kept ringing and ringing. He wished someone would turn it off so he could go back to sleep.

JD sat bolt upright, startled out of his dream. The fire had died down to coals and the house was chilly and quiet. He'd probably missed a phone call.

He'd done that before, worked the noise of the phone into a dream instead of waking up. Just as he'd known he would, he felt pasty and hung over. He looked at his watch. It was only 6:30. He sank back on the couch, wishing he could go back to sleep and knowing it was impossible.

What if he had missed her phone call? He stood up. He needed to stop this. He was making himself miserable, and there was no point in it. If she wanted to acknowledge his apology, she would, in her own good time. He decided to go get a shower, see if that would clear his head.

He was at the top of the stairs when he saw headlights through the arched window above his front door. Somebody was pulling into his driveway. He headed back downstairs and opened the door. Maggie was standing there. She looked up at him as if she'd been caught. "I was here a few minutes ago," she said, "and there was no answer. I was on my way home, but then I thought I should leave you a note or something so I came back."

"You want to come in?" JD asked.

"I just wanted to let you know I got this," she answered. She held up a Ziploc bag with the remains of his note in it.

"What the hell happened?" he asked.

"My dog ate it," Maggie said. That made JD laugh. "But I got most of what it said," she went on. "And I wanted to tell you . . ." Her voice trailed off.

"Look," he said, "I am really sorry. I should have listened to you right away. I should have caught it myself long before you had to deal with it. I learned something very important from this. From you."

"Thank you," she said, her voice soft.

"Won't you please come in?" he asked. She shook her head, just a tiny motion, and he realized with a sudden sharp pang what the real problem was. "It's okay," he said gently. "You can trust me."

She shook her head again, her eyes glistening in the light that spilled through the open front door. She took a deep breath. "I can't."

The way she said it nearly broke his heart. "Tell you what," he offered, "how about you invite me over for an after Christmas dinner drink?"

A slight smile curled the corner of her mouth. "My dog puked in the kitchen."

"Finally, a kitchen achievement I don't feel compelled to outdo."

She did the most unexpected thing. She giggled. The sound filled him with delight. Without thinking, he reached out and brushed a stray curl off her cheek. He caught himself instantly, but as he pulled his hand back, she touched it just briefly, her finger on the outer edge of his palm. "How about you come over for an after Christmas dinner drink?" she asked.

"Nothing would please me more," he answered.

30

Mac felt stupid. His whole life he wanted to see Times Square on New Year's Eve, and finally he gets there and what happens? He can't handle it. He pretended it was the cold, and Albie pretended she believed him. But he couldn't take the crowd. It was worse than scary. The people weren't people anymore, they were one big wild animal, noisy and out of control. He felt too hot and dry all over. Even though he was breathing he felt like he couldn't breathe. Albie said why didn't they go back to her apartment and watch on TV. She acted liked he was doing her a favor, but he knew she could see he was scared.

They got to her place and he flopped down on the couch. Albie looked at him but didn't say anything. She turned on the TV and then went and got a soda for him. Mac picked up the can. "This isn't even sugar-free. This is proof we're having a pity party."

"Everyone needs something to toast the New Year with," she answered. "I hope you're not disappointed to be spending it with me rather than that little crust of bread fellow."

"He's a jerk," Mac said.

"I noticed we haven't seen much of him since the synagogue incident."

"He acts like that was my fault even though it was his idea. He won't even talk to me." Mac took a sip of soda. "Not like I want him to."

"He's very screwed up," Albie agreed. "I hope you don't believe there's something you can do about that."

They watched the TV, waiting for something interesting to happen. "Albie?" Mac hated when his voice came out like a little kid's.

"Hmm?" she answered. She sounded sleepy.

"Did my dad ever love my mom?"

She sat up like he'd startled her. "Rather an unexpected question."

Mac looked at her. "Never mind," he said.

"Don't jump to conclusions," she said thoughtfully. "In truth, I'm not sure I know how to answer that."

Mac looked back at the TV. "They never fought or anything. But I don't think he felt the same way about her as he did about me."

"One wouldn't expect him to show his love for the two of you in the same way."

"Yeah," Mac said, "but I never saw him kvell over her."

"You never saw him what?" Albie laughed.

"Kvell," Mac said seriously. "It was one of his Yiddish words."

"And it means?"

Mac always had a hard time conveying Yiddish meanings. "Once, when we were in Washington Square Park—before he died . . ."

"Clearly," Albie said.

Mac gave her a look. "There was this couple. The girl was totally ignoring the guy and he didn't even notice. He was looking at her like he couldn't believe he won the prize. Or like he was her goofy dog or something."

"Ah," Albie said, "I get it. Some Yiddish words are quite onomatopoetic. Some aren't."

Mac continued. "I said the guy looked really stupid. And Dad said he was kvelling over his girlfriend. Then he said it was a mistake to ever feel like that about a woman."

"Why would he say that?"

"I thought because it made you look like such a jerk, but Dad said it was because it always wore off and then you'd regret what a mess you made out of your life. He said not to worry, though, cause very few people ever fall in love like that."

"So what makes you ask about this now?"

Mac turned up the volume on the TV. It was nearly midnight, and the crowd in Times Square sounded like a storm. "That's how JD looks at Mom. And he only does it when he thinks nobody's looking."

The countdown started on the TV and the phone rang at the same time. Albie went to answer it. Mac figured it was his mother and listened for Albie to call him. But she didn't. She was flirting with someone. It made Mac feel weird, so he stopped listening. When she came back he asked, "Your Japanese sweetheart call to wish you a Happy New Year?"

"Indeed."

He thought she'd say more, but she didn't. He couldn't remember Albie ever being quiet like this. "What's his name again?" he finally asked.

"Sakura."

"Is that like Mike or something in English?"

"In Japanese names have meanings."

"So what does Sakura mean?"

Albie took a long time before answering. "Cherry blossom."

"Cherry blossom?" Mac repeated, confused. "That's a strange name for a guy."

"Indeed it is," Albie agreed.

Mac's eyes opened wide. "He's not a guy, is he?"

"No," Albie said. "He isn't."

Mac struggled for something to say. "Does Mom know?"

"Certainly not," Albie replied. "Do you think I'm daft?"

"Mom would be cool about it." Mac didn't actually know if that was true, but it felt like the right thing to say.

"Mom would be cold about it," Albie said. "Can you just imagine how jealous she'd be if she knew I had another woman?"

Mac opened his mouth, but the question didn't want to come out. "Do you think my mother's gay?"

"Heavens no," Albie said, amused. "She's just so sure nobody could actually love her that she's terrified about one of us loving someone else."

Mac took another drink of soda and stared at the TV. "Why is it so hard for her to want to be happy?"

"Happiness is like a helium balloon," Albie answered. "It's great fun when you have hold of it, but you never get to keep it for long. We all learn that the hard way. For some people it deflates slowly and they have time to adjust to the loss. But for other people it gets whipped away by the wind in a way that hurts so badly they don't want to risk grabbing for it again. There's no right or wrong to it."

"So what am I supposed to tell Mom? I mean about you and Sakura. I don't want to lie."

"Of course not," Albie agreed. "So if she happens to ask, 'Do you think Albie's special someone is a woman?' you should say, why as a matter of fact, she is."

Mac shot her a look. "She's not going to ask that."

"Well then," Albie got up and stretched, "we don't have a problem, do we?"

ɾ   ɾ   ɾ

Vee and Maggie found themselves trying to think of something interesting to do on New Years Eve, since they never got beyond planning to spend it together. In an ill-considered compromise, they finally decided to walk around town and see who was at First Night. They ran into people they knew volunteering at various events, but even JD was too busy to pay attention to them. In desperation, when midnight approached they went to watch the Locals Only Comedy Line-up in the auditorium of St. Agnes'. This was listed on the program as 'The Ultimate First Night Event'. It wasn't until they were seated in the back of the room that they figured out this was one of those cases where ultimate meant last. Since it would just be too pitiful to go home before twelve, they decided to stick it out. Vee's cell phone rang and she stepped outside to answer in gratitude, even though she didn't recognize the number.

"Vidalia?" The voice on the other end didn't wait for her to speak.

"You call me that just to piss me off."

"Of course," Albie answered. "Happy New Year."

"You called to wish me a Happy New Year?"

"Don't be silly. We may have a situation."

"Is Mac okay?"

"Not that kind of situation, thank goodness. This is potentially of a pleasant nature."

"More pleasant than you moving halfway around the world?"

"It seems MacDonald has seen hints of the possibility for a liaison between his mother and your police chief."

Vee snorted. "Unless MacDonald's got some other mother I don't know about, I want some of what you're drinking."

"I trust his judgment," Albie said. "Your job is to wise her up."

Vee finished the call and went back into the auditorium. She caught Maggie's eye and waved her over. "Let's go," she whispered. "We need to do something to salvage this night."

Maggie looked at her. "You think there's still a bingo game going somewhere?"

"You are a sorry excuse for an SWF."

"Just in case I wasn't painfully aware of that," Maggie sighed, "the fact that I'm here with you on New Years Eve might be a big clue."

"I got it!" Vee snapped her fingers. "Why don't we invite JD back to your place for drinks when he gets off duty?"

"Was I supposed to think that was spontaneous?" Maggie asked. "Because it was so incredibly lame you could be up there on stage with the comedian."

"What do you have against JD?" Vee demanded. "Don't you think he's cute?"

"Cute?" Maggie asked. "Cute implies harmless."

"Don't you ever wonder why he's so mysterious? We could get him drunk and see what we can find out about him."

"We already know stuff," Maggie said. "Like that he's from the South."

Vee looked at her suspiciously. "Do you have proof?"

"He married his sister, didn't he?"

"Accidental sisters don't count," Vee insisted.

"Fine," Maggie finally gave in. "Even sober he's more fun than we're having here."

☙ ☙ ☙

The last thing Maggie remembered was going into the den to rest for a minute. The next thing she knew, Vee was complaining loudly to someone and trying to wake her up. She thought she heard JD's voice. When Maggie sat up, not quite awake, she was alone. She could hear Vee and JD in the kitchen. She stumbled in there. They were at the table, a bottle of Jack Daniels and two glasses between them.

"Well, look what the dog dragged in," Vee said.

"It's cat," Maggie crabbed at her. "Look what the *cat* dragged in."

"Cats usually drag in something that's still alive. Dogs, on the other hand, drag in dead bunnies and old shoes and all kinds of crap."

"Happy New Year," JD said, nodding toward the clock. It was somewhere past 2 AM.

"Yup," Maggie replied, pulling out a chair and flopping down.

"I think our friend needs to join the game," he said to Vee.

"What game?" Maggie asked.

Vee got up and went to the cabinet for another glass. "We're playing 'No Shit'."

Maggie made a face. "Pass."

"You don't even know what it is," Vee protested.

Maggie pointed to the bottle on the table. "I know I don't drink whiskey."

"Not a problem," JD said brightly. "You're allowed the poison of your choice."

Vee opened the freezer. "All you got in here is flavored stuff. Real women do not drink flavored vodka."

"That could be true," JD said. "Madame Yaskagya loves that stuff." He looked at Maggie. "You in or not?"

"Somebody tell me what's involved."

"You need to start with a loading dose," Vee said. She poured some pear vodka into Maggie's glass. "Drink this and be quiet. It was my turn when you so rudely interrupted." She splashed a generous shot of Jack Daniels into JD's glass.

"Yours too," he insisted.

She shrugged and poured some for herself. "Bottoms up," she ordered.

"That's not how it goes," JD objected.

"It's my game," Vee said. "I say how it goes."

"That's not a game," Maggie pointed out. "That's the same as real life."

JD threw back his whiskey and held out his glass. "Fill 'er up. Sometimes I make my own rules, too."

"No shit," Vee began, "I am a southern boy."

JD nodded. "I suppose you could say that. I was born in Kentucky."

"Kentucky?" Maggie said incredulously.

"What's so amazing about Kentucky?" he asked.

Vee held her hand out toward Maggie. "Pay up," she demanded.

JD looked from one to the other. "You two had money on this?"

"How come you don't have an accent?" Maggie asked.

"I didn't say I was *from* Kentucky," JD pointed out. "I just said I was born there."

Maggie made an obnoxious game show buzzer noise. "Wrong answer. That would be like me saying I was French just because I was born in Paris."

"You were?" Vee asked.

"No, of course not," Maggie said impatiently. "I was making a point."

"Actually, you would be French if you were born there," JD said.

"But I grew up in America. So even if I was French, it wouldn't count," Maggie insisted.

"I grew up in western Maryland."

Vee made a triumphant noise.

"That is *not* the South," Maggie said.

"I beg to differ," JD said. "It's below the Mason-Dixon line."

Maggie looked at them. "I bet you two fixed this up so you could split the winnings."

JD turned to Vee. "How much are the winnings?"

"Five bucks," she said. "And you're not getting half."

"Madame," JD said, "you insult me."

Maggie rolled her eyes. "Took you long enough to figure that out."

"Another round!" Vee declared, and refilled their glasses.

"I don't want any more," Maggie groaned.

"I don't need any more either," JD agreed.

"First one to finish gets to ask me a question," Vee said.

"I get to ask you questions all the time," Maggie pointed out.

"This time I'll tell the truth."

"What if there's nothing I want to know?"

"I got one," JD said. "You ever been married?"

"Drink up!" Vee commanded. He downed his whiskey. "Nope. Never been married."

"Had a serious boyfriend?"

"You aren't following the rules!" Vee protested.

"Have you?"

"Damn, you're persistent," Vee said. She poured him more whiskey.

"I can't drink all that," he complained. "I'll puke."

"The price of wisdom," Maggie said. JD threw back the whiskey and gagged a little. "That was very unmanly," Maggie pointed out.

"So have you?" He coughed. "Had a serious boyfriend?"

"Yes," Vee snapped indignantly.

"You ever think about getting married?"

"Let me clarify something for you," Vee said. "Whoever said the mass of men lead lives of quiet desperation was a man *and* a fool."

"I think that might be redundant," Maggie said. JD gave her an evil look.

Vee ignored them both. "The mass of men lead lives of *noisy* desperation. Always whining and moaning about how *bad* they got it and how life never treats them *fair* and nothing is ever their fault. They're always halfway pissed off about something and watch out if you don't laugh at their stupid jokes. What do I need that for? Put up all day with a mess of dumb-ass students and shit-for-brains administrators and then have to listen to that? People say all men want is sex, but you take any man over thirty, he just thinks sex is a time-out from talking about himself. When a woman gets married, she shouldn't even bother with a dress, she should just buy herself a ginormous earring, cause all she's doing is agreeing to spend the rest of her life as one big ear."

"Thanks for clearing that up," JD said.

"You're welcome," she snapped.

"So Miss Maggie May," JD began.

Maggie looked at him with disbelief. "You're drunk."

"Yes, Ma'am, I believe I am."

"No shit," Maggie said. "JD stands for . . ."

"Take a drink!" Vee scolded.

Maggie screwed up her face and slugged back the remaining vodka in her glass. For a minute it felt like every inch of guts between her belly button and her neck was struggling to take flight. The pain gradually passed, her eyes watered a bit, and then she felt a nice warm buzz.

"Ah," JD said pleasantly. "Looks like she's going to survive."

"I think my insides just turned to sea cucumber."

"Ask your question," Vee commanded.

"No, shit, I call myself JD because . . ."

JD turned to Vee. "Ump, that's not a question."

"Just shut up and tell her what JD stands for," Vee demanded.

"If I shut up, I can't tell her anything."

"You, sir, are prevaricating," Maggie said sternly.

"True enough," he admitted, and took a long swig straight from the bottle.

"Cut that out!" Maggie said. "You are not allowed to die of alcohol poisoning on my property."

"Pass," he gasped.

"I know!" Vee said triumphantly. "John Doe!"

"Good guess," he said, "but no."

"James Dean?" Maggie asked. He shook his head. Maggie pointed at the bottle of whiskey. "Jack Daniels!" she said, full of glee. JD grinned at her wickedly.

"Okay, okay!" Vee exclaimed. "I've got one!" Maggie and JD both looked at her glass. She chugged some whiskey like a trooper, then took a deep breath. "No shit, I grew up . . ."

"You already know where I grew up," JD pointed out. "I just told you."

"I haven't grown up yet," Maggie said.

Vee reached over and poured a substantial amount of vodka into Maggie's glass. "Required procedure," she said.

Maggie looked at her balefully and took a drink. She began coughing. JD reached over and thumped her back. She shoved his arm away. "Cut it out," she gasped. "You're compromising my dignity."

"So why would you rather die than say where you grew up?" JD asked.

Maggie wiped her eyes with the back of her hand. Her face went blank. "I grew up here," she said without looking at either of them. "In this house. There was no garage then. And where my bedroom is now, there was a screen porch. I used to sleep out there in the summer." The room was suddenly very quiet. "Somebody say something."

"We need a toast!" JD said.

Maggie raised her glass. "To an unpredictable, remarkable new year!" She and Vee clicked their glasses and drank.

"Hey," Vee said to JD, "you're not drinking."

"I don't like that toast," he said churlishly.

"You make one then," Maggie said.

He thought about it so long it started to look like he'd forgotten what he was trying to do. "I know," he finally said. "To the randomness of events."

"That's a stupid toast," Maggie said. They all clinked glasses and drank again. "That's it," Maggie said. "I quit."

"You can't quit," JD protested. "A person can only quit when they're winning." He looked at Vee for confirmation.

"I can quit whenever I want," Maggie said. "This is my house."

"That kind of attitude makes you a bad hostess," JD pointed out.

"If you don't like it, you can leave," she offered.

"That's rude."

"You're rude," Maggie said. "And bossy."

JD stood up. "Here we go again. I'm outta here."

"Let me help you with your jacket," Maggie said. She picked it up off the back of his chair and held it for him. He nearly fell over trying to put his arm into the left sleeve. "How about we call someone to take you home?" Maggie asked.

"I'm fine," he said roughly. "I can make it on my own." He stumbled out of the kitchen.

They stood and watched him weave his way to the front door and then struggle to close it behind him. "I should call the station and have somebody pick him up," Vee said.

"Nah," Maggie said. "Let's bet how far he gets before he falls over."

Vee looked at her. "You are a cold woman."

"It's like an experiment. We can see if his blood alcohol level is high enough to act like antifreeze." They went to the living room window to watch his progress toward the street.

"I really think I better call somebody before he tries to drive," Vee said.

Maggie held up her hand. JD's keys were dangling from it. "Somehow these seem to have fallen out of his jacket pocket," she said.

"Look," Vee said, pointing out the window. "He's walking right past his car. Well, tripping past it." She pointed to the keys in Maggie's hand. "You got his house key on there?"

Maggie looked, trying to focus her eyes. "Could be," she replied with difficulty.

"He'll get mighty cold by morning," Vee said.

"Okay," Maggie sighed. "Call the station."

"I got a better idea," Vee said. She took out her phone.

"Who you calling?" Maggie asked.

Vee smiled. "Gamey. Runt's finally going to be good for something." Maggie could hear him yelling as soon as he answered. "Happy New Year," Vee interrupted. "Hey!" she yelled back. "Don't try that crap on me!" She listened for a moment. "Yeah?" she asked. "Well, you know what you get when an elephant shits out a mouse?" She hung up.

"Wait a minute," Maggie said. "You didn't ask him to do something about JD."

"Oh, yeah." Vee called back. "Go look out your window," she said, before Gamey could get started. There was a pause. "Yeah, that's him." She listened again. "Nothing. He did it all to himself." Another pause. "Yeah, that would be a good idea. We got his house keys if you need them." Pause. "He did not give her one! They're just on the same ring as his car keys." Pause. "Okay, then." She closed her phone. "Not our problem anymore."

r   r   r

Gamey pulled his car out of the alley, cursing. JD had made it a little over a block. He was still upright, but wobbling badly. In the few seconds it took Gamey to pull up next to him, he tripped twice. Gamey lowered the passenger side window and yelled. It took three tries before JD noticed the car moving slowly along next to him. "Evening," he said, with exaggerated sobriety. "Happy New Year."

"Get in the car," Gamey snarled.

JD leaned halfway through the open window. It was hard to imagine what was keeping him from falling the rest of the way in. "That's okay," he said, with a loving, beagle-eyed stare. "Doing just fine walking."

"Do me a favor," Gamey said, "and get in the car."

"No, no," JD insisted. "I wouldn't want to impose. You just go on about your business." He managed to extricate himself and stand up straight.

"Hey, asshole!" Gamey yelled. "What business you think I got out here in the cold at freakin' 4 AM? Get in the goddamn car!"

"Oh," JD said. "Okay." He messed up his first few tries at opening the door, then fell in, ending up in a heap on the front seat.

"Close the door," Gamey said impatiently. JD smiled at him sweetly and complied.

By the time they got the few blocks to JD's house, he was snoring oafishly, his head lolling against the back of his seat. Gamey managed to rouse him enough to get him into the house and up to his bedroom. He made a half-hearted attempt to put the big guy to bed, taking off his jacket and shoes, then gave up and left him on top the comforter.

On his way home Gamey thought better of just ditching JD. He wanted nothing more than to get back to the warmth of his own bed, but somebody should keep an eye on the big guy. It only took him a minute to figure out who. He pulled out his cell phone and called Martha. Everybody knew she got up early, but he sure as hell hoped this call wasn't the thing that woke her. She was plenty of bitch even when she got enough sleep to be jolly.

She answered on the second ring. "Do you know what time it is?" she demanded. "This better be damn important."

"I think we got a problem," Gamey said. "Our boy's been zapped by the pheromone wand." He answered Martha's questions with great patience, feeling generous now that he was off the hook.

31

Martha didn't see a need to rush right over to JD's. From the sound of things, he'd be a mess all day. She made a batch of biscuits and sawmill gravy, fried some bacon, and filled a big thermos with coffee. The coffee was not for JD. Even in his temporarily disabled state, he would never agree to drink coffee that had not been brewed to his specifications. She planned to stop at Maggie's when she finished with JD, and it was a safe assumption that any coffee she found there wouldn't be worth drinking.

She loaded everything into her car and set off, detouring so she could go through town to savor the cold, rosy quiet of early morning. There was something to be said for the pagan ritual of celebrating the turning-of-the-year, for believing, however briefly, in the purity and freshness of starting anew. Martha imagined the world momentarily holding its breath, taking a little rest before plunging back into the maelstrom of daily things. As if in complicity, nothing moved on the streets.

She parked in JD's driveway. His back door was unlocked, so she went in, banging it closed loudly behind her. She wanted to give him some warning in case he was lying around somewhere without clothes on. It was way too cold for that, but given Gamey's description of his state she wasn't taking anything for granted.

She was walking toward his front stairs when she heard the groaning. She doubled back and went into the short hallway that connected his kitchen and dining room. The powder room door was ajar. The lower half of one leg and a bare foot were sticking out. To Martha's relief, the leg was clad in jeans. She looked inside. JD was splayed out on the floor as if he'd been flung there by an angry giant. He had one arm over his face. "Go away," he whispered. "You smell like food."

"Quit moaning," Martha ordered. "A little bird told me you might be worshiping at the porcelain throne this morning. I brought you aspirin and greasy breakfast."

"Can't," he groaned.

"Nonsense," she said. "But first let's get you up off the floor." She climbed over him and wet a washcloth with cool water, then put it on his forehead. "Give that a few minutes."

"Ow," he said feebly.

"Cut it out or I'll have to throw you in the shower. You take any aspirin yet?"

"Won't help. Not that kind of pain."

"What hurts?"

"She's in my head," he moaned softly.

It took a minute for the words to sink in. "Oh, honey," Martha said, her voice full of concern, "we need to talk."

🐦 🐦 🐦

Maggie was on the living room couch closest to the front window. She let Vee have the couch in the darker part of the room. She wished Vee would give her credit for that, but she wished more that she would pass out. Everything hurt. She readjusted the bag of ice on her head. "Dying," she croaked.

For a while after that she was blissfully unaware, until someone slammed the kitchen door as they came into the house. She might have been too hung over to care, except that whoever it was brought a smell with them. It was normally a good smell, but today it was nauseating. "The world smells like pooh," Maggie whined.

"Bacon." It was Martha's voice. "I brought you girls greasy breakfast."

"Don't want any," Vee mumbled.

Martha stormed into Maggie's line of sight. "Get up," she commanded. "Time to eat."

"What are you doing here?" Vee sounded kind of alert.

Martha's voice was angry. "Gamey told me what happened last night."

"I'm not hungry," Maggie moaned. "I just want to die."

"Later," Vee said shortly. "Keep it down," she said to Martha. "She's got the spins."

"I am really disappointed in the two of you." Martha was full of reproach. "Aren't you a little old to be making this kind of mess out of yourselves?"

"Go away," Maggie said ineffectually.

"Sit up," Martha said. "Breakfast time."

"If I projectile vomit, may I be excused?" Vee asked.

Through the slit of one eye Maggie watched Martha put a gaily colored runner on the coffee table. She opened her picnic hamper, which had a decidedly evil aspect, and began laying out breakfast with annoying efficiency. Maggie turned her face to the sofa. Everything made noise as Martha set it out—clicking cutlery, plastic lids unvacuuming off tubs, paper plates being judgmentally slapped on the table. "Rise and shine," Martha called, way too loud.

"You can't use that word around me," Vee protested weakly.

"Oh, cut the crap," Martha replied. "If I was in the mood to insult you, I'd have plenty of ammunition without resorting to dated racial slurs."

Maggie exerted some energy to try and sit up. It was useless. The few inches she managed to lift her head felt precipitous. She eased herself back down with extreme caution.

"Here." Martha held a piece of bacon under Maggie's nose. "Open your mouth. Salt and fat. Best thing for a hangover."

"What about me?" Vee demanded. "Don't I get breakfast in bed?"

"You," Martha turned to her, "are sitting up. Something tells me you are not nearly as hung over as our friend here."

Vee grinned. "You bring any Bloody Marys?"

"How about you come in the kitchen and help me find some mugs?"

"Tell me you brought coffee," Vee said. Martha reached into her basket and pulled out the thermos. "If you got a masseuse in there, I just might have to marry you."

Martha motioned toward the kitchen with her head. "Come on."

Vee followed her and stood aside as she slammed through the motions of pouring coffee. "What crawled up your butt and died?" she finally asked.

"What are you doing, Vee?" Martha's tone, like bad wine, had an aftertaste.

"About what?"

"Why is it they're both sick as dogs and you're bright as the first crocus of spring?"

"They," Vee said thoughtfully. "You mean Maggie and Jack Daniels?" Martha just stared at her. "I fraternize with college students. I happen to be wise to the ways of stupid drinking games."

"Wise enough to suggest them."

"Sue me," Vee said, opening the fridge and fruitlessly looking for something to drink.

"Back off," Martha said, her voice as hard as stone. "You don't know what you're screwing around with."

Vee slammed the refrigerator shut. "Why don't you tell me?"

"Which one do you care about?"

"What kind of crappy ass question is that? I care about them both."

Martha circled her to get to the sink. "I don't think so," she finally said, looking at Vee like she was throwing down a dare.

"What kind of bullshit is that?" Vee didn't wait for an answer before turning her back and resuming her hunt through the fridge.

"Look," Martha said, "just don't mess with them, okay?"

Vee closed the refrigerator a second time, and stood staring at Martha, her hand on her hip. "Would it be a crime if they discovered they liked each other?" she finally asked.

"No," Martha said. "But it could very well be a tragedy."

"Oh, stop," Vee sighed. "It's too early in the day for melodrama."

"Vee, can you just take my word that this is a lot more complicated than you realize?"

"No," Vee said simply. "She is my friend. He is my friend. They are both alone and lonely. Where is the harm in cutting down the brush so they can see the path between them?"

"What if they're alone and happier that way?"

"Open your eyes," Vee snapped. "Which one of them do you think is the happy one?"

"It's just not your version of happy."

"How do you know my version of happy?" Vee asked angrily. "When did you ever doubt your own superiority enough to ask?"

Martha jabbed her finger into the air between them. "You have no idea what you're messing with. She's better off the way she is."

"Why?" Vee asked. "So she can dry up into an old prune? Like I'm gonna do? Like you almost did before Daniel came along and put a little juice in you?"

"Leave him out of it."

"Who, Daniel?" Vee was confused.

"JD."

Vee's eyes narrowed. "That's the real problem, isn't it? We're playing with your boyfriend. Who'd he have before she came to town? Just me and his secret stash of nookie. No competition for you. But pinecone wreaths and chocolate chip cookies don't give you much of an advantage over a real woman, do they?"

"Forget it," Martha said. "You don't understand."

"I'm inviting you to help me understand. My guess is that's not happening because you don't have a real answer."

"I've got all the answers," Martha said angrily. "It's just none of your damn business."

"Go screw with somebody else," Vee said, walking over to finish fixing the coffee. "Better yet, go screw yourself."

"You are not the only one who cares about her," Martha hissed as she pushed past Vee and flung open the kitchen door. "If you believe nothing else, believe that."

Vee watched Martha disappear around the corner of the garage before she closed the door, very quietly. She stalled a few minutes before bringing the coffee into the other room so her hands had a chance to stop shaking. Nothing like a good strong adrenaline rush, she thought, to clear out the last cobwebs of a hangover.

Maggie struggled to sit up when she saw Vee. "Where's my Bloody Mary?" she asked.

"Far as I can tell," Vee said, "she got on her broom and left."

32

January second was always a letdown as far as Maggie was concerned. Even when New Year's day was nothing special, January second managed to be less. This year it dawned rainy and cold. Mac wouldn't be home from New York until dinnertime, so it was the perfect day to get lost in an easy read, something with large type and lots of dialogue. In her previous life, Maggie only ever read meaningful things that expanded her horizons. Now every trip to Dooley Books was an adventure.

She parked behind the bookstore and went in the back door. A new Maurice Sendak book caught her eye in the Children's Section. When Mac was a toddler she thought Sendak's monsters would frighten him. Albie brought the books home anyway. They were Mac's favorites, as if he already knew life would be full of lurking things.

As she got near the front of the store she saw JD at the magazine rack, and her blood pressure went up. Vee hinted that the reason she was upset had something to do with him. It had to be his damn nosiness again. Maggie stalked across the store, determined to tell him off.

He looked up at the last minute. "Hello," he said pleasantly. Maggie glared at him. JD looked over his shoulder, as if that look couldn't be for him. "Have I offended you?" he asked.

"I am not a suitable topic for your curiosity." She enunciated each word.

JD was startled by her intensity. "Can we go somewhere and talk about whatever's bothering you?"

"You've already done enough talking. Especially where I'm concerned."

"I think your reaction is a little out of proportion. I asked Martha a few questions about your background. I'm sorry if it appears anybody betrayed any confidences."

"Why do you care about my background?"

"I was curious why you left town all by yourself when you were just a teenager. And then suddenly you show up again after all these years. I'd like to understand more about you."

"I'm not a crime scene," Maggie said. "Get over it." She started to walk away.

"Hey," he called, "Ms. Mystery."

When Maggie turned back, she was enraged. "I am not an object for you to ridicule."

"Whoa," he said, losing his smile. "Lighten up."

She strode over to him and grabbed the front of his shirt. "Do not . . ." she began.

JD spoke with cold authority. "Put your hand down." Maggie let go and started to turn away. "Hold it," JD said. "We're going to step outside now and have an adult conversation."

"I don't think so," Maggie said.

"You have just publicly assaulted a police offer. I am offering you an opportunity to resolve this situation before I take further action. You want to take advantage of that offer, walk outside now. If you choose not to, I will arrest you."

Maggie's heart was pounding. It had been a long time since she had disliked anyone as intensely as she disliked this man. "Arrest me," she said.

"You're a real piece of work, you know that?" JD shook his head and walked away.

"Wait a minute," she said to his back. "Tell me the truth. Why are you really so determined to find out about me?"

When he turned back toward her it was clear he was working hard to reduce the tension between them. "Come get a cup of coffee with me and I'll tell you."

"What's our basis?"

"I don't understand what you're asking."

"Cop and victim?"

"If you recall, I was the victim."

Maggie continued as if he hadn't interrupted. "Social worker and project? Confessor and penitent?"

"Friends?" he asked.

"No. We are definitely not friends."

"Fine," he said. "Satisfy my curiosity. Your secrets will be safe with me."

Maggie led the way out onto Main Street. Then she stopped. "Maybe this isn't such a good idea," she said.

"We're just having coffee. Look," he opened his jacket, "I'm unarmed."

"Fine," Maggie answered, and started up the hill toward the General Store.

"I do have a reason for some paranoia," JD offered. "I did a DMV check and there's no Maggie or Margaret Rifkin with a Pennsylvania driver's license."

"So?" she said.

"So you obviously have a driver's license. It must be in some other name." Maggie didn't answer. "You don't think that's a big red flag that you're hiding something?"

"That's melodramatic crap," Maggie said. "What do you really want?"

JD stopped walking and looked at her. His breath formed little clouds. "What are you so afraid of?" he asked gently.

"The pain of human contact. There. Now you feel better?"

"Okay," he continued. "Then this town's not big enough for the two of us."

That finally made her smile. "Can we just go to the General Store and have a cup of coffee?" she asked.

"Sure," he said. "But Dutch. That way, you won't feel entitled to demand anything from me later."

Lola/Mercedes looked up as they walked in. JD gestured at a door behind the counter and she nodded. He led Maggie into a small room, barely large enough to hold the table and chairs that were in there. "So," Maggie asked, "where's the rubber hose?"

JD pulled out a chair for her. Maggie took off her jacket and sat while Lola/Mercedes brought them coffee. Nobody said anything. Maggie had that same feeling she used to get in Mother Superior's office, wondering how to maintain her impudence while staying just this side of the line. Lola/Mercedes left, closing the door.

JD spoke first. "I believe I owe you a secret from our game the other night."

"You don't owe me anything."

He pulled out his wallet. Maggie watched while he slipped out a plastic card and flipped it across the table to her. She looked down at it. "Your driver's license?"

"Take a good look at it."

She picked it up. It had JD's picture, but the name on it was Thomas Charles. "Your name is Thomas? So why make such a big deal about JD, if it's just a nickname?"

"Because once I made a secret out of it, it took on a life of its own. You want to know what it stands for?"

"Now that I'm sober, I'm not sure it makes a difference."

"It was the designation assigned to me by Family Services."

Maggie thought about this. "Are you telling me it stands for juvenile delinquent?"

"Yup."

"And were you?"

"Yup."

"How bad?"

"Bad enough to get sent away."

Maggie considered this. "That doesn't tell me very much. What did you do?"

"I set my house on fire."

"Okay," Maggie said, "I'm hooked."

"When I was nine years old. With my father inside. It was just the two of us. My mother split when I was little. No doubt him being a mean son-of-a-bitch had something to do with that, but I'm willing to guess he got worse once she deserted us. Even when he was sober he'd beat me and bust things up just because he felt like it. One night he came home falling down drunk and threw me into a wall, and that's when I decided to do it. I figured it would be just like TV. I'd already almost done it once by accident, back when I started smoking. I used to snag his old butts and then hide in the basement and smoke."

"You started smoking when you were nine?" Maggie asked in disbelief.

"Eight." JD corrected her. "The time I almost set the house on fire by accident, I thought the match was out and I tossed it into the bucket next to the dryer, where we threw out the lint. The whole thing went up in flames, like that." He snapped his fingers.

"What did you do?"

"Nothing. I didn't *know* what to do. Luckily, it was a metal bucket and there wasn't much in there. It burned itself out. But it gave me the idea. I started saving lint, thinking about when I would do it. Not if, when." Maggie said nothing. "Every time he beat me up, I thought about it. And then finally, the night came that I had enough. It wasn't even a particularly bad beating, I'd just had enough. So I waited for him to go to sleep. I was planning to put all that saved lint under his bed. I imagined the flames engulfing the bed, taking him away forever. That's the thing about kids and death, you know? It isn't real for them. It means going away forever, but forever is just until somebody wishes you back again.

"But then the time came to do it and I couldn't. I was too afraid. I used to go into his room all the time when he was sleeping off a drunk to steal his change. I knew how not to make a sound. But this time was different. What if he woke up and caught me?"

"What happened?" Maggie asked quietly.

"I piled up the lint in his doorway. I put three matches on it, just to be sure. And then I ran outside. It seemed like forever, but finally I saw the smoke and flames through his bedroom window. And then I heard the fire truck. I heard it for a long time, getting louder and louder."

"And you didn't run away?"

"I was rooted to the spot."

Maggie looked out the window at the parking lot full of dirty, trampled snow. She took a deep breath and looked JD squarely in the eye. "Did he die?"

JD shook his head. "He woke up. He was the one who called the fire department. He got some second-degree burns trying to put it out before they got there. And mild smoke inhalation."

"And he turned you in?"

JD made a rueful face. "One of the firemen came over and told me how lucky I was, that my father was going to be okay. At that point the firemen assumed it started from smoking in bed. But he always caught me sooner or later, so I was sure it would just be a matter of time before he figured out what really happened. I was afraid of what he'd do. So I told the guy the truth, that I started the fire because I wanted to kill my father. I figured they'd ask me why and after I explained they'd take me somewhere he couldn't get me."

"And they didn't?"

"In a sense they did. Those small towns on the far edge of nowhere, there are still people who believe a good beating is not only warranted now and then, it's what turns a boy into a man. In their minds, what I did was a sign I needed a stronger hand than his. So they put me in juvie. I was safe from him there, just not from much else. That's where I learned how to be good at being violent, to put all those skills he taught me to good use."

"And then Rebekah's father helped you find redemption." She could see from the split second of displeasure on his face that she had gotten to him. And still he persisted.

"That's one way to characterize it. Nobody ever checked if I was up to date on my shots. These are people who wouldn't buy livestock or take in a stray dog without checking on that. But an unwanted kid? Nobody cared. So I ended up with a bad case of measles, almost died. Rev was the chaplain. He came to see me every day in the hospital. When I pulled through he convinced them to let him take me home until I recovered. I'm sure he made a convincing plea about it being a last-ditch effort to save my soul or something like that. Nobody minded when he asked to make it a permanent arrangement."

"You must have been grateful."

"I was terrified. I couldn't imagine the burden of obligation that would come from letting people be nice to me all the time. How was I not going to mess it up? What would they expect when the time came to collect?"

Maggie nodded. She knew exactly what he was talking about. "And your father never raised any objections to any of this?"

JD shook his head. "He's dead. Rev made sure of that for me. He believed I'd never be able to heal unless I knew."

There was a long silence, long enough to become uncomfortable, except there was no tension. Finally, Maggie spoke. "So how does a child criminal get to be a police chief?"

"After Rev and Helen took me in, I stayed out of trouble. When I turned eighteen, Rev helped me get the record expunged."

"How can you not worry someone's going to find out and use it against you?"

JD smiled. "Anybody who might care already knows. I told them when I interviewed for the job."

Maggie finished her coffee. "I appreciate you taking me into your confidence. But I think I should get going now."

"You don't need to be afraid," he said.

"I'm not *afraid* of anything. Good for you that you found a way to make things simple."

"They're never simple," JD said. "Talking about it is just one way to make sure I never have to live on that edge again."

"But we didn't come here to talk about you, did we?"

JD took a sip of coffee. "That's completely your choice."

Suddenly, Maggie had an urgent question. "Did you ever get to ask your mother why she left you with him?"

"I never saw her again. She died while I was in juvie."

Maggie felt a grief she did not understand. "Did you at least get to go to her funeral?"

"I didn't know about it at the time. But it's not like it would have mattered to me. I barely remembered her. After living with Rev, I came to understand I was part of the underbelly of kids who get made by accident or out of sheer stupidity. She left me there because she didn't want me. Nobody wants those kids enough to show them even the rudimentary things they need to get by in life. So they make a mess of things trying to figure it out for themselves."

"And you decided to fix that when you grew up."

"It wasn't a conscious decision. Part of getting better is looking for some way to fix what's broken. The struggle to understand the rules is also a struggle to change them."

They sat in silence for a while. "Why keep the nickname?" Maggie asked. "It's almost like a pretense now."

"It reminds me of where I came from, that I faced it down and it lost its power."

"And how does this all translate into your curiosity about me?"

"It's not just curiosity. I see something in you that's reaching out for help."

"Really?" Maggie was almost amused. "Help with what?"

"You left town for reasons nobody will talk about. But you weren't a runaway. What could you have done that was so bad your parents felt they had to send you away like that?"

Maggie stared at him. Something had gone hard in her. "Not my parents. My father. My mother tried her own method of getting rid of me first. She put a gun to my head. Right here." She put her finger on her forehead, just above the bridge of her nose. JD's face went momentarily blank, as if the image inside his own head was more than he could stand to watch.

"She kept shouting at me to tell her the truth. The truth about what? I didn't know what she meant. But I was too afraid to ask. Then she started to spin the chamber on the gun and screamed crazy stuff at me. Part of me wanted to beg her, please don't kill me, please. But I knew she was nuts. Anything I said might make her do it. So I just stood there, trying not to breathe, not to move. It felt like forever. She was yelling about how he would never get the baby, that I was not going to help him get the baby, that she knew what I was doing. And then she cocked the trigger."

JD inhaled sharply. "I'm sorry," he said quietly.

Maggie was like a statue. "She was holding my arm, squeezing it really hard. She said this was my last chance to tell her the truth about him." She paused. "I couldn't even think about that, not while she had the gun in my face. But I knew the rumors. I'm sure he believed he was being discreet, but everywhere I went it felt like people were just waiting for me to leave so they could start talking. If it was that humiliating for me, imagine what it must have been like for her, on top of being crazy. And she was screaming at me, tell me the truth before I kill you. Those were her exact words. *Before* I kill you. Except, of course, she already knew the truth. She didn't want the truth, she wanted someone to punish." Maggie stopped and looked out the window again.

"I'm sorry," JD said. "How did you get away from her?"

"Doc walked in. Neither of us heard him coming, and he startled us. She turned the gun on him. As time would prove, that's who she really wanted to shoot all along. He hit her. Hard. And then he took the gun away from her. She was lying on the floor and laughing."

"I'm sorry," JD said again.

Maggie's voice was flat. "The world is full of people who have been through worse."

"Was the gun loaded?" JD asked.

"When Doc opened it there were five bullets and one empty chamber. She was playing her version of Russian roulette. Doc put me in the car and dumped me with Daniel with instructions as to how to get rid of me properly."

Her words hung in the air, covering everything with a fine frost. "Did you tell Daniel what happened?" JD asked.

Maggie's eyes bored into his, full of challenge. "Don't make it my fault."

"That's not what I meant," he said. "I'm sorry. It was a stupid question. I know that the first thing, sometimes the only thing, a child in that situation is taught is that they can't ever tell."

"I think what you fail to comprehend is that just because telling works for you doesn't make it the only solution. Some of us do just fine looking forward instead of looking back."

"You can't think about the future, or even the present, if there's a monster chasing you."

"You can once you know the monster will never catch you. I have a present and a future now, with my son. He's not part of that past unless someone brings him into it. I want to be clear that that's the reason I don't share my story. It would hurt him. He is never to know."

"You have my word."

"So now you answer my question," Maggie said. "What is the fascination?"

"Abused children are like vampires," JD answered. "We walk among the living, acting like them, and they fall for it. They don't actually see us, who we really are, even when they perceive that we're different. But when we encounter each other something resonates between us. If we can succeed in not killing each other, we can become friends of the soul."

She looked at him directly for a long time. "You are naive," she finally said. "You have no clue what you're asking for. We'd never survive." She stood up, took her jacket off the back of her chair, and left.

33

Once the holidays were over, there was an expectation, unvoiced but still pervasive, that the Boring Season had arrived. People focused on paying down their Christmas debt. When they did go out, it was only to rush through their errands, their moods as unpleasant as the weather. Common wisdom said this was the worst time of year to open a new business. But common wisdom never interfered with Madame Yaskagya's plans. She took advantage of the slow real estate market to quietly purchase a vacant storefront on Main Street. With so little foot traffic in town, most people weren't even aware something was going on behind the windows covered in white paper.

Madame kept a low profile. She worked as her own general contractor, driving to Northeast Philly to find other Russian immigrants to do her renovations. She paid forty bucks a day plus enough vodka to keep the men warm. She considered this a fair deal since nobody expected more than half a day's work out of men raised in Communist Russia, no matter how many hours they were on the job. Things were nearly complete before people figured out that whatever was going on involved Madame Yaskagya and her happy little band of baked goods.

When they did figure it out, though, the uproar was instantaneous. The locals were up in arms about the blight getting established right there in the center of town. What they didn't know was that Madame was going straight. She had a business plan, an accountant, and all the necessary permits. She treated her critics as petty aggravation, ignoring them and thus making them even more desperate to know what she had in mind. This was exactly what Madame had planned. She knew nothing built interest like a little mystery. This was important, since her real plan would never generate the kind of excitement people were making for themselves.

After the fire in the Henhouse, her girls were at loose ends. Looking to make the most of their talents for improving on nature's gifts, they decided cosmetology school was the perfect career move. Plus, they liked the idea of being able to stick together. As graduation approached they became increasingly distressed about having to bust up the group. It was Peaches Cobbler who came up with the idea of asking Madame to bankroll a nail salon for them. The profit margins, compared with what Madame was used to, were nonexistent. But Madame saw potential in the makeover idea, so once they increased her cut of the profits, they had a deal. The truth was she was damn bored with retirement and delighted to have all her girls back under one roof.

For those who hadn't done so well with their studies, Madame kept part of the shop as retail space. Lemon Meringue sold hand-knit scarves and felted purses in vaguely suggestive shapes. Key Lime and Cranberry Fool, who remained hopelessly fixated on S&M, became dealers of Brighton accessories. The tasteful designs had broad customer appeal, while satisfying the girls' obsession with leather and metal.

When it came time to choose a name for the business, Madame let everyone make a suggestion even though she had already made up her mind. "Vill be Scheherazade," she declared when they were all done.

"Shuh-herra-who?" Lemon demanded.

"Scheherazade Dream Spa. Ve tell you how to be husband's fantasy." Some of the girls weren't sure they liked it, but that didn't matter. Madame was in charge again.

Madame threw a lavish party for their Grand Opening. A private visit to the editor of *The Daily Intellectual* resulted in a nice color picture of Madame and her girls in their new venue on the front page of the Saturday Living Section. "Is not great money like whoring," Madame was quoted as saying. "But voman come here looking like old you, guaranteed she leave looking like girl her husband used to spend golf money to have." They booked up weeks in advance.

Madame's public reappearance had an unforeseen side effect. The first sign of trouble was an anonymous letter to the editor that showed up in the *Intellectual* entitled "The Morale (sic) Dilemma." It outlined, in very poetic terms, the Chipmunk's taste for exotic women's clothing and related paraphernalia. Then it asked the pivotal question: Who allowed such a creature to become a cultural icon and role model for impressionable children? No distinction was made between the Chipmunk character and the man who wore the costume.

Things still might have blown over except for the incendiary poster that mysteriously appeared on bulletin boards and telephone poles all over town. It was a grainy black and white photo of the permanently grinning Chipmunk head, with the caption, "Would You Want This Man Giving Candy to *Your* Children?" Seizing upon this as a potentially rich campaign issue, Mayor Frank appointed an investigative commission. To his dismay, they uncovered the fact that town mascot was a political role, and that Mayor Frank had, in fact, given a certain generous contributor a lifetime appointment some years before. Seeking to avoid further negative publicity, Mayor Frank had his people quietly identify leadership for a grass roots campaign to **Impeach the Rodent**.

In a matter of days, the streets of Dooleysburg were peppered with young mothers, rosy-cheeked toddlers in tow, badgering people to sign recall petitions. Local PTA presidents rallied their memberships to do door-to-door canvassing. Carl Bendz personally called Mayor Frank to express his displeasure. Mayor Frank, the health of his campaign war chest never far from his mind, assured Bendz all he had to do was lay low and let the whole thing blow over.

But this was the kind of storm that offered unexpected opportunities. There were women in town who made a career of noble causes, so long as their good works didn't interfere with a busy schedule of shopping, decorator appointments and workouts. Regrettably, Lillian Bendz had more than once dismissed these women when they approached her to support some pet project. Now, with the blitzkrieg efficiency of a direct marketing campaign, they excited enough public outcry to get the impeachment hearing put on Town Council's agenda immediately.

ɾ   ɾ   ɾ

Martha steered the car up the ramp another level in the Courthouse Garage. Usually there was more than enough parking. Tonight, though, every spot was taken. She continued to the roof level and found one of the last open spaces.

"I didn't realize civic responsibility could generate this much enthusiasm," Maggie said.

"Of course you didn't," Martha answered. "Having spent your adult life in New York City, you probably didn't even realize you were an American citizen."

"What is it I'm supposed to do here?"

"For crying out loud," Martha said with irritation. "You're supposed to *watch*. Not everything you do has to be meaningful. This is entertainment."

"So as your date do I get a special treatment too, since Daniel's on Town Council?"

"If all goes as planned," Martha said cryptically.

Over the past few days the *Intellectual* had been full of assurances that The Chipmunk would receive a fair hearing, but even Maggie knew tonight would be his swansong. The grand three-story Courthouse lobby was packed. The crowd hummed with anticipation. Martha took Maggie's arm and pulled her along toward the hearing chamber. People they annoyed as they brushed past quickly plastered on cordial expressions when they saw Martha. "You're a popular lady," Maggie whispered.

"Nonsense," Martha said. "It's good to be feared."

"I thought that honor belonged to Lillian Bendz."

"Why do you think they're all here tonight? They get to see both of them toppled off their thrones." She chiseled their way to the chamber doors.

"Hey," some man said, "the room's full. We gotta wait out here for the decision."

"Thanks," Martha said, opening the door and hustling Maggie inside. A bailiff leaning against the wall moved slightly, then saw Martha and waved them on. The benches on both sides of the aisle were filled, but people in the front row made space for them. Town Council was already seated at a big table facing the audience. They were having an animated debate, but the mikes were off. It sounded like they were hissing at each other.

"How revolting," Martha said. "Carol Ann looks like Sharon Stone."

"I think Sharon Stone's very pretty."

"Not her face," Martha said. "Remind me to tell Daniel they need a skirt on the front of the table."

The Council president banged his gavel furiously, even though the crowd was already waiting for something to happen. "There is only one matter on tonight's agenda," his voice rang out in the silence. "An article of impeachment has been brought against our town mascot. We have come, over the years, to value and revere our Chipmunk, the furry symbol of Dooleysburg's mischievous and lovable nature . . ."

"This is an impeachment," someone yelled from the back of the chamber, "not a eulogy!"

"I'm giving the executive summary," the president snapped.

"A procedural issue, if I may," Daniel interrupted. Martha nudged Maggie. "Does anybody know if it's appropriate to impeach an appointed function? I believe impeachment is intended for elected officials."

"I second that motion," Carol Ann said rapidly. Several Council members exchanged puzzled glances.

Maggie leaned over. "Whose side is Daniel on?"

"He's got a soft spot for the Chipmunk," Martha said.

"He get hit on the head with a Jolly Rancher?"

"Two free oil changes," Martha whispered.

Maggie turned to look at her. "You're joking, right?"

"Grow up, would you?" Martha answered, still paying attention to the proceedings. "This is the Game of Life."

"I can't believe people I count as friends can be bought for $79.95," Maggie said. Martha ignored her.

Things moved rapidly after that. Someone checked the web for more information on impeachment, and they finally found a definition that said it was the act of smearing a person. Council voted that on this basis proceedings could continue. Carol Ann got up and left, claiming a conflict of interest. Maggie noticed that she gave Daniel a tiny pat on the shoulder on her way out. Finally it was time for The Chipmunk to testify. There were a few minutes of confusion before everyone realized The Chipmunk was not present.

Without the promise of a showdown the indignation in the room turned flabby. Only two women went up to the microphone when the public was invited to provide comments, and as soon as the first one started talking about the trauma to her impressionable children people began slipping out the room. Daniel checked his watch and interrupted the speaker to make a motion that the proceedings be postponed until they could find the defendant. The motion was seconded and the hearing was adjourned. A brief paragraph buried near the obituaries in the next day's *Intellectual* reported that The Chipmunk had resigned. If anyone knew there was more to his refusal to appear in public than just bad attitude, they were not talking.

34

When the reports started coming in, nobody was willing to believe them. Officer Mike took the first one on a Saturday. It was witching hour, that time of day between when the shops closed and the dinner rush began. In cold weather, this was a daily interlude of general insanity. People ran red lights. Pedestrians jaywalked with the caution of sheep. Parents parked strollers full of packages or more precious cargo on the sidewalk while they ran into The General Store for "just one second." Keys got locked in cars. Children called the fire department in hysteria because they had cooked without permission and set greasy hamburgers aflame. Elderly women became convinced the worst had befallen their meandering cats. So when the line from Dispatch rang, the guys in the squad room just looked at each other. They played a tough game of chicken. On the second ring, Walter said, "It's not my turn."

"Give it a try," Joe Butts urged. "Maybe it'll be something new and different."

"Hey, Mikey," Walter said, "I think your mother's calling."

"Yeah, get Mikey to try it," Joe Butts said. "He'll try anything."

"That kind of joke is why old age has a bad reputation," Walter complained.

"For chrissake," Mikey said, "the phone's still ringing."

"So pick it up," Joe Butts and Walter said, almost in unison.

Mikey sighed disgustedly. "Officer Graden," he said, picking up his phone. He pulled a pad closer and began writing. "Yes, ma'am," he said a few times.

Walter and Joe Butts exchanged glances. Mikey was getting that funny look on his face. This wasn't necessarily unusual, but it held the promise of something good. The call dragged on. Joe Butts started making 'wrap it up' gestures.

The line from Dispatch rang again. "Whatever," Walter said, and picked up. It was a fender bender. They didn't need a detective. He told Dispatch to send a patrol car. Mikey finally got off the phone just as Walter finished.

"Well?" Joe Butts demanded.

"Seems we got a wildlife situation."

"Call Animal Control."

"That's what I thought at first. The lady kept going on about a chipmunk. I thought maybe she had varmints or something. But when I suggested Animal Control she went off the deep end. Started yelling how I wasn't taking her seriously."

"Can't imagine why," Walter said.

"Turns out it's not that kind of wildlife," Mikey explained. "It was *The* Chipmunk."

"You talking about our disgraced Chipmunk?" Joe Butts asked.

"If this call was real we won't be the only ones calling him that."

"What's he doing, playing with somebody's nuts?" Joe Butts asked. He and Walter guffawed.

"Yeah," Mikey answered. "According to this lady, his own. She says her sixteen-year-old daughter was coming home from town with a couple of girlfriends, this guy in a trench coat and the Chipmunk head blows out of the graveyard by the old First Presbyterian Church, opens the coat and waves a greeting at them."

"Any identifiers?" Walter asked.

"Yeah." Mikey looked at him. "A chipmunk head and a limp canoodle."

"Could be half the guys in Dooleysburg," Joe Butts said.

"Hey, it's thirty-eight degrees out. That kind of cold, it could be all the guys in Dooleysburg," Walter pointed out.

"Sure," Mikey said. "Except for the chipmunk head."

"Yeah," Walter said. "Except for that."

"You think old man Bendz goes in for that kind of stuff?" Joe Butts asked.

"Well," Mikey said, "after the impeachment thing he faded pretty quick from the public eye. Could be hurting for attention."

"Somebody's going to have to go ask him," Walter replied. "It's not like there are a whole mess of those chipmunk heads floating around. That was kind of a unique hobby."

"Yeah," Mikey said. "Not to mention he's a perv. He's probably kinked up tighter than a corkscrew after three months without the Henhouse."

"Okay," Joe Butts said, picking up his jacket. "I'm on it." He went out back and fired up a cruiser. What the hell was wrong with Bendz, he wondered. The guy launches a flotilla of bribes around town to kill the Chipmunk impeachment, then he turns around and does something stupid like this?

Joe Butts pulled out of the parking lot and turned on his flashing lights. It was bad enough he had to drag himself out in the cold to fix this. He wasn't about to spend half the night sitting in traffic. Plus, he hardly ever got to use the sweet V-8s they put in these buggies. He could hardly bear to drive one, his foot itched so bad to tromp on the gas pedal.

When he got out near Bendz's dealership he turned on his siren as well. There was not a snowball's chance in hell Bendz was still there at this hour, so if Butts created a big enough ruckus his brother might have the sense to call Bendz at home and warn him Joe was on the way. That would give him time to run around and hide stuff if need be. After all, there was only so much favor even Butts could get away with.

The head salesman was waiting out front for him. "Officer Butts," he extended his hand. "We were just getting ready to close up. What can we do for you tonight?"

"Boss around?" Butts asked.

"Afraid not."

"What time did he leave today?"

"If you don't mind," the salesman said, "I'll just go find your brother. He'd be the best one to know." Joe Butts gave a curt nod. "You want to wait inside? There's no coffee, but at least you can stay warm."

"Nope. Thanks. Fine out here."

The salesman disappeared. Joe Butts shuffled around, trying to keep his toes from going numb. Damn, he hated winter. The salesman returned, looking a little twitchy. "I'm sorry," he said. "It looks like your brother clocked out already too. Is there anything I can help you with?"

"No," Joe Butts shook his head.

"You want me to call Mr. Bendz at home?"

"That won't be necessary."

"Shall I tell him you stopped by when I see him on Monday?"

"No need," Joe Butts said. "I'll drive by his house now, see if he's around."

"Alrighty, then," the salesman said. "You have a good rest of your weekend. Anything else we can do for you, just let me know."

"Yup," Joe Butts said, getting back in the police car. Now be a good asswipe, he thought, and run in there and call your boss.

Joe Butts kept his lights and siren off on his way out to the Bendz place. He took his time, did a little sightseeing. It almost seemed a crime not to. How often did he get to ride around the countryside? He was gratified to see the gate was open when he arrived. How thoughtful. The house, at the top of the long curving driveway, was all lit up. He pulled up under the portico. The front door opened and Bendz stepped out.

"Evening," Joe Butts said.

"Officer," Bendz said, with that tinge to his voice.

"Like to have a word with you," Joe Butts said.

Bendz looked over the police cruiser, taking his time like it was a trade-in. "If I'm not mistaken," he said, "your jurisdiction is Dooleysburg."

Joe Butts looked at him with amused disbelief. "What are you getting at, Carl?"

"Well," Bendz said smugly, "we're in Salisbury Township here."

Joe Butts looked around. "Carl," he said, "I do believe you're right."

"So I guess you'll be moving on."

"Lillian home?" Joe Butts asked.

"She's indisposed," Bendz said firmly.

"Oh." Joe Butts started back to his car, then turned. "You might want to tell her to get disposed. That way, you won't have to wait for her to primp before she comes to bail you out."

"What are you talking about?"

"Since it seems you're not interested in talking unofficially with me, somebody official should be coming by shortly."

"For what?" Bendz demanded angrily.

"We got a complaint. Some whack job in a chipmunk head, or should I say *the* Chipmunk head, exposed himself to a bunch of teenage girls."

"Oh, for god's sake," Bendz said disgustedly. "Haven't you people had enough fun at my expense yet?"

"You know," Joe Butts walked back, "that's an interesting question. That's pretty much the same question I wanted to ask you."

Bendz was flabbergasted. "You think it was me?"

"You have an alibi?"

"I don't *need* a freaking alibi!"

"Not a lot of chipmunk heads out there."

The front door opened. The light from inside glowed around Bendz like a halo until Lillian stepped into it. "Carl," she remonstrated, "invite Officer Butts in. It's cold out here."

Bendz turned without a word and walked inside. Joe Butts followed him. "Ma'am," he said, as he passed Lillian.

"What's wrong?" she asked.

"This . . ." Bendz caught himself. "This man came by to ask me if I've been to town lately. Seems someone was flashing young girls."

Lillian looked at Joe Butts. "You can't be serious. Someone claims to have seen Carl doing that?"

Joe Butts avoided her eyes. He felt like the kid who just got asked to open his own desk after he ratted somebody else out for hiding dirty pictures. No wonder Bendz stayed married to this woman. "Not exactly," he finally said, shifting from one foot to the other.

"Then why *exactly* are you here?"

"It was The Chipmunk, ma'am. The perpetrator was wearing the chipmunk head."

"We don't have it."

"Ma'am?"

"The chipmunk head. It's not here. It hasn't been here for months."

"Lillian!" Bendz looked as if he might pass out. He actually clutched his chest. "What have you done?"

Joe Butts looked back and forth between the two of them.

"I didn't do anything," Lillian said. "When I was in the basement getting some Christmas things, back around Thanksgiving, the casket was out of place. Since you get so crazy when anyone touches it, I decided to put it back. But when I lifted it up it felt much too light. So I got your key and went back to check. It was empty."

Bendz started hyperventilating. "Why didn't you tell me?" he gasped.

Lillian's face changed expression like a time lapse video, as if she was considering all the different answers she'd made up to that question over the past few months. And then she got a serene smile. "Because I was so glad to have the damn thing out of the house."

🐓 🐓 🐓

The next time the Chipmunk appeared he got good press. Dusk remained his preferred time, small groups of adolescent girls his preferred prey. The guys from the detective squad were brainstorming how best to deploy themselves to intercept him when Mikey made an astute observation. "Did you notice," he asked, "that all the reports we took so far, the mother seems pretty upset but the daughter, the one who actually saw the incident, it doesn't seem to bother her all that much?"

"You think they're embarrassed to act scared in front of their friends?"

"We're talking about girls," JD said. "For the most part they wouldn't care."

"You know what I think?" Joe Butts said. "I think girls aren't what girls used to be. Thirty years ago, a girl cared about modesty."

JD laughed. "Thirty years ago on what planet?"

"Hear me out," Joe Butts continued. "So maybe modesty was the wrong word, but thirty years ago you still had some percentage of women who thought they should be virgins when they got married, which they planned to do before they went through the change."

"So now," Walter said, "the mothers, who were the daughters thirty years ago, are all worked up because this kind of stuff would have offended them, but the daughters . . ."

"The daughters learned all about salami in health class in middle school," Joe Butts finished for him.

"Hold on," JD said.

"Meaning what?" Mikey asked.

JD stood up. "Don't go there," he said sharply. "They're victims and this is a crime."

"He's got a point," Walter insisted. "Somebody who does this kind of stuff wants their victims to be shocked, upset. That's what makes it worth the risk. A young guy, he's going to know it won't work. Might even know these girls, know he's going to get laughed at."

"So he might do it once, as a joke, but you wouldn't have repeat performances."

"Exactly!" Walter gave his desk a satisfied slap. "So our Chipmunk is middle-aged!"

"Oh, good," JD said. "Now we've got him."

Everyone was quiet for a few minutes, thinking. Joe Butts broke the silence. "I dunno," he said. "We got over ten witnesses, and the only thing they can agree on is that the guy was naked and white. No age, no hair color, not even a good idea of his height or build."

"Maybe we've been asking about the wrong characteristics," Walter said.

"Walter," JD said, "you are a genius."

❦ ❦ ❦

The Pep Squad was assembled in the girls' locker room of St. Agnes of the Precious Lambs. It seemed like an odd place to be meeting with the Chief of Police, but this was an odd topic. He'd been talking for a while. A few of the girls still giggled, but most of them were just bored now. "We all want the same thing," he concluded, "which is to catch this creep. It appears he has a preference for cheerleaders, which makes it likely some of you will see him. But no one, and I repeat, *no one* is to go seeking him out."

Chrissie Carter turned to her friend Emily. "As if," she said, rolling her eyes. At the side of the room, Sister Fiacre noted this, one more minor transgression. She disapproved of all these girls, but the Carter girl was particularly frivolous. Her name, Chrissie, instead of the more formal and appropriate Christine, preordained her to be flighty and irresponsible.

JD raised his hand so that the small object he was holding was visible to everyone. "I'm asking you to carry one of these every time you go out. We'll provide as many as you need. Keep it readily accessible, and if you have an encounter use it as many times as you can. Then, if you have a cell phone, call the station immediately. Any questions?"

"Yeah." Chrissie stood up. As squad captain, she was used to having authority. "What is the big deal, really? It's not like *we* haven't seen enough of them before, and from what I hear, more impressive ones than his." The other girls laughed.

"I'd like to think," JD replied, "we can count on your help to catch him."

"It's not like flashers hurt anybody," another girl said in a challenging tone.

"If you mean physically, statistics say it's unlikely. But we can't assume that will be the case here. And remember, just because we find his behavior merely offensive doesn't mean it will have the same effect on everyone else."

"Yeah," someone said. "What if he flashed your grandmother?"

"She'd nail him with her handbag. She keeps a roll of nickels in the bottom."

Sister Fiacre stood up. "I think we've covered everything," she said sternly. "Thank you, Chief Charles."

"Thank you, Sister," he answered politely.

As they left the room, Emily turned to Chrissie. "I like the uniform. He's kind of hot for an old guy."

Katie joined them. "Yeah, but he's slow on the uptake. My mom had 'car trouble' twice, and he never took the hint. Plus, I heard he's doing that bitch from New York."

"You know who I think is hot?" Chrissie asked.

"The whole freaking school knows who you think is hot," Emily answered. Sister Fiacre came up behind them. "Right, Sister?" she asked.

"I will do you a favor and pretend I didn't hear that," Sister said sourly. Frivolous names, she repeated to herself.

35

Despite repeated visitations, the Chipmunk soon became back page news. Like most scandals, he seemed doomed to death by habituation. Advertisers were far more willing to buy space on a page where the *Intellectual* featured something about the unfolding Barry Manilow drama. The Ad department, a grandiose name for the middle-aged bald guy who managed sales and the part-time lady who did layouts, uncovered the story first. They took it straight to Editorial, who would have ignored them except for the sudden drop-off in ads being placed for the Manilow Valentine's Benefit Concert. An order went to the newsroom to find out what was up with the biggest social event in Dooleysburg history. This was interpreted as an order to find out what was up with Carl Bendz.

Bendz had been hiding from the press like he was taking a page from Jackie O. But as always it was his weakness of the flesh that did him in. He just couldn't give up his regular massages at the Golf and Cricket Club with Ionnis, the masseur of indeterminate Eastern European origin.

Ionnis was kneading that spot in the center of his back right now, the one that made him groan. Bendz felt like he was afloat in the middle of the room. He sighed deeply in satisfaction.

"Is coming Manilow?" Ionnis asked, hoping to maximize his tip with a little pleasant conversation.

Bendz stiffened as if somebody had just stuck an electrode in his armpit. "Who wants to know?" he demanded.

Ionnis, whose command of English was even worse than he pretended, pretty much lost it as soon as anybody got pissed off. The only word he was sure he understood was 'who'. "Manilow?" he offered.

Bendz sat bolt upright. "Manilow called here?"

"Manilow," Ionnis nodded. "Here."

"Damn!" Bendz said. "He must have been checking to see if we really canceled his booking. Was he upset?"

Ionnis frowned. It was times like this that he thought he should really start job hunting at one of those new resorts along the Baltic. Then he remembered the paradigm he always found so useful at fast food restaurants. He repeated the last few sounds he had heard. "He upset . . ."

Bendz hopped off the table and began storming around the room. He was babbling so fast probably even other Americans would have a hard time understanding him. But Ionnis wasn't trying. He was busy thinking about how in America he got the same pay whether the client danced around like a monkey or laid on the table like a flounder. He hoped Bendz would keep this up for the rest of his hour, but then the man got sloppy with his modesty towel. Ionnis covered his eyes.

The commotion stopped. "Sorry guy." Bendz came over and patted Ionnis on the arm. "You a big Manilow fan?" Ionnis, unwilling to uncover his eyes, nodded mutely. "Well, it is what it is," Bendz said. "They want to throw The Chipmunk out with the bathwater, they damn well better not expect me to pony up Barry Manilow."

"Ah," Ionnis repeated, "Barry Manilow."

"No!" Bendz said emphatically. "No Barry Manilow!"

Ionnis uncovered his eyes. "No Barry Manilow?" he asked, blinking.

Bendz leaned closer. "Our secret, pal," he said. "Let 'em dress up and have their fantasies about Barr-ree," he flapped his eyelashes. "Only a bunch of geriatric dollies would think a guy like him would give them the time of day. I can't wait to see the looks on their faces when they figure out there ain't gonna be no Barry Manilow."

"No Barry Manilow," Ionnis repeated. It was beginning to dawn on him that there might be something important about this phrase.

"Hey," Bendz said, "no repeating, okay?"

Ionnis understood 'okay,' although the rest of the sentence escaped him. "Okay," he nodded.

"Where's my pants?" Bendz looked around as if, after all these years, he couldn't recall where he got undressed. Luckily, pants was another word Ionnis grasped. He made the universal 'wait a minute' gesture and charged out to the locker room. Nothing would make him happier than to get the Crazy Man into his pants. He grabbed them and hurried back. Bendz reached into his pocket and pulled out a bill. He snapped it open in Ionnis's face. It was $100. Ionnis's eyes opened wide, as if they would grab the bill if only they knew how.

"Yeah," Bendz said, drawing the word out like a snake charmer. "You understand this language, don't you?" He held the bill out an instant longer, then snatched it back. "All you gotta do is keep quiet."

"Keep quiet," Ionnis echoed.

Bendz handed him the bill. "That's my man," he said, climbing back onto the massage table. He looked over his shoulder at the small clock on the towel cabinet. "Still got twenty minutes."

"Twenty minutes," Ionnis said, and proceeded to give Bendz the massage of his life.

When they were finished, Bendz melted his way to the sauna. He was just getting comfortable when the door opened and in walked the scumbag editor from *The Daily Intellectual.* Their eyes locked and then the editor turned and left. Bendz gave himself a mental pat on the back for staring the guy down.

Outside the door, the editor grabbed a robe and raced to the reception desk. "Where's the Hulk?" he demanded.

"Excuse me?" the receptionist asked.

"The Swede. The lump. The guy who gives massages. The one who only speaks grunt."

"Ionnis," she said coldly. "Right behind you."

The editor turned around. The guy had materialized out of nowhere. The editor pulled him into the locker room. "Listen," he said, "did you just give Bendz a massage?"

Ionnis believed he understood that one. He nodded.

"He say anything about the show?" Ionnis shrugged. It was a good all-purpose response. "He told you not to tell, didn't he?"

Ionnis shrugged again. The editor went to his locker and pulled out his wallet. He looked through it with something approaching sadness. Finally, he pulled out a bill and held it toward Ionnis. It was a twenty. Ionnis looked at him. People tipped after their massages. Since he hadn't touched this guy, Ionnis wasn't sure of the etiquette for this situation.

"Fine!" the editor snapped. He dug into his wallet again and pulled out another twenty. "This is as good as it gets!" he said hotly. "What'd he say about Barry Manilow?"

"Ah!" Ionnis's face lit up. "No Barry Manilow."

The editor looked as if he'd just found out his parents weren't married. "You wouldn't shit me, would you?" he demanded.

Ionnis nodded helpfully. "No Barry Manilow," he repeated.

The editor held out the money. "Here," he said.

Ionnis was a smart man, even if his language skills left something to be desired. So far he'd made some damn good money just for saying 'no Barry Manilow'. These two weren't the only ones who'd be interested. He went out to the reception area and flipped through the schedule, looking at his appointments. There it was, the name he was looking for. He got a piece of paper and copied down the phone number. Back in the privacy of his empty massage room, he took out his cell phone.

After two rings, she answered. "Mrs. Lillian?" he asked. "Is Ionnis." He listened for a moment. "No. No massage for you today. Maybe you come visit, I tell no Barry Manilow."

The editor of *The Daily Intellectual* suffered briefly over how to handle the Manilow situation. Journalistic standards required a corroborating source, but he felt a strong obligation to his public. With a flash of insight, he decided a letter to the editor could solve his dilemma. He wrote the letter himself, to assure a balanced perspective. Though nobody would confirm Carl Bendz had withdrawn funding for the Manilow Valentine's Benefit Concert, he wanted to present the possibility it might happen in a fair way. Then he raised the pivotal question—would Barry show if nobody guaranteed the take? He did a good job of representing both sides of the issue. So good, in fact, that if somebody wanted to assume the letter was written by Bendz himself, perhaps they could. He finished up by signing it 'Anonymous'. When he gave it a final read, it was such a good job he was disappointed he couldn't tell anybody he'd written it. But he was too much of a professional for that.

The letter brought an avalanche of replies. People wanted answers. Was Barry coming or not? What was the refund policy on tickets? Could people get their money back afterwards if they ate dinner, or had a few drinks and then Manilow didn't show? One or two letters raised the uncomfortable prospect that this might be just the beginning of the fallout from the impeachment, with darker things still to come. In the absence of real answers the town continued to prepare for the concert, but there was a touch of gloom over everything.

The staff at the *Intellectual* remained energized. There hadn't been a story this exciting in years. Even the volunteers walked around town with pads in hand. Anyone you stopped was happy to give an interview. Every few days someone called the Bendz residence or the car dealership to see if they could get a comment, without success. At one staff meeting some kid who had recently gotten his journalism degree suggested maybe they should call Manilow's organization. This was loudly rejected, and the kid got a private dressing down. Nobody at the *Intellectual* wanted this thing blown out of proportion.

Over at the police station the Manilow situation was seen as something of a gift. It was keeping the lack of progress on the Chipmunk case out of the news. It wasn't like the guys weren't still applying the full force of their intellect to catching the perpetrator. The case remained at the top of their daily briefing agenda, but every day their ideas got more absurd.

It was in the gloaming of an unseasonably warm evening that things started to get out of hand. Mikey picked up a call, and his face clouded over as he listened. By the time he thanked the caller and hung up JD was standing by his desk. "What is it?" he asked.

"Edmund over at the Courthouse." Edmund was the head of Courthouse security. "Says they've got a Channel 4 news van with all that giant video crap on top on their southeast corner."

"Parked or moving?"

"Parked, and the roaches are crawling."

"Something big going on at the Courthouse?" JD asked.

"Edmund says nothing big enough to make the Philly news. That's why he figured he'd better give us a call."

"Sounds like the fixings for an unhappy situation," JD said, thinking out loud. That was one of the things that endeared him to his men, the way he shared his ability to think. "Anybody want to guess what might have attracted our partners in the press all the way from Philadelphia?"

Joe Butts looked at him. "You think the Manilow thing is big enough?"

"One way to find out," JD said.

As if it read his mind, the phone rang. Joe Butts picked it up. "Let me see if the Chief's available." He put the call on hold. "Ask and ye shall receive. It's one of the TV reporters looking for a comment."

"You know I love it when you toy with me," JD said. "A comment on what?"

Joe Butts smiled wickedly. "Our inability to make progress on the Chipmunk case."

"Send it to my office," JD said. "No, wait. Better yet, have him bring his pretty little face over here. But no cameras. Tell him if he brings a camera in here he gets nothing."

In a matter of moments, the reporter was in JD's office. It seemed the mother of one of the Chipmunk's victims, frustrated by the lack of answers, had made an irate call to the station's news hotline. The station liked the story. If it took just a little longer to resolve the timing would be perfect for an upcoming ratings sweep. Not that anyone would ever want the police to delay catching a criminal just for ratings, the reporter was quick to assure JD. Then he asked for a quote.

"Sure," JD said. "We're pursuing a number of leads. This case is one of our highest priorities, and we'll continue to devote whatever resources are needed to solve it."

"Thanks!" The reporter seemed pleased. "Any chance I could get some footage?"

"Pack up and shove off before I decide I don't like you," JD said in a friendly tone.

The reporter pulled out a card. "I'd appreciate a call if anything breaks."

"I'll think about it," JD said, taking the card and tossing it on his desk. He stood up and offered his hand. The reporter shook it, then left. JD waited until he was sure the guy was out of the building before going back to the squad room.

"What the hell were you doing in there?" Joe Butts asked. "Guy looked like he just got off Santa's lap."

"People," JD said, "we've got a problem."

𝆖 𝆖 𝆖

Lillian Bendz used her characteristic determination to ignore the rumors about the Barry Manilow Benefit for as long as possible. She found it unacceptable that Ionnis expected her to come to the Club to find out what he knew, and whispered in the right ears to get him fired. Even so, the unhappy knowledge seemed intent on pursuing her. She picked up a call one morning that caller ID said was Picasso's Salon only to find the editor of *The Daily Intellectual* on the other end. Without even the briefest pleasantries, he asked her to corroborate a statement from Manilow's organization that the Valentine's Day booking was canceled. Lillian hung up without answering, her hands shaking so badly she nearly missed the phone cradle. This was it. Carl had betrayed her in the deepest, most treacherous way possible, not to mention exposing her to public ridicule for the second time in less than a year. This was the last straw, the straw that broke the camel's back; it was every trite cliché she could think of.

How could Carl take away her chance to bask in Barry Manilow's luminous glow, on stage, for the whole town to see? Barry would have kissed her cheek. He would have taken her hand and held it like a piece of rare porcelain. And, for a slight premium, he would have pretended to allow her to spontaneously choose her favorite song from his catalogue, which he would then sing to her, looking deeply into her eyes. Now the only thing they would all see was her disgrace.

She scrawled a note to the housekeeper in her cursive of rage, large slashing letters, directing the woman to pack her things for an extended absence. Then she put the note on Carl's bathroom vanity, so he would find it and be stuck making sure it got done. She took several thousand dollars in cash and everything else of value from her bedroom safe, stuffed it in her Vuitton overnight bag, and left the house.

36

Sitting in the opulent comfort of his ridiculously large house, Wesley Carter was beginning to appreciate the scope of his problem. As a fan of corny jokes, one of his favorites was the one about why hurricanes were named after women. But it wasn't funny now that it was a matter of personal anguish. Hurricane Lillian had blown in through his front door several days ago, and she showed no signs of abating. Like a Category 5 storm stalled over the warm waters of the Caribbean, her rage continued to grow until Wesley dared not risk leaving his bedroom. The problem was magnified at times like these, when he was hungry. Chrissie, the only member of the household able to get near Lillian without receiving a lashing, had brought him some dinner last night, but twelve hours was a long time in the life of a big man's stomach. And he knew, even through the muddle of his usual state, that things were not going to get better unless he did something. That knowledge, more than Lillian, more than hunger, was what made this situation unbearable.

There was a knock on his bedroom door. "Chrissie?" he called hopefully, even though he knew she was in school. The door opened, and Carol Ann walked in. "Oh." Wesley said, surprised. "Hello."

"I can't stand it," Carol Ann snapped. "It's like when I was a teenager, except I'm not worried about her stealing my boyfriends anymore. But otherwise, it's as bad as it ever was."

"We could ask her to leave," Wesley offered.

"Why do I even bother talking to you?" Carol Ann asked, and walked out before Wesley could answer.

It was just as well. He didn't have a clue why she bothered talking to him either. His job was to be dependably ineffective. It had worked for his marriage up to now. His mother-in-law was a constant background noise all the time, so having her in their house was merely an increase of several decibels. But this new problem, being expected to do something about it, posed all kinds of problems. Carol Ann hadn't married him just for his money or the chance to meld their family empires. Everything else being equal, she still would have walked away if she hadn't felt sure he could be relied on, no matter what the situation, to do nothing. He had polished this skill, honed it to weapons grade strength. This unpredicted requirement for him to take action was almost enough to ruin his appetite.

By mid-afternoon, things were looking up. Carol Ann had managed to lure her mother out of the house to look at drapery fabric, knowing Lillian would never allow domestic crisis to postpone decorating decisions. They came back in a decent mood, having shared a lighter moment at the expense of one of the unfortunates they'd encountered in town. Wesley, ever mindful of protocol, had their cocktails ready. Lillian's favorite was gin and Fresca. For Carol Ann, he made a rum and diet Coke.

He handed them their drinks before going to mix his own, then joined them in the mushroom and storm cloud gray family room. They were staring at the big TV. The distinctive evening news theme song filled the room. The anchor's head was so large on the screen it looked like he was getting ready to pop into the room. He was running through the list of teasers meant to hold the audience during the onslaught of commercials that opened every broadcast.

"Slow news night?" Wesley asked, sitting down.

"Shh!" Carol Ann hissed. Something in her voice made Wesley look over at the sofa where Lillian sat, transfixed. Her jaw was actually hanging slack as she stared at the TV. Wesley followed her gaze. There, in brilliant high definition, was the front of the Bendz estate, as seen from outside the gates.

"And finally," the news anchor intoned, "what makes a harmless mascot go bad? Stay tuned for our exclusive report on how a highly respected businessman and pillar of a local community may be involved in a child sex scandal." The theme song started up again.

Wesley picked up the remote. "We don't need to watch this," he said, feeling compelled to take the Carl role in this family drama. He clicked the TV off.

Carol Ann turned on him. "What are you doing, asshole?"

Lillian's face was white and pinched. "Turn the TV back on, Wesley."

"Mother," Carol Ann said, "breathe. Stay calm."

Lillian's voice was level. "Shut up."

They suffered through nearly the entire newscast in silence, waiting for the promised report. Wesley's internal monologue sounded pretty much like air hissing out of a leaking basketball. The story finally opened with an atmosphere shot of the Courthouse, one forlorn corner of large stones and an arched doorway. The eager young reporter who had interviewed JD was speaking directly to the camera, talking about how the model community of Dooleysburg harbored a serious threat. It sounded like the opening of a horror movie.

The shot of the Bendz front gate came on again. This time, the camera panned around to show Carl pulling into the driveway. He slowed, and the reporter stepped in front of his car, blocking his path. To his family's surprise, Carl stopped. The reporter ran around to Carl's window. "Mr. Bendz," he intoned, "Bob Frost from Action News." Wesley noticed that Carl's window was closed. He wondered if that might affect the interview. "Mr. Bendz," Frost began again, "what do you have to say about reports of the Dooleysburg Chipmunk exposing himself to several area young women?" Bendz stared straight ahead.

"At least the bastard isn't talking," Lillian said.

Frost unfurled a big sheet of paper. It was a blow-up of the Chipmunk poster that had incited Dooleysburg to action a few weeks earlier. Frost spoke to the camera in deep tones, emphasizing the seriousness of this matter. "Carl Bendz, proprietor of a local car dealership, and former Dooleysburg Chipmunk . . ."

"Wait a minute!" Bendz's head was sticking out of his window now. "Hold on!"

Frost turned back to the car. "Mr. Bendz, would you care to comment?"

"Bet your ass!" Bendz yelled. "The head is gone! It's been missing for months!"

Frost looked like someone had just offered him a choice bit of meat. "Are you telling this reporter you are not in possession of the Chipmunk head?"

Bendz mimicked him. "That's exactly what I'm telling this reporter."

"And have you made the local authorities aware of this?"

Bendz gave him a withering look. "Do you think they really give a damn?"

Lillian stood up. "Turn it off," she commanded, and marched from the room.

"You need to do something," Carol Ann said to her husband.

Wesley looked as if he had just skidded on roadkill in his bare feet. "About what?" he asked, stalling.

"About my parents!" Carol Ann snapped. "You've got to fix things."

"Why?"

"Why?" she repeated, astonished. "Why? Because if she divorces him, they split the ranch, stupid."

"So what?" Wesley asked. "You're an only child. You still get everything in the end."

"Everything minus lawyers' fees. Everything minus the loss he takes when he's forced to sell assets he undervalued for tax purposes so he can give her half the money. And what if he remarries? You think he's going to spend the rest of his life alone when he can buy any trophy between here and Antigua? You know what part of his share we'll see after my stepmommy gets done with it?" She softened her voice and put a hand on his arm. "And what about my mother? She'll never remarry. What if she decides to move in here permanently?"

"What are we going to do?" Wesley was near panic.

Carol Ann stood up. "I'm going to see if I can put her on ice for a while. You figure out some way to get us out of this mess."

𝆬 𝆬 𝆬

Wesley stood in the small paneled box of a room, trying to will away the light sweat that glazed his head. He didn't know his way around Conshohocken, and it had taken him longer to find the office than he expected. And now the agent was making him wait. Wesley was not accustomed to dealing with people who were not familiar with his station in life. If Carol Ann hadn't said this idea was a stroke of genius, he would leave right now. But considering it was his first stroke of genius in all the years they'd been married, he decided not to give up too easily.

"You can sit," the woman behind the desk said.

He wished she wouldn't talk to him. That way he could avoid the trouble of deciding if she was slutty or hot. It was a question he usually tried to ignore so he wouldn't have to think about his own frustrations, or about which category best described his wife and daughter.

"Over there." The receptionist indicated the vinyl chair with a flip of her head.

"No thanks," Wesley replied.

"He could be a while."

"He's already late. If he can't see me soon, we might have to call this off."

The receptionist looked surprised. Wesley felt bad he didn't even impress her enough to make her worry about him walking out. He regretted not considering hair plugs back when he still had enough hair to try them.

"Suit yourself," the woman said, with a shrug. Wesley sat down.

Not too many minutes later the door behind her desk opened and a sharply dressed man stepped out. He might have been Greek or Hispanic or some variety of Middle Eastern; he was swarthy, but beyond that it was impossible to tell. "Where's Carter?" he asked the receptionist, as if a large man was not sitting less than ten feet away. She used her head as a pointer again.

The agent stuck out his hand. "Hey," he said, "I'm Bernard. How you doing?"

"Fine," Wesley answered, grateful to be acknowledged.

"Can we get you something? Diet Coke? Coffee? Probably got some juice around here somewhere." Bernard began looking around without waiting for an answer. Fearful of what additional delays might happen if Bernard got distracted, Wesley insisted he wasn't thirsty. "So what can I do for you?" Bernard asked.

"I've been told," Wesley said formally, "that your firm is very successful at finding acts that—talent that—could pass for . . ."

"You mean impersonators," Bernard finished for him.

"Yes," Wesley said. "But tasteful."

"Who you looking for?" Bernard asked.

"Barry Manilow."

"Holy crap!" Bernard smacked him on the back. "You're from Dooleysburg, right?"

"Well, yes," Wesley said, somewhat nonplussed.

"Man, are you ever screwed," Bernard chuckled. "I mean, Manilow's a gentleman and all, but how could you people think he was going to show up on *contingency*?" Bernard broke into a full-out laugh. "I mean, you're lucky the guy didn't sue you for breach of contract."

Wesley drew himself up to his full height. "Be that as it may," he said. "It seems your agency might be in a position to provide a suitable alternative."

"My agency," Bernard looked around. "It's just me, bubba. You want a singer, you want a magician, see me. You need an exotic dancer, make an appointment with yours truly."

"No exotic dancers," Wesley said quickly.

"Too bad," Bernard said. "You don't get a better turnout than with that kind of talent."

"Nonetheless," Wesley was firm, "I'm inquiring whether you have an act that can fill Barry Manilow's shoes."

"Interesting way to put it," Bernard replied. "I wouldn't say my man fills his shoes, but he certainly sounds just like the original."

Wesley's face brightened so much he felt like his head kind of glowed. Then he remembered Carol Ann's orders. Try not to put on your 'kick me' sign until you've checked things out thoroughly, she said. He scowled. "How do I know this is a bona fide impostor?"

Bernard raised an eyebrow. "Come on," he said. "I'll let you listen." He took Wesley into the other room, a sort of studio. There was a small cluttered desk in one corner. Bernard pulled a stool out from behind it and dragged it over to an intimidating bank of equipment. He put on a pair of headphones and began fiddling with various dials and switches. Eventually he got up and handed the headphones to Wesley. Wesley settled himself on the stool and put on the headphones. Bernard adjusted some more controls. Wesley got a dreamy look for a moment, then ripped off the headphones.

"There a problem?" Bernard asked.

"'I Write the Songs' is the problem! You think I can't tell Neil Diamond from Barry Manilow?"

"Hey, dude, calm down. Look here." Bernard held out a CD case from Barry Manilow's greatest hits. Sure enough, "I Write the Songs" was listed there.

"Oh." Wesley colored slightly. "Okay."

"You want to hear more?"

"No." Wesley thought a moment. "So that was Barry Manilow?"

"You mean the actual singer? No, sir. That was my man."

"No kidding! He sounds just like the real thing."

Bernard kept his face composed. If he knew he needed to move fast before something else unkinked inside this guy's head, he did a good job of not showing it. "Not that I want to pressure you, but you only got a couple weeks before your show date and my man is very popular. If you want to sign him, you need to move on it."

"Of course," Wesley said.

Bernard went to the desk and picked up a folder. The contract had already been prepared. He brought it over to Wesley, who made an effort to pretend he was reading it, just like Carol Ann told him to do.

"You got any questions?" Bernard asked.

"He spells his name kind of funny." Wesley pointed to the page where the singer was identified as Barey Manilo.

"Come on," Bernard said. "You don't expect him to use the same exact name, do you?"

Wesley shrugged and signed two copies. There was one more thing Carol Ann had told him to do, he was sure of it. But for the life of him, he couldn't remember what.

❦ ❦ ❦

Wesley came into the family room. There was Lillian on her yoga mat, doing her morning stretches. He sighed audibly. He had heard other men use the sigh to communicate significant things, as a substitute for the longer, more tiring sentences that would otherwise be required to tell a woman she was to cease whatever she was doing and immediately tend to the man's desires. He had given up trying to master that kind of sigh years ago. For him, a sigh was just a sigh.

Lillian lay down and lifted one leg in the air. All Wesley wanted was to watch Regis and Kelly on his big screen TV. A man should not have to shower and shave in the morning only to find himself looking at his mother-in-law in a leotard and tights. And then, despite himself, he became fascinated by the contortions she could perform with her stick-figure legs. It was ironic, when you came right down to it, that at her age she could still fold herself into these kinds of shapes, and yet no human male would ever want to know what any of these postures might reveal. Who could blame the old man for some of his excesses? Wesley turned to leave the room.

"Wesley." Her voice was a command, even from the floor behind the sofa.

"Yes, Mother Bendz?"

She sat up. The couch between them created the impression that she was a disembodied head wearing a Hermes do-rag. "I wanted to thank you."

"You're welcome," he said, hoping that would cover whatever it was he had done. If he got away from Lillian now, he could make it back to his room before he missed his favorite part of the show, where Kelly gave Regis a hard time about something before they brought out the guests. He edged toward the door.

"It was very generous of you to find a replacement for Barry Manilow," she went on, oblivious to his distress. Wesley nodded. What good had it done, really? She was still here, wasn't she? "And then taking out those ads in *The Daily Intellectual*. That was a stroke of genius." Wesley began paying attention. Had she just called him a genius? "Only, why do you suppose they spelled the impersonator's name so oddly?"

"That's how he spells it. The paper called me to double check."

"Really." Lillian considered this.

"I think he's Filipino. You know, Manilo, like Manila." Lillian looked heavenward. Wesley wanted to kick himself. He always went too far. The Manila connection had sounded like a really good idea when he made it up.

"I don't suppose it matters," she finally said. "The unfortunate truth is that most people have not asked for refunds because they think it's worth an outrageously expensive ticket to see me get humiliated."

"Mother Bendz," he said, "how can you think that? You are universally admired."

"It's nice of you to say so. Nonetheless, I am not often treated with kindness."

Oh, god, no. She was going to cry. He could sense it the way dogs know about looming tornadoes. Do something, he screamed at himself. "Mother Bendz," he said quickly, "there's something I want to tell you. I was saving it for a surprise, but you look a little down."

She made that 'sob caught in your throat' noise.

"Mr. Manilo is going to call you up on stage and sing a song especially for you. It's part of the package. He's going to do, 'Can't Smile Without You,' just like the real Barry Manilow was supposed to."

Lillian's face screwed up like she'd just sucked on a lime. Wesley watched, helpless, as the tears began to slide down her cheeks. It figured she made a sound like a rusted hinge when she cried. He offered her the handkerchief he always kept in his pocket. As she took it from him, her face turned to the floor, he wondered if she would mind if he turned up the volume on the TV.

JD was just about done caramelizing the onions when he heard his cell phone. It took him a minute to remember where he'd left it. He turned off the stove and went to answer it. "Dammit, Mikey," he said, "you know I'm cooking tonight. Now the garlic's going to brown and I'll have to start all over again."

"I'm sorry, Chief." Like the rest of the squad, Mikey took JD's cooking seriously. "I'm at the Bendz place."

"Reporters again?"

"Nope. Been another break-in. Or maybe a reverse break-in."

"That's a new one," JD said. "What's a reverse break-in?"

"Not sure, actually. That's what Bendz is calling it, and he's not in the mood to explain."

"So now that you've ruined the *mire poix* and complained about Bendz, what is it exactly I can do for you?"

"Bendz wants you."

"Oh, you're too kind. Tell him I'm not that kind of guy."

"Chief, he's making everybody miserable."

"Put him on the phone."

Bendz's tone was a bit less condescending than usual. "Charles, I need to talk to you."

"I'm listening."

"Here. I want you to come to my place."

"Carl, I'm in the middle of making the best damn short ribs in the entire universe. Everybody says so. I've already messed up a critical step, which I will now have to repeat, much to my annoyance, because of this phone call."

"I'll buy you a goddamned prime rib dinner. Just get out here."

"Short ribs," JD muttered, "not prime rib. What is so important that you need me to drop everything and rush out there, when you're not even in my jurisdiction?"

Bendz lowered his voice. "It's about the Chipmunk."

JD stood straighter, even though he was alone. "Carl, you want to put a stopper in it until I read you Miranda?"

"Don't be a jerk. *I'm* not the Chipmunk. I was impeached, remember?"

"So, what, are you having a tender moment?"

"It's back."

JD got serious. "Back? In your house?"

"That's what I'm trying to tell you!"

"How'd it get there?"

"How the hell do I know? I get home, there's a mess of uniformed block-heads all over the place, and the damn head is sitting on my family room sofa."

"Well, they're not my blockheads. My blockheads only come when you call. So what brought law enforcement to your humble abode?"

"They said the alarm went off."

"So did it?"

"It would appear so."

"What do you mean, 'appear so'?"

"Inside garage door's been jimmied."

"How'd they get the outside garage door open?" That one stymied Bendz. Apparently nobody had considered it yet. "Anything missing?" JD asked.

"That's what I'm trying to tell you," Bendz hissed. "Nothing was touched. Nobody's figured out yet what's what, and I want you here when they finally do."

"What am I going to do that they can't?"

"Help me figure out who took the head just long enough to put the nails in my coffin."

"Put Mike back on the phone," JD said. Although it was supposed to be a secret, JD knew one of the nicknames the guys called him was the Nut Whisperer. He never bragged about it, but he was proud of his skill at reaching into the human mind and calming the trapped animal in there. He had a special finesse when it came to the rich and panicky. Still, there were short ribs to be made.

"JD?" Mikey finally got back on the phone.

"My famous short ribs at the shift changeover or I come out there to figure out what he's test driving these days. Your call."

"It's not like that, JD. I've never seen him this way before. I wouldn't have called you if it was just his usual crap. But I think maybe he snapped when the harpy moved out on him."

"Okay," JD sighed. "I'm on the way." He went back to the kitchen and threw the short rib fixings into the refrigerator.

37

Maggie always thought of the end of winter as a hollow time, as if the world had exhaled everything it had and now was stuck holding on for the new breath of spring. She felt odd about not working. She had nothing to show for her time, and yet all her freedom was eaten up by things she had ignored when she was busier. Sometimes she wondered if she wasn't prewired to always stress about something, so that when nothing real presented itself, her mind diligently created reasons for her to get unhinged anyway.

When Vee called for lunch, she was delighted. They hadn't seen much of each other since spring semester started. Vee was restricted by class schedules, office hours, articles to write and papers to grade. "I'll meet you at your house," Maggie said.

"Nuh," Vee answered. "I'll pick you up."

"You don't have to do that."

"Well, yeah, actually I do."

Maggie got concerned. "Is everything okay?"

"Oh, yeah," Vee said easily. "Everything's fine. We just got a little business to conduct before we go out."

"What sort of business?"

"Stop being a pain in the ass. You'll see when I pick you up."

Vee came in without knocking, as usual. She was carrying a gift bag, which she handed to Maggie.

"What's this?" Maggie wished she could stop feeling so uncomfortable whenever Vee did something nice for her.

"Go ahead and look," Vee said. "I won't stop liking you just because I brought you a present."

You can do this, Maggie thought. You can pretend to be normal and see what comes of it. She sat down on the sofa and reached into the bag. The first item was wrapped in pink tissue paper and covered with flower stickers. Maggie tore it open. Inside was a black strapless push-up bra. She looked at Vee as if she had just been presented with someone else's underwear, which she thought might be the case.

"Keep going." Vee nodded toward the bag.

"What else is in here? A G-string?"

Vee rolled her eyes. "Just open stuff up, would you?"

Maggie reluctantly took out the next tissue-wrapped parcel. It was very thin. She shook it. "Sounds like trouble," she said, tearing off the paper. It was pantyhose. "Just what I've always wanted."

"Turn the package over," Vee said. "There's something special about them."

Maggie took a look at the front of the package and dropped it on the floor, as if it had cooties.

"You don't like them," Vee said, disappointed.

"You got me crotchless pantyhose?"

Vee picked them up and put them on the coffee table. "I thought it was a nice idea."

"Don't put them there." Maggie snatched them off the table. "I eat food here occasionally."

"Until they get worn, the no crotch thing is just a concept, you know."

"And where exactly did you think I would wear them?"

"I had an idea, but now I'm reconsidering." Maggie sat back and waited. It looked like it was going to be a standoff. "You really don't have any girl skills at all, do you?" Vee finally said. "Finish looking in the bag."

Maggie reached in and felt a small envelope at the bottom of the bag. She opened it up. It was two tickets to the Valentine's Benefit at the Golf and Cricket Club. "How did you get these?" she demanded gleefully.

"Blackmail."

"This is great! I would be honored to go with you." Suddenly she got serious. "Vee," she began, "let's talk about this. I mean, the bra and the pantyhose. You are very special to me, but . . ."

"You are an idiot, you know that?"

"Fine," Maggie said, standing up. "Excuse me for jumping to conclusions. I mean, you give me tickets for a Valentine's Dance along with suggestive—no *erotic* underwear. Why would I think you're coming on to me?"

"Because you're a weirdo?"

"Oh, there's the pot calling the kettle black." Vee's eyes narrowed and she got that look on her face. "This is no time for your epithet sensitivity thing," Maggie argued. "I started my fight first. You have to wait for your turn till I'm done."

"I was *trying* to do something nice for you."

"Okay," Maggie said, a hint of conciliation in her tone. "Thank you. Since I obviously missed the point, what did you intend for me to do with this nice present?"

"Oh, I don't know. How about invite a *man* to the concert?"

Maggie plopped back down on the sofa. "A man?" she repeated. "Like who? I've got it!" she said suddenly. "I bet Carl Bendz doesn't have a date!"

"You are so remarkably thick it's like a gift."

"Not Gamey? He still hasn't recovered from Albie going over to the other side."

"You're going to make me say it, aren't you?" Maggie looked at Vee. They both knew what they were thinking, but it was like a game of ping-pong in a parallel universe, where they were trying to make each other hold on to the ball. "You could ask him," Vee finally said.

"I cannot ask him." Maggie stood up and started stuffing the goodies back into the bag.

"Why not?"

"Oh, I don't know," she said sarcastically. "Pride?"

"Honey, I don't know about where you came from . . ." Vee realized what she was saying. "Okay, I do know where you came from, and I agree it was screwed up. But where I came from, which is closer to where he comes from, Valentine's dances are a Sadie Hawkins occasion."

"Sadie Hawkins? Wasn't she the woman from the Grand Ole Opry who wore the hat with the price tag hanging off it?"

"That was Minnie Pearl. Sadie Hawkins originated the tradition in which ladies invite men to a celebration."

"Ladies don't do that in Dooleysburg. Besides, that's not my pride issue."

"I don't understand," Vee said, out of patience. "You're attractive single people, the only ones in this town with the intellectual capacity to keep up with each other. Why can't you spend an evening together?"

"Let's see. How about because he's a control freak who doesn't respect me enough to stop interfering in decisions I have the right to make myself?"

Vee got a wicked gleam in her eye. "So take control," she said. "You can figure out how to run the show."

"I cannot believe you give me a pair of crotchless pantyhose and think that will empower me to show JD who's boss."

"You know what I think?" Vee asked.

"Hardly ever."

"I think you're scared. I think you're afraid he'll turn you down. You don't have to wear the pantyhose. Just invite him to the dance."

"Fine," Maggie said, accepting the challenge. "I will."

38

Maggie sat in her living room, waiting for JD to pick her up. Part of her was amused that age had not made this one bit more comfortable than it used to be. At least now she had Mac, who was trying to distract her with small talk. When the knock came at the back door, Mac offered to get it. Maggie was grateful. The strappy, spiky shoes she'd reluctantly bought for tonight were already a challenge. She heard the low exchange of male voices from the kitchen, and then Mac called, "Mom! JD's here."

She got up. If she could get into forward motion she barely tottered. "What's with using the back door?" she asked, coming into the kitchen.

"I got some insider information that you'd appreciate having to walk as little as possible," JD smiled.

Maggie couldn't help noticing he was sizing her up. "No flowers?" she asked.

"I'm sorry," he began. "I didn't realize . . ."

"I'm busting you," she said.

"Mom," Mac said, "be nice."

They went out and followed the walk around the garage. Parked in her driveway was the smallest sports car she had ever seen. "Is this new?" Maggie asked, filled with dismay at the prospect of trying to get in or out of it gracefully.

"Sure is," JD answered.

"Does your fairy godmother show up at some point and turn it into a car?"

"So you like it," JD said.

"It looks like a sneaker."

"Thanks," he said, opening her door. "That was good for my ego."

"You really care what people think about your car?" she asked, climbing in.

"Most people," he replied. "Just not you."

"Getting in here is like the reverse of being born," she commented as he got in on the driver's side. "You fold yourself all up and stuff yourself into a tight space."

"I like my car."

"Okay," she said. "I won't pick on your car anymore." They drove a few blocks in silence. "So when you got rid of your pickup truck, did you save the shotgun rack?"

"This is going to be a long night," he said. "Why don't you save some for later?"

"Fine." Maggie started rummaging around in her evening bag. It didn't hold that much, but she kept rifling it. She looked over at JD. She was being incredibly obvious, but he wasn't rising to the bait. She finally exclaimed, "Damn!"

"If it would help," he said, "I can turn on the interior light."

"Never mind," she replied. "It looks like I forgot them."

"Forgot what?"

"My panties." She wasn't sure what kind of response she expected, but it wasn't the one she got.

"Is that a problem?" he asked. "You're wearing pantyhose, right?"

"Yeah," she agreed. "But they're crotchless."

This time he didn't answer. They stopped behind a line of traffic at a red light. In the glare from the oncoming headlights she could see he was leaning back against his headrest with his eyes closed. He swallowed hard.

"You okay?" she asked.

"Sweet Jesus," he said softly. "I can't believe you just did that to me."

There was no further conversation until they reached the Golf and Cricket Club. From the foot of the drive, they could see red and white flashing lights hanging from every conceivable overhang. "I like the carnival feel," Maggie said.

"Courtesy of Madame Yaskagya," JD said. "Rumor has it she still does a brisk business in the private rooms."

"Hey," Maggie said, "the sign for valet parking is over there."

"I know," JD answered, heading up a different driveway.

"I thought I was going to get some consideration for my shoes," she said.

JD took his eyes off the road for a moment and looked at her. It must have been a trick of the light, but he looked almost feral. "I haven't forgotten your shoes," he said. "Believe me."

"Tell you what," she bargained, "if you valet, I'll pick up the tip."

"I was hoping you'd get the tip either way."

She looked at him with disdain. "If you're having a hard time getting laid, I have a helpful pointer for you."

"I'm sorry," he said, not sounding sorry. "The shoes seem to have done something to my sense of propriety."

"I doubt it," she said. "I'm guessing you bottom out on a regular basis without any help."

"Tell you what," he said, pulling up at the front entrance by means of the alternate driveway, "why don't we avoid the talking part and just stick to the seduction?"

"Did someone indicate you were going to get seduced tonight?"

JD looked at her. "Forgive me," he said. "My mistake, confusing your confidences about your lack of undergarments with seduction. Stay there," he added. "I'll get your door."

"That's not necessary."

JD sighed. "Would you please just try being receptive to a nice gesture here and there? Who knows? You might afford me the opportunity to be something other than a pig. Or alternatively, we can have a miserable frigging evening."

Maggie didn't answer. He got out of the car and opened her door. She tried to do the ladylike thing about getting out, though she'd only ever seen it done successfully on TV. She was pretty sure the basic move, keeping one's knees pressed together while raising them toward the chest and rotating on one's butt like it was a ball bearing, was something only Lamaze instructors could do. She gave up and used one leg to lever herself out of the car. It still would have been a fairly graceful move, except that JD was standing right there, in her way. "Excuse me," she said with attitude.

Instead of moving, he took her arm and slid her along the car, out of the way so he could shut the door. And then he just stayed there, in front of her. She could feel something powerful flowing from him. It was unavoidable. She realized she was breathing heavy. She also realized he was waiting for her to make the next move. He was too close for her to see his face, but she imagined he was quite satisfied with himself. She brushed up against him, just for spite, and was about to begin serious contact when he stepped back without warning. She wasn't prepared. He reached out to steady her so she didn't fall. Then he grinned wickedly and said, "Let the games begin."

✒   ✒   ✒

As they climbed the stairs to the front entrance of the Club, Maggie was glad she had practiced walking in these shoes. At least on perfectly flat surfaces she'd be okay. But on anything else, it was going to be harder than she ever imagined. The problem wasn't merely having to balance. It was that the stiletto heels were likely to catch in any small space on the ground. Having to stay aware of this at all times provided yet another reason why prostitutes deserved to get paid.

"You want a hand?" JD asked.

For once, she let reason guide her. "Yes."

"You in serious jeopardy?"

"Yes, but I have my pride."

He offered her an elbow. "Should you feel the need for something more substantial, let me know."

"You mean like the hospital lift?"

He looked at her, startled. "I was thinking about an arm around your waist."

She took his elbow. "This will do."

They walked through the double doors and into the oversized foyer. The cocktail hour was already in progress. The doormen checking tickets just nodded at them. JD handed his car keys to one of them without bothering to give instructions. A waiter with a tray of champagne flutes walked over. JD took one and passed it to Maggie.

"Nothing for you?" she asked.

"Champagne goes to my head," he said. "Makes me giggly."

"I'd like to see that," she said.

"Can I get you something from the bar, sir?" the waiter asked.

"Yes," JD said pleasantly. "Glenlivet neat, please."

"Yes, sir." The waiter hurried away.

"All the peons are lining up at the bar to get their own drinks. Does everybody in this town cater to you?"

"Maybe not right off the bat," he said. "But you'd be surprised how motivational their first ticket generally is."

"Are you telling me you take bribes?"

"Nah." He smiled down at her. "I just try to save as many people as possible from Butts."

"Why don't you do something about him? You're the boss."

JD looked serious for a moment. "There's a wide and twisting line that separates good from bad. It's not always obvious which side someone falls on."

Maggie was about to ask for more detail when the first of JD's admirers walked up. JD tried to introduce Maggie, but the woman clearly had no interest. The waiter arrived with JD's drink and Maggie took it. She leaned against JD's arm and when he looked over she handed him the drink. Before he could even thank her, another woman came over. It was like JD had a receiving line. Maggie gave up and glanced around the room. There were a few stray loners, but she had no desire to join them. The night was warm and gentle, so she decided to go outside. As she passed a waiter, she took a second glass of champagne off his tray. With both hands full, she went out the tall French doors to the patio.

In the ballroom the music had just been part of the underlying hum. Out here it was much more obvious. Maggie walked to the edge of the patio, and sure enough, there were speakers set in the shrubs. The atmosphere was helped by romantic lighting. No doubt this patio was designed as a venue for all those married grown-ups inside who wanted someplace to fondle and test-drive each other's spouses.

But for the moment Maggie had the patio to herself. She made a slow circuit of the perimeter. It afforded views of the golf course and the gracious homes surrounding it. She took her time. It wasn't like she had anything else to do. The moon was nearly full, and the landscape looked like something from a Victorian illustration. She drained her first glass of champagne and set it down on the short stone wall that edged the patio. As she lifted the second, she sensed him coming close. It was extraordinary. She had none of the animal dread she always felt when other people came up behind her. All she felt was that flow of energy.

She didn't turn around. It felt good to have him standing so close. His breathing changed as he leaned into her. He bent his head until his face was near her neck and inhaled lightly. His voice was faint as he said, "You smell incredible." Maggie couldn't answer. He put his mouth to her ear and whispered, so that she could feel his words as he spoke. The vibrations shook her insides. "If you want me," he breathed, "all you have to do is turn around." Maggie pivoted slowly until she faced him. For an electric eternity he stood close enough so that she could feel the contours of his body beneath his tux, but he didn't touch her. Finally she realized, once again, he was waiting for her to make the next move. She put her mouth up to him. He grazed her lips with his, more light friction than kiss. Then he did it again. And again. When she began to groan, he finally gave her a real kiss. All the tension that had been building went into it. Unlike Gary, JD used his tongue gently, to tease her.

And then he stopped. He took the champagne glass from her hand and set it down on the ledge. "Dance with me," he breathed.

She had lost track of the music. She listened now. The song was the Spanish ballad "Besame Mucho". "This singer's voice is like honeyed wine," she said softly.

"It's Raul Malo," JD answered. He held her and they moved gracefully in the moonlight. Maggie listened to the lyrics. "Besame," Raul sang, "besame mucho. Como si fuera esta noche la ultima vez."

"I requested this so we could dance to it."

She pulled back slightly and looked at him. "Do you know what he's saying?"

"He translates it. Listen."

Maggie did. "Love me forever," Raul Malo sang.

"That's not exactly correct," she said, resting her head near JD's shoulder.

"There's something incredibly romantic about this song," JD said.

Maggie refrained from answering, from telling him what the lyrics really said.

A genteel gong sounded from the speakers. "You have the tickets?" JD asked as they moved toward the doors.

"I think they're in my evening bag. Does it really matter? They already let us in."

"Take a look," he said. "It's reserved seating. Our table number is on the tickets."

Maggie looked quickly through her small bag, and then again, more intently. "I don't know what I did with them. Maybe I left them at home?"

"Don't worry about it," he said. "Someone will have a list."

𝓇   𝓇   𝓇

"Is there anything else you could have *possibly* fucked up tonight?" Carol Ann snarled at Wesley.

"Your family sponsored this," he said helplessly. "How did I know they were going to insist we bring our tickets?"

"This is just wonderful," she snapped. "My mother gets to sit alone up front with the strangers who were wait-listed for a better table, and we're in the back with the overflow. I can't wait to see which other losers forgot their tickets tonight. I'm sure we'll have the best company in the whole place."

Wesley didn't think there was anyone present, ticketless or not, who could be a less desirable dinner companion than his mother-in-law, but he was wise enough not to say so. "I still don't understand why they won't just let us sit there."

"You are such an asshole!" Carol Ann stormed. She seemed intent on continuing for a while so Wesley set his mind to stupor. Like an armadillo, he was capable of maintaining a defensive posture indefinitely. Sometimes, as he watched rage do its grotesquerie on his wife's face, he felt like he was in a trance. He followed her to the overflow table at the back of the room. He had the presence of mind to pull her chair out for her. But any goodwill he earned from the gesture was lost when their tablemates sat down.

"Evening," JD said, as he pulled out Maggie's chair.

"Oh, my god," Carol Ann moaned.

"Evening," Wesley responded pleasantly.

Maggie didn't answer. She picked up the menu from her plate. "This looks good," she said to no one in particular. "And I'm hungry."

"Maybe you should go eat something right now," Carol Ann said, looking pointedly at JD. "No need to wait for the food."

"That's okay," JD said. "When the meal is really special it's worth the wait."

Carol Ann threw her napkin on her plate. "I need a drink," she said. She stormed off toward the bar.

"What was that all about?" Maggie asked.

"Maybe she's a little upset that dinner's not being served until after the show," JD said.

"You've got to be kidding," Maggie responded. "We've got to sit through Barely Manilow before we get to eat?"

"It's Barey," Wesley said politely. "Not Barely."

JD leaned over to Maggie. "Try a little kindness," he whispered. "You'd be surprised how well he responds to it."

"I wonder where they found him?" Maggie asked.

"I found him," Wesley said proudly. "Right in Conshohocken."

"In Conshohocken?" Maggie asked, in a pleasant conversational tone. "Local bar?"

Wesley rolled his eyes. "*He's* not from there. His *agent* is there. I listened to a demo. He sounds just like the real thing."

"Wow," Maggie said innocently. "Wouldn't it be a bitch if his agent played an actual Manilow recording for you and now you have no idea what we're really going to get?" Wesley looked devastated. Odd metallic noises started coming from the sound system. "Ah," Maggie said. "Here comes the recording now." Stop it, JD mouthed at her.

Carol Ann returned just as the introduction began. It was loud, silencing the room. The same deep generic voice used by the local theater read a list of Barey Manilo's accomplishments. The curtains in front of the portable stage remained closed.

"That is a bit of an unusual introduction," Wesley said nervously.

Carol Ann looked at Wesley as if wishing some remarkable form of suffering on him. "You better hope this show improves fast," she said.

Barey sang his first few bars, live. He sounded just like the real thing. He stopped and launched into friendly patter. He was charming, talking about the beautiful grounds of the club, the attentive service he'd received since arriving, the historic significance of Dooleysburg and what an honor it was to appear here. When he paused, there was enthusiastic applause. As it died down he said, "But you didn't bring me here to chat." With a trilling piano introduction, he launched into "Mandy," one of the real Manilow's greatest hits, except that he used the name Lillian. His delivery was flawless.

Had anyone cared to look at Lillian, they would have seen she was near ecstasy. This impersonator sounded exactly like the Barry Manilow of her dreams, and he was singing to her. She swayed ever so slightly, with the transfixed grace of a charmed snake.

The applause got stronger as the curtain began to open. Then, as the people up close got their first glimpse of the singer, the applause quickly subsided. The Faux Manilow was sitting behind a baby grand that mostly obscured him. The only things showing, between the legs of the piano, were his own hairy calves and naked feet. As the curtain opened fully, the platform where the piano was mounted started to rotate. There was the hint of a gasp as those closest to the stage saw him in full figure. After a moment, the entire audience could see him, completely naked. The platform moved until his back faced the crowd.

Lillian buried her head in her hands at the sight of his naked ass, missing the moment when Manilo stood up and turned around to take a bow. All she was aware of was the sound of the audience reacting, a mixture of gruff male laughter and feminine revulsion overlaid with an unmistakable hoot of derision.

ᵣ   ᵣ   ᵣ

Lillian went sweeping past the overflow table to the ladies' room. Carol Ann stood up, glaring at Wesley as if she wanted to burn a hole in his head, if only she could spare the time. She raced after her mother. Maggie expected Wesley to act like a dog that anticipated a beating. Instead, he began looking around the table expectantly, trying to figure out where he could affiliate next.

JD leaned over. "What do you say we get out of here?"

"Sure," Maggie whispered back. "But first I have to pee."

"You can pee at my place."

"How about in your car? Because that's where it's likely to happen if I don't go now."

"I'm pretty sure it's an urban legend that women can't hold on."

"The stakes are kind of high if you're wrong."

JD leaned closer. "You can't leave me here with him."

Maggie stole a glance at Wesley. JD was right. If either of them made eye contact with him, he was likely to follow them home. "Go get the car," she whispered. "I'll meet you."

She walked into the ladies' room with a certain amount of dread. As badly as she needed to use the facilities, she had no desire to witness whatever drama was taking place in there. She could hear Carol Ann and Lillian, locked in the handicapped stall. In between the occasional ladylike muffled sniff, Lillian was going on about how she'd never be able to show her face in town again. Carol Ann was making comforting noises that still managed to sound both insincere and bored.

Maggie went into the stall farthest from them and took care of business as fast as she could. She was at the sink washing her hands when the door to the handicapped stall opened and Carol Ann looked out. Her face hardened and she walked up to the next sink. "I presume you find this sufficiently amusing," she said coldly.

"No," Maggie said. "I don't take pleasure in seeing anyone get upset."

"So it was just coincidence that you had to use the bathroom right after my mother and I came in here?"

"Give it a rest," Maggie said. "We're leaving and I had to pee."

Lillian's voice came plaintively from behind the stall door. "I'm sure you're not the only one who'll be leaving early."

Despite herself, Maggie felt bad for Lillian. "There doesn't seem to be any kind of mass exodus going on," she said. "JD just isn't feeling himself."

"Why should he, when he has someone to do it for him?" Carol Ann sniped.

"I do hope it's nothing serious," Lillian said from behind her door.

"I don't think so," Maggie said. "He seemed to be overcome with a sudden stiffness." Carol Ann's eyes bugged in wordless fury. "And he feels pretty hot."

"Tell him to hang on until tomorrow and I'll stop by and make sure he gets whatever he needs," Carol Ann said arrogantly.

"I'll bet that thought alone would cure the stiffness," Maggie answered.

"If he doesn't fall asleep from boredom," Carol Ann said, "ask him to show you that thing I taught him to do with his tongue."

Maggie walked out of the ladies' room. She wasn't going to get mad. Carol Ann had done her a favor, reminding her about what she already knew, that it would be a mistake to let things go any farther with JD. Just because the wildness in her had begun listening to him, that was no reason to forget that she had to keep away.

She went out the front door of the Club, trying to maintain her dignity despite her spike-heeled gait. JD was leaning against his clown car, watching her. As she got close he said, "You should wear shoes like that more often. They do something incredible to the way you walk."

"Is it true?" Maggie asked.

JD looked amused. "You might need to tell me what you're talking about."

"Did you bang Carol Ann Carter?"

"Bang?" He smirked. "That's a rather archaic term."

"Did you wave your magic wand and propagate all her wishes? Dip your wick in her wax?"

"Okay, okay." He held up his hand. "Yes. Along with every other male creature in this town higher than reptiles on the evolutionary scale."

"Did you have to go to Carol Ann? I mean, couldn't somebody at the Henhouse have taken care of you?"

JD was amused. "I'm the Chief of Police. I can't patronize the local whorehouse."

"No. Just the local whore. And what's that thing you supposedly do with your tongue?"

JD laughed. "That was Gamey's dog."

"You are a pig."

"Perhaps," he said. "But you're wondering, deep down inside, if there isn't a chance I'm telling the truth about the dog, aren't you?" Maggie had to laugh. Then she turned away.

"Hey," he said. "Where you going?"

"I'll find my own way home."

JD grabbed her arm. "Okay, wait a minute," he said, suddenly sounding very sober. "Why do you think she hates you so much? I haven't gone near her since that first day I saw you. Seriously." He lifted her hand and kissed her palm.

"Stop it." She pulled away.

He was too fast for her. He moved around her, using his hips to pin her to the car. He rocked into her gently. "If you tell me to stop again," he said softly, "I will." Still moving against her, he put a hand on her ribs and slowly slid it upward.

Maggie forced herself to remember there was a problem here. She caught his hand. "Wait a minute," she said. "If she's doing everything that moves and you're doing her, you're probably carrying a buffet of STDs."

"Nope. I'm clean. I get tested twice a year. It's an SOP at the department."

"You expect me to believe that? SOP 52—Adequate Sanitary Precautions Following Relations with C. A. Carter."

"No, goofball. We check for bloodborne pathogens in case we need emergency care, and so we can donate blood for each other."

"Oh." She was quiet for a moment.

"Come on," he said gently. "Let me take you home. My home."

"I'm kind of not in the mood anymore."

He sighed. "That's okay. We can go back to my place and just have a nightcap."

"Nightcap?" she said. "You make fun of me for using the word 'bang' and then you use nightcap?"

"Would you just get in my car?" he asked. "Please?"

"Where did you do it? With Carol Ann? In your itty bitty car?"

JD laughed. "I didn't have my itty bitty car then. But did you ever try to do it in a car?"

"Nobody in New York has a car. And taxis are too expensive."

"Take my word for it," he replied. "It's not worth the effort."

"So where then?"

JD gave up for the moment. "Everywhere. Her house, my house, her father's house."

"I don't want to do it somewhere you did it with her."

"Okay," JD said softly. "I promise, we'll do it someplace where I can be your virgin."

r r r

It only took Carl Bendz a few minutes to get to the Golf and Cricket Club after Carol Ann called. He stood at the ostentatious entrance to the bar, looking across the room at Lillian. She was on a barstool, uncharacteristically hunched, staring into her drink or what was left of it. If she looked up, she would see him in the mirror. But she didn't.

She was so thin. Like one of those joke dogs, he thought, the kind that's bred to look like hide stretched over a skeleton. Why does she do that to herself, he wondered. She didn't even look like a woman anymore.

He had her coat, the full-length sable, draped over his arm. He'd picked it up from the checkroom on his way in. Only he, and perhaps their daughter, would realize that she brought this coat tonight in the hope, however unrealistic, of having her picture taken with the real Barry Manilow. He walked across the room to where she was sitting. "Hey," he said.

She looked at him sideways, without raising her head, then looked away. If she was surprised to see him, it didn't show. From the look of her, this was not her first drink. He glanced around, prepared to wave the bartender away, but the Club hired only the best, and this guy had already scoped out the situation and busied himself at the far end of the bar.

"Lillian," he said, "put your coat on. I'll take you home."

"Whose home, Carl?" she asked. "Your home? Carol Ann's home? I don't have a home."

He was about to respond with something sharp, tell her not to be an ass, when he realized the redness in her eyes was from crying. It was his big weakness, the one thing that never failed to crack his shell, when one of his women cried. He had to give Lillian some admiration here. She knew this about him, and even so, she never used it just for the sake of taking advantage. Putting her coat on a stool, he sat down next to her. He looked from the coat to her expensive dress, to the diamonds glittering in her jewelry. "It hasn't all been bad, has it?" he asked.

"Not after I finally accepted the fact that you're in love with a car lot," she said.

Don't forget the whores, he thought. He considered that it might not sound as funny out loud. "I'm sorry about your show," he said instead.

Lillian took a deep, shuddering breath, fighting not to dissolve into tears. "I'm ruined."

"Ah, people will talk about it for a while, then they'll get over it. Something else will come along to distract them before you know it."

"This is probably good enough to get picked up by the wire services. Especially once the *Intellectual* tells their version of it."

"It won't be in the *Intellectual*," Carl said.

"Of course it will! That simpleton of an editor was here tonight! I donated his goddamn ticket myself!"

"I'm telling, you," Carl said simply, "it won be in the *Intellectual*."

Realization slowly swept across Lillian's face. "What did it cost you?"

"I gave my granddaughter a Humvee," he replied. "Don't you think you're worth more to me than she is?"

"Thank you, Carl," Lillian said quietly.

He stood up and handed over her coat. "Come on," he said. "Let's go home."

ɾ   ɾ   ɾ

JD pulled into his driveway. This time Maggie waited for him to come around and get her door. He led the way inside, stopping in the small mudroom to take off his shoes.

"You want me to take off my shoes too?" she asked.

He looked her up and down slowly, savoring her. "Those shoes can have the run of my house." Taking her hand, he led her into the kitchen. "I've got some candles," he began.

"No," she muttered, pulling him toward her. "I want to see you." She dropped her purse on the table, and kissed him hard. He only held the kiss for a minute and then stepped back. She ripped open his shirt, sending fancy studs flying. He stood there, breathing hard. Maggie stepped close again. This time she put her mouth to his ear and exhaled the slightest whisper of breath. He groaned. With her mouth, she followed the vibrations of that sound, kissing his neck and then the base of his throat while her hand slid over his chest and belly. He was more muscular and yet softer than she had imagined. She slowed herself down, then noticed that his hands were clenched. He was using everything he had to hold back. With one motion, she pushed his shirt and jacket off his shoulders and then stepped back as he freed himself from them and stood before her, naked from the waist up. "My god," she whispered, "you're so beautiful."

He looked at her, a look with something archetypal in it. Gently he turned her around and started kissing the back of her neck, slowly, starting behind her ear and working his way down. He wrapped his left arm around her waist to hold her upright. Then he released the comb holding her hair, letting the curls fall loose around her shoulders. He unzipped her dress and slid his right hand inside, tentatively at first. When she didn't protest, he raised his hand, caressing her through the satiny fabric of her bra. Gently, insistently, he began exploring her. Suddenly he removed his hand. "Don't stop," she moaned.

Holding her tight against him, JD slid his hand down the open back of her dress. With no warning, he slipped it between her legs. Maggie inhaled sharply. "Oh my god," he groaned.

He began stroking her, very lightly at first, gradually increasing the pressure. Maggie was helpless. She had no choice but to lean into him. Suddenly she gasped, "Stop. I can't stand up anymore." JD stepped back.

Maggie turned around. She unbuttoned his trousers. He kissed her while he slid out of them. She reached for him, but he caught her hand. "No," he said, his voice hoarse. "I can't let you do that yet." He started to slip her dress off her shoulders. This time, she stopped him.

"My game tonight," she said. "My rules." She put her hand on his chest. He held her gaze as he allowed her to push him down onto a chair.

Neither of them moved, and then JD said softly, "Take it off."

Maggie did nothing for a long moment. She wanted him to wait until his suffering became exquisite. When she was sure, she began, one shoulder at a time, to pull off her dress. He watched briefly, and then closed his eyes, swallowing hard.

"Look at me," she commanded softly.

JD's eyes were barely open, focused on her. She took her time removing the dress, finally leaving it, a puddle of silk, on the floor. She started to take off the pantyhose.

"Don't," he said.

She stood before him, just beyond his reach, and slowly removed her bra. She closed her eyes, swaying slightly. When she opened them again, he was watching her, waiting. Now that she was looking at him, he began exploring her with his eyes. It made her groan.

"I want you now," she demanded.

JD smiled slightly, still in control, always in control. "Come here," he whispered. When Maggie got close, he pulled her down on top of him. With one swift thrust he was deep inside, making her gasp. JD kissed her, hard. She couldn't hold still. She opened her eyes, just for a moment, and he was still watching her.

"You go first," he breathed.

Maggie didn't know what he meant. He waited a moment, then used his hands to guide her into a rhythmic, hypnotic motion. Her body took over. "What does it feel like," she murmured, "inside of me?"

JD did not answer right away. "It feels silky," he finally whispered. "Slippery. And hot. Hotter than any woman I have ever had. Like it's near the core of the earth inside you."

Maggie let go of control for an instant, and flowed with the sensation. Then she held herself tighter around him and leaning toward his ear, whispered, "Now?"

"Stop," he pleaded. "I'm trying to . . ." and then he moved convulsively. "I'm trying to hold on for you." This simple statement triggered sensations so sharp and lovely that for the first time in her life, Maggie existed only as what she felt. There was nothing here she could control. She went lost within the spiral of an evolutionary dance.

Only after she arched her back and writhed did JD begin to move. Maggie was helpless as she lost control again and again, until finally, exhausted, she began to drift back to the kitchen and the night. Then JD let himself go. With a sound so guttural it came from somewhere below his heart, he lifted them both into the air and exploded inside her. Listening to the song of her body, she moved on him, drawing his orgasm out beyond the limits of anything he could have imagined, almost beyond what he could endure. The sound of him was like the cry of sailors bashing themselves into oblivion at the feet of the Sirens. Maggie was stunned by the power and mystery of his pleasure. When he stopped moving they collapsed into each other, sweaty and heaving for breath, commingled. JD raised her face and kissed her gently. "I think I could love you," he whispered.

Maggie began to tremble. It was not the sort of shaking that came from being cold. It began somewhere deep inside, as if her foundation had been built on a fault line. It grew in intensity until it ripped her away from JD. She raced into the powder room, stumbling on her ridiculous heels.

It was quiet for a while, then JD heard the water come on. He was getting cold. He went and knocked softly on the door. "Hey," he said quietly. "You okay?"

"I want my clothes," Maggie answered.

He gathered up her things, finding them suddenly flimsy and inadequate, unequal to the task of protecting her. He went to the hall closet and pulled out his favorite hoodie. Then he knocked on the bathroom door again. "I have your stuff."

She opened the door from behind, so that all he saw was her hand. At the last minute he felt awkward about giving her his sweatshirt and held on to it.

He was waiting in the kitchen when she came out some minutes later. He'd put his trousers back on, with a clean tee shirt from the laundry room. "Can I get you anything?" he asked.

"I want to go home." Her voice was flat, somehow childlike.

"Sure," he said, his tone careful. He hoped for the explanation he somehow knew would never come. "Take this," he said, putting the hoodie around her shoulders.

Maggie didn't answer. He put his tux jacket back on and held the kitchen door open for her. He could see her retreating farther and farther into herself. By the time they got to his car he was questioning whether he'd totally mis-read things somehow. He started the car, then asked, "What happened back there?"

She looked at him, confused, or maybe preoccupied. "Have you forgotten already?"

He refused to be derailed. "That wasn't just sex. That was communion. I know you felt it. And then suddenly you got scared."

"I didn't get scared."

"You were shaking. And you ran off to the bathroom in a panic."

"I was wet," she said shortly. "It's not good to be wet. I just went to get cleaned up."

"Does that always happen?"

"I don't know what you're talking about," she snapped.

"Okay," he answered. "I'll stop. I just hope some day you can trust me enough to tell me. I can wait. I know I have to earn your confidence."

Maggie looked at him without patience. "You're being a jerk," she said, and from the look on her face it was clear she was tempted to call him worse than that. "If you don't want to take me home, I can walk."

JD put the car in gear and backed out of the driveway. They rode the blocks to her house in strained silence. He pulled around behind her garage. Before he could turn off the car, she opened her door and got out. She started to take off his hoodie.

"Keep it," he said. "It's cold out. I'll pick it up tomorrow."

"No need," she said, dropping it on the seat of his car.

"Hey," JD gave it one last shot, "I'd like to see you again."

Maggie closed the car door without answering.

39

Perhaps if the spell of unseasonably warm weather hadn't continued so long, Chrissie wouldn't have gone through with the idea. Later, she would decide that was it, the weather was behind her obsession with the plan. The first couple of times she suggested it, Katie and Emily were totally against it. Chrissie wasn't surprised. After all, Nathaniel wasn't exactly the kind of boy you brought home to mother. She kept at it, though, knowing she would eventually wear her friends down, like water dripping mercilessly on a stone.

"I don't get it," Emily finally said. "What do you need us for? It's your car and your body. You want to give the token black guy a ride, you're already in the driver's seat any way you look at it."

"What is the big deal with helping me out a little?" Chrissie asked irritably.

"Don't you feel even a little bad about using people?" Emily asked.

"He's not just some guy with a great body," Chrissie insisted. "He is going to *be* somebody. He's smart, he's funny, he really thinks about things when you talk to him."

Emily looked at Katie. "Do you believe it? She has a crush on him."

"Stop being a jerk," Chrissie said, but without malice.

Katie always capitulated first. "If I do this," she said, "what's in it for me?"

"I can see if he has a friend."

"Yeah, right," Katie snorted.

Chrissie hesitated. "You can use my Prada bag."

Katie considered this. "Nope," she said. "I want the Hummer."

Chrissie looked as if she was facing Sophie's choice. "My grandfather would kill me."

"How's he going to know?"

"Trust me, he'll find out."

"I'll only use it after dark. North of Salisbury Township."

"It won't matter," Chrissie said. "You might as well drive it around town at noon."

"Forget it, then," Katie said.

"King of Prussia Mall," Chrissie gave in. "We all go together, I drive out past Chalfont, and then you take it from there."

"This Saturday," Katie bargained.

Chrissie thought about this. "But Saturday is when Nathaniel said he can hang out."

"Nope," Katie insisted. "We go to the mall this Saturday or the deal is off." They stared at each other.

"This is getting boring," Emily said, out of patience. "He lives in Norristown, which is on the way to the mall anyway. We'll go there first and then pick him up on the way home."

Chrissie hugged her. "You're a genius! You're coming too, right?" The girls all knew nobody stood a chance of getting permission to go anywhere outside of town unless Emily came along. Parents always assumed her mature, tranquil demeanor meant she had good judgment. They never figured her for the brains of the operation.

"Prada bag," Emily said archly.

"For one day," Chrissie replied.

"Screw you," Emily laughed.

"Em," Chrissie pleaded, "I've only used it twice."

Emily pulled out her phone. She scrolled through her messages until she found what she was looking for, then turned the phone around so Chrissie could read the screen. Chrissie's mouth dropped open. "Why is he asking *you* to get together on Saturday?" she demanded.

"Because god's gift to St. Agnes football needs some help from the calculus freak," Emily said smugly. "So we both have something the other one wants."

"Fine," Chrissie said, accepting defeat with minimal grace. "Prada bag. But I have visiting rights."

☞   ☞   ☞

Chrissie could not believe her luck. Nathaniel and the weather were both cooperating. It was so warm for early March that people were walking around in summer clothes. She insisted on driving once they picked up Nathaniel, but Katie didn't seem to care. She was beat from walking around the mall and happy to sit in the back seat with Emily.

The only weirdness of the day was when they had to stop at Nathaniel's house. Chrissie hadn't expected something quite so *downscale*. The town where he lived felt more like a miniature city, a really poor one. Even though it was Saturday afternoon there were only a few stores open. And almost nobody was outside. The people they did see reminded her of hyenas, hanging around waiting for something to get killed so they could fight over the carcass. There was a huge courthouse in the center of town, much bigger than the one in Dooleysburg, probably because they had to handle lots more crimes. It had a big green dome on top, but there were chunks missing out of it, like it was the partially rebuilt Death Star.

And Nathaniel's mother kept acting like they came for a visit, offering them food and stuff. All Chrissie wanted was to get out of there, but good manners were a big deal to Nathaniel, so Chrissie knew it would be stupid to insult his mother. That meant they had to wait around and have something to drink. By the time they managed to get out of his house she was cranky.

None of that mattered now, though. They were in Gorge Park, on their way to the Cliff View Overlook. She had promised Nathaniel a special surprise, and she was ready to deliver. But first she had to show him the Overlook. As far as he knew, that's why they were here. She turned left onto a dirt road. It was full of deep ruts and she had to go slow. At the end was a small parking lot. "We're here," she said, pulling in.

The only other car in the lot was a crummy old Chevy Blazer. It looked like it was held together with bumper stickers. "I bet somebody junked that here," Katie said.

"Are you kidding?" Emily asked. "Out here in the boonies that's probably somebody's vacation home."

Chrissie wished they'd cut it out. What if Nathaniel's mother drove an old junk? But she had a bigger problem right now. The Blazer was in the hiding spot, the only one that couldn't be seen from the road. She spun past it and took the next best place, behind a big rock. With no leaves this time of year, it was the only other cover out here. She turned off the engine.

Nathaniel looked around. "This is the Cliff View Overlook?" he asked.

"No, silly," Chrissie giggled. She knew her girly act annoyed Emily. Too bad. "We have to get out and walk."

"Okay," Nathaniel grinned. "I'm game."

"Big game," Chrissie heard Katie say under her breath. She hoped Nathaniel didn't hear.

They got out and Chrissie opened the back of the Hummer. There was a blanket over the stuff they got at the mall. She reached under one corner and pulled out two backpack-style coolers. "Here," she said, handing one to Katie. She hefted the other one herself.

"Let me get that." Nathaniel took the pack from her. "This is heavy," he said. "What's in here?"

"I thought we could have a picnic," Chrissie said innocently.

"It's a bit late for a picnic, don't you think?"

She loved his Caribbean accent. "Not a whole picnic. Just some snacks and drinks."

"It will be getting dark soon. Won't the park be closing?"

"I don't think so." Chrissie shook her head, eyes wide.

Nathaniel shrugged and set off with her toward the rutted entrance to the lot. Emily rolled her eyes at Katie as they followed behind. "I thought he was supposed to be smart."

"He's innocent," Katie said. "Naïve. Pure. She loves the challenge."

One thing Chrissie had told the truth about was the awesome view. People called The Overlook the Grand Canyon of Bucks County, and they weren't exaggerating. It was a short hike to the edge of a steep cliff that had an iron fence all along the edge. The land fell away in front of them. Far, far below a roiling creek curved around the far side of the gash in the earth. The fence was sturdy and as tall as Nathaniel. They walked up to it and looked through the bars to the drop-off. "Okay," Nathaniel said. "This is pretty scary."

"This is nothing," Chrissie said. "You're totally safe here. There's a better place where the fence ends. We can go down there."

Chrissie hurried ahead. The light would be fading soon. She didn't want to give him a chance to think about this. With the end of the fence in sight she charged forward, grabbed the last post, and swung herself over the edge of the cliff face. There was a shuffling sound of something sliding on dry leaves.

Nathaniel ran to the spot where she'd vanished. He dropped the cooler pack and leaned over the edge, holding tight to the fence post. "Are you all right?" he called.

"Come on down," she called back. "There's a big ledge here."

"I'm not convinced that's a good idea," he said firmly. "Come back up. We can have our picnic right here."

Katie and Emily caught up with him. "If you're not going down," Katie said, "move out of the way." She kneeled down and dropped her cooler pack over the edge, then scrambled past him. Emily followed. There was utter silence. Nathaniel stood alone on the brink of the drop.

"Hey," Chrissie's voice suddenly called. "Get down here. And don't forget the cooler."

Nathaniel grabbed a strap of the cooler and, saying a rapid prayer, slid over the edge. He landed on a big flat piece of rock covered in dead leaves. There was just enough room for the four of them to sit comfortably. The place where they'd come over the edge was five or six feet above them, but there were plenty of crevices and a few roots they could use to climb back up.

Chrissie took the pack from him and unzipped it. She pulled out a bottle of Wild Turkey. "You like bourbon?" she asked. Nathaniel shook his head. "You ever try it?" He shook his head again. "First time for everything," she said.

"No thanks," he said politely.

Next she pulled out a six-pack of beer. She held a can out to him. Nathaniel shook his head again. "Come on," she said. "You at least have to try."

"Not today," he said. "But don't let me stop you."

Chrissie opened the bourbon and took a swig. Her eyes watered, but she kept it down. She popped the tab on a can of beer and took a long sip. "Here," she gasped, handing the bourbon to Katie. The bottle went around once and came back to Chrissie.

She turned to Nathaniel. "You need to take a turn."

He seemed amused. "I don't think so."

"Come on," Chrissie harassed him. "Don't be a wuss."

"My mother and I are Baptists," Nathaniel replied. "We don't drink alcohol."

"If you're Baptist, what are you doing at a Catholic school?" Emily asked.

"I believe the proper term is, I'm a 'ringer'."

"That's what I heard," Katie said, "that Father Curran bought us a football player."

"What about Father Curran's touching scholarship fundraising speech? I thought the money was for a deserving scholar who wanted a Catholic education," Emily said.

Nathaniel shrugged "I don't mind the Catholic part. And I like playing football."

Chrissie took a long chug of beer. "I'm cold," she shivered.

"Oh," Emily said, with enough sarcasm in her voice for everyone to hear, "what a good thing we brought a blanket."

Chrissie glanced at her. "Hand it over."

"Perhaps we can share?" Nathaniel suggested.

"Good idea," Chrissie said, shaking open the blanket and wrapping it around both of them.

"Anyone else cold?" Nathaniel asked.

"No," Chrissie answered. If Nathaniel wasn't going to drink she could revise the plan. They didn't need to sit out here until the cooler was empty. The girls had access to booze whenever they wanted in the snug comfort of each other's homes as long as they were careful to do it in a way that allowed their parents to pretend they didn't notice. Chrissie gave Katie The Look. It was getting dark, but Katie didn't miss it. She stood up, "I need to tinkle."

"It's kind of dark now," Chrissie said. "Maybe you should take Em along."

"What for?" Emily asked. The other two looked at her, stunned. She stared stubbornly back at them.

"You can hold the flashlight for me," Katie said.

"Yeah," Chrissie added, "and watch out for someone who wants to stab her in the back."

"Actually, it's getting kind of chilly out here." Emily emphasized the word 'chilly' as she stood up. "How about giving us the car keys?"

"You can head back if you want," Chrissie said, not bothering to keep the anger out of her voice, "but you're not getting the keys. We'll be there in a few minutes."

Katie turned and quickly climbed up the wall. Emily glared at Chrissie for several long seconds, then followed. "Hurry up!" she hissed as she climbed past Chrissie's head. When she pulled herself over the top of the ledge, Katie was standing there with a sour expression on her face.

"You look like one of the nuns," Emily said.

"You shouldn't have done that."

"Why not?" Emily countered. "What's she going to do, stamp her little foot and get pissy with me?"

"We had a bargain. Holding out for the keys wasn't part of it. Friends don't do that kind of stuff to each other."

"Friends don't do *this* kind of stuff to each other." Emily waved her arm to indicate the dark, barren forest. "Don't you ever get tired of standing around holding the bag for her?" Katie didn't answer. Emily aimed the flashlight into the trees beyond the path. "Do you have to piss or not?" she demanded, and set off into the woods.

r   r   r

Chrissie snuggled close to Nathaniel. "Warm me up," she said. Nathaniel leaned over and kissed her. There was nothing tentative about it. Suddenly he was all biological imperative, not good breeding. Chrissie squirmed slightly under the pressure of his mouth. Nathaniel gave her a moment to breathe, then put his arm behind her head and kissed her again, hard. This time there was tongue in it. "Wow," she said. "You don't mess around."

"Your friend asked us to hurry," he responded.

"Screw her," Chrissie said.

Nathaniel chuckled. "Tonight or some other time?"

Chrissie pulled back. "That's not funny," she pouted.

"My mistake," Nathaniel said. "I wasn't sure of the extent of my obligations."

"What's that supposed to mean?" Chrissie demanded. "You think I'm some kind of chore?"

"I think you're a fine girl, and this will be a privilege. But I wasn't under the impression you were looking for a commitment."

Chrissie was furious. "I don't need any favors!"

"Shh," Nathaniel said.

"Who are you to tell me to be quiet?"

He lifted his head to listen. "I thought I heard something."

Chrissie looked at him coldly. "Now you want to play Blair Witch? You are a sorry piece of work." Nathaniel frowned and gestured for her to be quiet. Chrissie strained to listen. "I don't hear anything," she said. Nathaniel stood up, tensed like a coiled snake, and then bolted up the rock wall.

"Freaking great," Chrissie said to the empty ledge. She scrambled up the wall after him. As her head came even with the top, Nathaniel turned and waved at her to stay down. "Yeah, right," she muttered, and then had a flash of paranoia. She felt her pocket. The keys were still there. At least he wasn't trying to steal the Hummer. She scrambled over the top of the ledge. "Katie?" she called. "Emily?"

"Please!" Nathaniel whispered. "Keep quiet a moment!"

"Over here!" a muffled voice called. Chrissie gave Nathaniel a contemptuous glare and started off in the direction of the voice. Nathaniel grabbed her arm. "Please wait," he said.

"Go to hell," Chrissie said. She tromped off into the woods, even though she pretty much couldn't see where she was going. "Katie?" she called again. There was no answer. "Katie? This isn't funny. Come on, you guys." A stick snapped behind her, and she turned quickly. It was only Nathaniel. "Piss off," she said to him.

"Something's not right," he said.

"Yeah, I know," she replied sarcastically. "I took a mama's boy into the woods after dark." She went a little farther off the path into the woods. "Emily," she called again, "where the hell are you?"

Without warning there was a sound of heavy crashing off to the right, as if multiple people were running through the brush, and then just as suddenly everything went silent. And then there was a scream. Chrissie and Nathaniel ran toward the sound. It was Katie. She had fallen right near the edge of the cliff. She managed to stop herself from going over by grabbing a sapling, but she was thrashing around in panic, looking like she might lose her hold any second.

"Hold still!" Nathaniel yelled. She ignored him. She was screaming something. He laid face down on the ground, and anchoring one arm around a smallish tree, used the other to grab her across the chest. She tried to claw at him. "It's Nathaniel!" he yelled. "Just hold still!" He rolled onto his back, using his weight to pull her up to safer ground.

"They have Emily!" she was sobbing. "I got away, but they still have Emily!"

"What?" Chrissie asked. "Who? Who has Emily?"

"I think she means us," a voice said.

Everything got very still as Nathaniel and the girls looked around. And then a flashlight popped on, illuminating the place where the voice came from, momentarily blinding everyone. The flashlight was being held at Emily's waist, and it pointed up, directly at her head. Someone was holding her from behind, with a hand clamped over her mouth. Her sweatshirt was torn and her nose was bleeding. Her eyes were open, but not focusing on anything. "Well, look at that," the voice said. "She didn't want you, but she's rolling around on the ground with a nigger."

"Get up," another voice said from nearby in the trees. "They're from Dooleysburg."

Nathaniel slowly got to his feet. "Why don't you show yourself?" he said.

"You know how I know they're from Dooleysburg?" the voice continued. "Because the ho didn't want me, but she's ready to give it to him."

Two more flashlights shone out from the trees, directly into Nathaniel's face. Nathaniel cringed, then lowered his hands and stared at the lights. "What is it you want?" he asked.

"What is it you got?"

"You looking to bargain with us?" a third voice said, and then laughed. "Cause we could just cut you up and take whatever we want."

"Sure," Nathaniel said. "But you could have done that already, and you didn't. That means you're not stupid men."

"They're not men," Katie whispered. "They're our age."

"Nobody's seen you yet," Nathaniel continued. "You could turn off your lights and go, and nobody will ever hear about this."

"Coulda done that without all this trouble," the second voice said.

"Hey, Snow White," the third voice said, "what are you doing in the woods with the Ace of Spades? Why don't you come over here and meet a real man?"

"Maybe some other time," Chrissie said.

"The Hummer," the second voice said. "Hand over the keys to the Hummer."

"Give them the keys," Katie urged quietly.

"How many Hummers like that you think are riding around Bucks County?" Chrissie asked. "If I don't show up home with that thing in an hour, every cop in the county will be looking for you. You won't even get a decent ride before they catch you."

"Jesus, Mary and Joseph," Nathaniel said.

"Well it's true," Chrissie said. She turned back to the voices. "Ask for something else."

"We're not playing frickin' magic genie, ho," the second voice said. "Maybe we just need to go ahead with the original plan."

"There's beer," Nathaniel said. "A couple of six packs. And some Wild Turkey."

"Where?" said the one holding Emily.

"Down there," Nathaniel pointed. "On the ledge."

"Go get it." The flashlight beam waved briefly.

"How do I know you won't take off with the girls?"

"You don't," the voice holding the flashlight said.

"Send one of the girls," the third voice said.

Chrissie and Katie looked at each other. "Go," Nathaniel said harshly to Chrissie. It took her a few trips, since she couldn't get up the wall with a full pack. When she was done she hoisted herself up onto the ground. "That's all of it," she said.

"Put it over there," the third voice said, waving his light in Emily's direction. "Next to your friend."

"I'll do it," Nathaniel said.

As he passed Chrissie she whispered, "I tried to make a call. There's no signal."

Nathaniel stacked everything in his arms so he could make one trip. He backed away rapidly after he put it down.

"What the hell is that?" the third voice asked. The fierce beam of a halogen light was several hundred yards away, moving rapidly in their direction. The boys turned off their flashlights abruptly, plunging the group into darkness. There was a confused panic and the sound of people crashing through the underbrush. Nathaniel was shouting not to move, to stay away from the cliff. Then the screaming started. It was one of the girls.

"Emily!" Chrissie called. She bumped into Katie and Nathaniel as the three of them headed toward the sound, and then tripped and fell on top of Emily. "It's okay," she said loudly. "You're okay now! We're here with you!" Emily continued to scream. "Please stop," Chrissie said, starting to cry herself. "Please make her stop," she said to Nathaniel.

Over the noise of Emily's screaming, they could hear, once again, the sound of someone running heavily through the woods. The high-powered light was coming at them. There was a moment of stunned silence, and then Katie began to scream as well. "Oh, shit," Nathaniel said. "Please don't let this get any worse."

"Nobody move!" a new voice bellowed. It was deeper and more authoritative than the previous voices. The light, pointed in their direction now, illuminated the tableau of terrified teenagers. "What's going on here?" the latest intruder demanded.

"We got lost," Chrissie said immediately. "In the woods."

"You!" the voice ordered, pointing the beam at Nathaniel. "Move away from those girls." Nathaniel stood up slowly. "Hands over your head!" the voice ordered.

Nathaniel did as he was told. The beam of light moved suddenly, dropping to the ground near Nathaniel. Without warning, he was hit from behind. He fell to his knees and his face was shoved to the ground. Someone kneed him in the back, then he felt his wrists being handcuffed behind him. Whoever it was picked the light up again. "Get up!" the voiced ordered. Nathaniel had a hard time doing that without his hands, and he tripped, stumbling a few feet closer to the edge of the cliff.

"Stop!" Chrissie yelled. "He didn't do anything!"

"What happened here?" the voiced demanded, pointing the light at Emily.

"I told you, we got lost. She tripped and fell."

"What was all the screaming about?"

"She got scared. She thought she was going to fall down the cliff."

"Who are *you*?" Katie asked suddenly.

"Park ranger," the voice said. "I was down in the station and saw lights moving around up here, so I came up to investigate. That Humvee in the parking lot belong to you?"

"Yes, sir," Chrissie said, sounding young and scared.

"What are you doing up here at night?" he demanded. "Drinking?"

"No, sir."

He shone the light around on the ground, looking for evidence they were lying. There was none. "So what are you doing up here?"

"Nathaniel here," Chrissie pointed to him, "is an exchange student. Since the weather was so nice, we wanted to show him the Overlook. Except it got dark a lot faster than we expected, and we didn't have any flashlights, and we got lost out here, and then we were scared we'd fall over the cliff."

"I just saw flashlights," the ranger said.

"Oh, we had them," Chrissie said, "but we had to . . . you know, and I was holding the lights while everybody did their business, and then I heard Emily scream and I panicked and dropped them. They're around here somewhere."

"So you're telling me he wasn't bothering you?" He waved his light at Nathaniel.

"No, sir," Chrissie said sweetly. "He's our friend."

The ranger shone his light on each of them in turn, as if inviting them to disagree. Nobody said a word. "Come on," he said gruffly. "I'll take you back to your vehicle. If we don't see your flashlights along the way, it's your loss."

"Thank you, sir," Chrissie said. "What about the handcuffs?"

"I'll take them off when we get to the parking lot." He didn't wait for anyone to protest, grabbing Nathaniel roughly by the arm and taking off. "Everybody stay together," he ordered. Nathaniel stumbled and fell. They waited while he struggled to stand up. Emily started to cry again quietly. "I could take you all in and call your parents," the ranger said. "There's a good reason this park closes at sunset. I hope by now you figured out what that is. But if I catch you up here after closing again, you're not getting another break."

"Yes, sir," Chrissie said meekly.

They crossed the rutted road into the parking lot. The Hummer was there, as was the ranger's SUV. The Chevy Blazer was gone. "Thank you, sir," Chrissie said.

"I'll wait until you're out of here," he said. Chrissie pulled the keys from her pocket and pressed the button to unlock the doors. The Hummer beeped and flashed its lights in welcome. She opened the driver's side door and climbed in. The ranger walked around to the passenger side and finally unlocked Nathaniel's handcuffs. Then he shone the light onto the front passenger door, moving it back and forth as if he was reading something. He looked up and tapped on the window, motioning to Chrissie. When she came around the car he pointed the light at the front passenger door again. "What's this?" he demanded.

On the side of the SUV, somebody had scratched, "Nigg-r lov-r". Instead of the "e" in each word there was a swastika. Chrissie started to cry. "My grandfather's going to kill me."

"Okay," he said, impatiently, "nobody's leaving until I know what really happened tonight."

"Nothing," Chrissie insisted. "I already told you."

"I think we better go over to the state police barracks," he said.

"No," Chrissie begged. "Please." Katie started crying too. "We made a really bad mistake getting lost out there in the dark. But I promise we'll never do it again. Please."

"Was this on your vehicle when you came here?"

Chrissie nodded, sniffling. "We took Nathaniel to the mall today. We wanted him to see all the stuff they don't have where he comes from. Somebody did that while we were inside."

The ranger pulled a pad and pen from his pocket. "What are your names?" he asked. They told him. He turned to Chrissie. "You have any ID?" She nodded and got out her driver's license. He copied down the information. "Here's want you're going to do," he said. "You're going to take your friends home, and then I want you to go straight home and stay there. Don't ever come back here at night. Maybe don't ever come back here at all."

"Yes, sir," Chrissie said. "Thank you, sir." They got in the car, Nathaniel up front with Chrissie, Emily and Katie in the back. Chrissie flipped the switch that automatically locked all their doors, and drove with extreme caution to the park exit. They continued through the darkened countryside and then down the steep curving road that ended at Route 32. Once they were in familiar territory, she began to relax. "That was a real shitstorm, wasn't it?" she asked.

"What the hell is wrong with you?" Emily shouted. "Why didn't you tell him what happened?"

"I did," Chrissie said nonchalantly. "I told him a version of what happened."

"You lied," Emily said angrily. "We could have all been killed, and you lied about it."

"Don't be such a drama queen. Those guys weren't going to hurt anybody."

"You don't know that. They weren't holding you!" Emily started crying again.

"Look," Chrissie said, "the only bad thing that happened was we got a little scared. The real problem is, how am I going to explain my car to my grandfather? When he sees it, that's when I'll really need to worry about getting killed."

"Is that all you ever worry about?" Katie demanded.

"It's plenty," Chrissie said. She glanced over at Nathaniel. In the light from the dashboard she could see that his jaw was clenched. "Are you okay?" she asked, not sounding as if the question was of any real importance.

"Are we near a town?" he asked.

"Not really," she answered. "Why?"

"I need to use a phone."

She pulled hers out. "Here," she said. "Use mine."

"No, thank you," he said stiffly. "I prefer to use a public phone."

Chrissie was losing patience. "What for?"

"I want to make a call."

"Don't tell me you were scared," she said mockingly. "You want to go sit in the back with the other girls?"

"Just drop me someplace where I can find a phone," he said, cold. "I'll make my own way home."

"Not a problem," she snapped. "I had no idea you would be such a drag." She drove on with determination, looking for some place to ditch him.

40

JD sat in the back room of Scheherazade Dream Spa. The lipstick-red vibrating chair wasn't as comfortable as he remembered, but leave it to Madame Yaskagya to find a place to use it. She walked in and put two small glasses of tea in silver holders on her desk. "You vant schnapps?" she asked, in her deep voice.

"No thanks," JD answered.

"You vant I turn on massage function?"

"Maybe later," JD said pleasantly. "Right now, I hope you'll forgive my abruptness, but I have some business to conduct."

Madame settled in her chair. "Is not like old days," she said. "Ve do 100% legal now."

"Somebody trying to shake you down?" JD asked solicitously.

"Still choirboy." Madame shook her head slightly. "Is not crime no more, you know. You vant ve do a little favor? The girls all happy to see you. For old time's sake." She reached over and patted JD's arm.

"Not that I'm ungrateful," he said. "Just, you know, that thing about contagion I've always had."

"Hah!" Madame said haughtily. "Ve still test, every month."

"Like a version of team building?" JD asked.

"Paid in advance," she answered. "Four more months on contract. After that, every voman for herself. You vant certified, now is your time."

"Well, I appreciate the offer," JD said. "But I think I'm okay for now."

"So vat I can do for you?"

JD reached into his jacket and pulled out an envelope. "I was hoping you might be able to help me make an ID." He spread some photos on her desk. They were candids of the Chipmunk in full flash.

Madame looked at him. "Tell me," she said quizzically. "You can get pictures, vhy you don't just arrest the imbecile?"

"We didn't take these," JD explained. "He likes cheerleaders, so we went around to all the pep squads and gave the girls disposable cameras. When they turned the cameras in, these were the best of the photos."

Madame opened her desk drawer and took out a pair of reading glasses. She put them on and carefully examined the photos, taking her time, lifting some to look at them more closely. When she was done she took off her glasses and turned to JD. "This is not Chipmunk."

"Are you sure? What if he dyed his hair to disguise himself?"

"Is not Bendz," she said simply. "This one has a stiffie."

JD was sorry he had a mouthful of tea. "Carl Bendz never got an erection?"

"No," Madame said. "Pink feathers, high heels, girls tried everything. Cheap bastard always took a discount, like vas girls' fault."

"Okay, okay." JD waved his hand before she could go any further. "Any idea who this might be, then?"

"Is nobody ever came to my house," she said.

JD was surprised. "Are you sure?"

"Sure I'm sure," she said. "Could be any Tom, Dick or Harry." A satisfied grin spread slowly over JD's face. He took Madame's hand and kissed it. She sighed and fanned herself melodramatically. "Such a gentleman."

"And you, my dear, are a genius."

ɼ   ɼ   ɼ

Harry Butts walked dejectedly into his house. It had been a bad day, a terrible day. Today was their quarterly review of inventory and sales figures, and the results didn't make Bendz happy. Not that Harry had any way to influence the sales numbers, but that didn't stop Bendz from taking things out on him. His title might be Showroom Coordinator, but his job was whipping boy. Bendz would be chewing him out for days, criticizing every move he made, throwing stuff at him, small stuff, sure, but stuff nonetheless.

He put his mail down on the credenza, then stopped. There was no moon tonight, and it was utterly dark in his house, but he sensed something was different. He didn't hear anything, but he felt like he was having that thing animals get. Up till now, he always figured people made that up, but this was real. Harry Butts froze like a scared squirrel. If he had a sharper intellect, he might have appreciated the irony in that.

"Who's there?" he finally asked. His voice squeaked a little. A lamp snapped on next to his favorite chair. JD Charles was sitting there. "Chief Charles!" Harry's breath, which he hadn't realized he was holding, released explosively. "You scared the crap out of me!"

"Ought to get a timer, Harry. Need to leave some lights on when you're not around, scare off the burglars. And nobody likes to come home to a dark house."

"What are you doing here?"

"Now there's an interesting question," JD said. "What do you think might bring me here?" Harry made a puzzled face. "Come on over here," JD said. "There's something I want to show you."

That's when Harry noticed the Chief was holding one of those Kodak type envelopes, except this one didn't have any brand name on it. He walked over reluctantly.

"Have a seat," the chief said. His tone was kind of unfriendly. "I have some pictures here I want you to look at." Harry nodded. "You need your glasses or anything?" Harry shook his head. He swallowed. He hoped the 'glunk' sound it made wasn't as loud to the chief as it was to him.

JD took a small stack of photos out of the envelope and handed them to Harry. "Had to have these done at the state lab," he said. "Not the kind of thing you can take to the local drugstore. So these are only copies. They kept the originals at the lab." Harry took the pictures, but continued to stare at JD. "Go ahead," JD urged. "Have a look."

Harry looked at the first shot for just an instant, then rapidly shuffled through the deck, his hands trembling. It didn't take him long to finish. "Chief Charles," he looked up, his face reddening, "these are very offensive."

"Yeah," JD said. "I thought so too. As did a number of teenage girls around town, including the ones who took these pictures."

Harry swallowed again. "So why are you showing them to me?"

"Ah," JD said. "Good question. See, between the Chipmunk head and the trench coat, there's not a whole lot we can use to identify this guy. He planned that pretty carefully, wouldn't you say?" Harry shrugged. "Matter of fact," JD continued, "there's only one thing on these pictures you could say for sure was his. Want to guess what that might be?"

"I dunno," Harry said dully.

"Look again," JD said. "Maybe it'll come to you."

Harry barely glanced at the first photo, then looked away. JD got up and stood over him. "Here," he said, taking the pictures from Harry's hand, "let me help you. See right there?" He pointed. "The guy covered up everything but his tool. Which kind of makes sense in light of his objective, don't you think?" Harry did not respond. "What do you think, Harry?" JD demanded again, anger creeping into his tone.

Harry looked at him defiantly. "You got nothing," he said. "You want to search my place for the Chipmunk head? Go on. I got nothing to hide."

"Yeah," JD said. "Shortly after a group of victims took these pictures, the head was returned. We checked it for prints."

"You can't get prints off fur." Harry halted abruptly. Oh, man.

JD leaned over him. "Well, that's right," he said evenly. "Interesting that you knew that bit of trivia." Harry shrugged. He'd be keeping his mouth shut from here on out. He clamped his lips firmly.

JD went back to his chair. "Now you or I," he began, "we're certainly not in a position to name a man from that part of his anatomy. Might catch a glimpse of somebody's now and then in the john, but etiquette and decorum dictate that you try not to look, and what you see at the urinal stays at the urinal." He put the pictures back in their envelope. "Not to mention that if you were to see one in the condition it appears in these photos, most likely you'd hightail it out of there. So I asked myself, who's a local expert on stiff dicks? And you know what I realized?" Harry shook his head, but his eyes looked like he was watching space aliens preparing to give him a colonoscopy. "Madame Yaskagya!" JD slapped the arm of his chair, as if to punctuate his own brilliance. "Madame Yaskagya knows every shlong in Bucks County by name! She never forgets a face, so to speak."

Harry waved his finger irately in the chief's direction. "I never been to Madame Yaskagya's! Not even since she's doing nails!" he shouted.

JD said nothing. He waited quietly until even the dust motes had settled. "Well, you see, Harry," he finally said, "that's the thing. When you stake out a whorehouse, you take as much notice of who never goes in as the regulars. Now, I didn't mention this to your brother, but me and the rest of the guys, we couldn't recall ever seeing you go in there." Harry nodded energetically. "Which is why, when Madame said this was somebody she never saw before, that didn't leave a lot of players on the field."

Harry began to cry, great shaking sobs. JD waited for them to subside. "Now Harry," he finally continued, "you did a pretty good job covering your tracks. At this point, you know I've got you, and I know I've got you, but these photos, they'd be worthless in court. So the only way I could really get you is if you confess, but I have to read you your rights first or your confession won't hold up in court either. So far, you haven't confessed anything, so how about you continue to keep your mouth shut?" Harry nodded.

JD leaned back. "The thing I like best about Dooleysburg," he said, "is how it kind of got lost in time. Sure, people buy the latest clothes, and kids listen to new music and there's always a little bit of the drug of choice changing hands that I can't seem to get on top of, but the stuff that made America the best place in the world fifty years ago, that's survived here somehow. People fall in love and stay married even after the magic wears off. They know their neighbors, and like them. They watch out for each others' kids, and take good care of their own. I think that's what matters to me the most," he said thoughtfully. "That this is a good, safe place to raise kids." Harry had calmed down to the occasion sniffle by now.

JD sat forward suddenly. "Except when some crackpot wants to wave his willie in girls' faces. When that happens, my own personal Brigadoon gets tainted, you know what I mean? No," he held up his hand. "You're not supposed to answer, remember?" Harry nodded. "So we need a solution," JD said. "And our solution is, you're going to leave."

Harry looked like he didn't understand. "Leave?" he asked.

JD nodded. "Yup. As in, go live somewhere else. And keep yourself in your pants, because if you ever do anything like this again, I'll make sure I get proof."

"No!" Harry panicked. "Chief, please!"

"Shut up," JD said evenly.

Harry ignored him. "It's not like you think! I didn't do it to bother those girls! It don't give me any kind of thrill! It made me feel terrible. I couldn't even get it up without Viagra, I felt so bad!"

"Aw, for chrissakes, Harry. I told you to keep your mouth shut."

Harry was crying again. "I just wanted to get even," he sniveled. "Just for once, to let him know how it feels to be the one getting picked on." He looked up forlornly. "If you knew the things he says to me, the things he makes me do, you'd understand."

"I doubt it," JD said. "I'm not much for whacking off in public."

"Don't you see?" Harry pleaded. "That Chipmunk was the only way to get him. You could do whatever to his wife and family, short of hurting them, and he'd just throw money at them to make it all better. Hell, you could blow up his car dealerships and he'd just take the insurance and beat us up until he was back in business. But that Chipmunk, he really believed being town mascot made him something. Did you know he had a special box made just to keep it in? Red mahogany, nice brass hinges, all lined with silk?"

JD looked at him with something like disgust. "So what?"

"I know," Harry said. "You think I'm bad for hitting a man when he's down."

"I think you're bad for breaking and entering, theft, multiple counts of indecent exposure, breaking and entering again, and acting stupid."

"Please don't make me leave," Harry begged.

"I can't make you do jack shit," JD said, aggravated. "Even horses' asses have constitutional rights. But I thought you'd welcome the chance to get away from this."

Harry shook his head. "Look at this." He indicated the room in general. "Look at this house, look at everything I got. Dooleysburg ain't great just because people do a good job of raising kids here. You think I don't know I'm stupid? Where else you think I could go and be able to live like I'm just as good as everybody else? Sure, Carl's an SOB and he makes me do things I'm not proud of. But he takes care of me, and he will until the day I die."

"Okay," JD stood up. "Show's over."

"You gonna let me stay?"

JD got in his face. "I'm gonna be watching you closer than a Rottweiler on a T-bone. Don't step out of this house, don't even brush your teeth or wipe your ass without asking yourself, would Chief Charles be okay with this? You got it?"

Harry nodded like a child. JD stepped back and Harry stood up. "Thank you, JD," he said, tearing up again.

"I mean it Harry. You put so much as one toe over the line, and I'll personally dump you in Jersey."

"I won't let you down, Chief." Harry held out his hand.

JD looked at it. "No thanks," he said, and walked to the front door.

41

Maggie hadn't answered the phone in days. If Mac picked up a call for her, she wouldn't take it. She was consumed with figuring out some way to reverse the gyrations of fate she feared she had put in motion. She wasn't even sure, exactly, what she'd done. She only knew that she felt out of sync with reality. Mac noticed it, whatever it was. His anxiety came across as a gentle solicitousness that made her feel like she'd failed him too. She was relieved he had to go to school and work, that he couldn't sit around trying not to watch her, trying not to show he was worried about what was causing her affliction.

It was midmorning when the doorbell rang. The house was so quiet that Maggie and Penelope both jumped at the sound, and then they both reacted the same way, edgy, but drawn to the front door. The bell rang again. With Pavlovian obedience, Maggie opened the door. Too late, she realized she should have checked first. JD was standing there. She tried to close the door. JD blocked it with his arm. "Stop," he said, tense but controlled. "I just want to talk."

"Talk," Maggie said.

An incapacitating spell couldn't have been more effective at stealing his words. He stood there, helpless, his arm still against the door. Maggie turned away. "Please stop," he said.

"I assume at least some of those calls were you," Maggie began, without emotion. "Clearly I didn't answer, which was intended to communicate something to you. Clearly you weren't interested in hearing that message."

"Maybe I have something important enough to say that I needed to ignore that message."

"Then say it."

"Whatever I did," he began with difficulty, "I'm sorry. I mean that. Give me a chance to fix it. Just give me a clue what I need to change and I'll change it. I've tried for days now to figure out what it was, and I can't. But this hurts. Really hurts, really bad." His eyes grew dark. "And I don't like it."

Maggie shook her head. Her tone was remote. "You didn't do anything."

"What is it, then?" he demanded.

"I made a mistake. I'm sorry it involved you. But you're making this more than it is. We went on a date. We had a good time."

"That's it? A night of fun, thanks, good-bye?"

"What is the big deal?" Maggie asked. "Men do it all the time."

"That's bullshit!" JD exploded. "You can't lie like this! You were there, really there. You enjoyed yourself. You enjoyed me! You were *involved*." Without warning, his whole demeanor changed. He softened, and looked as if he might reach out to her. She stepped back slightly. "You might not care now," JD said, "but you cared then, in the moment. And then I told you I cared too, and something happened. What was it?"

When she spoke she sounded, for the briefest instant, lost. "Nothing happened."

He reached for her hand, then thought better of it. "Maggie, it wasn't just the incident when she pulled the gun on you, was it? What did someone do to frighten you so badly?"

"There is nothing to tell," she said.

"There is something," he insisted gently. "But you're not allowed to tell me, are you?" When she didn't answer, he continued. "Those are the rules, aren't they? If you want to stay safe."

"No," she replied, her voice hollow. "Those are the rules if you want to stay alive."

"You needed to believe that," he answered softly, "for a lot of years. But it's only a habit now. You can let it go."

"Stop this," she said, closing up like a clam that just exhaled some irritating sand. "This isn't necessary."

"You know what's not necessary? That poisonous moat of isolation you hide behind. The anger you wear all the time, like a suit of armor. Don't get me wrong. I believe you needed it to survive once, but after awhile, I think you started to like the nice cozy fit. And now you're so wrapped up in it nobody's going to be allowed to be essential enough to make you take it off."

"You are right that I am damaged," she said, without emotion. "You just don't like the fact that I'm not helpless. You don't like that I am probably tougher than anyone you know. I can take care of myself, and my son, and anybody else who needs it. I never learned to be generous or kind. I only learned to survive. You don't want to see that about me. No man ever does. I'm a beacon for men who want to be gallant, and it disappoints them when they see I can fight my own crusades. You want me to take off my armor? There is no place safe enough."

JD looked so sad. "Let me be that place. Can't you just give me a chance?"

"Always the hopeless romantic," she replied. "I particularly enjoyed your analogy about abused children being like vampires. Abused children are not like vampires. They're like deer. They come to the side of the road and see destruction speeding toward them, and sometimes they just act on stupid impulse and run in front of it. And sometimes they stop and wait, assess their choices. Then, at the last minute they race in front of the car anyway, because that's the decision they've made. But every now and then they have enough sense to turn around and disappear back into the woods. You want to know your mistake? It's not anything you did. It's what you will do, if I give you the opportunity."

JD removed his arm from the door. "Maggie," he pleaded, "you have to trust me."

"No," she said. "You will hurt me. In a devastating way, when I least expect it. This is my last chance to stand by the side of the road and decide to turn back. Otherwise, I'll never see it coming. I won't defend myself. You will do me irreparable harm."

JD looked off down the street and took a deep breath. Then he looked back at her. "When Martha told me I was a pompous fool for thinking I could get close to you, she said it was because you'd already been done irreparable harm. That's what made me a fool, thinking I would be able to do anything to salvage you. I disagreed with her then, and I disagree with her now. Please," he said brokenly, "let me help you. I think you're buried so deep you can't even remember what you were afraid of in the first place."

Maggie shook her head. "Don't do this," she whispered. "You don't have a clue what you're messing with."

"Neither do you," he snapped.

"Yeah," she said simply, closing the door. "I know."

ꞁ ꞁ ꞁ

Vee took a sip of her coffee and slammed the mug down on the table. "Shit's cold," she said angrily. A moment ago they'd been sitting here in the General Store as if everything was just the same as always. Now things were suddenly out of control. "So what was it?" she demanded. "You went to the dance with him to get even?"

Maggie looked stunned, which only made Vee angrier. When she answered her voice was raspy, like she'd just had the wind knocked out of her. "I went to the dance with him—I asked him to go to the dance with me—because you told me to."

Vee's tone dripped sarcasm. "And you thought I suggested that, why? So you could rip his heart out?"

For a moment Maggie looked confused. Then the door on the blast furnace of her own rage blew open. "I didn't think about why you suggested it. I just did what you said because you were my friend and I trusted you."

"Hold on, back up," Vee said. "I am your friend. That's why we're having this discussion."

Maggie shook her head, eyes narrowed. "No. You are his friend and your friend. If I'm in the mix at all, I'm a distant third."

"Can't I be watching out for both of you?"

"Not when you're watching out for both of *you*."

"I don't even know what you're talking about," Vee said, dismissively.

"No, I guess you wouldn't," Maggie spat. "How could you?"

Vee's look was stormy. "Why don't you just tell me?"

"You used me." It came out too fast, as if Maggie hadn't had a chance to consider it. And then it lay there, like some pulsing embryonic monster they were both too horrified to touch.

Vee took a deep breath. She was too angry to give in, but she cared about what was at stake. "I just wanted my friend to be happy."

"Which friend would that be?"

"Both of you. Was that a crime?"

"How do you think it feels to know I was your gift to him?"

Vee was startled. "You got it all wrong. You were my gifts to each other."

"You just assumed setting me up for him would make both of us happy?"

Vee ran out of patience. "Might have made both of you happy if you weren't such a self-centered girl."

Maggie stood up to leave. Then she leaned back down and lowered her voice. "Don't you mean it might have made me happy if I was you?" she asked. "That's really what this was all about, wasn't it?" When Vee didn't answer, she continued. "You're the one who wanted him, who always wanted him, but that wasn't compatible with your vision of yourself. How could you fall in love with a classic, nice white southern boy and still respect yourself in the morning? So you used me as your surrogate."

"You are wrong," Vee said coldly.

Maggie looked at Vee a long moment, her eyes filled with acrimony. "You could at least show me the courtesy of being honest," she said, then walked out.

Vee stared down into her cold mug of coffee. She was afraid that if she tried to move she would cry. What if some of what Maggie accused her of was true? She never stopped to consider that Maggie, having access to something she herself wanted so badly but would never take, might have her own reasons for not wanting it at all. She couldn't begin to think what this mistake might have cost her. She put her head in her hands and sobbed like a baby.

42

Maggie sat on Martha's hiding stool and watched Daniel push paint around. "Why do you do that?" she demanded.

Daniel looked at her oddly. "Paint?"

"Pretend to paint. Don't you ever grieve for all the time you could have spent making real art while you sit here and whore yourself by pretending to paint?"

Daniel didn't answer immediately. "You want to tell me what you're really mad about?" he finally asked.

"You used to do that when I was fourteen."

"That's because you used to act like this when you were fourteen."

"I'm not acting."

"No, but you're very upset about something, and instead of dealing with it, you're just lashing out."

Now it was Maggie's turn to be pensive. Daniel waited her out. "How did you find out they were dead? You didn't read about it in the paper, did you?"

Daniel didn't need to ask to know she was referring to her parents. "It was an even smaller town then. The cops came looking for me because they didn't know where else to go."

"What did they tell you?"

"What is it you want to know?" he asked.

Maggie paused a long time. "Why do you think she did it?"

"There was no why," Daniel said, with conviction. "If you believe nothing else, believe that. She wasn't capable of intent. She operated purely on impulse. That was part of her illness." He paused to let this sink in. "People said your father was just in the wrong place at the wrong time. The truth is, so was she. She had no more control over herself than he did."

Maggie tried to make sense of this. It didn't want to fit. "Was she drunk?" she asked.

"According to the autopsy results, she wasn't under the influence of anything."

"So she just decided to kill him and his nurse and then herself."

Daniel said quietly, "She probably didn't decide anything. She was that bad by then."

"If that's true, he would have known it."

Daniel sighed. "I can't say what he knew. Nobody can."

"That's why he let her get loose," she said with conviction. "He wanted them both put out of their misery. If I had been willing to help him, he might have made a different choice."

"I would like to think, although I cannot speak from firsthand experience, that parents give children life as a gift, not as an obligation."

Maggie laughed humorlessly. "How very modern of you. It wasn't so long ago, even around here, that parents had children pretty much by accident and only allowed them to live because of the value of their labor."

"Just because you weren't planned doesn't mean they didn't want you. She wasn't always ill."

"When he wrote to me, did you know?" Maggie asked.

"No," Daniel said, taken off guard. "Did he write often?"

"Only that one time, the summer before college. When he asked me to come back."

Daniel waited for her to continue. When she didn't, he said, "I think you made the right choice, for whatever that's worth."

"Why do you think he wanted me to come back, Daniel?" It was part challenge, part plea.

"The potential reasons are pretty obvious, aren't they? More than likely, he felt bad about sending you away. More than likely, he loved you, in his own way."

"And what's less than likely?"

Daniel hesitated. "Maybe he wanted to make whatever amends he could."

"Come on, Daniel. He wanted to apologize? And finally be a father to me? How about he wanted me to take her off his hands? You think that selfish son-of-a-bitch wanted to spend the rest of his life burdened with her?"

"Does it make you feel better to believe that?"

"Nothing makes me feel better," she snapped.

"Then let me give you a little wisdom from the vantage of age. Hatred requires a great deal of maintenance. It's a waste of your energy."

"I don't hate them. I don't hate anyone. It was a mistake to come back, that's all. You know why? Because you can heal yourself, you can get past whatever it is and make a new, whole life. You can even forgive. But the one thing that's unbearable is when you have to lie to protect the person who hurt you. Somebody brutalizes you, and you have to cover for them. It's a sore that won't heal. And I stupidly returned to the scene of the crime. Every single one of you was complicit in making me lie about it." Daniel did not look at her. "Come on," she taunted him. "You knew that she was insane."

"Not then," he insisted. "Not that early on."

"So you want me to believe you didn't know why he had you desert me at a crappy hotel in New York?"

Daniel shook his head. "I respected him enough not to mortify him by asking. It didn't take a genius to figure out it was for your own good."

"She pulled a gun on me." Maggie's voice was devoid of emotion. "And after Doc took the gun away, after he got me out of the house, the whole time he was bringing me over to you he didn't say anything to me. Not, are you okay, not, I'm sorry. Nothing. I was fifteen years old."

"I'm sorry."

"The loyal henchman," Maggie said harshly. "Did you help him find women too? Your models, maybe? Tender young things, for the slow times between student nurses."

"It was a long time ago," Daniel said quietly. "All of us made choices. The ones you made saved your life."

"No," Maggie corrected him. "My choices made my life. There was nothing before that to save."

Daniel looked like he might cry. "I'm sorry I was unsuccessful at showing you, but I cared. I never knew how bad it really was, but even if I had I can't honestly tell you I would have had the courage to do anything but what I did. It's not part of who I am, to know how to really help people." He wiped his forehead with his hand. "I'm sorry I let you down. When you came back I had this fantasy, and I admit it was a fantasy, that we could be like family. Because that's how I always felt about you."

"It was a mistake coming back here. I'm remembering things I thought I'd managed to forget. I don't know what to do with all this mad."

"Look at it for what it is and then let it go."

"That was how he managed, wasn't it? Discard the things that don't please you, especially if they're ugly. I'm not sure he proved the success of that approach."

Daniel looked at her. "This may be hard for you to fathom right now," he said, "but there comes a time when people have had enough. It's a bigger philosophical question than I can answer whether it's right or wrong."

"Is that why you had them cremated?" she asked. "Because you thought it might be suicide?"

"That's *your* Catholic stuff," Daniel replied. "I didn't want them buried together. I couldn't see condemning your father to spending eternity next to her. He'd already done his time in hell."

Maggie got up and turned away. Something about Daniel trying to find her father some relief for the rest of eternity made her furious.

"Come with me," Daniel said. "I have something to show you." Without waiting for an answer, he went down the basement stairs. After a slight hesitation, Maggie followed. There were random pieces of framing material lying around, the remains of a still life on top of a draped table. Daniel went behind the furnace and pulled out a large canvas covered in heavy fabric. He uncovered it and turned the painting to face Maggie.

She knew the scene instantly. "This is Mac and me in Central Park. When did you do this?"

"Just after Mac's first birthday. Your father commissioned it."

"That's creepy," Maggie said. "You were watching us?"

"No," Daniel said. "I had no idea where you were by then. I painted this from a photo."

"He took the photo?"

"Yup."

A tightness under Maggie's breastbone was making it hard to breathe. "He was watching me? After Mac was born?"

"He was always watching you."

She sat back down. "I don't understand."

"Sure you do," Daniel said. "You're a parent now."

Maggie focused on the portrait. That was a good time for her, when Mac was that age. She was astonished by his beauty, the miracle of him as he began to walk and talk. When she was pregnant, when he was a newborn, she had been terrified of what she might do. By the time he was a toddler, she knew he was safe from the monster that might lurk within her, that she would do nothing to harm him. This portrait was before she cut off the jet-black curls of his baby hair. His eyes, tropical blue, were fringed in black lashes, and Daniel had captured the dimple in his left cheek.

They were blowing bubbles. Mac's lips were pursed to blow at the soapy wand in Maggie's hand. She couldn't help studying herself, frozen in a moment of unselfconscious delight. Somehow the woman in the painting wasn't reconciling with her concept of herself. "You took some license here," she said.

"Nonsense," Daniel replied. "That's a perfect likeness of you."

"Even a dozen years ago I didn't look like that."

Daniel raised his eyebrows. "If anyone else said that I would assume they were fishing for compliments. But you really don't believe you look like this, do you?"

"No. I don't see myself like that."

"You mean beautiful? Or looking like her?"

Maggie felt a shock of betrayal. "Are you saying I look like my mother?"

"Absolutely," Daniel said. "You got his mind, but her looks."

"Why did he keep her?" The question had slipped out, and now it suffocated the space between them. "She was crazy before she was an alcoholic. He knew it. Why didn't he put her somewhere?"

Daniel shook his head. "It wasn't the sort of thing we talked to each other about. It's hard for me to imagine he ever talked about it."

"Maybe he felt guilty," Maggie said. "That would be nice, to know he paid for his excesses somehow."

Daniel looked at her before answering. "Maybe he loved her."

"No," she said, with a note of violence in her voice. "He didn't love anybody."

"How can you be sure?"

"Spying on me and my son from a safe distance doesn't make him a parent."

"Maybe he thought that's how you wanted things."

"How can you say that to me? Don't try to make it my fault!"

"Okay, okay," Daniel said, his tone conciliatory.

"It's not okay!" she snapped. "I walk around with this dark shadow looming over my head, and the shadow is all anyone ever sees."

"If that's true, maybe it's because the dark shadow is rage."

"I'm entitled!"

"You make a choice, like always. You want the rage, you can have it. But at the expense of letting anyone see anything else about you."

"So what would you recommend?" Maggie asked angrily. "I've spent my life pretending nothing happened. It didn't cure me."

"Think about this. Maybe if he chose you, she would have destroyed you altogether. Maybe it was his way of protecting you."

"I don't accept that."

"Is that because you find utility in staying mad?"

If Maggie showed her fury, that would only make Daniel think he was right. She evened out her voice. "He could have done more than just leave me alone to deal with her. It was every day. After school, at dinner most nights, on weekends while he supposedly devoted himself to his patients. And all that time he was actually off living his real life." Her face hardened. "He used me. He didn't even care that I couldn't do it right. As long as somebody was there, he didn't have to be."

"Suppose that's true," Daniel said. "Which quite likely it is. What does it get you to hang on to it now?" When she didn't answer, he continued. "You might just be better off if you decide to forgive."

"*Forgive* him?" Maggie repeated, incredulous. "What did he ever do to earn forgiveness?"

"How about being a frail, screwed up, average human being? Okay, so he never went the extra step for the people he should have protected . . ."

"While going out of his way to be a hero to strangers. Don't forget that."

"No," Daniel said. "I haven't."

"He's gone. What do I get for forgiving him now?"

"Maybe that would let you begin to figure out how to forgive the rest of us. Lower the standards a little and come on board the mother ship. Maybe you can even begin to forgive yourself in the bargain."

Maggie shook her head. "Forgive myself for what?"

Daniel got up. "What would you like me to do with the painting? It's yours, you know. He paid for it."

"I don't want it," Maggie said. "I hate what it says about my father, that he felt so guilty and still couldn't make the effort. I don't want anything from him."

"Take it for me, then."

"Why?" she demanded. "Does it make you feel bad to know it's down here? Does it remind you about the part you played? Maybe that's what finally made you human, having it down here haunting you. You deal with it." She was about to get up when Martha walked in. Neither Maggie nor Daniel was able to look at her.

"Well," Martha said evenly, "what little drama have I interrupted today?"

"No drama," Maggie said coldly. "I'm leaving."

"Don't leave on my account," Martha said. "You're welcome to stay if you and Daniel have something more you'd like to discuss."

"Town," Maggie said. "I'm leaving town. I'm going to find somewhere we fit in better."

"I can't say I'm surprised," Martha said. "You haven't been happy for a while."

"Nonsense!" Daniel exploded. "When are you finally going to stop?" Both women looked at him, surprised. "You can't keep running away!" he continued. "If you don't start learning how to manage now, what will you do if things get really hard?"

Maggie laughed. "What do you know about how I manage when things get hard? Those are big words from somebody who never had any balls of his own."

"Hold on!" Martha interrupted. "Whatever's going on here, ramp it back."

"Tell her," Maggie demanded. "Tell her how you never had the courage to protect me." Daniel looked at her helplessly. "I'm sorry," Maggie said abruptly. "This was a mistake. It was a mistake for me to come here to try to explain to you." She hurried up the stairs.

"I've lost her again," Daniel said brokenly.

Martha walked over and put her arms around him. "Try to remember that what you're losing is the fantasy. She was never who you imagined. She's right that there's nothing here that can heal her. You can't hold yourself responsible for that. You know you can't fix every tragedy that washes up near you."

"She's not a random problem," Daniel said. "I am at least partially to blame for what happened to her."

"You're only taking your turn on the rack."

"What does that mean?" Daniel asked.

"She's coming apart at the seams. She's alienating everyone. First it was JD, then Vee, and now you. I'm sorry, Daniel, but I don't think there's anything you can do about it."

"I'm worried about her," he said sadly. "And Mac too."

Martha patted his back. "I know," she said. "But I'm more worried about you." She walked over and started rewrapping the portrait.

43

Third period was Resource. In the beginning of the school year Morsel always hung around Mac during Resource. This annoyed Mac at first. He wanted to use Resource to do homework. Morsel thought Mac was totally missing the point, and eventually Mac counted on Morsel being around. But like everything else, that changed after the incident at the synagogue.

Now Mac usually spent Resource in the library, where the other smart kids hung out. And he learned how to skulk around the building without looking suspicious, so if he felt like going someplace, he didn't need a pass. The only place he never went anymore was the auditorium. Nobody said it, but everybody knew that the auditorium was for losers.

Today Mac was alone. Jayme was on a field trip, and if Robbie and the older kids were in the building somewhere, Mac couldn't find them. It felt strange being alone now. He used to think he didn't mind, but that was only because he didn't know how it felt to be on the inside. That's when he suddenly realized how Morsel must have felt when Mac got new friends. It made Mac feel bad, realizing he ditched Morsel like that even if he didn't do it on purpose. It kind of explained stuff too. Mac had no idea how to fix things, but he felt like he should try. He went to the auditorium. Morsel was sitting in the middle of the room, in a pool of empty seats. Mac went over. "Hey," he said quietly, "what's up?"

Morsel looked at him. "What do you want?" he asked.

"Just wondering what you were up to."

"Nothing," Morsel replied.

"Want to hang out?" Mac asked.

"Nope," Morsel said.

"Come on," Mac said.

"You know what?" Morsel said. "Piss off."

Mac walked away. So what if Morsel didn't want to be his friend? Only, why did it hurt so bad? He sat down a few rows away. When he glanced up, Morsel was scowling at him. Mac pretended not to notice and opened a book. A few seconds later, he looked up and Morsel was standing in the row in front of him, still glaring. "You want something?" Mac asked.

"Yeah," Morsel said. "I want you to get the hell outta here."

"What's it to you?"

Morsel was so angry his voice cracked. "You got the whole rest of the goddamn school to be in. Me, I got right here. It's bad enough I gotta see you at the deli and around Gamey's house. I don't want to have to look at your ugly face here, too."

"Fine," Mac said, with the same cool easiness the older boys used. He picked up his stuff and left, careful to look all relaxed. He hadn't gotten far when he realized he had nowhere to go. Without friends around there was no good place to be. Then he realized there was one more place to try.

❦   ❦   ❦

Mr. Don looked up as Mac walked into the band room. "Rifkin," he challenged, "do you have a pass?"

"Nope," Mac said.

"Well then, haul yourself back to wherever it is you are supposed to be."

"You could give me a pass."

"Not if you got here illegally." Mr. Don looked at him. "But you know that."

"There anything I could help you with?" Mac asked.

"I can find something," Mr. Don said, "so long as we're clear you're not going to wander in here without a pass again." Mac nodded. Mr. Don pointed to a stack of plastic containers. "I need those moved. Don't try to pick up more than one at a time. They're filled with sheet music. Weigh about a ton apiece."

Mac went over and lifted a container. "You weren't kidding," he grunted.

"Hey," Mr. Don said, "if it's too heavy, take stuff out and move it in stages."

Mac was about to open the top container when the alarm began. It was a sound he hadn't heard before, piercing like a siren, but with an ominous bass note. "What is that?" he asked.

Mr. Don looked a little freaked out. "It's a new alarm system. It's not supposed to be live yet."

"Oh," Mac said, relieved. "So what kind of drill is it?"

Mr. Don's sounded like he was having a hard time staying calm. "There's no drill scheduled for this morning. You need to leave the building. Now."

Mac looked at him. "Why?"

"This alarm indicates intruders in the building. Get out. NOW."

"What about you?" Mac asked.

Mr. Don talked normally. "You need to follow my instructions. Do what I tell you and leave now." Mac started toward the door. "Not that way," Mr. Don said, his voice louder now. "Use the doors that go outside."

"That'll set off the alarm."

"Go!" Mr. Don yelled. "Just get as far away from the building as you can. Head for . . ." He stopped. There was an unusual noise out in the hall. Mr. Don looked at Mac. He spoke quietly, but his voice sounded strange. "Evacuate the building *now.*"

Mac started to go. The doors to the Band Room flew open, and he saw what was making that sound. It wasn't really what he expected gunfire to sound like. It almost wasn't loud at all.

"Run!" Mr. Don screamed.

r r r

The doorbell was ringing wildly, as if a delivery of maniacs had just arrived. Having learned her lesson from the confrontation with JD, Maggie checked through the fanlight before answering. It was Vee. She had taken off her hair extensions. What was left of her hair, her real hair, Maggie assumed, was sectioned off into tidy squares all over her head. Each patch of fuzz was twisted into a small knot with a pigtail extruding out the end.

More unsettling than her hairstyle was how she was acting. She was wilder than a cat in a paper bag. She punctuated her jitters by jabbing the doorbell. Maggie couldn't read the expression on her face, but she recognized Vee's agitation. She opened the door. "You want to come in?" she asked.

Vee stopped in front of her and put a shaking hand on the doorjamb. "Have you seen the news?" she asked.

"On TV?" It was a dumb question, but Maggie was trying to ignore the feeling she was getting.

"I was doing notes for my class. Wednesday's my late day this semester. And I heard a breaking report."

Maggie's stomach hurt. "What? What was it?"

"The school," Vee said with unnatural calm. "Something terrible is happening at the high school."

Maggie ran into the den and turned on the TV. They watched for a few minutes in stunned silence. Aerial footage showed the school surrounded from a distance by police and emergency vehicles. There was a dark smear of smoke rising from the rear of the building. Other than that, there wasn't much to see. The anchorman's calm, droning voice burned like drops of acid on the rawness of their fear. He kept repeating the same things, snippets devoid of real content, all useless to a parent at a time like this. 'Mrs. Rifkin,' Maggie willed him to say, 'your child is safe.' Instead, he kept announcing things like, 'law enforcement is in the process of securing the building.'

Maggie felt lightheaded. "I have to go."

"There's no point," Vee replied, trying to sound in control. "You'll learn more by staying here and watching the news. You know they won't let you near there."

"They will if people are hurt." She grabbed her jacket. "Come on," she insisted.

"You're not going to be able to find him," Vee said quietly.

"I know that," Maggie snapped. "I might be able to help someone else."

Vee stared at her a moment, then asked, "You want your black bag or something?"

Maggie took a deep breath. Her face was set, hard. "How much do you know?"

"Enough."

"Everyone else knows too?"

"Everyone who matters. Including JD."

"Good," Maggie said. "Then he'll know I can help."

Vee drove. It took about ten minutes to get near the school's rural location. Maggie tried to find information on the car radio, but the music and banter were like sandpaper on her nerves and she snapped the radio off. Nobody else was on the road. The countryside seemed poisoned with stillness, the sky an apocalyptic gray, as if ready for the storm at the end of the world.

A little more than a mile from the school they were blocked by two state police cars with all their lights flashing parked diagonally across the road. They were facing opposite directions, ready to take off in immediate pursuit if need be. Policemen in flak gear stood nearby, looking like ominous characters from a science fiction movie. One came toward them. He carried an assault rifle pointed at the ground. He motioned briskly for them to stop.

"Slow way down," Maggie ordered. "That thing's loaded, and if he's jumpy enough he'll shoot anything that moves." As Vee inched the car forward the cop raised the rifle barrel to hip level. "Stop," Maggie ordered. "Turn off the car and put your hands on the steering wheel where he can see them."

"Maybe I should hold them up in the air?"

Maggie looked at Vee. This was one of those stupid moments that could only happen in real life, she thought. Vee's eyes were open so wide their dark irises were completely surrounded by white. With her new short hairstyle she looked like Buckwheat from the "Our Gang" comedies. "You need to put your extensions back on," Maggie said. Vee looked at her, speechless.

They jumped at the sharp tap on Maggie's window. The cop had knocked on it with the butt of his rifle. He motioned for her to lower the window. "You can't go through here," he said. "You have to turn back."

"Officer, I'm aware of what happened at the school . . ."

"Go home, ma'am. No one's being allowed any closer." Then he softened slightly. "You have a kid in the school?"

"My son."

"You need to stay at home. That's where they'll try to reach you if they need you." Unless I had a damn cell phone, Maggie thought. "Keep your TV on. They'll be giving updates to the local news."

"I'm a trauma surgeon," Maggie said. "May I show you some credentials?"

"I'm sorry, ma'am. My orders are nobody goes through. Unless they sent for you, you need to turn around."

"I respect that," Maggie said calmly. "But I need to let them know I'm available. Is Chief Charles down there? Dooleysburg PD."

"I wouldn't know, ma'am."

"Well, then, I suggest you check." She spoke with her operating room voice.

The cop nodded. A badge and rifle were no match for a surgeon's ego. "Your name?"

"Margaret MacDonald. Dr. Margaret MacDonald."

He went back to his car. It took several minutes before he returned. "Ma'am . . . Doctor, the Chief says for you to go home. He says as soon as they find out about your son he'll get word to you, so stay there and wait." He softened for a moment. "Sorry."

"How many injuries are there?" she asked evenly. "How serious are they?"

"They're still assessing that."

"And how many medical personnel are there?"

"I couldn't say."

"Officer," she looked pointedly at him, as if making sure she could identify him later, "I strongly suggest you go back to your car and call the Chief again. Tell him I'm asking if he's prepared to let some kid die because he refused available medical assistance. *Explain* to him that I am here in my professional capacity."

The cop walked back to his car. In a few minutes he returned. "Your friend can't stay," he said. "You'll have to come wait in my car."

"What did the Chief say?" Maggie asked.

"They're entering the school now. There appear to be multiple injuries. Nobody knows how serious yet. There were one or more explosions as well as an attack with firearms. They have to go slow until they can determine if there are any remote triggers or undetonated material. As soon as the school is secure, they'll send someone to bring you in."

"Thank you," Maggie said. As she began to get out the car, Vee grabbed her hand and pulled her over. She gave her the best hug she could manage with the car's front console between them. "I'm praying for you," she whispered. Jim

Morrison's voice blew through Maggie's mind. "You CANNOT petition the Lord with prayer!" he roared.

🙞 🙞 🙞

The wait seemed forever, but an EMT finally showed up to drive Maggie to the school. The state trooper opened the back door of the cruiser and Maggie walked quickly to the EMT's car. As she got in, he asked, "You bring anything with you?"

"I'm not currently practicing," she said. "I took a sabbatical and moved here to raise my son in peace." He looked at her, surprised. "What kind of support do you have down there?" she continued, detached.

"A few of the local squads. More on the way. It's a mess. They just let us into the lobby. They haven't secured the rest of the building yet. If the rest is as bad as the lobby, we might not have much to do."

"I've seen bad before," Maggie said. "Fatalities?"

"Seven dead so far. There's a few with less severe injuries, and at least one who's not going to make it. That's just in the front entry. Bastards had semi-automatics, and at least one of them had dumdums. We already used up all our morphine. We're waiting for more."

The school parking lot looked like what it was, a disaster scene. There were state police cars, local police cars, county sheriff's cars, ambulances and fire trucks. There was still smoke rising from the rear of the building. Numerous people in uniforms were milling around, many of them in bulletproof vests and helmets with visors. It made Maggie think how futile it all was, an army of protection after the damage was done. One of the futuristic cops halted them at the parking lot entrance before allowing them to pass. As soon as the EMT parked the car, Maggie jumped out. "Hey," he called after her, "What's your cell number? I'll let you know when the morphine gets here."

"Can't use phones in there," a nearby cop said, "until they confirm the building isn't wired." Maggie started toward the door. "Where you think you're going?" the cop said.

"I'm medical personnel."

"You need an escort."

"I'll come with you," the EMT said, getting out of his car.

The lobby was both not as bad and far worse than Maggie expected. Despite the number of casualties, it was fairly quiet. Someone was crying at the far end, and two policemen near the door were having a tense conversation. Children's bodies sprawled lifeless on the floor, savage chunks torn from their heads or chests. Children Mac's age. Some of whom, no doubt, he knew. Had known.

This realization began to allow that other possibility to creep into Maggie's thoughts, the one that would send her screaming, terrified, through the building in search of her own baby. She forced a heavy door closed on that part of her mind, turning off her feelings and yielding to the Observer, that rational function which, through years of training, had learned to use all her skills and knowledge without requiring her participation.

She walked up to the nearest police officer. It was impossible to tell who was who when they were all in riot gear. "I'm the doctor from town," she said. "Where should I go first?"

"Everybody in here's been checked out," he said. "EMT over there is triaging those two." He pointed across the lobby. "Haven't found any other survivors so far."

Maggie walked over. Both girls were conscious and crying. One's legs looked badly torn up. The other was bloodied in a way that indicated it was as much due to smearing as actual wounds. "What have you got here?" Maggie asked.

The EMT looked up. He was from the squad where Mac had volunteered. He squinted at her. "Aren't you somebody's mother?" he asked.

"I'm a surgeon," she said. "What can I do to help?"

"These two were lucky." He indicated the girls. "They're not as bad as they look. We're gonna get them out of here as soon as we stabilize a few bones and they'll be okay. But there's a guy around the corner who's in bad shape. Maybe you can take a look."

"What kind of supplies do you have?" Maggie asked.

He held up a box of rubber gloves. Maggie looked at him in disbelief. "That's it?"

"I wasn't near my station when the call came in. Somebody'll be here in a minute with our gear."

"Make sure he finds me when he gets here." The EMT nodded. Maggie took two gloves out of the box and put them on as she started to walk away.

"Doctor?" one of the girls said. Her voice was heartbreaking. Maggie walked back and squatted down next to her.

"Yes?"

The girl was shivering. "Principal . . ." She stopped, and it took her a moment to start again. "Mr. Babson . . . he saved our life."

Maggie looked at the EMT. "Get a blanket on her. She's in shock."

"Yeah," he said, "I already sent for some. I think she's talking about the guy around the corner. The one you were going to look at."

Maggie got up and went in the direction the EMT had pointed. Babson was on the floor. From the pattern of destruction on his shirt, he'd taken part of a round of automatic weapons fire in the gut. Maggie didn't bother to examine his wounds. Even a cursory visual made it clear he'd been nearly cut in half. She knelt to see if he still had a pulse. Babson opened his eyes and looked right at her. The surprise nearly knocked her over. "It hurts," he whispered.

"Okay," she said gently. It's not supposed to hurt, she thought. Not when someone is this bad. "I'm going to get you something for the pain." She stood up and hurried back to the EMT in the lobby. "He's conscious," she said, controlling her voice for the sake of the girls.

"You're kidding," the EMT said.

"Do you have anything I can give him?" she asked.

He shook his head. "I heard there's morphine on the way."

"Yeah," she said, distracted. "Do you have a radio?" The EMT shook his head. Maggie looked around. One of the girls was holding a cell phone. "Can I use that?" Maggie asked.

"We can't," the girl said. "They told us not to use our phones until they check out the building, because if there are any more bombs, cell phones could cause problems."

"Is Mr. Babson going to be okay?" the other girl asked tearfully. "He got shot trying to stop them so we could get away."

"I'll do everything I can," Maggie replied. She turned back to the EMT. "As soon as that morphine gets here, get it to me."

"Where you going?" he asked. "No place is secure yet except right here."

"I'm just going to stay with him." She began to walk away, then turned back. "Can I have your cell phone?" she asked. The girl handed it to her hesitantly.

"Don't forget," the EMT said. "Don't use it until we get an all clear."

"Yeah," Maggie said. "I won't forget." She put the phone in her pocket and changed her gloves, out of habit. Then she went back around the corner and knelt down on the floor next to Babson again. "Help is on the way," she said softly.

Babson squeezed his eyes in response and a tear ran down the side of his face. "Will you tell my wife I love her?" he struggled to ask, his breathing ragged.

"Of course," Maggie said. She couldn't believe he could get enough air to talk. She thought about all the stupid clichés she'd seen over the years on TV, about how somebody always told the dying person they should rest and save their breath. What a load of bullshit. The man had, at most, a few more minutes to live. The only thing she could offer him for his pain was some small reassurance that when he disappeared forever, he would not go unheard. She leaned close to his ear. "What else?" she whispered.

"She wanted to go to Hawaii," he managed to choke out.

"Let's take her there, then," Maggie said gently. She took his big, fat hand in both of hers. Ignoring the smears of blood on it, she began patting it, as if he were a child. "I bet you love Kauai, don't you?" He did not respond. "You know where you are? You're on the north side of Kauai, the side with those big, beautiful green cliffs. There she is. On the beach. She's wearing your favorite swimsuit, you know which one I mean?" Babson grimaced. "She's waving at you. You've made her so happy. She loves you very much."

Maggie held his hand longer than she had to, until she realized someone was standing over her. It was the EMT from the lobby. He was holding out a syringe.

Maggie gently laid Babson's hand on his chest. "Save it for someone else," she said, standing up. "And make sure you put something over him so no kids see him this way." The EMT nodded and went off. Maggie stayed a moment longer, composing herself for the next wave of horror. She had seen enough in her career to know it would hit, without warning, in its own time.

Another EMT came out of an intersecting corridor and ran over. "Are you the surgeon from town?" Maggie nodded. "Can you come with me please?"

"What is it?" she asked.

"They've secured a few of the corridors. There are kids we might be able to help."

Maggie took off after him at a controlled run. "We need supplies," she said.

"I've got some stuff there." They turned a corner and came to the next station on the carnage road, a small group of bloodied, fallen children. They worked rapidly, figuring out which children they might be able to hold on to long enough for the stretchers to arrive. As soon as more help got there, Maggie and her new partner moved on.

As they got deeper into the building, finding broken children scattered about like rag dolls, Maggie had to make herself ignore the decorations on the walls, the trophies and art projects. A few hours ago these things had been such an unimportant piece of some child's life they were destined for the attic or the trash. Now they would be thrust into greatness, the failed talisman of a vanished child. Which of these children had some parent foolishly believed they could afford to temporarily dislike when they left the house this morning because of a forgotten chore, or a bad grade, or a nasty crack? Make sure you always have clean underwear on, Doc used to say. You never know when you might end up in an accident.

"Dr. Rifkin?" A voice behind her shoulder interrupted her thoughts. Maggie turned around. "They need you in the band room." Maggie stripped off the soiled rubber gloves she was wearing and dropped them on the floor before hurrying off toward F wing.

ɼ   ɼ   ɼ

From the heavy double door, Maggie could see Mr. Don lying on the low stage at the front of the room. He appeared unconscious. As she got closer, one of the paramedics stood up. "How bad is he?" she asked.

"Two entry wounds in the back, one of them pretty close to his spine. No exit wounds."

"Do you have him immobilized?" Maggie asked.

"We're working on it. But he's out. He hasn't moved."

Maggie went over and knelt down next to Mr. Don. His pulse and breathing were stable. She was about to ask someone for a clean pair of gloves when he coughed and began struggling to sit up. Maggie quickly took his head between her hands and held it still. "It's okay," she said calmly. "You've been hurt. You have to try not to move. We're getting you help."

Mr. Don gradually opened his eyes. It took him a while to focus. "Mrs. Rifkin?" he asked, confused.

"I'm going to let go of your head, but you have to stay still. Otherwise, I'm going to have to restrain you." Mr. Don tried to nod. "No nodding," Maggie said sternly.

"Okay," he gasped.

Maggie gently released his head. "Can you breathe okay?" she asked.

"I can't feel anything," he said, beginning to sound panicky.

"You're in shock," Maggie said. She touched his hand. "You can feel that, can't you?" she asked.

Mr. Don closed his eyes. "Yeah," he said. He smiled a little.

"Hey." Maggie looked up. JD was standing over them. He was in a bullet-proof vest, but he'd taken off his helmet. "How's he doing?"

"Ask him yourself," Maggie said.

JD leaned over. "Don?" he began. "Can you tell me what happened?"

"No," Mr. Don said, sounding exhausted. "Can you tell me?"

"Somebody with guns and explosives carried out an assault on the school," JD said. "Looks like you got shot."

"Anybody else get hurt?" Mr. Don asked.

"Some," JD said. "We're still assessing the situation. New alarm system seems to have worked pretty well, though. A whole lot of the kids and most of the staff got out."

"That's good," Mr. Don sighed. "That's good." He was quiet for a minute. "What's that I smell?" he asked weakly.

JD looked at Maggie before answering. "Seems like they took a special liking to your band room. They blew up the bleachers and part of the back wall." He leaned closer. "Don," he asked, "were there any kids in here when you were attacked?"

Mr. Don began to shake his head. Maggie stopped him. "I don't think so," he said faintly. "I can't remember."

"Okay," JD said. "Not a problem." Maggie looked at JD. "It could be days before we get them all accounted for," he said softly. "You okay to stay here until they can move him?"

"As long as I'm not needed elsewhere."

He put a hand on her shoulder. "There were somewhere north of a thousand people in this building this morning," he said. "So far, we've found less than thirty who were in the line of fire. The odds are in Mac's favor."

The Observer freed the tiniest bubble of Maggie to answer him. "I know," she said, before turning back to Mr. Don. JD walked away. When she glanced up again, he was across the room near the rubble of the bleachers, talking to some other policemen.

"Mrs. Rifkin?"

Maggie looked down at Mr. Don. He was drifting in and out of consciousness. "Yes?"

"Where's MacDonald?"

"We don't know," she answered. "There hasn't been time to find all the children yet."

"Did he make it out?"

Maggie took a deep breath. "We don't know, Mr. Don. We're still looking."

"Because I told him to run."

Maggie's eyes opened wide, but she controlled her voice. "You told him to run. So he was with you?"

Mr. Don nodded. Maggie forgot to restrain his head. "Did they get him too?" he asked.

"Where did you tell him to run to?" Maggie asked calmly.

"Out the back door. Near the bleachers."

ᵣ ᵣ ᵣ

"Staties always have to run the show." The guy from the Sheriff's Department was bitching.

"Hey," Walter said, "there's enough mess to go around, don't you think?" The sheriff's guy made a disgusted face and walked away. "Nothing like a good tragedy to separate the men from the assholes," Walter said to JD.

"So what's next on the agenda?" JD asked the small group standing near the remains of the bleachers. Before anyone could answer, Hugh Masekela's unmistakable trumpet blared at them from somewhere nearby. Walter stared over JD's shoulder as if he'd just seen a ghost. JD whipped around. Maggie was no more than ten feet away, her face a mask of distress. She moved a cell phone away from her ear and closed it. Then she flipped it open and dialed again. Hugh Masekela's dulcet tones filled the quiet. They were coming from somewhere under the rubble. When the music stopped, Maggie closed the phone, then opened it again. JD strode over to her. "Stop."

"That's his phone ringing," she said in a monotone.

"Don't come any closer," JD ordered. He turned back to the assembled policemen. "Get me a crew and something to brace the wall." There was an interminable moment of general paralysis, and then people scrambled. JD looked at Maggie. "I'll get him for you," he said softly. Maggie nodded, too frightened to speak.

☞ ☞ ☞

Maybe it only took a few minutes for them to get to her son, but Maggie had lost the ability to judge time. She stayed back far enough to keep out of the way, using the last of her self-control to keep from pawing through the wreckage on the floor. They uncovered his arm first. It was not moving. They braced up the debris and began to carefully remove the rest of the load on top of him. Maggie couldn't see everything, but it looked like a beam had wedged over him, supporting a section of wall that was in turn keeping a pile of concrete from crushing him.

JD squatted down. That's when Maggie got a view of the body splayed in front of him, unmoving. "Look out," she said, trying to get closer.

JD held up his hand without turning around. "Not yet," he said, with calm authority. He took Mac's pulse while the rest of the crew continued to clear space around him. Then he began to carefully check Mac out. When he turned to Maggie, she felt his unnatural calm. "Come on over," he said. "Watch where you step, and don't touch anything." Maggie hadn't realized she was holding her own breath until she saw Mac's chest rise and fall. She exhaled loudly and gulped more air.

"We can't move him yet," JD said. She nodded. He waited until Maggie was kneeling next to him. "It looks like he has a head injury."

Maggie carefully leaned over her son. The hair on the right side of his head was caked with blood. Very delicately, she lifted it. There was a hole in his head, above his right ear. "It's a bullet wound," she said, her voice lifeless and flat. "At close range."

"Hey," JD said. There were tears in his eyes. "He's breathing on his own and his pulse is strong. Those are good signs."

Although she was looking straight at JD, she was seeing something else. "If he doesn't come back to me," she said, her eyes empty, "I will cease to exist."

"I'm going to radio for a Medevac," he said, standing up.

Maggie nodded blankly. "I'll just hold his hand until help gets here."

44

Lillian had just picked Chrissie up for their Wednesday appointment. There'd been no waiting this time, which Lillian took as a positive sign. She resisted the urge to ask what had become of the black boy, deciding to take his absence as satisfactory evidence that this particular diversion had run its course.

As they were pulling away from the curb, her cell phone rang. It was Carol Ann, and she wasn't making sense. She insisted that Lillian bring Chrissie home immediately. Despite Lillian suggesting she explain herself, she wouldn't give any further information. "We're having our roots done today," Lillian finally said, exasperated. "Do you know how long we'll have to wait for another appointment if we cancel now? That receptionist at Picasso's is a vengeful bitch. We'll only be a few hours. Whatever it is, I'm sure it can wait." Without giving Carol Ann a chance to protest, she hung up. Her phone rang again immediately. It was Carol Ann's number.

"Better answer it, Grams," Chrissie said. "You know if she doesn't get her way with you now you'll pay for it later."

Lillian sighed and flipped open her phone. "Yes?" she said icily.

"Lillian." It was Carl. "Screw your hair. Bring her back here now."

For the first time in forty-odd years, Lillian heard something in Carl's voice she did not know how to control. "What's going on?" she demanded.

"Would you please just do what I ask this one time?" he said and hung up.

🐦 🐦 🐦

The cops were crawling around Carol Ann's living room like maggots on a carcass, Bendz thought. They were waiting to question his granddaughter. His granddaughter, for chrissake! Like that little girl could have had anything to do with something like this. He fought to control his indignation. The front door opened and JD Charles walked in. "Hey!" Bendz exploded off the couch. "What the hell is going on! I want details!"

"Sit down," State Police Captain Bradford ordered.

"Take it easy, Carl," JD said.

Bendz raised his hands. "I'm taking it as easy as I can. Tell me what's going on."

"You know what happened over at the high school this morning?"

"We filled him in," Bradford said.

"What's that got to do with my granddaughter?" Bendz demanded.

JD looked at Bradford, then back at Bendz. "Whoever did it escaped with the evacuating kids. We found clothing and weapons they left behind."

"You think it was kids that did this?" Bendz asked, disbelieving.

"We're not ready to make any conclusions," JD said. "But whoever it was, they fit in with the crowd running out of that building."

Bendz had a hard time asking the next question. "You think my grand-daughter was involved?" His voice was full of quiet anxiety.

Bradford looked at JD. JD nodded. The captain produced a piece of paper. "This is a copy," he said. He held it out for Bendz to see. "The original was in the pocket of one of the overcoats we found near the weapons." In sharp block print it said, "Kill th- Nigg-rs". The "e" in each word had been replaced with a swastika. Bendz put his head in his hands.

"You recognize this?" Captain Bradford asked.

Bendz nodded without looking up. When nobody else spoke, he raised his head. "Somebody scratched something like it on her front passenger door. A few weeks ago."

"You report it to the police?"

Bendz shook his head. "She was at King of Prussia Mall the day it happened. She said she had no idea it was even there. Her mother saw it the next morn-ing. We just assumed it was some asshole at the mall, vandalizing cars. Took it into my place, and they compounded it out."

"You get a picture before you fixed it?" Bradford asked.

Bendz shook his head again. It took a few moments before the pieces of the puzzle began to assemble themselves for him. "Wait a minute," he said. "Some-body must have reported it, or you guys wouldn't be here. My granddaughter was in school all day today!" His voice sounded panicky. "We can prove that!"

"We just want to talk to her," Captain Bradford said.

"Come on, Charles," Bendz said. "You know she'd never be part of anything like this."

JD looked at the captain, then turned to Bendz. "A few weeks ago a park ranger filed an incident report with the State barracks up in Peachtree Town-ship. It involved three Caucasian girls and an African American boy, up in the Cliff View section of Gorge Park. The ranger suspected there might have been an attempted assault, but nobody was talking. He escorted the kids back to their vehicle, which was the only one in the parking lot. They were out there after dark, which is unusual for this time of year, but again, nobody would say anything. So he got some ID and told them to go home. Then he thought better of it, and put in a report just in case someone's parents decided to complain later. Your granddaughter was one of the girls, and the tags on the vehicle match her Humvee. The ranger reported a racial slur scratched onto the front passenger door of the car. The manner in which it was written matches what we have here."

Bendz squeezed his eyes shut tight. "Do I need to get a lawyer?"

"That's up to you," he said. "But Carl, time is of the essence. We need her to tell us the truth." Bendz nodded.

ɾ ɾ ɾ

As soon as they turned onto Carol Ann's cul de sac Lillian knew something was desperately wrong. An army of police cars was parked around the house. "Grams," Chrissie gasped, "what's going on?"

Lillian shook her head. "Nobody would say." She pulled the SUV over to the curb and put it in park. She looked hard at her granddaughter. "This is your chance. Tell me, whatever it is. If we need to go away before anyone sees us, we can still do that."

"Grams," Chrissie said, and for once she didn't try to sound sweet or sincere or any of the myriad other ways she had learned to manipulate adults, "I swear I don't know what's going on."

Lillian put her hand on her granddaughter's arm. "I love you, Chrissie. In the deepest, most fearful way possible. Do not let me walk blindly into this."

Chrissie started to cry. "Everybody was texting about something awful that happened at Dooleysburg High this morning, people getting shot and blowing stuff up. That's all I know."

"And do you have a clue why anyone would think you might have been involved?" Chrissie shook her head, her eyes wide with fear. "Okay," Lillian said, in charge once more. "Then we walk in there and act as dumb as posts. You got it?" Chrissie nodded.

They drove the rest of the way to the house in silence. When they walked in the front door, Chrissie was telling her grandmother the latest gossip. Lillian was proud of her ability to carry this off.

"Look at her," Bradford said under his breath to JD. "You can smell the fear all the way across the room."

ɾ ɾ ɾ

Once Chrissie described the Chevy Blazer, checking the owner's identity with Motor Vehicles was only a formality. Everyone from Peachtree Barracks knew the old truck, and that Kenny Robison drove it. Kenny's old man ditched the family years ago, and it was generally accepted that in the war between his talent as a drummer and his taste for trouble, trouble was going to win. So everyone was surprised when a call to Mammon High verified he'd been in school all day. He was already headed home, so Bradford put together a team to go to his house. He was not happy that Chief Charles wanted to go along, and he said so. For starters, he didn't believe Charles was impartial. And he didn't like Charles' reputation for meting out his own justice. This was already too damn risky without a freelancer on board. Charles agreed with everything he said, then asked if Bradford wouldn't feel more comfortable being able to keep an eye on him. Bradford was pissed he got outsmarted, but he let Charles tag along.

The team got to Robison's house before he did. By the time he arrived they had the house secured and the mother seated, terrified and weepy, on the living room sofa. The kid walked in and they had him on the floor before the front door closed. They frisked him and cuffed him. They emptied his pockets and put everything on the front hall table. There were no weapons. Two of the officers lifted him by his arms and walked him over to the sofa, where they sat him next to his mother. One look at her, and the kid started talking without waiting to be asked. His voice was cold and flat, like he was reading his homework.

"It was Eric Sloan," he said. "The dude's crazy. We used to talk about what we could do to those kids from Dooleysburg, but we were just screwing around. You know, taking their expensive cars for a ride and stuff like that. Then when they beat us at the band competition, he started making up some really scary stuff." He stopped and took a breath. "But he was full of shit, too. He was always trying to impress us, talking about mean stuff him and his old man did to animals or black people, and you knew it was total bullshit. His old man's so drunk all the time he doesn't even get off the couch. So when Eric started talking about how he had guns and nasty shit he got off the Internet, nobody paid attention." Kenny stopped again. "Then this morning he showed up here before school and said, 'Today's the day,' and I said, 'The day for what?' and he said, 'Today's the day we slaughter some rich kids and niggers.' And I said, 'What are you talking about?' and he said, 'We're going to Dooleysburg High, teach a few people a lesson.'" Kenny looked at them like the most important thing on his mind might be changing the channel on TV. "I told him get the fuck out of here. He called me a pussy. So I punched him. Then he started yelling stuff. And he was wearing this big coat I never saw before, and he opened it to show me this gun he had under there, like the ones you see in video games. He said maybe he should kill me first." Kenny's mother started crying in earnest.

"You think you should've called somebody?" JD asked.

Kenny shrugged. "Don't make a difference now, does it?"

"So he just left?" Bradford asked.

"Yeah," Kenny said. "I told him to stop being stupid. I said he should go put that shit back in his house or wherever he was hiding it and meet me at school."

"And you figured he would do that," Bradford asked.

Kenny looked him right in the eye. It was steel meeting steel. "He has no balls. He never did anything on his own, without me to tell him. So yeah, I figured if I didn't go along he wasn't going to do anything."

"What about when he didn't show up in school?"

"Him and Joey cut school all the time."

"Who's Joey?"

"Joey Shea. He moved here a few years ago, and him and Eric got to be friends because they're in the same homeroom every year. Joey's even crazier than Eric, but he's so wasted all the time he never gets off his ass to do anything."

"Until today," JD said. Bradford gave him a look.

"We need their addresses," Bradford said. "And a list of the other places they might be."

"They're like Siamese twins," Kenny's mother said. "If you find one you'll find the other. Eric called here looking for Kenny about an hour ago. I said he was in school, why wasn't Eric, and he hung up on me."

Bradford gave Kenny a look. "You talk to them?"

"Eric called my cell."

Only Bradford's flared nostrils gave away the depth of his rage. "What'd he say?"

"He was high. I could hear Joey too. They were laughing and screaming stuff. Eric said be sure and turn on the news as soon as I got home."

"How long ago was this?"

Kenny shrugged. "Maybe half an hour ago."

"Where were they?"

"Joey's."

"Where does Joey live?" Bradford asked.

"It's in my address book," Kenny's mother said. "In the kitchen."

"I'll keep her company," JD said. He followed her while she got the address, watched as she copied it onto a piece of paper. When she went back into the living room, he stayed behind.

Once they had the address, Captain Bradford left a couple of men in the house with orders to keep the kid and his mother away from the phone. He knew he was going to be in deep shit when the DA's office found out he didn't read anybody their rights before talking to them. At some point before the day was out, they'd get a search warrant and toss the kid's house. If he was telling the truth, they wouldn't find anything except maybe a little weed, and he'd get to walk away. Bradford didn't want to think about how big his problem would be if the kid wasn't clean. But for now he wanted the shooters. Who knew what else they had in mind? The problem with kids was they did crazy shit because they hadn't figured out yet just how long and awful the rest of their lives were going to be with something like this following them around.

Bradford walked out onto the front lawn. The usual circus of local law enforcement had arrived. He called everybody over and did a briefing. When he was done, he looked around for his team leads. That's when he noticed Chief Charles was missing. "Where's Charles?" he exploded. Nobody answered. "Somebody find Charles," he said, pissed.

One of the Dooleysburg cops spoke up. "I couldn't say for sure, but maybe he went to the hospital."

"What the hell for?" Bradford demanded.

"The kid who got shot in the head? The one they airlifted to Philly? That's his girlfriend's son."

"Goddammit!" Bradford roared, sprinting for his car.

⌐　⌐　⌐

JD flipped open the cell phone. There was a huge old maple at the curb, and he stayed behind it. He had run all the way, in his heavy flak jacket and helmet, but he was so pumped on adrenaline he was barely out of breath. If the kids were in the house, they weren't watching or they'd have shot at him before he got behind the tree.

He had Kenny's phone. He'd taken it off the front hall table on his way out of the house. He scrolled through the directory now until he found Eric. "Hey," an adolescent voice answered.

"Eric, don't hang up," JD spoke quickly. "This is Chief Charles from the Dooleysburg Police. I just want to talk."

"What are you doing with Kenny's phone?"

"I borrowed it."

"Where are you?"

"I'm in front of the house."

There was a pause. "I don't see you."

"I'm behind the big tree so you can't take a shot at me. But you can see there's nobody else out here."

Eric immediately got hysterical. "I didn't shoot anybody!"

"Okay," JD said. "But you need to come talk to people, tell them what happened."

"We can't!"

"Joey in there with you?" There was no answer. It sounded like somebody was crying. "Talk to me, Eric," JD said. "I want to help."

"I think Joey's dead," he blubbered.

"Why?" JD asked. "What happened?"

"He locked himself in the bedroom upstairs. I think he shot himself."

"Come on out and I'll help you, Eric."

"You come out first," Eric cried. "Where I can see you."

"I can't do that Eric. You might shoot me."

"If I come out, *you'll* shoot *me*."

"Tell you what," JD said. "I'll throw my weapon on the ground. Watch the tree." He reached under his flak jacket and took his service revolver off his belt. He tossed it wide, onto the front lawn, where it lay in full sight of house. "Did you see that?" he asked.

"Yeah."

JD switched the phone to his other hand and took the small semi-automatic out of his shoulder holster. He put it in his pocket. "Now you can come out," he said.

"No," Eric said. "I don't think so."

JD heard something in Eric's voice that raised his alarm level. The kid wasn't sounding quite as scared anymore. "Okay, Eric," JD said. "Are you hungry?"

"What do you mean? Like my last meal or something?"

"Nope. Just thought you might like something to eat." Off in the distance, JD heard the faint whine of sirens. Christ, Bradford, he thought, turn them off. He covered the phone, but it was just a matter of time before the kid heard them too. He weighed his options. "Eric," he finally said, "do you hear what I hear?"

"What are you talking about?"

"Sirens. I hear sirens. Soon every cop in Bucks County is going to be right here, outside the front door. You surrender to me now and I'll take care of you."

"I didn't *do* anything!"

"So tell me what happened."

"What are you talking about?"

"Somebody must have pissed you off pretty bad."

"What do you know? You don't know anything!" Eric's voice was all fury.

"Hey, buddy, I'm asking, right?"

There was no answer for several moments. JD waited. "Rich bastards," Eric muttered.

"What's that?" JD prodded. "You want to teach them a lesson?"

"Even the black kid's got it better than me. You want to tell me what makes it right that he's riding around in a Humvee while white kids are mopping the goddamn floor at Wendy's just to buy cigarettes?"

"What black kid is that, Eric?"

"The one who's screwing the blonde bitch!"

JD slowed his breathing. "Eric," he said, "you got the wrong school."

"What the fuck you talking about?" Eric screamed.

"Those kids don't go to Dooleysburg. That black kid doesn't even live around here."

"Fuck you!" Eric hung up.

ɾ   ɾ   ɾ

The first of the police cars turned onto the street. An instant after JD saw it, his own cell phone rang. He put Kenny's phone away and pulled out his own. "What the fuck are you doing?" Bradford thundered in his ear.

"What the fuck are *you* doing?" JD yelled back. "Turn off the goddamn sirens. The kid's already on the edge. Just take it down a few notches and we'll wait him out." Bradford's car began to slow. "And for crying out loud, don't park within range!"

Bradford stopped several houses down, where his car was shielded by a high hedge. "What do you think he's got in there?"

"Could be a damn rocket launcher for all I know. I got a bad feeling he thinks he's got nothing left to lose. He says Joey locked himself in the upstairs bedroom, and he thinks he killed himself."

"Jesus," Bradford said. "You still got him on the line?"

"No. Thanks to you and your big-ass sirens, he hung up."

"Try to call him again."

"Not yet. Get your people around the house. Then I'll try to talk him out, and if that doesn't work, we can teargas him."

"How much time you think we got?"

"How much you need?"

"I got some snipers on the way from Philly."

"I don't think that's in play. This kid's not going to last that long. We need to bring this down ourselves, one way or the other."

"Hey, Charles?"

"Yeah?"

"This is not about your girlfriend's kid. You understand me?" JD said nothing. "There is potentially one, maybe two mass murderers in that house. Our first priority is to protect the public. Our second is to see justice served, which means these kids get a fair trial, and *if* they are found guilty, a court of law decides their punishment. Not some small town cop with an axe to grind." He paused. "I don't hear you."

"Yes, sir," JD said.

"Because I'll risk my life to protect yours, but if you step over that line, I will hang you out to dry."

"Yes, sir."

"And don't forget, if your girlfriend's kid makes it, he's going to need you around to help him put the pieces back together."

JD snapped his phone closed.

🐦 🐦 🐦

Maggie continued her circuit of the waiting room. She stood, she sat, she paced. If all was going well, they were about halfway through Mac's surgery now. Which meant she had a couple of hours left to go. She began the cycle again. There was a family on the far side of the room. They seemed to cringe and shrink into their chairs whenever her path took her near them. That didn't slow her down.

As she came near her own side of the room Vee looked up. "You're scaring those nice people," she said.

"There is no such thing as nice people," Maggie said. She raised her hands. "Look at me. I'm a mess."

"You want me to find you some clean clothes?"

"No." Maggie shook her head. "I'm doing Jackie Kennedy."

"How about some coffee?" Vee offered.

"Do I look like I need *coffee*?"

"I was hoping it would be like giving Ritalin to a hyperactive kid."

"I feel nauseous," Maggie said.

"You need to save some energy," Vee said. "You know this is going to be a long haul."

"It's like my body wants to make sure my mind doesn't relax for even a second."

The doors at the far end of the waiting room opened. A young woman in scrubs walked in. She went over to the other group. "Dr. Rifkin?" she asked.

Maggie looked at Vee wildly. Everything in the room had suddenly gone crystalline sharp, as if her eyes were on red alert. She couldn't catch her breath. She could feel something beginning to rip open inside her. "It's too soon."

Vee jumped up and grabbed her. She forced her to sit down, then sat next to her with an arm around Maggie's shoulders, rocking slightly. Maggie could hear Vee crying softly. "Our father," Vee whispered, "who art in heaven, hallowed be thy name . . ."

"Dr. Rifkin?" The young woman came over. "I'm Dr. Spencer. I'm on rotation in neurosurgery."

Maggie wanted to scream, just tell me! But all that would come out was a faint, "Yes?"

"Your son isn't out of the woods yet. But I thought you'd like to know they got the bullet out. It's a small caliber, probably a .22. The entry wound looked bad because he was shot at close range. But there's reason to hope the damage will not be nearly as severe as it might have been. If there's such a thing as good news in a case like this, this is it. There's a chance they'll be able to preserve most of the right hemisphere."

Vee jumped up and got in the woman's face. She was so furious it was a wonder her tears weren't sizzling on her cheeks. "They already told us that! They knew that from the pictures or films or whatever the hell you call them that they took before surgery!"

"Oh." The woman backed away.

Vee was not done with her yet. "You just came out here and scared the living shit out of us so you could show off, didn't you?"

"I . . ." Dr. Spencer looked like she just figured out there was a bear in the cave. "I'll let you know if there's further news." She scurried away. Maggie started shaking uncontrollably.

"Wait a minute," Vee yelled. "As long as you sashayed your pseudo-doctor ass out here, you might as well make yourself useful. Go get this woman something clean to put on so she doesn't have to sit here looking like a poster child for some Third World civil war. And hurry the hell up," Vee added as she sat back down. "Fucking interns," she muttered.

"I could never tolerate them." Maggie said, standing up.

"Where you think you're going?" Vee demanded.

"I think I'm ready to puke now. You keep praying."

🐦 🐦 🐦

Kenny's cell phone rang. "Yeah," JD answered it.

"What're you guys doing out there?"

"Waiting for you, Eric. We're prepared to wait as long as you like."

Eric hung up. JD called Bradford. "Time's running out," he said. "He's getting antsy."

"You know what I been wondering?" Bradford asked.

"What?"

"What are you gonna do if you gotta take a leak? You're stuck behind that tree. You step out, the kid's gonna off you."

"Guess I'll just have to drop trow right here and you get to admire my sweet ass."

"That used to really bother me when I was a kid," Bradford continued. "Especially Star Trek. Years and years of space travel, and nobody ever takes a bio break. They show them eating, they show them drinking. Where's all that stuff go?"

"Where no man has gone before?"

Kenny's cell phone rang again. Before he answered it, JD asked Bradford, "You positioned to cover me yet?"

"Mostly," Bradford said. "Just don't do anything stupid. No grandstanding."

JD hung up and switched phones. "Yeah?" he said.

"I can wait a long time," Eric said. His voice sounded edgy, slightly hysterical.

"I know you can," JD said. "I've heard you're a tough kid."

"Liar!"

"Eric, come on. My feet are starting to hurt."

"Who gives a shit about your feet!"

"Eric, I'd like to reach an agreement. I know you're scared. I want to keep you alive."

"You don't care about me!" Eric started to cry. "You're laughing at me!"

"No Eric. I do not consider you someone to be laughed at." JD heard a voice in the background. It was yelling something, but it sounded far away. "Who is that, Eric?" It sounded like maybe the voice was yelling hang up. "Eric, is that Joey? Is Joey still with you?" The phone went dead.

JD called Bradford on his own cell. "Looks like it's crying time," he said.

"We're ready."

"There might be two of them after all. Somebody was yelling at him in the background."

"We'll put two canisters in the downstairs windows on either side of the front door. See what that flushes out."

"Just remember," JD said, "he's mine."

"Hey buddy. Why don't you just stay behind your tree?"

"No. Cover me. I want to take him."

"Alive."

"Alive," JD agreed.

"Cause we're the good guys. We don't kill people for revenge."

"Believe it or not, Bradford, I'm still not convinced he's the one."

"Okay. We got the back of the house covered. We'll put a few canisters in there too just for good measure. The place is set pretty far back from the street, so give it a good count of ten before you come out."

"Yeah," JD said.

"Hey, you know what?" Bradford asked.

"What?"

"You're on a roll. You're treed like a squirrel, and you got a town mascot who's squirrelly, going around introducing his little fellow to the ladies. It's like you got a theme going."

"He was a chipmunk, asshole." JD hung up and took out his semi-automatic. He heard the nearly simultaneous thuds of the teargas being launched. He counted to ten and stepped out from behind the tree. There was heavy smoke pouring from the downstairs windows. He took a few strides toward the house. It was stupid to leave himself out in the open, but truth be told, he didn't much care. It had been a long time since he felt this desolate, this willing to put himself in the hands of fate.

The front door opened. JD saw a dark shape emerging from the smoke. He heard the blast almost at the same time he felt the rain of shotgun pellets. At this distance, the shot wouldn't have done much damage anyway, but what reached him bounced off his flak jacket. He turned slightly to call, "Hold your fire!" and just as he did, he saw the flash from the upstairs window. Something incredibly powerful slammed into him, right where his left shoulder became his chest. It didn't hurt the way he expected it to. But it was true, what they said about how you become a detached observer. He saw his body flying toward a hard landing on the ground at the same time his right hand squeezed the trigger and sprayed the front of the house with bullets. The dark shadow at the front door fell, while at the same time he heard gunfire all around him and saw the upstairs window blowing out. And then, stupendously, although he was no longer hearing anything, the whole roof and most of the top floor of the house exploded into brilliant orange flames. JD was vaguely aware of large chunks of burning stuff raining down, and then he peacefully went to sleep.

45

By the time Vee brought the car around from the parking garage, Maggie felt composed, not the shaking mess she'd been when the pediatric neurosurgeon gave her Mac's prognosis. It was, as she should have expected, as she would have delivered herself if their roles were reversed, no prognosis at all. Mac was right on that cusp of adolescence, when it was impossible to predict whether the brain plasticity that enabled children to make miraculous recoveries still existed inside his head. Nothing to do but wait until he woke up and see who was inhabiting his skull now. He might develop a seizure disorder. He might have significant personality changes. He was likely to have some physical impairments. How many times had she delivered similarly devastating messages, never allowing anyone's suffering to pierce her armor?

Maggie got into Vee's car. Like a post-op patient crouching over an incision in a pointless effort to avoid further pain, Maggie was guarding her soul. She said nothing as Vee navigated Market Street. When they took a left onto the 676 ramp they ran into traffic. "Always ties up," Vee remarked, as if conversation might hold some power to restore normalcy. "These people congregate here every damn night like it's an assignment." Maggie did not answer.

They continued east on 676, Vee cutting in and out of the lanes as if something would be gained by being the first to merge onto Route 95. They went up that ramp and descended into a mass of taillights. The congestion was too heavy for Vee to weave through and she had to content herself with cursing under her breath and flicking on her turn signal from time to time.

Traffic finally opened up as they passed the oil refinery at the north end of Port Richmond. That was the same moment the roar of grief came from deep in Maggie's gut and tore its way out of her throat. Even as she gave vent to it, she thought what an odd experience this was. Here she was howling with despair, and yet she was completely separate from herself, intellectual capacity resting like a butterfly on the wretched creature in the front seat of the car. As her cries became more uncontrolled, she floated up above herself, looking down on her rocking body. She wasn't thinking how to comfort it, she was just puzzled by what it was doing.

Vee glanced over as she changed lanes once again. "You go right ahead and scream," she said. "Scream until it's all out of you. Nobody but me's going to hear you."

Maggie moved as if her body was following some ancient imprint for grieving. She had neither need nor power to direct it. The clawed, dark hand of grief reached into her gut trying to forcibly rip out her soul. She crossed her arms over her chest and pressed hard, trying to contain herself within herself before the pain emptied her completely. If she eased up on the pressure she thought her being might just burst out of her and spurt irretrievably away, like the blood from a severed artery. Vee drove on, implacable. It was several miles before Maggie was too hoarse to scream anymore. She continued to rock for a while, moaning quietly now and then.

"You want me to pull over somewhere?" Vee asked.

"He shouldn't have died," Maggie whispered hoarsely.

"Honey, he's not dead," Vee said forcefully. "Don't think like that. Don't give up on him." When Maggie didn't answer, she continued. "You are not going to let go of hope now."

"Gary," Maggie breathed fiercely. "Gary shouldn't have died. We never would have left New York if he didn't die."

"You think this was somebody's fault?" Vee asked. "That make you feel better? To believe if we only made different choices we could get in charge of what happens to us?"

"No," Maggie said. She didn't know what she believed.

"But you think you could've stopped this somehow?" Vee glanced over.

"I didn't love him enough. Any of them. I didn't love any of them enough."

"Stop being so unkind to yourself. Love does not protect people. All it does is give them some strength to face the next thing life throws their way. Bad shit happens in life because being alive is risky. We're all doing exactly the same thing, just trying to hold on to the people around us and stay afloat somehow. This is not your time to think about giving up."

"I am so tired of living in the spaces between tragedies," Maggie said, exhausted. "I am tired of bad luck."

"It's true you've had some mighty bad luck," Vee said cautiously. "But you need to realize sometimes you put yourself in harm's way. You take unnecessary risks."

"How can you say that?" Maggie shouted. "How can you say that to me now, today?"

"Because you need to know so you can stop," Vee replied gently. "You take those risks because you don't notice you're in danger. You have no clue how to take care of yourself."

Neither of them spoke after that. They continued on the highway until they reached the New Hope exit, where they got onto local roads. Maggie began fishing around in her purse.

"What are you looking for?" Vee asked.

"I borrowed a cell phone from a girl at the school this morning. I forgot to give it back."

"I'm sure she'll forgive you."

"Can I just borrow yours?"

Vee took a deep breath. "Reception's pretty bad right here. Who do you need to call?"

Maggie caught on instantly. She was too raw not to. "Why can't I call JD?" she asked with a fearsome quietude. "I want to tell him about Mac." Vee didn't answer. "Why can't I call JD?" Maggie yelled.

Vee pulled into the small parking lot of a local winery and turned off the car. "Get a handle on yourself," she said. "I can't talk to you when you're like this."

Maggie braced herself against the back of her seat. Breathe, she thought. Just live through the next ten seconds. Swallow life in small doses, the way medieval princes used to increase their tolerance for poison so it wouldn't kill them. "I'm ready," she finally said.

Vee looked out her window, then at Maggie. "I tried to call JD while we were at the hospital and couldn't get him. So I called the station. I talked to Walter." Maggie stared straight ahead. "JD was with the task force that went after the kids who did it. They think it was just a couple of boys. They got them." Vee paused, trying to judge how much more Maggie could take. Maggie's gaze was hollow, like her eyes had been popped in place by a taxidermist. "They're dead," Vee said. "The boys who did it."

"JD," Maggie said.

"JD is alive." When she heard this Maggie realized she'd already forgotten her own order to breathe. Vee tried to speak and choked. She took a shuddering breath and started again. "But probably not for long. He got shot in the upper left chest. Bullet went through his flak jacket. Walter didn't know any other details. Just that it's really bad."

Maggie sagged against her seat. Her voice was frighteningly calm. "Take me to him."

"Honey, you've got to get some rest. You have your own struggle ahead of you." She patted Maggie's arm. It was like touching stone.

"Take me to him," Maggie said again.

"You re a mess," Vee said. "Nobody's going to let you into the ICU."

"Take me to him," Maggie said with cold, quiet force. "This may be my only chance to tell him I'm sorry. Stop wasting time."

Vee started the car and took off. The road curved like a snake in motion, and she went fast enough that she could feel the car slip at the edge of control. Maggie drew her legs up to her chest and hugged her knees, curled up against her window. They finally came to a straight stretch of road. Vee glanced at Maggie. "It was easier when you were screaming," she said.

Maggie looked at her dully. "I'm praying."

Vee reached over and put her hand on Maggie's leg. Maggie did not react. Vee left her hand there most of the rest of the way home, as if seeking her own comfort.

ɾ   ɾ   ɾ

Maggie stood near the telemetry station. One of the nurses had spotted her on her way to JD's bed. The scrubs she was wearing and her purposeful stride had gotten her this far, but it had no effect on this particular bitch. "Only immediate family," she told Maggie with authority.

Are you pissed because I got your spot on the blow-job line-up? Maggie wanted to demand. But she listened to the tiny remnant of reason left in her head. As much as Maggie might hate her at the moment, the nurse was just trying to protect JD.

"I'm sorry," the nurse said. "If you don't leave I'm going to have to call Security."

"Call the attending instead," Maggie said.

"Why would I do that?"

"I'm one of the doctors who was at the school today. The one whose son got part of his head blown off. If I had a hotline to God, I would ask him to explain to you personally why you are going to let me sit with Chief Charles. But I don't, so the attending will have to do."

The nurse looked her up and down. "You can't go in like that."

"This has been a record holder of a bad day." Maggie was exhausted. "Get me a gown, get me some scrubs, put me in a fucking hazmat suit. Whatever you want. Just let me in there."

"I'm going to make a call," the nurse said. "If you stay where you are, it will be to the attending. If you move one inch closer to his bed, it will be to Security."

She walked to the desk. Maggie looked at the clock. She would give her ten minutes. She craned her neck to watch JD. Same way she watched Mac less than two hours before. Helpless. Today, at this moment, she was grateful they were alive and breathing. By tomorrow or the next day, that would not be enough, and the hope and gratitude would begin to drain off her like water off a melting block of ice, slowly at first, but then with increasing speed and volume, until there was nothing left. She tried to close her mind's eye.

"Hello," someone said beside her.

Maggie was startled. She'd been so deep inside herself she hadn't noticed the older man walk up next to her. She nodded.

"I'm Dr. Burns. House staff. You wanted to see me?" He spoke calmly and softly.

He's using the emergency lunatic address system, Maggie thought. "Thank you for coming." She let her exhaustion bleed into her voice.

"You were involved in the incident at the high school yesterday?"

This shook Maggie up. Had a day already passed since the world blew into deadly sharp fragments? "My son was one of the children who got shot."

"I'm sorry," he replied. "Did he make it?"

"Barely. He's at Children's Hospital. I was on my way home to get stuff so I can stay down there when I heard about JD. Chief Charles."

"How do you know him?"

Maggie was out of patience. She wanted to deliver the kind of cutting remark she usually used to mow people out of her way. Instead she sighed. "If you were a local, you'd know."

He shook his head. "I live up in Allentown."

"We were very close," Maggie said. "I would like to sit with him."

"He's very sick. You know standard procedure is only immediate family."

Maggie looked around. "Do you see any family here?"

"They've been notified."

"Who did you notify?" she insisted. "His wife's parents? He has no other family."

The doctor paused. "I guess you knew him pretty well?" The use of the past tense did not escape her.

"We were lovers," she said. "I called the station on my way here. I know he already arrested twice. Is he going to make it? In your opinion."

He hesitated. "I can't give you a call one way or the other."

"Please," Maggie said. "If everybody did their jobs like they were supposed to, anything inside him that could be repaired was repaired, to the extent possible. Now all anybody can do is hope it will all decide to work again. But he's lost so much blood his body is doing stuff that could kill him despite your efforts. Please just let me hold his hand for a while." She paused, willing herself to say the rest of it before she lost her courage. "Don't let him die alone."

"Okay," the doctor relented. "But you shouldn't stay too long."

"I won't," Maggie said tiredly. "I have to get back to my son."

"I'm sorry," the doctor said. "How's he doing?"

Maggie drifted off for a moment. "By tomorrow I could lose them both," she said softly. "This happened to him because he was trying to catch whoever hurt my son."

"He was doing his job. I'm sure if he could, he'd tell you that himself."

"Let me stay with him as long as I can. With luck, he'll make it until his family gets here." Her eyes moved only from JD to the monitors and back again.

"We'll get you a clean gown," the doctor said. "You know the rules."

She nodded. Then she asked the question she'd been dreading. "The bullet wasn't a dum-dum, was it?"

"No. But it was armor piercing. It did a lot of damage."

"Cardiac involvement?"

"Not directly," the doctor answered. "But as you said, he had significant blood loss. He arrested once on the way over and again on the table. I hear they put up a real fight to hold on to him. Nobody wanted to let him go."

"No," she whispered. "There's nobody around here who would want to do that."

"So many people showed up to give blood for him they had to tell a bunch of them to come back tomorrow." Maggie nodded. She was tired of talking. All she wanted to do was curl up on a bed between Mac and JD and die along with them.

ʳ ʳ ʳ

Maggie pulled her chair close to the bed. She watched JD for a few minutes, then got up and kissed his forehead. "I'm sorry," she whispered. She moved her mouth closer to his ear. "I'm sorry I hurt you. I could try to love you. I will try to love you. Please don't die." She looked up at the monitors. There was no change. Even though she knew that sort of thing didn't happen in real life, she was still devastated that he showed no response to her voice. She sat back down and took his hand. She laid her head next to him and closed her eyes and waited.

46

When Morsel didn't come home, Gamey tried not to panic. The kid left him a message earlier in the day that he was fine, he didn't get hurt. So Gamey figured it was business as usual. But when he got home and there was no sign of the kid, he knew something wasn't right. He never felt anything like this before, but he just knew.

He held out a couple hours, hoping Morsel would show up. When he couldn't take it anymore he called the station. "I need to report a missing kid," he told the cop who took his call. He figured they'd ask a few questions. He wasn't prepared for the official treatment. They put him through to some special unit and started giving him the third degree. "Listen!" he finally blurted out. "The kid left me a message. He's okay." Once they heard that, and that Gamey had no official responsibility, they dumped him like a smelly sack of fish parts.

Gamey spent the rest of the night driving around town trying to pick up Morsel's trail. It was no use. Nobody was on the streets. Every kid within miles knew enough to head for shelter. What hurt Gamey deep inside was how Morsel didn't come looking to be safe with him.

The start of the new day only made things worse. The afternoon crew showed up at the deli, and Gamey snarled at them for answers. They didn't have any. He filled Morsel's voice mail and didn't get a call back. He closed up and went home and threw around as many things as he could without doing real damage. When he was finally exhausted, he got into what was left of his van, the metal hull full of dents from the crash at the synagogue, and drove over to the police station. Only, once he got there he didn't know what to do next. Charles was his inside connection. Which of those other clowns would take pity on him? He sat outside in the dark, waiting for inspiration.

Eventually the shift change started. Two cops came out. Nobody was joking around tonight. They got into their cars and left. Then Joe Butts walked out the back door. Gamey hopped out of the van and scurried over. Butts did a double take, surprised by the sound. "Don't shoot!" Gamey yelled. "It's me, Roland Gamey!"

"What the hell you doing out here in the middle of the night?"

"Please," Gamey said. "I need help."

"What kind of help?" Butts asked suspiciously.

"It's the kid. You know, the one that was living with me. Morsel." Butts didn't respond. "He's gone," Gamey continued. "Just took off after the mess at the school. Left me a voice mail to tell me he was okay, didn't get hurt, and then never showed up home."

"File a report," Butts replied.

"I tried. They told me I got no standing."

"So ask the parents to file a report."

"I would," Gamey said, "if I knew where to find them. I checked the old man's place, and he's long gone. And I got no clue where to find the old lady. All I know is she lives in Northeast somewhere."

"What do you think I can do?"

"Please, Butts." Gamey didn't even know he could beg until he heard that whiny voice come out of his mouth. "This is killing me. I can't eat, I can't sleep, I can't think about nothing for two minutes without worrying, is he okay? Is he alive? Does he need help? Please."

Butts shook his head. "Sorry. Not my province."

Gamey caught his arm as he started to walk away. "Butts, all I'm asking is for you to help me find the kid, make sure he's all right. Anything you want in return is yours. You name it. Anything."

Butts shook Gamey off. "I told you," he said gruffly. "You're barking up the wrong tree."

"Charles would find a way!" Gamey shouted.

"So go ask him," Butts said.

Gamey stood in the middle of the parking lot and watched Butts get in his car, watched his taillights come on, watched him pull out and head toward the exit, thinking the whole time, he'll change his mind. He watched the taillights go down the street and out of sight. He waited some more. A pair of headlights came from that direction, and his heart beat fast as they got closer. They passed the station and kept going. Gamey began to cry.

He got back in the van and headed to the deli. He couldn't go back to that empty house. That's what you get, he told himself. You had a fine life. And then you had to go and screw it up, get yourself a kid. Now everything the kid had touched was tainted, proof that he was gone.

Gamey parked behind the deli. The damn dog started howling. Good old Oscar Mayer. Piece of shit would lick the ankles of anybody who broke into the place, but he couldn't shut his yap at the thought of Gamey. Gamey went around and opened the front door so Oscar Mayer could hoist himself outside for a piss. Then he walked into the back room and sat down without turning on the lights. He was probably there a good half hour when the stupid-ass dog started howling again. Gamey went to let him in. When he opened the front door, Joe Butts was standing there, Oscar Mayer singing at his feet. "Quite a watchdog you got," Butts said.

Gamey didn't know how to answer. Was the guy actually looking for donuts after what he pulled tonight? "Something I can do for you?" he asked.

"Nah," Butts replied. "Something I can do for you." He handed Gamey an envelope. "Police report," he said. Gamey stared at him. "Take a look," Butts added.

Gamey opened the envelope. It was a report of a car stolen from Northeast last October, found in the parking lot near Tuohy's Costume Shop. The car belonged to a Renee Bazewski. "Same last name as the kid," Gamey said, his lips moving as he read.

"It's his old lady," Butts said. "The incident when he quote, unquote borrowed her car last fall. Could be she still resides at that address."

Gamey was afraid he was going to cry again. "Thank you, Officer Butts," he said. "I don't know how to tell you what this means to me."

"Forget it," Butts said, turning away. "We all been through enough for one lifetime. Good luck finding your kid."

🐓 🐓 🐓

Gamey drove south on Route 309. He had every intention of starting out at the crack of dawn, but somehow it got to be 2 PM before he hit the road. He was feeling a little twitchy. He wasn't a fan of the city. That had to be what was putting him off. A few miles from where MapQuest said she lived, his hands got sweaty and his heart started doing a jazz number. He thought about turning the van around, but he knew if he did he would never get up the courage to try again.

He crossed Stenton Avenue. It was like crossing the border into another country, just not the one he had imagined. It looked pretty average for being where all those murders, car thefts and other disasters he saw on the nightly news happened. The two-story brick rowhomes reminded him of old-fashioned army barracks. There were a few people on the street, nobody remarkable. Gamey was a little disappointed things weren't more dramatic.

He took the third right after the graveyard, like it showed on the map. He was losing his courage again. Then he saw the parking spot. There was still money on the meter. Nobody in their right mind would pass up a spot like that. He pulled up nice and tight next to the car in front, then, turning the steering wheel with only one finger, swung backwards. At the instant his passenger side mirror was even with the rear fender of the other car he cut the wheel hard, and eased into the spot like it was made for him. With a sigh of satisfaction, he straightened out his wheels, put the van in park and turned off the ignition.

That's when he started to wonder what the hell he was doing. His problem was he was too damn greedy. He could never pass up that penny on the sidewalk, the six-pack of soda the cashier didn't see on the bottom rack of the shopping cart, the dollar bill an old lady dropped when she was putting away her change. Now his greed got him parked here when common sense was yelling at him to go home.

Movement in his rearview mirror caught his eye. A bus was stopped at the intersection behind him and people were getting out. Most of them were black. This neighborhood, older than the rowhomes he just passed, must have been pretty upscale in its better days. The houses had fieldstone fronts and large porches with mullioned windows. But the area was spotty now. Some of the places were dilapidated, others still looked cared for.

Gamey checked the nearby house numbers. Her place was a little ways up the block. A few of the people from the bus walked past. Gamey hoped maybe one of them was her so he could watch her go in, get a feel what she was like. No such luck. He was all alone on the street now. In his great parking spot. Which he would have to leave with money on the meter if he drove away. He got out of the van, making sure it was locked before he walked away.

Her house was about halfway to the next corner. He took his time getting there, like it made a difference. The porch was a little out of square and the steps needed to be repointed. There was an old couch on the porch with a blanket on it that somebody had made by hand. He considered turning back again, but at the last minute he saw himself sitting in his kitchen alone, pissed that he didn't make at least one attempt. He climbed the steps. It wasn't until he knocked, hard, that he wondered what he might say to whoever answered. He didn't have to worry about it long. A large woman opened the door and stood there, staring down at him like he was asking to be squashed. "Yeah?" she said.

"Mrs. Bazewski?" His voice cracked.

She took a minute to answer. "You're him, aren't you?"

Gamey shrunk down even further. He hoped there was some chance "him" might be somebody else. "I'm Roland Gamey," he offered sheepishly.

"Come on in." She turned around and walked into the house, like she knew he would follow. Which he did. They went back to the kitchen. "You want something to drink?"

"Nah," he said. "I don't drink during the day."

She looked at him like she couldn't believe he was such a dope. "I meant like coffee. Or water."

That's not what Gamey expected. "Nah."

"Okay," she said. "Sit down."

Gamey settled into a chair. "He tell you about me?"

"The old man," she said cryptically. Gamey looked confused. "When you took him home on Halloween, his father called. Bastard was afraid you were going to come looking for support money, wanted to make sure I'd ante up my share. Told me the kid was going to live with some freaky little man." She nodded. "No offense, of course."

"What do you mean, no offense?" Gamey barked. Then he remembered his mission. "Never mind."

"He don't want to see you."

"I kind of figured," Gamey said. "I thought maybe you could give him a message."

"Won't matter."

"It might," he insisted.

She poured herself a cup of coffee and fixed it with Sweet'N Low and non-dairy creamer. While she was busy, Gamey looked around. The place smelled of stale cigarette smoke, but it was spotless. Nothing too nice, but all of it polished and tidy. She sat down across the table from him. "Maybe you should get on with it," she said.

He opened his mouth, then stopped. He couldn't call the kid Morsel to her face. But it was the only name he knew. He never even bothered to look at the paperwork when he hired him. "The boy," he finally began, "well, I don't know how to say this, you being his mother and all, but he means a lot to me."

"Not that much," she said hotly.

Gamey was stunned. "How can you say that?" he demanded.

"You people, you all got money and fancy houses. You live easy. What do you know about people like us? What do you care?"

"That is an unfair assessment," Gamey answered. He drew himself up straight, careful to remain seated. "What do you know of how I treated the boy?"

"I know what Marcel tells me," she said decisively.

"Who?" Gamey asked.

"Marcel," she said, looking at him like he just asked what planet they were on.

"Marcel," Gamey repeated, almost to himself. Of course. The pieces of the puzzle suddenly fell into place. "So tell me," he continued, "why exactly was it that you let him stay with your ex? You must have known the guy was a slug. And the boy, Marcel, he thinks very highly of you. How do you just send a kid away like that?"

"You got no right to judge me!" she snapped.

"No, ma'am," Gamey agreed. "I'm just curious."

"He has a job already, you know. At a diner in Cheltenham. He's going to start saving money, and he'll be plenty happy. Why can't you just let well enough alone?"

"I would like to give your son a future."

"You're so damn smart, aren't you? What if he's not that kind of boy? What if all you'll ever do for him is fill his head with dreams that won't do anything except make him hate what he is?"

"I think you had those same dreams for him," Gamey said, enjoying the delicacy of the moment before cashing in. "My guess is, you let him stay with your ex-husband when you left because you wanted him to be in a good school."

"That's not a crime."

"Nope," he agreed. "The crime is that even after that sacrifice, even after you left your boy with that scumbag, those good schools didn't do a damn thing for him."

To his chagrin, Mrs. Bazewski began to cry. Not big, honking sobs, but dignified tears, which made it even worse. "They passed him along year after year," she said, her voice husky, "like a hot potato. At first I thought it was him, that they couldn't wait to get rid of him. After a while I figured out it was because it would mess up their numbers if they held him back. They didn't give a damn what was right for him."

"Mrs. B.," Gamey said, feeling like he could take certain liberties now, "you convince him to come back to me, and I'll take good care of him."

"You know what I think, Mr. Roland Gamey? I think you should stop hoping you got the magic answer that'll turn him into something he's not."

Gamey started to panic. He couldn't go back to living his life alone. "Is it the money?" he asked. "You like that he's bringing in some cash? You name a price, and we'll talk." She started bawling in earnest. "Okay, okay," Gamey said in a rush. "Forget I mentioned it."

"No," she shook her head. "It's not only the money, but the money's nice."

"What else?"

"I been living alone for years. Marcel's a good kid. He can be a pain in the ass, but his heart's in the right place. He's good company."

"Yeah," Gamey said sympathetically.

A chill fell on the conversation. "So why should he come live with you?" she demanded. "I'm lonely too, and I'm blood to him."

This was more of a conversation than Gamey was counting on. He raised his hands in surrender. "I got no answers," he finally said. "I was just hoping to get him back."

Mrs. B. wiped her eyes and nose with a napkin. "It's up to him," she said.

There was a gust of air as the front door opened, and then they heard it slam. They froze as if caught in a criminal act. Morsel walked into the kitchen. "Hey!" he demanded. "What are you doing here?" Then he noticed his mother. "What did you say to her?" He was furious.

"Marcel," Mrs. Bazewski said, "mind your manners. This man is a guest in our home."

"That's right," Morsel said roughly. "This is my home, the kind of place where people like me belong."

"Siddown," Gamey growled.

Morsel and his mother both looked startled. "Who you talking to?" Morsel said, failing to sound tough.

"You heard me," Gamey commanded. "Sit your ass down." He reached over and pulled another chair out from the table. Morsel sat. Mrs. Bazewski looked fascinated by the mystery unfolding between this pint-sized man and her quart-sized son. She lit a cigarette, her hands shaking slightly.

"You're wasting your time," Morsel said, angry. "I ain't going back there."

"What are you afraid of?" Gamey challenged him.

Morsel gave him a mean look. "They all think what happened to him is because of me."

"Nobody's blaming you," Gamey said.

"The hell they're not," Morsel insisted.

"Trust me," Gamey assured him. And then he saw it, what the kid was hiding, same as he'd been doing for years. Gamey picked up Mrs. Bazewski's cigarette pack and tossed it on the table in front of him. "What does that say?" he demanded.

Morsel looked at Gamey like he was an idiot. "Newport Lights."

Gamey looked around, irritated. The place was too frickin' tidy. He got up and opened a cabinet. There was a container of Quaker Oats. He grabbed it and stomped back, slamming it down on the table. "What does this say?" he demanded.

"Quaker Oatmeal."

"Read it exactly!"

"Quaker Oatmeal!" Morsel shouted angrily.

Gamey got in his face. "It don't say 'oatmeal'."

"Who gives a shit what it says!" Morsel shouted. He began to cry.

"Leave him be!" Mrs. Bazewski ordered.

"Kid," Gamey ignored her, "you come back with me, I'll help you, whatever it takes."

"Stop it!" Mrs. Bazewski yelled. "You people parade through life thinking your money means you know what it takes." She started to cry again as well. "How many times you think you can break his heart before I can't fix it anymore?"

Gamey opened his mouth, but nothing came out. It was like somebody just touched him with a magic wand. He looked at Morsel's mother. "We are not enemies," he said respectfully.

She wiped her eyes and sniffed. "Don't make him promises you can't keep. He can have a good honest life with me."

"Yes, ma'am," Gamey said. "But I swear to you, if he comes home with me I will not give up until we find a way for him to learn how to read."

Mrs. Bazewski took a deep, shuddering breath. "Marcel," she said with difficulty, "pack your things. It's time to go home."

47

Maggie stood by the window of Mac's room, trying not to think. His doctor had been in again, today as every day. At this point, he didn't have much left to say. A few days ago he stopped saying time would tell, because time was telling loud and clear. It was taking too long. The most significant damage, it turned out, was from the entry wound. The gun had been close enough to Mac's head that pieces of his skull were blown into the brain tissue. The gun had been pointing upward when it was fired, so the bullet itself skimmed over the surface of his brain for the most part. They'd kept a close watch on him to make sure there was no swelling that would damage his brain by crushing it against his skull. Everything indicated he would recover. But he wasn't waking up. And he should have been awake by now.

There was no explanation why he was still unconscious, except that sometimes these things happened. Maggie had seen the words, "Dx—persistent vegetative state" often enough to know that sometimes you just got unlucky. She gave his doctor credit for still showing up each day. One of the reasons she chose trauma surgery for her specialty was so she wouldn't have to deal with families day after day, watch as initial reserves of hope got drained away and the bad news hardened around them like concrete.

Vee would be here soon. She showed up every day as soon as she was done with her classes. Maggie knew she should be grateful, but she was starting to dread these visits more than the doctor's. Vee remained so fucking hopeful. Maggie couldn't face the task of convincing her the time was coming to think about giving up. She was just hanging on now, waiting for Albie to get here from Japan. She knew Albie was due to arrive soon, but she'd lost track of the date, the same as she'd lost track of all the life that continued normally outside the hospital walls.

She walked over to the side of Mac's bed. Lying there, his head bandaged, it was difficult to remember him as the funny, wise boy who had been the focus of her existence. He looked so different. Maggie realized she'd never seen his face, even during peaceful sleep, so expressionless, so blank, just a set of features with no one inside.

r *r* *r*

Albie blew into Mac's room like a warrior returning in triumph, ready to take charge of things at home again. On the ride from the airport Vee had been clear and at the same time vague. She had some apprehension, it seemed, though she wouldn't come out and say so, that things might not come to a good end. Albie simply would not accept that. She knew she could fix this, as she had always fixed everything in Mac's life. Nothing else was conceivable.

Maggie got up from her seat near the bed. She walked toward Albie tentatively, as if she were hollow and in danger of imploding. Albie just looked at her. They couldn't risk anything else.

"This was not your fault," Albie said.

"I figured out what I forgot to teach him," Maggie whispered. "I forgot to teach him to be afraid."

Albie walked to Mac's bed. She leaned over and spoke softly into his ear telling him why, exactly, he would be returning to them. Nobody in the room seemed to be breathing. Then she reached into her bag and pulled out a beat-up old copy of *Where the Wild Things Are*.

"I had no idea you saved that," Maggie said.

Albie glanced at her. "I should think you wouldn't," she said. "I took enough pains to hide it." She pulled a chair up next to the bed, made herself comfortable and began to read. She read the book exactly as she always had, and the paths her voice had made in Maggie's memory so many years ago lit up like they'd only been waiting all these years to be rekindled. Albie even misread the name of the little boy in the book, calling him Mac instead of Max, like she always used to. Except now he was lost for real with the wild things, perhaps in and out of years. Albie finished the story. She flipped back to the beginning and read it again. And then again. Her voice did not vary in the least from one reading to the next.

Vee walked in quietly and took Maggie's arm. She spoke in a hush, as if they were witnessing something sacred. "Come on," she said. "Let's go get some coffee." Maggie didn't particularly want coffee, but she couldn't watch this much longer.

Nobody paid attention to how long they were gone, but when they came back Albie was still at it. She was right where they had left her, still reading calmly, with the same familiar intonations. The only change, so slight that only Maggie could see it, was the panic deep behind her eyes.

r *r* *r*

Albie stood idly in front of the elevator. Vee had gone ahead of her to bail the car out of the garage. She was probably already double-parked downstairs. But Albie was not quite ready yet. It took several deep breaths before she was able to push the down button.

When she got to the lobby, Vee was right outside the door. Albie got into the car. Vee was uncharacteristically quiet. Albie was uncharacteristically forbearing about it. They rode that way for several miles.

Without warning, Vee started. "It's funny," she said, her voice sounding almost like she was talking to herself, "a tragedy like this happens, and you think you're doing okay. But you're only coated in shock, like that Ice Age man they found in a glacier. And then the shock starts to fall off you. It's just little bits at first, but then it starts coming away in slabs and chunks, until a big hunk falls away and some of you gets exposed to reality. And still, somehow, you carry on. I mean, even when you're in a daze, you still manage. At least you hang on to the illusion you're managing. And then some little thing happens, just enough to put a pinhole in you. And you feel it and you think, after all those big hits of pain, what's one little pinhole? But you're like a balloon, and that one pinhole is enough to blow you all to hell. Makes you realize the whole time you were just holding your breath." She started to cry. "I think my heart is going to break."

"It can't be time to give up on him already?" Albie asked quietly. Vee shook her head. Albie took a deep breath before speaking. "But we need to start preparing her for it, don't we?" Vee nodded, crying. "He's not on life support," Albie said tightly. "It'll be a cold day in hell before she'll give them permission to starve him."

"He'll decide to go on his own." Vee's voice broke.

"Why would you think such a thing?" Albie asked.

Vee took a minute to get herself under control. "It's his little dog," she answered. "She stopped eating the day before yesterday. She won't even take any water. It's like she knows."

❦ ❦ ❦

Albie came into the room first. "Where is she?" Maggie asked, her voice low and conspiratorial.

"She's on her way," Albie answered. "Don't get your panties all in a twist." Maggie started for the door. "Get back here!" Albie hissed. "I swear, you would have given away the invasion of Normandy. Just sit down like everything's the same as usual."

Maggie sat down in her chair for a second, then popped up and walked to the window. She nearly jumped when Vee finally came in, a huge Burberry bag under her arm. "Did anybody give you a hard time?" she asked.

"Why would anyone give me a hard time?" Vee asked.

"Oh, I don't know," Maggie said. "Because you're carrying a bag the size of an expedition tent? And it's wriggling?"

"Dog needed room to move," Vee said. "But this is Philadelphia. Nobody's going to hassle a woman of color with a large bag and an attitude." She set the bag down on Mac's bed and pulled Penelope out. The little dog leapt out of her hands and scrambled up to Mac's face. Nobody breathed. Penelope furiously licked Mac's cheek. Nothing happened. Maggie turned from the bed. "Take her away," she said quietly.

"Come Penelope," Albie said, forgetting herself. The little dog instantly collapsed, like a stuffed toy.

"Wait a minute," Vee said. "Let me try something." She took the dog and set her down near Mac's hand. Penelope laid there, not showing any inclination to move. Vee lifted Mac's hand to put it on Penelope's head. The dog mistook the gesture. She gently took his finger between her teeth and shook her head back and forth, pulling on his finger. "Look," Vee said. "She remembers that trick he taught her."

Maggie turned back to the bed, and as the three of them watched, Mac's stomach began a slow ripple that grew visibly in intensity. It went on for several seconds, and then he belched. When the nurse ran in to see what all the noise was about, she wasn't sure how to react to the sight of three grown women hooting and screaming and jumping around the room.

❦ ❦ ❦

Maggie still dreaded these little talks with Mac's doctor, even though the news was so much better these days. Mac was going to be discharged to rehab soon. Once he finally started to wake up, his progress had been remarkable. Still, there was no question he had a long way to go. Maggie already knew what today's lecture would be. It was always a variation on the same theme. Time will tell. Still too early to know about potential personality changes. The fact that he took so long to come out of his coma may be an indicator of things to come. Every reason to be hopeful, but nobody can know right now.

What is there to know? Maggie wanted to demand. Even if you could undo everything that has been done, make him whole again in every way, it might all be an illusion. What is the half-life of tragedy?

48

There was Lillian, reading the *Intellectual* again. She had become obsessed
with it. Well, maybe it was more correct to say she was obsessed with anything
to do with the tragedy. At first it just seemed like morbid curiosity, something
Bendz could relate to. But it developed into a consuming need to understand
what had torn the high school apart. It was like she thought some explanation
would eventually make the reality tolerable. While life slowly resumed its daily
tone for most of Dooleysburg, Lillian was like one of the walking wounded,
like she had suffered a personal loss.

Bendz watched this change come over his wife with a new kind of frustra-
tion, different from the comfortably familiar displeasure they'd shared over
the years. It was born out of his inability to arouse any kind of interest out
of her. This was not like when she used to stonewall him. She really didn't
care anymore, about anything. She was that same flat calm all the time. He
found himself doing the lowest kinds of stunts just in the hopes of pissing her
off. He'd welcome her being mad at him. Anything. He just wanted her to act
alive again.

Bendz thought maybe she felt the tragedy so deeply because of Chrissie. But
when he suggested they spend some time with their granddaughter, Lillian
flatly refused. He noticed other changes as well. Her grooming was as impec-
cable as ever, but she stopped doing her yoga. And one morning he actually
caught her wearing two different socks. The worst part was he didn't know
this new Lillian. For all the years they'd been married, she had been a particular kind of person. Whatever that person lacked in kindness and consideration
she more than made up for by always being the woman he married. Bendz
hoped that woman would return soon.

"Lillian," he said this morning, exasperated, "what is it with you?"

She put the paper down and took a deep breath. "I feel so helpless, Carl."

"Helpless about what?"

"I don't know." She shrugged and picked up the paper again.

"Hey, hey, hey!" he yelled. "Don't do that! Look at me here!"

She looked up. "Yes?"

"What do you think you're going to find, always looking for news about what happened? It ain't gonna change. There's no explanation anybody's going to come up with so that it'll make sense. Crazy kids, dead people, a big hole in the back of the school. It is what it is."

"They're going to have a Healing Ceremony," she said quietly.

"What the hell is that?"

"Nobody's sure yet. They just decided to do it. Have everyone come out to the football field and be together."

"Ooh," he said, prancing around. "Let's sing songs and hold hands and all be friends."

"'Maybe," she said, not paying attention to him. "They haven't figured it out yet. They're asking for suggestions."

"What a crock of shit."

"Is it?" Her cheeks colored just a little. "Do you have a better idea about how to try to get life back to normal?" She turned back to the paper.

☙ ☙ ☙

The longer Lillian's funk went on, the more it consumed Bendz. It held his attention in a way none of the other things she'd tried in all the years they'd been together had done. The only way he knew how to respond was get annoyed. At least his annoyance got Lillian to move. When he wasn't annoyed with her, she just kind of haunted the house or rooted herself somewhere, like a plant, with her brain turned off.

So when she asked him, out of the blue, to run an errand for her, Bendz was so grateful he agreed. She wanted sticky buns. Not just any sticky buns. She wanted the ones from the wholesale place on Route 616. "You want me to go all the way out there?" Bendz demanded, never far from the sharp edge of his own irritation. "In fifteen minutes I could go into town and get you nice fresh ones. I could pick up a phone and get some made custom, for chrissake. Why do you need day-old grocery store buns?"

"Never mind," she'd replied emptily, looking off into space at nothing.

"Fine," he'd snapped. "I'm going." And he did, but he was fed up with things he didn't understand, and his driving showed it. He weaved a little over the line, making the driver on his left honk repeatedly, which only pissed him off more. Exiting onto 616, still distracted, he didn't bother checking over his shoulder before pulling into traffic. He heard a deafening blare, like Gabriel's horn blowing right in his ear. He was driving directly into the path of a huge container truck. There was nowhere to get out of the way. Thanks to local politics, funding never got approved to connect this stretch of the highway to anything, and eventually the earthmovers packed up and went home, leaving the freeway to end right here. Bendz couldn't even pull off onto the shoulder, because there was no shoulder. The lane he was in ended at a bridge abutment. So those were his choices—death by bridge abutment or death by big truck.

Bendz did notice it was true there was absolute calm right before the end. But he didn't get any video of his life flashing before his eyes. All he got were the big green letters on the side of the truck. "Mr. John," they said. And then relatively smaller, but really not small, "Your sanitary solution." And finally, "Septic pumping."

In the few seconds he had left, Bendz felt gravely disappointed that this was how he was going to go. Had he really been so vile that he deserved to be creamed by a honey wagon? To have to depend on some guy in protective gear to make sure all his parts got picked out of the sludge and shipped on to his final resting place? What if the fellow had poor quality standards? Would the parts he missed end up sanitized and mixed into a batch of Hydro-Green, leaving him to be sprayed into eternal suburban hell?

At the absolute last moment the truck careened to the left, giving Carl just enough room to swerve around the abutment. He made it under the bridge and pulled up short on the loose gravel on the far side. His heart was pounding, and his hands shook as he put the car in park. He felt like he could use a good cry. He would not have been surprised if a shaft of golden light poured down directly from heaven and through his windshield at this very moment. No question he had just been the recipient of divine intervention. When his breathing was back to normal, he eased the car onto the highway. Maybe, he thought, he should think of some way to say thanks.

⌐ ⌐ ⌐

It was shortly after this near-miss and its resultant epiphany that Bendz came up with his plan. He had no idea where it came from, but he recognized its brilliance immediately and made an appointment to discuss it with Mayor Frank. Bendz got to the mayor's office exactly three minutes past his appointment time, proud that he hadn't lost his touch. The mayor greeted him personally and ushered Bendz into his office.

"Frankie," Bendz said effusively, sitting down, "how's life been treating you?"

"Can't complain," the Mayor answered, holding up his end of their little ritual.

"And the wife?" Bendz asked. "She good?"

Frank raised his hands, palms up, to indicate so-so. "This school thing's been pretty tough on her."

"I know what you mean," Bendz said. "Lillian too. I can't figure it out. Wasn't like one of those kids was hers."

"It's the whole death thing," Mayor Frank said. "These women, they dye their hair, they do their exercise classes, something starts to sag, they get it lifted back up again." Bendz nodded. "As long as life cooperates they can pretend their number will never be up."

"Life sure didn't cooperate this time."

"No sir," Mayor Frank agreed, "it sure didn't."

"So I'm here to say, what can we do about it?" Bendz continued.

Mayor Frank looked happy. "You want to contribute to the Healing Ceremony?"

"Bet your ass!" Bendz slapped the desk. Somehow an envelope had appeared in his hand. "I tell you what, Frankie," he said. "That Healing Ceremony was a stroke of pure genius." He tapped the edge of the envelope on the desk. A respectable sum of folding money was visible through its glassine window. "Bendz Automotive has already sent an official contribution. But I'd like to do something a little more personal as well. Maybe a brief appearance?"

"Aw, Carl," Mayor Frank said, shaking his head. "I can't. Not on this one."

"Come on," Bendz cajoled him. "For Lillian."

"I'm sorry," Mayor Frank said.

"Frankie, this is my town. I know what people need to get back on their feet."

"Look Carl, you and me go all the way back. I know it was not you in that Chipmunk head going around town waving it at teenage girls. Your own granddaughter, for chrissake."

"You know me, Frankie. That was not me."

"But not everybody knows you like I do. I don't see The Chipmunk in the game plan."

Carl sighed deeply. "I can do something else."

Mayor Frank shook his head. "Even so. I'm sorry."

"Please, my friend," Bendz said. "Reconsider." He reached into his shirt pocket and took out a car key, which he dropped into the envelope.

"Carl!" Mayor Frank said. "I am not for sale."

"How can you imagine I would think such at thing?" Bendz demanded. "All I'm asking is a chance to redeem myself. In front of the town. In front of Lillian."

"We can't have any shenanigans."

"Absolutely not."

"All we got is speeches and singing. You got to let me see your speech ahead of time. I don't like it, you change it. We get to the day before, I don't like it, all bets are off."

"Frank, you are the best friend a man could ask for." Bendz slipped the envelope deftly under his side of the desk blotter.

"I meant what I said about not being for sale," Mayor Frank said.

"I respect that," Bendz replied, standing up. Mayor Frank stood also. They shook hands. "You won't regret this decision," Bendz said. "I promise I won't let you down." Mayor Frank nodded. Bendz turned and headed for the door.

"Just a minute," Mayor Frank said. "You left your envelope."

"What envelope?" Bendz asked. He reached for the doorknob.

"Hold it," Mayor Frank said. Bendz froze. "That key. What was that for?"

"Oh, that was just a token," Bendz said. "Come on over to the lot and see Harry. You can trade it in for whatever kind of key suits you."

🐓 🐓 🐓

Bendz peeked around the edge of the huge canvas sheet covering the back of the temporary stage. "Looks like Woodstock," he said to the young cop next to him.

"Yeah," the guy replied, "except everybody's got clothes on."

"They're all staring at the stage with that same dumb look. Like something wonderful's going to happen up there."

The cop glared at him. "You know what?" he said. "If you really are as big an asshole as everybody says, don't go up there. Because if you are, and you do, I'm personally gonna take you down. And when I'm done, I'm gonna feed your remains to every angry son-of-a-bitch in that crowd." Bendz craned his neck to get a better view. "You hear me?" the cop demanded.

"Yeah," Bendz said. "How many people you figure are out there? About a thousand?"

"Mr. Bendz?" The dame who'd been running around with the mike walked up to him. "Can you go sit behind the curtain, please? We're about to begin."

Bendz took his assigned seat in the waiting area. It took a lot of heated discussion before he agreed to be offstage when the ceremonies started. He was only listed in the program as "Guest Speaker". The first guy up was the priest from St. Agnes. Bendz half-listened as the priest did his mumbo-jumbo. Then there was singing. Next was Mayor Frank. As usual, he went on for half a lifetime. Bendz was pretty sure there was a deep undercurrent of snoring mixed in with the applause from the crowd. He started to fidget. He should have brought a magazine. Mayor Frank finally finished, then they had to listen to the rabbi. These guys were going on like they were getting paid by the hour. The lady in charge walked by. "Hey!" Carl hissed. "You got a newspaper? It's a little slow back here." He winked at her.

She looked at him with something approaching disgust. "You're up next."

Bendz watched her walk away. Good thing she had a paying job, he thought, cause she sure wouldn't be able to make living off that ass.

Finally the boss lady came over and handed him some papers. It was his approved speech, double-spaced in great big letters so even an idiot could read it. "Come on," she said, marching off ahead of him. Carl folded the speech and stuck it under his chair. Then he took his real speech out of his inside pocket. He walked around the side of the stage and up the stairs. As the crowd saw him their expectant hush became a stony silence. He might be the Guest Speaker, but he was an unwelcome guest.

He took his time getting to center stage. He put his papers on the podium and smoothed them out. He made a big deal of taking his eyeglass case from his pocket, removing the glasses from it, and making sure they were at just the right spot on his nose. He cleared his throat. He was just about ready when the boss lady made one of those noises at him from the side of the stage. "I am not a cat!" he exclaimed. His voice boomed out over the crowd.

"You forgot your speech," she whispered loudly, waving the papers.

He pointed to the podium. This time he covered the mike before answering. "I got what I need," he said. She didn't look happy, but that wasn't his problem. He uncovered the mike.

"Good afternoon," he began. The crowd did not respond. He waited a minute to see if they'd change their minds, then continued. "You might be wondering why I'm up here today. I know I'm nobody's hero." He looked around. The boss lady looked like she just discovered a load in her pantyhose.

"Here we are," he continued, turning the act of looking around into a grand gesture. "We are Dooleysburg, and we have been hurt. Maybe you are here today trying to pretend you can put that behind you. Well I say, don't try." The crowd started shifting in their seats.

"Carl!" Mayor Frank hissed from the row of chairs behind him, "this is not your approved speech!" Bendz didn't bother to turn around.

"I'm not going to pretend I can forget either. You know why?" he continued. "Because some of us have lost more than others, but there is not a single one of you out there who hasn't lost something." He paused. "My deepest, most heartfelt condolences to those who have lost someone they love." In his first draft he offered to do whatever he could to help, but he realized some fool might turn up at the showroom looking to convert that sentiment into a discount, so he deleted it. "And to those who have lost a friend, or a special teacher, or suffered an injury, my heart goes out to you as well. But for all of us who were lucky enough to escape direct harm, let's stop making believe we didn't get hurt too. Let's *not* bury the memory of what has been done to us. Dooleysburg is a family. Families should always know they have each other when they are hurt. Let us *not* be afraid to cry. Someone has broken into our lives, robbed us of our peace and safety, and vandalized our hearts. Let us remember, always, because that is the proof they cannot break our spirit!" He looked up at the crowd. He had them now, all right. They were crying, they were blowing their noses, they were holding on to their neighbors for dear life. Time to show them who was their leader, even without a head.

"There's a song. It might be too old for some of you to know, but it's based on a psalm or a prayer or something like that. It goes, 'To everything there is a season, and a time to every purpose under heaven.' Well, this is your time and your season. This is the kind of speech you'll probably be bored to sit through at your graduation, when all you can think about is getting out of those polyester gowns so you can go party." At last there was a little laughter. "So I'll keep this brief. I just want to add to that wonderful song or prayer or whatever that to every glimmer of hope, no matter how faint, there is a beam of light. You are those light beams. And that school," he pointed behind the crowd, "is your lantern. That's the place, for now, where the light from each of you adds up to create a glow so brilliant, so powerful that NO ONE will ever put it out!" He was interrupted by spontaneous applause. He waited for it to die down.

"Well, someone tried to destroy your lights and your lantern. We all know, sadly, that this isn't the first time something like this has happened. There are too many places in our world where people do stupid, terrible things every day. But I can tell you, with absolute certainty, that this will be the last time anything like this ever happens in Dooleysburg. Whatever it takes, we are committed to making this town, and this school, places of shelter for every single one of our lights. So get on in there, and start glowing! Glow brighter and stronger than you have ever done before, and show the whole world that nobody should ever be foolish enough again to believe they can extinguish you!" Bendz removed his glasses and swiped the back of his hand across his eyes, just like the note he had written to himself in the margin reminded him to. To his amazement, he had to wipe his eyes again before he could go on. He turned to the assembled dignitaries behind him. "Whatever it takes," he said, "you keep these children safe. And all the kids who'll come after them." He put his glasses back on.

"Okay," he said. "So I just talked a lot about you and this town and what all that means. By now you're probably asking yourself, what's all this to him? Here's this rich old guy, you might even be thinking, who's maybe a little bit crazy." His first draft had some oblique references to his various hobbies as well, but he had deleted those. "Well, I'll tell you what all this means to me. My Lillian, my beautiful wife Lillian," he scanned the crowd, but couldn't find her, "this has broken her heart. We were only blessed with one child of our own, but the children of Dooleysburg, they were her children too. She saw the potential in each and every one of them."

Deep in the crowd, Martha elbowed Daniel. "Potential household help," she whispered, laughing and crying at the same time.

"And so, when I say I want to see our children grow up safe, I've got some skin in this game too. More than skin. I'm putting my money where my mouth is." He pulled an envelope from his pocket. "I have a check here for $100,000. I'm giving this check to Mayor Frank Romano, in front of all of you," Mayor Frank flinched, "as seed money for a fund, named for my Lillian, but in honor of all of you. This money will be used to protect our children, and to help them heal. Now sure, some of this money will have to go for increased security, but part of it, and I want this to be a substantial part, is to be dedicated to stuff for kids, stuff that will help them feel safe and help them believe that Dooleysburg is their home in every sense of the word, a great place to live. So we don't forget that's why we all came here in the first place, we're going to call this 'Lillian's Dooleysburg Sunshine Fund'."

The crowd loved it. They gave him a standing ovation. Bendz walked off the stage in a daze while they were still clapping. He went around behind the canvas, and there was Lillian. She stood there, just looking at him. For a moment it was forty years ago in her eyes, and he saw her seeing the man she had thought she would worship for the rest of her life. "Lillian," he said, astonished, "I made myself cry."

She took his hand. "What do you feel like doing now, dear?"

"Oh, I don't really care," he said, "so long as we do it together."

49

JD sat in the Adirondack chair, a real one, weathered by countless summers. He pushed aside some dried pine needles with the heel of his sneaker. Writers who talked about soft beds of pine needles carpeting the forest floor neglected to mention there was a reason they were called "needles". He and Rev took great joy in watching each new crop of barefoot tourists do their fire dance across the needles on their first trip down to the dock every year.

Although he couldn't see it, occasionally he heard the river out there in front of him, where the old pines stopped abruptly and the land sloped down to the shore. If he had the energy, it was only a short walk to the wooden steps and dock he had helped build when he was about Mac's age. But he didn't need to check to be sure they were still there. Everything Rev made was dependable and permanent. When JD first understood that, he was sure it was due to some kind of magic. Rev believed the things he counted on would not go away, and they didn't. It made JD understand Rev's trust in God.

JD pulled the blanket up close to his chin. He got cold easily now, partially because of inactivity and partially because of everything his body had been through. Knowing why it happened didn't make it any less unpleasant. Back when his biggest problem was trying to get out from under the panic that always threatened to explode into rage, Rev taught him a way to get outside the immediate sensations in his muscles and gut. He said it was a way of taking control by letting go. That didn't make sense to him, but it worked, and he still used it now.

He cleared his mind and focused all his attention on a sailboat he imagined out there on the water. It was going against the wind, so that it had to tack, gliding back and forth in a zigzag pattern that somehow enabled it to move forward. He took deep, controlled breaths. There was nothing but that boat, and all his other thoughts became background noise. For a brief instant, it worked and his mind cleared completely. Then, as always happened, new thoughts slithered in, beckoning until he gave in and followed one.

He opened his eyes. Rev owned this acre of riverfront less than forty miles from Annapolis. He and Helen, Rebekah's parents, had bought the land when they were first married. There was a tiny little house on it then, and over the years JD had helped him add to it until it became the perfect place to live when they retired.

The stillness was fractured by the sound of Rev approaching from the house. JD had to laugh. Rev, like the fog, usually moved on little cat feet. No doubt he was making all that noise so he wouldn't startle JD. "I've brought you some herb tea," he said.

"Herb tea," JD said. "Oh, yum."

"You're welcome."

"Did you use my 'Invalid' mug?"

"Helen said it was in the dishwasher, so I used your 'Smart Mouth' mug instead." He put it on the arm of JD's chair. "We need to leave for physical therapy in half an hour. You need anything?"

"Yeah," JD said. "Real coffee."

"I would think after making it this far without caffeine, you'd be grateful to be free of the demon."

"I have yet to hear of anyone losing their immortal soul to coffee."

"I was more concerned about your earthly health and welfare."

"You know," JD pointed out, "if none of the other things I've been through killed me, I don't think we really need to worry about a little caffeine."

Rev sat down in the chair next to him. "You have quite a fan club, it seems." He held up the day's delivery of cards.

"Umm," JD said, without much interest.

"Don't even want to take a look?"

"I'll go through them after therapy."

"Funny," Rev said, "in the beginning you couldn't wait to see what came every day."

JD made a smile that was partly grimace. "If things are a little slow for you, you could read them to me and see if that makes you happy."

"You know," Rev said comfortably, "when you begged off last Christmas, we were hopeful you'd finally found someone. With a child," he added. "That's usually why people want to stay home for Christmas, when there's a child to celebrate with." JD didn't take the bait. "Perhaps you're a bit disappointed because you haven't received a card from her?"

"You're assuming there's a her."

"It's not a groundless assumption, you know. There was a woman who stayed with you that first night in the hospital."

"Someone spent the night?" JD was annoyed he sounded like a hopeful teenager.

"Helen and I drove up as soon as they called. We got to the hospital around 6 AM. I was furious that nobody had called right away, that they'd waited hours to notify us. I was bawling out the nurses about taking a chance you might've died alone, and one of them said a woman had been with you most of the night. Held onto your hand even after she fell asleep, left an hour or so before we arrived."

"I had no idea," JD said. Could it have been her? Even though her own child was fighting for his life in another hospital at the same time? It didn't make sense. And yet, he wanted it to be true so bad it made his chest ache. He closed his eyes. He still tired so easily. He'd finally learned to give in and drowse. It was easier than struggling to stay in control all the time. He closed his eyes.

Rev treated this, like everything else about the healing process, as something to be expected. He waited a little while to see if JD would rejoin the conversation, then got up and walked over. JD heard him, even though he barely made a sound. He tucked the blanket under JD's chin with great tenderness. JD smiled without opening his eyes. Here he was, a full-grown man, and there were still few things as comforting as a father's love.

*   *   *

In the car on the way to physical therapy, JD negotiated a deal. He usually couldn't stand to let Rev drive. The man's extreme caution made him nuts. Since he had no choice in the matter now, in exchange for the promise of real coffee he agreed to relax while Rev drove.

"So what's your mystery woman like?"

The question caught JD off guard. He considered how to answer. "She's different."

"Different how?"

JD made a noncommittal gesture. "She's from New York. Actually grew up in Dooleysburg, though I had a hard time getting her to admit it."

"Can't blame her for that," Rev said. "So what kind of friendship do you have that she spends the night at your hospital bedside and then doesn't even attempt to contact you during your recovery?"

"It's complicated."

"You mean she's complicated."

JD sighed. "Pretty much, yeah."

"Good. You need somebody complicated. The truth is, Rebekah was no match for you."

"That's not fair," JD said. "She was a good woman."

"That she was," Rev said. "And I'd trade my own life without a second thought if it meant we could have her back. That doesn't mean she was right for you."

"*What* was in your Wheaties this morning? I loved her," JD protested.

"Yes, you did," Rev said. "Probably more than she loved you. Not to be unkind."

"Be sure to let me know when you're being unkind, so I can see the difference."

"Is this woman intelligent? You need someone who can give you a run for your money."

"She's a doctor. A surgeon."

"And?"

"Her name is Maggie, she's a widow, and she's got a son, almost fifteen. She moved back to Dooleysburg after her husband died," JD said quietly, "because she wanted a safe place to raise her kid."

Rev glanced over at him. "Tell me he didn't get shot."

JD swallowed hard. "And then buried under the rubble in the explosion."

Rev's voice was even, controlled. "I'm sorry."

"But he made it," JD said. "Mostly. There's brain damage, but they're hopeful he'll recover pretty well."

"You decided you were in love with her before or after?"

"What's that supposed to mean?"

"Ever since you found yourself, you've been on a mission to save the world, one messed up kid at a time."

"I fell in love with her before her son got hurt."

"Ah," Rev said, pausing while he changed lanes. "So *she's* the messed up kid." JD did not answer. "How bad is she?"

"Obviously, she's very functional."

"What's the but?"

"She's mad as . . . heck." JD caught himself. Even now he tried never to break Rev's rule about cussing.

"That what caught your eye?"

"No, that's just a nuisance. She caught my eye because she's an enigma. Figuring her out is like trying to put together a puzzle without the picture from the box."

"And she has a kid."

"And she has a kid, a good kid. She must have something right going inside, to raise a good kid."

"You say that like maybe you haven't seen proof yet."

JD took a deep breath. "I saw it at the school that day. When other people needed her, she gave everything she had, even though she was terrified for her son."

"And in the absence of disaster? How does she do then?" JD didn't answer. "You're in over your head aren't you?"

"Maybe."

"She was abused?"

"So it would seem. Her mother was alcoholic or psychotic. Probably both. Her father pretty much left her to deal with it all. She got out of the house when she was fifteen, after her mother pulled a gun on her."

Rev shook his head. "And we pretend we're civilized creatures."

"Yeah," JD said. "Half the town must have known something was wrong. It's a small town, and it was even smaller then. And nobody ever raised a finger to help her."

🐓   🐓   🐓

JD sat across the table from Rev. He couldn't help wondering if Rev had chosen this place because it looked like the coffee would be lousy. But at this point JD almost didn't care how bad the coffee was. From the moment the waitress took their order, he'd been in a state of raw anticipation. He purposely waited to ask for his coffee until after their sandwiches arrived, knowing he would not eat another bite once he got it.

Now the waitress was carrying his mug to the table. The coffee sloshed a little as she walked. JD fought the urge to jump up and take it from her. "You look like a kid waiting for his Christmas orange," Rev chuckled.

"She's spilling some," JD said, his voice full of yearning. He felt like he was trapped in a slow motion dream. A customer at another table said something to the waitress and she stopped. "So close and yet so far," JD said wistfully. Finally she finished her landing pattern and put the mug down in front of him.

"Better go get the pot for his refill now," Rev said to her.

JD ignored them, as well as everything else around him. He blew across the top of the mug, sending the wavy column of steam slightly off course. He inhaled, getting just a hint of the dark, complex essence he would have brewed at home. He took a sip, slurping like an oenophile.

"Is it good?" Rev asked.

"Diner coffee."

"Drink your fill," Rev advised him. "You won't be getting any more once we leave."

"I never took you for a cruel man," JD replied.

"Nor I you."

JD lowered the mug. "What's that supposed to mean?"

Rev suddenly looked very serious. "When you came to us many people already counted you as lost. Others thought I was foolish for bringing such a dangerous child into my household." JD did not interrupt. "Do you remember that when you finally recovered from the measles, I took you out to get you some clothes?" JD really wasn't sure, but he nodded anyway. "We went to the mall. When we were done, we got on the escalator to go down to the parking garage. There was a boy in front of us, eight or nine years old. Do you remember now?" JD shook his head, amused. There was no point trying to fool the old man. Rev continued. "He was wearing baggy pants, canvas ones with big pockets. There was a loose piece of metal right at ankle height. It caught on that boy's pants, but of course the escalator kept going. His leg was trapped, and he started to fall. That's the kind of accident where kids lose fingers. Before I could even react, you reached out and grabbed him. You were as scrawny as a string bean, and weak from being so sick. But you held on to him so tight he didn't fall and his pants ripped free. You did it reflexively, without thinking."

JD sipped his coffee. "I honestly don't remember any of that."

"No," Rev said, "which doesn't surprise me, because that's how you are about helping people. It comes naturally to you. But it showed me that you could be saved. It showed that me that someone, somewhere, had treated you with enough kindness to let you build that fragile bridge to the rest of humanity."

JD swallowed hard. "It was you."

Rev took a sip of water. "Thomas," he began painfully, "there is no way for me to say this but to say it. You appear to be in love with this woman. You need to ask yourself why."

JD looked at him, bemused. "Why does anybody fall in love?"

"It's not a general question," Rev pointed out. "It's specific to you and specific to her. What is it about this woman that has you captivated?"

"She's smart, she's tough, she's funny."

"She's damaged." JD put his coffee cup down harder than he meant to. Rev went on. "Like you were, like something deep inside you will always be. You are yin and yang."

"Suppose you're right," JD challenged him. "Suppose that is what first appealed to me. So what?"

"Suppose that is what will always appeal to you? Suppose you need her to stay damaged to sustain your love? Do you care enough for her to walk away from that?"

"You make me sound like a junkie."

"We are all junkies of one sort or another, Thomas. Those of us who are lucky enough to be aware try to contain our addictions, to stay away from those things capable of destroying us."

"Come on," JD said shortly. "You're making way too much out of this."

"Am I?" Rev asked. "Forgive me then."

Forgive me, my ass, JD thought. "You saved me. You don't think I can pass it on?"

"You were a child," Rev said, "still young enough to heal."

"That's crap," JD answered, throwing his crumpled napkin onto his half-eaten sandwich. "People grow and change their whole lives."

"Absolutely," Rev said. "Couldn't agree more."

"So what's your point?" JD demanded.

"Even God can't close up the Grand Canyon, Thomas. And he's smart enough not to die trying."

JD moved his plate away. He was losing his temper, and he knew Rev knew it as well. He worked at controlling his voice. "You've never even met her. Yet you assume she's damaged beyond repair."

Rev let this sit out there. "Thomas," he finally said, "you are my son in every vital sense of that word. I won't deny that makes me likely to judge anything that threatens you more harshly than it may deserve. But I am speaking from the heart when I tell you that I believe anything you do now to fix this woman will be like chalk on concrete. You no longer have the option of changing the shape of the concrete. It's already set."

"She's not concrete," JD said painfully. "She's fragile."

"That's the essential contradiction, isn't it?" Rev replied. "That even something as hard as concrete can be fragile. She has a terrible, fundamental fault in her somewhere, a structural weakness you may not ever see unless circumstances force it to crack."

"You're referring to nearly losing her son?"

"Perhaps," Rev said thoughtfully. "Though frankly, I would be more concerned about someone accidentally putting his weight on her the wrong way. Sometimes loving someone means choosing to protect them from our own good intentions." They did not speak for some time, Rev watching JD, and JD staring out the window. Finally Rev asked, "Would you prefer to go now?"

"Yeah," JD said. He didn't bother to finish his coffee.

50

Mac and Mr. Don both ended up in the Rehab Center at the same time. Mr. Don had significant spinal damage, and he was bitter that he would never walk again. Mac had some serious losses in his responsiveness and memory, and his left arm had to be restrained thanks to its unpleasant tendency to act of its own accord. They spent most of their free time together, finding a comfort in their common anger and grief that they would not share with people who were still whole. Mr. Don was sensitive, though, to the need for something new to grow now between Mac and his mother, so when Vee showed up most afternoons with Maggie, he would invite her back to his room for a while to watch the soaps. It wasn't long before the soaps became the primary reason for Vee's afternoon visits.

On a particularly beautiful spring afternoon, Maggie and Mac sat in the sunny Common Room. Mac was determined to catch up with his schoolwork. Maggie was amazed how much his ability to focus his attention had already improved. She, on the other hand, could barely read at all. Her eyes kept moving over the same paragraph while the reader in her head tried harder and harder to make her listen.

"Is everything okay?" Mac asked. "You look kind of antsy."

"I'm just having a hard time sitting still today."

"Okay." Mac picked up his notebook, but it was like his question had released a spring inside Maggie. She closed and opened her book repeatedly. Her foot started tapping. She catapulted from her chair and paced back and forth to the window.

"Mom," Mac asked, "what's up?"

"It's funny," she replied. "I just get these bursts of energy. No particular reason. They just happen at the most unusual times. Usually I just go with it, you know? I mean, what's the point of forcing yourself to stay in bed just because it's the middle of the night if you get this pop! and you can get all kinds of stuff done?"

"Oh," Mac said.

"Wait until you see the house!" she grinned. "It's so clean you won't believe it's ours."

"Okay."

"So I was thinking, would you mind if we left a little early today?"

Mac looked at her. "You can't go yet. Vee and Mr. Don are watching their soaps."

"So?" she asked. "What's the big deal if they miss a little?"

"Mom," Mac cracked up, "they're *watching* their *soaps*."

Maggie's brow creased momentarily, and then she finally connected the dots. "Oh." She sat down clumsily, as if a puppeteer had let her strings go slack. "You mean . . ."

Mac grinned. "Yup."

"She never told me." Maggie looked at him. "Did Mr. Don say something to you?"

"No."

"Well, then, what makes you think . . ."

"Guys know these things."

Maggie was even more stunned to hear this. Her son had hooked into the flow of secret guy communications? What else was there about his world she would be excluded from?

🐓   🐓   🐓

When Vee and Mr. Don came back to the Common Room, Maggie could see immediately that Mac was right. Their relationship had developed so gradually there hadn't even been any signs to miss. Out in the parking lot, Maggie turned to Vee. "I'm very happy for you," she said, feeling awkward.

Vee looked at her with a smile that could neutralize a power outage. "Me too," she said.

"He's a good man."

"And I'm making him better."

"You are hopeless," Maggie said. Vee turned to go to her car. "Wait." Vee walked back. Maggie's voice was strained. "I never said thank you," Maggie struggled to speak, "for everything, and you've done so much for me. I'm sorry."

"You have nothing to be sorry for."

"I'm sorry, Vee." She looked away. "I hurt you. I sent you away. And you came to help me anyway, and you've been with me this whole time and you never once threw it up to me, what I did." She looked up again. "I don't know why you put up with me, but thank you."

"You poor thing," Vee said. "Didn't anybody ever let you know that in this world where we all screw up every day, love is mostly forgiveness?" Maggie did not answer. "Come here." Vee didn't wait, enfolding her in a big hug. Maggie was stiff, not sure what to do. "It's okay, honey," Vee said softly. "I won't hurt you." Only then did Maggie almost relax.

ꝑ   ꝑ   ꝑ

Morsel locked the front door of the deli. So far, it was okay being back. Better than he expected. Gamey let him be in charge sometimes. Like tonight, he was closing up all by himself. And no more crap about going to school. He walked by the slicer, and out of habit, he put a finger on it. Then he took the corner of his apron and polished off the fingerprint. It made him happy now to make things shine, keep the place spiffed up. Gamey had come all the way to Northeast to bring him back. He had a stake here now.

He went into the back room. The place looked good. The boxes were stacked neatly, the shelves were all sorted out. The big grill and hood, though still blackened in places, were clean. Some of the kids who'd been around a long time quit when he came back with his new attitude. Not right away, but when they figured out there'd be no more greasing up the floor for oil skating or placing hairs in the takeout for a laugh. Gamey was upset to see them go, but Morsel told him it was a good thing. He found new kids, ones who didn't mind working or following orders. When a man started going to work because he felt proud, and not just for fun, that was the kind of crew he needed.

He turned off the lights. Only thing left to do was take out the garbage. He lifted the bag out of the can and carried it carefully an inch or so above the floor, because dragging it could cause leakage. He went out the back door, locking up behind himself. The air was soft, but it still got dark early, and it was deep night outside.

He started for the dumpster and jumped. Someone was standing there. She came into the circle of light from the back door, and he saw it was Jayme Campbell. He took a step back, as if she was a hive of bees. "What do you want?" he asked suspiciously.

"I just want to talk to you."

"Why?"

She hesitated. "I need to ask you a favor."

"Get lost," Morsel snarled.

"Wait," Jayme said. "Please. This isn't just for me."

"Screw off," Morsel said, but he stayed there, listening.

"Look . . ." She stopped. "Do you know who those kids were? The ones who did it?"

"Yeah," he said. "Some freaks from Mammon."

"Not just any freaks. They were some of the kids we beat in the band adjudication."

"What do you mean?" Morsel asked with disbelief. "They blew up a school and killed people because of a band trophy?"

Jayme shrugged. "I know. It sounds stupid."

"It is stupid!"

"I saw Chief Charles," she said. "In the General Store."

"Was he weird?"

"Who, Chief Charles? He looks kind of skinny. And old. He joked around a little, though, like he used to when we were hanging out in town and he'd come over to spy on us. He said he'll come to school to talk to everyone once he starts getting around again."

"Were you scared? About talking to him?"

"Yeah. Pretty much."

"So what's all this got to do with me?" Morsel asked.

"I wanted to ask him how Mac is doing. I figured he'd know. But I was scared. I mean, one day you think you might be in love with someone, and then somebody tries to blow their head off. What if he's not the same anymore? I don't know what I'm supposed to say or how I'm supposed to act."

"You mean when you see him?"

Jayme nodded. "So when we ran out of things to say, and Chief Charles was going to leave, I asked him. He said we should go visit Mac at rehab. And Mr. Gamey was there too, with the Chief, and he said Mac's mom told him Mac feels bad nobody comes to see him."

"Wait a minute," Morsel said. "Are you telling me Gamey was getting coffee at the General Store?"

"Yeah," she replied. "And then Chief Charles asked Mr. Gamey . . ."

"Hold it," he interrupted. "Gamey was paying money for somebody else's coffee?"

"I guess," she said indifferently. "So he said . . ."

"What's the matter with my coffee?"

"It probably tastes like piss," she said. "Anyway . . ."

"Nah," Morsel said. "My coffee's good. I bet he was trying to make time with the Spanish chick."

"Would you just shut up and listen to me?"

"Yeah, I bet that's it. There's two of them exactly the same, you know? So he must figure he's got better odds because if he screws up with one, he's still got the same one to try with again, only her sister."

"You're such a loser," Jayme said, furious. "No wonder you think what happened to him was your fault. Oh," she stopped suddenly. "I wasn't supposed to say that."

"It don't matter now," Morsel said flatly.

Jayme came closer. "It really wasn't your fault, you know." Morsel looked at her, willing her to go on. "They wanted to get him. That's what the Chief said. I asked him why, and he said it was a hate crime, and hate crimes don't make any sense, but that they remembered Mac and that kind of made him a target. Like a place to focus their hate." Morsel wiped his eyes and nose with the back of his hand. Maybe the night air was getting to him. "In a way," Jayme continued quietly, "when you think about it, you probably saved a whole lot of people's lives. I mean, if you told him to hang out with you in Resource, there were, like a hundred kids in there. Can you imagine how many more of us they would have killed if they didn't find Mac right away and went into the auditorium?"

"It don't matter," Morsel said. "Nothing's ever going to be the same anyway."

"I bet it matters to all the kids who are still alive." She finally came fully out of the shadows and walked up to him. He could see then that she was crying a little. "I'm sorry," she said softly. "I'm sorry we were so crappy to you. You know, when life is normal, you do all kinds of mean stuff without even thinking about it. And then something terrible happens and you realize all the bad things you've done. It makes you really ashamed."

"Yeah," Morsel said. "I know how that feels."

"So will you come to see him with me? That was the favor I came to ask you."

"What if he don't want to see me?"

"Then he'll throw us out, right? But what if he really does want to see us and we don't go because we're scared and we let him down?"

🍂 🍂 🍂

Now that Mac was doing better, Maggie suddenly saw life going on around her again. She felt like Persephone emerging from the cold, dark bowels of the earth, to see, once again, the progress of the days. She started to think about JD, that he had been home for awhile, and she hadn't gotten over to see him. With Mac in rehab she had lots of free time in the evening, so she didn't have an excuse. Soon imagining her reunion with JD became her focus every moment she wasn't forced to pay attention to something in the present. She began finding excuses to avoid Vee and Martha, who both wanted to spend way too much time with her anyway. They were a distraction. She decided she would cook dinner for JD, something extraordinary. She would put all her energy into learning to cook, and he would be pleased. Once she had a plan, she was so happy she felt giddy.

She spent hours going through cookbooks. She read them with the same concentration she used to have for medical texts. She bought them, she took them out of the library, she looked for recipes in magazines. But everything seemed old and outdated. Mac suggested she should try the Internet. One of the librarians in town showed her how to do searches, and she was so fascinated that she bought a laptop so she wouldn't have to stop when the library closed. Sometimes she became so engrossed that when she looked out the window the sky was getting light and she realized she hadn't made it to bed. It wasn't like the missing sleep made a difference, though. She felt more energized than ever. She hardly needed to eat anymore, and her mind flew from idea to idea with the speed and focus of a laser. She had so much to be happy about she was filled with elation.

She finally decided she would make beef stew. It would be the most remarkable beef stew he had ever eaten. She stopped at Erin go Braise and used her gift certificate to buy a crockpot. It took her three days to get all the ingredients, as she went to a different specialty store for each. Then she prepared them with exquisite care and put them in the crockpot, turning it on before she left for rehab. Vee came home with her late that afternoon. Before Maggie even unlocked the door, they smelled it, rich and intense. "What is that?" Vee demanded as they walked into the kitchen. "It smells like real food visited this house!"

"Here," Maggie said, feeling oddly shy. She scooped some stew out of the crockpot. "Taste this."

Vee blew on it impatiently then took a dainty bite. She expressed her appreciation mostly with sounds. "You're going to invite me to stay for dinner, aren't you?"

Maggie blushed. "Actually, I made this for JD." She added quickly, "You should take as much as you want, though. I'm sure he'll get sick of it before he can eat it all and he'll end up throwing some out . . ." She stopped. Vee was staring at her. "What?"

"This is very brave of you. Especially you. I know you're scared. I'm proud of you for taking a chance." Maggie felt awkward. "There's something else," Vee said. "You need to be prepared. He's not who he used to be."

Maggie's stomach seized up. "I thought he was doing okay," she said.

"The problem isn't physical. It's in his spirit."

Maggie felt relief stream through her. That's okay, she thought. That's to be expected. She knew it was nothing she and her pot of stew couldn't fix.

🪶 🪶 🪶

The crockpot of stew was more unwieldy than Maggie expected. She felt like a juggler trying to manage it and wasn't sure she'd make it from his driveway to the front of the house. The door to the mudroom was ajar, so she went in. He was sitting at the kitchen table and looked up. "Sorry," she said, walking in from the mudroom. She couldn't believe she was out of breath. "I didn't want to barge in or anything, but my hands are full." She put the crockpot on the table.

JD nodded. He didn't even smile. He looked like hell, though there was nothing obvious that said, here's proof something horrible happened to this man. Maggie felt an edge of pain in the back of her throat, as if something sharp was fighting to tear its way out. She pointed to the crockpot. Trying to keep her voice light, she said, "Believe it or not, I learned how to cook. At least a little. I made you beef stew."

JD finally spoke. "Thanks," he said. "I'm not very hungry right now."

"That's okay," Maggie answered, struggling to cover whatever it was that was making it so hard to swallow. "I'll put it in the refrigerator for later. You can heat it up when you want some." An awkward silence filled the room as she put away the stew.

When she turned back to the table, JD was still looking at her. It took all her courage to walk over and sit in the chair closest to him. Maybe it was his silence that made the words start pouring out of her. "I'm so sorry," she began. "For everything. For what happened to you. Especially everything that happened because of me." His eyes bored into hers, but he didn't reply. Maggie's heart was pounding. She felt like she was trapped on a rollercoaster and if she jumped off now that would be even worse than hurtling onward. "I can't ever apologize enough for what I did to you." She had to stop until that pain in the back of her throat let up a little. "I was afraid. I am afraid. There was a chance— no, a likelihood that I would start to depend on you, and I didn't know what to do with that. I've never been able to trust anyone. Even the people who start out caring about me go away eventually, and I don't know why, I don't know what I do to cause it, but I'm willing to do whatever it takes to make it stop. I want to be someone people can love. I want to be someone you can love. I can learn." She was talking faster and faster. "I'm sorry. I'm just so sorry."

JD made a gesture with his hand, indicating she should stop. When he spoke his voice was even, not emotionless, but simply reflective of a well thought out conviction. "Maggie," he said, "go away."

Maggie couldn't breathe. She couldn't think. A wild coldness flooded her head. She stood up. Her legs felt like they were her enemies. "Okay," she said, and left.

51

Maggie stood over her sleeping son and hugged herself to stop the shaking. Tonight had been wild and violent. Mac fell asleep easily enough, giving her false hope. And then, as she started to doze in the guest room across the hall, the screaming began. In the seconds it took to fill the syringe, he was already bashing himself against his door so furiously she could barely open it. She started to panic about what he might do to himself if she couldn't give him the shot, get him sedated. She finally managed to push her way into the room, but there was no way to get near him with the needle. At one point, he shoved her so hard she flew across the room, crashing into the dresser before she fell to the floor. As she was struggling to her feet, JD appeared. He grabbed Mac from behind and pinned his arms, but it was a terrible fight for him to hang on long enough for Maggie to give the injection, and nearly as hard to hold Mac down on the bed until the sedative took effect.

Maggie tucked the comforter around Mac's shoulders. She worried about the heavy doses of medication she was giving him. She nurtured a hope, however false, that as the nights grew shorter they would get easier for him, since this only came upon him, like a possession, when he slept. At any rate, the shot would last until morning. She stood next to his bed, loath to leave the sight of him resting peacefully. Finally she walked out into the hall, closing the door gently behind her.

In the dim ambient light she could see JD leaning against the wall outside Mac's room, more shadow than shape. He was bent over, holding his shoulder. "Are you okay?" she asked.

He said, "No," his voice so weak she could barely hear it.

"Are you having chest pain?"

"Yes," he gasped.

"Like it's your heart?"

He shook his head. "No. It's from the shoulder. I think I'm going to be sick."

Maggie gently pushed his head down. The pain was making him tense up, which in turn was only making the pain worse. She put her fingers on his neck. His pulse was racing, but it was strong. "You need to try to relax," she told him.

"It hurts so bad I think I might pass out."

Maggie grabbed a chair from the guest room and dragged it out into the hall. "Sit down," she said. "Put your head between your knees and try to relax until it passes." She rubbed his back, very lightly, until she heard his breathing slow down. She took his pulse again. Almost normal. "I think you're going to be okay."

He sat up slowly and leaned back in the chair. "Jesus," he said, exhausted, "that was terrible."

"I guess you haven't tested your limits yet."

"No," he winced, "I think I just did."

"Not quite ready to put the cape and boots back on?" she asked.

"Stop," he said, without humor.

"We should get some ice on your shoulder to minimize any inflammation from this. Stay here and I'll bring some up." He nodded. "I mean it. Don't try to move yet."

Maggie went to the kitchen. She felt so helpless. Everywhere she turned was one more thing she couldn't fix. She was not prepared for failure after failure. She filled the teakettle and put it on the stove, thinking it was a stupid gesture. Who boiled water for tea on the stove anymore? She couldn't decide whether to leave it there while she made an icepack, or take it off. While she was deliberating, JD walked in.

"Don't make herb tea," he said. Maggie turned off the water. His hair was longer than usual, and he needed a shave. He looked more interesting this way, but his uncharacteristic lack of attention to his grooming disturbed her.

"What are you doing down here?" Maggie said. "I told you not to move."

"I was afraid you were going to call an ambulance."

"That's not how I operate," she said, aggravated. "Unless it's an emergency, I'm not going to substitute my judgment for yours." Then she noticed how weak he looked. It took the steam out of her. "You're all pale and sweaty," she said. "Sit down." She was surprised when he listened. She got a Ziploc bag and put in some ice and water. Wrapping it in a kitchen towel, she handed it to him. "You know," she said, "you really should go to the hospital and get checked out."

"I'm not having a heart attack."

"There's no harm in being sure."

He looked at her dispassionately. "Do you really think it makes a difference?"

"Of course it does. You could die."

He laughed humorlessly. "That's not the kind of concern for me it once was."

"It's not unusual for someone who's been through what you have to feel that way," Maggie said. "But it doesn't change anything."

"I've made whatever peace I intend to make. I'm done." He put the makeshift icepack on the table.

"You need more ice?" Maggie asked. She reached for the bag and bumped against the back of a chair, wincing sharply. JD surprised her, moving with his old speed and grace. He lifted her shirt. Her side and back were nearly covered with a huge yellow-purple bruise. "What do you think you're doing?" she demanded, pulling her shirt back down. JD grabbed her wrist and pushed up her sleeve. More bruises. She yanked her arm away and stepped out of his reach.

His face was hard. "He threw you down the stairs, didn't he?"

"No," she said, furiously. "He did not throw me down the stairs."

"You have bruising consistent with domestic violence."

"Stop it. He's a child."

"He's stronger than you are, Maggie. You've got to get some help."

"I'm managing."

"What about him? You're not being fair to him. He needs help to get beyond the damage that's been done to his brain. You think you're protecting him, but you're only allowing his disability to worsen."

"Don't do this again," she said, trying to hide her panic. "Don't come into our lives and impose your own solutions without even looking at the facts or caring what you're doing to us."

"What facts are those?"

"These are night terrors. This is his way of working out all the horror that's happened to him. He's fine during the day." She stopped. The look on JD's face clearly said he didn't believe her. "It's true," she insisted. "He's even happy most of the time, despite everything he's been through."

"Why didn't you call someone for help with the 'night terrors', then?"

"Who would you have had me call?"

His eyes narrowed. "What's wrong with you? People lose their tempers and say things in anger. Nothing is as literal as you're determined to make it."

"Please," Maggie said, without energy. "I can't spar with you anymore. I'm at the thin edge of my spirit. Just tell me what you want to tell me and be done with it."

"Do you really not get it?" he said roughly. He ran a hand through his hair. "Look, lots of people care about you. All your friends are worried. Any one of them would have been here if you gave them the slightest sign. But nobody knows how to approach you. They're all afraid of doing the wrong thing."

"Come on," Maggie said dismissively. "Let's not make excuses. There's a world of pain between worrying about someone and making the sacrifices to do something about it."

"You could have called me."

Maggie looked at him angrily. "No," she said. "I don't think so. You talk a good game, but you're not interested in the long haul. You pop up out of nowhere, do your hero thing, give orders, and walk away without ever looking back to see what kind of mess you've left behind."

"Where do you get these ideas?"

"Are you telling me it's my fault you left us to our own devices?" He didn't answer her. "Are you?" Her voice was rising. "I came to you. And you told me to go away. It didn't sound conditional."

"You didn't even put up a fight," he snapped.

"You don't get to blame me for that," she said. "You can't just say things and then expect me to assume you don't mean them. If that's what you're doing, I don't have any way to know what's true and what isn't. I can't find reality." She waited while JD took a deep breath, trying to figure out how far to push. After all, she knew she should be grateful he was here tonight. But she didn't feel like stopping. "Go ahead." She waved toward the door. "You're not obligated to stay here."

"There's a sick child upstairs who appears to be beating the crap out of you. If this were any other domestic violence case, I wouldn't walk away." He paused. "You need to get help."

"No, we don't. You don't understand."

"What if he really hurts you?" JD asked. "What if you die in your next 'accidental' fall down the stairs? What will happen to him then?"

"It's not like that," she insisted. "You're jumping to conclusions."

"He's hurting you. And there's a good chance, from what I saw, that he'll hurt himself."

"We just need to ride this out. It will pass."

JD rubbed his hand over his face, exhausted. "Cut it out," he finally said. "Nobody ever wants to face this kind of news, but you know better. Brain injuries can cause personality changes. Don't handicap him further by putting your head in the sand."

"Would you listen to me?" She was beginning to feel helpless against the force of his will. "This is how he's working things out in the least painful way he can. He doesn't even remember any of this when he's awake. I got these bruises before I had medication to get him through the night."

"Maggie," he demanded, "where are you getting the drugs to treat him? You're not even licensed in this state." She didn't answer. JD shook his head. "You think it's wise to treat him with bootleg drugs?"

"They're not bootleg."

"Look what happened tonight."

"That's not what happened tonight." She was wearing down. "I wanted to see if he was making progress, so I held off for a few hours." Suddenly her head whipped around, as if she'd been startled. "Did you see that?" she asked.

"What?"

She shook her head slightly. "Something just outside my peripheral vision. Some dark thing moved."

"I didn't see anything. Maybe it was a bug."

She shook her head again. She tried to keep her voice level, but she couldn't entirely conceal what she felt. "It scared me."

He looked around. "There's nothing there." He watched her. "You know," he said calmly, "you probably haven't been sleeping right. And you look like you're not eating much either. Maybe you're beginning to hallucinate?"

There it was. Her deepest fear, that her fate was already determined, her story written. How old was her mother when she went crazy? It was so hard to remember things anymore. Even dumb things. What year was the American Revolution?

"What's that?" JD asked quizzically.

Oh, god, she hadn't even realized she was talking out loud.

"You need to get some sleep," he said. "You're dreaming with your eyes open."

Maggie said nothing. She was too smart for that. Everyone knew that trick, to push you and push you until you fought back so they could say that proved you were crazy. That's all sanity was, being the one in power. Bend like the willow. Survive the storm. "You're right," she said. She took a deep breath. Divert attention. "So how does one ask for help?"

JD looked pained. "You just ask, dammit. Take your chances. How do you not understand that human beings screw up and forgive each other all the time?"

Maggie didn't answer. That's right, she thought. It's my fault. Always my fault. The bubble of rage in her gut twisted and pulled to break free. "I think we better get you home," she said calmly. "You're welcome to come back tomorrow and see for yourself that everything's okay." The Observer gave approval. Control access, it advised. Ask for help you don't need so your enemy thinks he knows your weakness.

"No." JD's jaw was clenched. "I can't leave you here alone with him. There's too much risk he'll hurt you, or himself. I'll stay upstairs in the spare room."

"Suit yourself," she said. She held her calm for a moment, but his sneakiness bothered her. She raised her voice. "Remember, you have no authority here. Whether you believe me or not, you better not go behind my back. No secret plans."

"Maggie, if he needs help, you're not doing him any good by hiding him."

"Stop it!" She recognized that note of fraudulent calm in his voice, like he was coaxing a wild dog into the open so he could trap it. "This is *my* life. This is *my* son. Stop thinking you know better than I do, or that I'm lying to you, or that you have all the right answers."

"Okay." He stood up. "I'm sorry. Is it okay if I stay the night?"

She thought hard. If she said no, would he really leave? "People will talk," she said.

JD walked toward the stairs. "Leave the back door unlocked," he said. "In case I need to call somebody."

Maggie stayed in the kitchen. She put away the things she'd taken out for tea and cleaned up the icepack. She would not sleep tonight, not with the enemy right here in her house, upstairs near her son. Cold in her limbs and with her head buzzing as if she'd had too much coffee, she turned off the lights and headed down the short hall to her room. Only then did she realize that she didn't know how JD had ended up in Mac's bedroom in the first place.

❦ ❦ ❦

JD woke early. He laid in bed and watched the brilliant late spring sun begin to paint its ascent on the next block. It annoyed him that no matter what kind of devastation people suffered, they were ultimately hardwired to notice the world's beauty. It was like aesthetics were just one more of nature's sly tricks to get humans to stick around when life became too disagreeable.

He'd slept in his clothes, thinking he might have to jump out of bed to respond to the siren of Mac's screams. But as Maggie predicted, the rest of the night had been quiet. Now he felt stiff and sore, and his shoulder hurt like a bitch. He hobbled to the bathroom and rummaged around until he found some Tylenol and an unopened toothbrush. At least cleaning up helped him feel slightly more capable of facing things. When he finished, he peeked in on Mac, who was sleeping soundly. JD left his door open a crack so he could listen for anything unusual, and went downstairs.

He was surprised the kitchen was so well stocked until he realized Gamey kept bringing stuff in and nobody was eating it. He went through the refrigerator and found onions and peppers, eggs and cheddar cheese. He wasn't hungry himself, but he decided to make a frittata. He could stick it in the oven and if nobody woke up for a while, it could sit around.

It felt good to be messing around in the kitchen again. He hadn't cooked anything in a long time. In their desire to show how much they cared, people had nearly interred him in an avalanche of homemade food. Mikey eventually saved him by enforcing a schedule. Then someone started a rumor that JD had invited them to stay and eat with him. It wasn't true, because he rarely felt like either eating or socializing, but the only way to defuse the situation was to invite whoever was on the schedule to join him. In the end, that did a lot more for his recovery than the food.

He found the cast iron skillet, the one he had seasoned himself before cooking dinner here last fall. He put it on the stove so he could brown the onion and peppers before sticking the frittata in to bake. He was surprised how unwieldy it was to chop things with his left arm partially out of commission. His technique suffered for it, but he was pretty sure nobody here would notice. When he was done, he made himself a cup of coffee and went into the den to relax. He couldn't believe how tired he was just from making breakfast.

He leaned back on the couch and put his feet up on the coffee table. You had to give it to the woman, she knew how to find the most comfortable furniture he'd ever sat on. He closed his eyes and drowsed a little. He hardly needed these little naps anymore. While that was a good sign physically, it meant he was going to have to start thinking about what to do with the rest of his life. Whatever normal was going to look like, it would have to be a different version from before. But at least he could still get there, to some kind of normal. That might not be true for the boy upstairs. His road to normal might be blocked forever.

JD sat up and took a sip of coffee. Amidst the magazines on the coffee table was a laptop. He turned it on. It was connected to a network. He opened up the connections and had a good laugh. Dr. Maggie the technophobe was taking a free ride on Gamey's wireless. But she hadn't been sophisticated enough to put passwords on anything. He went into her browser history. All the websites she'd visited recently were in Spanish. His own Spanish was pretty rudimentary, but hers was probably pretty good after years of practicing medicine in a New York City hospital. Anyway, it wasn't hard to figure out what she was doing. The word 'farmacia' appeared frequently. So this was how she was getting the drugs to treat Mac.

The frittata smelled done. He shut down the computer and went to take the pan out of the oven. As the frittata cooled, he started looking for something special he could make to go with it, something that might interest her enough to eat. Buried in the back of the refrigerator, he found an unopened Trenton Pork Roll. This was the real thing, capable of luring the most reluctant sleeper out of bed with its savory, tangy scent as it fried. Gamey probably drove over to the factory in Trenton to get this himself, his way of showing how much he cared.

JD slid the frittata onto a large plate and wiped the skillet out with a paper towel. He looked down the hall to Maggie's door. It was still closed. He knew she needed to sleep, but he hoped the cooking smells would rouse her. He was worried that if Mac woke up before she did, he wouldn't know how to handle him alone. He was still trying to decide if he should go wake her when he heard Mac thundering down the stairs. "Hey, Mom," he yelled, "what smells so good?" His voice had lost most of the boyish quality JD remembered.

Mac came whipping around the corner. He saw JD and stopped. Then, with the sloppy affection of a Labrador puppy, he raced over and hugged JD hard with his good arm. JD winced from the crush on his shoulder, but no force on earth could have made him pull away. He only hesitated an instant before he returned the hug with his own good arm. Mac's left arm started trembling and he self-consciously pulled away.

"Hey," JD said, pointing to his own shoulder, "we're a matched set."

Mac's face was one huge grin. "How you doing?" he asked.

"I'm good," JD fibbed. "How about you? You must have grown four inches." It was remarkable, he thought, what a body could go through and not get blown off the course of its genetic map.

"Yeah," Mac said. "All my clothes are too small."

"Well, we'll have to take you out and get you new ones."

"That would be cool," Mac said. "Mom's been stalling."

Too late, JD realized his mistake. "We'll leave it up to her," he said. "She's the expert on when you'll be ready to go out. Don't want to risk your recovery over fashion."

"Oh, it's not that," Mac said. "She just hates to go shopping." He sat down at the table. JD watched him surreptitiously. So far, except for the left arm, everything appeared normal. "You like shopping?" Mac asked.

JD turned back to the stove. Time to flip the pork roll. "It's not what I do for fun," he said, "but I don't mind it. When I was your age, Rev was the one who always took me. Helen claimed she didn't know the first thing about dressing boys, but I think she was just embarrassed about figuring out what size drawers I needed."

Mac laughed. "Mom's not embarrassed about stuff like that."

"I suppose not," JD said. "It's good to have a parent who doesn't embarrass easily. Rev's like that too."

"That's your wife's father?"

JD smiled. "Rev and Helen started out as Rebekah's parents, but even before she died they were my parents too."

"You mean like stepparents?"

"No, I mean like the real thing." He turned off the flame and moved the pork roll to a serving plate. "Nature intended for birth parents and real parents to be the same thing. If it doesn't turn out that way and you're lucky, you can find your real parents somewhere else." He brought the food to the table. "That's how it worked out for me." Mac got up to help set the table. "You okay to do that?" JD asked.

"Sure," Mac shrugged. "Why not?" JD served them both. Mac inhaled two helpings before speaking again. "When did you get here?" he asked.

"Last night," JD said. He decided to test. "I thought you might have seen me come in."

"Nope," Mac said. "Mom said you were staying with you wife's parents until you got better."

So Maggie hadn't told him JD was back in town. He knew he should leave things alone, at least until he understood better, but this was like the hole where a tooth had been extracted. He couldn't resist poking at it even though it hurt. "You been sleeping okay?" he asked.

"Sure," Mac said. "Why?"

"It's just that when I saw your mom last night, she looked . . ." He had almost said 'pretty beat up,' but caught himself. "She looked really worn out."

"Yeah," Mac said, his face clouding. "I'm kind of glad you're here. I'm getting worried about her. She doesn't want anybody to visit. I think something's not right."

"What do you think it is?" It was a leading question, but JD was feeling reckless.

Mac was very serious. "Besides being tired all the time, she's been falling a lot."

"You mean tripping over stuff?"

"That's what's weird. I've never actually seen her fall, but she's got all these bruises. A couple of weeks ago she told me she fell down the stairs. She says it happens at night." He sounded scared. "Do you think she started walking in her sleep?"

JD looked at him, trying to detect some sign he was lying. There wasn't any. "I think she's just been under a lot of stress lately," he finally said.

"Why would she be under a lot of stress now, when I'm getting better?"

"Sometimes people don't show it until they know everything's going to be okay."

Mac got up and put his plate in the sink. "Are you going to stick around and help out?"

JD felt on the spot. "If she wants me to."

"I want you to." Mac blushed. "I can't even wash dishes with only one hand."

"Don't give me that crap," JD joked. "A real man can single-handedly load a dishwasher."

Mac didn't laugh. He turned and looked out the kitchen window. There was a subtle shift in his posture. Then he turned back and looked down at the floor. "I had time to run."

JD sat very still, quietly waiting. When the silence stretched out too far, he said, "I didn't know that."

"Yeah," Mac continued. "The first shots came when they opened the door and Mr. Don got hit right away. One minute he was yelling at me to run, and then he was just lying there. I didn't know what to do, but I didn't want to just leave him like that. Then they came in, so I ended up running anyway, only it was too late." Again JD waited calmly. Finally Mac looked at him. "Do you think it was stupid waiting around like that? It didn't even work."

JD shook his head. "I don't think you were being stupid. You took a calculated risk. You paid for it, but you did it because you wanted to save another human being's life. You demonstrated the best motives a man can have. For what it's worth, I'm proud of you."

For an instant, Mac grinned. And then his face contorted, and from somewhere deep within him a great gasping sob began. He cried violently for several minutes. Finally he slowed down. JD tossed him a dishtowel and he wiped his face. "I couldn't do that if Mom was here," he said, his voice still sounding broken.

"Don't worry about Mom," JD said. "I've got her covered."

r r r

The first thing Maggie heard when she woke up was the sound of her son and JD laughing. It made her feel edgy. She got out of bed and dressed quickly. When she went out to the kitchen, she thought they both looked guilty. "Hey," she said by way of a general greeting.

"Morning," JD said.

"Morning, Mom," Mac replied.

"You guys have breakfast already?"

JD indicated the clock. "We were beginning to think about lunch."

"I can take over from here," Maggie said. "If you'd like to get home."

"Sure." JD got up from the table and took his coffee cup to the sink.

"I'll wash that," Maggie said.

Mac grinned wickedly. "She must really want to get rid of you if she's offering to do your dishes." He looked from one of them to the other. "Guess I'll go get my shower now."

Maggie waited until she heard the water running upstairs. "I heard you talking with him," she lied. JD just looked at her.

"There are things he needs to talk about, Maggie."

"He has me," she said harshly. "He can talk to me."

Her tone was unreasonable, but JD stayed calm. "He needed to ask if what happened to him might have somehow been his fault."

"That's bullshit," Maggie spat. "How could it be his fault?"

"Because that's what kids think in the face of inexplicable tragedy." She stared at him. "I gave him an answer he could handle," he continued. "There's no comfort in calling it a random act. That only makes it clear how hazardous life really is."

"Don't lead him to believe it's any better if he has his own personal hero."

JD put on his jacket. "I'm not a hero," he said tersely. He turned on her without warning. "What version of the truth would you have preferred me to give him?"

"There's only one."

He shook his head in frustrated fury. "Is it so important to you to be everything to him that you would have me hurt him even more?"

Maggie didn't answer. Where was the place for JD between her and Mac? Wherever you let him make it, the Observer answered. She turned to JD. "Before you head out," she began, "I was wondering. Why did you show up here last night? And how did you get in?"

JD looked at her with an expression that might have been disbelief. From the way she was talking it was hard to believe she'd been in the room a moment ago. There was no sign of her anger. "I used Morsel's key. The one you gave him to deliver groceries."

"Morsel gave you the key?" She heard her voice rising.

"No. I didn't say he gave me the key. I said I used it."

"I'm tired," she exhaled. "Don't fence with me."

"Martha got it off him. I wasn't supposed to tell you. Morsel heard Mac screaming. He's heard it before, but last night he was home alone and it really scared him. So he called Martha. She came over and heard it too. She asked him for your key because she figured, like the rest of us, that if she came knocking at your door you'd send her away."

"Martha came in here?" Maggie asked, feeling strange. "Last night?" JD nodded. "I don't want her in here."

"Maggie," JD said, "cut it out. She wanted to help you. After she heard what was going on, she called the station."

Maggie reached for a chair and sat down hard. "What was she thinking?"

JD was out of patience. "She was thinking you and your child were in danger."

"She had no right! What if somebody misunderstood? They would take him away!"

"Well, they didn't. Mikey talked to her and called me. Your son's still here. Everything worked out fine." Maggie stood up and started pacing. She could feel the risk, right there beside her, waiting in the shadows. It was like a trap had been set, and though she narrowly avoided it this time, it had sprung right next to her head. "Calm down," JD said. "You're getting all worked up over nothing. You're no good to your son if you're a mess."

"Don't bring her in here again," she said sharply. "And don't send someone to take him away. You saw him just now. He's almost there, he's almost whole again. You've been through the system. You know what gets done to a child in the name of protecting him. Even if they just keep him until they figure out they made a mistake, it could break him. He's too fragile." She stopped. She would not show fear. It was too much like an invitation to fate.

She couldn't read JD's face. She was barely capable of seeing the primary colors of emotion let alone something as complex as he was feeling now. He reached into his pocket and slapped her house key on the kitchen counter. "I'll be back tonight," he said. "You can decide whether or not to let me in." He left, letting the door slam behind him.

Maggie stood looking at the door. That's right, the Observer said. We don't need them near your son.

52

JD realized he should go up to Mac's room. It was earlier than Mac usually went to bed, but it had been a long, exhausting day. He'd gotten Maggie's permission to take Mac out for some "guy" fun. They'd gone fishing at the state park. In all likelihood, neither of them would have posed a threat to the fish even with two hands. But in their current single-handed state their lack of skill reduced them to making fun of each other until their hilarity annoyed the serious fishermen and they had to leave.

Then JD decided he was hungry for some authentic Pennsylvania cooking. Mac, whose experience of Pennsylvania cooking consisted mainly of Gamey's Deli and his mother's efforts, couldn't imagine why anyone would intentionally eat it. So JD took him on a road trip to Lancaster County. Mac was fascinated by the glimpses they got of the Pennsylvania Dutch lifestyle, the horses and buggies, the classic farms powered by windmills. They stopped at a smorgasbord, and Mac filled himself with fried chicken, pot roast, creamed cabbage, mashed potatoes and shoo-fly pie. Stuffed and exhausted, they stumbled into the house in the early evening. Maggie wasn't home. Her note said Vee insisted they should go out and she'd be back before bedtime.

JD wanted nothing more than to nod off on the couch. That's what made him realize he'd better keep Mac awake until Maggie got back and gave him his shot. Tired to the bone, he dragged himself upstairs. Mac had taken a shower and was lying in bed reading. "Feel like talking?" JD asked.

"You missing me already?" Mac teased him.

JD sat at the foot of the bed. He made a summary judgment to go for the truth. "I'd like you to stay awake until your mother gets home, if you can."

"I think I'm ready to stop having the shots," Mac said.

JD shook his head. "I'm not the one to decide that."

"You know why she gives them to me, don't you?"

"I do," JD said, thoughtfully. "Do you?"

Mac took his time answering. "I think they're for the nightmares."

"Do you remember the nightmares? Can you tell me about them?"

"No," Mac said. "But when I have one I feel really bad the next morning."

"Bad like you've had a workout?"

"No." He shook his head. "Bad like I did something I shouldn't have." His face showed the struggle going on inside him. "Why should I feel bad? I'm not the one who hurt people." There was a long pause while Mac worked up the courage to say what he had to. "You killed him because of me, didn't you? Just say it."

JD exhaled. "I killed him because I didn't have a choice." His eyes got glassy. "That was how my job worked out that day. In order to protect the public I had to kill a child."

Neither of them spoke for a while. "Is that the real reason you're not going back to work?" Mac asked.

"Maybe," JD said. "Maybe not. I'm not really sure. I haven't decided what I'm going to do yet."

"Are you spending time here like a kind of penance?"

"No, MacDonald," JD said. "I care about you. If I didn't, I wouldn't be here. I do not believe I need to even the score somehow for what I did. There is no equity in life."

They were silent again. "Are you glad he's dead?" Mac asked.

"No," JD answered sadly. "It's not the kind of thing you ever feel glad about."

Mac's voice got hard. "I am. He killed people. He was trying to kill you. And me."

"Yes, he was. And I'm glad we're all safe from him." JD considered his words before going on. "But whether I killed him or not, his life was already over."

"You mean because he got caught."

"No. His life was over the moment he made up his mind to do this thing. He became one of those people who are the prisoner of the wild thing inside them. Some people who have a wild thing inside are lucky enough to learn how to control it. But others can't, and once the wild thing takes over they do something they can't live with. Then whatever good was inside them has to deal with it, and guilt ends up making them the wild thing's prisoner whether they're in jail or not. Once that happens there's almost no hope for a real life."

Mac struggled with this. "Is that what you were thinking about when you shot him?"

"No. I was thinking about how to get him under control. And I was scared. Then he shot at me and I shot back. It's what I'm trained to do. He would have shot at anybody if he had the chance. He made his decisions."

Mac was quiet a long time. "If you really believe that's how it is, like killing a man-eating tiger to protect innocent people, do you forgive yourself?"

JD smiled sadly. "I'm trying."

"That's how I feel," Mac said. "Like I should, but I'm not there yet."

🐓 🐓 🐓

Maggie felt bad when she saw JD's car in her driveway. She wanted to get home before they did. She parked quickly and hurried into the house. They were up in Mac's room. She went into her bathroom and prepared his medication. Then she went upstairs, tapped on his door and walked in. They looked surprised to see her. The syringe in her hand made her feel evil. "I have your shot," she said.

"That's okay," Mac said. "I'm going to try to sleep without it tonight."

Maggie looked from him to JD. They had a secret. She could see it. That should be her sitting on her son's bed sharing his confidences. She was careful to keep any hint of annoyance out of her voice. "Sometimes you have trouble sleeping," she said.

"I'll be okay."

"What if you have a bad dream?"

"I think he'll be fine," JD said.

Maggie turned abruptly and left. When JD came downstairs a few minutes later, she was waiting for him. "You encouraged him to do that."

"I think it might be time."

"What if you're wrong?" she demanded. "You saw what happens. Why would you want to subject him to that?"

"I read somewhere that even nightmares can be healing," he replied. "And I believe he's strong enough now to handle it."

Maggie left the room without saying anything else.

🐓 🐓 🐓

The next morning, JD was already in the kitchen when Mac came down. He kept working on whatever he was preparing.

"I did it, didn't I?" Mac asked quietly.

JD took a while to answer. "How do you feel?"

"Did I make it through the night?" Mac persisted.

"Yeah, buddy, as far as I can tell, you did."

Mac watched him chopping for a minute. "You don't seem very happy about it."

JD finally turned around. "I'm sorry. I am extremely happy about it. It's great that you're getting well." He turned back to what he was doing.

Mac went over to the refrigerator and poked around inside. Eventually he emerged with a bottle of juice in his hand and a hunk of cheese in his mouth. "Hey," he said, chewing, "are you almost done?"

"What's up?" JD asked.

"I wanted some help with my workout."

"I just need a minute," JD said, indicating the food on the cutting board.

Mac took the bottle of juice down to the basement. JD came down a few minutes later. Mac was trying to hold a three-pound weight in his left hand while he did his exercises. He was still warming up, and he kept dropping the weight. JD stood back by the stairs. Mac saw him in the big mirror on the wall, the one where he used to watch himself play the drums. But he didn't make eye contact. He continued his warm-ups, struggling to get his left hand to stay closed around the weight.

Taking measured breaths, he began the rest of his routine. He was only on his first set of repetitions when his arm started going wild. His hand was finally holding onto the weight, but he couldn't get control over the arm. He got more and more frustrated. JD just stood there, still watching in the mirror.

Mac made a furious animal sound and threw the weight across the room. It slammed into the mirror and a section of the glass shattered. "I'm never going to get better," he yelled.

"Looks like you still got pretty good aim," JD replied.

Mac began to cry. "It's too hard."

JD walked over to the closet where the cleaning supplies were and took out the broom. Walking back to Mac, he said, "Getting better doesn't happen all at once. You'll keep getting better right up till you make the mistake of thinking you've come as far as you can."

"That's bullshit!" Mac lashed out.

"I'm saying it because I believe it," JD said. "You want to be angry, you want to be sad, I'm with you. You want to give up, you're on your own."

Mac stared at him with rage. "You don't know what it's like! You got hurt, but not as bad as me!"

JD held the broom out to him. "Go clean up the mess you made."

"Kiss my ass!" Mac shouted. JD just stood there, holding out the broom. Mac began to cry harder.

They both heard Maggie at the same moment. She was standing on the bottom step. "Give me the broom," she said harshly to JD.

JD looked at Mac. Mac looked back at him with razor eyes. He did not look at his mother. "I'll do it," he snapped. Clenching his jaw, he struggled to take the broom in his left hand. No one else moved, a tableau frozen in pain, until he finally succeeded.

As it got closer to the day when Mac was supposed to return to school, several things became clear to Maggie. Most of them had to do with JD. He was incredibly controlling. For starters, even though Mac seemed past whatever had been causing his night terrors, JD still hung around every night. While he went somewhere for at least part of each day, he was always back well before dinner time, and just came into the house and started cooking like he belonged there. He was always telling them what to do, especially Mac. He was good-natured about it, of course, but there he was, every time she turned around, as if he had been endowed with all the answers. It was painful to watch how Mac waited for JD's agreement to confirm everything, including Maggie's opinions.

This wasn't healthy for Mac. What role did JD play in their lives, really? For him this was, at best, a temporary investment, a solicitude born of obligation, or perhaps pity. Maggie became more and more convinced of what she needed to do. It would be difficult for them all at first, but she believed that in the end Mac would understand how it was for the best. She just couldn't let things continue the way they were. JD's constant presence made it impossible for her to concentrate or get things done. How could she ever show her son he could depend on her when she couldn't even complete simple tasks? Clearly she needed to do something about JD's interference in their lives. She would be polite about it, and kind. After all, she was grateful for all his help. But now it was time to let JD know she and her son were ready to get on with their lives. She was sure he would understand.

🐦 🐦 🐦

The night before Mac started back to school, the weather turned unexpectedly cold. The wind blew from the north, and the leaves turned upside down, showing their silvery undersides as if they knew they had to protect their glossy green tops from the stinging rain that would fall. JD bought a bottle of champagne to go with dinner. Maggie decided Mac shouldn't have any, then drank far too much herself. By the time dinner was over, she was sloshed. She laid her head down on her arms while Mac and JD cleared the table. "Hey," JD said, "why don't you go into the den and relax?" There he was again, suggesting what she should do. She wanted to put up a fight, but she was too tired. Eventually they left her sitting there while they went off to do whatever it was that they did in the evening.

Maggie roused herself after awhile and went into the den. She wasn't aware she had been dozing until she heard JD coming down the stairs. As he walked in, she picked up the remote and pointed it at the television.

"Mind if I hang around awhile and watch with you?" he asked.

"Actually," she said, daggers in her voice, "I do. Mind."

JD looked taken aback. "Okay," he said. "No problem."

"Well, yes," she snapped, "there is a problem."

"Looks like I'm about to hear what it is."

"Please don't demean this by trying to make it into a joke," Maggie said sharply.

"Sorry," JD said.

"Have a seat," Maggie commanded, standing up. JD raised his eyebrows, but sat at the end of the couch. She could see now that the champagne had taken its toll on him as well. She decided to go easy on him. "I don't want you to think I'm ungrateful. You've been a great help to us. But we can't keep imposing on you."

"I don't mind."

"Well, I mind."

"This is all a little abrupt. Have I done something to offend you?"

"Sorry," she said, not sounding it. "I probably should have tried to soften this somehow, but it's difficult to find the right way to say it."

"Sounds like you're doing okay." JD stood up.

"Now you're insulted," she said.

"Oh," he said sarcastically, "that's not what you had in mind?"

"Why are you blaming me?" she demanded.

"What was my crime this time around?" he shot back.

"He's my son. He does fine with one adult in the house."

"That's why I stuck around," JD said. "So he could have one."

"Okay," Maggie said. "This isn't going anywhere. You can still be his pal. We just don't need you to move in here."

"Maggie," JD tried to take her arm, but she pulled away. "I'm sorry. I'm making stupid cracks instead of telling you what I really feel. I would like to help you take care of your son. I would like to help you take care of yourself."

"I don't want to be one of your good works," she said roughly.

"You are not a charity project for me. I have a great deal of respect for you."

"Open your eyes." Her voice was harsh. "I am the result of an experiment, what happens when a sane person is raised in an insane milieu."

"Maybe that's why it doesn't come naturally to you to understand love. But I've never met anyone so goddamned determined not to try."

"That would be so convenient for you, wouldn't it? But guess what? I understand perfectly well what love is. Did you ever consider that maybe you're the one who doesn't understand?"

'Trust me," he said. "I know what love is. I just never realized before it could be so tangled up in jealousy that it could wreak havoc."

"That's naïve," Maggie said dismissively. "Humans are hardwired to destroy anything that comes between them and who they love."

"Is that what this is?" JD's eyes narrowed. "You're willing to put your son at risk for the sake of owning him? It's so important to you to be the center of his universe that you don't even care if that harms him?"

When Maggie spoke, her voice was emotionless. "You deceived yourself into believing you're an essential part of our lives. But you know what you really are? You're a control freak looking for some destabilized family to take over. Too bad for you, because you're looking in the wrong place. We don't need you. In fact, we're too strong for you." She looked at him with disgust. "Get out."

"That's it?" he asked, his voice getting sharp. "You figure now that it's convenient for you, you can just cut me loose?"

"I was hoping this wouldn't have to get ugly," Maggie said. "But we have nothing more to say to each other. Why don't you just get out of here while you still have some dignity?" She walked past him.

JD grabbed her from behind so hard he pulled her off balance. She stumbled backwards, trying to find her footing. Before she could, he threw her down on the couch. She caught a glimpse of his face as he forced himself down on top of her, and it was not a face she recognized. She tried to hit him, scratch him, distract him long enough to get away, but his bad arm was not nearly as bad as she believed. He used it to pin her hands together by the wrist. With his other hand he pulled down her shorts. "Don't do this," she hissed at him, full of venom. He forced his knee between her legs. "If you care about Mac," she spat, "don't do this. Not here. Not where he might see his hero with his ass hanging out like the white trash he really is." JD slapped her, not too hard, mostly intended as a further insult. She turned her face away from him. "I won't cry," she whispered. "I don't cry. Nothing can make me cry."

"Look at me!" he ordered her.

She kept her face turned away. "Just get it over with," she whispered. "Just rape me or kill me or whatever it is that monster inside of you needs to do and then leave us alone." JD let go of her hands and began to cry. Maggie closed her eyes. She had no sense of how long they laid there like that, and then he got up. She listened to him go out the back door.

She stayed on the couch a little longer, her head aching from champagne and rage and who knew what else, and then stood up and straightened out her shorts and put the pillows back in place on the couch. This might have been expected, she realized. Doc always warned her about how she blindly drove people into the red zone of their anger. He told her too many times that she was stupid about crossing boundaries, that she never made the effort to think about what she was doing to other people. The Observer, which had no expectations and was always fair, confirmed that she still had not learned. In the end, all she got was what she asked for, but she continued to ask for it anyway. It was nobody's fault but her own that she always paid the consequences. At least JD had finally started communicating in a way she understood. She took a quick shower and went to bed.

53

When Maggie woke up, Mac was already banging around the kitchen. She looked at her alarm clock. It wasn't even supposed to go off for another five minutes, so she could only imagine what time he'd gotten up. She threw on her robe and went out there. "Hey," she asked, "aren't you a little early?"

"I'm okay," he said. "Where's JD? His door was open, and his bed was already made."

Maggie felt surprisingly calm. "He wasn't feeling great last night, so he thought he'd go home, try to get some sleep there."

"Is he okay?"

"Yes, honey," she said. "He's fine. You want me to make your lunch?"

"Nah," he said. "I already took care of it." Mac looked at her. "I was thinking, would it be okay if I took the bus?"

Maggie shook her head. "I don't think that's a great idea."

"Why not?"

"It's your first day back. Let me bring you in, make sure you get settled okay. You know, just give you a hand."

"No pun intended."

"Mac."

"No, really." His eyes were all seriousness now. "If I'm going to go in there and get my life back to normal, I should just do it."

"But what if . . ."

"I know. I know some people are going to be weird. But the sooner they see I'm okay, the sooner it will stop."

"And what if you get tired, or you just don't feel like dealing with it?"

"What were you planning to do, follow me around all day with a box of tissues and a huggie bear? If I need anything, I'll call."

Maggie closed her eyes. What would a real mother do, what would a real mother do, she repeated to herself like a mantra. "Okay," she said. "If I let you ride the bus, will you call me as soon as you get there?"

"No," Mac said.

"How will I know you're okay?"

"Can I have a hug?" he asked.

Maggie felt whatever was strong inside her begin to give way. I can't let go, she thought. I'm too scared to do this. He walked over and she held on to him tightly. He was taller than she was now. Soon he will be beyond you in all the important ways, the Observer noted. "I love you, baby," she said softly.

"I love you too, Mom."

She loosened her grip. "Are you sure you'll be okay?"

"Sure," he said. "Don't be scared, all right?"

"I'll try."

"Good girl." He laughed and patted her on the head.

ɼ ɼ ɼ

Maggie watched out the window as Mac went down the front walk and across the street to the bus stop. He was the first one there. He was like a strand of kelp, she thought, bending to the currents around him, never allowing his roots to be ripped from the solid ocean floor. Within a few minutes, Morsel came around the far side of Gamey's and joined him. Maggie heard he'd finally decided to return to school. He walked up to Mac, the disparity in their heights now almost comical. She could see from his gestures that he was offering to take Mac's book bag. Mac shook his head. Then he said something that made Morsel punch him in the arm. Morsel instantly looked horrified. And then Mac punched him back. They both started laughing. The rest of the kids were arriving now, but the bus pulled up and blocked Maggie's view. When it pulled away, the street was empty.

Maggie realized the sharp crystal of anxiety in the pit of her stomach was growing. Sending her son back into the world was only the first hard thing she had to get through today. She still had to go to JD and confront what had happened last night. She got into the shower, trying to compose a script in her mind for a scene she had no idea how to play. She had to help him understand what had happened between them. It was her responsibility.

By the time she was ready to leave, her hands were shaking. As she backed into the alley, she focused her mind on driving carefully. She needed to control her growing fear. She drove the few blocks to JD's house with exquisite caution. She pulled into his driveway. His car wasn't there. She got out anyway, praying his car would be inside the garage. She looked through the windows. The garage was empty, except for some yard equipment.

She got back in her car. Her hands continued to shake. She backed out of his driveway, waiting until she was sure there was no oncoming traffic. She would go into town and check at the station. He had to be there.

The closer she got, the slower she drove. She turned into the parking lot with infinite care. As if in a bad horror movie, the building seemed to elongate, so that it took forever to get to the back. Under the shade tree in the far corner was his car. Her relief was so powerful it made her fingers numb. She got out of her car as carefully as she had driven, and walked around to the front of the station. She walked right past Reception and down the hall to the squad room. Joe Butts was at the desk closest to the door. He looked up when she came in, and Maggie had a painful moment as discomfort and embarrassment played rapidly across his face.

Walter was sitting at his desk in the far corner. "Maggie," he said. "How're you doing?"

"I'm good, thanks, Walter. How about you?"

"Can't complain. How's your son?"

"He started back to school this morning. I was pretty scared about it, but he seems to know what he's doing."

"That's good," Walter said. "That's really good. I'm glad to hear it."

Maggie turned to Butts. "Joe," she said. "How are you doing?"

"Something we can do for you, Mrs. Rifkin?"

"Yes," she said. His attitude was not lost on her. "I'd like to see JD."

"Chief's not here," Butts said.

"His car's out back."

"Yeah," Butts said.

"But he's not here."

"Nope."

Walter was looking back and forth between them like this was a distressing tennis match.

"So where is he?"

"Couldn't say."

"Why not?"

Butts lost his temper. "Because I don't know," he snapped.

"So why's his car here?"

"You saying I'm lying to you?"

"Why's his car here?" Maggie persisted.

"He left it here so we could keep an eye on it."

"Why?" She was beginning to panic. "Why did he need you to keep an eye on it?"

"Because," Butts spoke as if to an idiot, "he was going away for a while."

"Where?" Her voice was rising.

"I don't really know."

"Well, who does know?" She felt her guts constricting inside her.

Butts knew he had the upper hand. He shrugged. "He didn't even know himself. Just said he needed to get away for a while."

Maggie could feel herself beginning to separate, like what happened in the car after Mac got shot. Part of her was panicky and screaming. The rest was the Observer. "Tell me where he went." She thought the Observer was talking until she heard the shakiness in her voice.

Butts stood up and started to come around his desk. "Why can't you leave him alone?"

"What is it to you?" Maggie asked, her voice full of acid. "You have a crush on him too, like the rest of this fucked up town?"

Butts' face turned red. He pointed a finger at her, jabbing it as he spoke. "You know what, lady? There are plenty of people think he was trying to get himself killed when he went after that kid. Why do you suppose that was? Huh? Who hurt him so bad he wanted to die?"

"Hey, Joe, come on." Walter stood up.

Maggie backed away. "That's not true," she said, but she sounded like she didn't believe herself.

"And what happens when he finally fights his way back? Tell me that. Tell me what happened between you and him that made him decide he had to run away."

"Joe!" Walter raised his voice. "That's enough!" He turned to Maggie. "He didn't go yet," he said. "He's home packing. He said he'd call here when he's ready to go to the train."

"Thank you," Maggie said softly. She moved quickly to the door, determined to make it out before her legs collapsed under her.

ɾ   ɾ   ɾ

Maggie drove like a madwoman back to JD's. She pulled into his driveway and flew out of her car, tripping on the way to his back door. It was locked. She ran around front. That door was locked too. She hammered on the bell, then pounded furiously on the door. No answer. She ran back around to the kitchen door and started pounding again. She was breathing so hard her chest hurt. She could not let this happen. She was just mad last night. She didn't mean it. It was all her fault. She had to see him so he could understand that going away was a mistake.

She kicked the door. She felt insane. She drew back her fist, then stopped. Morsel knew how to break into houses. What would he do? He wouldn't mess up his hand. She pulled off her shoe and smashed it against one of the small glass panes. Nothing happened. She tried again, and the pane held firm. She began pounding with the heel of her shoe, full of fury. Suddenly there was a crash, more noise than she would have expected, and pieces of glass went flying into the vestibule. She put her shoe back on and reached through the broken window to unlock the door. The Observer was curious about what she thought she might do next. As if toying with a trapped mouse, it casually urged her to look for a more reasonable path. Maggie forced herself to ignore the voice and go into the kitchen.

There was no sign of him. But thanks to the grace of old plumbing, she heard the shower running upstairs. She was so relieved she almost laughed. He was still here. She had no idea what to do next. So she sat and waited. As if nothing was amiss. As if someone would be coming along any time now to bake apple pies.

She listened to the water coursing through the pipes. It was almost hypnotic. Or maybe it was just exhaustion that tranquilized her. And then her mind catapulted out of neutral. The shower had been running for a long time. She must have been here at least ten minutes already. The clock on the stove said 9:55. The next train out of Dooleysburg would leave at 10:30. If JD planned to be on it, he would have to leave soon. She would give him five more minutes.

It was a hard five minutes. Sometimes it stretched out so far it clouded the horizon, and then, within an instant, a minute or two would be gone. Through it all, the sound of the shower went on and on, filling a bucket of dread. Suddenly she couldn't take any more. She ran up the stairs, following the sound of the shower into JD's bedroom at the far end of the hall. But she lost her momentum as she got near the closed bathroom door. She hesitated, then knocked. No answer. "JD?" she called, knocking again. An image of him, sudden and real, slumped unconscious on the floor of the shower jammed into her head. She could see the water streaming down the walls, his face slack and partially submerged. She called him again, in a panic, and twisted the knob. The door was unlocked.

She threw the door open and then stopped. Across the room, JD stood in the shower, but not under the water. His back was to her, his head cradled on his good arm. The hot water had partially fogged the shower door, so she couldn't be sure what was happening. As she slowly walked closer, his shoulders shook and she realized he was crying. She felt helpless. She had nothing in her lifetime's worth of experience that showed her what to do for this kind of need.

Then the moment passed and she saw him as no different from any other wounded man. She grabbed a towel from the bar on the wall. Opening the shower door, she turned off the water. "JD," she said softly, "I'm here."

He did not respond. The Observer, if Maggie had been attending to it, would have told her to back off. Instead, she kicked off her shoes and stepped into the shower. She began to dry him off, gently. He held very still. She dried his neck and shoulders, taking great care with his left side. Then she dried his back and knelt down to dry his legs. He didn't acknowledge her, but he also didn't tell her to stop. Finally she took his arm and moved him gently away from the wall. "Turn around," she said.

He did, and she was devastated. Even Maggie, who had no aptitude for reading what others were feeling, could not escape the grief on his face. She did not know what to say. She handed him the towel, which he wrapped around his waist. "I have to leave you, Maggie," he whispered.

Maggie felt a sharp, choking sensation in her throat, like she was trying to swallow a piece of corroded pipe. Her eyes burned. "Why?" she pleaded. "Why now? Haven't we been through enough?"

"You were right," he said hoarsely. "Back when you told me to go away because you knew sooner or later I would do something to hurt you, you were right. I knew it then. I knew it even before you said it."

She shook her head mutely. She wanted to pull those words back, to have never planted them in his mind, where they'd taken full advantage of the opportunity to grow and writhe and seethe inside him. Even though, somehow, she'd known this was coming, she had no idea how to stop it. The only thing she knew for sure was that she was not likely to survive. The Observer was intrigued that she had the capacity to understand this.

JD tried to turn away from her. Maggie could feel the panic rising up, cutting off her air, suffocating her. She had to reach beyond it. There had to be an opening somewhere. She imagined him demanding her to choose between him and her demons. She could read his mind. She took the sort of deep breath one might take before plunging into a torrent. She reached out, eyes closed, and embraced him. She clung to him with the fierce energy of a drowning person.

"Maggie?" he asked. "What are you doing?"

She couldn't talk. She opened her eyes. She tried to speak and choked. He pulled away and held her by her upper arms, maintaining the distance between them. "Last night," he began, and then had to stop. He fought his way back into control. "You know I have to go," he whispered. Maggie shook her head. JD's confusion morphed into anger. "Don't do this," he said. "You can't pretend it didn't happen."

"I don't understand." She sounded lost.

"Dammit!" he said. "Last night." He started crying again.

She shook her head. "You were just angry. I made you angry. You didn't force me to do anything, you didn't do anything wrong . . ."

"Stop it!" he commanded. "I wanted to hurt you so you would do what I wanted." He stopped and calmed down. "You are like an addiction for me. The more I can't have you, the more I suffer."

"But you can have me!"

"Not on these terms. It will destroy both of us."

"Name your terms!"

"Poor Maggie," he said, gently. "You hold yourself so carelessly over the abyss. You would let yourself fall to your own destruction to keep me, wouldn't you? I can't let you do that. If you do, you will destroy me as well." He almost lost it again. "You were right all along. You said I would do you irreparable harm. You sensed the violence that's always there, just below my surface. But me? I never saw it. It was just my wallow. I didn't even think about what it would mean to drag you down into it. You and Mac, you could have owned my heart. But who knows what I would have done to you for it?"

"It doesn't matter," she whispered. "Please."

"No." He shook his head. "Don't treat yourself like this."

"It's not me!" she pleaded. "Terrible things have happened to me."

"And I'm one of them."

"No!" she insisted. Probably, the Observer said, indifferent.

"Don't you see that you keep putting yourself in harm's way? That's why you want me."

"It's my choice!"

"And you taught your son to do it too."

Maggie covered her ears. "Stop!" she shouted.

"No," he said. "Now you'll listen to me. I thought you wanted me to save you, save Mac, but the truth is that's not what you're looking for. You look in your internal mirror and you say, what is that? What is that thing? You don't recognize it as yourself, and you certainly don't recognize it as anything of value. So you make choices to destroy it. You make choices to make others help you destroy it. I can't do that. I can't be that brutal, sadistic thing you use to destroy yourself. You saw the weapon inside me and tried to push me away when you were still able to. But I wouldn't go, and I insisted on coming back and coming back until it was too late. And now I have to save you from me. I'm sorry I hung on too long."

"You could take care of Mac," she said.

"No," he replied, "that's your job."

"I'm sorry, I'm sorry." She sounded like a child. "I'll do better. Please don't leave me." She clung to him again.

"If you really love me," he said sadly, "let me go." He kissed her cheek.

Maggie felt the wetness. She felt a cold, cold breeze on the back of her neck. It gave her chills, and then her head started to shake involuntarily. Her breathing got shallow and her field of vision narrowed.

"Maggie?" JD shook her slightly. Her eyes were not focusing. "What's going on?" JD shook her harder.

"Stop," she said. "Stop shaking me."

"I'm not." He tried to hold on to her. "It's you. You're shaking all over."

"I'm wet," she said, her teeth chattering. "My clothes are wet." As she spoke, her voice became panicky. "My clothes are wet! I shouldn't be wet." She struggled to break his grip. She needed to run away.

"Here," he said. "We'll get them off." Maggie was as stiff as an unjointed doll. The Observer watched as JD efficiently stripped off her clothes.

When she was down to her underwear JD pulled her out of the shower and wrapped her in a towel, rubbing her hard as he dried her off, trying to warm her. She continued to shake so violently he was briefly afraid she was having a seizure. He held her slightly away so he could see her eyes. They were watching something so terrifying that he took an involuntary look over his shoulder. The only thing there was the shower door, drops of water slowly trickling down, coalescing, joining into ever bigger globes until, doomed by their own weight, they skittered toward the floor and fractured apart.

JD led Maggie out of the bathroom. He put her into his bed, wrapping the comforter around her. "Frozen Margarita," he said. "You're so cold you're nearly blue. Stay here under the covers. I need to throw your clothes in the dryer, and I'll make you something hot to drink. I'll be right back." He waited a minute, and when Maggie did not respond, he left the room.

In her mind, she was not there for the time JD was gone. She was not anywhere. When he came back with a steaming cup of tea, she had to work hard to make herself return. He set the cup down on the night table and put an arm behind her to help her sit up.

"Holy shit," he said, "you're like a corpse." He climbed into bed beside her and held her to him, rubbing her arms, trying to warm her up.

Finally the shivering subsided a little. "Thank you," she murmured. "I was cold."

"What was that all about?" he asked.

"Nothing," she said, her voice weak. "I was just cold."

"Tell me what happened," JD whispered. "You were terrified."

Maggie was confused. "I got cold."

"I'm a cop," he said. "I know when people are scared. Tell me what scared you."

She stiffened. "Nothing scared me," she answered. "I got cold."

"Okay," he said. He pulled her up tight against him.

"Stop!" she said, sounding panicky again.

JD held his hands up in the air. "Sorry," he said. "You be in charge."

"I'm no good at touching," Maggie said. "I can't let anybody touch me."

"You need to warm up," he said. "I'm afraid you're going into shock."

Maggie moved closer to him then, very gradually, until her body was next to his. She couldn't find a comfortable place to put her head, so she finally laid it on his shoulder. But it was his left shoulder, and she knew she was hurting him, so she didn't protest as he shifted slightly underneath her, moving her head lower down on his chest. When he was still again, she could hear his heart beating, right below her ear. It was odd, she thought, drifting now, how different this heart sounded from the thousands she had listened to during her life, as if there was a message here for her. It made her feel sleepy. Just as she was on the edge of letting go, she heard JD talking, very softly. "Maggie," he said, "can you feel me breathing?"

"Yes." Her voice was the merest whisper.

"Breathe with me." It was too much trouble. She was too sleepy. "Come on," he urged her quietly. "Slow breath in. Long breath out. Don't think about anything but the breathing. Clear your mind. Just breathe."

"Are you trying to hypnotize me?" she asked groggily.

"Shh," he said. "I need you to follow me somewhere. I need you not to be afraid." He paused a moment, breathing slowly with her, leading her. "Can you do that for me?"

"Yes," Maggie said, so relaxed it came out sounding like a faint hiss of air.

"Good. Let's just keep breathing for a while."

Maggie floated. The Observer was watching, but quietly, also resting. Maggie felt like she was totally in control. The Observer would not think anything she didn't want it to. All Maggie wanted now was to please JD, to do whatever he asked.

"Maggie," his voice came from far away, "take me back. Take me back to when you were a little girl." Maggie was quiet. "Tell me what was nice."

"Swimming in the lake. Swimming was nice. There were fireworks on July fourth."

"What else was nice?"

"Daniel was nice."

"What about school? Was school nice?"

"The uniforms made her mad. Every morning she had to iron it and make sure the shoes were clean, or the nuns would notice. If they thought she wasn't doing a good job, they might call Doc and then Doc would be mad. She didn't want Doc to be mad at her. Doc would hit her if she made him mad. But the work made her mad. So she told Margaret to do the work."

"Who didn't like all that work?" JD asked from far away.

"The mother."

"Did you make her mad?"

Maggie's voice was very small. "Margaret made her mad. She didn't mean to."

"It's okay," JD said. He began lightly scratching her back, moving his hand in gentle circles until she relaxed again.

Sometime later, Maggie gradually became aware that JD was calling her. She wanted to roll over, but she couldn't move. "Are you floating now?" he asked.

"Yes." She felt very relaxed.

"Let's talk some more about when you were a little girl."

"Okay." Maggie's voice sounded syrupy.

"Tell me about when you were happy."

"When Doc took me to the office on Saturday. Everyone acted like I was special. I'm going to be a doctor when I grow up."

"Everyone was nice to you at Doc's office."

"Yes."

"But people weren't always nice to you."

"No."

"Tell me about that."

Maggie did not want to, but she had no choice. It was too hard not to do what JD said. He was being so nice. She wanted him to be nice to her. She didn't want to make him mad too, like other people got mad. She thought about when people weren't nice. She remembered when she was eight or nine. The other children thought she was scary. Grown-ups didn't like her because she always said the truth, even when it embarrassed them. She didn't mean to make people mad at her. When she did, it was always by mistake. But it happened anyway. "The other kids were mean," she said.

"What did they do?"

"Carol Ann had a doll. The soft rubber kind, shaped like a bowling pin, and when you squeeze it, the eyes and tongue and ears pop out of its head. She wrote, 'Margaret' on it. When Sister wasn't looking, she would pull it out and squeeze it and everyone would look at me and laugh."

"And nobody ever stopped her?"

"The kids thought it was funny."

"What about the grown-ups? Didn't they care?"

"You mustn't cry. No matter what they do, you mustn't cry."

"Maybe they didn't know."

"They knew. Grown-ups always know."

"Did you tell them?" Maggie stiffened. JD's voice got very quiet. "It's okay," he said, starting to scratch her back again. "Let's float for a while."

Maggie relaxed. She was drifting again. "You can't tell them," she mumbled. "You know what will happen if you tell them." She drifted for a while, and then JD was back with her.

"Tell me about when you got in all the trouble," he said. Maggie did not answer. "Do you remember getting in trouble?"

"No," she said groggily.

"When you got very wet."

"I don't remember," Maggie said.

"Okay," JD said. "Tell me a story about a little girl who comes home wet and what happens to her."

Maggie was quiet. She tried to think of the story. You had to stay quiet in the classroom, or Sister would slap your hands with her ruler. It was spring-time. It was warm enough to go to school without a coat some days, but it still got dark early, especially when the weather was bad. Today started out warm and sunny, but after lunch the sky got all dark, like the clouds were rolling in dirt. Margaret was glad to come inside from the playground after lunch. Halfway through catechism, the storm began. She was in first grade then. She knew she was different already, but the other kids didn't know yet.

"Who was so angry with you, Maggie?" JD's voice distracted her, but not quite enough to bring her out.

It took her a while to decide where she was looking from. "Mother," she finally said.

"Did you know she would be so angry?"

"You couldn't know. Sometimes she would not be angry. Sometimes she didn't care."

"What happened this time?"

"I don't know."

They rested quietly. "Tell me about the day," JD began.

"The kids were in religion class and the sky got really dark." Maggie spoke in a monotone, as if she were a child who had just learned to read and did not recognize the emotion clues embedded in the story. "Then there was thunder and lightning. Some of the kids started to cry. The little girl wanted to cry too, but Sister told them to stop behaving like babies, so Margaret didn't cry. First there was hail, and then a lot of wind, and then some tree branches hit the window. Some of the children screamed, so Sister smacked some desks with her ruler and the children stopped. Then the rain came. It sounded like stones when it hit the windows. And it rained and rained until the last bell rang. Some people went to the coat closet, but most of them didn't. Everybody was scared.

"When they went out into the foyer, some of the mothers were there. Usu-ally the kids just walked home, but the storm was bad and the mothers came to take the children home."

"Was your mother there?"

Maggie paused. "Margaret's mother was not there."

"Were you scared to go home alone?"

"Margaret was not allowed to leave. Sister said it was too dangerous to go out with the lightning and the trees falling, so no one could leave until a mother came to take them home."

"So you waited."

"Yes. Margaret waited."

"Did everyone's mother come?"

"No. Some of the other mothers took someone else home."

"But no one took you."

"Margaret wasn't friends with other children. Her mother was not friends with the mothers. Margaret tried to look at the mothers when they took the other kids home, but they wouldn't look back at her. She was invisible."

"So what happened to her?"

"Sister told her to wait by the door. Then Sister went away and Margaret stood there and waited and waited, like she was supposed to."

"Were you scared then?"

"Margaret always did what she was told when she was little."

"Did anybody else come?"

"No."

"It must have gotten pretty late."

"It was almost dark out, but the streetlights weren't on yet. The janitor came to lock the doors. 'What're you doing here?' he asked. 'Sister told me to wait until my mother comes to get me,' Margaret said. He said, 'Don't look like she's coming. You want to come to the office and call her?' Margaret didn't know her phone number, but she was afraid to say so. She was supposed to know it, but she was scared and she forgot it. So she said, 'No.' The janitor said, 'I have to lock up. But I'll be back soon, and then you can come home with me.'"

"What happened then?" JD asked, very gently.

"Margaret didn't want to go with him. She told him Sister said she had to stay there."

JD's voice seemed very far away. "What did he do?"

"Mother Superior came by on her way out, and the janitor went away. She asked Margaret why she was still there. Margaret told her Sister said she had to stay until Margaret's mother came. Mother Superior said it was very late, and Margaret should go home."

"And did you?"

"Margaret went outside. She was very scared. It was dark and cold and raining very hard." Maggie shook slightly as she spoke. "Margaret walked down the school steps. She tried to take her time. Sister always punished children for running. But she was too scared, so she started to run. She ran fast, but she was so scared she didn't know if she was going the right way. Then she heard a noise in the bushes, right next to her, and she started running again and it was so dark she couldn't see anything, but she kept running. Then she tripped and fell off the curb and landed in a cold, cold puddle, deep water going fast into a drain. All her things, her picture of the red cardinal, and her spelling work and her lunch box went all over the place and some of her things got sucked into the drain and she just sat there in the cold water, crying and crying. There was too much water and she couldn't get up. Some of her favorite things were gone down the drain."

"So what did she do?"

"Nobody came. She waited and nobody came. So she stopped crying and picked up the stuff that was left. She was wet all over and her knees were scraped up and they hurt. And she was so cold."

"But she was okay."

"No," she said eerily. "My shoes. I was scared about my shoes. They were too wet. They squished every time I walked. They would never believe it was an accident. They would think Margaret did it on purpose. She hated those ugly gray lace-up shoes like the nuns wore. The girls were allowed to wear pretty shoes with their uniforms. All the other girls had them. Carol Ann had shiny patent leather ones. But Doc said the gray shoes were more practical and they were cheaper, so that's what Margaret had to get. I pitched a fit about it. I said I would throw them away if he made me wear them. Doc got very mad when Margaret said that, so *she* got really mad at Margaret too. She gave Margaret a beating for making Doc mad. She would think I ruined them on purpose."

"She? You mean your mother?"

"Yes."

"So you were afraid to let your mother know about the shoes."

"Yes."

"But you went home anyway."

"Where else could the girl go? She was scared."

"What happened when she got there?"

"She ran the rest of the way. She fell down a couple more times but she was so scared of the dark she just kept going. It took a long time."

"Was she waiting for Margaret to get home? The mother? Was she worried?"

Maggie tried to think about this. "Nobody worried about Margaret," she finally said.

"So what happened when you got home?"

"The house was dark. Margaret was still scared of the storm outside, and she was scared of the dark inside too, but she was also glad. If the house was dark, maybe she would get a chance to fix everything before the mother found out."

"Margaret went into the back door, into the mud room. She would squeeze all the water out of things and then hide them in her closet. They would be good as new tomorrow. So she took off her blouse and her jumper and she held them over the washtub and squeezed and squeezed. She didn't do a very good job, because she was too little and the water ran down her arms and onto the floor, but she got out all the water she could. Then she took off her shoes and socks. She put her socks in the hamper, because that's where dirty socks go."

"And her shoes?"

"Her shoes were bad. There was too much water in them. Squeezing didn't help. It was dirty water. It was making a mess in the tub and all over Margaret, and what if the mother came in and caught her? So Margaret decided to take the shoes upstairs and put them in the closet with the rest of the uniform and tomorrow she could pretend they were fine."

"So that's what you did?"

"I started to go upstairs, but the house was so dark I couldn't see anything. So I switched on the living room light." Maggie stopped suddenly.

"What did you see?" JD urged her softly.

"Margaret was behind the couch. She could see over the back of it, and the coffee table had bottles and dirty glasses and a full ashtray." Maggie shuddered.

"What else do you see?" JD asked gently.

"She was sleeping on the couch. The light woke her up." Maggie took a deep breath. Her voice got high and tense. "She looks like a monster. Her hair is all a mess, and the makeup around her eyes and her lipstick are all smeary. She's yelling at me, but I can't hear what she's saying because I'm too scared. Her yells are smashing into me. I back up. And all I'm wearing are my undershirt and panties, and I'm so embarrassed, because we don't see each other like that in our house, and I am so ugly and now she will hate me even more. I need to cover myself up before she sees me. I hold up my hands to cover myself and she sees everything." Maggie's voice got very strained. "She sees the uniform all a mess, and the shoes."

Maggie stopped and lay there quietly. She saw nothing. She did not see JD pinch the bridge of his nose, hard. Maggie continued. "She grabbed my arm, and then she grabbed one of the shoes and she started to hit me with the shoe. She hit my face and my arm and my back and all over." Her voice was even now.

"Were you crying?" JD asked, his voice filled with a sharp-edged foreboding.

"No," Maggie said. "I was not crying. Margaret was crying. But she stopped, when her tooth came out. She thought her nose was running, but when she tried to wipe it, there was blood. Then she saw there was blood on her under-shirt, and that made her cry again. 'You're getting blood all over everything!' the mother screamed, and she pulled Margaret out to the back porch and yelled at her to stay there and locked the door."

"Margaret is safe now," JD said.

"No," Maggie said. "She is not safe. She is crying. She is sitting on the back porch and someone might come by and see her like this, crying in her underwear, and she will be so ashamed." She began to rock slightly.

"Let me bring someone to take care of you," JD said helplessly.

"Yes," Maggie said. "Here is Annabelle."

"Will Annabelle help you?" JD asked.

"Yes," Maggie said, almost sounding happy. "Annabelle is lost too. No one wants her."

"Is she your friend?"

"Yes. She is the kitten," Maggie said. "She is Margaret's secret. When no one is looking, they play in the garden together, behind the rain barrels. Margaret saves some dinner for her. That's why the mother says she is so fat, because she takes extra food. She hides it in her napkin, and puts her napkin in her pocket and brings the food out behind the rain barrels for Annabelle." Maggie took a deep breath. "Annabelle is cold too. We'll cuddle up very tight together, so we can stay warm. Wait Annabelle!" she suddenly called. "Wait! Don't go away!"

"What's the matter?" JD asked. "Where is Annabelle going?"

"Oh, no," Maggie said anxiously. "Oh, no. She is trying to get away. Ow! She scratched my arm!"

"What happened? What scared her?"

"Doc," Maggie whispered. "She hears Doc coming."

"Can you tell him you need help?"

"No. The mother told us to stay here. Be quiet!" she ordered. "So he won't notice us."

"What does he say when he sees you?" JD asked.

"He is very angry. Now Margaret is really scared. She has made Doc angry too. 'How did this happen?' he asked, but Margaret will not tell him. 'Get up,' he says. 'I have to stay here,' Margaret whispers. Doc pulls her up by her arm and takes her into the house. They go through the mudroom and into the kitchen. 'Get in here!' he yells. The mother comes into the kitchen. Doc lets go of Margaret. 'You did this to her?' he asks, and the mother doesn't say anything, she just takes a puff on her cigarette." Maggie stopped suddenly. JD did not breathe.

When Maggie started again, her voice was without intonation. "Doc hits the mother," she continued. "He hits her so hard, she gets a cut on her cheek and she falls against the refrigerator. Her cigarette goes across the room and lands on the table, near the napkins, and nobody notices except Margaret. But Margaret is afraid to move. So if the cigarette starts a fire and the house burns down, that will be her fault too. Doc picks the mother up by the front of her dress, and he starts to shake her, and her head goes back and forth like she's a broken puppet. He is madder than the mother ever gets. 'If you ever do anything like this to her again, if you ever lay a hand on her again, I will put you in the nuthouse, where you belong!' he shouts. 'Do you understand?' The mother laughs at him. So he hits her again. 'I mean it,' he says, and then he just lets go and the mother falls on the floor. 'Come with me,' he says to Margaret, and she goes with him upstairs and into the bathroom. It hurts when Doc touches her face and he tells her to be still, he has to clean her up. 'Put on your nightgown and get in bed,' he says. 'What about my kitten?' Margaret asks. 'She can take care of herself,' Doc says. He is still very mad."

"Is that it?" JD asked.

"Is that what?"

"Does the mother ever hit her again?"

"Not until she is big enough to hit back."

JD exhaled. "So Margaret is safe now?"

"Yes," Maggie said. "Now Margaret is safe."

JD began to lightly scratch her back again. "Let's rest for a while."

"That's good," Maggie said. "We need to rest."

𝓇   𝓇   𝓇

"Maggie." JD's voice was soft, almost a singsong. "Are you still cold?"

When Maggie answered, her voice was that of a little girl. "Where is Annabelle?"

"Hm?" JD responded.

"Where is my kitten? Where is Annabelle?" Her voice changed to a strange, raspy alto. "Come here," she continued. "Do you have Annabelle?" the childish voice asked. "Come with me," the alto voice answered. "I have something to show you."

Margaret followed Mother off the back porch. Her face felt stiff and it hurt in places. It was much later than she usually woke up. The sun looked like it was Saturday morning outside, not a school day. "Am I going to be late for school?" she asked. Mother did not turn around or answer. She just kept walking toward the back of the yard until she reached the white picket fence around the garden.

The fence was almost as tall as Margaret's chest, but it only came up to the top of Mother's thigh. She turned around. "Come along," she said. Margaret did not move. "Do you want to see or not?" Mother asked. Mother did not make surprises for her. Maybe this was something special.

Mother opened the gate and walked inside. Margaret followed her. They went along the border of the garden, passing the lettuce and the broccoli, the freshly turned earth where the beets had just been planted, and then to the very back, where the earth was still waiting to be prepared for the later season vegetables, the tomatoes and peppers and beans. Behind that were the two barrels where Doc collected the rain that he used to water the garden. After yesterday's storm, the barrels were really full.

Mother stood by the barrels. "Come here," she said again. "Closer." Margaret came over, walking slow. "Would you like to be surprised?" she asked. Margaret nodded. She wasn't sure, but she didn't want to make Mother mad.

There was an upside-down bucket behind the barrels. Mother stuck her hand under it and Margaret heard a desperate mewling. Margaret's stomach hurt. Mother's eyes were staring at her so hard that when she smiled she looked like a witch. "Can you guess what I have here?" she asked. Margaret shook her head. "Are you sure?" Mother asked again. "Because you know what happens to little girls who lie."

"Annabelle?" Margaret whispered.

"Annabelle?" Mother repeated. "Who is Annabelle?"

"My kitten," Margaret breathed.

Mother pulled her hand out. She had Annabelle squeezed tight in her fist.

"Stop!" Margaret said. "You're hurting her!"

"Do you love her?" Mother asked. Margaret nodded yes. "I can't hear you!" Mother said. Margaret started to cry. "No crying!" Mother shouted. "Do you love her?"

"Yes!" Margaret yelled. Mother took her hand holding the kitten and plunged it into one of the rainwater barrels. "Stop!" Margaret screamed.

Mother took her hand out of the barrel. Annabelle was screaming too. She scratched at Mother's hand and made it bleed. "Do you love her?" Mother asked again.

"Yes!" Margaret screamed.

Mother plunged her hand back in the rain barrel. Margaret was crying too hard to yell anything. "Do you want me to stop?" Mother asked. Margaret shook her head yes. "What do you have to do to make me stop?" Mother asked.

Margaret was too afraid to think.

Mother lifted her hand out of the barrel just long enough for Annabelle to cry, then she put it back in again. "Are you going to tell your father on me again?" Mother asked.

Margaret shook her head as hard as she could.

"Are you sure?" Mother asked. "You have to be sure."

"I'm sure!" Margaret screamed.

Mother lifted her hand out of the barrel and threw Annabelle at Margaret. Margaret tried to grab her, but Annabelle clawed at her arms and scratched her chest. Margaret dropped her and Annabelle ran away.

Margaret ran toward Mother. "I hate you!" she screamed, pounding on Mother. Mother grabbed her wrists and held them tight in one hand. With her other hand she forced Margaret's head toward the barrel. Margaret could not scream; she could not breathe. She tried to hold her head back. That made everything worse.

"Look," Mother said. "Look what you've done."

Mother forced her face into the barrel. Margaret pushed hard against Mother's hand. What if her face went in the water? She was going to hold her breath, but then she saw it in the water. It looked like a baby, but not like a real baby. It was too little, and its head was too big. Its arms and legs were too skinny. Margaret started to scream. Mother was going to put her face in the water and kill her like that baby thing! Mother pushed her hard and her face went into the cold water, but it was not like swimming, she was not ready and she breathed and water came up her nose and into her mouth and it hurt, it hurt, it hurt. It burned all inside her. And then Mother pulled her face out of the water. Margaret was coughing and choking and crying. Mother was saying something, but Margaret didn't care.

"Be quiet!" Mother said in her witchy voice. Margaret tried to stop coughing. "Do you want me to put you in the barrel like that baby?"

Margaret shook her head. She started to cry again.

"If you ever tell him, that's what I will do" Mother gave Margaret's neck a shake. "He thinks it's a sin to get rid of a baby. But it's his sin, not mine. He's the one who hit me. And yours. You made him do it. You shouldn't have told. Now the sin is on you."

Margaret made a scary sound because she was trying so hard to breathe. The hurt places on her face were burning.

"Stop it," Mother warned her. "Don't ever cry again. If you cry, he will know something's the matter. And then you'll have to tell him about the baby. But you can't do that, can you, Babykiller?"

Margaret closed her mouth tight so no sound would come out. She tried to shake her head, but Mother's hand on the back of her neck was like a claw.

"You'll never cry again, will you?" Mother asked.

Margaret didn't say yes or no. She didn't want Mother to put her face back in the barrel.

"Remember," Mother said. "You made him hit me. You are the Babykiller." She let go of Margaret's neck and pushed her away. Then she picked up the bucket and scooped the dead baby out of the water. "This is your fault," she said. "If you ever stop being careful he'll find out you did this." She took the bucket and went away into the house.

Margaret didn't want to be here, but she didn't know where to go. She was too afraid to go back in the house with Mother. She wanted to cry, but now she knew she must never do that again. Maybe if she was very quiet magic would happen and Annabelle would come back. So she stayed hiding behind the rain barrels. After a while she started thinking about other things and she forgot that she wanted to cry. Then her knees started to hurt. She was very cold in her nightgown. What if a neighbor came and saw her? So she decided she had to go inside.

She was very quiet. She needed to sneak past Mother. But then she saw that Mother was on her couch, asleep, with her bottles on the table. Margaret went upstairs to her room. Her uniform and her shoes were still wet, but she got dressed in them because this was a school day. Then she sat on her bed. Nothing happened for a very long time. It got dark out. She heard Doc come home. Then she heard him walking up the stairs. He opened her door and the light came in from the hallway. "Why are you sitting there like that?" he asked.

Margaret did not answer.

"Everything go okay today?" he asked.

Margaret stared at him. She knew all about sins. They were studying for First Holy Communion at school. She did not want to go to Purgatory like the baby thing, or spend all eternity with the Devil.

"Margaret," Doc said, "what happened with your mother, it would be best if we never speak about it. Just put it to the back of your mind and try to forget it. Do you understand?"

Margaret nodded.

🦅　🦅　🦅

"Hey, Maggie." JD was standing over her. "Time to wake up." Maggie was having a hard time remembering where she was. She sat up. "Hey," he said. "It's okay. Remember, your clothes got wet?"

She rubbed her face with her hands. "What time is it?"

"Here, I've got your clothes. Everything's dry now."

"Okay," she said, taking her stuff. He started to turn away. "JD?" she said, "What happened?"

"You fell asleep for a while. But it's time for you to get home now. I figured you'd want to be there when Mac gets home from his first day back at school."

"Oh," Maggie said, feeling stupid. How could she have forgotten about that? "Of course. Thanks." He left the room and she dressed quickly. When she got downstairs, he was in the kitchen. He had a brush and dustpan, and he was dumping the broken glass from the vestibule window into the trash. "I'm sorry," Maggie said. "I did that."

"Don't worry about it."

"No, really. Just send me the bill."

"Forget it," he said. "It'll take me three minutes to fix it." He took her purse from the table and handed it to her. "Keys in here?" he asked.

"You in a hurry to get rid of me?" she replied, hoping it sounded like a joke.

"Nope." He shook his head.

She began to walk to the door, then stopped. Turning to look at him, she asked softly, "Was it a dream?"

"What's that?"

"Nothing," she said. She felt totally disoriented. It was as if the day had somehow come unglued from the calendar and couldn't match itself back up with anywhere it belonged. Without saying anything else, she went out and got in her car. She was most of the way home before she glanced at the clock on the dashboard. It was only 11:30.

54

It was nearly five when Mac came in the door. He had stayed for band practice, even though it was his first day back at school, even though Mr. Don was still in rehab, even though nobody would have held it against him if he'd chosen not to. When he left in the morning, before all of Maggie's energy was focused on trying to keep her weight off the sharp edge of the razor blade on which she now balanced, she had not wanted him to stay for practice. Now she barely noticed he was late.

The surrealistic dream she had at JD's house seemed to have infiltrated her reality even though she couldn't remember it. The only thing that displaced it was a growing apprehension that JD might still have gone away. Somewhere during the afternoon she realized he never said anything about changing his mind. The phone hadn't rung. If he still wanted to be with them, he would have been here starting dinner by now.

Maggie went to the kitchen when she heard Mac come in. His head was already in the refrigerator. "How did everything go?" she asked.

He stepped back and closed the fridge. She could tell from the way he looked at her that she didn't sound right. "It was cool," he said, still staring at her.

"That's it?" she asked, trying to lighten things up. "It was cool?"

"Sure."

"Nobody baked you a cake or anything?" she joked feebly.

"Nah," he said, opening the fridge again. "It wasn't a big deal."

Maggie realized this was true. Ten weeks ago represented a whole different era in the timeline of a teenager. Except for the kids who had been directly traumatized, life had long since returned to an energetic hormone-fueled hum. Even the band kids had settled back into a comforting routine. The Board of Ed provided a trailer for their practices, and the substitute filling in for Mr. Don took his role seriously.

"How was band practice?" Maggie asked.

Mac was stuffing a square of American cheese into his mouth. "I was kind of nervous about going. But Morsel kept giving me a hard time until I finally went."

"Did people act uncomfortable?"

"Yeah," he said, pulling out a chair and sitting down at the table. "When I first walked in, everybody got quiet. That really spooked me. Then Jayme got up and came over and walked to the drums with me. Everybody was watching. I sat down and then I knew I had to pick up the drumsticks." He stopped and took a deep breath. "Jayme handed me one and then she put the other one in my left hand and wrapped my fingers around it. I was really afraid I'd drop it."

"Did you?"

"No. And then she went back to her chair and everybody just kind of rustled around like they were getting ready to play, and then the sub held up his baton and we started."

"How'd you do?"

Mac looked at her and his face glowed. "I started to play and everybody else stopped, like they got some kind of cue. So then I stopped too. And they all started to clap. So I started to play again. And then somebody stood up, so they all stood up and they kept clapping."

Maggie sat down at the table with him. "And you kept playing?" she asked, even though the words hurt as she said them.

"Hell yes," Mac grinned. "It was the worst I've ever played in my whole life and I got a standing ovation. Why wouldn't I keep playing?"

🎵 🎵 🎵

Sometime later Maggie realized she had to make something for dinner. If JD hadn't shown up by now, he wasn't going to. She pulled a package of lasagna out of the freezer and stuck it in the oven without reading the instructions. Then she sat down at the table and rested her head on her arms. The spine-scraping blare of the smoke detector woke her. There was black smoke coming out of the vents at the back of the stove, and her eyes were tearing. "Shit!" she yelled, and leapt to open the oven door.

"Stop!" a deep masculine voice yelled. It took her a moment to realize it was Mac. "Don't open the door yet, just turn the oven off!" Maggie did not move. Mac reached around her and shut off the oven. Then he grabbed a box of baking soda from the overhead cabinet. He struggled to open it. Maggie did not try to help. Finally, he managed to pull the pour spout off. Opening the oven door, he threw baking soda onto the flaming foil tray of lasagna. "Why didn't you take the top off before you put it in?" he demanded.

"I'm sorry," Maggie said.

"You can't put paper in the oven."

"I know. I'm sorry."

Mac looked at her. "Are you okay?"

"Yes," she said. "Everything's fine. I just screwed up."

"Where's JD?" he asked. "He usually shows up by now."

There it was. The dreaded question. The one she couldn't answer, because she didn't know the answer. Except that it was all her fault. Now she would have to break Mac's heart, as well as her own. "JD's not coming," she said softly.

"Oh," Mac said. "Okay. You mind if I go hang out with Morsel?"

"No," she said, feeling hollow. "That's fine."

ɾ   ɾ   ɾ

Mac was spending a lot of time with Morsel again. He was still kind of weirded out that somehow Morsel and Jayme had become friends. It seemed unnatural, like a fairy tale where the princess decides to become friends with the toad instead of turning it into a prince. But he had to admit it was working out. It saved him from having to choose between them. What was even more strange was that girls loved Morsel now. Somehow, while Mac was absent from school, he'd become a kind of folk hero.

It was too bad the one he picked for a girlfriend made Mac so uncomfortable. From the back, she kind of looked like Jayme, with the same long blonde hair. But she was totally boring. All she cared about was herself and whatever trendy thing caught her attention. Jayme told him people pretended she was okay because of her car. They figured they could ignore her if they got a chance to ride around in it. Since Mac was getting that chance, he knew they were wrong. But as long as he was with Jayme he really didn't mind what they ended up doing.

Today Morsel decided they needed to go for a walk in the woods behind Milton's Retreat. But as soon as the girlfriend parked her fire engine red Hummer in the castle's lot Morsel said, "Catch you later," and the two of them disappeared. It didn't look like they were coming back any time soon. Mac was relieved that Jayme didn't think it was a big deal. She took his hand, the good one, and led him into the woods, to a small clearing surrounded by trees and thick undergrowth. He wondered how she knew about this spot, but decided it was better not to ask. They sat on a fallen log. Mac figured some kind of making out came next, he just wasn't sure how to get there.

"I'm sorry about your arm," Jayme said.

"Yeah," he replied. "Me too."

And then, without warning, Jayme reached over and very gently touched the right side of his head. His hair had grown back, so it didn't look like anything had happened to him if you ignored his arm. "Can I see?" Jayme asked. "I mean, where you got shot?"

Mac shrugged. It wasn't something he would've asked someone, but lots of things Jayme did seemed inexplicable to him. She took his silence for consent. Very gingerly, she moved his hair aside, then stood up to look closer. She lost her balance. She leaned into him, and he could feel her breasts against his shoulder and the right side of his chest. He took a deep breath, thinking that would help him stay in control. It only made him dizzier. She touched the spot softly with her lips.

Mac knew what was coming next. Jayme was still leaning against him, holding his hand. He could smell her shampoo. At least he thought it was her shampoo. Then she got so close he had to close his eyes, and that was when it happened. Her lips were on his mouth. They felt really soft on the outside, but firm underneath, maybe like what hot dogs would feel like if they were velvety instead of slimy and you pressed them against your mouth instead of taking a bite. Mac felt like a whole packet of Pop Rocks was going off in his stomach. Only it wasn't his stomach, exactly. It was lower down, just not *there.* Jayme stopped kissing him for a minute, and he was actually relieved. He needed to breathe and swallow. Only he didn't open his eyes, and the next thing he knew, she was kissing him again, but this time on the neck, right under his ear. He felt sparklers going off inside his head. This felt so good! He grabbed her and kissed her hard on the mouth. He was starting to get a boner and he didn't care if she figured it out.

꙳   ꙳   ꙳

Maggie was tired. She had anticipated that once Mac was back in school, she would be able to relax. Instead, she seemed incapable of shutting down, ever. If only she could sleep. But every time she tried, she was unsuccessful. Or at least that's how it felt. She would finally fall off, exhausted, only to be awakened with a shock that bolted her upright from her bed, some wraith of madness striking and disappearing before she could even crash through the wall of consciousness. Then, too fatigued to remain standing, she would collapse back onto the bed as if someone had unplugged her. The cycle kept repeating until her brain used up whatever chemicals enabled her to fall asleep in the first place. Then she would roam the house like a specter, no longer of the world of the living, but having no other place to light. At one point, fairly early on in the process, when the Observer had still been functioning it said, "You are very depressed. You should tell someone." It was a relief that there was no one to tell. Mac was already so thoroughly assimilated back into his own life that he was rarely around. That was the way it was supposed to be. He was meant to grow up, to grow beyond her, to be whole and enmeshed in his own universe. Healthy children outgrew their need for parents.

They could do just fine with adult friends. Normal adult friends. JD could be Mac's friend.

The more she thought about this, the more it seemed like a really good idea. It was so hard to think anymore, to follow some train of thought to a destination, any destination. But this thought was whole and complete, and it did not go away. So she clung to it. If JD and Mac were together maybe that would bring her peace. She focused on this, as she had been unable to focus on anything else for the past few days. She did not notice the shift in angle or color of the sunlight as the day progressed, nor was she affected anymore by the numbers on the clock. She paced around, mostly in a way that was physically driven, without intent. And occasionally she would find her way back to her comforting thought.

Today, as the afternoon wore on, she became more and more tired. She sat now and then, only to be impelled from whatever perch she had taken and thrown back into her pacing. She needed to rest, she had to rest, she wanted to go to the place where she could get a firm grip on her comforting thought. She went into the bathroom and opened the medicine cabinet. One by one, she examined the containers, removing those that met the criteria. Labeled in Spanish and English, purchased over the Internet, prescribed for MacDonald Rifkin by Dr. Margaret MacDonald, who had once been enough in touch with reality to maintain a current medical license and DEA number, there was everything an injured mind could need. Oxycontin, Prozac, Xanax, Ambien, generics for various sedatives, anxiolytics, painkillers. She lined the pill bottles up on the front edge of her sink. Most of them were still full. You shouldn't think about this, the Observer said. Or maybe it said, what are you waiting for? Maybe it was the voice of Mother. Just take the pills.

ɾ   ɾ   ɾ

Morsel's new girlfriend, Chrissie, pulled her red Humvee up to the entrance of the alley. "Get out here," she commanded.

"Why?" Morsel asked crossly. "You can't take us to our houses?"

"No," she said, picking at one of her acrylic fingernails. "I can't back this thing up in tight spaces."

"Fine," Morsel said, as if it wasn't, and hopped out. Mac was about to follow when Jayme grabbed his right arm. She leaned over and planted a kiss on his mouth. To his surprise, her mouth was open and the kiss was kind of sloppy. He generally thought spit was gross. In fact, that was one of the reasons he'd avoided taking up a wind instrument. And yet, somehow this kiss was making him get hard. He opened his door and jumped out. "See ya," he said, slamming the door, desperately hoping his jeans were baggy enough to provide adequate cover. Chrissie gunned the engine and pulled away, not waiting for Jayme to move into the front seat.

"Your new girlfriend is a pretty big bitch," Mac said conversationally.

"Really?" Morsel asked. "I didn't notice. She doesn't have much to say, you know, with her mouth full most of the time."

Mac looked at him in disbelief. "Nuh-uh," he said. "You got fellatio?"

"I got *what*?" Morsel said incredulously. "What the hell is that?"

"Never mind," Mac said, blushing.

"Hey," Morsel asked, "did you get any?"

"Any what?"

"You know." He rolled his eyes.

"We just kissed a little."

"What a loser," Morsel replied. "You should use the gimp thing. What's the point in having it if you don't get full value?" They walked toward their houses. "You want to stay over again?" Morsel asked.

"Sure," Mac said. "Just let me go tell my mom."

"So when she kissed you," Morsel said, pointing to the vicinity of Mac's left side, "did your arm spaz out?"

"What?" That stopped Mac in his tracks.

"Your arm, dude. Did it fly all over the place and shake?"

"Shut up, jerk."

"Hey," Morsel said, "don't get mad. I think the arm thing is pretty cool."

Mac gave him a withering look. "You would. You're not stuck with it for the rest of your life."

"You don't get it," Morsel said. "It's still your arm, you know? It's still part of you. It's like me being short because nobody ever got my back fixed. I could hate it, but it's just who I am. If I hate it, I hate me."

ɾ ɾ ɾ

Mac walked in the back door. Penelope ran over and jumped up on him. "Hey, girl," he said, scratching her head. He pushed her down, which only made her more determined to jump up. They tussled for a few minutes before Mac called, "Mom?" The house seemed awfully quiet, but things had been like that lately. He didn't just want to tell his mom he was sleeping over at Morsel's, he kind of wanted to check up on her. She was being wifty lately. Sometimes when he talked to her, it was like she was looking at something inside her own head instead of at him. The past few days especially, he'd begun to notice that they'd be talking about one thing and she'd answer as if they were talking about something else. And he heard her, walking around at night. He guessed maybe things had been pretty hard on her. Maybe he shouldn't sleep over at Morsel's after all.

"Come on, girl," he said to Penelope, and led her out onto the patio so she could roam around the fenced side yard. There was no sign of his mother out there, even though it was a beautiful day. He went back inside via the den and then through the living room. The house was *too* quiet. It made him feel prickly and jumpy, as if he was in a movie and the evil thing was waiting around the corner. "Mom?" he yelled. She had to be in here somewhere. The house was open, and her car was in the garage.

He went back into the kitchen. "Mom?" he called again, his voice rising. When there was no answer, he went down the short hall to her bedroom. The door was open. The blankets on her bed were tossed around like a big pile of meringue. He went over quietly, suspecting she was sleeping under there. Sometimes lately she dozed off at unusual times. But her bed was empty. He turned around and saw that she'd left the light on in her bathroom. He walked over to turn it off, and from the doorway saw the pill bottles, a lot of them, lined up along the front of her sink, their caps neatly beside them.

He had a hard time breathing. His insides felt as if somebody had just yanked hard on a string and drawn them all up into a knot. "Mom!" he shouted, and his voice cracked. He ran back through the downstairs, shouting for her in near hysteria, looking around wildly to make sure he hadn't missed her body lying somewhere. She wasn't there. He was crying, and it was still hard to breathe, but he didn't care. Everything looked sharp and distinct and crystal clear, like nothing would ever connect again with anything else on the planet. "Mom!" he screamed running up the stairs.

His bedroom door was open. He ran inside. There she was, on his bed. Her arms were flung out at strange angles. From the door, he couldn't see if she was breathing, and he wasn't sure what else to look for. "Mom!" he screamed again, and grabbed her shoulder with his good hand. He began shaking her as hard as he could. "Wake up!" he yelled in a panic.

"What?" Maggie said groggily.

"Wake up!" he screamed. "You have to get up! You have to walk around!"

"Mac?" She sat up, trying to get her eyes to focus. "Stop it!" She pulled away from him, still half asleep.

"What did you do?" he yelled.

"I'm sorry," she said. "I'm sorry, okay? I just got really tired. I fell asleep on your bed. I'm sorry."

"With the pills!" he screamed. "What did you do with the pills?"

"What?" she asked, confused. She finally noticed he was crying. "What's wrong? Mac, what's wrong?"

He straightened up and backed away from her. "What did you do with the pills?"

"The pills. What pills?"

"The pills in your bathroom! I saw the bottles all lined up on your sink. How many did you take?"

The realization appeared to dawn on her slowly. "I didn't take any."

"Don't lie to me, Mom." He was starting to shake. "Don't do it."

Maggie stood up unsteadily. "Mac, I swear, I didn't take any."

"Then why are the bottles all out?" he demanded.

Maggie looked like she was having a really hard time thinking. "I swear, I would never do that to you." Even as she said it, it sounded like an empty promise. "I just took all that stuff out because I was going to get rid of it." Mac looked at her without answering. "Really," she continued. "You can check. They're still full. I didn't take anything. I got that stuff when you got hurt, just in case you needed it. I was checking to see what we had. I didn't take anything."

"Really?" He still wasn't sure he should believe her, despite how badly he wanted there to be a simple explanation.

"It's the truth," she said. "Go have a look."

"Okay," he said warily. "Come on." He took her by the hand as if she were the child and led her downstairs. In her bathroom, he began picking up the bottles, lifting and tilting them, trying to judge what might be missing. They were, indeed, mostly full. "We don't need this stuff anymore, do we?" he asked. "I'm all better."

Maggie made an effort to look nonchalant. "It's not hurting anything to have them here."

"I don't want them here anymore." He took the plunge. "I'm afraid. I'm afraid you'll hurt yourself."

Maggie looked like she was struggling to find enough pieces of herself to approximate a whole. When she spoke, it was clear that whatever pieces she had found fit together badly, and it looked like it was painful to hold them in place. "I promise I won't hurt myself."

"You don't need these."

"No," she said, clearly wanting to please him. "I don't need these."

Mac emptied the first few bottles into the toilet. Maggie made no effort to stop him even though she looked like she felt trapped. He picked up the next couple of bottles with his good hand and stopped. "Go ahead," she urged him, her eyes hollow.

When he had finished, Mac threw the empty bottles into the wastebasket. "Come on," he said, taking her hand again. "You need to take a nap."

"Yes," Maggie said. "That would be good."

He led her to her bed, where she lay down without protest. He covered her up. "I think I should call JD," he said. "I think he could come help us."

"No." Maggie sounded far away. "JD's gone."

"What do you mean?" This didn't make any sense to Mac.

She yawned. "JD went away. Nobody will say where."

"Mom," Mac said, "is that what messed you up so bad?"

"He wanted me to prove I was human," Maggie said softly. "I couldn't do it. So he went away."

"Poor Mom," Mac said. "It's not your fault."

Something somewhere might have reminded her that she should be comforting him. "He still cares about you," she said. "It's just that he never wants to see me again."

"Sure he does," Mac said soothingly.

"No he doesn't," she said. "I don't even know where to find him."

Mac didn't know whether to laugh or cry. "Mom," he said in disbelief, "we can just call his cell phone."

"And then he could come take care of you. Would you like that?" she asked. "Would that be okay?" Mac did not say anything. Maggie drifted toward sleep for a short time before the demon woke her up again. "I could go away, and then it could be just the two of you."

"Don't say that!" Mac was angry. "I don't want him instead of you!"

"You know what?" she said sleepily.

"What?" Mac asked, hoping it was something he could bear to hear.

"I kept you home when you were sick because I was selfish. That's the truth. I was hoping you'd get better, but I had no idea if keeping you here would be better for you or not. I was just afraid that if I let anybody else decide they'd take you away from me. And I loved you too much to let you go. I would have rather had you for the rest of your life damaged than take a chance of not having you at all, of letting some strangers take you. Nobody ever loved me like that." She rolled over, and this time the exhaustion finally won out. Still, it felt like a lifetime to Mac until she fell asleep. He was so scared he felt the sharp edges of every single second that passed. Even after he was sure she was sleeping all he could do was sit, curled up like an armadillo, in the chair across from her bed.

Then he realized what he had to do. He left her room as quietly as possible, leaving the door ajar so he could hear if anything happened. When he got to the kitchen he took his out his phone and scrolled to JD's number.

"Hello?" JD said on the third ring.

Mac thought he was hoping the phone wouldn't go to voice mail, but now that he heard JD's voice, he couldn't speak. What he wanted to do was shout, "What did you do to my mother, you bastard?" but the words wouldn't come out. Nothing would.

"Hello?" JD said again. And then, after a moment, "Mac, I can see it's you. Talk to me, buddy." Mac was still not able to say anything. "Come on, Mac," JD said, a note of uncertainty creeping into his voice. "Tell me what's wrong." Mac opened his mouth to talk, but instead started crying uncontrollably, noisy little kid sobs. "All right," JD said, all even and composed. "Come on. Just tell me what's going on."

"Where are you?" Mac finally managed to choke out.

"Are you okay?" JD sounded concerned, but Mac didn't respond, so he continued. "I'm sorry I left without saying goodbye." He took a deep breath and let it out. "I just thought it would be easier on all of us if we had some time to heal ourselves. Please don't think I did this in any way because of you. I care very much about you." The words hung in the air, trite and ineffectual, like something out of a divorce primer. "I'm sorry I disappointed you this way."

There was a long pause. The fury kept building up inside Mac until it was finally ready to explode. "You asshole!" he screamed, his newly hatched man's voice cracking under the weight of his rage. "What did you do to my mother? You said you would help take care of her!"

"MacDonald," JD's voice was hard, "tell me, right now, what is going on."

"She's going to kill herself," Mac sobbed.

"Where are you?" JD was nearly shouting now. "Please. Just talk to me. Tell me where you are. I'll get help to you."

"We're home," Mac sobbed. "We're at home."

"Are you alone with her? Is she armed?" This was a whole new source of terror for Mac. He hadn't even considered that possibility. "What's she doing?" JD demanded.

"She's sleeping now," Mac said. "I'm afraid she's going to hurt herself."

"Are you okay there, for a few minutes?"

Mac kept crying. "She's not okay. Something's really wrong."

"I'm sending an ambulance."

"No!" Mac shouted. "Don't do that! Just come over!"

"Are you going to be all right for a few minutes? Just for a few minutes," JD said. "Can you hang on until I can get you help?"

"Where are you?" Mac asked again, crying.

"I'm not close," JD said. "I'm not close enough to get to you. We need to get someone over there to help."

"Don't call the police!" Mac screamed in a panic. "She's sleeping now. She didn't hurt herself yet. Just get here before she wakes up!"

"Okay," JD said calmly. "I'm going to send somebody to stay with you. Just stay right there. But you have to promise me. If you have any reason, no matter how small, to think you might need help before somebody gets there, you call 911. Don't feel funny, don't feel guilty. Just do it."

"Are you coming?"

"Help is coming, buddy. Just hang tight."

Mac hung up. He went back into Maggie's room and stood over her bed. He watched her, not certain what to do. He didn't want to stay here. He didn't want to be in charge. But he was afraid of what might happen if he left. Or even if he left her with anyone else.

55

Maggie came out to the kitchen shortly after the sun came up. JD was waiting for her there. She looked disoriented and groggy.

"What are you doing here?" she challenged him.

"How are you?" he asked quietly, shocked at her appearance.

"Where's Mac?" she demanded.

"I asked Martha and Daniel to keep him for a few days."

"No!" she shouted. "No! Don't take him away!"

"Maggie," JD tried to calm her, "he's only hanging out at their place. It's okay."

Maggie looked as if she heard him, but not really. Her responses were delayed, like she was someone trying to understand a foreign language in which she was not really fluent and she might or might not grasp what he meant. "Don't send him away," she repeated mournfully.

"I won't send him away." JD tried to sound reassuring. "I know you won't hurt him."

Maggie was watching JD carefully. She raised her hand as if to touch his face, and then drew back, like she'd suddenly noticed something unhealthy about him. "Why are you here?" she demanded.

"We were worried about you. Mac and me," he clarified hastily, hoping to stave off additional paranoia. He pulled out a chair. "How about something to eat?" he offered. "Mac says you haven't eaten in a while. I can make you some breakfast. Or some coffee." He shut up. He was beginning to babble.

"You were up all night." This was a statement, not a question.

"Yes," he said. "Most of it. It took a while for me to get back to town, and then I needed to talk with him. With Mac. When he left, I just wanted to be awake in case you needed anything."

"You look tired. You sit," she commanded.

He smiled softly. "Okay, doc." He meant it as a gentle joke, realizing the connotations too late. It was careless of him, and he feared it might have an effect like removing a plug from the bottom of a dam. Out would pour Maggie, all the venomous pain she had so carefully withheld, everything that had fueled her for so long.

"You're just like him," she said awfully. "Go away. You go away. You all go away."

JD wanted desperately to explain. "I didn't want to go away because of you. I knew I had to go away to save you. From me."

"Liar," she said simply. "Say the truth."

JD felt as if she'd hit him. "I'm sorry," he began again. "You're right. I also went away to save me. It wasn't your fault I lost control. I was obsessed with you. Until I met you, I had myself convinced I had exorcised my ugliness, gotten rid of the part of me that enjoys letting go of control, that's capable of hurting people without regard to the consequences. But it's just like any other addiction. It's hard-wired into my brain. And your rage," he continued sadly, "the engine that drives everything you do, calls out the monster in me. Once it happened a first time, I knew I had to leave you. I couldn't take the chance of hurting you even more. Not after everything you've been through. But I thought that before I went, I could at least help you get to the bottom of your mystery. I didn't want to leave you without that. I thought it would make you strong enough to keep on going the way you always have, without anyone."

"You're all the same. You all think I should go on without anyone. No one can stand to love me."

"Oh, Maggie," he said sadly, "that's not what I meant." He watched her fight for what she wanted to say.

"He wrote me a letter, you know. He wanted me to come home. I never answered him."

"One letter, Maggie? You're willing to beat yourself to death because the best he ever did was one lousy letter?"

"I wanted to see him again. I thought I would get a chance to see him again."

"But you didn't want to come home."

"Can't you see?" she demanded, sounding somewhat hysterical. "I was afraid he just wanted me to take the load off him, to take care of her again."

JD realized this was the first time he had ever heard her admit to being afraid of anything. "It's okay," he tried to calm her. "You don't need to think about this anymore. There's every chance you were right, you know, that he was just a selfish man who took whatever suited him from other people."

"No," she said sharply. "Daniel showed me the picture. The one of me and Mac in the park. Why would Doc want a picture like that? Except if he loved me." When JD did not answer, she leveled a cold, remote gaze at him. "When I believed Doc couldn't love anybody, it didn't matter that he didn't love me. Then Mac got hurt, and I saw it. I saw the truth about Doc. I kept Mac here, even though I had no idea if that would hurt him, because I loved him too much to let him go, because I would have rather had him broken than not at all. That's why Doc kept her here. My mother. He kept her here even though she destroyed her own child. Even though he knew she would eventually destroy him. Because he loved her that much. He let her kill them both because he loved her. He couldn't bear the thought of letting her go alone, of going on without her. Because that's what love is."

JD tried to hold his voice even. He was fighting hard for control. "Your father's version of love, at least."

The storm in Maggie picked up again with terrifying fury. "I killed him!"

"No you didn't!"

"The same way I kill everything that loves me. He wanted to let me know he loved me and I sent him away!" She began to move erratically around the room. "That's why he let her have a gun!" She laughed, and it was a frightening sound. "I wanted her to die. But not him. Not him too."

"Don't do this," JD pleaded. "You were the victim. This was never something you could fix. You would only have sacrificed your life trying."

"That's how she knew!" Maggie shouted. "She knows he loved other people! Maybe he was ready to love her!"

It took JD a moment to realize Maggie was referring to herself in the third person. "You're not sure of that, are you?" he asked softly.

Maggie howled as if someone had just touched her skin with acid. "She made a mistake! She believed he couldn't love anyone!" She was moving around now in a totally uncontrolled way, banging into things wildly. Hurting herself like a trapped bird. "That's why she never answered him, why she sent him away!"

"Maggie," JD said, trying to catch her, "you have to stop this. You're hurting yourself for no reason."

The words flew from her as if launched. "What do you know? Do you even know the worst thing someone can do to a child?"

"Maybe I don't," JD said, trying to keep his voice level. "Tell me what that is."

She laughed at him. "You think it's abuse, don't you? You think it's the one who hurts you who does the worst thing. You're all so stupid," she said venomously. "He made *me* lie to protect *her*. He made *me* pretend everything was okay! There is nothing more destructive you can do to a child than that!"

"He had to make a terrible choice," JD said gently.

"What kind of terrible choice?" Her voice cracked. "He knew there was no hope for her. She drank because she was crazy, not the other way around."

"And what would he have done with her?" JD pushed on. "Put her away somewhere? People can't always do that with someone they love. You, of all people, know that."

Without warning, she halted her flight and grabbed him by the arms. Her grip was brutally strong, like being held in the clutches of an angry man. This unharnessed strength finally forced JD to look at the precariousness of her sanity. Maggie's wild-eyed stare didn't hold any recognition. She suddenly let go of him and slid away. She began to laugh, with an inhuman fury. "That's the joke. He didn't love her more. He just loved her. Like when I couldn't send Mac away. Because I loved him. That's how he felt about her. But not about me. He sent me away just fine."

"Look at me," JD commanded. She wouldn't. He talked anyway. "You were a kid. Kids have unrealistic expectations, and they can be very unforgiving. Yes, he deserted you at the worst possible time in your life. But he had nothing to give you. He wasn't prepared to change anything."

Her breath caught in a hiccup as she tried to speak. "What if he was sorry?" she asked brokenly. "What if he changed his mind? What if he finally decided he loved me instead? And I wouldn't give him the chance."

"Maggie, please," JD begged. "Please stop hurting yourself. You'll never know why he wanted you to come home."

"Why did he choose her? What was wrong with me?"

JD spoke very gently. "Maybe he just thought you were the stronger one, that you were the one who could make it without him. There are no simple rules for choosing between the people you love in an impossible situation. If you choose wrong, you will surely lose one or both. If you choose right, the outcome is likely to be the same."

She stopped for an instant, stood completely still. When she spoke, her words came out in gasps. "You were willing to die because you thought he was going to die." JD did not answer. She forced herself to continue. "You chose Mac instead of me."

JD was angrier than he realized. It was not until he spoke that he saw it, but he didn't let that stop him. "I knew if I killed that boy you might never forgive me. But I also knew Mac would be safe. And who knows? Maybe I wanted revenge." He closed his eyes for a moment before continuing. "I wanted to protect your son because he needed me."

"*He* needed you?"

"Come on, Maggie," he said harshly. "I don't love him more than I love you. I just had to choose." The instant he let himself say it, he was sorry. But, as always, it was too late. The words were out there, with an existence of their own. He looked at Maggie, at what was left of her. He might as well have shot her. He watched what remained of her soul bleed out of her eyes. In an instant she was gone, so far beyond his reach that it didn't matter that they were mere feet apart in the same room. "Maggie," JD said despairingly, trying to take her arm, "I'm sorry."

She turned away from him. "That's what *he* wanted to tell her." She began stalking around the kitchen, crashing into things without stopping, without feeling the pain. "He wanted to tell Margaret he was sorry. He wanted to explain. She sent him away." Her voice was a monotone.

JD put himself in her path. "Stop, Maggie," he commanded. "Listen to me." She did, actually, for a brief moment. "Don't do this to yourself," he pleaded. "You don't need to do this."

The moment of lucidity sizzled away and she was off again, moving, crashing. "You see, he wanted her to come home. He wanted to show Margaret he loved her. Someone was going to finally love Margaret and she threw him away."

JD couldn't take it anymore. "That's enough!" he yelled, grabbing her by the arms. She looked at him without recognition, the same way she might notice a fly had lighted upon the wall. "*I love you.*" He shook her slightly. "*I love Margaret.*"

"No!" She broke loose with so much force it pushed him backward. "Nobody loves Margaret!" she shouted. "I told you that!" She turned and blindly started for the hallway to the front of the house. She bashed into the doorjamb so hard she literally rebounded, then kept going. He heard the crash of something heavy falling in the living room. There were a few seconds of silence, suddenly pierced by a lunatic wail. JD ran toward the sound.

Maggie was curled up on the living room floor like a creature under attack. The coffee table was upended where she had crashed into it, and magazines and pieces of broken ceramics were scattered about. He sat down on the floor next to her and she curled into herself even farther. He tried to hold her, but she resisted with incredible strength. It was as if, sensing that her ties to the world were being severed, she was clinging to the earth itself.

JD fought to get his own panic and guilt under control. This, he finally saw, is where his hubris had landed them. He had hammered away at her defenses without caring that the wall he wanted to break down, the one she worked so hard to defend, was between her and this cataclysmic firestorm of pain. His conceit about his power to heal her had succeeded only in forcing her here, to the edge of the abyss. Now, one wrong breath and she would be gone. This went far beyond even his most heroic imaginings. And the moments left between salvation and madness were hemorrhaging away. If he let her fall into the void, eventually some expert might be able to bring back the tattered shreds of who she used to be, but those would not be anyone he recognized.

And she had known what he was capable of doing to her, had tried to save herself, had even tried to warn him. Like all things grown up wild and unprotected, she had retained the ability to see impending danger from a long way off, and knew that if it couldn't be bluffed away, the only alternative was to hold on tight for the duration of the battle. JD the crusader, convinced of the nobility of his mission, never saw that the conflict itself was his consuming passion, that victory was the only prize that really interested him. Now that her defenses had been breached, he had no clue what to do with this child who had never been given enough human contact to enable her to endure.

Here was the irreparable harm she had tried to warn him about. What did he have to offer her? His love? How many powerful people in her life had used that word, love, like the cover of darkness, to inflict terrible damage and then slip away unpunished? Her one fragile bridge to humanity, to her son, had been brutally ripped from her by the torrent of fate, and she had neither the tools nor the knowledge to rebuild it. JD finally realized the totality of what he had done. He had helped Mac to rebuild that bridge to himself instead of to her, reaping himself a share of vengeance in the deal.

Now she was howling away her spirit. When she was done, she would be empty. If he let this go on to its end all that remained would be the empty shell of the creature that survived. The Maggie of his fantasies had never existed and never would. But the Maggie of realities, the one he could have loved if he had only been wise enough, was also ceasing to exist, slipping beyond his reach.

"Maggie," JD said very softly, "I need to tell you something." She gave no sign that she heard him. He could only hope she might be listening. "You are a miracle. You started with nothing and you made yourself into an incredible human being. You saved lives, you comforted countless people. And you are the best mother I have ever known." He started to cry. "I'm sorry I made you feel like less than that. I was just being proud, and stubborn. But Mac didn't call me to come back because he wanted me. He wanted me to help him save you."

If this was having an effect, it wasn't obvious. JD felt panic taking over. He focused all his attention on the nothing inside his eyelids. What he saw there was Rev, trying to warn him. Too late, he saw that this had never been about her. It had always been about him. All the damage he had already done, all the rest he was capable of doing, was merely a display of his own strength, the gorilla beating its chest in the jungle to make all the other creatures cower. And she had known, back when she was still capable of defending herself. If there was any chance left now of saving her, this had to be about her. He had to find a way to give her control. He tried to focus on the things she had told him, searching for the beginning of the fracture. When he recognized it, he also saw the only person who could possibly save her. "Maggie," he said softly, "we need to go back to garden."

"No!" she wailed.

He lay down on the floor next to her. She immediately curled away, as if he had thrown salt on her raw flesh. He used his good arm to hold her close, despite her resistance, and with his other hand he gently began rubbing her head, so lightly she might not even have sensed it. He had seen Rev do this with infants right before he baptized them, had watched their terror at being held out over emptiness by a strange face gradually melt into a transfixed state of relaxation. He increased the pressure of his fingertips slightly, letting her slowly become aware. She gradually quieted. After several minutes, he gently moved closer. "I'm going to help you," he said very softly. In his experience sliding underneath the layers of paranoia and panic, only a whisper could be heard above the howling of souls on their way to being lost. This time was just a little different. The panic was partially his own.

JD tightened his grip, knowing what would come next. "Maggie," he began softly, "there is no garage. It's just the garden there now, and the rain barrels. It's time to go back to the garden."

"No!" she screamed, fighting to get up. He held her down.

"I'm with you," he kept repeating. "We're just standing on the screen porch, looking. I'm behind you, protecting you. Can you feel me here?" He felt her body stiffen. "Don't be scared," he whispered. "I'm not going to go away. Can you see the garden?" Maggie did not answer. "It's morning," he continued, "and it's quiet out there now. The storm is over." She still didn't acknowledge what he was saying, but he felt he had her attention. "Come on," he said gently, "it's time for us to go into the back yard."

"No!" She started shaking. "She'll hurt me!"

He waited for her to quiet a bit, then held her close again. "Let's go down the steps now. Together."

She began to shiver again. "I can't. My clothes are wet."

He was about to repeat that he was there to protect her when he finally saw the full truth. "No, they are not wet," he said firmly. "You are Maggie now. This is your garden and there is nothing in it that is stronger than you. Nothing here can hurt you."

Maggie was very, very scared. What if he was wrong? She walked slowly into the yard, stopping every few feet, waiting for the Observer to attack. When it didn't come, she walked a few feet more, advancing slowly until she was beside the picket fence. The fence came to the top of her thigh.

"Can you see her?" JD whispered. "Can you see Margaret?"

"No," Maggie said. "She's hiding."

"Yes," he said softly. "But she's there. She's in that garden, alone and scared and badly hurt. You need to go help her."

Sure enough, there was a little girl crouched down behind the rain barrels. Her nightgown was filthy. There were the streaks of dried tears in the dirt on her cheeks, but she was not crying now. Her face was terribly swollen and bruised, her bottom lip badly cut. Maggie walked a little closer to her, then stopped. She was too scared to go any farther.

"Go on, Maggie," JD said softly. "Go to her."

"The mother will hurt us," Maggie said pitifully.

"Not this time," JD whispered. "Not ever again. Go to the little girl." Maggie went closer. "Don't be frightened," JD urged her.

"She doesn't want me," Maggie said. "She's angry."

"She doesn't want any grown-ups. Grown-ups hurt her. Is she crying now?"

"No. She will never cry again so the things she loves won't have to die. She doesn't want me to come near her."

"Not yet," JD said. "First you have to get her to trust you."

Maggie's voice rose. "I can't do that."

"You can," JD said firmly. "Help her understand that once she comes to you, she will be safe forever. You will never let anyone hurt her again. You will be her real mother."

"I don't know how." Maggie's voice was heartrending.

JD closed his eyes. He spoke as if the words came from somewhere else. "If you let her in," he said finally, "she will teach you how." He paused. "Go to her," he urged gently.

"She doesn't want me. She doesn't want a mother anymore."

"Pick her up," JD said.

"I can't!" Maggie said, panicky. "I can't pick her up! She's ugly! She hates me!"

"Look again," JD said softly. "She looks just like Mac, doesn't she? When he was little?"

"Yes," Maggie whispered. She was surprised she hadn't noticed this before. It made her feel calmer.

"She's beautiful, Maggie. And she loves you."

Maggie walked closer. The little girl stood up very slowly, like she was thinking about running away. Maggie carefully reached out toward her, and when the little girl came closer Maggie lifted her to safety. The little girl held on tighter than Mac ever had for just an instant, and then she was gone. "Where is she?" Maggie cried, terrified. "I've lost her!"

"No you haven't," JD said. "She's with you now. She's finally whole. She'll never be lost again."

Maggie began to cry, slowly and quietly. There were just tears at first, slipping down her cheeks. Gradually, the intensity built into sobs of mourning. Very, very carefully, JD held her.

56

Maggie sat in the grandstand, waiting for the Labor Day Parade to begin. "I feel lucky that we arrived in time to see The Chipmunk's swan song last year," she said to Martha, "though I can't wait to see Gamey's big surprise."

"Whatever it may be, you'll see it pretty good from up here."

"Yeah. Last year we were down on the bottom riser with the peons."

"Well, now you know you've arrived, don't you?"

"Do you know why they call them peons?" Daniel asked.

Vee turned on him, ready for a hostile engagement. "The word comes from the Latin root for foot soldier."

"Oh," he said pleasantly. "Never mind."

Martha turned to Maggie. She was about to make a rude observation about the crowd, but she stopped suddenly. "Come back here," she said evenly. "This is not the time to be watching the show inside your head."

"Is it that obvious?" Maggie asked.

"Your pupils are the size of poppy seeds. Are you tired?"

Maggie nodded. "A little, but not too bad."

"Don't indulge yourself right now," Martha said. "This is public time." As was Martha's way, she got directly to the point. Maggie had grown to admire that about her.

"I really appreciate everything," Maggie said quietly. "You know, that you and Daniel have done to take care of Mac and me these last few months."

"That's what real family is for. It makes us happy to see you getting strong again," Martha replied. She put her arm around Maggie.

"I'm better than I was before," Maggie said. "I'm not brittle."

"No," Martha agreed. "Things just didn't turn out the way you expected, did they?"

Maggie sighed. "Great works of fiction demand tragic endings. Someone or something needs to be destroyed or suffer a horrific loss. Only in real life people have to stick around and do the hard, dirty work of dealing with the mess." She paused before continuing. When she spoke, her voice was so quiet that

Martha had to strain to hear her. "We were like matter and anti-matter weren't we? Destined to collide, with cataclysmic results."

"If you wanted me to listen to you get all meaningful," Martha said, "you should've brought along some beer."

Maggie had to laugh. Then she heard the first faint sounds of the marching band. It was still at least a block away, but the crowd rumbled in anticipation. Distracted by the general excitement, Maggie did not see him until the last minute, a strong figure in a black tee shirt and a baseball cap. The sight of him gave her a yearning that was physically painful. From this distance she realized it was only her imagination that made her believe she could see the small embroidered patches of the Dooleysburg Police Department logo on his cap and chest. He began climbing up the far end of the viewing stand without looking up. He got to a relatively uncrowded spot at the other end of the risers a couple of rows below where she was and sat down, leaning his elbows on his knees and apparently focusing on the parade. As she watched him, her heart hurt from pounding so hard. It felt as if it were thrashing against the walls of her chest, trying to get out so it could reach him.

Maggie turned her attention back to the parade. The band was still somewhere down the street, playing a standard Sousa-type marching song. She forced herself to concentrate, trying to figure out the affiliation of the group in front of the viewing stand. They appeared to be ladies somehow involved with canning. Suddenly she was aware of someone standing behind her. "I didn't see you when I first sat down," he said. "Shove over. You can make more room than that." She scooched over closer to Martha, and JD stepped over the riser and sat down next to her. They both watched in silence for a few minutes.

"I'm glad you could make it," Maggie said softly, without taking her eyes off the parade. "You look good in black." She finally glanced over and JD smiled at her. His thigh was next to hers. She could feel the heat of him through the fabric of his jeans. She didn't flinch. "I got scared," she said matter of factly.

"Bad music?" he asked. When she didn't respond to the joke, he looked at her. "I'm sorry," he said. "That was inconsiderate. You want to tell me about it?"

"Not a whole lot to tell beyond the usual. Things have been going well for a while. So I'm just afraid of what will happen to destroy that."

JD took a deep breath. "I could lie to you," he said. "But quite likely something unpleasant will happen, sooner or later. That's what being alive means. Shit happens. You need to remember it will happen whether you've enjoyed the interludes or not. If you choose not to, maybe it doesn't hurt quite so bad when things go wrong. Less contrast, you know? So I guess you could say those of us who enjoy the interludes just have a heightened tolerance for risk."

Maggie wasn't sure any of this was making things better, so she changed the subject. "I appreciate all the time you've been spending with Mac."

"You know about that?" JD asked.

"We don't need lies," Maggie said. "Of course he tells me about the stuff you guys do." She turned her attention back to the parade.

JD made a noise like he was clearing his throat.

"Look," Martha said, pointing to the twirlers who were coming into view. "You can't see their thongs this year. Guess The Chipmunk isn't paying for their uniforms any more."

JD produced another fusillade of odd noises. This time, Maggie looked at him. His face was bright red. "Are you okay?" she asked with concern. "Do you want me to get you some water?" He shook his head. Without thinking, she automatically reached for his wrist to take his pulse.

"Maggie," he stopped her hand, "I'm fine. I'm just blushing."

"Blushing?" she laughed. "Are you having an impure thought?"

He cleared his throat again. "I was trying to figure out how to ask if I could hold your hand."

"JD," she said, "that's so sweet." She leaned closer and laced her fingers through his.

He nodded at something a few rows down the stands. "Carol Ann is sending you a poison dart."

Maggie didn't bother to look. "Shall I flip her the bird?"

"That would be rather immature."

"I've decided to embrace my immaturity."

"I know," he said, suddenly pinning her with a direct gaze. "You could forgive me, you know."

"Stop it," she said, not unkindly.

"You could go out with me." He looked toward the street again. "On a real date. Let me take you to an incredible dinner."

"No."

"A concert? A movie?"

"No."

"Is there anything I will ever be able to do to earn your trust back?" he asked.

"I trust you, sweetie," she said simply.

"We live in Pennsylvania. We could go bowling. I could find us a cow pie bingo within a two-hour drive."

"You need to be patient," she said. "I'm still learning how to crawl and you want me to fly."

"When you're ready to fly, will you fly with me?"

"Is Carol Ann still watching us?" she asked.

"Yeah, she's trying to be cool about it, but I think I see some spittle flying out of the side of her mouth whenever she turns her head."

"Do something," Maggie said.

"Like what?" JD asked.

"Something to make her even more jealous."

JD lifted her hand to his lips and kissed the back of it. He could feel her re-flexively stiffen and then immediately begin to work on relaxing.

"I'm sorry," she said softly.

He smiled. "Don't be. We'll get there."

"So after I'm finally all grown up, will you still love me, Pygmalion?"

He smiled at her. "I will always love you. The question is, will I be able to stand you?"

Maggie turned her attention back to the parade. She watched for a while before the feeling of JD's eyes on her was an unbearable distraction. "What?" she finally turned to him. "Do I have food on my face or something? You're staring at me."

"I was just thinking that you are perfect, woman as god intended her to be, beautiful and flawed."

"Knucklehead," she replied, turning her attention back to the parade.

"So I was thinking," JD said, "if you're determined about no dates, can I just come to your house and sit and kvell at you?"

"Kvell," Maggie cracked up. "You get that from Miles Standish?"

"I got it from your son," he said. "It's Yiddish for moon, gape. Get all googly-eyed."

"Moon at me here," she said. JD looked away. Maggie suddenly realized this had become serious. "JD," she asked quietly, "what is it you want? Really want?"

"Please just tell me how long I have to wait. That's all I'm asking. I will wait as long as you want, but the pain would be easier to bear if I knew how long that might be."

Maggie took a deep breath. "Until you fail me," she said simply. "I need to know how badly it will hurt, to figure out if I can survive."

"Then I will be waiting forever," he replied, "because I will not fail you again." He looked at the parade. He was squinting as if the sun was in his eyes, although it was behind them.

Maggie watched him intently. "I believe you," she finally whispered.

"But that's not enough, is it?" he asked. She shook her head. "And what is it you want?" he asked forlornly.

"I want the time and space I need to become a completely whole person."

"Okay," he nodded. "I understand."

"And once I have achieved that, I would like to spend the rest of my life with you, if you'll still have me." She looked away after she said it, for fear that she would cry.

"Look at me," he whispered. She forced herself to turn back to him. "However you want it," he said softly. "I am here for as long as you want me, on your terms."

"Hey!" Vee snapped. "Eyes front! Here comes the band!" As the Dooleysburg High Marching Unit approached the grandstand, the first person to come into view was Mr. Don, his motorized wheelchair festooned for the occasion.

"Yoo hoo!" Vee stood up and shouted. "Mr. Don, honey! Up here!" Mr. Don flashed her a thumbs-up, momentarily removing his hand from the chair's controls and causing a minor hiccup in the procession. Vee was bouncing up and down with excitement. The stands actually felt as if they were rocking slightly, though it might only have been an illusion. Nonetheless, she was causing some consternation amid the surrounding townsfolk.

"Vee, honey?" JD began. "Could we maybe have a little decorum?"

A surly-looking fellow a few rows below them turned around, and, with a most unpleasant expression on his face, snarled, "Sit down, asshole!"

Vee pointed a finger toward his face. "How would you like me to rip you a new one?" she shouted. Then she resumed waving her arms wildly, hooting like a maniac.

"See?" Maggie said to JD. "Decorum is not all that big a part of our culture either."

Martha patted Vee's arm. "Sit down, Vidalia," she said. "You're behaving like Pepe le Pew."

"You're just envious," Vee replied, but at least she sat down.

"Hey." JD leaned across to talk to Vee. "That's quite a chair Gamey got Don."

"It's just a lease," Vee said dismissively. "The best the little freak would do is get him a loaner."

"Maybe he's counting on Don walking again," JD said helpfully.

"Gamey had old man Bendz negotiate the terms. They agreed to a mileage limit."

The band pulled up even with the viewing stand. Mr. Don doffed his hat to the judges and the band launched into the school's fight song. Even though there were no other bands competing today, Mr. Don was taking things quite seriously. He had clearly communicated that to his musicians. They solemnly concentrated on playing their instruments, marking time with brief nods of their heads. When the song was over, they silently marched on to the corner of the street and then stood in place as an expectant hush fell over the crowd. Even Vee kept herself under control.

Into the quiet stepped the new Gamey Deli Marching Club, led by a majestic Genoa salami the size of a very small man. Armed with a drum major's baton, the salami was guiding a procession of marching deli items. The youngest kids, from the junior sports league, were dressed as pepperoncini, their bright green wrinkled pepper shapes topped with bobbing stems. The middle-sized sports kids were slices of tomato and onion. There were a couple of varieties of cheese in size places, and then the serious players, the meats. There was ham, bologna, capicola. Bringing up the rear were the tallest kids, dressed as torpedo rolls. The foam costumes made it impossible to identify any specific child. "I hope nobody spoils in this heat," Martha said.

All the marchers wore identical tights and shoes, which struck the only false note. The tights were red and white striped, as if the costume designer had stumbled into Munchkinland for inspiration. The shoes, which, truth be told, would have been a challenge under any circumstances, were a clear rip-off of Mickey Mouse, with large clunky yellow insteps and fake foam cuffs. The Mickey theme continued on the kids' hands, which were covered with puffy white three-fingered gloves. In the eerie silence left by the sudden cessation of the band's playing, the shuffling clump of children marching in unison had the effect of a dream, the rhythmic whooshing reminiscent of the sound of the pulse in a sleeper's ear.

The assorted cold cuts and fixings lined up directly in front of the judges, facing the viewing stand. They stood for a moment, decorously posed. Without warning, the marching band, under Mr. Don's direction, launched enthusiastically into a song. It took a few bars before becoming recognizable. "Wow," Daniel said. "I didn't realize there *was* a marching band arrangement of 'Like a Virgin'."

In response to the music the various deli items began lifting their right legs in unison, keeping perfect time. Then half of them, the taller half, began pivoting around, carefully changing position while maintaining straight lines. As the routine became increasingly complex, the meats and cheeses had difficulty executing the precision moves in their cumbersome shoes. Nonetheless, everyone kept time to the music, displaying the grace of a Busby Berkley routine. The brass section of the band reached a crescendo, clearly feeling Madonna's lyrics and, with a flourish, the lunchmeat and toppings assumed their final pose. Only when they stopped moving did it become evident to the crowd that they had sorted themselves into Italian hoagies, each torpedo roll fronted by layers of cold cuts, cheese and condiments. In keeping with his commitment to kosher-style, Gamey had reserved one sandwich as cheese only. As the last chorus of the song played, the kids kept their places, holding their gloved hands upright from the elbow, manically rotating their wrists in classic Bob Fosse style. Maggie's head whipped around as she scanned the line of torpedo rolls.

"Something wrong?" Daniel asked, watching her.

"I can't tell which one is Mac," she replied, still searching.

"Of course not," Daniel said. "They're all dressed the same."

"No," she said excitedly. "You don't understand! They're all doing jazz hands. Both hands. He's using both hands! He's using his left arm!"

Next to her, JD smiled. "He wanted to surprise you."

Suddenly the music stopped and the hoagies, in unison, fell to their knees. The crowd went wild. On the bleachers, everyone rose to a standing ovation, and the roar vibrated the metal of the benches. If anyone rued the end of the Chipmunk era, it was sensibly kept private.

♪   ♪   ♪

It was a long day for Mac, but Monday was his night to e-mail Albie. Despite being tired, he booted up his laptop and sat down with it on his bed. He opened a new message and began.

Hey Albie—

Today was the Labor Day Parade. I think Gamey's hoagie idea was good. Nobody even talked about The Chipmunk anymore after they saw us. People really liked the dance part, but next year I'm going to ask for a different Ham. The one I had this year was a real pain in the ass. He never learned his moves, right up until the last minute, and he kept shoving our Cheese and picking on the little Peppers. I know what you're thinking. Well, forget it. Telling on people is not something the Rifkins do. Besides, ever since Gamey saved Morsel's immortal soul, he thinks every spoiled brat is just a 'poor troubled child'. He'd probably just give the kid a bag of Fritos or something.

Here's another secret. You have to promise not to tell this one either. Though since Mom doesn't have e-mail, I guess there's nobody for you to tell. Mr. Don told me Vee is going to have a shotgun wedding. I'm actually not sure how that's different from a regular wedding. You'd think they'd want to stay away from anything to do with guns, but whatever. Maybe it has something to do with him taking her last name instead of the other way around, though my bet is he'd do just about anything to get rid of Dickerman. Anyway, Mr. Don sounded happy about it when he told me, so I guess it'll be okay.

Mr. Don is still working with me a lot on the drums. I kind of don't want to play anymore cause of my arm, but that freaks out the old folks, so I just go along with it all. He says since he knows he'll never get his legs back, my arm gets the benefit of his Freudian displacement. I looked that up on the net, and it was something totally strange, which shouldn't surprise me, since it has to do with Freud. So I figure it must be his idea of a joke. Anyway, he says because I'm a kid and my brain isn't completely set in its ways yet like an old fart's, if I keep working at it, my arm might come back. Maybe he's right, because I can pick up my drumstick with my left hand now, and I hardly ever drop it any-more. That's a secret too, for now.

Now here's the big one. At the parade today, JD was sitting with Mom in the grandstand. And *they were holding hands*. Swear to god. They probably thought nobody saw. What a couple of blockheads. *Everybody* saw. Then we went to Daniel's for a picnic after the parade, and everybody kept grinning at me, like I had something to do with it. It was totally weird, the two of them pretending like nothing was going on when he's kvelling at her every time her back is turned and she's making puppy eyes at him when she thinks nobody's looking. Martha says Mom is testing JD's patience. I think she's probably test-ing a whole lot more than that, because he's eating a ton of shit from her and not giving any back. I asked him about it, if it doesn't make him mad, and he told me not to worry, he's not going anywhere. I'm not going to get my hopes up or anything, but he could be okay for a father.

I'm pretty tired now so I'm going to go. Say hey to Sakura for me.

Old MacDonald

Acknowledgments

Dear Reader,

Thank you for coming along on this journey with me, and more importantly, with my characters. I know the ride hasn't been totally smooth. But my very first acknowledgment goes to you, because a book is nothing but a power tool for the mind, stuck in the "off" position until you come along and turn it "on" with your imagination. Without you, there is no inner eye to see the words turn into a story. I am very grateful to you.

I will admit that my motives, when I first began the work of creating a novel, were purely selfish. My day job involves contributing to the much larger goal of finding a cure for cancer, and since I'm not the one with the brilliant scientific mind, I am always working as part of a team. This is a struggle for me. I like things to go my way. They often don't. Consequently, I'm not unfamiliar with the experience of having a bad day. And so, I started thinking about something to do in my spare time that I could accomplish all on my own. I know! I thought in my naïveté. I'll write a book! As I have discovered, I could not have been more wrong. Forget about that silly concept of doing it in your spare time. I still have my day job. Only now I have a night job, too. Forget the concept of spare time.

And you really can't write a book all on your own. Maybe you can write a good draft. But it takes the eyes and ears and wit of a number of gifted people before your finished product might qualify as good. I would like to try to thank some of those people here. Let me apologize in advance that I won't possibly be able to name everyone. That's how many people it takes. But the generosity and enthusiasm of friends and colleagues along the way was sometimes the only thing that tipped the scale between this story becoming a book or staying reams of scribbled-up pages on my bedroom floor.

First and foremost, there aren't enough grateful words for me to give my husband, Rich Grote. He put up with hours of me babbling story at him, and read and listened to numerous drafts. He was incredibly gracious about overlooking those occasions when he came upon me laughing maniacally or crying hysterically as I perpetrated some evil or other upon my beloved characters, and always made a flawless call about whether I needed a refill on my coffee or it was time to change up to a glass of wine. But most importantly, he believed in this book from the very beginning, in the importance of my writing it, and rewriting it, and getting it into print. I am honored that he revised one of his most beautiful paintings for me to use as a cover, and then put hours into doing all the behind-the-scenes work on cover production and websites and the kinds of stuff my brain simply refuses to understand. Thank you, honey.

It is also difficult for me to find the best words to express my gratitude to the gifted fantasy writer Gregory Frost. I have never stopped believing some power beyond my understanding directed me to my first-ever writing class, Greg's "Beginnings and Endings." At the time I was stuck as to how to handle both, and had planned to take a full-fledged night course on the subject. But then the friend who was going to come with me decided she'd rather take quilting, which I already knew how to do, and I didn't feel like taking a 9-week night class alone. So I signed up for Greg's one-afternoon workshop instead. What I learned in those three hours was not only enough to get me jump-started on my beginning (which, it turns out, lots of people write after the rest of the book is at least partway done), but also how to begin to identify all the other things I didn't know. Greg has remained a generous teacher, mentor and friend ever since, and if anybody out there thinks you'd like help recognizing your own intuitive approach to solving some of the mysteries of writing, find a class with Greg. Any class, anywhere. You won't be sorry. And in the meantime, read his books. I've whiled away many a stormy night with the *Shadowbridge* duology.

I'm also feeling kind of at a loss for the right words to acknowledge Doug Gordon of P. M. Gordon Associates. Doug came to the Dooleysburg adventure somewhat later in the game, but his generosity, guidance and contributions have been every bit as essential to the book. I had been trying, without success, to understand some of the complexities of book publishing until I met Doug, and I can't thank him enough for all his help, patience and good humor.

I owe an enormous debt of gratitude to all my first readers. Many of them also happen to be wonderful friends, which makes me feel doubly blessed. Sometimes they had difficult things to tell me about early drafts of this book, and they found the courage to do it. Sometimes they just wanted to give me encouragement. But each and every one of them motivated me to keep going, to try to make this book the best I possibly could. To Christine Weiser, publisher of *Philadelphia Stories*, a special thanks for reading the very first draft and making lots of helpful comments. My thanks as well to those members of the PS Workshop, especially Helen Mallon and Carla Spataro, who read early excerpts and helped me come to terms with the fact that a main character who is too tough to like is not someone readers are going to be willing to invest their time in.

I also want to acknowledge beloved friend David Frame, who was a faithful cheerleader for my writing. We still miss him dearly. And thank you to his beautiful wife, Paula, who also read the book and shared her confidence in it.

Thanks as well to first readers Laureen Talenti, Julie Senecoff, Ann Sonntag and Stephanie Donado; to Claudine Wolk for not only reading the book in draft form, but for also giving lots of good advice about getting published; to George Tuohy for demanding more each time he finished reading the portion I'd just written; to Raphaele Mary and Mary Newman, respected colleagues from my other world who were willing to join me in this one; and to Barbara Szymaszek, who devoted hours of her time to helping me make sure I got everything right. From each of you, the excitement and generous praise was oftentimes the fuel that kept my engine going.

My thanks as well to those friends who haven't yet read the book, but have made it clear they're with me one hundred percent in this venture. Too many times for me to count, I have been carried over a rough spot by a random act of kindness from Andrea Campbell-Czekaj. And to Barbara Kraskian, Ellen Gotthardt, Nancy Widener, Hillary Dietz, Cindy Zacharias, Esther Huffman, Jane Rosenblum, Mark Czekaj, Mark and Mary Stranix, and Miro and Kelly Kamenik, you are all incredible. I appreciate your support and humor more than you can imagine.

There is another group of people, professional writers and professionals in the publishing industry, who read some or all of this book and consistently urged me to keep working toward getting it published. I would especially like to thank Jackie Cantor, Sara Crowe and Linda Fairstein for their generous encouragement, and Pam Houston, Robert Olen Butler and Michael Neff for their thoughtful and helpful comments.

Last but never least, a big embarrassing hug and kiss to my son Matthew, whose forays into the off-limits boxes in the basement yielded some stories of mine so old and forgotten they were printed with a dot matrix printer on that old continuous-feed computer paper I don't think is even made anymore. He hid them in his room only long enough to read them, then brought them to me and said, "You're a pretty good writer, you know. I think you need to keep going and see how this all ends." All my kids are rather spectacular, but how lucky for Dooleysburg that I have a kid like him.

CPSIA information can be obtained at www.ICGtesting.com
Printed in the USA
BVOW011959140911

271250BV00003B/4/P